# BEN ELTON OMNIBUS

# STARK
# GRIDLOCK

# Ben Elton

WARNER BOOKS

A *Warner* Book

This omnibus edition first published in Great Britain
by Warner Books in 2000

*Ben Elton Omnibus* Copyright © Ben Elton 2000

Previously published separately:

*Stark* first published in Great Britain by Sphere Books Ltd 1989
Reprinted 1989 (twenty-three times), 1990 (five times), 1991
Reprinted by Warner Books 1992, 1993 (twice), 1996, 1997, 1998,
1999 (twice), 2000
Copyright © Ben Elton 1989

*Gridlock* first published in Great Britain by Macdonald & Co (Publishers) Ltd 1991
Published by Sphere Books Ltd 1992
Reprinted by Warner Books 1993
Reprinted 1994, 1996, 1997, 1998, 1999, 2000
Copyright © Ben Elton 1991

The moral right of the author has been asserted.

A CIP catalogue record for this book is available from the British Library.

ISBN 0 7515 3144 8

Printed and bound in Great Britain by Clays Ltd, St Ives plc

Warner Books
A Division of
Little, Brown and Company (UK)
Brettenham House
Lancaster Place
London WC2E 7EN

# STARK

# BREAKFAST IN CARLO

Carlton is a little coastal town some miles south of Perth in Western Australia. They're a strange contrast those two towns. Perth is home to a higher density of millionaires than any other city in the world, but just down the road in Carlton people hang kind of looser. Certainly the place has its fair share of bread-heads and hustlers, but it's still got a laid back feel. Boats and cafés and taking it easy are the things a visitor carries away in the memory.

Perth gets up in the morning and says, 'OK let's do it, let's make money, let's get on with a load of really high-powered stuff right now!'

Some mornings Carlton doesn't get up.

It's a nice place to holiday in, or retire to, so actually quite a bit of money is made there in a gentle kind of way, a lot of it by a man called Silvester (or Sly) Moorcock. Sly lived in Perth, he was one of that city's many self-made rich, smug bastards, and finding the need to get further into property for tax reasons, he had bought up all the old granny duplex's and made Carlton (or Carlo to its friends), one of his many possessions. Some of it he knocked down, some of it he rented out. Some of it looked as if he'd got half-way through knocking it down but then changed his mind and decided to rent it out. Such a place was occupied by Colin.

Yes, Sly owned Carlo, but he didn't rule the roost — not in Colin's little part of town anyway. All right, so Sly could have evicted Colin. Also, if Colin had had a job, Sly could have made him redundant. He could have impounded his possessions and done him for non-payment of rent. But so what? Colin didn't really own anything anyway and when it's time to move on, it's time to move on.

No, Sly didn't bother Colin overmuch. So the guy was a billionaire, what could he *really* do to you? Nothing. In the searing heat and natural abundance of a Carlton summer, Colin had much more pressing enemies than Sly. Let's face it, Sly was unlikely to appear as if from nowhere, on Colin's bread-board and make him feel like throwing up. He wasn't going to creep into the fridge and hide in the folded spout of the milk carton so that when Colin popped back the spout wings, there he would be! all horrid and scuttley! Then, off like a bullet, but not before he'd shocked Colin into dropping the milk and ruined Colin's day.

Sly Moorcock was more powerful than God in Carlton, but Colin had never had to throw the butter away because he'd found Sly having a fuck in it – it takes a special kind of bastard to make you do that. Colin's enemies were cockroaches, he had no time to worry about billionaires.

## COCKIES

Cockroaches have an extraordinary physical resilience. You can smash one to bits on your living room floor leaving it in numerous cockroachie pieces and a little later when you have steeled yourself to clearing it up, it's gone! It's cleaned *itself* up! Some say that other cockroaches have simply come and carried it away to have for their dinner but this is not true. Cockroaches are definitely bionic, they can rebuild themselves. If you put the shattered corpse of one in the bin, it will wait until you are gone and then slowly pull itself back together again, gluing on its head with its own horrid goo. Then, when it is ready, a born-again cockie, bigger, scarier and somehow managing to have more legs than it started off with, it will scuttle out, refreshed, from a mound of potato peelings making obscene gestures at you with its little cockroach fist.

Nothing is more deflating than being sneered at by a cockroach. It is said that cockroaches would survive a nuclear war better than anything. They would brush off fall-out like they brush off being smashed to bits with a shoe.

As Colin lay in bed, watching with distaste the phoenix of a new cockie rising out of the ruin of its dead self, it seemed to him eminently likely that in the barren aftermath of the final folly; when the poison winds blow cruelly over the rotting debris of us, the previous top dogs, cockroaches will inherit the earth. After all, they had clearly already inherited Carlton. Colin was thinking of charging them rent.

Perhaps, he thought, the government had been conducting secret nuclear tests and the holocaust had already come to Western Australia.

## POMMIE POSEUR

Colin was a pom. He'd lived in Oz since he was thirteen but that doesn't make any difference, if you're a pom, you're a pom. The Aussies have a strange double standard when it comes to poms. For instance, they are fairly happy to cheer Lady Di and have a Union Jack on their flag, but that doesn't stop most of them calling you a whingeing pommie wanker if you happen to remark that it's hot when the mercury's pushing 40 °C.

Colin did not care. However hot it was Colin always thought he was cool – small and cool. He was one of those rare people who try to be cool and somehow manage in the process to be a bit cool – not much, but a bit. He was so unashamed about his pretensions that they kind of worked. For instance, despite living in Oz, he managed to speak in an accent that was situated somewhere in the mid-Atlantic, half-way between Britain and the USA – having arrived at this location via some pretty groovy forties movies and some equally crucial rock lyrics. By rights this should have been horrible, marking Colin down as the worst kind of poseur, but it didn't. It almost did, but it didn't.

Probably it didn't because Colin wouldn't have minded being considered a poseur, in fact he would have thought

3

being called a poseur quite an interesting pose. Everybody poses, the coolest people pose most of all, they just make it seem natural. Colin had a picture on his damp patch of Brando in *The Wild One*, dressed in leather, leaning on his Triumph with a little peaked cap on his head, tilted to one side, looking slightly off-camera with an expression on his face that seemed to be saying: 'Listen, I may be sensitive, confused and inarticulate but I could still beat seventeen types of shit out of you, OK?' Now *that* was posing, but nobody minded because it was Brando. He remained cool, even though he was an utter poseur with a damp patch behind him.

It's all a question of confidence. Colin never had any money, but he acted like he was loaded. Poverty was always a temporary problem for Colin. His present period had lasted about twenty-five years.

His clothes were piss-poor but he wore them with aplomb. He would practise things like opening and lighting his Zippo lighter with just one hand and throwing cigarettes up in the air and catching them in his mouth. Strangely this did not make him look like a total wanker – it nearly did, but not quite. There was a tiny degree of charm in the way Colin accepted his many failures with the same easy confidence that he greeted his few successes. When Colin missed his mouth with the fag he acted the same as if he'd scored a hit. When he burned his thumb with the lighter he yelped with pain in a manner that suggested that pretty soon anyone who was anyone would be burning their fingers on Zippo's and yelping with pain. Colin's surname was Dobson. Being aware that James Dean would never have been cast in *'Rebel'* if his name had been Colin Dobson, Colin called himself CD. Since the advent of compact discs this had given Colin an opportunity to do his great joke about being perfect, clear and flawless. Astonishingly he managed to deliver this without sounding like the biggest dickhead in history. He came a very close second.

4

# BREAKFAST THOUGHTS

CD got out from under his grey duvet and lit a fag, he missed his mouth twice which delayed the evil moment of lighting up by about ten seconds. This was good, CD was trying to introduce a programme of starting later in the day and even ten seconds counted. His problem was he didn't want to give up, he really liked smoking, he was one of that ever dwindling group of people who still thought it looked cool. Like most committed smokers, he worried about it all the time. Unfortunately, whenever he found himself dwelling on the proven dangers of the weed he got so uptight he had to have a fag.

'Catch 22,' he would say, throwing one up towards his mouth. Which was ironic really because he probably hadn't caught twenty-two in his entire life.

As CD fished about in the dirty clothes bag for a pair of pants that had only been worn once, he thought his morning thoughts. He thought, as he thought every morning, that it was time to go to the launderette. He thought, as he always did, that it was time to get a new toothbrush. The bristles on his present one were flattened so far back that they were parted in the middle. He had a toothbrush that looked like the top of Oscar Wilde's head.

He hoped, as he always did, that the state of the exterior of the kettle did not reflect upon its internal cleanliness. Logic, of course, insists that the outside of a kettle is an entirely separate entity to the inside, but none the less the thick, greasy, dusty gunge that coated the whole thing was a bit disquieting.

Yet again, as CD wandered through to the kitchen, he tried to gather together the resolve to throw away all his crockery apart from one bowl and one dinner plate. It was, after all, nearly two months since he had done a proper wash-up, his life was a series of mini wash-ups. A plate in the evening for toast, a bowl in the morning for Weetabix. The rest of the pile just sat in the sink laying low his spirits whenever he looked at it. In a world crowded with tiny bummers there is little more depressing than an ancient sinkful of scummy washing-up.

Of course, CD conceded, the alternative to junking it would be to wash it all up, but what false hopes lay in that cheating dream? CD knew that doing the washing-up just meant a brief, transitory illusion. A cruel glimpse of an unattainable civilization where one plucked a mug or a plate at will from the tempting gleaming pile – squandered resources – and made each new coffee in a fresh cup. A paradise soon lost, and in an obscenely brief time, the pile is back, only this time it seems bigger, scummier, even more teetering.

CD considered himself an ecologically concerned person. And yet, like everybody else, he would sooner use a clean cup than wash up a dirty one.

There was a cocky struggling in the water, wriggling, what looked to be its last wriggle. Knowing cockies it probably had a set of scuba gear. CD stared at it in a morning trance, the dirty cockie in the dirty washing-up in the dirty little house that was owned by Sly Moorcock.

# DINNER IN LOS ANGELES

Sly Moorcock himself was feeling pretty elated. It had been years since he had genuinely appreciated any of the things that his enormous success had brought him. The thrill of acquiring and consuming had long since faded for Sly. He would never recapture those early joys and he knew it. None the less, as the car left the airport he was feeling good enough to at least enjoy the memory of them.

'Welcome to Los Angeles,' the chauffeur said, 'I believe you'll find we have some gorgeous weather laid on for you.'

Sly grabbed his chance, 'If I want a disc jockey, kid, I'll buy a radio station. Drive the car.' Sly grinned to himself, he had been acting like a rich, arrogant bastard for so many years now he'd forgotten how good it could feel.

Being rude is one of the principal hobbies of the wealthy. Not very rude, just a bit rude, constantly brusque and impatient, implying that one's own life is much more important than that of the person you are talking to. This attitude is at its most satisfying when applied to pretty girls at hotel receptions. Sly remembered nostalgically the warm masculine glow and the tremendous erection that had consumed him the first time he had really flexed his muscles in this manner.

'I'm sorry, Sir, but the room isn't ready yet, perhaps you would like to . . .'

'What I'd *like*, dear, is my room, *right* now, OK lovely? I don't care how you do it poppet, but do it. *You* may have time to polish your nails young lady, but I have a business to run.'

There was something monumentally saucy about a pretty girl in a prim little outfit, with her first name pinned to her tit,

7

hating you so bad that she'd like to kill you and not being able to do a thing about it. The same game could be played with some airline hostesses.

But on the whole those thrills were history for Sly. He had had to learn the hard way that the difference between being poor and not being poor is far greater than the difference between being rich and being stupidly rich. Being able to own a swimming pool is physical pleasure, being able to own hundreds of them is just an abstract idea. Sly had only one dick, only one stomach. There was only so much he could do for them, and yet each day he worked harder to get more of what he didn't need and couldn't use.

## EMPIRE-BUILDING

What fun it had been, back in the early seventies when Sly had done his first major deals. Then it had seemed to him that there was an almost frontier, empire-building spirit to his corporate battles. As if he too was using guts, balls and naked cunning to build a new Jerusalem, just like those early Aussie pioneers in their slouch hats and broken boots. How fondly he remembered the days when, with flares flapping round his ankles and kipper tie a foot across, he had lost a friend every time he picked up the phone.

Sly had been one of the very first corporate raiders. He had really been a part of developing the whole craft – or art form as Sly preferred to put it. Even twenty years later he often dwelt fondly on how amazingly clever he had been.

It had started in a pub. Sly was having a beer with an old friend from school and the old friend from school was very upset about his family pie-making business.

'We should never have moved into ham and cheese,' the old friend from school was saying, 'ham and cheese is a poof's pie. I told Dad, I said, "Dad, ham and cheese is a poof's pie. The great Australian bloke is not going to take kindly to having to build the best bloody country in the world on ham and cheese pie."'

'He wants meat,' sympathized Sly.

'Of course he wants meat,' the old friend from school said, 'you can't surf all day and root all night on ham and cheese.'

## EASY AS PIE

The meat pie plays a significant part in Australian culture. It is far and away that country's most popular snack, it fills the same place in their hearts and tums that fish and chips used to fill for the British. It is often referred to as a 'rats coffin' and the recipe has not changed since it was first discovered being used as part of the lining for Pandora's box. Consisting of pastry so greasy if you drop one on the floor it will stop the boards creaking, and a substance called 'meat' which is made of minced string in gravy.

This horrendous creation, taken almost obligatorily with a squirt of tomato sauce, is delicious. Delicious in a way that only truly awful, stupefyingly, unhealthy food can be. Delicious in a way that vegetables (or indeed anything that is good for you) can only dream of being. Hence it has so far withstood all efforts to ponce it up.

This had been Sly's old school-friend's dad's mistake. He had tried to ponce up the great Australian pie. He did not understand the most important rule of yummy snacks. That they are not yummy *despite* being so awful, they are yummy *because* they are so awful . . .

'It's not as if we put peas or carrots in them,' the old school-friend protested. But secretly he was ashamed, he knew that he and his father were in the wrong. Ham and cheese is a poof's pie.

'Not to worry, old school-friend,' said Sly, who always had trouble with people's names. 'Your dad's company's still in great nick, you're very big in doughnuts, you dominate the mock-cream fancies market, and your apple turnover, turnover is the fastest in WA. Christ almighty, heart disease is one of the biggest killers in Australia, that's a statistic you and your dad can be proud of.'

9

'Oh sure, no worries,' said the friend, 'I'm not saying we're in trouble, I mean in real terms the company's fine, but a cock-up like that hits your share confidence. Market-wise we're at a bit of a low ebb.' And that was when Sly had his brilliant idea.

The next day he quit his job as runner for the fast-growing Tyron Organization and went to his bank to borrow a lot of money. He had stumbled upon a fascinating situation, a healthy company with extremely valuable assets, which was temporarily depressed on the market. My, my, my said the spider to the fly.

On the strength of the information he had got from his old school-friend, Sly bought a majority holding in the friend's family firm at a bargain price and took over as boss. Now a lesser maverick than Sly might have stopped there, content to be the new head of a successful bakery. Remembering the incident only as a stern warning never to chat pies with pals. But Sly was destined to be more than a baker, he wanted to be a bastard. So he smashed the company up, flogging the Cream-Horn machine to one rival, the Viennese Twirl twirler to another. Before long there was nothing left of his old friend's family firm and Sly was sitting on the foothills of what would one day become a mountain of cash.

Sly soon realized that it did not take a ham and cheese debacle to render healthy companies temporarily vulnerable. So erratic is the stock-market that at a time of depressed trading, any concern, even a very successful one, can find itself laid open. Suddenly, the mere hard assets of a company, the carpets, the typewriters, the amusing stickers that say 'you don't have to be mad to work here but it helps', if sold off separately, can add up to a considerably greater value than the sum total of the share value quoted on the index.

The fact that these companies are going concerns that make things and create jobs, is entirely immaterial to the business of asset-stripping. This is scorched earth capitalism, you buy something, smash it up, flog the bits and move on. Then the predator, faced with the question of what to do with the money he or she has made, will probably do it all over again. Cutting a swathe through jobs and dreams, growing bigger and more destructive with every deal.

## GOLDEN BOY

An even more curious side to this strange way of making a living is the way in which it is regarded socially. Sly found himself lauded and held up as a role model to other young Australians. Far from being seen as a vandal whose job was destroying other people's jobs purely for personal gain, he was presented as someone who created work, bringing money into the state and helping to keep the wheels of commerce turning. His youthful good looks made him popular with all and he quickly found himself regarding women in the way he regarded companies: things to be used and discarded, he would take from them what he desired and move on. Astonishingly, this too won Sly not contempt and condemnation, but jovial respect. It seemed that not only was this man a brilliant operator, but also he was a hell of a lad to boot. Curiously, this side of things had become rather irritating for Sly. He liked power and it is quite difficult to experience power if all gives way before you. You can't push people round if they're already bending over backwards, it gets boring. Even the sex began to get on his nerves – even with people bending over backwards. Sly was a fantastically successful individual, but he could not be said to have had a fulfilling personal life.

## CITY OF ANGELS

And that's why it felt so good to feel good again. As Sly glided in from L A airport, minor irritations, like deep personal discontent, were forgotten. He had the thrill again. The thrill of being, irrationally, pointlessly and idiotically rich. He felt like he'd arrived, and the reason for this childlike elation was a dinner invitation. Silvester Moorcock had been invited to dinner.

Nothing very special about that of course, he'd had dinner before, often. Admittedly, this time he would be dining with some of the richest and most powerful men in the world, but once you've eaten smoked salmon mousse out of the bottom of a Penthouse Pet you have high standards as to what makes a meal swing.

It was not the invitation, but what the invitation represented that made Sly hug himself with excitement that night (normally he would have paid someone to do this for him, but he'd been in a hurry at the airport and anyway, it was a very private moment). Sly knew that he was about to be accepted into a club. An exclusive club. So exclusive a club in fact that it had no name and no membership list. It had no premises and you could not apply to join. A person simply drifted into membership having achieved the required qualifications. These qualifications being truly enormous wealth and the social conscience of a dog caught short on a croquet lawn. It was, and is of course, rare to find the former, without the latter.

The venue for the meal was unpretentious enough. A private room in a restaurant in Los Angeles. With certain obvious exceptions, the super-rich are a fairly faceless bunch and do not feel over-paranoid about going out in society, especially a society that provides itself with its own private police force, as Beverly Hills does.

If Los Angeles ever had a town planner, all the movie stars should club together and get him a guide dog. Whoever it was he must have designed the place while his brain was in a meeting. The town is a mess, worse than the suburbs of Perth, thought Sly as he limo'd through the streets. Streets that looked as if someone had dropped a load of buildings on either side and by coincidence they had all landed the right way up.

Los Angeles, like Sly's native Western Australia, suffered from too much space and too much sunshine. For years and years developers had simply spread out, leaving one shit heap and building another a hundred metres further on, creating hundreds of square miles of depressing, low-rise sprawl.

When the oil runs out LA will be completely finished as a city, millions will starve to death. For most people the nearest shop would be five or six hours walk away and, since in areas like Beverly Hills you quite literally get picked up by the law for walking, most people have forgotten how to do it.

Sly's limo purred up outside 'California Dreaming', a restaurant which made a virtue out of what it called its 'exclusive pricing policy'. The motto was, 'If you want to eat here, be prepared to sell your house.' The idea being to keep out scum and riff-raff. It didn't keep out scum and riff-raff of course, it just kept out people who did not have a ridiculous amount of money.

Probably about a twentieth of the world's ready cash was represented round the table that night so, not surprisingly, the food was good. Not good enough, of course; it would have been the same quality if only a twenty thousandth of the world's wealth had been present, or even, horrible thought, a twenty millionth.

This must be one of the principal blights on the horizon of the super-rich: the fact that luxury and quality is finite. Paying a million pounds for a meal would not make it worth a million pounds; it would not make it ten thousand times better than one that cost a hundred pounds; it would probably not even be twice as good. The earth only has so much bounty to offer and inventing ever larger and more notional prices for that bounty does not change its real value. One day, of course, if there is any justice, heaven will prove to be a store-house of new and unimagined luxuries. The guiltless will scoff great mounds of ambrosia, washing it down with jugfuls of nectar, but it is unlikely that any of the mega-mega-rich will be invited to that particular blow-out.

One presumes that billionaires are not stupid people, they cannot be unaware of the paradox of their great wealth. 'Just what am I working for!' they must shout rhetorically at their art collections, full of art which secretly they don't like. They

13

know the answer of course. They have long since exceeded any possibility of conventional satisfaction. They are working to fuck up the world for everyone else.

## THE CLUB

And so Sly joined the club, although club is far too small a word to describe it. For the first time Sly, now a bona fide billionaire bastard, was to take his place at a cabinet meeting of the World Government of Money – or convivial dinner party of like-minded colleagues as they would have preferred to put it. In his wanderings around the upper echelons of society, Sly had often heard hints and rumours regarding a shadowy super-elite, a group wielding almost incomprehensible power who were preparing some secret and terrible purpose. Now it seemed he was being asked to take part.

Of course it was not quorate, by no means all the billionaires who were in on the conspiracy were present. They were dotted about the world, joylessly going about their business of fucking things up for everyone else. Their presence was not essential, for the Government of Money is not like a conventional government. It has no debating chamber, nor specific list of representatives. No official documents guarantee its legality. Indeed, many of the people round the table would have strenuously denied that it was a government at all and perhaps even half-believed their denials. But it is a government, as powerful as any. An invisible, amorphous, multi-headed dictatorship of money.

And it had a plan.

As Sly entered the restaurant, thrilled and excited, he had no idea what that plan was, or where it was leading to. As it happened, it was leading to hell and beyond. Sly's life was about to change utterly. That evening he was to be indoctrinated into the Stark Conspiracy.

# FOR THOSE IN PERIL
# FROM THE SEA

Some characters in this narrative will loom large, being directly connected, either for or against the great conspiracy which Sly was to join that night. Others must come and go for they are only indirectly connected, but are no less a part of it for that. For the influence of Sly and people like him is impossible to calculate, their tentacles spread across the globe. Sly lived in Oz, he was eating in Los Angeles, but his money was everywhere. His bucks had assumed a life of their own, they were out there doing things of which Sly knew very little and cared even less. Just as long as they went forth and multiplied it was fine by him. His bucks were animals that he had let off the leash. They ran about the world in an uncontrolled frenzy, bursting into the lives of people that Sly would never meet nor think of.

For example, as Sly entered the restaurant in Los Angeles some of his money was floating off the coast of Britain. Of course Sly was aware that a few of his bucks had found a temporary home as a majority holding in a Belgian waste disposal group, his brokers always consulted him before making a share purchase. But what did that tell Sly? nothing about reality. Certainly Sly knew about the company's collateral, its profit and loss curve, its disposable assets, its history on industrial relations and the chances of an injection of public funds should it hit the skids. But that was all he knew. He saw his investment purely and simply as a device by which to make money. What the company actually did was a matter of supreme indifference to him.

He did not know about Captain Robertson; he did not know about the great toilet irony; he did not know about the Pastel family on holiday . . .

## BRASS IN MUCK

Captain Robertson was a sad and bitter man. All his life he had wanted to be master of a ship. And what sort of ship did he end up being master of? a sludger. Scarcely a dashing or romantic command.

'What do you do for a living mate?'

'I lug shit up the Thames and dump it in the North Sea.' Captain Robertson would occasionally try to cheer himself up. 'It's a rotten job but then people have to do toilet,' he would say to himself as yet another great steaming slick slid out of the bowels of his barge and began its slow journey back to Britain.

Of course he was right, people *do* have to do toilet. Even the most rabidly concerned environmentalist would be unlikely to volunteer to cork their bot. But it doesn't have to end up dumped virtually raw in the North Sea. It can in fact be processed and used as fertilizer. It could be re-eaten via a nice healthy cauliflower rather than a deformed fish. But perhaps this would be too long-winded a route by which people – like Sly's bucks – could go forth and multiply.

The situation is quite ironic really because people are normally so fastidious about their bathroom hygiene. They are happy to invest in a foaming blue-flush which, although costly, is guaranteed to produce a sparkling bowl and lemon-scented toilet freshness that the whole family will enjoy. However, anything that happens beyond the U-bend is somebody else's business.

## THE PASTEL FAMILY ON HOLIDAY

The Pastels had had a lovely day wandering around in the freezing rain and the whole family were getting peckish.

'Now then, kids,' said Mr Pastel, 'I'll tell you what we're

16

going to have for our tea ... Mussels, that's what, just like your mother and I had on our honeymoon.'

So they did, they had mussels and the whole family got the utter and total shits, because the mussels weren't just like on the honeymoon, since then the world had changed and the mussels with it.

Mussels and oysters feed by filtering tiny particles out of the sea water. These days that includes chemical wastes, agricultural poison and heavy metals. Also an awful lot of bacteria and viruses from human excreta, which cooking and cleaning does not always remove (cooking and cleaning the mussels that is, very few people cook and clean their excreta). Poor Mummy Pastel ended up with acute viral gastroenteritis and died, but we've all got to go sometime.

Sly didn't know Mrs Pastel, she didn't know him, but they were bound together in life and death by money.

# COURT, HIPPIES AND LOVE
# AT FIRST SIGHT

Anyway, back to CD who had just finished his Weetabix, well, finished the part he was going to eat. He was not a very good eater, especially when he was uptight and this morning was a bummer because he had to go to court, which for sure is the kind of thing to ruin a guy's day.

He took some care in selecting what to wear. He had a pretty minimal wardrobe, but you have to make the effort if you're appearing in court. After some thought he selected a pair of pretend Levis with a designer tear on the knee (he'd actually done it on a nail but in the world of being groovy you take your luck where you find it). He also wore his metal-tipped cowboy boots, an ace shirt which had metal tips on the collar, an ecologically sound tie with a picture of a steaming whale carcass on it and the slogan 'Stop the bloody whaling', and a sports jacket. CD still turned up the lapels of his sports jacket, even though no one else had done this since 1978. To this ensemble he added his droopy, mirrored shades.

I cannot see, CD thought to himself, eyeing his reflection in the broken wardrobe door he used for a mirror, any judge trying to deny that I am looking *good*, I mean *bitching*. Perhaps he couldn't see because he had his shades on.

However, whatever the judge thought of it, and however prejudicial the mirrored shades may have been to his sentence, CD was later to thank his lucky stars that he had elected to go to court strutting like an ace king of teenage cool, because it was at the court that he met Rachel. And when a

18

guy meets the girl of his dreams he should for def' be wearing his pretend torn Levis, metal-tipped boots and shades.

So love found CD at the Carlton Criminal Court. An unlikely location being as how the place was about as romantic as anal warts. The Old Bailey it was not, no ancient oak and dignity for the Carlo crim' processing plant, just veneered chipboard and nineteen-year-old coppers showing off.

CD hated young coppers. Getting busted by someone who could be your dad was one thing, but getting pushed around by a couple of teenage casuals was quite another. Older cops were all right on the whole. For a start they were bored with their jobs and wanted to get home for their tea. Also, their egos were sufficiently well-developed not to need massaging on every piss-poor little bust they made. The problem with some young coppers is that they're exactly the same as the blokes they're called upon to nick. Putting them in uniform doesn't make any difference.

It was CD's contempt for this type of cop, the smug, strutting, government sponsored juvenile delinquents, that got him the black eye.

'Just because you've got a big shiny uniform doesn't mean you've got a big shiny dick,' he had remarked casually to the walking zit who had collared him . . . and there he was, in the gutter going 'No, please, please, don't hit me again, please.'

CD's crime was to paint CND symbols in the middle of the road. The straight white lines were already there so it seemed silly not to complete the pattern. It wasn't the sort of thing CD was wont to do under normal circumstances. He was an intelligent bloke and he knew that this action would not reduce the nuclear arsenal by so much as one radioactive pea-shooter. What's more, he was extremely dubious as to the propaganda value of his protest. It was difficult to imagine an average punter walking along the street, seeing the symbols, slapping his forehead as if to say, how could I have been so blind and shouting 'of course, that's it! We must ban the bomb'. It just wasn't going to happen that way.

Although CD was unquestionably against the bomb, this

was not the reason for his crime. He had actually committed it because he was drunk and because he wanted to go to bed with the girl from the day-centre for peace studies, and painting tarmac was her idea of a romantic evening.

## KAREN THE HIPPY

'I really think it will be a valid statement,' this insanely deluded girl had whined. 'It will prove to people that there *is* an opposition, that they don't *have* to sit down and take it.'

Looking back on the whole incident, CD was at a loss to work out why he had conceived a desire for this monumentally stupid person. Thinking about it in retrospect he wouldn't have thought it could be done.

It wasn't that Karen was unattractive, she was very attractive in a wet kind of way. She had an immense mass of highly frizzed hair and was very tactile.

'He was sad and uptight and scared so I gave him a cuddle and I think it helped,' she would say with stupefying complacency. Karen was under the erroneous impression that she had a soothing, calming personality and was therefore an immense pillar of slightly mystical womanly strength to those who knew her.

Worse than that, she was one of that large group of men and women who are convinced that they can give massages, forcing them on any acquaintance who unwisely admits to anything from a slight headache to being about to attempt suicide. This type of 'massage' consists exclusively of grabbing the subject's shoulders from behind and kneading away as if making pastry. The idea being that every muscle in the subject's body instantly dissolves into a warm fluidity, releasing years of built-up twentieth century tension.

In reality the victim sits there, gritting their teeth, suppressing their fury and probably laying the groundwork for an enormous ulcer. Karen normally spoke in a kind of highly sincere, little girly voice that made you want to kill. It was meant to imply the pure simplicity of true knowledge and self-awareness. In fact it implied grounds for justifiable homicide.

'I think it would be really nice and pretty to have the peace group outside, away from man-made structures because I think that would be very ironic and apt.' Why were the people who wanted the right things usually such wankers? CD had thought when he met Karen. Surely it didn't have to be that way. If it did it definitely knackered any possibility of ever gaining mass popular support for anything.

CD thought back to the lads he had been at school with. He felt fairly confident that it would take something more convincing than the offer of a massage from Karen to turn them onto an alternative culture. The appropriation of radical thinking by lazy, self-obsessed hippies is a public relations disaster that could cost the earth.

CD met Karen at a benefit concert to support a women's peace camp situated outside some mysterious US communications installation up in the Northern Territory. This was a pretty good cause and he was there partly because he was happy to support it, but mainly he was there because he had worked behind the bar and it was twenty-five bucks. That particular gig was the easiest money CD had made in quite a while. It had been organized and published by Karen and people like Karen, hence for the first hour there was only them, CD and the band there. The hippies had spent so much time discussing whether sausage-rolls were offensive to non-meat-eaters they had forgotten to put their poster up in the community bookshop. Karen was fairly outraged.

'I really don't understand people, right?' she whined, 'I mean, it's *their* world, too, right?'

Later on eight people turned up and the banner fell down. It was hung up behind the band, a big picture of a skeleton in a US steel helmet.

'It's brilliant, isn't it,' Karen said as she hung it back up. 'Jill did it. If only more people could see it I'm sure they would understand better what we're trying to say.'

Finally Karen started the bopping. She did this after

spending half an hour wandering round saying, 'Why aren't people bopping? God, people are so boring.'

Four people danced, and watching them CD could scarcely keep his dinner down. He himself was no great dancer, but at least, he thought, I have the decency not to flaunt it.

CD considered ageing hippy dancing to be one of the most embarrassing forms of movement in the world. The problem is that the people involved see it as a form of self-expression rather than as a jolly thing to do. They believe this so strongly that they feel honour-bound to express themselves even when there is nothing to express – which is always. The result is that they hop slowly about the dance floor gyrating and waving their arms with an expression of concentration and delight on their faces. Matched only in intensity by the horror on the faces of anyone unfortunate enough to witness the revolting display.

None the less, as CD stood behind the bar sipping a beer, for some reason he conceived a horrid little desire to try and get a bit of a feel-up off the one in the middle whom he knew to be called Karen.

Maybe it was divine intervention because, of course, if he hadn't made his move he would never have got involved in the painting expedition, he would never have found himself in court for vandalism, and so he would not have met Rachel. God works in mysterious ways.

## COURT

The judge fined him a hundred and fifty bucks plus costs. This was an unexpectedly harsh blow. CD had reckoned on maybe seventy-five. Perhaps it was the tie. If you want a judge to like you, don't wear a picture of a filleted whale carcass to court. On the other hand, maybe it was CD suggesting that the judge should not come crying to him when he got nuked to bollocks and beyond. Maybe it was a combination of the two, plus the shades and the trousers and the boots. Some people would call CD plucky; most people would call him an utter pratt – either way he was undeniably prone to displays of pointless bravado which always made everything worse.

Whatever it was, the fine was a lot. Too much for CD who was, as always, terminally short of cash. He tried a desperate plea in mitigation. If all else fails, tell the truth . . .

'Your Majesty,' he said, trying to look honest, 'the truth of the matter is, I agree with you, painting symbols on the road was a pointless act of vandalism. But, can I level with you, your Highness?' CD attempted to make his tone ingratiatingly man to mannish. 'There was this chick, right? and she's a bit of a peace freak and I wanted to impress her so I could well . . . do the business, right? Anyway . . .'

CD's fine was increased to two hundred and fifty.


## FALLING IN LOVE WITH RACHEL

Rachel was up for a driving offence. She had some highly credible ancient old car, bright red with white-wall tyres, jacked-up rear suspension and reflecting glass on all the windows except the front one. It was a car that almost seemed to be pleading with the cops: 'pull me over, I must be doing *something* wrong'.

On this occasion it was thirty kilometres over the limit in a built-up area, plus a baldish offside rear tyre. Three demerits on a licence that was already feeling the strain. Mind you, it would have been worse had Rachel not made careful preparations.

Rachel was most striking to look at, a natural red-head with pale skin that led her to wear huge hats for eleven months of the year. It wasn't that she was particularly beautiful but she was vivacious, and those men that did fancy her fancied her a lot. Rachel was an all or nothing type of girl in her looks, her opinions and her car.

She had come to court in a smart two-piece suit borrowed from her mother. Her hair was an elaborate coiffure and she carried a brief-case. The whole ensemble was designed to suggest a serious-minded, conservative young woman for whom driving was essential. She looked like Margaret Thatcher and it clearly worked because she got off pretty lightly. On hearing her sentence Rachel thanked the judge and took her wig off. This wasn't to show off but because it was ninety in the shade. However, not surprisingly the judge totally did his nut and considered doing her for contempt. Reason returned when he caught the amused eye of the journo from the *Carlo Times*. He decided he could do without wigs becoming the basis for another debate on civil liberties. Like all judges, secretly this one wished he had lived in some earlier age. He just bet Judge Jeffries didn't have to deal with some cub hack plastering 'COME OFF IT JEFF, WHY DON'T YA!' across the front of two thousand advertising freebies. You couldn't win any more, thought the judge. What was the betting this little bitch could come up with some damn religion where wigs were compulsory for women up on driving offences.

Rachel walked free.

Situated just behind the court was a pub called the Dancing Cockatoo. This pub has a jolly sign which inevitably led the Aussies, with their natural wit, to call it the Pissed Parrot. It was here that most of the ne'er-do-wells, shop-lifters, peace freaks and prostitutes found themselves after their encounters with the fearful majesty of the law.

And it was to the Pissed Parrot that CD had gone to drown his sorrows and to wonder where he was going to raise two hundred and fifty bucks. Shortly after which, Rachel entered and ordered a gin and tonic. She was wondering about getting a less flamboyant car. Both of them had gone to court alone, neither of them needed their hands holding, and there they sat, alone.

Except that within the space of a casual glance CD was no longer alone. He was with Rachel, far away from the Pissed Parrot, walking hand-in-hand, laughing in the rain, having their first ever row about something silly and then making up in a variety of interesting positions and locations and then not being able to remember what the row had been about in the first place. He fancied this girl like mad, he fancied her purely and spiritually. This girl clearly oozed with character, intelligence and . . . lots of other things like that. This, CD knew, was what had captured his heart so suddenly. Obviously he desperately wanted to root her as well but, CD assured himself, that wasn't the only thing.

He *had* to make a move. Never would such a conversation opener exist again. They were fellow lags, joined by that invisible fellowship that unites the criminal fraternity. Comrades, forced together against a hostile world. Normally when you go up to a strange girl and try to start up a conversation, reflected CD, it's bloody obvious that you're making a play for them. But this was different. This time he had the perfect opener, plus endless opportunities for idle chatter, casually getting to know each other through their shared experiences under the majesty of the law. One thing CD was certain of, he resolved to be himself (whatever he thought that was). His recent experience of pretending to be a committed peace-nik had led him to near financial ruin and he hadn't even got a root. CD determined that this time there would be no lying or deceit, she would have to accept him for what he was.

'So you got done for trying to ban the bomb,' said Rachel from across the pub, 'I think that's really great.'

'What? Oh yeah.' CD replied, 'I'm a pretty committed peace-nik.' He was nothing if not adaptable.

Rachel was interested. 'I've been wondering about all that stuff myself,' she said. 'I used to go out with an American sailor, he was OK but his mates were real dags. Totally war obsessed.'

'Yeah well, maybe it's not their fault, it's all indoctrination isn't it?' said CD magnanimously.

'No way!' replied Rachel. 'People have to make their own decisions.'

'Oh yeah, that's true too,' conceded CD hurriedly.

'That's why I think what you did was good,' said Rachel, 'You have to decide what you're into, and go for it . . .'

This had always been Rachel's way. During her brief punk phase she had dyed her beautiful red hair mauve and her father had cried. She hadn't even wanted to do it much but what was the point of being a punk if you didn't dye your hair? CD's crime interested Rachel because it was self-expression for a purpose. For a long time she had been uncomfortably aware that she was wasting her time and that she didn't really care about anything. She was interested in someone who did.

CD, sadly, was, to coin a phrase, interested in one thing and he was desperately trying to think of a good line to edge him towards it . . . 'By the way, my name's CD. You look fantastic in that suit.' As he said it he knew it was a mistake. This girl was into peace, she was a thinker, he couldn't blagg her with cheap flattery. He might just as well have marched straight up and asked her to sleep with him.

'Sorry, what a stupid thing to say. I might just as well have marched right up and asked you to sleep with me.' What was he saying! If the suit line was a mistake, this was a disaster! Seldom had a chat-up situation been so ineptly handled. CD had to recoup the situation. Quickly he reminded himself that he was cool. He reminded himself that he was, after all, wearing cowboy boots with metal tips, pretend torn trousers and shades – a combination little short of sexual dynamite. He had started badly but all he needed to do was to stay cool and let his trousers do the talking.

'OK it's like this, I have just taken a pretty heavy rap for defending world peace and I'm confused. Now if you don't let me start again, swearing that you have forgotten all that has passed between us so far, I'm going to kill myself. The choice is yours.'

'It's a free country,' she said.

'Got her!!' thought CD, 'torn jeans, they can't resist it.'

# MORE DINNER IN LOS ANGELES

As Sly took his seat his sense of satisfaction had not left him, how could it? Now he was really at the very centre of everything that mattered. He had been accepted, accepted as a colleague – a colleague in a great conspiracy. But what was the plan? Sly had no idea for what secret and shadowy purpose the group had come together. Certainly to make money; colossal, unimaginable, utterly meaningless sums of money, of that he was certain. They were there to make money.

He was wrong.

But he had to wait to find out. For these slavering corporate predators prided themselves on being civilized. Business must wait until after dinner.

There were no menus at 'California Dreaming'. You ordered what you wanted. Sly, in a mood of jolly bravado, ordered swan. It had always intrigued him that in England apparently only royalty are allowed to eat swan. On this very special night Sly felt like a king himself and reckoned he deserved a slab of Her Maj's exclusive tucker.

The *maître d'* – a svelte figure who gracefully exuded that peculiarly Californian air of superiority that made one embarrassed that one was not oneself a homosexual – accepted Sly's order with a rather deflating matter-of-factness. His manner suggested that he rarely took orders for anything *but* swan. That tiny flick of his eyebrows seemed to say 'if just one more person asks me for swan I shall go and work for Col. Saunders'.

It's a strange thing about waiters, because while Sly could happily have faced down a corporate takeover bid from

Ghengis Khan, that one bloke's offhand acceptance of his magnificent self-indulgence made Sly feel like a piece of shit.

In the kitchen, the *maître d'* hastily consulted with the cook. They decided against pigeon because there was a good chance he'd recognize it. The same reason ruled out grouse. Eventually the chef had a brain-wave and slaughtered the cat. Poor Tiddles yielded a goodish portion of tough, light brown meat which the chef pan-fried in garlic butter and mushrooms. A lady guest in the public section of the restaurant had arrived in a beautiful coat layered with hundreds of ostrich feathers. A couple of these discreetly pruned, plus a duck's beak, completed the picture and Sly was duly served his swan.

'To tell you the truth it tastes worse than a dead cat,' said Sly in reply to the polite enquiry from his neighbour.

As it happened, the talk about the table was far too interesting for Sly to worry overmuch about what he was eating. Conversation normally bored Sly, he always felt like he knew what people were going to say. This made him very irritating to talk to as he never let anyone finish a sentence. He would normally say 'Yeah, yeah, yeah, yeah, yeah' at machine gun speed within five seconds of anybody saying anything. This, of course, meant that Sly never learnt anything. If somebody were to shout at Sly, 'Sly, the building we are standing in is on fire' Sly would probably say, 'Yeah, yeah, yeah' and burn to death.

That evening, however, Sly did not feel his usual need to forcibly stamp his personality on the gathering. He did not do his normal thing of wriggling with discomfort until he was able to prise open an opportunity to say something wry, witty, pithy or tough, just to show everyone what an impressive bloke he was. For instance, he never felt happy at major political dinners until he had contradicted the Prime Minister. It didn't matter what he said, just as long as he scored a point. His proudest moment to date had come at a dinner party in Canberra, when the Prime Minister, commenting on the

28

primitive Australian economy, had said: 'Us Aussies are still riding on the sheep's back.'

Quick as a flash Sly responded, 'You stick it in what you like Bob, just leaves more birds for the rest of us.' This had got a huge laugh and firmly established in Sly's mind the idea that he should go into politics. He was, in his own opinion, a top-class racon-fucking-teur.

But that night at 'California Dreaming' Sly was definitely prepared to sit quiet and listen. After all, these were not politicos – vain little scumbags with a small talent for middle management. The men Sly was facing (for there were no women at the dinner) were men of real power: power that would last. What did they want? What were they doing dining together? When would he learn of the great plan, whatever it might be? Perhaps the unofficial chair of the evening sensed Sly's tension for, as the coffee came round, he made the introductions.

## ATTILA THE HAMBURGER SALESMAN

'Gentlemen, few of you have had the opportunity to meet our Australian friend socially,' said the fat, affable American who had recently sold his eighty billionth hamburger. 'Although,' he added chuckling, 'he's burnt a few of your asses in the futures market.'

Sly flushed with pride, it is very rare that the mega-rich receive genuine praise. If you crap on people for a living you can't really expect a great many heart-felt tributes to come your way. So it was particularly gratifying that this important and brilliant man should treat him with such friendly esteem.

And Tex Slampacker *was* a brilliant man. His insight into the human soul had made his hamburger marketing uncannily successful. He had elevated the manipulation of people through retail outlets into an art form. It was said of Slampacker that he could sell shit if he wanted to, which was, of course, exactly what he did.

His outlets are the same all across the world, identical in

every detail. Frontier forts of an occupying army riding rough-shod over the myriad ancient cultures that they have colonized; sneering at the quirky individualism of their subject races; laughing at those who waste time considering choice and variety when they could be making money. From the deepest depths of Islam to the heart of Christendom, the Slampacker invasion is complete. Napoleon couldn't hold Moscow but Slampacker could and did.

Richard the Lionheart was halted long before he saw the gates of Jerusalem; Slampacker just walked right in without a fight. Life-styles and customs that had stood for centuries, fiercely resisting the attempts of foreign powers to subvert them, had fallen to Slampacker in a decade.

Tex Slampacker knew no French (except of course the words franc and centime) but had he known any, the phrase *vive la différence* would have completely mystified him.

## COMING TO THE POINT

'Let me fill Mr Moorcock in on our principal concerns at this point in time, gentlemen,' said the burger king, 'because, as you are all well aware, the day is fast approaching when action must be taken and we are very much hoping that Mr Moorcock will be joining us in our endeavours.' As Tex Slampacker rose to speak Sly felt an incredible expectant thrill. More than ever now, the enormous potential of the evening hit him. Here he was amongst the very biggest players in the world, the Yanks, the Japs, the Arabs ... Clearly something was afoot and he, Sly Moorcock, the Aussie street kid made good, was to be a part of it. Countless billions must be involved, the power and influence that sort of money represented was mind-boggling. It must be global, that was obvious thought Sly feverishly as Slampacker wiped his brow. God knew what ... What the hell were they planning to do ...? Buy the Society Union, maybe that was it!! Christ this lot could afford it, *and* make it pay.

Suddenly Sly was sweating. Brief-cases and computer

terminals had appeared on the table. Shadowy figures materialized from nowhere to guard the doors ... The situation was colossal, the potential for profit beyond computation ... Slampacker, the first man ever to make a million dollars in under five seconds was addressing them all for *his* benefit! The utter strangeness of the situation almost enveloped Sly. All these predators, all these mavericks, men dedicated to personal and individual gain, joined together in one room! Conspiring! What could it possibly be about?

'Gentlemen,' said Slampacker. 'Fourteen individual species of butterfly have become extinct since this meal began.'

There was a significant pause during which Sly tried to work out what he presumed was some tortuous Yankee metaphor. It wasn't. Sly could scarcely believe his ears but Slampacker, a gung-ho, hard as nails mega-cynic, began to talk like some kind of damn hippy. He spoke of the ozone layer. He spoke of the greenhouse effect. He dwelt at great, and what Sly considered unnecessary, length on the various types of waste that are floating about in the world's water system. He seemed particularly concerned about trees. Slampacker, a man whose never-ending need for beef pasture had made him responsible for cutting down more trees than all the shipbuilders, furniture-makers and carpenters in history put together, spoke with dull passion on the subject of the destruction of the forests.

Sly itched to shout 'who gives a fuck' at him, but the atmosphere was wrong, people were listening and, to Sly's astonishment, they looked scared. Eventually, to Sly's relief, one or two around the table began to shift about a bit and fidget.

'Good,' thought Sly, 'somebody's going to tell the fat old bastard to save his hang-ups for his shrink.'

But, to Sly's further aggravation, those who wished to chip in clearly wished to do so because they felt that Slampacker was not pitching the case strongly enough. Various world-class money men, men who Sly would have bet a chain of breweries cared more about hair restoration than reforestation, started to whine about the death of trees. And it wasn't just trees either. They were worried about a mystery virus that had made an eighth of the world's moles impotent for Christ's sake! One fellow seemed to be almost pervertedly interested in a mystery fungus that had appeared under the wings of sea birds.

Sly squirmed with annoyance. All the way from WA to hear some arsehole waffle on about a gull's armpits? Somebody's going to skin up a doobie in a minute and they'll all start singing 'Blowing in the Wind', he reflected bitterly. Bottling up his boredom and disappointment Sly sat waiting for a moment when he could decently take his leave.

# LOVE AND CONFUSION

Of course, if Sly thought he was experiencing frustration, he should have tried sitting in CD's trousers.

CD was definitely surprised. He had thought he'd been in love before but clearly he hadn't. Nothing he had experienced so far in life had prepared him for the gutful of emotions he had been at the mercy of since that moment at the Pissed Parrot. It was extraordinary. At first he thought he must be ill.

CD could not understand it, all that stuff that claims to be about love; mushy stories; wet songs; unpleasant childlike cartoon figures holding hands and saying, 'Love is doing the washing-up even when it's not your turn'. These things CD now discovered had absolutely nothing whatsoever to do with love as he was currently experiencing it. In the world of pulp publishing, pop charts and greeting cards, even when love hurts it usually hurts in a nice and tasteful way; yearning glances; attractive anguish and broken hearts. The truth is, it's a pain in the guts.

And that was another thing. Why is it that the heart has been singled out as the seat of all emotions? OK so it occasionally misses a beat, but what's that compared to the long sleepless hours of dull stomach ache? The guts are unquestionably the seat of the emotions, that's where CD felt the pain. But of course it wouldn't look so good on the Valentine cards; eight feet of small intestine with an arrow through it or a cute little cartoon figure feeling queazy and saying 'Love is wanting to go to the lavatory'.

CD had been prepared by countless juke boxes to feel exhilarated, tearful, turned on by love, he certainly had not expected to feel sick. It was as if he had gone mad. He was acting in a way that he despised himself for. It was fifteen years since he had tried his hand at poetry. He had thought that shameful, inexcusable episode in his life was over and forgotten forever. There is absolutely no excuse for amateur poetry writing, it should be against the law. Teenagers, CD reluctantly accepted, should be allowed a brief foray into this repulsive, self-indulgent activity. After all, every kid in the world goes through a period when they are under the impression that they are the only person who has ever suffered, the only person who has ever really truly understood confusion and rejection, and exam revision and acne. Obviously this horrid time needs an outlet other than vandalism and hence, while it lasts, every kid is clearly entitled to pen the occasional teen-anguished epic. But these should be decently burnt within a year and the habit soon dropped. At the age of fifteen CD had decided to ditch poetry to leave more time for masturbation and had never had cause to regret the decision.

But now what had happened? Here he was trying to find a rhyme for 'Rachel' and coming up with 'bagel'. Sitting there, alone, his eyes prickling, his guts churning, trying to write something that should it ever get out would force him to commit suicide out of sheer embarrassment.

And this was not the only alarming symptom. Everything was changing, CD was definitely not the same person he had been a week before. Conversations had become a means to bring the subject round to how much he loved this girl. He didn't want to do it, it just seemed to happen.

'Are you going to watch the footie then, CD?'

'Yeah, maybe, you know I've met this girl called Rachel. I think she'd like footie. She's an extraordinary girl, you know I really think I'm in love and I don't know whether to be happy or sad or what.'

He felt an absurd affection, even loyalty, for Carlo Criminal Court, where he had first set eyes on her. He had bought a copy of 'Money for Nothing' which had been on the juke box in the Pissed Parrot when he had tried to make conversation. It was ridiculous but when he played it, which was often, he always felt he had to listen to the very end or somehow he was letting her down. She would never know, and she certainly wouldn't care, but he still had to listen to every bloody note.

It was so weird he had only met her on a couple of occasions and yet now he thought about her literally all the time, constructing little fantasies to himself as he wandered about. Lacking almost any knowledge of Rachel at all he filled in the gaps himself. Sometimes she was Doris Day, a happy little housewife with whom CD would share the domestic chores and construct a normal life. In this dream he even had a proper job and kids were on the way. She was chirpy, devoted and, of course, insatiably saucy. Other times she was a tough, committed alternative woman intellectually brilliant, artistically innovative, courageous, combative and, of course, insatiably saucy.

These fantasy characters bore no relation to the real Rachel and, of course, they did not need to for CD had fallen in love with her whatever she was really like and it only remained to discover what he had let himself in for. This was one thing CD did know about love: it can happen regardless of personality. How often had he noticed couples who seemed totally mismatched struggling through their lives together. Couples that made you say 'I never would have thought he was her type', and yet there they were, a Zen Buddhist and a female mud-wrestler applying for a mortgage and looking at curtain material. CD was discovering now for himself that love is not logical. He didn't know anything about Rachel, why was he so certain that she was perfect? And why when, as he knew he must, he discovered that she was not perfect, did he know he would forgive her? Clearly because love hates logic, it cannot be planned, it cannot be created and it cannot be stopped. It will, at all times, do its own thing like a hippy on the dance floor or a back-packer's bottom when it gets to India. One thing was clear, if there's a part of the body less involved with love than the heart, it is the head.

This is why CD was in such a state of disarray. He was a cleverish, cynical person, and he was out of control. Captain Love had taken command of the ship and CD was heading for the rocks.

Clearly it was time to form a plan. CD could not go on listening to 'Money for Nothing' and having trouble with his bowels for ever. He had seen Rachel once since the encounter at the Pissed Parrot and it had not been a conspicuous success. All he had done was crack jokes and try to catch another tantalizing glimpse through the tiny gap that gaped between the second and third buttons of her blouse. One of the great male delusions is the belief that girls are unaware when they are being ogled. No one has ever managed to discreetly eye a cleavage. You might as well put out bunting saying 'I am getting a stiffy'. On the other hand taking a sneak peak doesn't necessarily mean that the peeker is falling in love. Blokes do it on instinct. So despite being acutely conscious of his staring, Rachel remained unaware of the immense turmoil that she was causing in CD's stomach and in his trousers.

Poor CD. Most girls suffer the subliminal harrassment of being ogled in silence but Rachel was made of sterner stuff. She could handle the embarrassment of confrontation.

'Stop staring at my boobs!' she had snapped and CD had never felt so mortified in all his life. For the rest of the evening he had been in danger of cricking his neck in his efforts to demonstrate that he was staring at the ceiling.

But, CD was an optimist, he reckoned that there were grounds for hope, after all, they already had quite an intense relationship. So far Rachel had embarrassed him, made him feel sick and turned him into a bore, there was certainly an emotional bond developing which he felt he could build on. What he needed was a plan.

## A PLAN(ISH)

CD decided to pull himself together and concentrate. It was clear to him that a degree of serendipity was going to be required to nudge along the essential process of wooing the gorgeous Rachel. This was obvious from one glance at the differentials. She was a love goddess; she was the font from which all beauty flowed; she was a sexual weapons system waiting for a crazy man to push her button – and he was a pratt.

Playing an honest hand CD was destined for disaster on the courtship front, so he was going to have to lie. He recalled that at their first meeting at the Pissed Parrot, Rachel had expressed interest in his bullshit about peace freak connections. So a committed 'citizen of the world' approach seemed to be the clearest route up her dress. This was fine as far as CD was concerned. He did not care who he pretended to be. He was so obsessively hot for Rachel's action that he would have gone on a diet and claimed to be Mother Theresa if it had promised even the chance of a feel-up.

As it happened there would be no element of hypocrisy in the little charade CD was planning that could besmirch the purity of his horrendous horniness. CD was hip to all the principles held dear by the peace lot, he just felt that clothes-wise a small thermonuclear blast would definitely improve their appearance. After all, there isn't really much you can do with a tie-dye T-shirt except atomize it into oblivion so that it may never return to offend the eye.

Reflecting on these reflections, CD determined that if he had to play a bit of a hippy, it would at least be a tastily dressed one. He would show Rachel that a concern for the future of the planet and crucial threads were not mutually exclusive. It was possible to desire peace on earth and not look like you'd been dragged through a puddle on the way to a jumble sale. Who could tell, maybe besides making Rachel his own for all eternity he would do those hippies some good!

As he dressed, CD stared out of the window to the place where Dave used to play when CD had first come to live in his little duplex. CD didn't know Dave. Dave was not destined to play any part in the story of Stark. In fact he was already dead. But his story is connected, as all stories are. He

37

was, like CD and Rachel and poor Mrs Pastel, a tiny piece of the same giant jigsaw; a bit player in the same titanic tragedy for which Stark believed itself to have a solution.

# DAVE AND BILL: AN
# INVOLUNTARY KILLING

Dave was killed by Bill.

They never even met, but Bill killed Dave as surely as if he'd shot him in the skull. Obviously Bill never meant to do it, but few of the terrible things done in the world are meant.

## DULL

It happened this way. Bill had given his life to nylon – he was very into nylon. Some people are into leather or PVC, Bill was into nylon. Not wearing it, you understand, or stretching it tight across the buttocks of a close friend and popping his thumb through at the point of least resistance. It was the structure of nylon which fascinated Bill. It needs a special type of person to be seriously into hydrocarbons. Basically you need to be very dull. Not dull in the way that is normally classed as dull, the sports bore or the person who reads the books about the SAS that you can buy reduced at station bookstalls . . .

'Oh yes, it's the most rigorous training in the world. Apparently they were put on full standby red-alert mode maximum kill facility alert, the moment the Home Secretary got the news.'

Much duller than that, dull to the point where it is almost a creative act. Those who met Bill often wondered if they were missing something . . . 'I suppose I'm very stupid,' they would say, 'but I really don't see the fascination.'

Any single-mindedness is obviously in danger of being dull.

Single-mindedness about something that is already dull is clearly double dull. The problem is that a dull person remorselessly pursuing a dull idea can appear a bit like a clever and inspired person who can see something that others can not. The well-adjusted observer begins to doubt his or her critical faculties and asks if perhaps there might not be something in it after all. This can be a bit worrying in the case of the various political and religious maniacs who want everyone to think the way they do. But in Bill's case, it was not worrying, just very very dull.

If you went for a drink with Bill he would somehow work the conversation round to carbon research. His only other skill besides carbon research was working the conversation round to carbon research and, it has to be said, he was pretty good at it.

'Fancy a drink, Bill?'

'I'd rather do a bit of carbon research.'

But Bill was all right, he bored people but he didn't eat them. The world and its spouse had no reason to regret Bill's birth. Not, that is, until he killed Dave.

The chain of events that put Bill on the path to murder started right back when he was at school. He was a total and utter fart as a kid, thin, farty and dull, dull, dull. The sort of kid who was 'really incredibly into science' and used this as a substitute for a personality. Every class has a couple. They take great pride in carrying sciencey things in the pockets of their blazers. Electrical screwdrivers, conversion tables, bits of wire. Their conversation is monumentally dull because they feel the need to announce their scientific obsessions in even the most commonplace sentences. If they did not do this they would cease to exist and be marked absent on the register.

'Is that your chair, Jenkins?'

'Specifically and fundamentally,' replies Jenkins, 'you would not be a hundred and eighty degrees off in presuming the affirmative.' And then Jenkins would look pleased and slightly embarrassed as if having delivered rather a good joke.

Bill and his ilk are awkward kids; always grinning and

40

getting taller. They go around at break-time offering to prove by equation that one and one equals three, but then get it all wrong.

As they grow older these people get into Deep Purple and Bowie and grow their hair in greasy mops. They start drinking cider and blackcurrant and go to university and say things like: 'Last night we got what I believe is technically described as rat-arsed.'

Inevitably, as a recreational subsection of their dullness, they become Real Ale bores and they are the most boring of all Real Ale bores because they can tell you the specific gravity of the beer they are drinking. Worse, they know what specific gravity is.

Such a fellow killed Dave.

Dave, who was not remotely boring and, were you lucky enough to meet him, would keep you enthralled for hours. Not that that makes any difference to the crime. If Dave had killed Bill it would have been just as wrong, but he didn't. Bill killed Dave.

## THE SUBLIME AND THE RIDICULOUS

Bill was actually pretty bright. Whereas most science farties end up as computer programmers, he was destined for bigger things. He took three pure science 'A' levels and went to university determined to get into nylon. It was in the middle of Bill's second year – during his brief dissolute phase, when he seemed to be paying more attention to the Silly Buggers Society than to nylon – that Dave was born.

On the same night that Bill tried gamely to walk the length of the student union bar with a full half-pint of Real Ale balanced on his head and a radish up his arse, at the same moment, far away, Dave drew his first breath. Talk about the sublime and the ridiculous.

Ironically it was also that evening, the evening bloody murder began to creep slowly into Bill's life, that he found love. The killer met his moll. He met her upstairs at the student union, in the smaller Bistro Bar – so called because you could buy wine there. Her name was Jane and Bill boldly asked to sit beside her, remembering too late to remove the radish. Jane had witnessed his earlier cavortings and pretended to be totally contemptuous of them, but really she thought the whole thing pretty exciting stuff. This was because Jane was nearly as dull as Bill – her idea of a rave was a Cadbury's Creme Egg. She thought Bill sophisticated and a proper hoot. So worldly and romantic with his extensive knowledge of early Bowie and nylon and the future calendar of the Silly Buggers Soc': 'We're going to dress up in girls' nighties and push a double bed up the High Street to raise money for cancer.'

And so it was that on the night Bill got his first ever girlfriend – a night of fumbling and snogging and that triumphant feeling of having grown up – on that night of all nights, Dave was born and Dave was doomed. Bill the nice, dull, git with the brand new, dull, bossy girlfriend, was to be his nemesis. There would be a terrible bloody murder; a frenzy of panic, agony and desperate violence, a moment's shocked disbelief and it would be over. Dave was twenty-one years younger than Bill. It's hard to say why but somehow this made what happened all the sadder.

## MODERN BIRTH

These days giving birth underwater is very fashionable, middle-class mums will travel to France and spend a fortune so that some hippy French doctor can grab them by the tits in the shallow end of a school swimming pool. The theory seems to be that the warm water is highly reminiscent of the womb, so you drop your sprog in the pool to comfort it. Of course, your average womb hasn't normally had a class full of little boys pissing in it a few hours earlier and the acoustics of a cold meat storehouse. Also few wombs are lined with luminous white tiles and administered by a bloke who's a dead spit of Adolf Hitler, except for the mop and bucket.

None the less, apparently the awesome transition from Mum's tum to big bad world is less traumatic if done via the local baths.

Dave's family had been giving birth underwater for generations. But not for them the sanitized safety of a whirlpool bath and a French quack with a degree in being groovy. There were no doctors present at this birth, just two midwives, not professionals, friends, but friends who had done it before lots of times. There wouldn't be a problem. No birth is easy but as they go this one wasn't too bad. Dave's mum heaved and strained, the midwives coaxed and prodded about a bit to help ease him out and eventually he came, breech born, head last, but in perfect nick. The umbilical cord was broken pretty sharpish, as is necessary, and the midwives swam Dave to the surface in order that he might take his first breath. This is how dolphins are born.

## DEATH OF A STRANGER

Very little is known about dolphins – by humans that is, probably dolphins themselves know a little more. However, enough can certainly be guessed at for them to be raised far above the level of 'dumb animal'. Their intelligence, ability to communicate and social interaction are so clear that it seems reasonable to assume that they also possess personalities, feelings and emotions. Despite the genocide that has been wreaked upon them, they still seem to bear humanity no ill will. In fact, there are countless stories of dolphins aiding humans in distress. Documented instances of them warding off sharks at their own personal risk and also of nudging the unconscious survivors of shipwrecks to the shore. These, like the practise of midwifery, are not fanciful human inventions but the facts regarding another race of beings.

One day Dave was swimming about minding his own business, when he was caught in a fishing net which, despite possessing a phenomenally sophisticated sonar system, he had not noticed. After a brief and desperate period of thrashing about helplessly, Dave drowned, unable to get to the surface for the oxygen he required.

The net was made of a revolutionary new nylon that is lighter and stronger than previous nets. It is also undetectable by dolphin radar. Bill had been pleased with the development. He had been a crucial cog in the research team that had come up with a very slightly more efficient and profitable way of going fishing. You can't stop progress and, after all, it's only a few dolphins.

# THE PURSUIT OF LOVE.
# THE DINNER GOES ON

### DREAM DATE

He picked Rachel up in a cab. CD did not drive and Rachel wanted to drink. The memory of her recent bust and straining licence was fresh in her mind and she was taking no risks.

CD was wearing a cream three-piece suit, wide lapels and slightly flared trousers. Flares keep threatening to make a comeback and so to CD's mind he looked five minutes ahead of the next fashion, rather than ten years behind the last one. CD was a true optimist.

He had added a CND stud earring for style, also to confirm his character as a committed activist and finally because he believed it made him look swarthy and romantic. His aftershave was seriously whiffy and the cowboy boots, newly polished (right round to the heels as well) were a walking dream.

'CD,' he said to himself as he contemplated his reflection in the broken wardrobe door, 'you are a love rocket, primed, charged and already requesting flight clearance from mission control.' He was, indeed, a true optimist.

When Rachel opened the door CD nearly lost his cool and blasted off there and then. She was orgasmic! Sauciness beyond his wildest dreams! – and CD had had some pretty wild dreams. She had on a little black cocktail number and the baddest suede, pointy, red shoes you ever saw. CD nearly flipped when he noticed they too had metal tips. Was this a sign? Of course it was; they were as one. Rachel wore nothing else, no jacket, no tights, it was a real hot night and it was getting hotter by degrees as CD's mercury threatened to burst out of the top of his tube.

'No rush, the guy's meter's running,' said CD who was in much the same position himself.

'I'm ready,' replied Rachel.

CD nearly fell over – down boy, down! This was more than he had dared hope for! What sort of phrase was that to use at eight-thirty! The temptress, the teasing, taunting, tempting sauce bucket! Clearly she wanted him, that much was obvious, wanted him badly. 'I'm ready,' she had said . . . God that was fast work, this lady wanted it *all* and she wanted it *now*. Why else would she put it that way? She could have said anything . . . she could have said . . . uhm 'we can leave immediately' or . . . well anything, but no, she said 'I'm ready.' Said it? she *breathed* it. If that wasn't the old green light to oblivion thought CD, he was a stupid wanker. And, of course, he was right. It wasn't and he was.


## TURNING GREEN IN LA

It was, without doubt, the longest dinner it had ever been Sly's misfortune to attend.

Festel had begun to speak, the head of a Norwegian chemical consortium. Here was a man with a monumental contempt for the common good. A man proud of his record that despite the numerous compensation claims that resulted from him putting poorly tested drugs on the market he had never paid out a single penny. He remained oblivious to the anguish of gangs of mothers holding up babies with no legs or torsos.

It was widely believed that Festel had personally arranged the framing and imprisonment of an employee who had threatened to expose the way his company rushed drugs onto the market. And yet, to Sly's astonishment and anger, this same man suddenly seemed to have turned into a sort of wood-nymph, Pan-like figure, desperately concerned for the pastoral balance of the planet. He pointed out that fifteen million trees were felled every twenty-four hours in India alone. The resulting soil erosion was almost visibly creating deserts. What was more, without the forests there was a terrible danger of catastrophic flash-flooding.

India? Sly was at a loss to understand why he had flown all the way to L A to whine on about trees in India . . . Bastard probably owns property in Delhi, he thought.

Trunk spoke next. Trunk was a car man. He had been a colossus in motoring for over thirty years. Hence few had been closer to the vanguard in the battle against legislation on lead-free motoring than he. Trunk had fought it tooth and nail, lobbying politicians, obstructing research, deliberately encouraging his own technicians to distort their findings in order to produce ambiguous results. This, despite being well aware all along of the terrible toll that lead emissions take on growing bodies and minds. Trunk's motive in all this had been the fear that other manufacturers might not take on the cost of the retooling required and of the slightly more sophisticated engines. He could be left on his own with the other bastards selling slightly cheaper cars. Rather than risk this, he had tried to stop the whole idea. This was the metal of the man Sly now heard bleating on about sneezing seals and how some damn mammal or other was choking on its own phlegm.

Sly knew all this, he read his Sunday colour supplements, everybody knew about pollution, so what? One thing was for sure, if he had come half-way round the world to be asked to join some damn top-snob, green charity whinge for tax loss purposes, he would tell them to stuff it up their arseholes.

Lord Playing, the British tobacco giant, spoke up. Here was a man who was presently denying, on his mother's grave, that his company had been sure about the connection between tobacco and lung cancer since the mid-fifties. Denying that he had personally suppressed the findings and harrassed independent researchers. But now this same cynical man was shouting down Festel claiming that it was the salination caused by the rise in the water-tables that was the most terrifying aspect of the death of the forests.

'And where is the oxygen to come from, without trees?' the tobacco king added.

The whole evening sounded more like a gaggle of green Euro MPs having a whinge than a cabinet meeting of the World Government of Money. It wasn't that Sly disapproved of worrying about the environment – he didn't like having to swim round clusters of old rubber johnnies when he went for a dip in the sea, any more than the next fellow. But what had it got to do with *them*? Jesus, if they wanted a donation why hadn't they written to him? Sly was no longer simply disappointed, he was angry. If there was one thing Sly couldn't stand it was whingers.


## A QUESTION OF PRINCIPLE

In the cab Rachel had asked if CD was a vegetarian. It was a very tricky moment. What to reply? CD loved meat, his idea of vegetables was tomato ketchup. He was the sort of bloke who reckons not fishing out the bit of gherkin in your hamburger counts as eating your greens. But what did Rachel think? Was she a veggie? She was into peace, but that wasn't conclusive. Jesus had been into peace but he never said anything about having to eat rabbit food or multi-grain when you fancied a hot dog. What should he say? People were very touchy on this subject. If he said no would she throw red paint over him and say she refused to share the same cab as a murderer? Those animal rights activists did not mess around. He didn't want the first time Rachel visited his place to be when she came round to put dog shit through his letter box. CD knew these people. Once, at a folk concert, he left his jacket on a seat and some bastard had written on it in lipstick: 'There used to be a dumb animal inside this leather jacket. There still is.' The annoying thing had been it was only imitation leather. Served him right for going to a folk concert of course.

But, how to answer? Maybe she wasn't a true fanatic, maybe she was a conscience-stricken would-be veg, that was worse. That would mean a mind-numbing, tedious six-hour discussion on degrees of personal responsibility.

'Well, I'm prepared to wear leather shoes but I wouldn't personally harpoon a whale.'

'I'm *basically* a vegetarian, it's just I get this *craving* for half a pound of bacon every morning.'

There were so many opinions on the subject, so many chasmic pitfalls to be circumnavigated. It's all a question of degrees. Some people are quite happy to eat a raw chicken stuffed with a couple of shoals of fish but consider it an offence against God to toy with a chop. Others would eat anything, great steaks dripping with blood, raw suchi, sausages, bloater, black pudding, haggis, unwary family pets, anything, and yet would call the police if they caught you even considering veal.

'You know how they make it don't you? They tear the baby cow foetus from the mother then artificially fatten it by feeding it napalm and electrocute its testicles to make the meat whiter, then cut its head off and stuff it up its arsehole *while it's still alive*!!!!'

People just take their pick on the subject of vegginess, draw their line where they feel like it. It's not about conventional morals. Hitler, after all was a veggie, but he didn't mind cooking Jews. There is absolutely no logic on the subject, but you cross people at your peril.

'Are you a vegetarian?' she had said it so simply, so casually, as if it was of no consequence.

No consequence! Ha! As CD squirmed and writhed and desperately tried to compute the chances of various answers being acceptable, he knew that his entire sex life could be hanging on his reply.

'Because I fancy a hamburger,' Rachel continued.

He could have kissed her.

Neither of them had much money and there was only an hour until the film and so they decided to dine at

Slampackers. They did this knowing that it would probably make them feel sick, knowing that the stuff had much the same effect on the complexion as napalm had on North Vietnam and also knowing that it was absolutely delicious and they could just fancy one.

## CRUSHED IGUANA

They studied the enticing menu, with its dazzling array of choices. Cheeseburger, cheeseburger with salad and sauce, double cheeseburger with twice the salad and twice the sauce. Curiously there was no Iguana or fruit-fly on the menu. No open-ended list of as yet undiscovered life forms but, indirectly, that was what CD and Rachel were consuming.

Thousands of miles from where Rachel and CD stood there had once lived an Iguana. Had that Iguana still been alive it would have wept to see that facile menu (obviously being alive wouldn't have been enough, it would have had to have been able to read, and speak English . . . and Iguana probably don't cry anyway, but whatever . . .).

The Iguana, and millions like it, and millions more unlike it, for a tropical rain forest contains a wider variety of life forms than any other environment – with the possible exception of a sleeping bag at a rock festival – all these life forms had died in the service of Slampacker. They had been consumed along with the slice of gherkin smothered in secret recipe sauce.

Iggy had been chewing a fly when he first felt a tremendous rumbling. At first he thought that the fly must have disagreed with him and that he himself was responsible. But then the rumbling got louder and more terrible and Iggy realized in his little lizardy brain, that something was wrong. He knew his own bottom and no way was it capable of producing flatulence that was clearly going to feature on the Richter scale. This, Iggy sensed, was an approaching disaster, and of course he was right, which was no comfort at all. Being right is not as good as being alive. Suddenly Iggy found himself surrounded by plummeting species. Species which he had never seen before. Shaken from the various life levels that the forest houses were many creatures as yet undiscovered by humankind. Creatures that never would be.

They don't cut down trees anymore, it's too slow. They blow them up, or push them over with bulldozers. This was how Iggy and his host of little forest pals — whom Beatrix Potter would probably have called things like Simon and Jemima — met their ends, under bulldozers. For such is the demand for beef that the global hamburger addiction has fuelled that the rain-forests, which provide oxygen and change the weather, are being bulldozed down to create short-life pastures.

Besides the obvious undesirous side-effects, can be added the fact that much of science and medicine is derived from plant and animal research. It's just possible that the undiscovered cure for cancer went splat the day Slampacker sent Iggy to join Dave the dolphin and Mrs Pastel.

## IDENTIFYING THE ENEMY

Sly's mind was in a spin. He wanted to punch their faces and shout: 'Shut the fuck up about the environment!!'

Tex Slampacker could see that Sly was irritated by the discussion. 'Look here, boy,' he barked, 'you know my burgers?'

Sly did indeed know them for although he could have afforded to eat an elephant full of caviar every lunch-time without going to the cash machine, he still secretly craved Slampackers and scoffed plenty.

'Well, hell, we all know what the damn boxes are doing to the ozone layer, Christ I wish we'd never developed the damn things,' he continued. 'But we *did* and those boxes mean I don't have to pay anyone to wash up dirty plates. I am faced with a cruel choice, gentlemen. Voluntarily cut my profits by re-introducing crockery, or subject the world to the risk of skin cancer.'

Tex Slampacker was deeply affected by this awesome moral confusion. Just framing the phrase 'voluntarily cut my profits' had felt like swearing in church. He was a hard man, not easily upset, but some things offended his conscience.

## CASE FOR THE DEFENCE

That was it for Sly, he'd heard enough. He jumped to his feet. He was angry now. To think he had respected this man. 'Cruel choice, Mr Slampacker? Cruel choice?' he snapped, surveying the assembled company with that famous Aussie squint. This was his money-making look and with it Sly could have sheared the wool off a sheep's scrotum if he'd thought there was enough on it for an egg cosy. 'Forgive me, mates,' he said, fist in hand, the good old boy, teaching the high-brows horse sense, 'but I see no choice here, I see no dilemma. Clearly we have a question of morality to face, gentlemen, and I hope we're men enough to take it on.'

It would be a brave bookmaker who would have taken odds on that one but Sly wasn't leaving room for hecklers. 'Look we're all bloody sorry about the trees, of course we are, but people want the wood for Christ's sake! What can we do? You don't force them to buy your damn burgers!! The laws of a free market economy are sacred and we are guardians of those laws. Strewth, mates, you can't bugger about with market forces, that's social engineering, gentlemen, Brave New 1984 and all that. Your average bloke doesn't want some little Hitler from the ministry telling him what he can and can't buy! What he can and can't make! For sure it's a shame about the sneezing seals, and the birds with mouldy armpits, and the ozone layer, a bloody shame, and Christ if anyone's passing the hat round I'm in for 10K towards cancer research, no worries, but you can't stop progress and progress is market-ing . . .'

The faces around the table remained inscrutable, Sly had no idea how they were taking his little lecture but he didn't care. He wasn't closing *his* aerosol factory until it stopped making a profit. 'Listen, Mr Slampacker,' he continued, 'if you didn't use those boxes some other bugger would and then where would you be? I'll tell you, mate, hanging out in the sun to dry with the wombats using your hat for a toilet. Meantime the ozone layer's still fucked and the other bastard's building a private dermatological ward to get the malignant melanomas chopped out of his arse. Gentlemen, we can't weaken, it would be a crime to interfere with the sacred laws of free enterprise simply to protect the environment. Do that and what do you get for an encore? I'll tell you, some green cop telling you you can't take a piss in your back garden because it upsets the ants.'

Sly would have continued but to his astonishment he found himself interrupted by warm applause. He had thought that he was speaking against the mood of the meeting. Now he discovered that he had captured it perfectly.

'Young man, you speak for all of us here and also those who attend in spirit,' said Slampacker. 'We are all of us engaged in one activity or another that is destroying the environment, we don't like it, we wish we weren't, but in the long run, what can we do?'

There was a brief silence during which around the world the acid rain fell, the nitrates seeped through the soil into the rivers, the greenhouse effect melted the ice caps and the kids breathed the lead from the leaded petrol. Sly realized that he was amongst friends. They weren't wimping on the problem they were merely recognizing it. What next? he wondered.

## CONNECTIONS

And well Sly might have wondered for the problem was so clear, so terrible. The earth was dying. To be more specific, the earth was being killed. Done to death by its fond owners. Killed by the pursuit of money. For the men gathered around the table it was so utterly frustrating to have inherited the earth and then have the damn thing die on you. And, of course, its death would mean their death, everybody's death.

53

Like it or not, the human race, powerful though it is, remains only a part of the astonishingly complex chain of beings that makes up life on earth. It is not an island and cannot survive without the other life forces; the life forces that create the oxygen and food, that clean the water and protect us from the sun, the forces that bind the soil together and prevent the deserts spreading across the whole globe; the forces that keep the ice caps from melting and drowning us all.

It's all connections. If dung beetles didn't eat cow shit, we'd be knee-deep in flies by now. Eating cow shit is a dirty job, but somebody's got to do it. Luckily, either by divine plan or cosmic coincidence, at the dawn of creation the dung beetle said, 'Oh, for God's sake, *I'll* eat the cow shit, if no one else will.' But the dung beetle, like all other forms of life, depends on all other forms of life. From micro-organisms to Great White whales, it's a chain. Break that chain and all the money in the world will not save you from the ecological Armageddon that will engulf us all. So, what was to be done?

They were coming to that, they had a solution. They'd been working on it for a while. Everyone had a part to play, including Sly.

'Mr Moorcock,' said Slampacker, leaning back in his chair, 'I'd like to tell you, if I may, about the Stark Conspiracy.'

# LOVE AMONG THE
# RADICALS

During the meal at Slampackers, such as it was, CD told Rachel about the film he had thought they might go and see. As a preliminary to establishing his character as an active peace campaigner, he had chosen a movie he'd read about recently in a groovy-ish mag. At the time he had marked it down as the sort of film which he would rather be forced to eat than watch, but in the present circumstances it suited his purpose . . .

'It's about the parallels between the way men run countries and the way they run their personal lives. I mean, the parallel between pricks and missiles is a bit laboured these days but I suppose maybe that's because it's true.' CD was desperately hoping that Rachel had not read the review he'd read. She hadn't, and he would have been gratified to know that she was thinking that he seemed an interesting sort of bloke, a bit intense maybe, but a cut above the usual dag.

In this respect at least, CD's plan was working. Rachel had always been a bit of a closet radical – she liked the feeling of talking about something that mattered. And so they finished their delicious Slampackers, except for the horrible bit of gherkin which they had both fished out, and went to the movie. As they had both suspected, it was well meaning but bloody awful. Its principles were presented with such horrible monolithic certainty that it would have turned Ghandi pro nuke. Afterwards the director gave a short speech. He did this after every performance of the two-week run at the little arts cinema.

'Some people,' the director said with what he believed to be a knowing smile, 'can't see that missiles are penis extensions. Oh yeah? Well I don't know what's going to come flying towards us when some man pushes the button but it certainly won't be a fifty-foot flying cunt.' This, the director considered, was not only a brilliant and conclusive point but also a hilarious joke and his personal favourite. Although, in fact, he would not have known a joke if he had found one hanging off his earring.

'I think he was being cynical. You know, talking like an idiot in order to make an astute point,' said CD putting on a brave face. He would have put pink icing and a cherry on it if he had thought it would get him any closer to Rachel's affections.

'I think he was talking like an idiot because he is an idiot,' replied Rachel. And CD, who agreed with her entirely, had to think about cold porridge and vinegar for five minutes to stop his monumental desire becoming too obvious.

## RADICALLY INEFFECTUAL

In the weeks that followed they went to a benefit concert together, and a discussion group, and looked around the community bookshop and generally became a recognized feature of alternative haunts. All the time with CD anxiously impressing on Rachel what a committed, worthwhile individual he was. He need not have tried so hard. She liked him, it was his mates that annoyed her. Limpish, tired individuals, endlessly discussing how screwed up the world is, without apparently having very much intention of doing anything about it.

'They're dull, Colin,' CD could not get her to call him CD. 'Your friends are dull. They're not going to save the world.'

CD could only shrug, beginning to wonder whether in constructing the fiction that the people from the community bookshop and local theatre collective were his soul mates, he might not have made a mistake. Right from the beginning he had pretended that he knew them all much better than he did.

'Hi, Todd,' he had said, casually to the bloke at the peace bookshop the first time he had taken Rachel down there. CD had checked out the name beforehand, he knew that if you address someone with sufficient familiarity the chances are very good that they will presume that they know you, especially if the person is a hippy. The plan had worked perfectly, except for the fact that Todd had turned out to be a bit of a boring wanker and CD now had to live with the fact that Rachel thought he was Todd's mate. CD, sensing his tactical error, had decided to try and distance himself from the wet types he had pretended to be so close to. There would be no more 'Hi Todds'. He intended to remodel himself as a hard, practical man, looking for hard, practical solutions. He was even considering buying a pen-knife. That was his plan anyway, unfortunately the whole thing was ruined by the return of the dreadful Karen.

## THE RETURN OF THE DREADFUL KAREN

CD had been innocently sitting in a café with Rachel when suddenly and without warning he and his cappuccino were enveloped by a mass of frizzy hair.

'Hi-i-i-i,' Karen cooed, and then demanded, 'Hug please.'

It made him ill to do it but CD was obliged to provide a weak little squeeze. Uninvited Karen plonked herself down, bags and hair everywhere. She liked to effect the attitude of always being in a slightly scatty rush, as if a great many people depended on her.

'Can't stop,' she said, stopping. 'Christ CD haven't seen you since we got busted painting the road, what a night, man!'

'Since *I* got busted,' replied CD, his heart sinking. He desperately hoped that Rachel had forgotten that he had slightly exaggerated his crime when they had first met, claiming that he had been arrested for trying to break into a US naval installation to prove that any terrorist could steal an atom bomb.

'Was that the same night you tried to break into the naval installation?' asked Rachel.

'Is this your new lady?' said Karen, giving Rachel what was intended to be a smile of radiant sisterly love.

If there was one thing that Rachel hated it was the term 'lady'. 'Why don't you bring your lady?': May I introduce my lady. Rachel would almost have preferred anything; girlfriend, bird, she would rather have been someone's casual fuck than their 'lady'. May I introduce my casual fuck . . .

'No,' answered CD, 'this is Rachel, a friend of mine.'

'I *see*,' said Karen with a touch of girlish innuendo, as if to suggest that CD was concealing all sorts of delicious secrets but that she wouldn't pry. 'CD and I were nearly an item ourselves, weren't we?' she confided in a nauseating frank manner which was designed to suggest a modern woman who combined independence and vulnerability in equal measures. Karen stared at people when she spoke to them, at least they thought she was staring at them. She thought she had a disarmingly frank and open countenance.

CD wished that the floor would open up and swallow him, even if it had been eating garlic and hadn't brushed its teeth for three days.

'You look a bit uptight, love. You need a hug,' Karen said. Then she delivered her knockout punch. 'I know, I'll give you a massage.' It was a vicious blow and she delivered it below the belt. CD was down, the umpire was counting him out. He dragged himself back from the brink and hit back.

'Uhm, listen uhm . . . Oh yeah, Karen isn't it? We really have to go, maybe catch you, whenever, OK?' It was good, but not good enough. As he rose the waiter brought the food they had ordered.

'Now, you're really untogether, CD, are you sure you're OK . . . Oh wow, no you're *not*, I mean are these shoulders tense or what? . . .' The claws descended on his shoulders and began to knead away like he was tomorrow's croissant.

At that moment CD discovered what Rachel and most

58

women learn young, that if someone forceful decides they want to touch you, and they present it as an act of friendship, it is almost impossible to stop them. CD and Rachel had been enjoying Sunday brunch at a café, it was a lovely jolly morning despite the heat. CD had been contented, basking in the light of Rachel's radiant sauciness and now the dark shadow of a wet hippy had fallen upon his happy idyll.

His food sneered up at him — it's extremely difficult to tackle waffles and maple syrup when someone is trying to wring your neck. CD did not know it but the solution to his problem was very close. Not the problem of Karen, of course, she was insoluble, like the hairs she had left in his coffee. Nor indeed the problem of how to persuade Rachel to let him have a go at her, that was a toughie too. Just the problem of how to deal with maple syrup. Because thousands of miles away, a highly-trained team of specialists were working to make problems with maple syrup a thing of the past. Working, in fact to make maple syrup a thing of the past.

## DIE BACK DIPLOMACY

The crack unit was headed up by Wayne Strongman, a tough, two-fisted career diplomat who carried a personal phone like it was a side arm, and wore a laminated ID on his pyjamas.

His job at present was stone-walling the Canadians on the problem of US acid rain destroying the Canadian maple trees. Negative diplomacy it was called — a job he knew well. He had been a top trouble-shooter in the Republican Party Damage Control Group for the last two elections. What Wayne Strongman didn't know about twisting a statistic could be written on the back of a stockbroker's tax return.

'The point is,' he said with the quiet assurance that had made him such a feared prosecuting attorney and such a deeply loathed dinner party guest, 'that your people have not been able to establish a *direct* and *proven* correlation.'

Henri Le Conte, Strongman's opposite number, lost his rag.

59

'I *beg* your bugger-up pardon!!' he said.

Got him, thought Strongman ... An angry man at a conference table is a wide open target, he is a man saying, 'here is my ass, kick it'. Le Conte rose to the bait, shouting:

'And when every fuck maple tree in Quebec is bastard dead! Then you won't need damn all bugger correlation! Is that it!' (It is a strange thing about second languages, no matter how well the foreigner learns them, perhaps to the point where technically they speak better than a native, no one is ever capable of swearing properly in any language other than their own. Le Conte was a French-Canadian and, as he himself often lamented in his strong French accent ... 'I never know when I need a bugger, or where to put my bollocks.')

Now Strongman was staring at him passively. It enraged Le Conte ...

'How much proof is required hell bloody! Do the owners of your factories and power stations have to come to Canada and chop down the fuck trees themselves!!'

There was an embarrassed silence which Strongman allowed to linger one beat into being seriously uncomfortable. His team knew well enough not to break an embarrassed silence. 'Sometimes it's what you *don't* say,' he often told them. Strongman had sent innocent men to the electric chair with a well-timed theatrical pause.

'Henri,' he said dispassionately to the red-faced French-Canadian. 'I can understand you being upset. Clearly it's not just a matter of lost revenue, to you guys the maple tree is your national symbol.' That was the way, play it soft for a moment ... but just a moment, just long enough for them to register that you're being conciliatory – then hit them. 'But frankly, I find the implications of your outburst deeply offensive. I can only presume you feel that we on the US team are a bunch of dumb and unprincipled ecological vandals.' He continued quickly, before Le Conte could agree with this. 'Well, let me tell you Mister, you're barking up the wrong damn maple tree! Do you think we don't have maples in

Ontario? New England? US kids got a sweet-tooth too! If we can verify for *certain* what's killing the damn things, well you may rest assured, Sir, that the United States government will pursue it to hell and beyond and nail it to the wall, by crikey! But before I start closing factories; before I start putting men out of work and forcing their families onto welfare, by Heaven, I'm going to be as sure of my ground as an old pig and that's *hog* sure!!'

He had just made up the 'old pig' metaphor. Strongman liked inventing pretend colloquialisms, it confused foreigners.

'Mr Strongman,' said Le Conte, badly wanting to kill him. '82 per cent of the trees in the Beauce-Megantic region are showing signs of pollution. It's sulphur dioxide from *your* factories. Ten years from now we will have no trees left. This is a world emergency . . . Quebec produces over two-thirds of the world's maple syrup. We've cut our acid rain, you've got to cut yours.'

'We can't be sure. The connection isn't proven,' said Strongman, reasonable again. 'Believe me, our top men, the best, are on this thing. We're chasing it Henri, oh yeah, we're chasing it like a pan-fried Tennessee whore with the clap, and that's *finger licking* chasing.' That was a good one, thought Strongman, they'd laugh about that tonight. He couldn't help but notice the secretary's admiring glance. Who knows, maybe . . . Anyway he'd certainly waffled that dumb French kayak's maple syrup right up his sweet backside, you bet he had.

Le Conte, a native of Quebec, wanted to cry. With great sadness he called upon his science officer to present the Canadian argument yet again.

The negotiation machine would continue to produce bullshit at a comparable rate to the industrial production of acid rain. The US/Canadian dialogue had been going on for so long it would certainly outlive the trees. It takes a maple tree about five years to perish from a phenomenon known as 'die back'. They die from the top down. Like a balding man, their branches recede. The syrup farmer taps his trees each year and watches them die by inches, becoming poor, sad, shabby shadows of their once mighty selves. This disaster is, of course, not confined to maple trees but is beginning to affect the majority of all the trees in the world.


## THE FHAGWASH

The waffles had gone cold and CD's shoulders were numb. Finally, Karen released him.

'Anyway, I really have got to get my act together,' said Karen, turning down a non-existent invitation to hang around. 'Boogaloo and Rhumtitty are probably coming round for supper tonight or some other time. It's so difficult to cook for Yanyaroos.' Karen had a habit common to many people who pride themselves on possessing approachable and open personalities. She referred to people that she knew as if everyone knew them. Ostensibly this was because Karen believed that the world is actually full of love and that there are quite enough artificial barriers created between people without constructing extra ones.

'Karen, I don't know any of the people you're talking about,' CD had remarked on their one night together.

'Just because you don't know someone,' Karen replied, 'doesn't mean you can't be a friend of theirs.' She spoke with the same tone of happy confidence that Einstein must have used the first time he said $E = MC^2$. In actual fact, her habit of trumpeting the names of her acquaintants was her way of reassuring herself that she had friends. Unfortunately the effect of this habit, on someone who did not know better, would clearly be to presume that CD and Karen were not only mates, but that they shared much the same circle of friends.

Obviously this was distastrous for CD. After all he had only just made his decision that he must quickly disassociate himself from Karen's type and suddenly, up pops Karen, blithely speaking as if she and CD balanced at the hub of the same social wheel. Worse still, it was a wheel which appeared to include Yanyaroos. CD was right to feel concern on this last point. There are a lot of Yanyaroos in WA and Rachel, like many, found it extremely difficult to understand the fascination. She could not, for the life of her, see how wearing a picture of a bearded, multimillionaire guru around your neck and dressing only in blue clothes could lead to spiritual enlightenment.

Strangely, another person who found Yanyarooism a pretty surprising phenomenon was Yoga Fhagwash, Chief Guru of the Yanyaroo cult, whose picture it was that hung on Karen's friends', Boogaloo's and Rhumtitty's, chests.

'I just don't understand it,' he would say to his aides and girlfriends, 'I tell all these middle-class white people to wear blue clothes and send me half their money . . . and they do!!!'

At first, the Yoga Fhagwash, unable to believe his luck, had tried to keep up appearances. Playing it all very spiritual, issuing poems and thoughts and mantras about enlightenment through denial. After a while, though, his confidence began to grow. He began to experiment with the credulity of his followers, suggesting for instance, that possessing twenty-five Rolls Royces was an intensely religious statement and what's more, not letting anyone else have a go in them maintained their purity and integrity.

To Fhagwash's relief and astonishment, there was no reaction. 'They don't seem to care,' he remarked in astonishment, while writhing in warm cocoa-butter on a water-bed full of champagne.

Rachel was convinced that originally the popularity of the cult had been based on its advocacy of free love. Fhagwash was a monumental root-rat himself and encouraged his disciples to go for it like a pack of rabbits on a weekend in Amsterdam. Yanyaroos were practically ordered to have it off willy nilly. This was what annoyed Rachel.

'I mean, it's like a never-ending adolescent fantasy with God saying how great you are for snogging. Well *yuk*!'

CD wasn't sure. He couldn't help thinking that if scripture

lessons at his school had been one long feel-up session there would have been a lot more converts to the Bible.

Since the advent of AIDS, of course, everything had changed. The Yoga Fhagwash had swung to the other extreme and gone completely ape mega-moral. The arch wick-dipper had become the arch party-pooper – possibly because he didn't want his source of income dying off. Fhagwash went rubber-glove mad. He had people putting a dustbin-liner over their heads before they washed their own faces. It wasn't long before his disciples were having to wrap themselves in cling film before making a telephone call. Soon, if they wanted to go out, they'd probably have to have themselves laminated.

The future of Yanyarooism lies in the balance. It is questionable whether people will want to give money to someone who says they can't have it off. Rachel was entirely indifferent to the future of the cult but one thing was for sure. If CD was thinking of going to dinner at Karen's, with Boogaloo and Rhumtitty, then he was going on his own.

## DENIAL

Karen was finally going. She got up and kissed CD.

For one appalling moment Rachel thought she was going to kiss her. Thankfully Karen confined herself to a squeeze of the shoulder which was still over-familiar considering it was based on an acquaintance of about fifteen minutes.

'Come round to dinner sometime, you must,' was her parting shot. 'Rash and Basil and Tish and Blossom said they might probably come round one evening or, if they don't, some other time.'

Another big, sloppy smacker delivered on the lips through a cloud of frizziness and she was gone.

There was a pause. Then CD spoke.

'I have never met that woman before in my life.'

# STARK CONSPIRATOR

## MAN WITH A MISSION

Sly had left the dinner in L A a changed man. Changed for ever. He flew home to Oz a fully committed member of the Stark Conspiracy.

## THE PROBLEM WITH ABORIGINALS

Unfortunately with trust came responsibilities. Sly had a specific role to play, a role which he knew would not be an easy one. He had been charged with acquiring the land. The consortium had done their homework and Western Australia was certainly far and away the best bet for the very detailed specifications necessary for their purposes – no doubt that was why Sly had been brought into the group at all. The clever bastards had already roughly picked out the bit of scrub that they wanted, which was almost convenient. Except, of course, for the Abs.

In his efforts to ingratiate himself with his new partners, Sly had spoken glibly of simply persuading the Abs to move on to greener pastures but in the back of his mind he knew it would be tougher than getting red wine chunder out of a duck down duvet. To say that Abs were a strange crew would, in Sly's opinion, be stretching the well-known Aussie talent for understatement to its limits. He knew kangaroos with more horse sense than an Ab. They were stubborn too, strange and stubborn, that was Abs, and on no subject were they stranger and stubborner than on the subject of land.

Land was an obsession with Aborigines. Of course, no one

could argue with a man being attached to the place he hung his hat. Sly himself had a little spread on the Swan River that was his pride and joy. It had a swimming pool the shape of Western Australia, an outdoor cocktail bar made of glass, with real fish inside it, and a genuine Henry Moore which Sly had bought unseen and had hastily had to plant a bunch of gum trees to hide the bloody monstrosity.

Beautiful land, beautifully appointed, but unlike some Abs he'd happily move on if he was paid enough. What was their problem? What were they protecting? Nothing, just a load of dust and rocks and empty bottles. It wasn't what was on the land, it was the land itself. For some reason specific bits of land had specific spiritual relevance. Sly thanked God he wasn't religious, he'd have bulldozed down Notre Dame if he'd thought there was half a barrel of oil underneath it.

Maybe the Abs have grown up, thought Sly in a brief moment of hope. Maybe they'd move after all! He'd give them good grazing country, access to a river, their own pub! But deep in his heart (which was not awfully deep), Sly knew they wouldn't. He could just see some bastard head man, standing leaning on his stick, staring straight through him – chewing his gums, through a huge, stupid, white beard that made him look like he was frenching a sheep. He wouldn't budge an inch. The bloody-minded old goat would fuck Sly off like he was Lord Muck with a million in his jeans, instead of some broke old derelict with a headful of lice.

These were Sly's bitter reflections as he sat in his first-class seat the morning after the dinner. It wouldn't have been so difficult a few years before but land rights had become a real big issue in the last decade or so. You couldn't just push people around anymore. You'd get every government sponsored bleeding-heart in the country down on your back. It was ridiculous, how were you supposed to run a country for the good of all if you kept worrying about people's damn rights?

Sly looked at the middle-aged hostess who was serving his champagne. Steel-grey crew cut, clearly a lesso, thought Sly.

That was equal rights for you! Sly could remember when air hostesses were a bunch of little spunks, every one. They'd lean over to pour your fizz in their cute white blouses and you'd get a tiny, tantalizing glimpse of the tops of their frilly little bras. Sexier than any full-on strip show that glimpse, thought Sly, because you knew the girl had class. They'd get sacked at twenty-eight of course, and why not? Why should people get a meal ticket for life at the expense of the consumer, he asked himself? What was a hostess *for* he'd like to know? Jesus, a machine could serve the fucking drinks and microwave the chops. A hostess was there to make the flight more bearable.

But *now* of course, that was called sex discrimination. No sackings on grounds of sex or age. These days you either got served by some boy faggot or a middle-aged hag who never married a captain because she was a muff-tucker. The only way to get a decent floor show was to fly a Far Eastern airline like Malaya or Singapore. Beautiful girls but could you trust the pilot? It wasn't that he was an ogler or anything like that, Sly assured himself, he'd never been a perv, *no way*!! It was just nice to look at pretty young girls, everyone knew that, so why couldn't these damn do-gooders admit it?

He wished he'd used his private jet.

Sly was getting pissed and working himself into a frenzy because he knew that what he had promised in Los Angeles would be very difficult to deliver. He just fervently hoped that when he headed north to scout around, the Aboriginals he would have to deal with would not be the spiritual type and would like a drink.

# THE COLLAPSE OF A DREAM

Sly may have been feeling bitter, but CD thought he was going to die. He was discovering that there are worse feelings than just being in love. There is something horribly worse, much worse than he could ever have imagined. Unrequited love. Two of the saddest words in the English language had laid CD as low as sure as if they'd been written on a brick and he'd been hit over the head with it.

The shock of learning how much he was capable of feeling made him scared and angry. He had always presumed that he was a fairly shallow sort of person, not wont to feel either joy or sorrow to any great degree, and now he discovered that he was at the mercy of feelings way way beyond his control. It was very confusing, he felt impotent, awash with emotions so palpable they seemed to have an actual physical form. The feeling that had dwelt in his guts for the last few weeks now seemed feather-light and gentle compared to the large piece of lead that somehow had managed to insert itself into his abdomen whilst he wasn't looking. Because . . .

She wasn't interested!

No, it wasn't anything to do with that Karen woman, Rachel had assured him in answer to his desperate protests . . . or any of the other people he had introduced her to. It was simply that she didn't feel that way about CD. Also she had had no idea that he felt that way about her either. She felt that they had just become very good friends, which was great. That was the way she wanted it. There was certainly no question of anything else. Just friends, that was all.

'I'm sorry, Rachel, I can't deal with that. It would be too much,' CD had said with dignity. Just friends! What a suggestion! What an insult to the strength of his feelings. Didn't she understand how much he loved her? Just friends! What did she think he was! You can't feel the things he was feeling and settle for 'just friends'!

'I'm an all or nothing sort of person,' he had said, looking at her with what he thought was an expression of boundless sorrow. 'Me and half-measures never did get along.' The eyes misty now, staring at hers with unrelenting frankness. In his anguish CD failed to recall that this trick did not work for Karen the hippy, and was unlikely to work for him. 'I have to have it all,' he added, switching his look to lean and handsome.

Rachel said, 'That's a shame, Colin. Oh well, I suppose that's it then.'

This was a surprise. One of the most irritating features of unrequited love is that hope springs eternal. CD had rather been hoping that Rachel would say, 'oh well, in that case, do you want me now or shall we wait till we can find a bed?'

Summoning up all of his dignity, which at that point took about a picosecond, CD rose to leave. 'I'm history Rachel. I'm outa here, yesterday's news. Maybe I'll travel, don't look for me tomorrow baby, because I'll be gone.'

'What about the casserole dish?'

'Keep it.' He slung his pretend leather jacket over his shoulder.

'It's mine. You've got it at your house.'

In a magnificent gesture CD walked out without a word, returning a few minutes later with a brand new casserole dish.

'See you,' said Rachel.

'Yeah, maybe,' CD replied with another portion of boundless sorrow. This time he really did leave. Walked out magnificently. Stood on the pavement in his torn jeans and burst into tears.

# HERO

He had no right to resent Rachel for not falling in love with
him. He knew that but, by God, he did and as he walked
home his anguish assumed ever more heroic proportions. He
was magnificent in his loneliness. He could do anything now
because he no longer cared. There was no greater force than a
man with nothing to lose, CD told himself. He could achieve
great things because all his achievements would mean nothing
to him. Nothing because he was nothing and nothing comes of
nothing. And when he had done all these great things, and
returned, tired or dead, the fruits of his terrible solitude
spread about him for all to see, then she would be sorry, then
she would realize what she had passed up. Then she would
weep and wish that things had been different. But he would
just smile at her – presuming he was still alive that is – smile
at her with infinite weariness etched in the lines of his lean,
craggy face and then turn away without a word . . . No wait,
maybe he would say . . . maybe he would say . . . well,
something brilliant about fucking casserole dishes anyway.

But for now it was definitely over. He had told her, that was
it, he had walked out of her life for ever and he was going to
stick to that. He would never speak to her again, that was the
only way. He knew it was the only way . . .

# HOPE SPRINGS ETERNAL

'Hi, Rachel, your friend and main man CD here, Colin to you.'

It was evening, hours after he had left her at the café with
the casserole dish. Not that he had held out that long. He'd
been trying since about three minutes after he got home but
she had been out.

'Oh, hi Colin, I wondered if you'd phone. I had to go to
Mum's. Promised to help her with the garden.'

This was scarcely the hours of anguished pacing along
pavements made strangely unfamiliar by her new isolation,
which was what CD had rather hoped Rachel had been up to

but, there you go. He wasn't quibbling, he'd recovered slightly. Hope springs eternal.

'Listen, I was just wondering if we could still be, you know, what we are at the moment, you know, just that,' he said.

'But of course, that's what I want, Colin,' replied Rachel, 'as long as you know that I meant what I said, I really did, and I do.'

'Oh yeah, of course, forget it, no problem, won't mention it again,' said CD. 'It'll be exactly the same as it was.'

'Great,' said Rachel, knowing that it would never be the same again.

Actually, although neither Rachel nor CD knew it, nothing was ever going to be the same again. Nothing in the whole world.

It was only early on in the southern summer but already it was very very hot, much hotter than usual. The times were definitely a-changing. It was definitely very very hot.

# ON THE BUSINESS OF STARK

Sly piloted his own four-seater light aircraft out of Perth and headed north east, up towards the Territory. It was a flight he normally enjoyed hugely, the place was so utterly enormous. It was what flying must have been like in the very early days, when you had the whole sky to yourself and could dodge and weave as you felt like it.

These days it was like playing space invaders with air traffic control. That wasn't flying, circling high in the stack, waiting in line to put down in a blanket of smog so thick you couldn't see the landing lights. Petrified to drop or rise by the width of a credit card because you'd probably get a jumbo in the face..

'Those passengers on the right of the plane should get a good view of the mountains and those on the left should just be able to make out a 747 full of terrified people pointing at you and screaming "get the fuck out of the way".'

Sly would not personally fly himself anywhere these days except over Oz. Maybe Africa would be all right but Sly wasn't going to go to Africa if he could help it. As far as he could see, the Third World was getting Thirder, soon they would have to start calling it the Fourth World, maybe even the Fifth. A continent full of poverty. What would be the point of going there?

## POOR BASTARDS

Actually, as he sat at the controls of his little plane, Sly was on a journey into poverty on the business of Stark. He was going to chat with some Abs, and you don't get much poorer than your average Ab'. That's why most people hate them, thought

Sly, they're so horribly poor. It gets on your nerves. Why do they have to hang around all the time being so poor? Why don't they fuck off and be poor somewhere else?

Lots of Aboriginals end up as piss-heads, causing people to say 'no wonder they're so poor, half of them are piss-heads'. It would, of course, make much more sense to say 'no wonder half of them are piss-heads, they're so poor'.

Australia is guilt-ridden by Aboriginal history and people get nasty when they feel guilty, they seek to find a scapegoat and often end up blaming the victims themselves . . .

'Jesus, mate, they're fucking rolling in it. Christ the government's so fucking wet it just spoon feeds them handouts and they piss the lot up against the wall.'

This, of course, is the way people deal with degradation the whole world over. Sympathy for victims is always counter-balanced by an equal and opposite feeling of resentment towards them. How often had Sly said:

'See that tramp. Wanted money for a meal. I gave him a buck of course . . . Ha, probably earns more than I do, probably got a fortune stuffed under his mattress.'

Sly never asked himself why someone with a fortune stuffed under his mattress would choose to sit in a gutter all day.

## PARADISE LOST

Sly was flying over Kalgoorkatta. They dug uranium there, Sly had a lot of money in it. It had been a hell of a battle to get the government to give the go-ahead. People were such a bunch of old women when it came to nuclear energy. It had cost the earth to prove how safe it was. Dinners, party donations, all expenses paid fact-finding luxury trips. Those high-minded political types did not sell themselves cheaply.

All Sly and his colleagues wanted was a tiny, tiny relaxation in the frankly impractical laws on how much uranium was produced. Also, it would be nice if there were less restrictions on who they were allowed to sell it to and, finally, it would make life easier if they did not have to ask so many embarrassing and impertinent questions as to what the buyer wanted it for. Just a small rationalization of these absurdly restrictive laws would net ten billion a year, which would of course generate some very juicy corporate tax, not to mention the jobs.

Besides this, the consortium argued, you can't stop progress. If they didn't do it someone else would. The Canadians were already doing it in fact. Yes, that had shocked those bastard greenies. Canada, land of the maple leaf and the acid rain protest was flogging uranium off the back of a barrow to just about any piss-poor, potential terrorist base of a country that could afford it.

Sly's mining consortium hadn't got everything it had wanted but they had got enough and Kalgoorkatta was by way of being a bit of a boom town. It was dangerous work and it certainly-screwed up the land a bit, but you can't make an omelette without breaking eggs.

Lots of eggs. What a mess it was! Until he flew over it Sly had never realized just how hellish a few hundred hectares of virtually unrestricted mining could look. It was a couple of years since he and the other members of the consortium had stood on the pretty hillside with the champagne and photographers, bleating on about it being a great day for Australia. Since then a good approximation of Hades had been produced. The land was scarred and smashed and poisoned. Soon it would also be empty. When that happened Sly and his friends would fence it in and move on. Land was there to be used.

## THE DESERT OAK

A couple of hundred years before the mines were laid, an Aboriginal man had used the land himself. He was on walkabout and thirsty. Aboriginals were often thirsty. This came from living in an enormous desert. The fellow in question was thirsty but he was cool. He was cool because he knew that all he needed to do was find a desert oak tree. It wasn't called a desert oak tree in those days of course, what the Aboriginal in question called it one can only guess at. Possibly, 'Sir' or perhaps 'darling', something appreciative certainly because this tree was going to save his life. You wouldn't have thought of it as a life-saver, not to look at certainly. No one, not even its mother, could have called it an inspiring or handsome tree. The desert oak was, and in fact still is, as a breed, a hugely unimpressive scrappy, crappy little tree. Its best friends would say so.

'Tree,' they would say, realizing that you have to be cruel to be kind, 'do not go entering yourself in any horticultural shows. You will only embarrass us all.'

But the desert oak can smile knowingly to itself, it has a secret. Because although on the surface it may be just a six-foot skinny streak of fibre with about ten leaves to its name, beneath the desert floor it is a very different story. For the desert oak can put down roots as deep as three hundred feet. In fact, as far as need be to reach water. Let there be no question about it, ugly as fuck though it is, root-wise the desert oak does not mess around. Still waters run deep and so do desert oaks. Other factors that make this tree remarkably together, as far as living in the desert goes, include its ability to 'die' at will. When times are hard, and let's face it they almost always are, for a tree in a desert, the top bit of the tree just switches off. Drops its leaves, shrivels up and pretends to be dead.

You wouldn't notice the change to look at it, of course. So unimpressive is the desert oak in full bloom that the difference between it stretching its branches and saying, 'God it's good to be alive and a tree today' and it pretending to be dead, is not marked. In fact, the two states are almost identical. None the less, that is what it does, on the surface the tree 'dies'. Underneath though, the search for water goes on and when that water is found, after what could be as much as fifteen or twenty years, the top bit comes back to life and blossoms into its full patheticness.

Possibly conscious of the trouble it has gone to to find

75

water, once found, the desert oak makes the most of it. It stores it, sucking up as much as it can up through its three hundred foot roots, and storing a few pints in its horrid, spindly little trunk.

And this is where the thirsty Aborigine comes in. Because the Aborigines have always known about these trees. They had worked out a way to get at that water without the tedious necessity of having to put down three hundred foot roots and pretend to be dead for twenty years themselves. What they used to do was this. They would make a little hole in the bark of the tree and put a twig in. Then they would sit under the twig with their mouths open and wait for the water to drip in.

This is what our man did, hundreds of years ago, on the site of what was to become the over-mined, useless uranium plant. And once he had drunk enough, he didn't just get up and piss off, leaving the tree to drip till it died. No, he removed the twig, got a bit of gum from the bark of a nearby eucalyptus, and bunged up the hole he'd made. This was the way it was done. You plugged up your hole.

The Aborigines were a Stone-Age society, one of the most primitive on earth. They had not even developed a simple television game show. But they knew that if you looked after the environment there was a good chance it would look after you.

Now Sly and his friends had taken what they wanted from the land just as the Aboriginal had done. But they had no intention of bunging up their hole. Too expensive, too much trouble.

The term 'primitive' is clearly a highly subjective one.

# PROTEST AND SURVIVE

CD had intended to change his entire policy regarding his pursuit of Rachel but he was not in a position to do so. Rachel liked the things they had been doing together just the way they were. The peace and ecology bit had really got in amongst her and she wanted to get more involved. As far as she was concerned, CD was inexorably linked with all this growing interest. That was what their relationship was based on and she liked it that way. After all, she knew plenty of blokes to drink and play pool with but there weren't many who'd schlepp 20K to a meeting about how much raw sewage was getting pumped into Perth's swimming waters.

## AUSSIE ADS

Today's schlepp was to a kind of protest bazaar at the naval installation thirty kilometres north of Carlton. For the previous six years there had been a permanent women's protest encamped close to the public jetty and this was a day of support. The US South Pacific fleet was coming in, which was always an occasion for excitement, horror or indifference, according to individual attitudes to US fleets.

CD and Rachel arrived a little late and the party was in full swing. The hippies were painting their children's faces, the police were pretending to be friendly and a small group of strippers and hostesses were waving their boobs about.

This was because the arrival of the fleet was a very special time for the clubs and strip joints of Perth. The owners would send down their dancing girls to hang adverts off the quay and bare their breasts as the ships came in. 'Come to the 301 Club and see bonza Aussie tits' the signs would say. The girls jumped up and down, jiggling their bonza Aussie tits as a kind of foretaste of what the lucky sailors could expect if they visited one of the clubs.

This, incidentally, is an example of classic Australian advertising. It tends to be abrupt and to the point. For instance, if a manufacturer has produced a sausage that he (or she) considers to be long and meaty, he will call the produce 'Long 'N' Meaty Saussies' and advertise it thus: ' "Long 'N' Meaty Saussies", they're long and meaty (and they're saussies).'

Half-way to the printers with the advertising copy, the manufacturer will realize that he has not pointed out that the saussies are Australian. He will immediately rename them 'Long 'N' Meaty Aussie Saussies' and proudly boast: ' "Long 'N' Meaty Aussie Saussies", they're long and meaty, and they're saussies, pure Aussie . . .'

After some thought he might add, 'eat 'em!' just to make the situation absolutely clear. It makes a change from the sort of ad where a picture of a lizard on a pyramid, basking in the sun, is supposed to make you desperate for a fag.


## THE ONE WORLD FESTIVAL

Anyway, the poor cold girls jiggled and the poor cold US sailors whooped and hollered from the decks of their ships, no doubt thinking that if the girls did this at the docks, what fabulous and exotic pleasures could be expected on paying twenty bucks to get into a club. None, sadly. Just more tit jiggling, minus the goose-pimples.

CD and Rachel arrived rather late.

'Look at those girls,' said CD, looking. 'Pretty gross, eh?' he added looking some more. 'I mean, just totally out of order,' he said as he took another long, hard look just to make sure it really was as offensive as he thought it was.

Rachel wasn't interested in the girls, gross or not. She was taking in the scene as a whole and experiencing a gutful of frustration and doubt. There, floating out on the high seas, was the US South Pacific fleet, looking, it had to be admitted, pretty hard. On the dock in opposition to this bay full of death-tech, stood the protesters, looking (it could not be denied) rather pathetic. Balloons, painted children's faces, acoustic guitars . . . 'I mean, for God's sake,' thought Rachel.

Anyone faced by a battle fleet is going to feel a sharp sense of scale. It can only add to the inadequacy to be surrounded by street theatre and kids with T-shirts saying 'I want to grow up, not blow up'.

'I hate the way people always feel they have to justify their principles by linking them to their snotty kids,' she said.

Rachel didn't like most kids very much. She found them selfish and demanding and socially inept. She certainly did not feel any need to lend substance to her hopes for a better world by harping mawkishly on the fate of the poor innocent kiddies. As far as she was concerned she was a poor innocent kiddie herself and would be till the day she died.

'It's so utterly yuk, bunging your own ideas on the chest of some revolting little sprog . . . We don't know what a kid wants anyway,' she moaned to CD, who was eating a vegetable samosa from a stall.

'Any one of these kids could be in the navy itself in fifteen years,' she continued, warming to her theme. 'I'm at this protest because *I* don't want to blow up. At least we know I haven't grown up to be an axe murderer. This lot might. They're probably more likely to actually. They reckon kids react against their parents' beliefs, and I'm not surprised,' said Rachel, staring around at the hippy throng. 'Wouldn't you turn into an axe murderer if your mother's idea of sweets was carrot cake?'

'Don't be so hard on everybody all the time,' said CD, who was enjoying his samosa and feeling benign. 'These people are cool. It's not their fault they've got poor dress sense . . .'

'Jesus, will you look at that fellah I just served,' said Rick the samosa maker, 'what *does* he look like!'

As it happened, CD believed himself to be effecting the casual elegance of an English gent abroad, strolling about on an early summer day. He was wearing a perfect linen suit and was the epitome of taste. Unfortunately he didn't have a perfect linen suit and certainly the old cricket trousers and chef's jacket were not an exact imitation.

Rick and his live-in friend, Judy, were convinced that CD must be drug squad.

'It's all so bloody pointless and *dull*,' Rachel moaned, 'nobody's *doing* anything.'

'Well, what the hell are you doing?' asked CD, who was vaguely experimenting with an idea that it might turn Rachel on if he was more butch and dominant. He toyed with the thought of adding, 'bitch', but mercifully reason prevailed.

'Nothing,' shouted Rachel, 'that's what makes me so angry. I'm not doing anything. I'm hanging around with a bunch of hippies, and hippies bore me shitless.'

'Hippies bore everybody shitless, Rachel, it's their job,' replied CD. 'Hippies even bore hippies shitless. That's why they take so many drugs, just to avoid having to talk to each other. They say it's to change their heads but it's not.'

'Well, it ought to be. If my head was as dull as that I'd want to change it,' said Rachel.

CD and Rachel stood in silence. CD trying to think of something dominant to say and Rachel reading a huge sign on one of the dock walls that said 'Perth Premium Gold – A regular drinking beer for a regular beer drinker'. Anyone who scorns Australian copywriting would scorn no further if they could have seen the effect that this advert was having on Rachel. Her whole soul cried out for a beer. Then somebody began to sing 'Blowing in the Wind'.

'Right, that's it,' she said. 'I'm going to the pub.'

But, just then there was a stirring in the crowd. Something interesting was happening on one of the ships. Rachel stayed to watch.

# THE *USS ENORMOUS*

The US Navy, in a monumentally optimistic bit of public relations, had opened up one of the warships to public inspection. The people of Carlo were to be allowed to take a look at the hardware to which they were hosts. What the thinking was behind the American decision is hard to say. Why people, nervous that their little town was being made into a prime nuclear target, should be less nervous for getting a closer look at the cause of their fears is a question not easily answered.

'And what you are standing on here, folks, is a United States warship, yes sirree. It's this little mother them Ruskis are going to be aiming at when they miss and hit your town.'

CD would have quite liked to have gone and had a look, although he wouldn't have admitted it. Actually, if he had gone, he would have been rather bored. The US Navy did not intend to give much away.

Second Lieutenant Kowalski was detailed to welcome the tourists aboard and escort them around those few sections of the ship that were not classified. He had been carefully chosen. Tall and splendid in his pure white uniform, he had an easy, open face and manner that made you just know he would defend democracy until his sabre broke. He dazzled his smitten audience of love-struck young women and death mad little boys, with a whirlwind of technology.

'This here is a US Naval 8.2 litre unload and distribution facility, manually operated by a single crewman.'

Moving on from the toilet the awestruck group were privileged to inspect an On-site Perimeter Confinement Safety Unit, or ship's rail. It was here that the excitement Rachel had observed from the shore occurred.

Through CD's second-hand binoculars she could see that two men had somehow managed to detach themselves from the group of sightseers and were scaling one of the sort of conning tower affairs that these ships seem to bristle with. One stopped only a few feet up but the other was tremendously nimble. He almost seemed to be running vertically. If he had been wearing a red and blue body stocking Rachel would have thought it was Spiderman. Having climbed as far as he could go – a good thirty feet above the shouting sailors – he attached himself to a satellite dish, managing to almost sit in it as if he was about to be stir-fried in an enormous wok. He raised his fist in a triumphant salute towards the protesters on the shore and then unfurled a twenty-five foot long banner that slashed about like a scythe in the strong wind. It was inscribed with the legend 'Nuclear Target'.

That was by no means the end of the entertainment, for suddenly there was a flash and a bang and all the shouting sailors dived for cover. It took another three bangs before they realized that these were not S S20s but simply fireworks let off by the other man, who had not climbed so far, to draw attention to the protest. The sailors, furious for having been duped, soon hauled the firework fellow down but it took twenty minutes for them to reach the one with the banner and bring him and his banner back to the deck. The protest was sufficiently dramatic for it to be shown on the news that evening. It wasn't much but it was something, and it was also undeniably exciting.

Watching from the shore, Rachel and CD did not know it but this was their first encounter with Walter and Zimmerman. They were soon to become comrades-in-arms against Stark.

# ZIMMERMAN AND WALTER

## ZIMMERMAN

Zimmerman's intense dislike of weapons of war had come upon him quite suddenly – literally in a flash. One moment he was walking through the jungle not decided on the subject either way, the next moment his private parts were hanging off a nearby tree and he knew he didn't like bombs. The doctors had done wonders, they fixed his legs, sewed his guts back together, but, sad to say, all the wonders of micro-surgery could not get his tackle down out of the tree.

A few months later Gough Whitlam brought the Australian Army home but it is said that for those who experienced the horrors, each one left a little piece of themselves out in Viet-nam. In Zimmerman's case it was his lunch-box. Ever since then he had never felt himself a whole member of society and, of course, he wasn't, because he no longer had a whole member with which to be social. He had not felt himself a part of what governments decided. He had not felt himself bound by their rules – basically, he hadn't felt himself.

Why had Zimmerman joined up in the first place? It was a question he often asked himself whilst contemplating the wreckage that lay inside his trousers. He could remember things quite clearly up until when he was about eighteen. It was about then that he had dropped a couple of tabs of acid and gone to see John Wayne in *The Green Berets*. He remembered that. But from then on it all got very confused. There were bangs and flashes and a series of very unpleasant experiences. Suddenly, it was three years later and he was being carried off an Army Medical Corps Hercules air transport. Sadly minus his hand luggage.

Since then Zimmerman had learnt that during the vague period of lights and bangs, he had turned into an exceptional soldier. Eventually becoming a commando. The army, it seemed, had trained him to do unspeakably horrid things very well indeed. They trained him diligently and his skills served them well. Zimmerman knew they had been pleased because they had given him a top combat medal of which he was proud.

Zimm had been very popular with his comrades. There was a good reason for this. They said he had guts. They were right, certainly he had guts and normally they were full of drugs. This made him very amenable. When someone was needed to creep down a suspicious looking hole, a hole which probably contained half the Vietcong Army, the others would shuffle their feet self-consciously and look shyly at Zimm.

'Zimm'll do it,' they would say to each other reassuringly.

'He's a real regular guy.'

By 'regular guy' they of course meant raving lunatic but were being tactful. When someone is stupid enough to risk his arse continually while others hide behind it, you let them.

Sad to say, by the time Zimm got back to Australia, his brain was fried. One thought was clear in his head though. One thought had sustained him throughout the long years since 'Nam. Zimmerman was going to save the world. That was what he spent his time doing, saving the world. That was what he was doing when he scaled the conning tower of the USS *Enormous* and unfurled his banner. He was saving the world.

He had been saving the world when he had broken into the tobacco company's laboratories and set all the dogs free. Certainly, the net result had been a bunch of Beagles wandering around half-starved and desperate for a ciggie but Zimm never thought his actions through very clearly. He just wanted to save the world, which seemed simple enough to him.

# WALTER

It was lucky then that Zimm's constant companion was Walter, a very together guy indeed. Extraordinarily together considering he was a hippy and hippies are not on the whole known for their togetherness. It was Walter who was with Zimm on the USS *Enormous* telling Zimm to cool it as they were led away by the military police. Walter always knew when Zimm was in danger of flying off the handle and exercising some of those terrible skills that the army had taken such pains to teach him. There were little tell-tale signs like veins bulging on his forehead, tiny codes in the things Zimm would say, like, 'I'm going to kill the dickhead in the white uniform.' Walter knew to pick up these hints and act on them.

Walter had a genuinely calming presence. When talking to him one really did get the impression that things were all right.

'Tell me things are all right, Walter.'

'They're all right.'

And, somehow, for a little while at least, they were. Of course, after a while Walter's cool could begin to irritate because there are times in every person's life when they want to fly off the handle. If the car explodes for instance, or you turn out to have an uncanny resemblance to an escaped psychopath and get wrongly sent to prison for a thousand years. Walter's response to disasters like that would be to say:

'It's OK, it's cool, try not to become uptight about it.'

This obviously could be pretty aggravating. But often Walter's calm, almost spiritual demeanour was a comfort to those who met him. Not the judges and police officers and representatives of chemical waste disposal firms, obviously. Nor the hire-purchase people to whom Walter would patiently explain that money exists only in their heads. But most people . . . well some people, found him calming – for a while anyway.

You needed to be calm to do the sort of things Walter was in the habit of doing. When you've sat in a tiny motorized dinghy with a shit scared Blue whale on one side of you, a seriously pissed off whaling fleet on the other side, ten foot waves underneath you and an explosive harpoon sailing over your head, you either learn to be cool or you go through a lot of pairs of trousers.

For Walter was green. He was as green as the contents of an Eskimo's hanky. He loved animals and plants and everything. (There was one plant that Walter particularly loved, although rolling it up and setting it on fire and sucking it to death was a funny way of showing it.) Walter also had a selfish motive for his green-ness, he firmly believed that peaceful co-existence with other life forms on the planet was the only way that the human race itself would survive.

A lot of people took the piss out of the sort of things Walter did. 'Oh wow, man,' they would say, 'Save the whale, yeah, and black lesbian disabled dwarfs for a nuclear free health food shop.' In fact, both Rachel and CD had been guilty of this type of comment in their time. But Walter knew that these people were wankers. Whales are the largest creatures left living on earth, the heart of a Blue whale is higher than a tall man and it weighs half a ton. The creature itself grows to a hundred feet and weighs a hundred and sixty tons. Everything pales in comparison to a creation of this awesome magnitude. What is the Taj Mahal or the Golden Gate Bridge to a living force with arteries so huge a child could crawl along them? Yet they were being wiped off the face of the earth to make soap.

'Listen, man, would you unpick the Bayeux Tapestry to get a reel of cotton?' Walter said at his trial. He got a thousand dollar fine.

## WALTER AND ZIMMERMAN

It was Walter who turned Zimmerman on to Eco stuff. He suggested to Zimm that he needed to channel his energies.

'Listen, man,' Walter would say, 'like, one day you're freeing Beagles, the next you're riding the bus all night defending old ladies ... I mean, cool, don't get me wrong, very cool. I just feel, like, we should, like ... you know, formalize our avenues of protest, right ...? Or does that sound a bit too much like heavy fascist mind control, and, like, pretty soon we'll be as bad as the people we're protesting against?'

'Well, it does a bit, man,' Zimmerman would reply.

None the less, despite the organizational pitfall of not wishing to get into any kind of fascist mind control thing, Walter and Zimmerman had sort of come to a conclusion as to what they were. They were Green Commandos. When they bothered to get up, and were straight, Zimm's horrifying military skills combined with Walter's ability to keep them in check, made them quite a team. They had saved animals, destroyed logging equipment, blocked up chemical waste pipes. Once they even burnt down a factory full of polystyrene packing bobbles. The little action of flying the peace banner over the ship was just a minor diversion for them.

Not so for Lieutenant Kowalski. He was a crazy man. He had never felt so insulted in his life. After all, here was the US Navy extending the hand of friendship and these two hippies had put a turd in it.

In fact, as the police escorted Walter and Zimm from the ship, a lot of people involved with the peace protest shook their heads critically. They strongly disapproved of confrontation, especially if it involved law-breaking.

'That's just silly,' they said, 'making people angry won't help.'

But Rachel felt it might help more than painting CND symbols on children's faces.

# BULLENS CREEK

Sly was flying much further north than Kalgoorkatta. He was heading up over the Great Sandy Desert. It was in this vast area of almost empty wilderness that he had been asked to secure the land required for the astonishing and immoral project that he was now a part of. He felt then, as he had felt on the jumbo the morning after his dinner, that this was going to be a lot more difficult than his fellow conspirators thought. The land requirements for the project were very specific, unfortunately they were also very contradictory. The two main points, ranking above all other considerations, were firstly that it had to be utterly remote and secondly, that good communications were essential. Great, thought Sly, a most ingenious paradox.

## STARK REQUIREMENTS

The need for isolation was obvious. The less people knew about what was going on the better. Mineral exploration and leisure development were to be the cover story and they would do at a casual glance. However, if someone started delving deeper and the real purpose of the site was discovered, well, Sly just hoped he had a convenient top-floor window to jump out of. Secrecy was the key, therefore, not only did the place have to be remote, but a contoured landscape was also considered essential – it is easier to undertake massive construction projects discreetly if you can hide behind a few hills. Also, an uneven terrain made electronic surveillance more difficult. Luckily most of the US spy satellites were pointing at the Soviet Union. The Americans were unlikely to bother the team Sly was now a member of. After all, Americans like multimillionaires. Their whole scene was hassling commies. Sly hoped so anyway because if some over zealous under-dog at the C I A or in the Pentagon did get on to them, no politico on earth would, or could, defend their actions. For the first time they would not be able to buy themselves out of trouble.

It was a salutary thought. Despite the enormous political clout that multimillionaires wielded, especially when organized in groups, so dark was their present purpose that were it to be revealed, even the most bent politicians in the world would be forced to turn and bite the hand that had fed it for so long. This was why privacy was essential. As has been said though, unfortunately, so were communications. The leisure cover story would not last long once things really got going. When the consortium moved it would have to move very fast indeed. Surprise would be the essence of success. If the world had more than a moment's warning, all might be lost. Hence they had to be able to assemble the personnel, the technology and the huge mass of hardware quickly. This could not be achieved with restricted access.

Anyway, the upshot of it all was that they were not actually spoilt for choice as to locations. The optimum spot seemed to be an area west of a place called Bullens Creek. It was hilly-ish, which is about as hilly as it gets in Western Australia, and it was utterly isolated apart from one road to Bullens. Bullens Creek itself, on the other hand, had just about sufficient communications for Stark's purposes. It had been fully integrated into the Telecom system five years previously. It was on the interstate highway and it had an airstrip. Also, it was only about five hundred miles north-west of Perth so what lines of communication there were would not be too stretched.

## DULLSVILLE WA

After a long dull flight, Sly landed at Bullens Creek airport.

Topol Bullen had been the first white man to find the creek, back in 1867. If at the time he had entertained any hopes that one day a thriving metropolis would grow up about the place, thus ensuring him and his name a kind of immortality, he had had it. Bullens Creek had started off tiny and tedious and gone downhill from there. Being the person after whom Bullens Creek was named is actually a slightly more anonymous thing than not having a place named after you at all. Even the people who live there have only half heard of it.

'Bullens Creek? Oh yeah, I think it's a little tiny town somewhere up towards the Territory. Come to think of it, buggered if I don't live there myself.'

Bullen himself never lived to discover that his name was to become a place that almost everybody in Australia had never heard of. He was killed by a camel whilst looking for his shorts, having had a dip in the creek he had just found. He had ridden the camel all the way from the coast and was under the impression that they had become friends. So had the camel, who was, therefore, rather surprised that on arriving at their first water for weeks, a meagre puddle dried almost completely in the appalling heat, Bullen had tethered it to a gum tree in order to get first slurp. Bullen's reasons for doing this were actually very sound. Camels can suck up literally gallons of water in a matter of seconds and Bullen, understandably, wanted to get in quick before the camel drained the puddle. The camel did not realize this however, and, thinking itself betrayed, broke its bindings in an anger of thirst and kicked Bullen out of the way, killing him in the process.

In fact, for quite a while, the place was called Camel Kick Creek, but eventually Bullens Creek prevailed – which is a shame because Camel Kick Creek is a much better name. The reason the name got changed was that there was a rather boring habit amongst the early white settlers of Australia. They liked to name places after very dull Victorians. During the same period, people in the USA were giving places terrifically exciting names like Tombstone, Deadwood,

Hangman's Tree and Death Gulch, but the old Aussies preferred things less colourful. For instance, there lies, almost bang in the middle of Australia, one of the largest monoliths in the world. An unfractured mass of glorious red sandstone that rises one and a half kilometres up from the flat desert floor and descends four kilometres beneath it. It has an astonishing, almost symmetrical shape and, according to the light, it changes colour from burning orange through fierce red to deep, cool purple. It is, of course, regarded with mystical awe by all who see it. The early Australians chose to call this wonder of the world 'Ayers Rock' after a dull Victorian administrator in a stupid hat – who happened to be chief secretary of South Australia.

It is, of course, a little unfair to make a comparison between Ayers Rock and Bullens Creek. In fact, the name of Bullens Creek was really rather apt because Bullens Creek is very boring and Bullen had been a very boring man. This was actually why he set out to stride across the Great Gibson and the Great Sandy Desert in the first place, he had got sick of people yawning at him when he talked about his theory. All the other explorers who set off on similar quests had great theories that people loved to listen to. Fascinating stuff about vast inland seas or a continent-sized oasis full of lush vegetation, fabulous rivers and endless free sex. Bullen's theory on the other hand was very dull indeed. He claimed that the vast hinterland of Australia was nothing but a dry, hot, flat desert with some dingos and a few broken bits of rock. He was right of course, but it was still a very boring theory. Had he ever made it back, people would have still yawned at him. After all, the only thing more boring than being dull is being dull and right.

Even the camel that got him was bored. 'What a dull drink,' it thought, and sauntered off, becoming one of the earliest of the domestic camels imported into Australia to return to the wild. Today, of course, there are herds of wild camels in the deserts of Oz but then it was quite a novelty – certainly more interesting than Bullen's Creek, anyway.

It was well over a hundred years since the camel had killed Bullen and that still ranked as the most exciting thing that had ever happened in the area.

What people do for diversion in isolated country towns is a bit of a mystery all over the world, although the physical similarities, hair-lips, low foreheads and high instance of mental disorder may go some way to solving the mystery. It used to be said that the best way to stop a girl getting pregnant in Bullens Creek was to castrate her brother.

Things definitely improved after they put in the airstrip and metalled the roads but once you've looked at the war memorial and said, 'Christ it's hot' a couple of times, you're still a bit stuck for raucous amusement.

One of the things they do in places like Bullens Creek is form dinner clubs. Sly was aware of this country habit and was relying on it to provide him with a medium whereby to ingratiate himself with the white locals. He felt that this would be a sensible preliminary to trying to negotiate with the aboriginal community.

Having parked his little plane, he strolled into the old shed, grandly titled the Airport Terminal, to get his paperwork sorted. Here, as he expected, he found a sign announcing the regular events which the town was looking forward to.

Royal Rotary Mouse – 2nd and 4th Mondays, venue – Queen Victoria Pub.
Grand Order Mason Sheep Shearers – Wednesday, venue – Queen Victoria Pub.
Lion Club Elks – 1st and 3rd Thursdays, venue – Queen Victoria . . . etc.

The fun went on and on. Scanning the lists of officers, Sly was struck by the number of times each name occurred, but in a different post. For instance, John Timpkiss might be the treasurer of the Elks and the secretary of the Mouses, whilst Phil Barcle was the opposite. Either lots of people in Bullens

Creek had the same name, or else all the clubs had the same members. The latter was, of course, the case. They could have just formed one big club but of course that wouldn't have been any fun. The variety provided endless diversion. It was a job sometimes for a bloke to figure out which stupid hat he was supposed to be wearing that night. Sly knew that since he was probably the most prominent visitor to Bullens Creek since the camel that got Bullen, he would be approached to address one of these institutions. That was fine by him. The sooner he started getting his story straight, the better.

# THE NERVE CENTRE OF ECOACTION

The place was real dark. Rachel wasn't scared of the dark, no, it wasn't the dark that she was scared of. It was not being able to see anything that she hated. She had already gone arse-over-tit twice, tripping on some form of creeper. The garden of Zimm and Walter's place definitely needed tending.

'We should tend that garden sometime,' Walter would observe.

'Man, it would take a Napalm strike to even make a dent in it,' Zimm replied. 'Doctor Livingstone is still in there looking for the source of the Nile.'

And so they let it go. It was getting increasingly difficult to get to the front door, as Rachel was discovering.

Country music was drifting through the darkness, whining, mournful music, straight-forward music. That was the great thing about country music, it did not mince words. The word 'obscure' is not in the country dictionary, foot-notes are not required. For instance, the country ballad writer wishing to suggest that he is low and blue because his baby is gone, would probably write something like. 'I'm low and blue because my baby is gone'.

This was how Zimm liked his music. Plain speaking was important to him, he hated hypocrisy. 'I want you out of my head and back in my bed before the morning comes', sang Lorreta Lynn as Rachel struggled up the path in the blackness, vegetation brushing her cheeks and deeply suspect substances underfoot. Just about every cat in Carlo shat in Walt and Zimm's garden. Walter thought it was OK because cats are clean shitters. They are always very careful to dig a shallow toilet and fill it in again afterwards. The problem obviously comes when the land has been so overcrapped that the surface is 100 per cent cat crap, which means the cat digs a hole in the crap, craps in it and then carefully pushes crap on top of it. A soul-destroying activity and one calculated to make any cat lower its personal standards.

There was no light inside the shack save the glow of a cigarette brightening with every draw and then dulling almost back into the blackness.

'Whoever you're looking for, they don't live here,' said a voice located just behind the cigarette.

'I'm looking for eighty-two King Edward the Seventh Empire Terrace. Have I got the right address?'

Whoever did the road naming in Australia was a serious empire freak. You'd be walking down some street in Sydney, half-Greek, half-Italian, half God knows what and the place is named after Queen Victoria. Zimm and Walter tried to get their street renamed Dead Abo Terrace and the local Freedom Association pushed a burning rag through their letter-box.

'You're here,' said the cigarette end, 'but you've got the wrong address. Like I said, whoever you want don't live here.'

'I'm looking for the two guys who got busted on the USS *Enormous* this morning.'

What happened next was an object lesson in why it was a bad idea to send confused young men off in a haze of drugs to fight a war that no one understands and can not be won, then bring them back, trained killers with fried brains and no bollocks. There was a split second of confusing movement. The cigarette end shot to within an inch of Rachel's face and she found herself pinned to a tree with her arms firmly clamped behind it. Her head was pushed right far back exposing her neck and although she could not be sure, she was conscious of the possibility that there might be a knife at her throat.

When her assailant spoke he sounded almost offended,

which struck Rachel as strange since she appeared to be the injured party. In fact Zimm was offended. He had a genuine persecution complex. He felt people did not respect him as a person. He felt they just saw him as a terrifying space case to be humoured, patronized and, if at all possible, avoided. He was, of course, right about this. It was a paradox of Zimm's sad mental condition that despite being pretty much a complete nutter, he could, on occasion, come up with an analysis as breathtakingly astute as this one.

'Oh man, I mean, what is the point, right?' he demanded, 'I mean, just what is the point? I mean, what am I, a non-person or something? Did they leave me out of the constitution, is that it? . . . Uhm, yeah, every guy and chick has a right not to be hassled in their own space, except Zimmerman . . . Like, if a dude was in court, right? The judge would say to him, "You are convicted of pulling someone's head off and eating it, have you anything to say before I bang you up in the slammer for ever? . . ." And the dude says, "It was only Zimmerman's head, your honour . . ." "Oh in that case you get a ten bucks reward and a new hat." *I said we weren't home!*'

Rachel sensed that with the last line her attacker had returned to the planet earth and some response was in order. However, even if her head hadn't been thrust right back, making speech pretty difficult, she would still probably have been at a loss for an appropriate remark.

Many people put Zimm's erratic speech patterns down to his terrible experiences in 'Nam, but in fact he had always been weird as anything speech-wise.

'I'll never understand you, son,' Mrs Zimmerman used to sigh – and she was right, she never did.

Just as Rachel was trying to decide whether kicking her assailant's shins would be a good or a bad idea, Walter turned on a lamp. It was a sixty watt bulb but after the darkness it made everyone blink. The light flooded out through the open French windows to the tree against which Rachel was pinned. She heard a gentle movement and then the light was gone. This was because Walter was now standing in the doorway and it fitted him perfectly. It was almost as if the doorway had been built around him, and what's more, by a carpenter who liked his doorways figure hugging. For Walter was huge, terrifyingly so – far bigger than he had looked at the docks. Rachel commended her soul to God. Zimmerman, at six foot two with his lean and wiry frame had been worrying enough, but his companion was the proverbial brick shithouse. A municipal version with fifteen sitters and a thirty yard trough. He was not fat, although the years had lent a certain dignity to his midriff, he was just huge. A shaggy bearded bear of a man in a smock and khaki shorts.

As it happened, Rachel need not have been afraid (of Walter, that is – she was still in the vice-like grip of a lunatic), because Walter was the gentlest of souls, Rachel could tell from his voice.

'Zimm, what are you doing, man?' Walter said. 'I mean, really, what are you doing? You have to cool it, you know? I mean, this is a terrible thing, pushing people around like that is a terrible thing. I just don't know what you think you're doing. If you do these terrible things, Zimm, you know I'm going to have to start thinking that you and I are on totally different wave-lengths. Like me on one wave-length and you on another wave-length, but a different one, not the same as mine at all. That's what I'm going to have to start thinking if you don't cool it.'

Despite her difficult situation, Rachel could not help but be impressed by the extraordinarily mellow quality of Walter's voice. It was a lovely calming voice. It made you think that things were going to be OK and she felt this despite the fact that Walter seemed to be talking almost complete drivel. She couldn't help but wonder what the effect would be if he ever said anything worth listening to.

Zimmerman, releasing Rachel, stepped back and was caught in what few rays of light managed to squeeze past Walter's huge frame by holding their breath and thinking thin. Rachel could now see that even without the voice, and despite his quite absurd size, Walter was definitely the one she'd prefer to meet on a dark night. Zimmerman looked like a piece of human granite. He wore the traditional Ozzie singlet, which is a baggy vest with very low cut armholes and his muscles looked like they had been painted on by Leonardo da Vinci. There wasn't sufficient fat on him to fry an egg (although the grease in his hair would have tempted Slampacker to open a franchise on his head). When you've been blown to bits, as Zimmerman had, you either train hard or you don't get better. Zimm had got better and then gone on getting better. From his shiny, greasy, biker-looking jeans to his short, greying beard, he was muscle and bone. Above the beard was a different story. He looked out to lunch – Mr and Mrs Sanity were clearly not at home to callers. His temples were quivering with riotous indignation and his deep-set eyes flashed about behind the long, sweaty strands of hair that fell forward from his centre parting. He was still mightily aggrieved.

'She said she's come about us getting busted on the boat this morning . . . I mean what *is* the point? All the cops are down at the Pig Pen thinking what shall we do this evening to justify the extortionate amount of bread the public pays us to be pigs? Shall we, like, go and catch a rapist or something? No, let's go hassle Zimmerman, that'll really make the streets safe for the kids to play in.'

'I'm not a police officer,' said Rachel. She could not bring herself to use such a monumentally dated and unfashionable expression as 'pig'. The fact that Zimmerman's mind had closed down in 1972 was his problem, not hers.

'So, what's the story, lady, where is it at?' said the mellow one.

Rachel was seriously beginning to regret having come. Not because of being half assaulted but because she seemed to have fallen in with yet more hippies. It was expressions like 'where's it at' that made Rachel suspicious. But she decided that she would have to persevere.

'I wished I'd been on the boat with you,' she said. 'I was one of the people on the quay waving a sign.'

'Man,' said Walter with what, for him, was a tone of excitement – which meant it would have anaesthetized an epileptic trapped in a stroboscope. 'You were one of the girls with their tits out? *I* wish you'd been on the boat with us.'

Rachel put Walter right. Walter admitted that although he abhorred sexism in every form, if it had to have a form, the form of a load of chicks waving their tits around didn't seem such a bad option to him. Rachel said she didn't think that Walter had thought this one through properly. Walter admitted that this might be true and promised to think about it really hard later in bed. Zimm said it was all one to him because he didn't have any bollocks anyway. Rachel thought this a pity, kind of like finding an E-Type in perfect condition, except the gear stick had been broken off. Introductions thus affected, Rachel went and got CD from the car and Zimm volunteered to make some tea.

# SPYING OUT THE LAND

## DINNER AND BULLSHIT

The sun had been down for hours but that didn't seem to make much difference in that baking summer of Stark. The Queen Victoria Pub's upstairs room was like the inside of a microwave. Dinner was over. What had started out as a summer salad had been reduced by heat and humidity to a sort of vegetable stew. The royal toast had been made and the beer was flowing, served in the curious Australian glass known as a pony, which is about the size of an egg cup. The point being that you drink in small units because if you leave your beer in the glass too long it will evaporate. Due to the climate, beer is served at almost zero degrees. A person freezes to the glass. In other countries you might complain about a bit of lipstick on the rim of your beer, in Australia you might find someone's lips.

'Gentlemen,' said the chief dingo, rising to his feet and calling order. 'The Royal Hatch of the Old, Stupid and Contemptible Dingo's (Bullens Creek chapel) have great pleasure in welcoming a self-made multimillionaire and good old all round Ozzie bloke, Silvester Moorcock.'

Sly rose to his feet amidst admiring applause. It did not disconcert Sly that he found himself addressing an audience who were all wearing false dingo ears. He considered himself lucky that it was not a Tuesday, in which case he would have been talking to the Chapel of the Charitable Chickens, which would have meant beaks, feathers and singing the 'Honourable cluck cluck song' on the stroke of each hour. Sly chose his words carefully, he wanted to win them over, to make them like and trust him so they would not start asking questions when he came to make his purchases. He gave them his best shot, his trusty 'Road to Success, I made it, you could make it too' speech:

'Listen, I'm pure Aussie, right? This is a great country and the honeypot is open to all. Christ, if a stupid bastard like me can get a pawful, anyone can,' – they loved the self-deprecatory stuff – 'I mean, any old pie-brained dickhead with no teeth and a wallet full of condoms way past the sell-by date can make it in the lucky country.' The older blokes were ecstatic.

'Sure, you need some talent and application,' he added, 'people who are not prepared to put the hours in need not expect to travel club-class . . .' Some of the audience attempted to nod intelligently at this – not a very advisable thing to do when you are wearing false dingo ears.

'You also need luck, of course you do,' Sly granted magnanimously. 'Christ, you got to be in the right place at the right time. The fellah with the goldmine isn't necessarily the best miner around but he's the fellah who found the gold, and good luck to him. Mind you, I don't say you can't *make* luck sometimes. Oh yes. That fellah who found the gold, well, chances are he was *looking* for that gold. Maybe he was the fellah who was prepared to go looking for gold in the hills that the mine expert said weren't worth touching. Maybe he just thought hell, maybe I'll get lucky . . .'

This meaningless tripe was slipping down pretty well with the fourth or fifth beer. The audience knew they weren't exactly listening to Abraham Lincoln but it was pleasant enough stuff. They liked the rugged frontier side of it and redneck anti-intellectualism. Actually it was a much cleverer speech than it sounded because Sly was getting around to a point. 'Listen, mates. There's more than one way to bite the tail off a kangaroo. Are you with me?'

They weren't but they didn't mind pretending. It was too hot to argue.

'What I'm saying is, if there ain't no gold to be found then dig for something else. I'm telling you, there isn't a hill in Australia that a profit can't be wrung out of if you think hard enough.'

Here, Sly lost his audience somewhat. Everyone in the room knew that their scrappy little hills had been surveyed to death and the only things ever found were a few old Ab' relics that a couple of archaeologists had got excited about for half an hour. But Sly pursued his theme of nothing ventured; nothing gained, with his usual force and charm so that when, just before he sat down, he announced his intention of taking another look at the whole area, he almost had people believing that he had a chance. After all, it was his time and money and if he *did* find something! Bullens Creek would become, figuratively speaking, a goldmine. Perhaps even literally! After all, look what this same man, Sly Moorcock, had done to Kalgoorkatta! Who could tell, maybe he would work the same magic in Bullens Creek.

By next morning reason had regained its throne. Nobody was planning swimming pools or European holidays, but Sly had laid a firm foundation for his story. They believed that he was going to take another look at the hills. Who cared? He was just a crazy bloke with more money than sense.

## A TRICKY PROBLEM

Sly headed towards the Yalurah community, peering over the top of the enormous cage-like steel 'roo bars that jutted out in front of his car. The land was owned by the Aboriginals that lived there. It had been granted back to them during the great land rights debate of the early eighties. Sly would have to play this negotiation very carefully. He could not be sure whether there were spiritual connotations to the place. He could not just say that there was an equally unattractive bit of useless scrub, just like the one the government had kindly granted them, fifty miles up the road and he'd give them a crate of scotch to piss off. The point was that the bit of scrub up the road might not have the same Dreamtime connections that the one they were on did.

Besides this, for all the fact that Sly claimed they were, Aboriginals were not stupid. If he wanted to get them out they were certain to ask themselves why he wanted them out. The conclusion that they were bound to come to was that the land was worth something. Now a few years ago that might have made them up-the-price but, no more than that. These days however, they were getting a touch more sophisticated. It was not unknown for Aboriginals to actually take an interest in mining themselves. Sly smiled as he remembered the awful crisis of principles that had beset the do-gooders and bleeding-hearts during the great uranium debate. For years these people had bleated on and on about Aboriginal self-determination; about giving them back control of their lives etc., etc. As if they wanted to do anything but drink anyway, thought Sly. Then along came the possibility of uranium on Aboriginal land and of course the same do-gooders were totally against more uranium mining but, unfortunately, some of their darling Abs weren't. The Aboriginals saw that finally they had a chance of grabbing some white man's money. It had been a delicious irony really. The do-gooders suddenly found themselves in the role of trying to tell the Abs what was good for them. The very thing they had been screaming about for donkeys years.

Anyway, Sly knew that if he gave the impression that he was desperate to acquire their land, the present occupants were bound to presume that he knew something that they didn't and hang on in until they found out what it was. It was a tricky little balancing act. He had to get the land off them while making them think that he didn't particularly want it.

Still, as Sly reflected, they *were* only Abs and he had ridden rough-shod through half the boardrooms in W A. He reckoned he could handle it.

## MAKING AN OFFER

The negotiations were not going well.

'Drink?' he said to the representatives of the community

that he sat facing – he had brought a splendid supply of the very best beers and spirits.

'We're dry here, mate,' said the old guy with a tone that directly translated as 'so fuck you'.

This was a big setback for Sly. If the place was dry it was going to be a damn sight tougher to manipulate them. Sly took a swig himself, not because he wanted any at all but because it was obvious that he was dealing with some fairly together people and he did not want them to think he had just been hoping to get them pissed.

'So it's no good hoping to get us pissed, mate,' the old bloke continued and Sly realized that although he did not particularly hate Abs in general, he sure as hell was starting to hate this wily old bastard.

'It's like this, Mr Culboon,' he said, forcing a smile. Sly explained that he was looking at a number of locations in Western Australia, of which this was only one, in an effort to find a suitable location for a business venture that he had in mind.

'Business venture, here? What are you going to do, sell white art to us Aboriginals?'

This was all Sly needed – a fucking comedian. He waited while the old boy got his laugh and then paused a little longer, eyeing the bare formica table, the rickety walls, the fat bellied children. Poverty hung about the place like they'd framed it and nailed it to the walls. These people did not have much to lose, it was time to assert himself.

'Listen, *mate*, you can sit and take the piss if you like, but while you're sodding me off, some other guy's walking off with a fat bank roll the size you wouldn't dream of.'

'I don't dream about bank rolls, big or small, mate. You do, I don't. Which I suppose is why you've got a brand new Toyoki and I've got a 1967 Holden, but, you're in my house so you'll watch your manners or you'll fuck off, OK?' The man was clearly a philosopher as well.

Sly was having to quickly revise all expectations of Mr Culboon, the head man who sat before him. He had looked such a clown to Sly but clearly he wasn't a clown at all.

'What do you want our land for, mate?' Mr Culboon asked.

'I don't want your land *particularly*,' Sly replied.

'Well, what are you doing here, then,' said Mr Culboon leaping on the point like a prosecution counsel, 'has my house suddenly become an in place for Perth money men?'

This wasn't getting Sly anywhere. He was in severe danger of wanting to strangle this Culboon fellah – which would certainly have soured future negotiations.

'I need some land, and as I say, this is one of the sites we're considering.'

'So, it's nothing to do with mining then?'

'Of course it's nothing to do with mining, Mr Culboon. Your scrappy little hills are a pile of shit and you know it. There's more minerals in a bottle of Perrier. You could dig for ever and you wouldn't come up with enough gold to fill your front teeth in. They're worthless, of course they are, or else why do you think the state government let you have them. You can be damn sure they weren't going to give you an oil-well.'

'So why do you want them then?'

Sly had to admit it was a fair question.

'Well, Mr Culboon, I'll tell you. Myself and my associates have formed a consortium called "Oasis" and we are investigating the possibility of setting up a desert vacation re-treat.'

There was an incredulous pause. Mr Culboon looked at the others in the room, they looked at him. Then they all looked out of the open doorway. They looked at the flies, the 'roo shit, the flat, shimmering boredom of a featureless bit of desert ringed by piss-poor, reddish little hills too steep to walk, too boring to climb. They looked at the one road – the road that ran from them to Bullens Creek and back again – a road that ran from nowhere to nowhere. Then they all looked at Sly.

'Vacation!!' spluttered Mr Culboon, and nearly wet himself.

Sly had to undergo the distinctly uncomfortable sensation

of a group of people from an alien culture – a culture towards which he had always felt massively superior – pissing themselves laughing at him. The noise of the laughter attracted some women from outside. They put their heads around the door and asked what the gag was.

'This fellah says he wants to turn our shithole into a vacation oasis!' said one of the men with tears in his eyes. The women howled.

'Ha, ha, so the beautiful people are coming are they?' a woman grinned. 'I can just see them getting off the plane saying, "mmm nice smell of dingo piss".'

They all howled some more, and more, and more. Sly felt that he was losing control of the conversation.

'Look!' he said, 'I'm perfectly serious and so's my money, so if you want to hear me out, fair enough, otherwise I'll fuck off now.'

'Fuck off now if you like,' said Mr Culboon, still laughing. Sly ignored him and continued.

'All we need is sunshine and you will agree that you've got plenty of that. We can't get planning permission on the coast anymore so we're looking inland. I'm talking a totally man-made environment here, pools, tennis courts, a theatre, discos, and, get this, a gambling licence. We are talking Las Vegas! Have you ever been to Ayers Rock? That's a totally self-contained holiday complex built out of the desert, what's the difference?'

'Ayers Rock,' said Mr Culboon who, one hopes, had resigned himself to the fact that he and Sly would never be friends.

'Well, exactly, the last thing your dedicated pleasure-seeker wants is a bloody great area of natural beauty that he's going to feel obliged to traipse all over. He wants to have fun! . . .' said Sly, getting down to business, 'we have various options of which, I repeat, this is only one. Now we have a one million dollar relocation budget for whoever happens to be living where we decide to build. There are ninety-seven of you, which works out at ten thousand dollars each to piss off. What do you say?'

People were taking him more seriously but Mr Culboon was very doubtful.

'A million bucks for a bunch of Abs? You must like this place mate.'

'We'd have to pay someone off wherever we went. And, besides,' Sly added piously, 'the consortium I represent are not unaware of the spiritual value of the land and wish you to be aware that this will be thematically integrated into the overall design of the complex.'

'How touching, a Dreamtime Cocktail bar, I reckon – and this folks is the very place where the dumb Abs drew their stupid pictures – that'll be your thematic integration, mate.'

'Look, *mate*, I'm not here to fight a race war. I'm here to do some business, and if you don't like it I'll take it elsewhere, all right?' Sly could see that a few of the faces did not look so anxious to laugh at him anymore.

'We'll think about it,' said Mr Culboon, 'give us a number where I can contact you.'

This was all Sly had hoped for and it was good enough. He reckoned that once he had gone they'd come round in the end. He was prepared to up the money, if necessary, but that Culboon was a clever bastard and he didn't want to appear over anxious.

## JUDGING A BOOK BY ITS COVER

Appearances are so deceptive especially when they cross a cultural divide. To Sly's white eyes, Mr Culboon had looked like a semi-savage. He had the traditional scars across his chest, deep and fearful. Plenty of ash got rubbed in them Sly had thought looking at the great welts that bubbled out of the old man's brown skin like surf in a sea of gravy. Also he had had his two front teeth removed, a practice which was utterly beyond Sly, it made the man look idiotic.

But really it's all a question of what you're used to. For instance, Mr Culboon and his wife both had big old floppy pot bellies. They were not a young couple and his especially hung like an enormous tea-bag across his belt. Neither he nor his wife were remotely self-conscious about this. Now the wife of one of Sly's principal business rivals in Perth, a woman called Dixie Tyron, had also been developing a gut like that, plus thighs with saddle-bags on them that flapped around like soft, quilted fins. She, unlike the Culboons, was not happy with them and had undergone a form of surgery recently developed in America, which involved injecting the fatty regions with some chemical which actually dissolves the fat, making it possible to suck it out. In comparison with this phenomenal self-mutilation, knocking out a tooth or two seemed merely eccentric.

When the whites first encountered the blacks in Australia, they were horrified to observe that they didn't seem to wash. This led them to conclude that they were uncouth, filthy creatures who barely knew how to look after themselves. In fact the exact opposite was the case. Their not washing, or rather not washing in the conventional Western manner, was a very sensible thing indeed. To a desert Aboriginal, water is used for one thing and one thing only, drinking. It is simply too scarce to get into the habit of using it for any other reason. They knew where it was, they protected it, they conserved it. Sometimes they worshipped it. What they did not do was put a rubber duck in it and splash it all over the place. Aborigines did wash, of course. They washed in smoke and heat, rubbing themselves down in their own sweat. All peoples adapt themselves to their environment. In the days before easily available heating fuel, the ancestors of those first Australian settlers had sewn themselves into their clothes for the winter.

# A CALL FROM OCKER TYRON

The morning Sly returned from Bullens Creek he was awakened by the phone ringing. Actually, 'ringing' is too dignified a word for the wet, simpering trill that was oozing listlessly round the room. It sounded like a small marsupial sitting in the bath and farting through a descant recorder. Sly hated the new phone tones. He could remember when a phone had sounded like a phone. 'Ring, ring,' that was something a man could answer with vigour and purpose. These days he felt like saying, 'I'm not picking you up until you ring properly'.

On this occasion he could not even find the phone – he did not actually know what it looked like. The apartment, as with all of Sly's properties, had been done out for him by an interior design team. Sly had told them he wanted a one-off shag den and so they had set out to create a relaxing atmosphere, free of tension, comfortly co-ordinated throughout, with everything blending in. The result had achieved just that and hence Sly could never find the phone. He stared about himself wildly for a moment and then, not for the first time in this situation, ran out to his car.

The interior of the car had not been designed by someone who wanted to be subtle and relaxing with everything blending perfectly. No, it had been designed by someone who wanted to suggest a rich, powerful man with no time to waste. 'Your quartz quadrophonic personal communication and data processing unit is located in your fully computerized, digitally automized, central console unit,' the salesman had said.

This meant the phone was between the seats and Sly was grateful for this simple arrangement. He jumped in, barking his shin on the car door. Somehow it is even more galling to knacker your leg on an Aston Martin that cost a hundred and fifty thousand dollars. This was a car that could withstand the impact of a two joint articulated road train, fully loaded with cans of lager. It had a roll cage a fat elephant could have used as a trampoline. It was so safe you could have used it as a nuclear fall-out shelter for Christ's sake and yet you could still bark your shin on it like the car was a Ford fucking Escort.

He picked up the quartz quadrophonic personal communication and data processing unit.

'Yeah.'

Sly was looking at his leg. For a moment there was nothing then, suddenly, as if by magic, a great glistening puddle of blood materialized. Quickly he hung the offending leg out of the window. Even multimillionaires don't like getting blood all over their soft, beige leather bucket seats. So, there he was, draped across the passenger seat, dripping leg hanging out of the window, gear stick trying to force its way through his back, about to have a phone call that was relevant to all life on the planet. If there is indeed a God, and if he really did make man in his own image, he must look a right dildo.

'Who's that?' said a rather unpleasant, gruff voice. Mind you, in fairness, the way Sly was feeling he would have found the voice unpleasant if Kiri Te Kanawa had rung him up.

'What do you mean, "who's that" arsehole? You rang me,' Sly replied, suddenly feeling nervous. He didn't like enigmatic calls. Sly hit the various telephonic security switches that had started flashing on the dashboard. He wanted the call taped, just in case it was blackmail. After all, he had had a creative and athletic evening with the Malaysian hostess on his last stop-over from the UK. Mind you, there was no law against peanut butter, or where you put it for that matter – it certainly tasted better than on Satay.

Sly also activated a signal distorter so no one could locate him from the position of his phone, a signal search so that later on, if desired, Sly could discover the location of the caller, a scrambler, in case a third party was listening in and finally, a frequency blocker on the off chance that someone had put a bomb under the car and the phone was the trigger. Sly had no reason whatsoever to presume that he needed any of these things but they advertised them in the magazines you get on airlines and Sly, as always, had been bored.

Of course, some people got off on this sort of thing because it made them feel like men. Sly was not this big an idiot. Ocker Tyron was though, and it was him on the other end of the line. He too had activated all his blocking, mixing, tracing and scrambling gear – consequently what was left of the line was pretty poor. Fifty grand each so that they could say 'pardon' at each other.

Without the 'pardons' the conversation went like this:

'Don't call me an arsehole, it's Ocker Tyron.'

'Oh no,' said Sly.

'Don't say, oh no, like that. What's the problem.'

'What do you mean, what's the problem? You're the problem, Ocker. We hate each other. You know it and I know it.'

Tyron was genuinely taken aback.

'Well, just because we hate each other doesn't mean we can't be friendly,' he said.

'What do you want, Ocker?'

'How did you get on with the Abs and the rednecks?' Ocker asked, knowing full well that Sly had got on crap and enjoying the knowledge.

Sly nearly fell off his seat, except that it's almost impossible to fall off a bucket seat in a car when you are leaning across it with one leg out of the window. He convulsively jerked though. Sadly he convulsively jerked with sufficient violence to release the handbrake – always put your car in gear on a slope. Sly spun round, or tried to, he had little room to manoeuvre. As it happens, he had little time either, in seconds the car had rolled into the gate post at the foot of the drive. All he succeeded in doing was agonizingly adding to the mess on his leg as the injured part dragged across the lock button on the door. One knackered leg, one knackered wing – the leg was worth slightly less.

'Shit!!'

'Yes, I rather thought that would surprise you,' Ocker Tyron sneered down the phone.

'Look, fuck off, Tyron. I'll phone you back.' Sly put the phone back in the fully computerized, digitally automized, central console unit. Jesus! What had happened? Five minutes earlier he had been asleep. Now he had a bleeding leg, a dented Aston, and worst of all he seemed to have breached the confidence and trust of the Stark consortium.

He went inside and had a cup of coffee. There was no point trying to avoid it, Ocker Tyron was on to him in some way and he had better find out what he knew and what he wanted.

Ocker Tyron was an old rival of Sly's. Sly had worked for Tyron years back, before he had pulled off his great pie scam. Ocker was a cliché-style Ozzie multimillionaire. A tough, boorish maverick. He and his exuberant wife, Dixie, styled themselves virtually as Australian royalty. He as the tough, powerful, elder statesman of national commerce and politics; she as a charity dispensing ambassador of goodwill.

Dixie had a peculiar talent for making many thousands of dollars worth of clothes look like she had bought them at Woolworths. This was her famous common touch (famous because it was often mentioned in her husband's newspapers) which she firmly believed endeared her to the honest folk of WA. In fact, of course, they would have liked to see her fry.

Sly hated them both.

'Tyron, it's Moorcock.'

Sly was struggling to keep his temper. Tyron had taken his revenge for the previous conversation by having his secretary leave Sly on hold for five minutes.

'Ah, Silvester, ready to have a civilized conversation now are we? Because I really don't have time for personal abuse.'

'Well, shut up then you stupid dickhead and get on with whatever it was you phoned me for.'

'The land project. You screwed it didn't you?'

'What do you know about the land project?' Sly turned on the lie detector and watched the blips on the screen. They weren't foolproof but it made Sly feel slightly better to flip it on. It was a bit like making an obscene gesture at the bastard behind his back.

'Oh, come off it, Sly, I know everything about Stark. You don't think I'm not involved do you? I'm worth twice as much as you.'

'They never mentioned it to me.'

Sly didn't know what to make of this. Had Tyron found out about the project and was he trying to muscle his way in on Sly's back? Perhaps he really was a member. Tyron was certainly richer than he – if differentials still meant anything at their exalted level.

'Of course they didn't mention it, we talk about this as little as possible. Slampacker called me to say that you were on board and that they'd asked you to find the land, and of course bung in your bucks . . .'

'Yeah, well, I'm finding the land aren't I? So why don't you stay out of it?' Sly was most disconcerted to learn that Ocker Tyron was a colleague in the project.

'I can't stay out of it, can I, old son? I'm assembling a great deal of the equipment, that's my job. Pretty soon I'm going to need somewhere to put it.' Ocker Tyron switched to scramble and dropped his voice. 'All this paraphernalia is rather difficult to pass off as harmless mining gear, you know. People notice things.'

Just talking about it made Sly's head swim.

'Are you sitting on the stuff now?'

'No, but it won't be long, fuel, power, control systems, the hardwear itself. I am going to need somewhere to put it. The stuff is scattered all over the world, but it's coming. Soon you and I are going to be nominal proprietors of a rather sophisticated installation. And so . . . we need the real estate.'

'Look, I'm getting on with it, OK? It isn't easy. What we're planning here is a disgustingly and immoral –'

'So what's new, love?' said Tyron. 'You just got Oz Businessman of the Year for being disgusting and immoral morning, noon and night . . .'

113

'Come off it, you know damn well that this is different. There's not a politician in the world we could buy off if they got a whiff of it. That's why I have to tread carefully. People own the land, I don't want to cause a stir.'

'Yes, well, if you can't do it, tell me and I'll do it, OK? Stay in touch,' and with that Ocker Tyron put down the phone.

Sly was left feeling absolutely livid. Tyron knew it and leant back in his huge chair happily. The voice of his secretary piped up.

'I have Mr Nagasyu on a secure line for you, sir . . .'

## NAGASYU, THE JOKE AND THE WHALES

Mr Nagasyu had got incomprehensibly rich with a very simple idea. He had noticed the huge Japanese success in making things smaller. People seemed to like their high-tech titchy. Determining to take advantage of this curious quirk, he had set about making things so small that they kept getting lost. Radios that you had to leave on, or you wouldn't be able to find them again, state of the art speakers and electric toothbrushes that could easily slip down between the cushions on a sofa. As Mr Nagasyu had guessed, Nagasyu products had constantly to be replaced and he became quite stupidly rich.

'Hullo, Mr Tyron,' he said, 'Slampacker tells me we have decided on the optimum location.'

'That's right, Mr Nagasyu,' Tyron replied. 'It only remains to acquire it, there are one or two small obstacles to be kicked aside.'

'Well, please to hurry up. I am sitting on some extremely embarrassing equipment.'

'Oh, I'm sure not,' said Tyron, trying to lighten things up. 'I heard a Jap's bollocks were his best feature.'

Luckily Nagasyu did not understand Western slang. Even if Tyron's joke had been funny, Nagasyu would not have got it. He did not possess a sense of humour nor did he aspire to one, which made him slightly better company than Ocker Tyron, who also did not possess a sense of humour but cracked gags all the time. Tyron did not do this because he was under the impression that he was any great hoot, he was a pretty realistic man and realized that his sense of humour was facile and uncouth. Tyron cracked gags as an exercise in power. Normally when he cracked one, he was surrounded by people who had to laugh, and they always did. Ocker was always struck by how silly people looked, simpering nervously at his childish comments. It was this kind of personal therapy that fortified Ocker Tyron's private contempt for the human race. A contempt that made him capable of doing the things he did. Unlike Tyron, Mr Nagasyu was possessed of a degree of style and sophistication. Nonetheless, despite their different personalities, Nagasyu was every bit as hard a man as Ocker Tyron and Nagasyu had wrought an easily comparable amount of damage on the fragile planet.

## HULLO YOUNG LOVERS

As it happened, Walter and Zimmerman had cause to know a little of Nagasyu's brutality. It was one of his ships that they had been shouting at when the harpoon had sailed over their heads and into the whale that they had been trying to protect.

They shouldn't really have had to be in such a dangerous position, because commercial whaling has finally been outlawed by international agreement. The task now is to restock the species and, of course, only the whales can do that. Unfortunately, there are so few of them left that it will require a level of whale sauciness liable to melt the ice caps. These are hot-blooded creatures and at one hundred and sixty tons they certainly know how to make the earth move. Still it has at least given the horny young whale a new and telling chat up line. 'Come on darling, we have a duty to restock the species.' Certainly beats, 'Look I just think it would be really beautiful, OK? Because I actually love you as a whale, you know? Not just as a sex object.'

Whales are quite shy and secretive about their love-making, which is no mean achievement when one considers that a

Blue whale gets to be about one hundred feet long. Anyone who has tried to keep things quiet with parents in the next room will sympathize with two shy young lovers trying to keep the noise down when their combined weight is over three hundred tons.

Unfortunately, despite the commercial ban, whales are not being politely left alone to do the business. Sad to say, Japan, Korea, Norway and Iceland still hunt and kill the tiny whale population that remains, bypassing the law by claiming that the cull continues for 'scientific' purposes. The real truth is that so spectacularly huge are these beasts and so efficient have hunting methods become, that despite the appallingly depleted numbers, it remains profitable to go after them.

Nothing kills passion faster than an exploding harpoon in the guts.

## MASTERMINDS

There is, of course, one truly intriguing whale question which it would be lovely to get an answer to. Whales have the largest brains on earth. What do they do with them? Let's face it, you don't need a brain that would get stuck in a lift in order to open your mouth and swim towards a load of stupid plankton.

What do whales do with their brains? Are they philosophers, struggling with the thorny questions of existence? saying to themselves, 'I know I think, therefore I am, but plankton do not think, therefore they are not, in which case, what have I been living off all these years?'

One of the things they certainly do with their brains is survive. They have survived for millions of years – or at least they did until people started sticking spears into them. The fact that they are not intellectually equipped to deal with this threat does not reflect adversely upon their intelligence. After all, if Albert Einstein had been mugged by Silvester Stallone, he would probably have got his head kicked in. It is to be profoundly hoped that Silvester Stallone is not, at the end of the day, able to claim intellectual superiority over Einstein.

Whales have been lounging about and eating plankton for

some fifty million years. Not a bad achievement, especially when compared to humankind's rather pathetic four hundred thousand. Maybe that's what whales do with their huge brains – they don't fuck things up.

It takes the human race to the very limits of its intellectual ability to fuck things up in the way it does. The brain-crunching effort that has gone into developing the technology to kill, destroy, poison and pollute, pushes our greatest minds to the very limits of their potential. Perhaps if they had been just a little bit cleverer they wouldn't have done any of those things in the first place.

Maybe you have to be really clever simply not to fuck things up. Perhaps Mummy and Daddy whale shake their heads sadly over little Timmy, saying in screechy whale talk:

'Poor Timmy is severely retarded, we'd better send him to a special school. He's working on a way to pollute the sea with high-level radioactive waste, and he's too thick to realize that this is stupid.'

Of course, not all creatures who have survived billenium have big brains. The Sea Cucumber, for instance, is nothing more than a machine for sucking sand – so no chance of 'O' levels there. Everyone has their way of getting by as age gives way to age. Ways that worked perfectly well, until the bad kid moved in on the block.

## TIME IS SHORT

Nagasyu didn't care how many whales he killed. He had bigger fish to fry.

'Time is short,' he barked down the phone at Tyron. 'Amongst other things I have assembled several square miles worth of solar energy panelling. I am anxious to unload, Mr Tyron. Are preparations for the Stark site going ahead smoothly?'

'Don't worry,' said Tyron with easy confidence.

He knew that if Sly Moorcock could not sort out those Abs, he damn well could.

# THE FIRST ENEMY
# OF STARK

At the offices of the *Financial Telegraph* in London, Linda Reeve was on the phone as well. You wouldn't really have thought it to look at her but Linda Reeve and the Great Blue whale had something in common. Something even more basic than that they were both mammals. More immediate than that, Linda, like the Blue whale, was largish with nice eyes. The most fundamental thing that Linda Reeve had in common with the Blue whale was that she too was in serious danger of becoming extinct.

Linda was talking to a colleague on the *Wall Street Examiner* in New York.

'Have you noticed, Chrissy? It's happened again, this time with Nagasyu?'

'What's happened again?' the voice crackled back irritably. It was still early in New York and Chrissy was trying to deal with the twin blows of a total smoking ban in her office plus it was de-caf' day for the coffee making thing. One of the strange things about life – which one day Chrissy intended to write a brilliant article about – was that despite the fact that she knew that caffeine and de-caf' day were strictly alternated, it always seemed to be de-caf' day. This, she presumed, was life.

The whole thing made Chrissy fume. Journalists giving up nicotine and caffeine! What price tradition? They'd start telling the truth next. Chrissy was a tough, independent New Yorker, totally unlike her rather stodgy English colleague. Small and dark and energetic, from a big New York Jewish family, she referred to herself as the runt of the litter. 'Not because I'm small,' she would say, 'but because I'm a girl . . . seven brothers. I think my father wanted his own platoon in the Israeli army.'

Linda knew Chrissy could be a little abrupt at times and so she was not put off by Chrissy's manner.

'What I was telling you about,' continued Linda, patiently – she was a quiet, persevering soul – 'another liquidation – a pretty big one. What are these people doing with the money they create?'

'Who knows,' said Chrissy, biting her nails and finding them a poor drug substitute. 'Home improvements. Mistresses. This is the free world remember, Linda. People are allowed to do what they like with their money.' The New Yorker thought Linda's observations interesting but nothing to get excited about. Certainly not on de-caf' day. 'You've got to get this thing out of your hair,' she continued, 'it's becoming a drag.'

'Home improvements, Chrissy? What is he doing? . . . uhm' Linda struggled to think of a witty illustration. 'Uhm . . . installing, something . . . uhm very very . . . expensive . . . in his home.' Poor Linda never had been a gagger. She returned to safer, drier territory. 'He's realized over ten billion yen and as far as I can see, he hasn't put it back in the market. Either he's sitting on it or he's bought something absolutely coloss'. Christmas, Chrissy! What can you buy for ten billion yen?'

'Look, Linda, he's worth fifty. Maybe he got religion and put it in the poor box.'

'Well I think it's worth a story.'

'Oh yeah,' replied Chrissy sarcastically. 'Real riveting stuff, Linda, "Man Spends His Money", sounds like a hell of a scoop. You go with it, pal, but I don't promise that the *Examiner* will pick up on the syndication.'

'Yes, I suppose it is a bit vague. Listen, I'll get back to you if I come up with anything else,' said Linda, brightly.

'I'll be holding my breath,' said Chrissy.

As Linda put the phone down on her friend she couldn't

help thinking that maybe Chrissy had a point. Chrissy was normally a pretty clear thinker. Linda had known her for a couple of years, although they had never actually managed to meet. There are not many women in financial journalism and each had noticed the other's articles. It had been Chrissy who had made contact, Linda would have been far too shy. Chrissy suggested that they might loosely stay in touch and swap ideas. Linda, who had few friends, had jumped at the idea. It had been fun, a real friendly chemistry had developed between dull Linda and the American live-wire.

Linda could not blame Chrissy for her dismissive attitude. After all, what did she have? Nothing, just some people choosing to get hold of a chunk of their own money. But there *were* a lot of them doing it and it *was* so much money. Linda just felt that something was going on. Maybe nothing bad, almost certainly nothing criminal, but something.

She thought it might be worth a piece on a new puritanism in the financial community. People wanting to return to a less speculative market; wanting their money close to them – almost under the mattress, so to speak. She searched the desk for her tiny Nagasyu word processor, finding it under a book. It certainly was an astonishing bit of technology, slim and beautifully designed. The only problem was you kept losing it.

'They probably want you to lose it', Linda and her colleagues would say to each other, but then laugh at the very idea.

She found the screen and began to write.

'One crash too many,' she headed it. 'Why is Tex Slampacker, the Tsar of all the burgers, pulling out of car production? Why has Ocker Tyron, the West Australian high-flyer, sold out of the Snowy River irrigation project? At home, the Duke of Cumberminster is no longer a major investor in the Channel Tunnel, he has taken his money and run, why? Today we learn that Mr Nagasyu, the Japanese microelectronics mogul, has realized yet another percentage of his enormous wealth. What has he done with it?' Linda was pleased, this was beginning to sound good.

'Of course,' the article continued, 'within the vast network of deals and counter-deals, none of these are world shattering questions, but none the less, in all of the above sell-offs, no other major player has stepped in to pick up the dumped assets and the national government has ended up making up the shortfall with public money. It is almost as if there is an orchestrated campaign to take hard currency out of the market-place. Almost as if the very people who built and benefit most from the absurd complications of super-capitalism have lost faith in it. Do they want their money in their pockets where it's safe? Perhaps the last crash was one too many. Maybe the monster bit its keepers just a little too hard this time.'

There was a fair bit more along these lines, detailing other interesting cases. Linda thought it was a nice, light, magazine type article.

Her editor didn't.

'This is little short of prying, Linda. Good Lord, a man's personal finances are his own affair,' he spoke as if she had disappointed him.

'I can take Tyron out of it, if you like,' Linda replied.

'The fact that we are published by Ocker Tyron is entirely irrelevant.' Now the editor was angry. 'I control editorial policy on this paper, and none other.' He spoke as if he almost believed it. Perhaps he actually did. There are, after all, none so blind as those who will not see. He continued in a more reasonable, almost placatory tone – perhaps he realized he was protesting a touch too much.

'Let me ask you this. If you go to the bank and empty your account, say you just walk out of that bank with a couple of thousand or whatever in your pocket, well, surely that's your business isn't it? You wouldn't thank me for prying into it would you? asking you what you wanted the money for and what you were going to do with it? It might be private – you might be having plastic surgery or something. Well, it's the same with your article. Not one of your people is pulling out of his own industry, they merely appear to be rationalizing the fringes of their operations.'

Linda was a bit taken aback, she hadn't thought of it as a moral thing. The editor softened further.

'I mean, stay on it, by all means, no harm there. But you're going to need a lot more than you've got at the moment before I'll even look at it. All the same, nice to see initiative. Oh, sorry about what I said about plastic surgery, by the way.'

As it happened, Linda had presumed that the comment had only been an example, nothing to do with her. Now of course she was worried – this is how a complex starts.

# SUPPING WITH THE DEVIL

## ARISTOS

Ocker Tyron sent for his half-brother, Aristos. He had been saving Aristos for something like this. Aristos was the classic talentless little brother, hanger-on, dickhead. He was twenty-eight and had either dropped out of or fucked up everything he had ever attempted. He smashed up expensive cars, spilt booze on expensive clothes, showed off at night clubs and apart from having access to a lot of cash was a complete and utter drag to be with. Dixie, Ocker's wife, perhaps recognizing a grosser version of herself, loathed him and constantly lobbied Ocker to drop the embarrassing little freeloader. But Ocker couldn't – his mother would not hear of it.

Aristos was the result of a brief second marriage that Mrs Tyron had leapt into with a Greek baker about a year after her first husband, Ocker's father, died.

Ocker's father's death loomed large in his legend. He always claimed that his father died of 'being decent'. This was Ocker's moral justification for being a professional bastard. He said that his dad had been an honest, friendly, fair-minded man, who knew nothing of the law of the jungle. This was why he had died poor, because he was taken advantage of, an innocent amongst the wolves.

This was all in fact complete rubbish. Old Mr Tyron had been a bitter, vicious, small-minded bigot who died poor because he was crap at his job. None the less, Ocker had used his father's untimely death to leave school and begin, with almost religious zeal, what was to be a life-long career of shitting on people.

Hence, by the time Aristos could talk, his big brother was already well on his way to building one of the largest business empires in Australia. This was Aristos' problem, old Mrs Tyron claimed, and Ocker had to take note because he idolized his mother. Not because he loved her, deep down he didn't, he didn't even particularly respect her. He idolized her because he thought it right and fitting that tough, self-made men such as himself should idolize their mothers – also, it drove his wife, Dixie, crazy. The problem for Ocker was that along with Mum came Aristos. Mrs Tyron believed that Aristos' stupendous lack of distinction was due to his being intimidated from an early age by Ocker's equally stupendous abilities and success. She contended that Ocker was indirectly responsible for his brother's condition.

'You were always there,' she would say, in defence of her baby, 'succeeding, winning. How could little Aristos be himself while he was standing in the big man's shadow?'

'I suppose I should apologize that we live in a two million buck house, is that it? That you can give twenty grand to the Methodists and make all those tight-arsed matrons green? Do you wish I had dropped dead lugging crates of lemonade for the Popso Brothers, like Dad? Then maybe little Aristos could be a well-balanced personality. Would you have preferred it that way!!'

'You leave your father's memory be!' Mrs Tyron would say, crocodile tears welling in her eyes. 'If he was here now he wouldn't let you talk to me like that, big as you are he'd belt you.'

If Dixie was around during one of these carbon-copy conversations she could never resist the opportunity to have a dig at Mother under the guise of standing up for her man.

'You shouldn't speak like that to Ocker,' she would declaim, false eyelashes flapping in time with her false loyalty, 'he works terribly hard for us. We all owe him a great deal.'

'Some of us more than others,' old Mrs Tyron would sneer significantly. It is a strange thing, but those who are linked to a person by ties of blood always feel that they have a greater claim over them than those that the person has chosen to share their lives with of their own free will. Hence Mrs Tyron firmly believed that she had more right to be in Ocker Tyron's life than had Dixie Tyron, despite the fact that Ocker had chosen to be with Dixie and, of course, he had not chosen his mother.

'Why, you're not even family,' old Mrs Tyron would say to the woman whom Ocker had pledged his life to in the sight of Jesus.

During these confrontations, the cause of all the trouble would normally be still snoring in his bed upstairs and this was bitter gall for Ocker. Aristos' very physical proximity filled Ocker with barely suppressed fury. There was something so utterly unmanly about a twenty-eight-year-old, healthy man living in his brother's house, hiding behind their mother. Most irritatingly pathetic of all was the fact that Aristos had even begun to learn his mother's excuses.

'I know I'm a passenger, Ocker,' he would whine in what he imagined was an ingratiating tone. 'But you know ... you've done so much, I just don't know where to begin. I suppose it would be different if you were an ordinary bloke, then maybe I wouldn't feel so bad. Then maybe I could get something together, you know?'

It would be impossible to exaggerate the feeling of impotent contempt that this kind of grim effort provoked in Ocker. It made him want to kill. That Aristos should be so witless as to believe that he could hoodwink Ocker with this poorly performed second-hand mix of pathos and flattery, somehow it was almost an insult. It was like when children try and manipulate you and their efforts are so transparent it makes you hate them.

To be fair to Aristos, it wasn't that he hadn't tried to take a place in the business, he had, a bit, but he was just a very untalented person.

But now Ocker had a little job which seemed tailor-made for Aristos. He needed someone who had a known connection with the Tyron organization and therefore could invoke its power and mystique, but who was also totally disown-able.

His mother aside, Ocker could easily drop Aristos if he had to. Everyone knew that Aristos was a frustrated dead loss, so if the shit did hit the fan it would be simple for Ocker to disclaim all knowledge of Aristos' actions. What's more, Aristos would be dealing with and seeking to manipulate people of perhaps even less talent and originality than he had. The set-up seemed perfect. Who could guess? Perhaps he would emerge from the experience a better and less irritating person.

## ARISTOS GETS A JOB

Aristos entered, trying to assume an air of brisk efficiency. He had on a beautiful Italian suit. Unfortunately he shared with his sister-in-law an inability to wear clothes so it looked like a bloody awful Australian suit. He wore shades. Aristos wore shades most of the time. He did this for anonymity. After all, as a major figure in society he needed to maintain some privacy. Actually, of course, the only time wearing shades is anonymous is in bright sunlight. Wearing sunglasses indoors is pretty much guaranteed to draw attention to you. Aristos knew this really, that was why he wore them.

'Yeah, I got the message to get my ass over here, on the car phone,' Aristos said pointlessly. But he liked people to know things like he had a car phone. Ocker knew already, all the company cars had car phones.

'I was actually en route, but you know, when you buzzed I just did a U-eee and burned straight back. So what goes down?'

Aristos was trying to be casual, but really he was very excited, touchingly thrilled to have been summoned to Ocker's office. Even if it was just for a bollocking it had still given him the chance to swish purposefully through the outer office with all the pretty girls saying, 'Hullo, Mr Tyron.'

'Can't stop, girls. Ocker buzzed me on the car phone, got to get my ass in there pronto.'

For a moment Aristos was the young dynamic trouble-shooter of the Tyron empire. He pictured himself as a daringly unconventional Mr Fixit. Gotta problem? Call Aristos. Sure he breaks rules but he gets results. It was a delicious fantasy and whatever Ocker actually wanted him for would not spoil it. What's more, he would be able to swish out again through all the outer offices with a look of gutsy concentration on his tanned, boyish features, giving the clear impression that he had been charged with some tough make or break assignment. Aristos just bet that any one of those pretty secretaries would give anything to be the first Mrs Aristos Tyron. No, it didn't really matter what Ocker wanted, he had been summoned, that was enough.

To Aristos' delight and astonishment Ocker did have a job for him. He was actually going to be given an important assignment. Aristos was so grateful he could have cried. Instead, as he always did when excited, he got carried away.

'Look this is terrific Ocko, really terrific. I mean, OK, I'm not saying I haven't got plenty on my plate at the moment, because for sure right? I have. But hey, pressure is something I'm used to handling right? I mean, you know that. Listen, Ocko, I've been thinking, we don't see enough of each other, what say we do some clubs, right? Just us guys, we could drink beer, talk . . .'

'Shut up, Aristos.'

'Sure. No problem.'

'There's a difficult and slightly unpleasant job I want doing,' Ocker said.

'So you need a difficult and slightly unpleasant guy,' Aristos replied, purposefully, not realizing what he was saying.

'The firm can't touch it directly, it's not entirely legitimate, so I want to sub-contract. You're going to be the liaison, OK?'

Liaison! Aristos could not believe it, he was going to be Ocker's liaison! And people said he was a dickhead! Yes, well, they were going to have to change their tunes a bit now, weren't they? now that he was a liaison. Maybe he could even have some cards and letterheads done.

'Aristos Tyron: Liaison'.

Ocker looked at his half-brother, wondering whether he could trust him and decided that even Aristos couldn't fuck up such a simple little assignment. It is strange that Ocker, who understood most things, especially regarding human weakness, actually did not fully understand just how stupid his little half-brother was. Sometimes he suspected it, but it just didn't seem possible.

As it happened, Ocker did not have much choice, he could not use any of his regular employees. In the unlikely event of trouble they would understandably not want to carry the can alone. Aristos had just the right combination of stupidity and family loyalty that meant he would probably even take a custodial sentence if he thought it looked cool and gained him his brother's respect.

'Officially, I and the Board know nothing whatsoever about it, right?'

'Right,' said Aristos, as if he knew everything about it.

Ocker handed Aristos an unpleasant leaflet with a flaming torch and a cross on the front and explained what he wanted his brother to do.

## ARISTOS' MISSION

It was an extremely hot morning. It was extremely hot every morning that summer, abnormally hot in fact. But Aristos had no time to consider the weather, he was busy liaising.

The shiny black Porsche purred through the slightly shabby suburb. Whenever it had to stop at the lights the occupant seemed to be rather impressively on the car phone. Clearly a high-flyer.

'At the third stroke the time will be . . .'

Aristos nodded thoughtfully as if receiving important news. After a few red lights he reckoned he had had enough of the speaking clock and decided to phone his mother.

'Mum, it's Arry. Guess what, I'm Ocker's liaison! Yeah, it's very hush hush, I'm on an important job. What do you think of that, eh?'

Mrs Tyron was delighted and immediately rang Ocker to express her approval.

'You're a good boy, Ocker, making your mother happy, giving Aristos such an important job. A liaison and all, it must be a very big responsibility.'

'Mum, I'm just using the little prick as a messenger, he has a company car he might as well make himself useful,' Ocker explained, beginning to wonder if enlisting Aristos' services had been such a good idea.

'Oh, Ocker,' chuckled Mother, 'you hate us to see your soft side, don't you? But underneath you're just a big sloppy teddy bear, aren't you?'

It took ten minutes of this infuriating gunk before Ocker could get his mother off the phone. Finally, with ill-concealed fury, the big sloppy teddy bear managed to get the receiver down.

## IN SEARCH OF THE NORSEMAN

'Mrs Gordon?' enquired Aristos with a winning smile – he could be quite personable when he wanted to.

'Uhm, well, yes,' she replied nervously, because the man was carrying a personal telephone and had sunglasses on. Obviously he was a policeman. Gordon was in trouble again. She *hated* it when Gordon was in trouble. There would be policemen, the local reporter, tearful Aboriginal women screaming abuse at her at the bus stop.

'Might I enquire, is your son Gordon Gordon in?'

Aristos could see the woman found him fairly awesome. He casually allowed his jacket to fall open revealing the bleeper and the computerized personal memo on his belt. Mrs Gordon thought one of these must be a new sort of weapon, which, had he known, would have made Aristos very happy, because that's what he always pretended they were. When he clipped his bleeper on in the morning he normally spent a moment or two zapping Klingons with it.

'Gordon Gordon, is he in?'

Mrs Gordon was no good at lying, especially when she was nervous.

'Uhm . . . I don't know . . . perhaps . . . no he's not. Is he in trouble? Those Aboriginals make up a lot of that stuff, you know, there's two sides to every story.'

'He's not in trouble. I just want to see him, I have an appointment, I phoned him yesterday.' He paused for a moment and then added, 'from my car phone.'

'Oh, I see, an appointment. Well, he's still in bed actually, it was Friday yesterday. Friday's his night. You'd better come in.'

Aristos entered making a tiny gesture to an imaginary minder that he should stay by the Porsche and watch the street. The hall was neat and tidy although there were jarring notes. A collection of baseball bats and night sticks for instance, two air pistols and a shot gun, an immaculate pair of red-brown sixteen hole Doc Martens, with red laces. Aristos had clearly come to the right place.

Upstairs, still sleeping, was the man that Aristos had come to see, Gordon Gordon, living proof that there is no God.

## BLOOD RELATIONS

There are actually quite a few skinheads in Perth and Gordon Gordon was one of the more prominent ones. Anyone unfortunate enough to have seen him lying there asleep, under his swastika bedspread, would have been surprised to learn that one of his principal creeds was a thing he called racial superiority. It is strange that Gordon, who had ready access to several mirrors, should be so enamoured of this idea. Because, if somewhere in the universe there does exist a race of tattooed, crop-headed Neanderthals, looking anything like Gordon, whoever they are superior to must be a pretty sad bunch indeed. Gordon Gordon was definitely no great advert for anything, least of all a master race. Looking at his thick neck and brutish forehead the term that sprung to mind was not so much 'racial purity' as 'in-breeding'.

So, where did Gordon come from? What was his 'race'? The one that he dreamt of fighting and dying for?

Well he'd be horrified to learn that recently scientists seem to have reached a consensus on where Gordon came from. They believe his earliest relatives lived in North Africa.

'That's rubbish, I am a fucking Norseman,' Gordon would no doubt claim, pointing to the crossed axes that hung on the wall above his bed.

But, sadly for Gordon, it's beginning to look as if we all came out of Africa. The new science of genetics has revealed that the differences between the various supposed human 'races' are truly only skin deep. Our lips may be slightly different, but our DNA is virtually identical. This points towards a common root for us all. Gordon Gordon, white supremacist and all round idiot, is a nigger.

What was it that turned Gordon Gordon into a Nazi? Surely not the fact that his first name is the same as his second? This could make a person a bit bitter, but surely is not justification for wanting to kill all the Jews and blacks and gays and commies in the world.

When people feel put upon or inadequate they search for someone to blame.

'It isn't my fault.'

It is a cliché, but none the less true, that Nazis are the most inadequate people of all. The proof of this is that they don't just blame other people for single worries in a moment of pique or angst, they blame other people for their entire lives. Everything bar nothing that is wrong in the life of a Nazi is someone else's fault.

Pissed off at work? Fucking Jews have got the best jobs, haven't they? Crowded pub? They let too many queers and scruffs in. Bus is late? Bastard blacks too lazy to drive properly aren't they?

In literally every area of a Nazi's life there is a seething, jealous, resentment. An obsessive, corrosive belief that they

131

are not getting what is rightfully theirs, and not getting it because of all the other bastards in the world.

## PROPOSITION

Gordon came downstairs to the sitting-room where Mrs Gordon was giving Aristos a cup of tea. Gordon thought Aristos looked like a wop and a poof. Aristos thought Gordon looked completely alarming. Gordon had on a Union Jack T-shirt, from which protruded brawny tattooed arms and a neck as thick as the head it supported. He looked like a dangerous thug and of course he was.

'Yeah?' said Gordon.

'Er, Mr Gordon,' said Aristos, trying to be casual and commanding. He held his portable telephone like a shield, it proved his power and superiority. Why didn't it ring? Why didn't it ring?

It rang. With a monumental effort Aristos managed not to jump.

'Excuse me,' he said casually, and turned on the phone, holding it to his ear.

'This is your Australian Telecom alarm call,' the computerized voice said.

'Listen,' Aristos snapped back at the machine, 'I told you to hold all calls. I am taking an important meeting . . . I don't care how many million . . . Sit on it till I can get to the computer in the Porsche. Just do it!!!' He finished with a flourish, adding as an inspired afterthought, 'You're all sacked.' He put the phone down and apologized to Gordon. Astonishingly the ploy had worked, Gordon was impressed.

'Get my breakfast on, Mum. I want to talk to this bloke.'

Mrs Gordon left and Gordon gave Aristos the look that he used when wishing to imply that he was listening but none the less he remained a hugely violent and unpredictable wild man so he was not to be messed with. Aristos wondered whether Gordon was ill. He seemed to be squinting and grimacing in a slightly alarming manner.

'I'm listening,' said Gordon.

Aristos explained that he had read Gordon's leaflet entitled 'Why The Norseman is The Superior Race' with interest and had found it, on the whole, a rattling good read. Gordon was not above the natural pride that any author feels when he hears his work well spoken of and made a tiny gesture as if to say that it was just a little thing he had thrown together. Unfortunately Gordon was a large and unco-ordinated man, so much so that even tiny gestures were unwise. When they had cleared up the tea cup, Aristos continued.

'Yes, I found your argument that the white man is naturally superior because he invented everything . . . uhm, very succinct.'

'Of course it's succinct. I wouldn't have had it printed if it wasn't succinct, would I?' said Gordon. 'I mean, your car, right? Who invented it?'

'Uhm . . .' replied Aristos.

'A white man of the Nordic race, that's who,' continued Gordon who, like all great orators, was given to asking rhetorical questions. 'It's the same with the airplane, and . . .' he glanced about for inspiration '. . . the electric fire. All invented by white men of the Nordic race, which proves his superiority over all other races.'

'Well, exactly,' agreed Aristos. 'Now, it said in your leaflet that you have formed a party, the . . .' he referred to the unpleasant leaflet that Ocker had given him, 'White Supremacy People's Fair Deal Party. It also suggests that your organization is not averse to a degree of direct action, is that the case?'

Gordon agreed that it was and Aristos got down to business. He explained that he personally was in sympathy with a great deal of what Gordon stood for and was, in fact, prepared to supply a certain amount of funding in return for . . .

'Who do you want thumped, Mr Tyron?' asked Gordon, who was not as thick as he looked, which was a shame really because if he had been as thick as he looked his system probably would have broken down under the intellectual strain of having to breathe. In which case, the world would be that one bit nicer a place to live in.

Aristos explained the delicate mission that Ocker had instructed him to explain. Assuring Gordon that all expenses would be taken care of, plus a handsome donation to the White Supremacy People's Fair Deal Party. Gordon thought the proposition sounded very tasty. However, he prided himself on being a fair-minded fellow and felt obliged to point out that the rich and powerful elite of Germany had thought that they could buy and use Hitler and that Hitler had ended up using and controlling them. Hence Gordon wished to make it quite clear from the outset that there was to be no whingeing if he, Gordon, ended up using and controlling Aristos plus all Aristos' Jewish capitalist friends.

Aristos agreed to risk it.

# TYRON'S METHODS

Enlisting the help of Gordon Gordon was not to be the only method Ocker Tyron was to employ to interfere with Sly's business. A week after Sly had visited Bullens Creek, Ocker started to turn the screw.

All day long the wasp-like little plane whizzed and buzzed about over the Aboriginal community. The pilot was good. He'd learnt his trade crop spraying. Now he was on a more obviously antisocial mission. He could get in real low before throttling back, so low that no matter how many times he did it, the people on the ground always felt that this time he really would crash into them. This form of harrassment was an old Tyron trick, and he wasn't the only one to have used it.

When the Northern Territory was discovered to be mineral rich, aerial buzzing had proved useful on more than one occasion. The reason it was required was that the territory had been developed much later and much more sparsely than the rest of the country and the Aboriginals had managed to hang on to their traditional life style in the bush. Getting them out was becoming increasingly difficult. It wasn't like the pioneer days when they could have been shot down. Even in Queensland hunting Aboriginals for sport had been illegal since 1927. These days they had some rights, so people like Tyron had to 'persuade' them to get off any decent land.

As the tatty shacks shook and rattled with the vibrations from the plane, the occupants cursed Sly.

'That bastard, Moorcock, wants us out right enough, he's not even waiting for an answer,' said Mr Culboon. 'Bastard.'

'Bastard.' His wife agreed.

Neither of them could understand the rush. What had they done to deserve this?

'Christ, who the hell would want to come to this dump on holiday anyway. Even the flies only come because there's plenty of shit.'

'Maybe he's got another reason for wanting us out,' said his wife.

'But there *can't* be anything. I mean, what could it be? The place has been surveyed. Like he said, if there was anything here they would never have given it to us. No, I reckon this is just his way of warning us not to think about raising the price.'

As it happened, the community had already taken the decision to accept Sly's offer. It was, after all, a great deal of money and there was nothing particularly wonderful about the hole they were living in.

Sly had made a big hit with the rednecks of Bullens Creek on his first visit. He would not be so popular the next time – not once it was realized that it was him who had provided the cash for a bunch of Abs to move to town and put down mortgages on some fairly decent properties.

Mr Culboon would have phoned Sly earlier but, as often happened, the fragile telephone link that existed between their community and the outside world, was knackered. Therefore, late in the afternoon, Mr Culboon set off for Bullens Creek to make the call.

He arrived in town at about the same time as Gordon and his legion. In the gathering dusk Mr Culboon did not notice the hired mini-bus full of unpleasant young men, and had he done, he would have avoided it. Mr Culboon had encountered enough racist thugs in his time not to wish to seek their company.

Gordon sat in the front seat of the van, resplendent in a combat jacket, camouflage trousers and tightly laced-up Doc Martens, sixteen holes, red laces, just like proper British skinheads wore. He was briefing his legions on the details of the operation.

'Storm-troopers, we are undertaking this operation in defence of race, culture and . . . uhm . . . well race and culture are good enough reasons to undertake an operation, in my opinion,' he said decisively.

The assembled storm-troopers agreed with this, although they would not have recognized culture if it sat on their faces and wiggled.

'Australia is a white man's continent, it is ours by right of conquest and we intend to have it all, which is what tonight's battle is all about.'

Gordon cut a ridiculous figure. A stupid, dull thug attempting to look like the leader of a crack fighting unit. On the other hand, he was no more ridiculous than the little gang he was addressing; stupid, dull thugs attempting to look like a crack fighting unit.

Unfortunately for the people of the little Bullens Creek community, they may have been a pretty pathetic bunch but they were a pretty pathetic bunch who had clubs, knives, petrol, darkness and cowardice on their side.

Mr Culboon got through to Sly.

'Listen, you bastard, Moorcock. You can have the place OK? I don't know what you want with our land and I don't care. It's yours, so you can call off your stupid plane, all right?'

'What plane?' said Sly, slightly surprised at Mr Culboon's aggressive tone. He did not deceive himself that he and Mr Culboon would ever be soul mates or bosom buddies but he felt naked abuse was unnecessary and said so.

'Oh yeah, mate. I suppose your fellah's just spending his day trying to piss us off for the fun of it,' Mr Culboon replied.

Sly was mystified but clearly Mr Culboon did not want to discuss it.

'Just get us the money, mate, all right? Then we'll be gone and I won't need to talk to you again.'

Mr Culboon slammed down the phone and went to get himself a beer. The community may have been dry but he was

137

in town now and it wasn't every day that a fellow and his wife got ten grand each for a useless bit of dirt.

As he entered the pub, Gordon and his gang were leaving, having consumed a certain degree of courage. They pushed past him contemptuously, forcing him to flatten himself against the wall or get trampled underfoot.

'Sorry about them, Mr Culboon,' said the bar person, who was a mate. 'Never seen such a bunch of wankers in my life.'

The bunch of wankers had spent their time in the pub being just loud enough to make everyone else in the pub feel uncomfortable. Mr Culboon was not surprised. If there was one thing he could not stand it was groups of young men. They didn't have to be as horrible as the lot that had just left. Any gang of young men made Mr Culboon want to spit. In his opinion, there should be a law stating that no more than three men between the ages of fifteen and thirty should be allowed to assemble together in a public place.

There is something strange and horrid which happens to even the most reasonable blokes when they go out with the 'the lads'. They rejoice in their collective strength. No longer are they scared, farty little sad acts who don't know who they are or what they are doing on earth. Suddenly they are cocks of the roost, they are unassailable, they have power and influence. On a train, in a pub, there they are, loud and arrogant. Lads. Confident in their numbers. Noisily flexing their muscles, making everyone around them feel small and impotent, causing normally liberal-minded people to bitterly wish a policeman would come along and put them all in the army for a hundred years.

Gordon, and his fellow members of the White Supremacy People's Fair Deal Party, got back into their van. They studied the map. There was only one road between Bullens Creek and the Aboriginal community, so even they were able to plan the route.

'Now all of you, watch it! All right?' said Gordon. 'We're going in to scare them, don't get carried away and do the business properly, OK? There'll be a right time for that when . . . uhm when the time is right . . . Yes . . .' he continued, well pleased with this powerful and stirring phrase, 'when the time is right. When will there be a right time for that!!' He shouted into the darkened mini-bus and his fellow crusaders dutifully and slightly drunkenly shouted back:

'When the time is right!'

'Exactly, mates, exactly.' Gordon did not really like referring to party members as 'mates'. It lent nothing to a speech and was scarcely calculated to inspire martial ardour but he had long been stuck for a suitable effective collective noun. The usual ones were 'comrades' or 'brothers' but they were both out. 'Comrades' sounded too fucking commie, and if there was one thing Gordon hated more than blacks it was commies. It will be remembered that Gordon considered himself a fair-minded soul and he realized that a black could not help being black. But a commie, well, a commie was a traitor to his race. The other option, 'brothers', Gordon had been forced to disregard as well. It sounded too fucking queer and if there was one thing Gordon hated more than commies, it was queers. The upshot of this linguistic puzzler was that he was obliged to try to stir his troops by addressing them as 'mates'.

In fact there was no need to stir the assembled gang, they were quite stirred enough already. The prospect of a quick, safe, vicious bit of brutality was really making their pulses race. This, plus a gutful of lager would have stirred a concrete cuppa.

## SCREAMS IN THE NIGHT

The bus pulled into the centre of the little cluster of buildings and the heralds of a new dawn all piled out and attacked a group of total strangers for no reason whatsoever.

They threw two petrol bombs at the general store and when the first people ran out to check out the commotion, they hit them with baseball bats. They shouted some things about killing niggers and they threw some anonymous leaflets about that said 'slavery or death, it's your choice'.

There were about three minutes of horrible shouting and screaming, running feet, calls for arms and torches, scurrying silhouettes in the flickering light of the burning store – then it was all over. Having managed to give one man a serious kicking, and before the people they were attacking could get organized, the Nordic knights all rushed back to their van and drove away.

'We did it! We did it!' shouted a jubilant Gordon Gordon. 'We really did the business.'

He did not know it, but they had been doing the business of Stark.

# A STEP TOWARDS
# EXTINCTION

## UNLOADING THE EMPIRE

That same night, Sly was also labouring over the business of
Stark. It had been soul-destroying work, dismantling even
relatively small sections of all that he had worked so hard to
create and make secure. But, he had no choice, he had his part
to play in the big scheme, like all the others. Quite apart from
acquiring the land, he had been charged with getting hold of
large quantities of uranium. This required a lot of money –
and a lot of money by Sly's standards was plenty.

The uranium was definitely a problem. He couldn't just
take it out of his own mines. His entire output was strictly
monitored. If the government got one whiff that he was
creaming any off they'd take him apart bit by bit and the game
would be up, for sure. It was so ridiculous, he was allowed by
law to flog the stuff to the French, yes, that was fine, no
problem there. And what did the French do with it? Blow it
up in the Pacific, that's what! Thus causing the Federal
Government endless embarrassment from cancer-ridden
environmentalists and luminous Aboriginals. It was so
frustrating, the Labour Party seemed to have no objection at
all to Sly putting the naughty bit in Froggy Exocets and yet he
wasn't allowed to hang on to a few tons of his *own* uranium for
his *own* personal use. The world was going mad.

All it meant was that Sly, who personally dug good, top-
grade Australian uranium, would have all the trouble of
acquiring the stuff on the world black market – probably

buying his own stuff back at ten times the price. Still, at least by getting the stuff off some shady character whose address was a portable fax machine, Sly was guaranteed discretion. The dealer Sly was using wanted ten million dollars in two dollar bills, this was not the kind of fellow likely to publish his memoirs. Anyway, the guy wasn't likely to live long, he positively glowed in the dark.

Sitting in front of a video screen as the dawn came up, unloading cash assets into the market, had been a strange experience. Some of the stuff he sold he didn't even know he had. Who would have thought he had a shit-dumping operation in the North Sea?

A couple of blips on the screen and he didn't anymore. Captain Robertson got himself a new invisible boss. It didn't make any difference, he still hated his job.

He was looking for smallish, easy to dispose of assets, stuff to chip away at. He did not want to unload any major conglomerates, it would be bound to attract attention. Stark had been very clear on that score. In fact he had been trying to discreetly break up his empire into more manageable chunks ever since he got back from the dinner in L A. His people had been pretty surprised.

'Sly,' his whole upper-management team had wailed, as if they were but one upper manager, 'you're laying us wide open. Putting out the cream and waiting for the cats. We're gonna get picked off bit by bit.' Of course they were right. According to every accepted business practice, Sly was inviting major losses. But he wasn't fighting for profits any more, he was fighting for his life. Unfortunately he could not confide this knowledge to his upper-management team and so he had to allow his upper-management team to think he was losing his grip.

One advantage of this piecemeal sell-off was that it made it much easier to unload assets discreetly. After all, if even Sly did not know that he owned half the stuff he was now selling, no one else would.

Actually, somebody else did. As a matter of fact somebody knew Sly's business better than he did; poor, dullish Linda Reeve of the London *Financial Telegraph*.

She had long been researching a book called *An Analysis of the Social Roots and Financial Strategies Pertaining to the Most Prominent Fifty Business Empires Constructed Since the Second World War* or *Megabuck: the Lives and Loves of the Top Half Hundred*, as her publishers wished to call the book.

It had been the detailed knowledge that this research afforded her that had enabled Linda to make the connections she had made regarding Nagasyu's diverse sell-offs and Slampacker's and the others that she had noticed.

It was eight o'clock in the evening in London and she was working late, nibbling a chocolate, staring with a puzzled frown at her VDU. It had been luck that she caught the first of Sly's dumps. The Prince of Wales had recently made a series of major speeches on the state of the North Sea. The death of Mrs Pastel from viral gastroenteritis, after eating a dodgy mussel, had given him the springboard he needed to try, yet again, to force environmental action on pollution. It was beginning to look as if local councils were going to have to pay far more to waste disposal contractors.

Clearly it was a situation from which an unscrupulous but legal killing could be made by any shit-dumper who wanted to double his prices for a 10 per cent improvement in the service he offered.

Hence the *Financial Telegraph* presumed that trading in waste companies would be fairly fierce. It was while putting together a small piece based on this assumption that a colleague of Linda's had remarked with surprise that a big player like Silvester Moorcock had elected to buck the trend and pull out of the business altogether. That very evening he had dumped every single share of the Belgian waste disposal conglomerate that he had been so heavily into.

Linda nearly missed it when her colleague made the

observation – her mind had been elsewhere. Linda had just been given a small box of chocolates by a cleaner whom Linda had helped with her accounts. It was the end of the day – choccy time so to speak – and there were four people in the room. The problem with chocolates is that they operate on a loss curve of massively diminishing returns. The first one out of the box, the strawberry cream say, is of far greater value than the last few left, the despised cracknels and nougats and such like. In fact, these chocolate lepers are often never eaten at all and are left forever, unable to be thrown away because they're still there, and yet never eaten because they're so horrid. Linda knew if she offered the chocs around the loss of the four best ones would halve the value of her box.

Of course she knew what she had to do, but she didn't like it. As Linda's colleague was telling her about Sly's sell-offs, Linda was watching both strawberry creams, a turkish delight and a soft caramel disappear. Luckily, neither of the lime barrels were touched or Linda seriously wouldn't have heard the momentous snippet. But, she did hear it and, still pursuing the half-formed theories that her editor had rejected so dismissively, Linda decided to take a little look at Sly. She rummaged through the huge mounds of books and papers that habitually covered her desk, finally locating her tiny Nagasyu keyboard.

Now, of course, there are tens of thousands of transactions going on at any one moment in the world markets and Sly's interests were so diverse that normally trying to pick up his trail would take months of painstaking research just to get a clear view of a single half-hour period. But, Linda had already done the research for her book. She had a computer program that detailed over 80 per cent of known Moorcock investments. She knew where most of his money was hiding. All she had to do was to instruct the computer to keep scanning the ever-shifting market until anything connected with Moorcock made a move.

She did not have to wait long.

It was extraordinary. Moorcock was undressing like a born

again naturist, selling off anything from ouija boards to weapons systems. All for ready cash too. Linda searched in vain for any corresponding reinvestment but found nothing.

She told herself not to get excited. She realized that the fact that she had gone looking for this, and had found it, would make her all the more anxious to prove that there was something in it. But there *must* be something in it. So much money was leaving the market but only through the big individual players. Middle-range investors, pension schemes, banks, etc., were not moving.

Something *had* to be going on amongst the big men but Linda did not believe that it was co-ordinated. Above all else, she knew that people like Slampacker, Moorcock, Tyron and Nagasyu would die before they would co-operate with each other.

But something was definitely going on, she thought, trying to clean her great big green glasses and getting chocolate on them. Had all the big men got the willies together? Had they all seen something coming that most people were too small to spot? Were we heading for the biggest crash ever and were the rats deserting the sinking ship? leaving small investors, pension funds and governments holding soon-to-be-worthless stock?

Selecting a horrid hard centre, she attempted to bite the chocolate off without eating the bit in the middle. No chance of course, she soon had half a Brazil nut in her mouth, which she hated.

Hero fantasies flicked across Linda's mind. Would she be the woman to predict the great crash? Would she ring the warning bell that cushioned the little fellow from the worst of it? She pictured silver-haired grannies thanking her brokenly for rescuing at least part of their pathetic savings and honest young lovers who would still be able to send the tots to good schools because of her prompt action. An MBE! . . . If she was right . . . But of course she wasn't. Linda pulled herself together. She had an interesting little anomaly that was all. There would be, without a doubt, some perfectly ordinary explanation. Still, she might as well ask. Linda reached for the phone.

The telephones in Sly's office complex did not trill, they rang. His whole body had jerked, he had nearly hit buy rather than sell mid-deal. He'd been trying to unload a plant that produced condensers for fridges and driers, instead he near as damn it purchased half a million ex-U S Army condoms. Sly could think of literally nothing more revolting than a second-hand condom.

Sly, of course, never answered the phone in his office but at that time of night he was the only person there and the thing kept ringing. Eventually he walked through about three secretaries' offices to where incoming calls were intercepted and picked up the phone.

'Sly Moorcock speaking.'

He was pretty surprised to find himself doing this but not half as surprised as Linda Reeve was to find herself speaking to the billionaire himself. She had known that somebody would be about because of the heavy trading, but she was astonished to find Sly running his own market stall.

'Uhm . . . Oh, right, Mr Moorcock, ahem, excuse me phoning like this . . .'

Sly didn't mind. He was in a kind of mischievous mood what with selling off all his stuff. 'That's O K. It's pretty late to call, but that's O K. Are you in bed?' Messing around with all his money had made Sly feel powerful and randy. It was very late, he just presumed the woman was a drunk gold-digger chancing her arm.

'What!!' said a shocked voice, to Sly's satisfaction.

'I said, are you in . . .'

'I'm phoning from London.'

Linda did not like his tone. She put on her firm voice. This was the voice that she always dreamt of using to the horrible young men whose job it was to hang off scaffolding all over London and make women feel uptight. Linda, although by no means particularly attractive, had a big bust. This one quirk of fate had meant that for her entire life, since the age of thirteen, the mere sight of scaffolding or road works had made her tense up and scurry along, blushing with anger and looking at her feet. Of course you don't need to have big tits to get intimidated, all women are scrutinized. All over any city, at any time of the day, there are women crossing roads to avoid the men hanging off scaffolding. They should add a bit to the road work warnings on the radio, 'and a lot of building in the High Street today so delays for motorists, and, of course, female pedestrians can expect to be biting their lips with anger and embarrassment as their bodies are assessed and commented on.'

On the phone Linda would be the toughie she would love to have been in the streets.

'I am not in bed, I am working, Mr Moorcock. My name is Linda Reeve, I'm with the *Financial Telegraph*.'

All Sly's smugness evaporated instantly. It wasn't that he was doing anything guilty, he just felt guilty and who could blame him? After all, he was personally involved in attempting to perpetrate one of the greatest moral outrages in history, including the invention of Pot Noodles. Anyone would feel guilty.

'Oh yeah, what do you want?'

Sly was making no further effort at flirtatious charm. He didn't care if it was Marilyn Monroe on the other end of the line, she was a journo and the last thing on earth he wanted right now was interest from journos.

'Uhm-uhm, we-we at-at the-the FT-FT,' Linda said, the line had suddenly got worse and she was trying to ignore the off-putting echo of her own voice coming back at her as it bounced around the globe.

'We were wondering why you're selling so much of your stuff-stuff.' She had not meant to put it as frankly as that, she had meant to speak briskly of 'asset stripping' and 'large scale dumps', but the echo, and the fact that she was actually talking to the man himself, had pretty much thrown her. Not half as much as she had thrown Sly though.

What the fuck did she have on him?

He was sufficiently shaken to make a big mistake. He started to deny something that clearly she had already established.

'Selling my stuff? Come on, what are you talking about?' Sly realized as he spoke that with this tack he would hang himself. The bitch wouldn't have phoned him if she didn't have something. Sly turned mid-sentence, 'Listen lady, I don't know who you are, or even why I'm talking to you, but you'd better get back to the woman's page, OK? Do some fashion stuff or something. Selling? I'm rationalizing, OK? Dodging and weaving, pulling out, putting in. Nobody hits a moving target and you can quote me. Now I've really got to . . .'

Sly's second mistake was trying to patronize Linda. He guessed it as he was doing it. People who got to work for the *Financial Telegraph*, especially women, couldn't be bullshitted as easily as that.

'Mr Moorcock,' replied Linda, now feeling a lot better, 'Mr Moorcock, you have dumped a ouija board factory, two local newspapers, a pharmaceutical lab, part of an oil-well, a chain of sweetshops, a TV station in Papua New Guinea, electronics, fertilizer, weapons, do I have to go on? And yet I cannot detect a single reinvestment. You must have over a hundred and fifty million Australian dollars in your wallet now.'

'Woah! Hang on a minute here, Ms Reeve,' snapped Sly, shaken. 'What is this? Snooping? We have laws you know . . .'

'The information is there for anyone who cares to look,' Linda interrupted, thrilled that she seemed to have got to him. 'I've done nothing wrong.'

Sly wanted to finish the conversation before he put his foot in it any further.

'The information is there, my dear, now it's up to you to interpret it. Let me give you a hint. I am a very rich man while you probably make no more than 20K sterling per annum. This is because I have ideas. I have ideas and you snoop. If I told you my ideas, maybe you'd be as rich as me, which is why I'm not going to tell you them. So far your facts are correct, I've flogged a few of my small holdings. But any peeping Tom could come up with that. Ring me back when you've figured out what I'm up to, baby. G'day from W A.'

He put the phone down and he was shaking.

His last shot had been good, Linda thought he sounded like a confident man with an idea to make money . . . maybe he was. On the other hand, she had definitely got to him at first, and there were the others . . . Her search would continue, to discover what, if anything, was going on and if there was one last edible choccy in the box.

# FACEFULL'S

It had been an unpleasant jolt but Sly wasn't over worried. He reckoned he had handled the situation pretty well and, after all, it was only a dumb pom journo. For the remainder of the night he carried on the lonely task of unloading his assets and by mid-morning on the following day he was close to fulfilling his financial obligations to Stark.

He decided he deserved a treat and so he went out for a burger. A burger in a public eatery. Sometimes he got like that, fed up with top-class food and top-class poncey people. Sometimes he liked to eat plain grub in lively, real places, served by spunky students in mini-skirts, working their way through college.

He liked to sit alone, away from the hundreds of people whose lives were in his hands. Anonymous, watching the world go by for a moment. He especially liked to watch the girls. Real girls. Girls who ignored him, girls who wore clothes rather than bait. Girls who had their own stuff to do. He was watching a group now, three of them, maybe they were from an office, they were so lively and unaffected. Why shouldn't they be? They got three hundred bucks at the end of each week and spent it. What was there to be affected about?

Sly had never really got used to mega-wealth. He was a bobby sox and apple pie man at heart. But, you can't fake it, you can't live a simple life when you've got a complex and enormous income, no matter how much you want to.

And so, occasionally, Sly would sneak out of the office just for a look at the real world – the one he had left behind when he first stitched up his friend's pie factory. He would sneak out to look at real girls and eat real food.

Actually, finding real food was becoming more and more difficult as Sly was about to discover. The yuppy decade had ruined simple food. Now every bank clerk thought he was a gourmet. Burger cuisine had arrived. Facefull's was the sort of place that would not let food alone, they had to ponce it up in some way or other. Sly could only presume that the reason for this was so that they could charge more for it.

'Ten bucks for a bit of fried chicken!'

'Well you're paying for the Chinese lettuce and the little miniature tomatoes, aren't you?'

Looking around him, Sly made a mental note to move into burger franchises and designer vegetables, but then he remembered that Stark was soon to make that part of his life a thing of the past.

He accepted a menu from a waitress in a huge T-shirt, belted at the waist to make a dress. In Sly's jaded mood she seemed to be a living embodiment of freshness and vitality. He smiled his winning smile. She thought, shit, the leerers never tip.

The menu was three squarc feet of laminated plastic. The thing flapped around like a sail in a transatlantic yacht race, you could have gone surfing on it.

The reason for the menu's great size was not because the selection was fabulously extensive. On the contrary, the choice was minimal, burgers, steaks, ribs, chicken and a thing called seafood, which was white and covered in breadcrumbs. The problem was that each dish apparently required a stomach turningly trite description, presumably so that the diner was left in no doubt about just how horrible the meal was going to be.

'Facefull's saucy prawns between the sheets. Gorgeous juicy prawns stretched temptingly between luscious layered squirts of the chef's own sauce! – Irresistible!'

Sly had never met the chef but he was damn sure that he could do without a squirt of his sauce.

Sly wanted a burger, so with incisive intuition he ordered a thing called 'The Facefull Burger: Just a plain facefull looking for a home! Juicy ground beef on sesame, a touch of mayo', a little exotic salad and oh, by the way, our fries are the best.'

This description was off-putting enough, but it sounded like gastronomic heaven compared with what Sly got. They had not mentioned Kiwi fruit, nor the avocado and they definitely hadn't warned him about the pine kernels. These were not the things a person wanted to have to scrape off his food when he fancies a plain burger. The touch of mayo' had become about a pint of sickly sweet slime. There were *currants* in the salad and the fries were thick cut and done in their jackets!

With sinking heart Sly realized that he was in a burger joint that was too trendy to peel its potatoes.

Sly went back to staring at the waitresses.

## THE ECOACTION TEAM

Linda Reeve, the dumb pom journo, was not going to be the only ripple in Sly's pond that day. Another one was drawing up outside the brasserie in a beautiful old red Holden with white-wall tyres.

The red-head in the huge hat, who was driving, turned to her companions.

'Colin, you stay here with Zimm, OK. Me and Walter will go in and talk to him,' said Rachel.

'Cool,' said CD, who clearly thought it wasn't. His idea of a great day out was not sitting in a car minding a half-mad bollockless psycho with a chip on his shoulder. On the other hand, CD was a reasonable guy and he realized that Zimmerman might be rather a liability in a fashionable eatery. Since Zimm's terrible injury he had developed a considerable empathy for bullocks and with it a deep hatred for anyone who served or ate veal. He didn't often go to restaurants, but when he did, there would be big trouble if he found veal on the menu.

'OK, I'll stay with Zimm,' he said.

'You stay where you like, kid,' said Zimm, 'I want a burger.'

So all four of them trooped in. The manager did not like the look of them, but the man in the shorts was so huge he decided to let discretion be the better part of valour. Had he looked a little closer he would have been more concerned about the tall, thin guy in the singlet.

Zimm's mind was racing and the place was liberally stuffed with large potted plants, and he was trying hard to hang on to himself. If he wasn't careful he would be back in the jungle once more and go for the nearest Asian businessman.

CD saw the signs and hustled him through, noting to his horror a couple of thick jowled arsehole young execs tucking into veal schnitzel and talking very loudly to show how cool and confident they were. Luckily Zimm did not notice the veal. The restaurant, pursuing their unswerving policy of fucking up food, had elected to put tinned apricots on top of it so Zimm thought they were eating ice cream sundaes.

Rachel and Walt spotted Sly at his corner table. They went over and stood in front of him.

'Yes,' said Sly, looking up, glad of the excuse to stop struggling with the crappy food. Sly was a cool hand and was not to be phased by a group of strange looking hippies approaching him, even if one of them was blocking out the sun. He presumed that they were there to persuade him to join a new religion. Besides, not fifteen feet away was a table full of his goons, sipping mineral water and just itching to kill someone.

'We got to talk to you about Bullens Creek, man,' Walter drawled. 'They hit the kids as well, you know, your thugs just hit whatever. How do you sleep, man?'

Sly felt he didn't deserve this. Twice in ten hours it had happened, first the journo bitch onto his sell-offs and now, strange giant hippies talking about Bullens Creek. The goons were getting up from their table but Sly waved them back, he needed to know what was going down.

Sly had not heard about the terrible racist attack on the Bullens Creek community – not many people had. The reason for this being that Ocker Tyron owned both local papers plus

153

one of the TV channels. News tends to be rather selectively reported when the people who are making it own the means of telling it.

'What's Bullens Creek to you, Mister?' said Sly.

There was something about Walter that made Sly take him seriously. It wasn't his size, not entirely anyway . . . there was a sort of monkish sincerity about him. Sly was always suspicious of true believers, you couldn't bribe them and hitting them didn't help. You had to talk to them. The lean one was even more disconcerting. Sly was a very practised judge of character and strength and this guy looked off the scale. Maybe he was just a very well-formed hippy but he looked kind of like a killer to Sly. And then . . . then there was the girl. She had something too, Sly couldn't put his finger on it. But he would have liked to.

He did not notice CD.

'Mr Culboon and his people were going to pay you, bastard, but you had to make sure didn't you? You're fucking scum, man, that's what you are.' Sly nearly fell off his seat! What the hell did this bunch of penniless looking hippies know about Culboon? Surely they weren't a group of eccentric billionaires who were in on Stark as well?

'You'd better sit down and explain what your problem is,' he said tersely. It was a corner table for four so there was only room for Walter. Zimm, Rachel and CD hovered . . .

'Your goons want to know whether you want them to take us,' Zimmerman said, eyeing the table around which Sly's men were sat. Zimm's arms hung loosely by his sides, the fingers alternately stretching and relaxing.

'Business associates,' said Sly, again waving his security back. 'Drink?'

'I don't drink with vicious, violent scum,' said Walter.

'Yeah, well me neither, normally,' said CD, 'but I'll have a Facefull Forcefield.'

He had always wanted to have a really enormous, extravagantly expensive cocktail and he wasn't going to miss the opportunity now one had presented itself. Faced with this collapse of solidarity, the other three said they'd have beers. Sly gave the order and behind the bar the Facefull Forcefield was prepared. This, like all the other cocktails, consisted of whisking up a load of fruit juice and cream, adding about one measure of mixed spirits, putting six straws and a small fruit salad on top and charging fifteen dollars for it. CD thought it was fantastic.

'What do you know about the Culboon business?' Sly asked.

'I know one thing, man. I know that although I am a completely committed man of peace, my friend Zimmerman is a war-crazed loon and he wants to kill you for what you did.'

Sly looked at Zimmerman. Zimmerman looked back and said:

'If you're not eating that can I finish your food?'

Sly gladly offered him the plate and prevailed upon Walter to explain himself. He learnt that Walter and Culboon were old friends and that he, Walter, had been distressed to get a call to say that a gang of Nazis had attacked the community.

'I mean, man, you know you guys are just utter pigs, right? The dude was coming round, he was cool to take your bread and split.'

Rachel squirmed in silent embarrassment at this awesome lexicon of completely unfashionable terms. CD thought it sounded great. Zimmerman wasn't listening, he was trying to decide whether there really was a tinned pear with cloves on top of his burger or whether he was suffering from LSD flash-back.

Walter continued in the same aggrieved terms:

'I mean, why can't people just be cool? First the plane all day, freaking all the kids out, then the fascists. I mean, just what is in your head, man? I'll tell you, bad shit, that's what. You have a head full of bad shit. You should see a doctor, yeah and what's more, you're going to need one when Zimmerman's finished with you.'

Walter turned to Zimm for confirmation but Zimm had his own problems. Were those tomatoes really only the size of grapes? They seemed to be, they certainly looked that way.

Then again, Zimmerman had once seen a huge pink dragon in a bikini emerge from the top of his commanding officer's head, so he was aware that appearances could be deceptive. But man, if they were real, those two little balls were just about the smallest tomatoes he had ever seen. After a while they started to remind him of something, and his eyes filled with tears.

Sly was very worried. What did they know? What were they talking about? Who the fuck were they? And why did the tough one look so homicidally upset?

'Look,' he said, 'I don't know what this is about. Sure I have an interest in Bullens but this is the first I've heard of any attack.'

This was too much for Rachel.

'Oh come on, Moorcock. First you offer a huge amount of money for their land, God knows why, then when they hesitate for one second they get beaten up. What do you take us for, a bunch of airheads?'

Sly decided not to answer that one. He was still confused but he was also relieved. They didn't know why he wanted the land, they didn't even seem interested.

'I mean, why the hell do you even want the land?' said Rachel.

For the first time, Sly found himself disliking the girl. Also, the tough hippy was beginning to look alarmingly volatile, he sure looked angry. Sly decided to try and take control.

'Look, I can see that it's going to be difficult to prove that I had nothing to do with this, but I didn't,' said Sly truthfully and firmly – although he was beginning to form a pretty sound theory about who had. Christ, Ocker Tyron was a vicious, stupid bastard. Why couldn't he have left things up to Sly?

The situation was tricky. Sly shot a glance at Zimmerman, who was obviously getting ready to explode. Sly had to allay their suspicions and stop them probing any further. He had to try and get the proof they needed to show that he had not been involved. The restaurant was nearly empty now. He produced a portable telephone and offered it to Rachel.

156

'Dial the Bullens Creek police station, here's the number.'

Rachel took the phone. CD was green with envy. He would have loved to have had a go on one of those phones.

'Ask for the chief, say it's Sly Moorcock calling.'

Rachel did this and having thus established that it really was the chief of Bullens Creek police, Sly took back the phone, motioning Rachel and Walter to lean in and listen close. He turned the volume on the phone up a little, but not too much. He definitely fancied Rachel and liked the idea of getting closer to her, Walter he would have to put up with.

'Hi Brad, Sly . . . Oh yeah, thanks, I enjoyed it too, the Dingo's sure know how to throw a rage. Listen, you know I'm taking an interest in land purchase round your way, lot of action, high investment, good for the town and all that. But, I heard you had some trouble out at the community. I don't like that Brad, what's the story?'

Rachel and Walter could hear the police chief's reply quite clearly. He was the exuberant, shouty, friendly type, if you were a white land-owner that is.

'Oh, no worries, Sly, definitely a one-off. Perth have picked up the ringleader, a known skinhead trouble-maker called Gordon Gordon. He'll do some time, no question. This is his umpteenth bust on similar charges, the little shit. I mean, Christ no one's in love with the Abs, but this guy's pathological. He just can't stop bashing them. They do over the odd country town, it's happened before. They put up posters and stuff about white Australia. Pathetic really, the fucking Japs own the place anyway. But don't you worry, Mr Moorcock, when he gets out, if he shows his face around here I'll hand him over to the Ab' women, they'll fucking eat him.'

Sly thanked the policeman, turned off the phone and put it away.

'Well,' said Sly, 'that's the story. Pretty disgusting stuff, in my opinion. Quite frankly I deeply resent you implying that I would be involved with a thug like that. Apart from anything else, what do you think it would do for my reputation?'

Walter and Rachel had to admit he had a point. He really

did seem to be genuinely surprised about the whole thing, which was hardly surprising really, since he was. Maybe it really had been a coincidence.

Sly reckoned he had convinced the girl and the huge hippy but the tough one was obviously still furious. Sly hoped they got him out before he blew. They didn't.

Zimmerman could bear it no longer. He had finally decided that what was on his plate was real and he did not like it.

'I mean, what's the point!' he shouted. 'I mean, what *is* the *point*!! You know, I mean, is it me or what? I rarely get a chance at decent food . . .'

Walter was a little hurt at this since he did most of the cooking at their place, but Zimmerman was too upset to worry about Walter's sensibilities.

'So when I do right? When I do get a stab at some groovy chow, what's happened to it, man? I mean, what has happened to it? I'll tell you, it has been *fucked up* man! That's what! You know, I mean, shit, like, tinned pears and sweet mayonnaise and skins on the chips!! I mean, man, what is the point? Can't anything be normal any more? Can't a groover just have a burger without having to scrape eight tons of shit out of it!! And what's with the tomatoes that remind me of my bollocks! Very tactful, man, I must say. Fuck you!'

Zimmerman walked out to polite applause from the few remaining guests. On the whole they agreed with every word he had said, although they had found the bit about his bollocks confusing.

'I'm glad somebody finally *said* something,' they all whispered to each other.

# DINNER NEAR SINGAPORE

Sly and Tyron shared a private plane to Nagasyu's private island off the coast of Singapore. They barely spoke for the whole journey, that is until five minutes before touch-down when Sly noticed an ominous grey frigate hanging around in the little harbour.

'Jesus,' he said, pointing, 'what the hell are the navy doing here?'

Tyron looked.

'That's not the navy,' he said, 'that's Nagasyu's.'

'He owns his own warship?' asked Sly in surprise.

'Four of them, and four M16s. He's a very big player, Silvester,' was the patronizing reply.

On landing, Sly was shown to his chalet by a uniformed and armed guard. This was a distinct change from the gay *maître d'* at 'California Dreaming'. Sly felt uncomfortable, he wished he'd brought a gun himself. Dinner was held under a beautiful South-East Asian sky, with the lights of Singapore City turning the vast canopy a fabulous dappled orange.

'Well, there's one thing I'll say for pollution,' said Tyron bluntly as they took their seats, 'it's certainly improved the views. The damn stuff's so thick the light just bounces back at us . . . and the heat,' he added more morosely. The terribly unnatural heat of that southern summer was scarcely relieved at all by the coming of night.

Even in the time that had elapsed between the dinner in Los Angeles and this, Sly's second session of the World Government of Money in Singapore, he could sense a gathering urgency in the proceedings. There was less preliminary chatter, people wanted to discuss the project and nothing else. Despite the fabulous tropical spread that Nagasyu had laid on, nobody felt like eating much. They picked at the odd irradiated bit of fruit but the atmosphere was too tense and edgy to really hop into it. Besides, a starlit picnic loses some of its charm when the waiters are packing machine guns and there's an armed warship in the bay. A lot of this security was, of course, to do with Nagasyu's own private operations and nothing to do with Stark but it all contributed to the general air of fatalistic doom.

'See about that sludge slick in the Eastern Atlantic?' Slampacker observed gloomily. 'Jesus, we weren't expecting those for years.'

Slampacker was still in the chair. He seemed to be the unofficial president of the board. Many of the other faces had changed though. Understandably, due to the location, there was a larger contingent of Asian billionaires. As with Los Angeles though, it didn't really matter who attended because any conclusion that the discussion produced would be instantly beamed to all interested parties.

'I've seen pictures,' Slampacker continued, 'yeuk! Green and yellow and red bubbling goo. The damn thing looked like one of my burgers with the lid taken off.' Slampacker spoke in English. Much to Sly's relief English remained the lingua franca despite the majority of the group being Asian. Tex Slampacker was referring to yet another man-made ecological disaster. A horrible, stinking, messy disaster – but that wasn't what worried him. It was the timing. It had come too early. He felt like a man who conscientiously plans his dental appointments and suddenly an unwise toffee pulls half a pound of metal out of his teeth.

## GOD'S SPIT AND THE DOMESDAY GROUP

In order to provide some parameters to their desperate rear-guard action some twenty years before, the Stark consortium (which Sly was discovering was much older than he had first thought) had set up a top secret research team to predict the point at which world eco-balance would become critical, and drastic final action would have to be taken. For example, they had known about the connection between aerosols and ozone a decade before public research reached the same conclusion. This was partly because the Domesday Group, as the research team was called, were far better funded than government research, and partly because with the edge that their extra knowledge gave them, Stark were able to perpetrate a highly effective disinformation campaign. Hence, holding back aerosol bans for ten years, causing countless cancers and making an awful lot of money.

The Domesday Group had also predicted the terrible slime slick to which Slampacker was referring. They had informed their masters that in the not-too-distant future, the pointless over-farming of the industrial world would cause large quantities of nitrates and phosphates to gather in the sea, caused by agricultural run-offs. These would eventually turn the sea into a kind of nutritional soup for the ever present microscopic algae which thrive on these elements. Having been given such a good free meal, these oxygen consuming algae would multiply rapidly and gel into a vast floating, slimy glob, doubling in mass every twenty-four hours and continuing to do so until they had used up all the available nutrients. The problem with this glob, apart from the obvious bummer of having two feet of scum covering part of the eastern Atlantic, is that these algae use up so much oxygen in their phenomenal reproduction that they stifle everything else in their bit of sea. A level of three million algae to a litre of water is fatal to marine life. Underneath the slime slick that had so upset Slampacker, levels were running at ten million a litre. That is a very overcrowded jug of water.

'God's Spit' as the Domesday Group had called their prediction, for obvious reasons, was one of thousands of documents that they had submitted to Stark over the years, and now, yet again, they had been proved right. God had spat on the ocean. But what was worrying Slampacker and his companions so much that night was the timing. This particular disaster had not been predicted for at least another five years – it had happened too early. As an isolated incident this would be acceptable but the Domesday Group were having to constantly revise their predictions backwards as events overtook them. Species of animals that were not meant to die out until mid-twenty-first century were already extinct. Trees were proving far less resilient against acid 'die back' than had been hoped.

This meant that the bottom line, Vanishing Point, the moment at which the world will cease to be able to sustain balanced life, was approaching much faster than had been expected.

'It is coming towards us quicker than we are going towards it,' Slampacker explained, unnecessarily.

The original Vanishing Point scenarios arrived at by the Domesday Group had been really quite optimistic. They reckoned we had three generations at least. They did not see a total breakdown happening until at least the second half of the twenty-first century. At the time the fledgling group that was to become the Stark consortium had taken great comfort from this, hoping that perhaps technology might come up with eco solutions that did not require them to take a drop in profit. Thus relieving them of the terrible necessity of having to intervene directly.

It should be remembered that the first article of the unwritten constitution of the notional World Government of Money is that under no circumstances should anyone be expected to take action that would reduce their profits, whatever the consequences of not taking action. Stark's central assumption being that there is no point in curtailing antisocial activities, because if you don't do it someone else will.

Unfortunately, ever since those heady, optimistic days, Armageddon had been getting closer. The consortium had already decided that the time had come to take drastic action even before Sly joined, now some alarmists in the group were beginning to wonder if they had made their move too late.

'That kind of speculation is quite pointless,' snapped Mai Wo, a small South-East Asian bloke who Sly knew well by reputation. He was much admired for managing to employ more labour for less cash than anyone else since the Pharaohs built the pyramids. Mai Wo brought the same calm logic to his assessment of the Armageddon plan.

'Whether we are too late or not is a non-variable, we cannot affect it,' he said, accepting a cheesy nibble from a waiter in a steel helmet with a small howitzer under his arm. 'We must presume that vanishing point is upon us and that we must act immediately. This we have done. So, let us put panic from our hearts, our shoulders to the wheel, and act as swiftly and as efficiently as we are capable of.'

He spoke as if they were embarking on some great public work, rather than the cruellest and most selfish plan imaginable. He made the others feel good about themselves. Possibly this was how he managed to persuade his enormous workforce to labour so philanthropically on his behalf – maybe it was because in his country trade unions were virtually illegal and the opposition were all in prison.

'Mr Mai Wo is, of course, absolutely right,' Slampacker said, 'and hence I have asked Professor Durf of our Armageddon Co-ordinating Group, to say a few words on what measures we are going to have to employ in order to accelerate our preparations to meet Vanishing Point when it hits us. Professor Durf . . .'

## PROFESSOR DURF AND THE AVALANCHE EFFECT

There was a smattering of polite applause as the dynamic young South African rose to his feet and fixed them with his one eye, the other one having been lost doing his national service. He claimed that he had lost it at the hands of a black soldier, which was true in a way. It had been a black orderly who had over-polished the floor of the officers' mess on which

Durf had skidded stabbing himself with a cocktail stick and thus fixing a small sausage to his left eye.

Durf was present at the dinner because, obviously, a group of people whose talents are centred around making money, could not operate the sort of project that they were planning on their own. Hence, over the years, a carefully selected and heavily controlled group of experts had been recruited to the team. All were shadowed and monitored, day and night, by a vast army of agents who had no idea what they were watching for. Just as most of those being watched, like the Domesday Group for instance, were completely in the dark as to the nature of the ultimate plan that they were unwitting parts of. Sad to say, science is no longer pure: commerce pays for it and commerce calls the tune. Domesday Group scientists produced results for their corporate masters just as they produced aerosols, defoliants and new methods of sticking sugar frosting to cereals. Professor Durf, head of the Armageddon Co-ordinating Group, was one of the handful of people outside the actual World Government of Money who knew the true nature of the plan; he was a part of it. Since the death of his predecessor, Professor Blakely, he was one of its principal architects.

Despite his central role in the Stark Conspiracy, there had been nothing sinister about Blakely's death. He had not been on the verge of spilling the beans – people just die, that's all. Although, with hindsight, the more thoughtful members of Stark realized that the cause of his death was chillingly ironic. He had been on a skiing holiday at Klosters in Switzerland and had been killed by an avalanche. Killed directly by an avalanche that is, but at one remove he was killed by the fires on the Mersey and the Thames and the Tyne.

Klosters used to be pretty safe, it still is, relatively, but none the less all over Europe the ski resorts are becoming ever more plagued by avalanches. In fact so bad has the problem become that whole Alpine villages are being forced to evacuate themselves when the warnings sound. Now one might say: more fool them, how stupid to build their Alpine villages in the paths of potential avalanches. The point is, of course, that for hundreds of years the villages have been perfectly safe. The thick tree cover on the mountain sides had anchored the snow to the ground, and that which did slip away was soon stopped and dispersed by the tough little high-flying forests. Not so anymore, unfortunately. Acid rain sweeping across Europe for a hundred years or more has dissipated the forests. The mountains are going bald. It is possible to filter the factories and power stations that produce the sulphur that turns the water to acid, but it's expensive, so of course it is not done. Little fir trees on frozen mountain tops do not carry a lot of weight when it comes to balancing market forces – but they carry a fuck of a lot of weight when an avalanche lands on your head.

Professor Durf was addressing the assembled party.

'Gentlemen, as you have been discussing, the Domesday Group no longer feel able to make a prediction as to when the world's chain of being will collapse under the pressure of having to generate capital. We may have two decades: we may have two minutes. The avalanche factor teaches us that we are simply not sophisticated enough to compute the myriad possible knock-on effects that could result from any one of the millions of environment shifting activities in which you and your colleagues are engaged.'

The 'avalanche factor' was a term coined in honour of Professor Blakely, whose death graphically demonstrated the fact that it is relatively easy to deduce a cause from an effect, but a mental nightmare to predict effects from causes. Who could possibly have figured out that a factory in Manchester would cause an avalanche? You'd need a brain the size of Heathrow airport. But, once it's happened, then it's comparatively easy to work backwards to the cause through a process of deduction. Causes do not become identified as causes until they have taken their effect. Meanwhile you've got a mountain on your head or an ocean completely covered in smokers' phlegm.

This was what the World Government of Money feared

most, the rogue eco-catastrophe, so unexpected, so obvious –
after the event. The unpredictable disaster that would cheat
them of their prize in the race for a solution to their
predicament. The avalanche factor.

'It is because of this terrible uncertainty,' continued
Professor Durf, 'that we have decided to reassess our
timetable. It would be most regrettable, I think you'll agree,
to achieve all that we have planned and then to die of skin
cancer or suffocation on the morning that we had decided to
push the button.'

This was a joke. Professor Durf was a smug fact-head. The
sort of idiot who would annoy a whole cinema full of people
by sighing and laughing loudly at the very scariest bits of a
horror film, then come out at the end saying, so that everyone
can hear, 'But it was absurd. It is a bio-physical impossibility
for anti-matter to transpose itself in that manner.'

One of the reasons that Professor Durf had been selected
for the project was that he had no friends and hence was less
likely to breach security in idle chatter.


## CRASH, BANG, WALLOP

Professor Durf continued:

'And so we have a problem, gentlemen, a very big problem.
Out of the blue – or perhaps these days I should say out of the
smog – the summer of Stark is upon us. It appears that we
have to act *now*. Unfortunately the astronomical costing of the
final stages of our project has always been computed as taking
place over a number of years, leaving time to slowly
accumulate spending capital and negotiate the prices of what
we need from strength. Each one of you have slowly begun
breaking up your resources and had intended to continue
doing so for the foreseeable future. Unfortunately, the
predictions of the Domesday Group and the fear of
avalanches, has made it a necessity that the final assemblage
takes place *immediately*, within months. No one in the
consortium makes the hardware required for Stark, only

166

governments do that. When we suddenly attempt to buy everything at once, we will force the prices sky high. We will create a sellers' market for the things we are trying to buy. In short, gentlemen, we won't be able to afford it.'

There was a nervous silence as the assembled company struggled with the meaning of the words 'can't afford'.

Durf was loving every minute of his brisk, bossy monologue. If he hadn't been an incredibly brainy person he would have been an officious one-eyed council clerk or something. Sly hated him. All right, Sly had decided to go along with the monstrous project because he could see the logic in it but Christ, you didn't have to enjoy it!

'Now hang on a minute,' interjected Tyron. 'What the hell is this "can't afford"? Why, if the Stark consortium were to liquify all its assets we could afford anything.'

'But of course, Mr Tyron,' replied the aggravating Durf, 'and, over years, it might even be possible for all of the members to do so, by bleeding small sections into the market piecemeal, as you have all been doing. But, let me ask you, Mr Tyron, if you wished to unload *all* of your holdings tomorrow, who would you sell to?'

'Well . . .' replied Tyron. But of course Durf, as usual, was only asking a rhetorical question.

'Mr Moorcock? Mr Slampacker? Mr Nagasyu? Lord Playing? Perhaps of course. But unfortunately at the same time *they* are trying to sell *their* companies to you. We all swap companies and no one comes out with a penny.'

The logic of Durf's point was beginning to sink in. He continued.

'Sure, a few of the Consortium would find buyers outside of Stark. Not all the money is in the conspiracy. But, a lot of the maverick, moveable, ready cash is. Basically, if we wanted to sell all the assets committed to Stark immediately – as we must, according to the Domesday Group – only Stark can afford to buy it. *Ipso facto*, we have an empasse.'

Well, there wasn't much anyone could say. This was, without a doubt, a bit of a blow.

'So, is that it?' said Sly. 'Nice meeting you all. Forget the whole thing?'

'Gentlemen,' said Durf, who was absolutely getting an erection from all this tension and attention, 'we have a solution to suggest to you. Mr Mai Wo, perhaps you would kindly explain.'

'Thank you, Professor Durf,' said the sanitized slave-owner, who was received warmly at the White House, Downing Street and any other centre of the civilized world he cared to visit.

'Gentlemen. We need to bring about a situation where the hardware we wish to purchase costs less than the capital that we are able to generate. The present market is buoyant, nobody can afford to buy us out and the things we need are hugely expensive.

'This, then, gentlemen is my suggestion. We *engineer* a crash. All together we begin to unload the very cream of our assets, creating a massive bear market. With the kind of mega-stock that we can load the shelf with, other lesser stock will become worthless. Who will buy John Citizen's meagre assets for a dollar when the mighty Slampacker group stocks are up for ten cents? Overnight a panic spiral of previously unknown proportions will develop. A vortex of selling will consume all the notional capital in the world. Small businesses, dependent on credit, will collapse. Little investors will go to the wall. As in previous crashes, only the very biggest will survive. Those with real assets, those who own the actual means of production will actually emerge even stronger because they will be all that's left. Us, gentlemen. Oh sure, on paper our fortunes will be cut by 90 per cent, but in *relative* terms, compared to the carnage around us, we will be richer than ever. Add to this the fact that the prices of the commodities that we wish to buy will also collapse in the general crash: governments will lose huge tax revenues as businesses go bankrupt and men are laid off: millions will turn to welfare, the politicians will be desperate to raise money. Then, gentlemen, it will be a *buyers'* market and *we* will be buying.

In the months following the collapse, which will be our site construction period, governments will be counting their pennies to buy food. I should imagine everything from solar panelling to orbital guidance satellites will be in the bargain bazaar.'

## DEATH WARRANT

Nobody could deny that deliberately creating a great depression was a pretty huge concept.

'Well, it's never been done before,' said Ocker.

'Exciting, isn't it?' said Slampacker.

'You mean,' interjected Sly, 'that the average bloke's last experience before the ecological vanishing point will be one of crippling world slump?'

'Exactly,' said Mr Mai Wo.

'No final party; nothing like that?'

'We have to create the right financial conditions for our purposes.'

Well, you learn something every day. Sly had thought he was a hard bastard. You couldn't help but be impressed though – the little git had it all worked out.

'Nobody likes this, Moorcock,' said Slampacker, his tone, for the first time, something other than cosy and benign. 'You got a better suggestion? The world's fucked, somebody has to do something. I didn't notice any of your "average blokes" refusing to buy my burgers, or aerosols or use the electricity from the acid power stations. We're all in this together, everyone in the world, right? We just happen to be in a position to do something about it. Let me tell you, son, when the time comes to stand before God, I shan't hang my head in shame, no sir! Not unless every other body and soul on this planet does likewise!'

Sly noticed that the assembled company were all glaring at him with some hostility. He realized that his compatriots were very sensitive to the moral issues of what they were involved in, which was hardly surprising since they were in the process of organizing the most bastard trick in history.

'Listen, Mr Slampacker. I'm just catching up here, OK? Just getting the parameters. You won't find me wanting, and frankly I resent the implication that you might. I was told that all our discussions were to be frank and open, that's all I'm trying to be. I'm getting the land aren't I?'

'We hope,' added Tyron.

'Acquiring thousands of acres of Aboriginal sacred sites, discreetly, is not easy, especially when people stick their noses in where —'

'Now hold on boys, hold on,' interrupted Slampacker, back to his old soapy tones. 'I'm sure you're doing a wonderful job, Sly, wonderful. Let's not fall out over silly things, after all, we have a long way to go together. Now then, I believe we were discussing all this financial wheeler-dealing, right?'

'Yes, and I have something to say on the subject,' said Sly. He hadn't been going to bring it up but he felt the need to say something more to prove he was a dedicated part of things. 'It may be nothing, but there's a stupid journo on my back. She's probably just fishing around but she's got all my withdrawals and rationalizations noted down in her damn filofax like a shopping list. Now I'm sure that —'

'What's her name?' Slampacker snapped, again losing his teddy bear quality.

'I don't know, I got rid of her as soon as I could. Linda something.'

'Linda Reeve?' interjected Mai Wo, a note of surprise in his voice.

Sly turned to Mai Wo in surprise. 'She's tailing your deals too?'

'Just a call. She'd noticed I was pulling out and not putting back. She has a theory that the big players are losing their nerve, but she thinks it's all unilateral action. She's not looking for a conspiracy.'

'Oh yeah and how long's that going to last?' Slampacker now looked a lot more like the sort of man who would order the destruction of an entire rain-forest. 'This bitch has phoned my people too.'

'This is a serious irritation.' Mai Wo used the word 'irritation' with a chilly detachment that would have made anyone who cared for Linda Reeve very nervous indeed. 'If any hint that we are working together were to emerge before we create our crash, it's just possible that the powers that be could act against us. Close the banks, suspend trading, etc. That would be most inconvenient.' Mai Wo's language was always mild. 'Irritation', 'inconvenient', he might have been discussing a parking fine, but he wasn't. And if any insurance broker who heard him had been asked to provide cover for Linda Reeve, even Stark wouldn't have been able to afford the premiums.

'We need to know what she knows, what she thinks and what she's said.' Slampacker clearly wanted to end discussions on the subject. 'She works for the *London Financial Telegraph*. You own that don't you, Ocker?'

'Yes, I own it. I own her boss and I own her. This situation is simply not a problem, we shouldn't even be discussing it. Tomorrow I will have my people look into it and deal with it. There'll be no need for anything drastic but you won't be hearing from her again.'

With that the discussion moved on to the other business at hand – Durf's plans for assembling and distributing the required hardware. It all hinged on Tyron and Sly as the consortium members closest to the centre of things. Sly was to carry on with the business of acquiring the land and having done so was to start with all haste, to prepare it. Meanwhile, Tyron would provide a dumping-off point for the equipment that must soon now begin flowing into Western Australia. He had a massive mining consideration which was all played out. It should be possible to store pretty limitless stuff there and pass it off as a consolidation point for Tyron Mining paraphernalia . . .

## A MAN WITH A FUTURE

Finally, the meeting ended. Sly decided not to stay. He

wanted a change of company. Nagasyu's people took him across to the city in a launch and he walked out into the hot streets in order to collect his thoughts. He needed to reconnect with reality. And yet, as he looked about himself; the buildings; the history; the milling crowds, he realized that Stark would soon become the new reality and all this would be a memory.

It was so difficult to comprehend. Sly tried to make himself grasp it. Make himself really take it seriously. As he wandered about he kept telling himself that he was looking at the past, like an old film. It was time to consider the future.

Who would he save? Who did he love enough? Who could he tell? Anyone? Who would he confide in and protect, and love for ever? No one, that was who. Sly didn't love anyone, that was the truth of it. He didn't love anyone and nobody loved him.

By God though, he could make somebody love him. Couldn't he just? With what he knew, with what he had to offer, he could make somebody love him till the end of time. But who?

# THE POST

Chrissy sat back on the sofa in her apartment and prepared to luxuriate over her letter. She loved getting mail and a letter was something to be savoured. Not work stuff obviously, although such is the instinctive pleasure of getting anything through the post that even that is better than nothing.

Perhaps it is something to do with the fact that when you're a kid, the only things you could ever get through the post were utterly exciting. Strange how childhood impressions linger, often remaining more pervasive than the experiences of later life. It's a pretty safe bet that 90 per cent of the mail any particular individual gets will be either dull, depressing or downright disastrous. The bills, the summonses, the junk . . .

But, very occasionally, comes that rare delight; a personal letter. And the remote possibility of that happy event is enough to make every trip to the mat to pick up the post a potential thrill, despite the near statistical certainty of disappointment. It seems that the distant echo of those childhood birthday cards, some containing book tokens and even postal orders, can still call to us from across the years. Old auntie what's-her-name would be pleased to know that her small, kind gesture so long ago had such a lifelong resonance.

## STUFF TO DO

Chrissy put the bill in the 'stuff to do' pile. She was very together about bills. At least she was very together about putting bills in the 'stuff to do' pile. After that things got a little looser. The 'stuff to do' pile was rarely less than an inch thick. It had a presence, that pile; a spirit of its own. Sometimes it seemed to be staring at Chrissy like some evil priest, gleefully reminding her of her inadequacy. It would mither her whenever she felt good, deliberately deflating her. After she'd finished an overdue article or done some research, she would glance across the room and there the pile would be, shouting, 'All right, fair enough, you've done that but what about me! You've *still* got loads of stuff to do in the "stuff to do" pile.'

The strange thing is that when she finally did attack the pile, it was so easy. Cheque-book, envelopes, stamps and in an hour it was over. The relief of an empty 'stuff to do' pile was one of the most lovely sights in the world. But, despite this knowledge – the knowledge that if she just got on with it it would be over in an instant – the pile always grew again. No matter how often she swore to deal with the bills more regularly, it always took a final reminder to make her tackle the pile. And so, for the want of a few minutes self-discipline, she allowed a terrible malignant beastie with fifteen envelope-shaped heads to live in the corner of her apartment.

## JUNK

Chrissy wasn't too bothered about the 'stuff to do' pile on the evening that she got the letter. Why, it was barely teetering yet, the venom that the monster spat was of little consequence whilst it had no final reminder to reproach her with. The pile could wait.

She tossed the junk mail in the bin, unopened. And in doing so, Chrissy unwittingly made a joke and a mockery of the lives, loves and endeavours of countless people whom she would never know. In that casual gesture she trampled upon an awesome human achievement and upon great sacrifices contributed by the natural world. Why didn't she stop to think? Why didn't she dare to care? What a bitch.

If only she could have seen them, seen their disappointment as she hurled their creation back in their honest faces. The person who cleared the land to plant the fir trees; the persons who planted and tore up the fir trees every second or third year; the drivers and the ships' captains who got the trees to the mill; the thousands who work in the mills and in the huge pulping plants and paper factories – if only Chrissy could have seen them she would have wept bitter tears of self reproach to have dismissed their lives so casually.

The copywriter? Did Chrissy not care that he had spent so many lonely hours trying to think of a tempting way to get her to accept ten days free home perusal of a fifteen volume history of the Wild West? The printer and the four colour offset litho process of which he was so proud – was his life to be just a pointless joke because of Chrissy? The animals and insects that were wiped out when billions of acres of forest and moorland were turned over to single crop, factory, fir tree farming. Did they give their lives in vain?

One can only hope and pray that those involved never discover that after the monumental worldwide effort and the truly awesome consumption of natural resources that went into bringing a piece of junk mail to Chrissy's door, she simply threw it away. Gone, gone, gone; all their hopes and dreams and sacrifices, rejected in that one contemptuous gesture. They must never know, for they would put up their arms in horror (or spindly leggy things in the case of the insects) and say, as Zimmerman would say, 'What *is* the point!? No, I mean really, what *is* the point?'

Over a year, as a moderately high-earner in the US – the country which wrote the original handbook on pointless consumption – Chrissy would receive between five hundred and a thousand bits of junk mail. Plus over a hundred 'free' newspapers, perhaps fifty cab firm cards and fifty offers from local estate agents to dispose of her property. She, like most people, threw the lot away unopened.

## LETTER FROM LONDON

Her letter was from Linda Reeve in London. Linda did not

often write but when she did it was normally something pretty good.

On glancing at the opening paragraph however, Chrissy felt a momentary irritation because it was immediately clear that Linda was still harping on about this business about Nagasyu and Tyron and Slampacker, and all the other assorted billionaires she was putting in her book. However, as Chrissy read on, despite herself, she began to wonder whether there might not be something in it. Linda had included a copy of the article which her editor had rejected, plus a series of less specific examples detailing withdrawals of smaller sums of money, or where some reinvestment had resulted. Chrissy had to admit that it read pretty well. Somewhere, somehow, in recent months, thirty billion U S dollars worth of stock had been converted into cash by a smallish group of individuals and simply disappeared.

In her article, Linda seemed to be suggesting that perhaps a collective fear was sweeping the upper echelons of the financial world and that some of the big men wanted their money where they could see it. But could they see it? Linda couldn't, and nor could Chrissy. It was unthinkable that they had simply put it in the bank. People used to watching their bucks divide and grow like amoeba were not going to put up with 7 per cent a year in a deposit account. And yet, none of those concerned had any major, high-profile project underway that would require heavy cash flow. Where had it gone?

Unlike Linda, who was deeply conservative, Chrissy was a bit of a radical. She did not have a very high opinion of the people she regularly studied and wrote about. Therefore, Chrissy did not have much time for Linda's theory about paranoia. These guys' religion was chasing money, they weren't just going to pull out. They'd screw everyone else in the world before they'd do that. So what was it? It would be wonderful if there was something illegal going on. Drugs would be terrific, but reason told her that this was out of the question. The people Linda mentioned were too big to bother to take risks like that. Arms seemed a possibility.

Perhaps it was a huge global arms syndicate! Linda had produced twenty-three names, that would be very big indeed for a syndicate, especially since all the people involved were big enough to play a lone hand.

It did look interesting, Chrissy couldn't deny it . . . Maybe she should take a look? On the other hand, maybe she should finish the article that she was writing about the aftermath of the unprecedently hot northern summer (suntan lotion and ice-cream futures were very big). Then again, she was long overdue to write to her sister in Wisconsin. Maybe she should do that . . . And she hadn't done her aerobic home workout in *seven months* – God she was definitely going to have a heart attack. Also, the toilet needed cleaning in the corner. The 'stuff to do' pile seemed to have grown, nothing had been added in the few minutes since she had last looked but it had definitely got bigger . . .

'OK,' it hissed at her maliciously, fluttering its papery arms, 'So there ain't no final bills, so what? How about that insurance form? Huh? And the new cheque card application? You still have that to do don't ya? And the register of voters, that's two weeks old already, do you want to get disenfranchised? You will be, if you don't do it! Come on, Chrissy, look at me! There is so much *stuff to do* in the "stuff to do" pile'.

## THE HONEST, DEDICATED JOURNO IS A RARE AND ENDANGERED SPECIES

The next day, during her first cup of coffee, Chrissy thought she'd ring Linda to apologize for being so dismissive on the phone before and say that having read the letter she now thought that perhaps there might be something in it.

Chrissy was hoping that she could persuade Linda to send the programs she had used for her book on the rich guys, down the line so that Chrissy too could pick up quickly on their movements wherever they were dealing. This would be stretching a pen-pal friendship quite a long way. After all, it would have taken Linda a very long time to put those programs together. Still, if Linda wanted Chrissy's help . . .

'Hello, Linda Reeve's phone,' the voice said.

'Hi, is Linda around?'

Looking back, Chrissy was sure that she had sensed something wrong even in that moment.

'Uhm, might I ask your business?'

'My name's Chrissy Waldorf, I'm on the *Wall Street Examiner*, we're friends.'

'Uhm . . . well, she's unavailable at the moment,' the man replied.

'Well, can you get her to call me?'

'Look, I'm awfully sorry, we're rather upset at this end, I'm afraid Linda's dead . . .'

Chrissy ran cold. Maybe there is something in sixth-sense, she felt like she'd known even before she picked up the phone. She did not reply, her mind was racing. The man on the other end clearly felt obliged to offer some further explanation – he had been doing it all morning.

'Dreadful business. It seems that she surprised a burglar and, well, uhm, he killed her . . .'

'A burglar?' said Chrissy, 'in her apartment?'

'Yes, that's right.'

'Did he get away with anything?'

The man at the other end was slightly put off that this was the American woman's first consideration. But, there you go, that was Yanks for you.

'I believe it was a very professional job. A great deal was –'

'Listen, are you at her desk?' Chrissy spoke urgently. Maybe poor Linda had been murdered coincidentally. First the letter, now this . . .

'Well, as a matter of fact I am but –'

'Will you do me a favour? Lock it, put everything inside and lock it right now and keep the key.'

The man at the other end explained that he would be happy to but that he saw no point as it had already been emptied and

178

the top had been completely cleared. All that remained was a half-empty box of chocolates and he didn't suppose that she wanted that. No, he didn't know who had done it. It had certainly been done when he arrived that morning. Perhaps the police . . .

Chrissy checked with the police. Then, posing as a relative, she checked with the editor. Neither knew who had emptied the desk. The editor thought perhaps relatives or one of Linda's colleagues, really he was very busy and everybody was very upset.

After that it was evening in Britain and Chrissy had to wait out the rest of the day and until early the next morning for London to wake up again. When it did she checked as best she could with the relatives, managing to contact Linda's mother. Mrs Reeve was clearly strung-out but hanging on. She believed that it was important that one contained oneself. Refusing to break down she dealt politely and clearly with Chrissy, who claimed to be a closer friend than she was. Unfortunately, Mrs Reeve knew nothing of who had emptied the desk, nor did any of Linda's colleagues that Chrissy managed to speak to. None of them were particularly interested either. It appeared that as far as anyone knew, Linda did not keep much of interest in her desk.

This was not the point as far as Chrissy was concerned. The point was that it had been emptied and nobody knew who had done it. Clearly a stranger had emptied it, hence obviously they thought she *might* have something of interest in it. Interesting enough to risk a search. Interesting enough, it seemed, to kill her.

The police report made it clear that the burglar was a professional. There had been a highly accomplished, no-nonsense entry, a swift, silent clear out, the lot. If that was the case, thought Chrissy, why had he killed her? Professional burglars are rarely murderers. You don't last long in a job if you start killing people. It's the one-off thug who normally panics and lashes out. The conviction was firmly growing in Chrissy's mind that this fellow had killed first and burgled afterwards.

# PRIVATE INVESTIGATIONS

## DISCOVERING MURDER

Linda's last letter to Chrissy, those few pieces of paper that Chrissy held in her hand, was, it seemed, the single and only piece of Linda's work left in existence. Chrissy felt cold even to think about it.

It had not been difficult to work this out. Chrissy had spoken a number of times to Linda's parents who were kind, helpful people. They had found out what she asked them to. Linda's flat, it seemed, still contained an awful lot of paper, love letters from Linda's one affair, bills, her attempts at poetry, but there were no papers relating to any aspect of Linda's work left whatsoever. Nothing, not a note, not an old article, not a floppy disc. Her entire career had disappeared.

'But I really can't see that it's at all sinister,' Linda's father, a quiet, sad voiced, ex-army officer, said. 'The police assure us that the burglars were very thorough. They really gutted and filleted the place. Even took the clocks, anything of value, the food mixer, the more expensive clothes, everything.'

Of course they did, Chrissy thought to herself. The only way to avoid arousing police suspicion was to make what was in fact a premeditated murder, appear to have been committed absolutely and indisputably for reasons of professional burglary.

Any burglar together enough to remove only the expensive clothes, is together enough to know that a girl's journalistic research is worthless to him . . . Unless, of course, it isn't.

That had been their mistake, that was what made Chrissy absolutely certain that something terribly wrong was going on.

They had constructed the façade of a serious, tidy, professional burglary in order that the police would presume that they could see at a glance what had been stolen. There was no ransacking here, no shadowy motive. It was all very clear, the police would not think to start looking for scraps of paper and note books that they did not even know existed. But Chrissy knew they existed. They must do, Linda was a very conscientious journalist. It was unthinkable that she would not have research data at home. Therefore, this supposedly pragmatic and professional burglar had taken the trouble to sort out and steal something he could not possibly want. The burglary *must* be a front, and what's more, a front based on the assumption that only the people who took out the contract on Linda were aware that her research was in some way compromising. This meant that Chrissy had a short start on the killers. Clearly they could not know that Linda had passed on the body of her research to Chrissy, or, Chrissy presumed, she would already be dead too. For the moment at least, although 'they' remained invisible to Chrissy, at least she was invisible to them.

Poor Colonel (retired) and Mrs Reeve were bewildered by Chrissy's questions, but it was obvious to them that this strange American girl thought that something was wrong.

'Look, if there's anything we can do . . .' the Colonel said, having to make an effort to keep his voice steady. 'Linda really was a marvellous sort, you know . . . terrific . . . really terrific. What I'm saying is, if you think that there's something, well, uhm, fishy in all this . . .?'

Chrissy reminded herself that the enemy had already killed once, killed a girl for reading a computer screen. She did not wish to provoke further tragedy.

'No, really, please forget it, Colonel. It's nothing, just a little project Linda and I were working on . . . about beetroot,' she added for some unknown reason. 'I suppose it's selfish of me, I just didn't want to have to re-do her work, that's all. Sorry . . .'

'Beetroot you say?' said Colonel Reeve absently, '. . . Linda never liked beetroot, but nobody does really, do they? I mean, not honestly. Stains the lettuce and puts you off . . .'

Chrissy excused herself as gently as she could and put the phone down, leaving the old Colonel thinking about beetroot and his dead daughter and trying not to cry.


## FOR THE LOVE OF A GOOD WOMAN

CD was also puzzled. He reckoned he understood Silvester Moorcock. He had more in common with him than the same taste in women. CD could spot a smooth operator when he saw one. After all, it took one to know one. Of course, CD acknowledged that there were differences between the two of them. For instance, Sly was worth several billion and CD had about forty bucks –but CD did not believe in getting hung up on minor details, they obscure the broader view.

Rachel and Walter had pretty much accepted Sly's protestations of innocence regarding the Nazi attack. After all, there was no reason for the Bullens Creek police chief to lie about it. But CD wondered why Sly had bothered to go to the extent of trying to prove it. After all, what were they to him?

CD pondered this question in the week or so after their meeting at Facefulls and the only explanation he could come up with was that Sly had something to hide. How, CD asked himself, would an entirely innocent multimillionaire react to being confronted by four penniless scruffs accusing him of promoting fascist race attacks for personal gain? Well, CD reckoned that there was a pretty strong chance that he would sue them. He might have them beaten up, he would certainly tell them to fuck off, what seemed unlikely was that he would ask them to join him for a drink and give the craziest one his hamburger. And yet this was exactly what had happened. The man had positively cooed at them, going to quite a bit of trouble to prove that he had not been involved in the attack. More than that, he had exposed to them what was clearly a rather dubious relationship with a police chief, purely in order to show some strange hippy that he had nothing to do with something. In CD's mind this suggested extremely strongly indeed that Sly *did* have something to do with it.

Love is a great motivator. CD still loved Rachel, truly and achingly. If only the strength of the love that people feel when it is reciprocated could be as intense and obsessive as the love we feel when it is not: then marriages would truly be made in heaven.

With every day it hurt more. The longing, the frustration; the frustration was definitely the worst. He absolutely ached to make love to Rachel, he would have done anything to see her naked. He would sit up long into the night tearfully whining to Zimm about it and drinking Zimm's home-brewed beer. CD was lucky to have such a willing confidante. Normally the ridiculously over-in-love are an utter and total drag to their friends and intimates, but Zimm loved hearing about CD's problems – it made him feel better about not having any balls.

Anyway, suffice it to say, CD had only got involved with the whole protest thing in order to endear himself to Rachel, first as a hippy and then following into association with Zimm and Walter and becoming an activist. He reckoned now he was in, he might as well go the whole hog. In for a penny, in for a pound, so to speak. If he could find something out, come up with something interesting, then maybe he would be worthy of her. Then maybe she would love him and let him up her dress.

She wouldn't, of course, the world doesn't work like that, but love is blind and hope springs eternal.

CD could not think what it was he might find out. Whether Silvester Moorcock was involved with Nazis perhaps? Why he wanted the land so much? Maybe nothing at all, but for the love of a good woman he was at least prepared to have a bash. He only had one lead; this skinhead bloke, therefore he would have to follow that.

# CONNECTIONS

Even before the terrible news of her death, Chrissy had been dubious about Linda's naïve contention that the various financial dealings that she had pinpointed were unconnected. Linda's theory that a kind of atmospheric change was occurring in the money markets and hence causing a bunch of people to act in exactly the same way, but independently, was far too airy-fairy an idea for Chrissy to give any credence to at all. In her mind, Linda could not have it both ways. If the various deals *were* unconnected, then they were of no significance. Conversely, if they were of significance then they *had* to be connected. Therefore, since, due to the manner of Linda's death Chrissy had already satisfied herself that something significant was going on, it had to follow that the various billionaires isolated in Linda's reserarch were, in fact, all in cahoots with one another. If this was the case then Linda had clearly stumbled on something enormous, which was why she had been killed.

A quick bit of mental arithmetic was enough to make Chrissy weak at the knees. A significant percentage of all the money in the world appeared to be working together. What's more, it was doing it in secret and it was prepared to kill to keep that secret. What the hell was going on? Chrissy's mind reeled at the possibilities. So far they had only released a tiny potential of their spending power. If they wanted to, collectively, these men had the power to purchase entire countries. Christ Almighty! Capitalist predators working together. It was contrary to the whole system. But what power they would have! They could buy out national debts, hold governments to ransom, close down whole economies if they wanted to. Had these people got bored with making cars and stereos and aerosols? were they going to start making history?

Clearly speculating as to what they were up to was fairly pointless. First of all she needed to firmly establish the connections. She did not have remotely enough at the moment to make any kind of case. And what if she did?

putting the murder aside, people were legally allowed to move their money about if they liked. It was what they were planning to do with it that she had to discover.

She knew that she could not say a word until she had something. Once you put your head above the parapet these people clearly shot at it. Maybe what they were planning would count as some kind of insurgency, treason perhaps? They were international figures – could one be treasonous against the whole world? Maybe the C I A were already on the case, it was certainly their territory, but these people were so enormous perhaps they owned the C I A? Maybe they owned the President? they certainly paid to get him elected. Chrissy realized that she had nothing and could trust no one. She was on her own.

She quit her job – she was freelance anyway – cashed in her stocks and shares and began to dig – to dig as secretively and as anonymously as she possibly could. She had no desire to share Linda's fate.

Using the names in Linda's letter, Chrissy began to try to trace the movements of the super-rich over the past few months, trying to establish that connection. It was tough, tough work, but not impossible. These were very high profile people. One useful source was the huge number of glossy magazines about money that had proliferated as the yuppy decade ran its course. They were basically gossip pretending to be theory and criticism, hence they chronicled peoples' movements when they could just to fill up the hundreds of useless shit pages that they published every month.

Hotels were another good source. It was comparatively simple for Chrissy, posing as a reporter from one of these appalling mags, to persuade publicity-minded managers to discreetly confide the names of the more illustrious members of the business community who saw fit to patronize their establishments. Also, Chrissy had a friend in American Diner. It was a big favour, but she managed to persuade him to divulge one or two details concerning where various Platinum cards had been active over short periods of time.

Eventually, hollow-eyed and a half a stone lighter, she pinpointed the evening in Los Angeles.

She was in a position to prove that at least fourteen of the names mentioned in Linda's letter had been in Los Angeles for less than ten hours on the same evening. Obviously this was not conclusive, L A is a pretty vital business centre, you would expect millionaires to congregate there. But it was all she had. Praying that they had not met at a private house, Chrissy started to contact all the major hotels and restaurants in L A. She chose Silvester Moorcock's name, they probably wouldn't bother phoning Australia to check him out.

'Hallo, my name is Patty, I am the personal assistant in the U S to Mr Silvester Moorcock, the Australian industrialist. I believe he dined at your establishment on the —th of the —th this year. We cannot locate a solid gold watch that was inscribed 'to Sly, stay real, Jimmy Carter'. It is of considerable sentimental value and Mr Moorcock wonders if he lost it that night and if you had found it. Obviously, if you had you would not have known who to send it on to.'

'I'm sorry Patty,' (this was L A remember), 'but we know of no watch.'

'Oh well, in that case I wonder if I have the correct establishment. Could you possibly check with the manager whether Mr Moorcock dined with you that night.'

Chrissy reckoned it was a pretty fair bet that you did not get to be manager of a top L A restaurant without remembering your billionaires. Time and again Chrissy stuck out. Many apologies but Mr Moorcock did not dine at so and so's that night . . .

'I would definitely have remembered, Patty, because that was the night King Hussein of Jordan took the upper-lounge room.'

Finally, to Chrissy's delight, her perseverance paid off. She dialled 'California Dreaming' and found herself speaking to a very superior *maître d'*, who remembered the night clearly.

'Yes, Ms, Mr Moorcock certainly dined with us that night. I recall Sir chose swan, a very wise choice for Sir to make, if I

186

might opine. However, I'm afraid we have no record of Sir's watch and may I assure you that our staff are utterly trust-worthy.'

Chrissy grabbed her chance.

'But of course. Mr Moorcock wanted me to make a point of mentioning the quality of the staff and the excellence of the swan. It's difficult these days to find an establishment that can properly accommodate such an important group of men.'

Chrissy was terrified that he would reply that Moorcock had dined alone, or with a lady friend or whatever. He didn't, she wanted to hug him.

'We do our very best, Ms, and I'm happy to say that our very best *is* the best. Mr Slampacker always honours us with his patronage when he entertains.'

She had it! A connection . . . Very gently Chrissy tried for more, she didn't want to be greedy but she had to get as much as she could.

'Catering must be hell I should think. So many cultures. I'll bet Mr Nagasyu wanted raw fish or something . . .'

'I do not recall what Mr Nagasyu ordered,' the *maître d'* said coldly. Clearly his suspicions had finally been aroused. He was wondering whether Chrissy was a gossip journalist, she would get no more out of him. But that was fine, she had got enough.


## A VISIT TO THE MASTER RACE

Chrissy's research had not been much fun but CD would have happily swapped it for the task that he had set himself. Taking a bus to Perth and then walking out to the suburbs to find a brutal thug who was on bail for criminal assault, was not CD's idea of a great evening.

He had taken great care to prepare himself for the part he had to play because he was well aware that if this Gordon Gordon fellow smelt a fraud, he would be in serious trouble. Getting your head kicked in type of trouble.

It had not taken him long to find out where the White

187

Supremacy People's Fair Deal Party hung out. A trip to the library to look up some old newspaper reports of Gordon's previous escapades had informed him that this unpleasant group of people frequented the Old Sydney Hotel. So that was where he was going. He had had his hair cut short – not a crop, more like a soldier would have it – and he wore a suit with a union jack tie left over from his brief mod-revival period.

His plan was to play a pom, and boldly approach Gordon, masquerading as a representative of British fascism.

He entered the pub, effecting an arrogant sneer that he hoped would suggest that he did not want trouble but if that was the way anyone wanted it, they could have it. CD was a small man but he knew how to walk tall. He needed to walking into a pub like the Old Sydney. It was what is called a 'Lingerie' pub, this being a place where you watch a semi-strip show which goes only as far as sexy lingerie. This prudish reticence does not indicate any fledgling moral principles on the part of the management, rather the local by-laws that forbid full on strips in the pubs. Apparently the strip club owners were threatening to put in dart boards and pool tables.

There were flags on the walls and various weapons, also a few sporting trophies and framed photos of long forgotten footie teams. The owner or brewer involved had clearly asked himself the question: 'What do men like?'

Basing his assumptions principally on his own tastes, the landlord had come up with the answers; wanking, war and sport. Hence it was along these lines that he had decided to theme his pub. Of course very soon his pub was full of war-mad wankers talking about sport. The boss often congratulated himself on his astute target marketing. It did make for a pretty unpleasant atmosphere, of course. If you stood at the bar you could almost feel the bitter and unfulfilled macho pretensions of the clientele – every one of whom by rights should have been a top mercenary in Angola or a football star.

CD spotted Gordon Gordon easily. He sat alone, watching the lingerie girl wear her lingerie. He was wearing his lingerie too, in a way. Inevitably it was a hot night and he was sat in his vest. He sat there with his muscles permanently flexed. He did not want people to know this of course, the idea being that the rippling state of his arms actually represented Gordon in a state of relaxation. His tattoos were a fairly comprehensive collection of daggers, eagles, flags and guns. He had a bunch of empty glasses in front of him. He didn't let them clear any away; he liked people to know how much he had drunk, which was plenty. His near-bald pate gleamed in the dullness as it reflected the changing coloured lights – they were the only bright thing in his head.

The management had thoughtfully provided these lights in order to add a touch of theatricality and glamour to a show which, when all was said and done, consisted of a girl walking around a stage in her underwear.

CD ordered a glass of water. This was a calculated part of his pose. Despite appearances to the contrary, he had to presume that Gordon was not a total imbecile. Organizing a political party, even a small and stupid one, must take at least a degree of native cunning. Therefore CD had determined to create a slightly more subtle persona than might be expected. There have, in the past, been police efforts to infiltrate organizations such as Gordon Gordon's. CD had to presume that Gordon would be ready for the obvious.

'Gordon Gordon?' He stood slightly behind the big thug, not a very convivial position from which to affect an introduction. At the very least it was extremely rude; at worst, deliberately putting Gordon at such a disadvantage hinted at potential violence. This was what CD wanted, it was nerve-racking and took a lot of bottle, but in the long run CD reckoned that it would be safer than trying to arse-lick the guy.

'You obviously know who I am, or you wouldn't be asking,' Gordon answered without turning around. He could occasionally play quite a cool hand and if he had had a completely different personality he might have been quite an acceptable member of society.

'So why don't you tell me what you want or fuck off,' he added.

189

CD moved around from behind, but Gordon did not look at him. He kept staring with bored detachment at the girl in the knickers. He was pretending to chew gum.

'I've come a long way to see you, Mr Gordon,' said CD, affecting his best laid-back cockney accent, hoping that Gordon would presume he was a cop.

'If you're going to do me, do me, mate. But watch your back when I get out, all right? If you're here for a chat, go and stuff it up your arse.'

Lots of Perth cops were ex-poms, and that, along with the suit and the studied arrogance, had done the trick.

'I'm not the filth, Mr Gordon, although I've done for a couple in my time. I represent the British race-warrior, white rock band 'Skrew, Fuk, Die and Kill'. I presume you've heard of them.'

Gordon turned for the first time to look at CD. He was suddenly very interested. He had all three of Skrew, Fuk, Die and Kill's albums, a tasteful little hat trick of two chord thrash-metal turkeys entitled respectively 'Final Solution', 'Blood on the Club' and 'JuFuker'. CD, of course, could not have known how much Gordon was into this band but he had presumed that Gordon would at least have heard of them. 'The Skrew', as their few fans referred to them, were four deeply violent and utterly talentless individuals whom the gutter-press had managed to raise from total obscurity to some vague international renown, without anyone hearing a note they played. A number of months previously there had been terrible scenes of violence in Europe when England had been playing in the Cup. The British press had gone bananas claiming that civilization would end immediately if the birch, the stocks, and death by stoning were not instantly re-introduced. In the midst of this, Skrew, Fuk, Die and Kill, who had not even been in Europe at the time, were delighted to find themselves picked up by sensation-hungry hacks as an example of the terrible spectre of resurgent fascism. Thus it was that a band, who until then could draw no more than a couple of hundred punters on their best night, suddenly found themselves instantly feared and famous, with questions being asked about them in parliament.

'What have you got to do with The Skrew?' asked Gordon eagerly. He was a true fan, he had even listened to both sides of the albums and had spent hours trying to decipher the lyrics.

'You're probably aware that they're fairly closely associated with the White British National Movement. I'm the party's international co-ordinator. May I join you, Mr Gordon?'

'All right, yeah, fine. The name's Gordon.'

'I'm aware of that, Mr Gordon,' said CD, happy of the chance to muddy their initial contact with a bit of confusion.

'No, call me Gordon, my first name's Gordon.'

'Oh, I'm sorry Mr . . .? uhm?'

'Gordon. Mr Gordon. My surname's Gordon too. Look my name's Gordon Gordon, all right, so call me Gordon, just Gordon, got it. Look, do you want a drink?' Gordon had been through this many times before and it was a source of deep annoyance to him.

'No thank you, I don't drink. We're under a lot of pressure at home, yids, reds, filth. I'm a prime target. I find it safer to stay completely in control. It is my belief that each pint knocks two dan off my black belt.' This was pushing the bullshit needle close to critical but CD believed rightly that Gordon was excited and wanted to believe in him.

'I'll come straight to the point, Gordon. The White British National Movement are anxious to start setting up some form of loose International. We see no reason why the Trotskyists should have a monopoly on co-operation.' It did not matter whether Gordon had heard of the Fourth International or not, CD knew it would sound convincing and it did. Gordon was thrilled, this was the sort of thing he dreamed of; being part of something big and strong and dignified, instead of just the dickhead who kept getting put in prison for hitting black people.

'Yes, well, the white race is racially . . .' Gordon would have liked to have spoken with the same confidence and articulacy as the pom but he wasn't up to it . . . 'the white race is racially . . . white . . . isn't it? I mean, that's what it's about, isn't it?'

'Exactly,' said CD, beginning to relax. 'Australia is very important to us. Europe's OK but, let's be honest, when all is said and done, they're a bunch of wops. Apart from the Germans, they're poor quality stuff, worse than the yanks in a ruck. Australia, on the other hand, produces the best fighting men in the world. Everyone knows that.'

Gordon swelled with pride. This was the sort of thing he could listen to all night. CD sipped his water, his eyes narrowed and he glanced about meaninglessly. He was attempting to give the impression that he was the sort of person who found it wise always to be aware of who was standing close by. It didn't work, Gordon thought perhaps the flashing coloured lights were bothering him. CD continued . . .

'Now then, the first move we are considering is some kind of cultural link. The Skrew have agreed to do an Australian tour as part of a recruitment drive. What we need is a man on this end. A man we can trust. A man who knows the local filth, who knows the top lefties, the wogs, everything. A bloke who can contain things if there's any real trouble, and of course provoke things if there isn't enough. You see, Gordon, most bands only require security but we also require provocation. Let's face it, if there's no trouble, nobody will know we were there.'

'I've got your drift, mate, no worries.' This was one of the most thrilling conversations Gordon Gordon had ever had.

'So we were wondering, Mr Gordon, if with all your extensive experience and local knowledge, whether it would be possible for you . . .'

Gordon's little piggy eyes were bright. He couldn't believe it, The Skrew . . . links with top pom Nazis . . . it was all his fantasies come true. CD was about to drop his bombshell.

'. . . to recommend someone for the job. We can't think of a single person who would be up to it.'

Even though he was dealing with a thug, CD almost felt sorry for Gordon, whose jaw dropped, increasing his already Neanderthal appearance, he was so disappointed he could have cried.

CD's tactics were clever. He knew that this fellow had told the police nothing of the attack on Bullens Creek other than that he had done it on principle. If there was any more to it than that, for instance if Silvester Moorcock was involved, Gordon Gordon wasn't telling, at the moment. CD had to get him to want CD's trust and goodwill more than any previous liaisons he had made. Gordon Gordon had to desperately want something that CD had.

CD wiggled the carrot.

'To tell you the truth, Mr Gordon,' he said, trying to sound hard and icy. 'We had originally considered asking you.'

Gordon started like a puppy, his eyes were pleading.

'Oh yes, the Grand Fascist Co-ordinating Counsel of the White National British Movement, Foreign Penetration Section,' in for a penny, in for a pound thought CD, 'and the band themselves, were very interested in asking you to take on this highly responsible job. A job which might eventually be seen as having played a small part in the inevitable world triumph of the Norse Peoples. A job, I might add, that would carry a not insignificant wage plus travel with the band and full expenses.' Gordon's tongue was nearly hanging out. 'But then there was the incident, wasn't there?'

'Incident? What incident! Who's been bad-mouthing me? I will fucking kill any man, woman or . . . man that has been bad-mouthing me!'

'Bullens Creek Abo' bash, Gordon. Bit of a mess, wasn't it? Bit of a cock-up don't you think? Can't afford cock-ups in this game, Gordon. You only get the one chance. What were you thinking of? Getting yourself busted over some meaningless, piss-poor little bunch of blacks. We thought you had plans, Gordon, we thought you were a bigger operator than that.'

'It wasn't my idea!' Gordon blurted. 'I was doing a job.'

CD had it! He *knew* there had been something more.

'Oh yes, Gordon? Well, that might change things considerably. Might. What's your story?'

CD was very surprised at what he heard. He would have bet money that Gordon would tell him that the multimillionaire Silvester Moorcock had employed Gordon and his thugs in order to try and intimidate the Aboriginals away from Bullens Creek. Instead he learnt that Aristos Tyron, the brother of a completely different multimillionaire, had put Gordon up to it, paid for the transport and made a very generous donation to party funds.

This was an exciting but confusing discovery. Gordon could help him no further; he did not know why Aristos Tyron should be interested in Bullens Creek; he did not know whether Tyron's important elder brother, Ocker, was involved. He had not, at any time, heard Silvester Moorcock mentioned in connection with Bullens Creek. All Gordon knew was that he had been asked to do the job, take the heat, and keep quiet about it – of course it didn't matter telling CD about it.

So that was it! CD took his leave, promising that the question of the job with the band would be reconsidered in the light of what Gordon had told him.

Outside CD hurried away as quickly as he could. It had been a pretty horrible experience but he was very pleased with himself. His next move would be much more pleasant and a lot more expensive. He would have to talk to Aristos Tyron.

## CRASH

Chrissy had now assembled what could perhaps be called the beginnings of a case. She was in a position to prove that some of the richest people in the world appeared to be slowly dumping their shares and pulling out of traditional areas of investment. As a financial analyst she could demonstrate that this was very strange behaviour and contrary to the interests of those involved. She was also able to prove that this same group of individuals, who were rivals in business and had no particular record of friendship, had all met together for dinner in Los Angeles. What's more, there were firm indications that a similar but partially different group had met later in Singapore. Finally, she could point out that her colleague, Linda Reeve, who had first picked up on the issue, and perhaps unwisely had allowed those she was trailing to know of her interest, had been murdered. No one knew by whom but the circumstantial evidence seemed to be mounting up.

That was her case, something and nothing. What to do next?

Chrissy was sitting speculating on this question, trying to come up with even one course of action apart from confronting those involved, which she firmly believed would mean her death. The only idea she could think of was taking her story to the C I A or the F B I. But who could be trusted? Anyone? And would they be interested? After all, even she didn't have the faintest idea what was behind it all. What's more, even though the sums involved were colossal, they had not yet reached the level for real mischief. It was the *potential* in this unholy alliance that she feared.

The morning that Chrissy was thinking about this, all over New York people began to fly. They began to fly downwards, because they had lost everything.

For this was the morning that the bottom dropped out of the market. This was the morning on which were recorded the largest single price drops in history. It was a Thursday. A Thursday that came to be known as 'Oh my God we're all going to starve to death Thursday'.

All over the world prices were plummeting and so were distraught financiers. The Stark consortium had made its move.

# WELCOME TO THE
# PLEASURE DOME

CD could feel it two streets away, coming up through his trouser legs even through the floor of the car, like someone was playing bass drum on the soles of his feet.

He shifted his position with what he believed to be a funky little movement. He clicked his fingers and the Zippo came alive in his hand. He lit up as if the world was watching him. Shielding the smoke against an imaginary wind, he pulled at it with an expression that suggested here was a man who was only really at home doing his stuff in bed, or doing his stuff on the dance floor. Another snap of the fingers and the Zip was dead. CD pocketed it. He knew he was looking good. Very good.

The reason for this excess of *joie de vivre* was that CD was filled with a delicious confidence. He knew where he was going and he knew what to expect when he got there. This time he would be hunting in a jungle he knew. At the Old Sydney he had penetrated a strange and dangerous world. A world filled with people whose dreams and expectations were very different to his own. War, pain and inflicting degradation were not CD's ideas of good fantasy fodder. Gordon Gordon's little world had been one that CD had entered with fear and reluctance. He had done it purely for the love of Rachel, that she would be proud of him and that maybe, just maybe, she would grant him access to her body; the single thing on earth which fascinated him most and was yet totally and entirely out of reach. An unknown country from which any traveller who returned would, in CD's opinion, be out of their minds.

Tonight, though, was different. He was on the same mission; to discover why a bunch of Perth Nazis had travelled five hundred miles to beat up black people. He was doing it for the same reason; in an attempt to prove worthy of and hence to win the love of the exquisite Rachel. But besides all that, CD reckoned it should be fun. He was strutting up town to shake his booty down to the ground and get down on it like the bitchin' motivatin' groove machine he knew himself to be.

## DICKHEADS ARE NEWS

It had not taken a very great deal of painstaking research for CD to pick up on the trail of Aristos Tyron. He was the kind of tedious git who turned up regularly in the gossip columns in sad identikit photos of the week's 'top parties'. CD found seven in just three weeks' worth of back numbers of the *Perth Daily News*. On close examination the pictures were definitely of different functions but, in fact, the editor might just as well have saved on the reporter's taxi fare and published the same photograph over and over, so similar were they. There he was, that gormless face, crushed in amongst other gormless faces. Bow ties and necklaces, arms about each others shoulders, huge fat mouths agape, apparently roaring with laughter at some fab elite gag that the poor, dull reader could never be a part of. All the photos suggested the same thing, that there exists somewhere a world where people are having the wildest sort of time pretty much constantly.

People have a tendency to presume that they are missing out on something. That they are missing out on some sort of key. A key to providing a better time than they are capable of providing for themselves. The other man's grass is astro-turf and it's *better*.

This is what gossip pages in newspapers depend on. They suggest that there is a mystical, club-centred world of pop stars and society beauties where a *better* time is being had. It is a strange theory, after all, there is no reason to presume that you will have a better time simply because you are standing about with a bunch of wankers and paying ten bucks for an orange juice.

But the photos suggest that there is. Those screaming faces that CD had looked at in the Carlo library; fat men, anorexic looking women. Those faces were saying, 'look at us, you'll never enjoy yourself this much'.

The photos do not record the event, they *are* the event. The photo is what matters, all that matters. As long as the photos are published, it's irrelevant what it was actually like in whichever pathetically fashionable disco they were taken.

Of course, those gormless, screaming fashion clones didn't actually have a better time than is had down at the local pub. But they *pretended* that they did, because that way, despite all the bordeom and the expense, there is a certain satisfaction, the satisfaction of being envied, of believing oneself to be special.

Getting your photo in the paper justifies any mind-numbingly stupid occupation. Ask a football thug.

## DISCO DOWN

CD loved it and he was really looking forward to his visit to The Shelter. The previous year, The Shelter had been called Hobo's and had been decorated with images of the great depression, tramps, breadlines, unemployed marchers, etc. Now it had been radically redesigned to represent nuclear Armageddon; huge mushroom clouds; flights of missiles; mock-ups of newspapers announcing World War Three, that kind of thing. The girls wore little costumes that glowed and banged on fluorescent tambourines.

'Party like there's no tomorrow' was written over the bar, which translated as 'please spend all of your money as quickly as you possibly can'.

CD had prepared his entrance carefully. He knew enough to know that, despite the efforts clubs like The Shelter make at exclusivity, they are there to make money. That is what the bouncers are trained to watch out for: money, or more importantly, the lack of it.

'Let the money in,' the manager would say to a new cave-man in a bow tie. 'Let the money in and let the tit in, because tit attracts money, all right? No paupers, and no dogs.'

But, looking like money is actually only a question of confidence. You can hire what is termed a 'luxury car' from a cab hire firm, for much the same price as an ordinary car. An extra 30 per cent gets you a nice Mercedes and a bloke with a hat.

CD had insisted on pre-paying for the journey which added a touch to the price, but it meant when he pulled up outside the club he could jump out immediately, shouting over his shoulder, 'Listen, Frank, take some time out, I'll get Janine to bleep you if I need wheels.'

CD turned to the bruiser in the bow tie.

'Hi, I'm here to meet Aristos, Aristos Tyron. Is he in yet? Hey, who cares? I hear this is the sort of place it's fun to wait around in.'

As it happens, CD needn't have tried quite so hard. There are about fifteen 'top' night-clubs competing for the city's night-clubbing business, and despite the manager's efforts, exclusivity was a bit of a myth really. Most places would let you in if you could afford a plastic bomber jacket, and, of course, are happy to pay the entrance fee.

CD paid it, but he wasn't happy. Twenty-five dollars was considerably more than he expected, they must have been charging by the decibel. As he walked into the flickering darkness, the sound hit him like a sweat-soaked brick. The lights flashed and scurried about the floor, walls and ceiling. An epileptic would not have made it through the door.

The SAS in Northern Ireland have long been working on a non-violent interrogation technique called sensory depriva-tion. The idea is that they subject the suspect to blinding lights and a confusion of high volume 'white' noise that so disorientates them they will divulge anything. As CD felt his way around the Shelter, he could not help feeling that the SAS could have just paid the twenty-five dollars admission and sat the suspect at the cocktail bar.

CD had been nursing a mineral water for about half an hour when Aristos arrived. CD introduced himself immediately as a journo from a London based trend mag called *Groovy Trousers*, which had recently won an award for the best laid out feature on whether Elvis is dead or not to be published that month. Aristos, being of course a complete media and fashion victim, had heard of it and ordered champagne. One of the signs of a club dickhead is somebody who does not say 'would you like a drink?' but asks 'would you like a glass of champagne?'

This is rendered even sadder in Australia because their superb wine-making industry has come up with many excellent champagnes that are similar to the French stuff in all but two vital areas. They do not come from Champagne, and they cost about the same as an ordinary bottle of wine. Hence an Aussie club dickhead wishing to gain the same effect (for what it's worth) that his European dickhead brother gets by asking 'would you like a glass of champagne?' has to ask, 'would you like a glass of *French* champagne?' Which of course translates as:

'I want you to know that I am quite deliberately paying forty bucks for something I could get for eight and which we will both swill down like we don't know we're drinking it.'

The French have long been involved in expensive legislation in order to stop the Aussies calling their wine 'champagne' and getting them to call it a 'champagne type fizzy wine' which, legally, they have a right to insist upon. So far, however, the Australian attitude seems to have been, 'OK, so invade us'. Hence, at the time of writing, it was possible to purchase an entire twelve bottle case of Great Western champagne for the price of a bottle of Moet and Chandon. Not surprisingly, people get quite pissed at Australian weddings.

As it turned out though, all the French efforts at a 'fair go' were soon to become irrelevant and the Australians and Californians were going to get the whole shooting match to themselves. The reason for this was that as Aristos Tyron was offering CD French champagne, thirteen thousand miles away in France in a little place about equidistance between the areas of Champagne and Cognac – two tiny districts that have given the world so much pleasure – in one of the numerous French nuclear power stations, a small, unseen hairline fracture was beginning to grow and was soon to render not one drop of French wine drinkable for at least a decade. Nor most of German wine, and Spanish and a great deal of Italian – British wine of course had never been drinkable in the first place.

So Aristos and CD sat in the mindless noise and light, shouting at the top of their voices to make themselves heard, swigging on a drink that was about to become a real world rarity. Both of them would have preferred a beer.

Screaming himself hoarse, CD bullshitted for half an hour or so about the celebs he was lined up to meet in Sydney and those he had just left in London. It is not difficult to convince somebody who wants to believe and, of course, Aristos desperately wanted to believe that an important and trendy journo was going to do an 'in depth' on him.

'Can we go somewhere a little more private, Mr Tyron?' CD suggested when he realized that his eye was wandering onto the dance floor where gangs of girls, rendered infinitely beautiful by the near darkness, were doing their funky stuff.

'Hey,' said Aristos, 'how many times do I have to say. It's Aristos, OK?'

'Oh yeah, sorry Aristos.' CD lit his cigarette like he was in a high wind and stared at Aristos through the smoke. 'You have a great attitude, you know that? Most of the big guys treat us media punks like shit. Oh, sure, they want the copy, they want the column inches. Yeah, they want all that. But, the guy putting the hours in, the man with the pen, he can go fuck himself. It's *Mr* Jagger, and *Mr* Bowie, even the politicians won't unwind, and who needs them.'

'Well, you know, Colin, I like you,' a delighted Aristos replied with massive condescension. 'Sure Mick and David can be brusque, but it's tough for them too you know?'

Aristos had done it again. No matter how much a person heard about Aristos, until they met him, they could never fully comprehend just how big a pratt he was.

'Yeah, I know it's tough being a tall poppy like Jagger or Bowie,' said CD, sucking his cigarette and talking as if they were discussing a couple of war veterans deserving of very special consideration, instead of two immensely rich and hugely envied people. Affecting sympathy for the super-fortunate and their goldfish bowl life-styles is one way of dealing with the horrendous jealousy everyone feels for them.

'Hey, let's get up the celebrity bar, and have some more French champagne. It's OK, I can get you in,' said Aristos.

Most large discos have a thing they call a celebrity bar. This is where local models, local football players and the managers' girlfriends go.

Aristos walked in casually, nodding towards CD 'Friend of mine,' he said to a waitress in a tutu who had not been going to ask. The music was about ten decibels quieter and they were able to talk, just.

'Listen,' said CD deciding he had better get the job done before his ears started bleeding. 'My editor wants me to get right behind the enigma that is Aristos Tyron. Your brother is a hugely successful man. Now we've been searching around, playing a hunch that you have a little bit more to do with that success than either of you lets on. Is that right?'

'Well . . .' said Aristos, because he didn't know what else to say.

'You know, I'm getting a picture here,' CD continued. 'Not the one that you and your brother want the world to see, but the picture *behind* the picture. Suppose Ocker Tyron needed a man to deal for him when he couldn't be personally involved. A man he had complete confidence in. Who better than the guy everybody thought was just a good time boy? A ladies' man? The fellah they all wrote off as just another fascinating, hard drinking, good lookin' sexual animal? Who better than Aristos Tyron, to be the liaison?'

Aristos could hardly believe his ears, this journalist was a genius. CD had lucked out in a big way. His casual use of the word 'liaison' had convinced Aristos that he deserved the description that CD was constructing – it was just what Ocker had called him.

'That's it. I'm his liaison, the silent right hand.'

CD flattered him some more and allowed him to order more French champagne. 'What kind of situation would you liaise in, then, Aristos? I mean, no names, no pack drill, but just an idea.'

'Woah! Woah there!' said Aristos with jolly, patronizing good nature. 'You don't think I'm going to spill me and my brother's business moves to the press, do you? Ha ha, I'm no fool, Colin. Have another drink.'

'Hey,' CD assured him, 'listen, you start doing that and I'm outta here anyway. Wow, that is big league stuff. I'll leave it to you, Aristos. What I don't know won't hurt me, right?'

'Right,' said Aristos with enthusiasm. He absolutely loved CD by this time.

'Besides,' continued CD soothingly, 'this is a fashion spread, remember. The sheep reading this, all the good-looking girls and that, they don't want to know the details, they wouldn't understand them . . . What they need is a kind of broad example, just a vague hint of what the big men get up to.' CD was gambling that Aristos would not have the wit to invent an example and would, instead, merely describe a real one and try to be non-specific. He was right.

'Well, you know,' said a drunken Aristos, 'supposing somebody wanted some people leant on, not hard you understand, but persuaded, and he didn't want to get involved. Well then, his liaison might find some people to help out.'

CD was so close he decided to take a calculated risk.

'But what on earth would he want in Bullens Creek?' he asked.

'Well, you know, it could be –' Aristos was suddenly nervous. 'What do you mean? What about Bullens Creek?'

'I said we'd been scratching around, Aristos,' CD decided to go for it, 'and after I talked to the White Supremacy lot . . .'

Finally Aristos began to wonder about this total stranger whom he had been buying drinks for. 'Look, what's going on? I don't know what you're talking about. What do you want to know?'

'Nothing.' CD was having one last chance at being soothing but he guessed the game was up. 'I just want to know why Tyron got you to send those Nazis to beat up the Aboriginals.'

'He didn't! He just asked me to —' suddenly, from some unknown part of Aristos' brain, a smidgeon of native cunning forced its way through his cotton wool brain. He called the manager and demanded a security guard while he hissed at CD, 'I never said a thing to you, mate, and if you say I did, even in the *Sheep Breeders' Gazette*, I'll sue you into oblivion.'

Aristos could not have found a better way of confirming absolutely everything that CD had come to find out. The guard arrived.

'I think this man has my wallet,' Aristos said. 'I don't want a scene, just turn out his pockets.'

The man did as he was told. CD didn't mind, his mission had been a complete success.

'No wallet, sir,' said the guard.

'And no tape recorder,' Aristos said in triumph. 'You've got nothing, mate. Throw him out.'

# HOUSE OF CARDS

And so the house of cards came tumbling down. That fragile global structure behind which we all shelter. A castle, built on shifting sands from little more than faith, hope and greed, came tumbling down with a crash that shook the world. A mighty crash indeed, considering that the castle was not made of anything of any substance. In fact, it was a castle that existed only in the minds of men. Constructed from nothing more solid than the financial pages in newspapers and the blips on a million computer screens. It was not a castle built from iron, or steel, nor cotton, oil or food. It did not fall because there was no more coal left or because all the cows and sheep had died. There was no physical reason for its collapse, because it was made of nothing at all. You couldn't touch it, smell it or climb it, but without its shelter, despite the appalling heat of the southern summer and the mildest ever winter in the north, the world turned suddenly cold.

## GOBBLEDEGOOK

Nobody really understood what was happening. Why should they, the global money industry is so phenomenally complex that it is doubtful whether anyone really follows it. When they do the financial bit on the television news it's normally at the end, just before the little jokesy item about a panda who can't get a hard on. The reason for this is probably because, as far as the average viewer is concerned, both items appear to be about equally relevant to them.

Nobody who lives in the real world, the world where things are made, and money is earned, has anything but the vaguest understanding of the utter gobbledegook they spout just before the panda gets his thirty seconds of fame. In fact it would probably make no less sense if they combined the items together . . .

'And now financial and zoological news. In New York, on the 100 point share market index, the panda's penis fell by six points to a record low, the Dow Jones rallied late in the day to raise some interest from Poo Poo, the gorgeous two-year-old lady panda who's causing all the excitement.'

Maybe the reason that the financial 'news' is delivered in such a deliberately incomprehensible manner is that what they are talking about is, in any real sense, meaningless. We are being brought an urgent daily update, a blow-by-blow account of something that exists only because people choose to believe in it. Entirely theoretical wealth.

At the beginning of the day a factory full of jars of jam might be worth a thousand pounds. At the end of the day; a day of 'good trading'; a day of 'rallies' and 'confidence', we might be told that the same factory is worth two thousand pounds.

What has happened? Only a few hours have passed. The factory has not changed. There is no more jam in it than there was. There has been no time for the new slogan 'Let him dip his finger into something fruity, Mum' to take effect. The slimmers' version still tastes bloody awful. Nothing has happened and yet the factory is 'worth' twice as much. Where has the extra cash come from? Nowhere, that's where. It doesn't exist. It is entirely theoretical and if people choose to dispute the theory, if they all choose at once to say 'but that's impossible. All right then, give me the cash . . .', the money would instantly disappear, like the puff of smoke it is.

This, of course, is how crashes occur.

The crash that Professor Durf set in motion was a whopper. People weren't even bothering to look at the paper before they jumped out of the window. They were plummeting like hailstones. In New York City it rained investors – the only things selling were concrete umbrellas. Financial news leapt up to be top story of the day. The panda with no stiffy got left on his own at the end of the programme.

More swiftly than ever before the repercussions spread. The dole queues began to lengthen as the factory gates began to close. The last puréed city gent had scarcely been scraped up when the first suicides due to mortgage foreclosure were reported.

# STRATEGIC DECISIONS

The morning after his visit to The Shelter CD's breakfast was even more cursory than usual. He'd run out of Wheaties so there was no need to wash up a plate. The papers were full of nothing but financial news so it wasn't worth lingering with a second coffee. CD liked a bit of popularism in his morning read and it was weeks since there had been a real good article about Joan Collins still having great tits despite being about seventy-five. Anyway, CD was in a hurry. He was anxious to tell Rachel and the others about what he had discovered. Mustn't hang about, he thought, could be very very important information he said to himself. But actually the main thing was he wanted them to know how clever he had been.

## PLANNING MEETING

'It seems to me,' said Walter, in his usual manner, i.e. as if he were about to explain the meaning of the universe, and what's more, he was going to be right. 'It seems to me, that we have to go and have a look. I mean we have a definite duty to try to dig what goes down, right? And, apart from anything else, right, it would be a trip. We could maybe take in some desert, cook up some lizard or something. It would be a vibe.'

As far as Rachel was concerned, Walter was not making too great a case for the journey. For a start, when it came to cooking up some lizard or something, she would definitely take something.

'It's hundreds and hundreds of miles, Walter. Your Aboriginal friends have sold up anyway, what's the point?

Whatever Moorcock wants it for, he's got it now. There's nothing we can do about it.'

CD was extremely brought down by Rachel's negative attitude. He considered that he had pulled off a pretty crucial piece of intelligence gathering. He realized now that a full-on sauce session with her whispering, 'my hero' in his ear and 'do it to me again, big boy' had perhaps been a touch over optimistic, but she might at least have said well done.

'You know, Rachel, you don't find things out without taking long shots. I mean, if anything *is* going on, they aren't exactly going to take an advert out in the paper,' he said, trying not to sound hurt but hoping that she would realize that he was.

'Well don't sulk about it, Colin,' she snapped, which was not the reaction he had been trying to provoke. Sometimes CD seriously wondered whether he was losing his touch.

'All I am saying is that it's a very long way to go in order to find out something we know already,' Rachel continued.

'Which is?' asked Walter.

'Well, that some bloody appalling thing is being done to another bit of land by a bunch of rich shits. I mean, it's obvious that whatever it is they're up to, it will be awful. But what are we supposed to do about it? Mount a picket in the desert? I mean, of course Colin's right, it's significant that Tyron is involved . . .'

'That is a mean combination, baby,' interrupted Walter. And even his phenomenally mellow tones could not reconcile Rachel to being called 'baby' especially when she was feeling defensive.

'Please don't call me "baby", Walter. I'm not going to discuss it any more if you call me baby.'

'Cool. No problem,' said Walter, effecting an aura of almost religious tolerance that made Rachel want to strangle him. 'Except, like, you know, it's only a word, but cool. If you don't like "baby" I have no hang up with that. I mean, really, no hang up at all. In fact, it's great. I'll just call you like, you know, something else, because –'

Rachel was about to give up but luckily Zimm had just returned to earth and was momentarily and uncharacteristically lucid.

'Hey, Walter, man, we were discussing the desert trip.'

'I know that, Zimm, but it's important that Rachel should feel relaxed about the language parameters we're employing here,' Walter replied.

'Well great but, you know, I think we should discuss the desert now, OK?'

'OK, Zimm, that's what we'll do.'

'Good.'

'I was just about to say to Rachel,' Walter resumed, 'that what CD had got here is kind of interesting, you know? I mean, Tyron and Moorcock together could fuck up the whole of Australia. They are very bad shit. But you know, like, if it was just another planetary rape, with full legal cover and state government backing, why the secrecy man? You know, why not just do what they normally do, you know. Like boast about it. Why don't they just shout "hey man, we're fucking up the world for its own good, so fuck you". I mean, they don't normally, like hide their light under a bushel, you know? Like, when they're going to give the world cancer, they want to get the credit, dig?'

'Yeah,' agreed Zimmerman. 'But this time. This time CD had to get down on the whole spy infiltration, James Bond bit.'

'Well, I'm glad somebody noticed,' interjected CD.

Zimmerman ignored him.

'Whatever they're hiding, I guess it's bad shit.'

'OK, OK,' said Rachel, 'maybe we should check it out. But your truck's off the road, right guys? Colin can't drive, which leaves my 1964 FC Holden volunteering for a five hundred mile drive. So before I sentence it to death I'm going to at least have one more try at confronting them to find out what they're up to.'

'Man, if he's hiding something all he has to do is bullshit you, I mean, these guys bullshit for a hobby. They like being investigated because they get to do some more bullshitting.'

'Yeah, well maybe he won't bother with me. After all, who am I? Nothing for him to worry about. Maybe he'll just say, "Oh yeah, I'm grinding up asbestos and throwing it in the wind, but I have government permission lady, so fuck you." In which case, we can protest about it here in Perth without totalling my car to find out.'

'You know, Rachel,' said Walter, 'I hope you're not turning into a possession head, that would be a bummer.'

Rachel managed to keep her temper, just. People who get through life dependent on other people's possessions are always the first to lecture you on how little possessions count. Walter was, in many ways, a lovely fellow, but he was also the sort who would finish off the last of your milk and when you complained, say 'oh come on man, it was only milk'.

Rachel decided to stick to the job in hand. 'I'll ask Moorcock rather than Tyron. At least we've met him. Better the devil you know . . .' And on such tiny decisions does the thread of life hang. Had she decided to go and see Tyron, he would, of course, have had her killed.

## FLIRTING WITH DEATH

Sly recognized Rachel immediately. It had been three weeks since their encounter at Facefulls. Three very busy weeks indeed for Sly. Like all members of the Consortium, he had played a large part in the terrible crash that Professor Durf had precipitated. First selling as quickly as he possibly could; then beginning to make the purchases that the group had designated as his responsibility. It had been a frantic time.

Besides this, Tyron was now beginning to report that the trickle of equipment and hardware that he was having to handle, looked like it was shortly to become a flood. On-site storage, even installation, was going to become an issue in a very short time and Sly had only just got rid of the last of the previous inhabitants. One vaguely satisfying thing was that, even in the short time since the crash, the money he had promised the Aboriginals had risen in value by over 20 per cent. Hard cash was appreciating fast as more and more people who had been rich on paper discovered that they didn't have a cent. Sly did not have a conscience as such but he didn't mind that old bastard Mr Colboon and his mates putting one over on the red-necks.

However, despite all these immediate considerations and the monumental size of the task in front of him, Sly recognized Rachel immediately. It was an inexplicable thing, but when Sly had been informed that a young woman was in reception without an appointment and wishing to discuss Bullens Creek, instead of feeling a little nervous, perhaps even scared, he had felt a twinge of excitement.

And there she was, and Sly knew that he was pleased to see her.

This was, of course, ridiculous. The last thing on earth he wanted at that moment was anyone taking any interest whatsoever in Bullens Creek. But none the less, he couldn't help it. He was pleased to see her. He walked round his desk and stood leaning against the front. 'So what's the story then, Miss . . .?' he said, trying to be commanding and sexy.

'Kelly, my name is Rachel Kelly, Mr Moorcock. I represent EcoAction. We are a group of environmentally concerned activists,' she replied, trying to be brusque and efficient, and maybe just a little bit sexy. After all, it never hurts to put out a bit.

'Environmental? I thought you were a Nazi hunter.'

'We'd like to know something of your intentions regarding the land that you have bought around Bullens Creek.'

'I'll tell you if you have dinner with me,' Sly surprised himself. He knew he was a smooth operator but even he had not expected that he would have the cool to try making a pass whilst being questioned about Bullens Creek. After all, Bullens Creek was a life and death project. Everything in the world was riding on it. On the other hand, Sly could not believe that this girl was onto anything. After all, it was understandable that environmentalists would be interested in any land purchases that he had made. Sly could not deny that now and then he had been personally responsible for fucking up some pretty large sections of Australia.

He thought all this in the time that it took Rachel to decide to say, 'Dinner? Love to. I'll call you next time I'm one hour away from death by starvation,' which she considered was a pretty good line. Rachel did not like being patronized or taken for granted, especially by someone whom, she was disgusted to discover, she found rather saucy.

'Great, that's all I need, a radical fem' greeny,' replied Sly.

'If your definition of a feminist is someone who doesn't go to dinner with creeps, there's a lot of us around.'

They were both enjoying the conversation.

'Go on, let me buy you dinner,' said Sly, trying a touch of innocent sincerity.

Rachel reminded herself that she was talking to Silvester Moorcock, one of the world's great vandals.

'No. Are you going to tell me what you're doing out in the desert or not? And I think I should warn you, we're a pretty sizeable organization. We have the funds and personnel to find out what we need to know.'

'Which is why last time you turned up with two burnt out hippies and a small bloke who wears his sunglasses indoors.'

Poor Rachel felt embarrassed for her friends, which is something that would weaken anyone's position in a power juggling conversation like this one. But she rallied strongly.

'Don't judge a book by its cover, Mr Moorcock. For instance, I've read that you're a powerful, self-assured, dominant man. I wouldn't have thought you were the sort who couldn't talk to a girl without getting a hard on . . .'

Sly looked! He didn't have one – but he looked! Just a twitch before checking himself, but it was enough; enough to make him look insecure; enough to make him look foolish. It was an extremely unfair gambit and Rachel knew it. A shocking thing to say, but then Rachel could be a shocking girl. Sly was angry, who wouldn't be. He tried to muster some cold dignity.

'All right, young lady. Thank you very much for the

cabaret, I am an extremely busy man, and don't have a lot of time to talk to foul-mouthed green freaks who —'

'Oh? You wanted to take me to dinner a minute ago.'

Sly was entirely unused to this. He knew hundreds of girls of Rachel's age, none of them cheeked him like she did. The difference of course was that all the other girls worked for him. Sly remembered why she had come to see him in the first place. He did not at all like the idea of a girl this intelligent, and with that much bottle, taking an interest in Bullens Creek. He decided to put masculine pride aside for a moment, and concentrate on allaying her suspicions.

'Before you go. You expressed an interest in Bullens Creek.' Sly spoke calmly as if they had just been exchanging comments about the weather, rather than exchanging insults.

'Well, my plans will shortly be made public, but I see no reason why I shouldn't share them with you first . . .'

Producing some carefully prepared mock plans and brochures, the same ones he had fobbed the planning people off with, he explained to Rachel the concept of the Oasis leisure complex. 'The central hotel will be entirely underground, and will be called 'The Ark'. This is because it will be a complete escape from the world. A place to recharge your batteries; a place for a new beginning.'

It all looked very convincing.

'Why all the secrecy then, for a hotel?'

'My dear, this isn't just a hotel,' said Sly, recovering his easy charm. 'This whole project is conceptually unique, a top security, totally safe, no hassle wind-down for the mega-rich. You can't call it just a hotel. That's like calling Elvis just a singer . . . I'm putting hundreds of millions into this scheme, you don't think I'm going to tell the world about it until I'm ready, do you?'

'You're telling me.'

'Rather that than have you demanding enquiries and sitting about with placards, getting the place a bad name before it starts.'

Rachel wondered. The brochures were all very glossy,

maybe . . . But then she remembered the Nazi attack; the obvious fact that it was a dumb place to build a hotel . . . Ocker Tyron's involvement.

'So this is just your little baby, is it?' she asked, fondling the brochures casually.

'Just mine. My risk, my profit.'

'No one else involved then? Nobody sharing the risks?'

Sly felt a slight chill, what was she getting at? She couldn't know anything, what could she possibly know? She was so young and poo looking. Christ he couldn't be scared of her. It was a perfectly reasonable question for an environmentalist to ask. His uranium interests, after all, were as part of a consortium.

'No, just me, I take my own risks love. It's the way I got rich.'

And Rachel knew he was lying. Even without the things that CD had found out, she would have known. Now they would have to go to the desert after all.

After Rachel had gone Sly sat thinking about her for a long time. He soon stopped worrying about her. He was certain that she couldn't possibly suspect anything. And if she did, how would she find out more, and who would she tell? He reminded himself that he was acting on behalf of an organization that represented a significant proportion of all the available wealth in the world, and she was a penniless greeny. But, insignificant or not, he couldn't get her out of his mind. She was so . . . well, so pretty, and so tough as well, and clever.

Sly's mind went back to the night of the dinner in Singapore when he had wandered about looking at that which was soon to be history. Suddenly he desperately wanted to tell the strange girl who had just left, all the terrible things that he knew. He longed to share the burden of the present with her; maybe even share the hope of a future. He didn't know her, but then he didn't really know any girl, not real ones, not ones he could love. Should he tell her? Should he make her love him by offering her a future? Sly pulled himself together. All

215

this was just idle fantasy, time to worry about companions later, the job had to be done first. Besides, she was a green activist for God's sake. The last person on earth Sly was going to share his huge and terrible secret with was a green activist . . .

The phone rang. It was Tyron. Great, thought Sly, sexual frustration and humiliation, followed by a chat with a fat, arrogant bastard. What a perfect day.

'Hello, Silvester. Are we on a secure line?' His tone was strangely conciliatory.

'We are now,' said Sly, flipping his scramble switch. 'What do you want?'

If Tyron noticed Sly's unfriendliness, he chose to ignore it, it was, after all, par for the course.

'Listen, Silvester, about the land you bought for us. Now you know at the time I was a little concerned that you might have problems?'

'I recall it very clearly,' said Sly, with open hostility.

'Well, I said nothing at the time, thought you might take it the wrong way, but I decided to uhm . . . help you, you know, just as a mate.'

'No, I don't know. What the fuck are you talking about, Tyron,' Sly barked, all the tension built up in the conversation with Rachel, beginning to come out.

'Look, I didn't realize those Abs would give in so quickly, so on the night that they decided to sell up –'

Sly interrupted him furiously.

'You organized a fucking program! You stupid bastard, you stuck a bunch of Neanderthals into the frame. Nazis for Christ sake! Couldn't you have used the mafia or something!!'

'Listen!' Tyron shouted back, he knew he was in the wrong, but you could take contrition only so far. 'I did it with them because there's no way it could ever get back to me. Everyone knows that lot are mad. If I'd used anybody else the law would have wanted a motive, but with them bashing blacks is a reason in itself!! You didn't seem to be getting any results, time is essential. Anyway, it hasn't rebounded has it? We got the land, the Nazi's in the slammer, and no one's any the wiser are they?'

'So why are you telling me?' said Sly, leaping on the obvious point.

Tyron's tone softened again slightly. 'Listen, I used that pig ignorant half-brother of mine. Everyone knows he's a law unto himself, so I thought even if the Nazi spills, no one will put it on me. Why should they? What motive do I have?'

'Get on with it.'

'Well it seems some reporter's been probing him and the silly bastard's admitted that he hinted that he was working as my liaison. Now it doesn't mean anything,' Tyron added quickly, 'after all, it's your land, nothing to do with me. All I wanted to know was whether anyone had been asking you questions about the deal, and that night in particular.'

Sly thought for a moment. He thought of the girl who had just left his office. He thought about the confidence with which Tyron had promised to deal with the business of the London journalist. He had never heard from her again.

'No,' he replied, 'no one's been asking me any questions.'

## THE SALT OF THE EARTH

Rachel apologized to CD and he nearly had to take a cold shower. None of them knew what was going on out in the desert, but it had to be something pretty bad. Either intimidation or deceit had marked every move in the game.

'Like I said,' said Walter, 'we might as well go and have a look.'

'All right, don't rub it in,' replied Rachel.

So they loaded up the Holden in preparation for the trip. Sleeping bags, food, cassettes – you cannot after all, drive five hundred miles without vibes – and they headed on up the highway.

There is an old expression, 'the salt of the earth'. This expression has always implied approval and goodwill.

Someone who is the salt of the earth is considered honest and trustworthy, even noble, in a rough and ready sort of way. They are always good company, reasonable, kind and considerate. They are unpretentious, quick to see the other person's point of view . . . in fact 'maddening bastard' would probably sum them up just as well.

Probably the reason the term 'salt of the earth' is used is because salt is an honest, wholesome, natural thing, traditionally in short supply. And this is the point; you could not want too much of it, just as one would not want to get caught in a room full of 'salt of the earth' type people. Such an abundance of hearty, straight-talkers, saying things like 'I'm a simple man, and I don't know much, but I do know this . . .' would drive anyone to the vom bucket.

As the little red Holden headed up through WA, its passengers could not help noticing that salt was no longer in short supply and was certainly no longer being viewed with such friendly eyes. There was salt all over the place, and wherever it was, it meant barren, parched and useless land. Land where no crop can grow and no animal can feed. Salt of the earth had come to mean complete ecological and economic breakdown.

The problem is called salinization and it means that too much salt is concentrated in the top-soil, attacking the vegetation that grows there. It occurs when the water-table rises, bringing more and more salt to the surface. The water then evaporates, leaving the minerals behind and the land becomes useless. Why is it that the water-table rises? The answer is simple; because all the trees have been cut down. The trees, with their deep roots, used to absorb the water before it could rise, leaving the salt far down below and allowing the water to continue its cycle harmlessly through their leaves hanging high above the ground. Now the trees are gone and Western Australia – like many hot parts of the world where surface evaporation is speedy and the forests have been cleared – faces a terrible problem with the salt of the earth.

This is the avalanche factor. Who would have thought that

cutting down trees to create agricultural land, would render that land terminally poisoned by salt within a few short years? These days, of course, the cause and effect are well-established, but the trees keep falling.

# ENCOUNTER AND DISCOVERY
# IN THE DESERT

On the afternoon that Rachel, CD, Walter and Zimmerman reached Bullens Creek, the crash was only a few weeks old. But, during that time, the whole world seemed to have grown a little poorer. It had been shocking how quickly the depression took a grip. The Social Welfare became the only growth industry. Well-heeled philanthropists were beginning to think about making soup.

Not in Bullens Creek though. Here it was boom time. The whole town was buzzing, there was work and money everywhere. This was because only a few miles away a vast new development was under construction – a development that was going to bring wealth and prosperity to the town, for time immemorial. The Silvester Moorcock Group, it seemed, was building the ultimate space-age leisure complex. The Oasis, an enormous and completely self-contained city haven, constructed around six massive underground hotels called the Arks. All to be made ready in treble-quick time, because when the depression ended, as at sometime it surely must, people were going to want a holiday.

No townsfolk were actually directly employed on the project but what with the hundreds of foreign workers, living in hastily constructed dormitories, plus the endless flow of traffic up and down the one highway, there were plenty of spin-offs.

'Well, if he is building hotels,' said Rachel, sitting stoically at the wheel, 'they're extremely big ones.'

They had hit the traffic jam at least ten kilometres out of

Bullens. Earth movers, mobile drills, articulated road trains; it was as if somebody was going to rebuild the world from scratch, and had decided to start the operation in Western Australia.

'Whoever heard of a traffic jam in the middle of the desert?' moaned CD. Tempers inside the car were beginning to fray, as indeed they would, stuck in a jam with knackered air-conditioning and a relentless, blazing sun turning up the heat degree by degree.

'Man, we have to accept the situation,' said Walter, 'that is the only way to deal with it. We are stuck, and we are hot. You know man? I mean, that's the way it is, all we have to do is educate ourselves to dig it. It's a Zen thing really.'

For a minute or two Rachel and CD tried to educate themselves to dig it. At least that is what Walter thought they were doing. In fact they were wondering whether they had the energy to tell Walter to go fuck himself or not. They both knew it was utterly unreasonable to blame him for his size but it was galling for the person taking up at least half the room to start preaching tolerance.

Zimmerman was thinking about something else. He got out of the car and stared about him, blackened into a silhouette by the blazing sun. The desert seemed to make him look taller and stronger. He was wearing his usual singlet and shorts and both Rachel and CD found themselves thinking more than ever that he looked extremely impressive. Such was Walter's ridiculous size that it was easy to ignore how well set-up crazy Zimm was. He was muscular and tanned. There were scars on his shoulders but they did not disfigure him. He had an expression of intense concentration on his lean, creased face. The beard, flecked with grey, was neatly trimmed – a contrast to his straggly hair and headband. Gone was his bored lope, now he moved amongst the stationary cars with an athletic grace that suggested a tremendous latent strength. Of course, Walter had told them that Zimm was a black belt Akido, a weapons and survival expert, but what can you tell sitting in a coffee bar? With a distant horizon stretching out all round them, and a huge empty sky overhead, Zimm grew more than ever to look like what he really was. Trouble.

CD thought to himself that it was a shame that Zimm was out of his mind. Rachel thought that it was a shame that he hadn't got any love tackle.

'Yo, Zimm,' called Walter, 'keep it together, you dig? Don't go eating any cars, we're on a mission here man. The last thing we want is to draw the heat.'

Zimmerman ignored him. He knew he was on a mission, he did not need reminding. That was why he was standing in the middle of a snarled highway in the burning sun, sniffing intently. It was so difficult to be sure. If you want to get a bearing on a trace smell it's best not to do it on a flat windless plain along with a thousand belching pipes.

'Do you think you should be shouting about us being on a mission then?' CD gently rebuked Walter.

'Oh yeah, man, that's true, you're right. Yeah.' CD had clearly given Walter cause for thought. He leant out of the window again and shouted at Zimm. 'Yo, Zimm man, like what I said about the mission, that was just a gas, OK? Like, as you know, we are not actually on a mission but just hanging out and digging things, right?' Walter turned to CD. 'I guess that pretty much makes things cool,' he said and CD could not work out whether he was taking the piss or not.

## CONFRONTATION

Zimmerman walked about fifty feet up between the two rows of huge, idling engines. The truckies stared down at him from their cabs. Zimmerman sniffed at the cargo of a lorry. He strolled on and sniffed at the back of a tanker.

'Hey, long-hair. Get your dumb face out of my cargo,' drawled a huge, mean-looking truckie through teeth clenched on a nasty, thin, little roll-up – a black one, made with liquorice papers. Zimmerman looked up at him. The man was driving a huge articulated double-fuel tanker, carrying the Murdoch Petroleum logo. His cab was about ten feet off the ground.

'You know something, fat man?' Zimm replied. He wasn't particularly anxious to be rude but this fellow appeared to address people by a single distinguishing characteristic so Zimm was simply falling into line. 'You know something, fat man –' he was about to continue with what he had intended to say but events overtook him.

'All right boy, don't say another word, just you keep quiet because you're going to need what breath you got.'

The big driver was very bored and he was very pleased indeed that this hippy had provided him with such a clear justification for some diversion. He climbed down from his cab. Unquestionably he was a big chap; as big as Walter but without the benign aura.

'I guess the best thing you could do is to give up smoking.' This had been what Zimm wanted to say, and he said it. He was a person who had dedicated himself to the preservation of life on earth and, within limits, this included enormous violent looking truckies. Therefore, he felt obliged to issue this warning. 'Because that ain't petrol you've got in the second tanker.'

But the truckie wasn't listening. He jumped down onto the tarmac, slightly denting it. 'How much money you got on you boy?' he asked, flexing his great heavy arms. 'Because these are your options, you hear? You've been sniffing round my load like some kind of damn thief, right? Then you march up and call me fat man, OK? Now you can't deny it, because I heard you. On top of that you start giving me that lung cancer shit –'

'It's got nothing to do with lung cancer,' replied Zimm.

'Don't you interrupt me, boy! Don't you fucking talk back on me!!' This fellow just loved being a bully. He smiled and continued. 'Now, the way I see it, all the things you done kind of makes you my property boy. You belong to me. Now, I'll tell you what I'm going to do. I am the top man, main moose-head charity organizer to raise money for the truck drivers' orphanage.'

'That's nice,' said Zimmerman, quickly treading on the cigarette butt end that the man dropped.

'Well, long-hair?' the truckie continued, clearly feeling the need to explain the softer side of his nature. 'Me and the boys reckon we leave so many fucking kids behind us on the road the least we can do is get them somewhere to stay.' He laughed coarsely at this.

Zimmerman's eyes narrowed with loathing. If there was one thing which bored and irritated Zimmerman, it was crude comments about sexual prowess.

'So, Mister,' the truckie continued, prodding Zimm hard. 'Either you hand over all you got, so's I can give it to the kids. Or, I'm afraid I shall be forced to flatten you.'

'I hates dudes who are like, terminal bastards, but lay some token charity trip on you because that makes it all right being pigs the rest of the time,' said Zimmerman.

The truckie reminded Zimm of the landlord of a pub in Carlo, who wouldn't serve Aboriginals. This same fellow proudly had a huge whiskey bottle on his bar which his customers were supposed to fill with money. Then he would have himself photographed handing it over to the local hospital. This guy had chucked out Zimm because of his hair and jeans. He had a sign up demanding 'smart dress' which means he would have served Hitler, but Jesus would have been barred for wearing sandals and a dress. The truckie didn't know of Zimm's aversion to self-serving charity, but he knew he had been called a bastard and a pig. He grabbed his Citizens Band radio.

'Ten four, brown bear, rubber duck, twice as nice, sex dog calling all rigs,' he barked into it, by way of an introduction. 'I got a long-hair here wants a pounding. I'd say six foot two, maybe twelve and a half, thirteen stone. There's a hundred bucks says I can knock him cold in under half a minute.' The traffic had been completely stationary for about an hour and so the prospect of a little diversion was most welcome. Word spread fast and pretty soon there were over a hundred hard-looking sports lovers crammed in amongst the trucks, waving money around.

Rachel, CD and Walter had also hurried along. They had

had a suspicion that the commotion might be something to do with Zimmerman and were most disconcerted to discover that they were right. Despite their earlier reflections on how hard Zimmerman had been looking, CD and Rachel had only to take one look at his opponent for their hearts to sink.

This was also the consensus attitude of the crowd. Nobody was offering money on the long-hair to win. The best CD heard was an offer to back Zimm to last forty-five seconds.

Then Walter spoke up. 'I'll take any bets on the hippy to win!' he shouted and was nearly crushed in the rush.

When everyone had finished their betting, a space was cleared, for what everyone expected to be a short fight. As the two opponents squared up to each other, Walter shouted to Zimm that Zimm was to forget for a moment that he was into love and a peace freak because it was important for him to win the fight. This was because if he didn't they would be over four hundred dollars in debt.

'OK,' said Zimm, 'but I want you to know that I don't really approve of this type of profiteering, Walter.'

Everyone had expected a short fight, but not as short as it turned out to be.

An old fellow who had been elected referee, informed the protagonists that he expected a clean fight and then Zimmerman hit the truck driver and the truck driver sat on the ground with a surprised expression and rolled over dead to the world.

There was a momentary pause and then pandemonium broke out. The crowd was convinced that the whole thing was a set up and that the big truckie had taken a fall. CD and Rachel could understand this. Zimm's victory had been so complete and so unlikely that even though they knew that it wasn't a set up, they almost believed that it was.

Walter stood on the bonnet of a cab, a disappointed expression on his face, and addressed the crowd.

'You know, man, like, uhm, I am speechless, I am just like totally, like . . . lost for words man. That anybody should feel, like that they have the right to lay this unbelievably heavy scene on us. I mean, you guys must all have some very bad shit in your heads, you know that? Very bad shit indeed. I think maybe you should look at your diets, maybe it's a diet thing and you should all go macrobiotic. Too much Ying, not enough Yang . . . or sometimes it's the other way around. Either way, it is one bad mother-fucker of a heavy trip, you dig?'

For the first time in his life, Walter found himself in the fairly unique position of having over one hundred truck drivers hating him all at once. They had not the faintest idea what he had been talking about, but some of them vaguely thought that he might have been suggesting that they go fuck their mothers, which was unacceptable. Truckies love their mothers. Mother-love, like some charity, is another of those catch-all excuses for unpleasant attitudes and behaviour.

'All right, so he shoots his business rivals and beats his wife . . . but he's wonderful to his mother.'

'Of course he is, and gives the earth to charity.'

Anyway, what with apparently trying to cheat them, and topping it with making improper and incestuous suggestions, Walter's life expectancy was now being computed in seconds . . . Zimmerman spoke up:

'I didn't do any fucking cheating, you red-neck slimes!' he barked. And even with their sensibilities dulled by spending twelve hours a day staring at a completely straight road through a desert, the assembled drivers could see that Zimmerman's feelings were hurt.

'So pick your best man!' he shouted. 'Pick your best *three* men,' he corrected himself, 'and let's do the thing again. Ref', shift the debris.' Zimm kicked the prostrate form of his defeated opponent. 'Start a pile.'

It would have taken about sixteen ref's to shift the sleeping beauty, but it wasn't necessary because Zimmerman's speech had succeeded where Walter's had failed. Nobody felt like picking up Zimmerman's challenge and so Walter started to pick up the winnings.

Back in the car, as the traffic started to move, Walter announced that they now had over a thousand dollars.

226

They crawled past the stricken double tanker which someone had driven to the side of the road. The still unconscious form of the driver had been propped up in the cab. He woke up in the middle of the night and started trying to think up a story that would cover the facts as he remembered them. How do you explain being beaten up by a hippy in front of a hundred of your peers?

## MISSILE FUEL

As they drove slowly towards town, Zimmerman was in a reflective mood.

'It just goes to show,' he remarked, 'that sometimes it ain't worth trying to do a guy a good turn.'

'You were trying to do him a good turn?' enquired CD, who remembered the whole thing rather differently.

'Sure, I was trying to tell him that I reckon one of the tubes he's hauling is carrying high octane rocket or missile fuel. You know, military grade stuff.' Zimmerman was rolling a cigarette and he was talking like he smelt missile fuel most days.

'Missile fuel?' asked CD, trying to adopt the same casual tone. 'You mean, the stuff they fuel missiles with?'

'Yeah.' Zimmerman borrowed CD's Zippo and lit his cigarette with one hand, producing that casual snap of the fingers which CD practised so diligently and which had so far eluded him. Zimmerman was sensing adventure and it was almost as if he was changing himself in order to meet it.

'What the hell is Silvester Moorcock doing shipping in missile fuel?' said Rachel, feeling a little scared.

'Well,' said Walter. 'You know, like it could be this, and like, it could be that, but I guess we have to entertain at least the possibility that you know man, it's . . . to fuel missiles.'

'It ain't to fill his lighter, man,' said Zimmerman, handing back CD his Zippo. 'Maybe I'm wrong, you know,' he continued, 'I haven't smelt it since 'Nam, but if that stuff's what I think it is, man, it burns like the sun. About a thimbleful would put this car into fucking orbit.'

There was a nervous pause.

'And it says petrol on the tank?' Rachel asked, breaking the silence. 'I mean, it doesn't say, "missile fuel for entirely innocent purposes" or anything like that?'

'It says petrol. And it isn't petrol,' said Zimmerman. And they drove on in silence.


## BOOM TOWN

Walter had already arranged for somewhere for them to stay in Bullens Creek. This was fortunate because absolutely everywhere was packed to the gunnels. It was a boom town. Excited, lively and full of pricks. Money was coming in fast and nobody was asking any questions. People didn't seem to mind if Moorcock blasted and dug their little part of the world to fuck and beyond. It is strange, but no matter how many millions of times in human history hindsight has revealed the most terminally appalling human errors, we still refuse to even attempt to develop foresight.

Walter had arranged for them to stay at Mr and Mrs Culboon's little place which they had bought a month previously for eight and half thousand, and was already worth fifty.

There was no way they could find a park so they left the Holden on the edge of town, along with the thousands of Toyota Nissan Landcruiser wankmobiles, and walked in.

It was like a gold rush town must have been back in the days of the old West. Everybody out on the street, half of them very very drunk.

'Maybe they're drinking the missile fuel,' remarked CD.

'I think we should maybe keep, like, kind of quiet about the missile fuel,' suggested Walter. And everybody agreed that this would be a sensible thing to do.

It was night now and on the horizon, towards what had recently been a tiny Aboriginal village, there was a tremendous ghostly glow that lit up the whole of the sky. Work on Oasis went on day and night. At present Moorcock's

228

builders were working off huge mobile generators flown in bit by bit. However, work was already under way to install enough cabling to buy in power from the eastern states.

Moorcock had been able to negotiate considerable federal co-operation. He was creating jobs and, like the people of Bullens, the legislature was anxious to see no evil. In fact, Australia was very proud that while the whole world staggered under the impact of a huge depression, her own home-grown entrepreneurs were rising to the challenge and risking their all instituting massive new projects.

The little self-appointed EcoAction team went into a pub, to get a better gauge of local opinion. It was just like outside in the streets, everybody was apeshit about the whole thing.

'It certainly is going to be a very big hotel,' remarked Rachel thoughtfully to the barperson, who was enthusing about the present and future prospects of the town.

'Bet it will still take an hour to get anything on room service,' said CD coolly, even though he had personally never ordered anything on room service in his life.

'Aw, c'mon, this ain't just a hotel! This is ultimate leisure,' the barman quoted. 'Like Disneyland times fifty plus the Gold Coast, this town is on the map. Yeah, we sure showed 'em. For a hundred years we were just a piss-poor bit of outback and now we're the only town in the world that ain't de-pressed.'

## HOSPITALITY

Mrs Culboon answered the door and invited them in.

'Nice to see you, Walt,' she said and clearly meant it. 'We've gone up in the world since you last came visiting.'

'Lovely, Maud,' replied Walter, looking around the sparsely furnished little duplex.

'All thanks to that bastard Moorcock, mate,' Mr Culboon entered with the beers.

'I still think building a bunch of hotels here is one of the

229

dumbest ideas anybody ever had, but there you go. It's his funeral,' he added philosophically.

'We think maybe he isn't building hotels, Johnny,' Walter replied, quietly sucking his beer. He then proceeded to explain to the Culboons the whole process of how their suspicions had grown, from lunch at Facefulls to the business with the suspected rocket fuel. When he had finished Mrs Culboon burst out laughing.

'By Christ, he nearly had even us believing in his Hotel Dingo piss, didn't he, Johnny? Don't it just go to show there's none so blind as those who will not see.' She wiped tears of amusement from her eyes. Nobody could really see what she found so funny. Mrs Culboon liked a good laugh.

'Walt don't know for sure it ain't hotels, he just reckons,' said Mr Culboon. 'Could be this way, could be that. Zimm hasn't smelt this fuel stuff in nearly God knows how many years. I mean, Christ, what else would the Moorcock bastard be doing in the desert? Fixing to start World War Three?'

'Well, we don't know, do we, Mr Culboon?' said Rachel. 'We just think that maybe we should try and check it out.'

'Ain't no harm I suppose,' Mr Culboon concluded after a pause for thought. 'Can only get done for trespassing I suppose. But I still say that the hotel business is the most likely explanation.'

Mrs Culboon shrieked again. CD wished she wouldn't do that.

'Johnny, what are you babbling about, you old fool. I guess the hotel business is the *least* likely explanation. Let me ask you this. Suppose we sold up and went travelling? Where would we go? I guess we ain't too likely to stretch and say to ourselves "my *my*, what I need is a few weeks relaxing in a huge hole in the ground in the middle of the desert". I guess that would really recharge our batteries, wouldn't it just.' Sarcasm was one of the principal weapons in Mrs Culboon's armoury, she liked it heavy. On the other hand, she undeniably made a strong case. Mr Culboon looked positively deflated.

And so, the next night, they all piled into the Culboon's pickup to drive out to the old community and take a closer look at what was going down.

# THE HEAT IS ON

The little EcoAction Direct Intervention/Urban Terrorist/ Green Commando/Whatthefuckarewedoinghere Unit, headed out into a velvet night. A night that was for all the world like an upturned pint of Guinness, with the creamy glow of Moorcock's floodlights hovering eerily on the horizon and the darkness above.

The sun was long gone and yet it was still hot. It had been hot for days, months, in fact the weather was second only to the crash as main news topic. The two combined made for a strange feeling that something was coming to an end. There had been a lot more religious nuts hanging out than usual. People's minds were turning to Apocalypse. The weather has always been a source of endless conversation but now the mantra had changed. The song did not remain the same. Whereas previously the comment had always been along the lines of 'bloody awful weather . . .'

Now people constantly moaned that it was 'funny' weather; it was not like it had been when they were young; it was no longer 'proper' weather. The strange thing was that even teenagers spoke in this manner.

In the Culboon's old pick-up they were sweating, the heat was making them nervous.

'Christ it's hot,' observed Mrs Culboon, without sarcasm.

## HOT HOUSE HUMANS

Professor Durf felt the same way. He and the Domesday Group had been watching the weather with increasing alarm, for some months. The speed of the deterioration had shocked them all.

The greenhouse effect, as every politician knows, is caused by the build-up of pollutants, which are held, floating at the top of the atmosphere, with no reason to disperse. This airborne shit slick provides no shade from the sun. The clear, pure, short-wave, solar rays pour through without a moment's pause. But once these rays have done their thing, heating up the earth's surface, the trouble starts, because the heat that then radiates upwards from the surface has changed. It is long-wave and it cannot, for some sad reason, get through the shit slick.

'The earth had a pretty good central heating system,' was the conclusion of the head of the Domesday Group, when he met Durf in New York. He was there in order to present Durf with yet more revised predictions as to the time the world had left to put its house in order. 'But we had to close the damn windows.'

'You're telling me what I already know,' snapped Durf. 'Jesus, kids in school know about the greenhouse effect. We've had heat waves before too. Maybe this is just a natural thing.'

'Yes, maybe,' the scientist replied, 'we can't be sure exactly what's going on but it's very hot isn't it, Professor Durf.'

'Listen. I know it's hot, tell me what's going to happen. Is this it? Are the damn ice-caps going to melt!' Durf was a planner, an organizer, he needed hard information, and he wasn't getting it.

'Yes, they're going to melt. Damn it they've been melting for years. I've been telling your people for years. I don't know how quickly but if something isn't done they'll go, Professor Durf, by God they'll go, like the ice in your damn drink!'

He was a worried and frustrated man, the head of the Domesday Group. He, like all those involved in Armageddon scenario research, was under the impression that the world's industrialists employed him that they might act upon the information that he gave them. And yet he saw no action; he saw no efforts at change. He might as well not have said a word. Actually, of course, action was being taken on his grim warnings, but not the kind of action that would have made him happy. He did not know about the divine pre-eminence of the profit motive. He did not know that a moral decision had been taken that market forces must come before the safety of the earth, no matter what the cost. He did not know about the grim rocket silos that were under construction ten thousand miles away in the deserts of Western Australia.

He tried again to impress upon Durf the urgency with which somebody had to start the process of depollution.

'Listen, Durf, you have influence, God knows I've written papers screaming blue murder, but it's the producers that count. The consumers just want their car and their cooker and their cheap fuel, they're sheep. We must influence those in power, the people that profit from the disinterest that the general population seem to be showing in their future. Professor Durf, the pig-headedness of the human race is on a collision course with the laws of physics. An irresistible force is about to meet an immovable object and we will not survive.'

'How long?' asked Durf again.

'I don't know!' the poor little scientist stressed yet again. Durf was being like the usual idiots, the people who acted as if science was a series of definite facts and scientists benign, all-seeing, all-knowing teachers. The truth was that every door that science opened revealed a corridor full of them, all barred and bolted.

This type of blind faith in science probably stems from popular science programmes on the telly when some utter smughead in a polo neck will explain the riddles of existence with a milk bottle, a ping pong ball and a lot of extremely expensive trips to foreign locations.

'It could be a decade or two, it could be tomorrow. I don't know,' continued the frustrated scientist. 'But I think very soon now. Very very soon.' There was real anguish and fear in his usually dispassionate voice. 'When are you people going to *do* something?'

# SHOTS IN THE DARK

Of course they were doing something and somebody else was taking a look at it. Or at least taking a look at an eight foot fence with six strands of razor wire running along the top of it. The EcoAction team had been driving cross-country, parallel to the wire for about half an hour and had come to the conclusion that the fence ran right the way around an enormous property, far bigger than the Aboriginal community spread. From where they stood, the glow of the working lights remained far away. There was no way they could discover anything at that distance.

'Oh man, this is beginning to look kind of sinister, you know? Like, this is a big fence just to guard a building site,' commented Walter, voicing their common thoughts.

'It does seem kind of heavy security for a holiday camp,' added CD.

'They ain't building no holiday camp here, mate,' said Mr Culboon. His wife shrieked with laughter, breaking the tension somewhat.

They had all been feeling rather thoughtful and solemn, but then Mrs Culboon always laughed at odd times.

'Of course they ain't you old fool! We knew that the first time the bloke came with his money, ha! Ten grand a head for a dingo's toilet, ha!' Dingos had clearly made a big impression on Mrs Culboon during her time of living at the Bullens Creek community.

'I reckon if he *is* building hotels, this bloody fence is to keep the guests *in*!!' And Mrs Culboon roared anew. She was not a woman who was easily frightened and the atmosphere had not got to her in the way that it had affected all of the others, except Zimmerman. She did not even flinch when they saw the lights of the car racing towards them.

'Oh my, oh lord!' she said cheerily, 'I reckon here comes the entertainments officer to inform us that there will be a dinner dance in the nuclear fall-out shelter.'

Her good humour was infectious and they watched the approaching lights with interest.

The ToyaNiski Bigdick Wankmobile pulled up with its lights on full beam, pointed straight at them. Its occupants stayed inside, someone spoke through a megaphone.

'Who are you and what do you want?' The voice was that of a man who liked playing at being a policeman.

Zimmerman did not like the vulnerability of the situation, the truck had not positioned itself in a friendly way. They were blinded, and exposed. 'Rachel and CD go right, Culboons go left,' he said quietly. 'Walter stay in the light and talk to them.'

Zimmerman knew that if they all deserted the light, whoever was in the truck would be spooked and who knew how they'd react. By keeping someone in the light Zimm had left their interrogators with a clear course of action.

'Stay in the light, all of you!' the amplified voice barked.

'Get into the darkness,' Zimmerman urged, and they all did, leaving Walter alone and blinking.

'Hey man, what's with all this giving orders scene, you know?' he asked sounding a little hurt. 'I mean, if like a bunch of peaceable people such as me and my compadres, can't even take in a moonlit drive without, well, being blinded and shouted at. Eventually we have to ask ourselves the vital question, like, what is the point? No, but really, I'm serious, I mean, what *is* the point?' Walter clearly felt he had put his case quite clearly.

'Everybody get back in the light, this is private property, you're all trespassers, we want to know why,' the voice insisted.

'No man, no way . . . *that* is private property, Fort Knox in there, this here's the desert and it belongs to the stars,' said Walter.

'You are almost three miles inside Moorcock/Ark Leisure Properties, this fence is just a dingo obstruction. You are all coming with us.' The voice was getting harder, more threatening. This was partly because its owner and his companion were peering about wondering where the hell the others had gone. They soon found out about one of them.

236

'Dingos!' shrieked Mrs Culboon. 'An eight foot fence for dingos, ha, ha, ha. Bionic dingos, maybe, with jet packs and pogo sticks and trampolines!!' The voice rang out of the darkness with delighted sarcasm. 'What do you reckon, mate? That the dogs have been rooting the kangaroos? That's the only way they're going to get over that fence. Unless, of course, they got some ropes and grappling hooks and stuff.' Mrs Culboon clearly felt that she had hit a rich vein of humour here and intended to milk it. 'Yeah, and after they've done that mate, they can mount a Dingo expedition to have a go at Everest or something, ha, ha, ha! . . .'

'Shut up you old bag!!' the voice was shaky now. 'Get in the light all of you or we shoot the guy with the beard!!'

This was a big surprise. Everyone knew that something was going on and that the people behind the lights were not just going to wave them on their way. But nobody had expected the stakes to rise quite so quickly.

'Jesus,' said a surprised Walter. 'This dude says he's going to kill me. I mean, man, that is just totally unnecessary.'

'We don't like boongs and we don't like hippies!' the megaphone crackled – 'boong' being an extremely rude word for Aboriginals. 'And you're on Moorcock property, so get in the fucking light.' To everyone's astonishment a shot rang out and a spurt of sand burst up at Walter's feet. Instinctively Rachel, CD and the Culboons moved back into the glare of the truck's headlamp.

'Now come on, mate, this is ridiculous,' said Mr Culboon. 'You can't shoot someone for trespassing, there wasn't even a warning sign.'

'Yeah! What's your man scared of?' shouted Mrs Culboon, the jolly sarcasm still heavily present in her tone. Mrs Culboon had lived over half a century in the lucky country, the country that her ancestors had first come to forty thousand years before. It had been half a century of abuse. In her life she had been confronted by bullying racist white men with guns more often than she could remember. Of course, it still scared her, but she had learnt to walk tall. Besides, she, like the others, did not actually believe that the man would shoot Walter.

'What's his problem?' she laughed. 'Does he think we're going to order too much room service in his hotels!! Ha, ha! Raid the mini-bars? Christ almighty lord, what goes on here? If the porters carry guns, I wouldn't want to meet the manager.'

'It does seem a bit over the top,' added CD. 'I mean, what's going on . . .'

'Where's the other one?' the voice shouted back, 'the one with the beard! Get in the light or we shoot!!'

The man's tone was becoming distinctly threatening. CD for one was beginning to take it seriously. He stepped forward.

'Look, come on, don't be silly, we'll just get back in our car and –'

The man doing the shouting was not the one doing the shooting. The trigger happy one was in the passenger seat, his pistol arm hanging out of the passenger window. Zimmerman was watching it with interest from his position crouched against the passenger door.

Zimmerman was back in the jungle, the danger of the situation clearing away the debris of the years. He was wondering if the fellow was left-handed or not. If he was, then Zimmerman could perhaps afford to let him loose off a few more warning shots, which was clearly the only option available to the man. Unless he actually was going to shoot Walter, which Zimm considered unlikely. But, if the man was right-handed, then he was taking a big risk firing with his left. It was possible that if Zimmerman hung around too long, one of his companions would catch an unfortunate stray . . .

'Dreadful accident . . . compensation . . . apologies all round, but they *were* trespassing and Abos were involved.'

Zimmerman did not need to be a cynic to believe that Moorcock was in thick with the local fuzz, especially since Zimm had actually heard Moorcock talking to the chief. All in all he reckoned it was time to finish the business and get out.

He broke the unfortunate man's arm and took the gun. Both guards were too surprised at the sight of the bearded apparition rearing up at them to say much. Zimm pointed the gun into the cab and spoke quietly to the others.

'Go get in the car everyone. It's time we had a beer and clearly this hotel isn't open for business yet.'

They did as he told them. CD and Rachel were amazed. This new gag cracking, arm breaking Zimmerman was a revelation to them. Even Mrs Colboon felt there was nothing more to say.

'Give me your gun man,' said Zimm to the driver.

'Oh now come on,' the driver replied, sounding a lot less coppish now he wasn't using a megaphone. 'Don't you think maybe this has gone far enough? Why don't you and your friends just get on out, don't come back and we'll just forget about everything.'

'Give me your gun man.' Zimmerman's tone did not change but now it was accompanied by the whimpering of the other guard whose arm was beginning to come out of shock.

'He broke my fucking arm!' he sobbed, 'give him the gun. He broke my fucking arm like a twig.'

The driver drew his pistol slowly and handed it over. Then Zimmerman made a search of the truck.

'Who were you expecting?' he asked, eyeing the extensive armoury, 'the Black Wizard of Thargon at the head of the Great Troll army?'

Luckily Zimmerman did not appear to expect an answer to this. He just shouldered two automatic rifles, a rifle with an infra-red telescopic sight and six stun grenades.

Then he shot out two of the tyres plus the radiator. 'Tear out the radio,' he said, looking in through the cab window. 'There isn't anything but shit in the charts these days anyway.'

'Oh come on, Mister, we're 20 K from base, you broke my mate's arm. They won't come looking for us till morning.'

'You trying to tell me you don't have to call in?' asked Zimmerman.

'We don't, honest, mate,' said the driver.

'Yeah, and I'm a teapot called Erika,' replied Zimm, presumably to show that he was dubious as to the driver's claim. 'I guess if that bastard Moorcock's got you goons, there's just kind of a small chance he's going to have a chopper. Which, if I leave you your rig, will be up my arse in about fifteen minutes.'

CD, standing by the car, debated briefly with himself whether to say something witty about not being prejudiced and that a chopper up the arse was fine between consenting adults using a condom. Wisely he decided that Zimm's mood was too volatile to risk interrupting him and he would save the gag for later.

Zimmerman shot the radio out of the dashboard with a burst of automatic fire, so sudden and so close that both men had unfortunate accidents. Which was a shame because, as it happened, the security set-up being very new, they were not supposed to report back and hence would not be missed until morning, meaning that they would have to spend the whole night, quite literally, in the shit.

Zimmerman loaded the ironmongery into the back of the Culboons' pick-up and suggested that they drove home.

'Maybe we should press on,' suggested CD, 'I mean, we're past the guards after all.'

'Yeah, I thought about it,' Zimmerman replied, 'but we'd never get the wheels through and it's 20 K into the middle. There and back that's quite a hike.'

'Well,' said Walter, 'I guess we should go home, smoke a little doobie and really try and concentrate.'

And on this contradiction in terms, they drove home.

# CONSPIRACY THEORIES

Ever since discovering that there definitely was some form of covert co-operation between the world's richest men, Chrissy had been casting desperately about, trying to find the vaguest hint as to what that co-operation might be. After all, it is not illegal for a large group of people to go out to dinner together. It might be boring if you get sat at the wrong end of the table, next to the wrong people. It might be annoying if you got lumbered trying to divide up the bill. Even more annoying if it is decided to just split the bill equally and you *know* that you only had a starter and that you didn't drink because you were driving. It might be all those things, but it is not illegal.

The tiny scraps of information that she did manage to pick up, simply added to the confusion. Using the information contained in Linda's final letter to her, she had been able to follow up one or two of the purchases that her target personalities had made during the first hours of the crash. But this had only made her more confused. For instance, the last thing that Slampacker had bought was a vast quantity of dried food, whilst Nagasyu was involved heavily in the jumble sale sell-off of the West European Space Group.

WESG had collapsed with the concentration of the satellite market, immediately following the crash. It had been hugely wealthy but only in the long-term. Being an entirely civil organization it had been able to concentrate purely on the commercial development of space, whilst both NASA and the Soviets had a huge military commitment. Unfortunately, the whole thing had been financed on credit, selling launch space for pay-loads that would not take flight for half a decade. With the whole sale cancelling most of these contracts, WESG found itself suddenly bankrupt. As it became apparent that the world was entering a decade of low consumer spending ability, all the new TV channels, private phone links, and mass satellite communication stuff had to be shelved. Nobody rents another TV channel when the cupboard's bare.

The Stark Consortium had been aware that this would happen and had jumped in early to asset-strip the agency. This had been the last major move that Chrissy had been able to observe, after that the transactions dried up. Unbeknownst to her, the reason for this was that Durf was now centralizing the preparations in order to speed things up. Obviously neither Durf, nor his assorted buyers, were in Linda's original computer program, so their dealings went unobserved.

But none the less, the few snippets she did uncover were enough to scare her even more deeply than she had been before. Chrissy was a good financial journalist, she understood money flow, she had even read parts of *Capital*. Of course, she did not agree with most of the social conclusions that Marx drew. She knew that the yuppies would do for themselves with cocaine, long before the dictatorship of the proletariat had time to inevitably succeed the dictatorship of the bourgeoisie. She didn't even know who the proletariat were anymore. On the other hand, she had always thought that there might be something in Marx's idea that war was an inevitable part of the money cycle. Money needed war. And somebody very rich was buying rockets. The time had come to seek advice.

## A LACK OF INTELLIGENCE

'That is the most preposterous lot of crap I have heard in all my years with the Agency,' CIA man Toole admonished, 'and I was the guy who wanted to poison Idi Amin by putting arsenic in his mistress's bidet.'

Chrissy had not really known what to expect, but going to Toole was the only thing she could remotely think of to do.

She supposed that maybe she had hoped that he would check the door and then inform her that the CIA were already on the case and that she could forget about it. Of course, Chrissy had no illusions about the extent of the CIA's knowledge about anything. Like all intelligence agencies, they knew what they stumbled on, unfortunately they could never believe what they stumbled on because it could be a plant, so they spent all day getting headaches, trying to double-think an opponent they were not sure existed.

But what could Chrissy do? Who could she turn to?

'I know it looks sort of weak but come on, Toole, we've known each other a long time. You're the only agency man I'd talk to. You know I'm not one to start at shadows.'

'Well, sure, but all this capitalist conspiracy stuff is pretty questionable you know, Chrissy,' Toole replied. 'I mean, maybe you should take it to the other side. It's kind of more their game you know. Our lot *like* capitalism, that's what we're here to defend. If there *is* anything in this, which of course there isn't, it is definitely a KGB brief, or maybe the Cubans. I can make a couple of calls if you want.'

'I'm not talking about capital *ism*, I'm talking about capital *ists*, a small group of them, who may be trying to screw the rest of us. Look, you have got to agree that I have the evidence that they were together and you've also got to agree that that is real strange. I mean *real* strange. Now what is the world financial situation at the moment?'

'It's in crisis, Chrissy, even the Agency can read the papers.'

'That's right, there is a world financial crisis. Decades of buying a new Hi-fi when you get bored with the record that's on it, has peaked. The credit boom is crashing about our ears. At any other time in history there'd probably be a war. That's what Marx said. The very nature of the system is growth, expansion and profit and the only way to keep that spiral moving upwards is to blow it apart with a war every now and then. Recreate demand, stimulate production, destroy old products, etc., etc. But it hasn't happened has it? In terms of major power against major power, there has never been a longer period of peace in history. Marx didn't know about nuclear weapons, he didn't know that the very next century after his, people would get scared of war, so the war he predicted hasn't happened, which leaves the world market in crisis . . .'

Toole interrupted her.

'Chrissy, are you suggesting that a group of well-known and respected businessmen are fixing to start their own war in order to recreate a market for their goods, because they're all good Marxists and he's told them how to keep capitalism on course?'

'I don't know,' Chrissy replied, angrily, 'it's just a suggestion. You try and explain what's going on here. My friend was murdered . . .'

'You think,' corrected Toole.

'She was murdered, whilst close to uncovering some kind of bizarre alliance between top money-biz fat cats. I pick up on the research and find that not only are they buying rocket fuel, but also half the West European Space Group . . .'

'Along with about a million other things, Chrissy,' Toole butted in again. 'Look, I'll do one thing for you and that is all. I'll call London and see if they know anything more about your friend's murder.'

Chrissy's knuckles were white with frustration. Toole adopted a kinder note.

'If you want my honest opinion, I'll tell you. I think you're probably on to something here. I agree that there are certain aspects that look a little strange, but no way in a billion years is this Marx business stuff cutting any ice with me, or anybody else. You're going to have to do a whole lot better theory-wise than that.'

'I haven't got any other damn theories!' Chrissy shouted. 'I have no idea what is going on!'

They parted; she to go and get a drink; he to make the one call that he had promised to make.

He was linked with an MI5 man called Carre. He knew him

pretty well and reckoned there was a good chance that he wasn't working for the Russians.

## KEEPING A SECRET

Secret Services are a bit of a puzzle really. In the light of the various unsavoury discoveries made about them since the war, it is becoming extremely difficult to find any satisfactory reason for why they exist at all.

It now seems fairly clear that for most of the time since the Second World War, the KGB have completely penetrated and totally compromised British Intelligence. And what good has it done them. They have not, as known, invaded Britain, or blown up any of Her Majesty's shipyards. They seem to have made no real profit out of their astonishing coup whatsoever. In fact, in the history of Britain, the audacious Russian penetration of our cloak and dagger boys will probably be deemed to have done little or no real damage at all, except perhaps to the egos of a few ex-public schoolboys. It has, on the other hand, sold an awful lot of novels. If the Soviets had thought to penetrate the West's publishing houses at the same time that they were penetrating its espionage organizations, they might today have all the hard currency that they so desperately need.

Of late the CIA has got the publishing bug and it almost seems that operatives are writing their memoirs before completing their first mission; with the result of blowing the gaff on past and present colleagues. The whole concept of espionage is so totally riddled with doubt and betrayal that the suspicion cannot be avoided that the entire charade is an utter waste of money.

Except of course it isn't, because the real purpose of national secret services is not to spy on foreigners but to spy on the people that pay for the thing in the first place; the population of the country in question. This is almost certainly the main job of the KGB and, if recently published memoirs are to be believed, is also the principal concern of MI5. The next

John Le Carré novel should be about Smiley trying to penetrate a bunch of vegetarian members of CND in Islington.

## THE GATHERING STORM

Chrissy went home more frustrated than ever, wishing that her friend, Linda, had never come up with her observations in the first place. She passed a news stand.

One of the placards announced that the heat in the southern hemisphere was now so severe that the rise in the sea level, due to the meltdown in Antarctica, was now a day to day reality. Coastal towns would soon no longer be safe and the whole of Egypt and Bangladesh were directly threatened. In the early eighties, scientists around the globe had predicted that within forty years the human race would face the most drastic climatic changes since civilization began. It was all happening much sooner than anybody had expected.

But Chrissy could not get worked up about it, she liked warm weather. She saw the second placard, it read:

DOUBLE EURO-NUKE TERROR; FRENCH REACTOR BLOWS; BRIT SUB FLOUNDERS.

Chrissy bought a paper and learnt of the dreadful events that had happened on the previous day. She could not help but smile. If the world wasn't careful it looked as if all her worries about money and the machinations of the world's billionaires would be entirely academic since there would no longer be any life on the planet to worry about.

## WARMING GLOW

The submarine in question, HMS *Dogged Endurance*, had hit trouble in a huge and unseasonal sea. The swell had been massive and Captain McEntoe had never seen the like before.

'It's those damn Americans mucking about with the weather,' he remarked, sucking on his pipe.

But it wasn't. It was just the sort of storm that only comes

246

very occasionally and nobody had really minded until the seas began to fill up with nuclear hardware which, once fractured, could poison extremely large areas for thousands of years.

HMS *Dogged Endurance* had been trying to leave harbour at its secret(ish) base in North Scotland when the weather had hit it and, despite its enormous power, the boat found itself drifting towards the rocks that formed the natural harbour. Three tugs had been called out immediately and had actually managed to get a rope onto the wallowing sub. However, to no avail and the side of the ship was breached on the fierce, craggy and soon-to-become extremely radioactive rocks of Scotland.

The weapons were not compromised but the small nuclear reactor, which powered *Dogged Endurance*, was. Within a matter of hours the major European frozen food companies were on the phones trying to get into the Pacific fish market.

The French power station was a much bigger disaster although, since the two incidents were only eight hundred miles apart, their effects became indistinguishable.

After the Chernobyl disaster the world was assured that with modern safety standards such terrible events were unlikely to happen again to a power station, even once in a thousand years. This, of course, was very little comfort because with the present proliferation of nuclear power it will not be long before there are a thousand nuclear power stations; which statistically suggests that one will go pop every year.

The disaster that Chrissy read about in New York made a large section of central France uninhabitable. Besides this, it cast a fall-out cloud that made all meat and vegetables, within a radius of five hundred miles, inedible. The argument for this form of power in the first place had been that it was cheap and clean. Of course, the cost of clearing up the appalling mess of this one disaster was uncomputable, and, with cancers running through many a generation, pretty open-ended.

# CLOAK AND DAGGER DETENTE

Toole went back to his office at the CIA New York station and phoned Carre in London.

Toole didn't like Carre. Carre was a boring snob and because he worked for MI5 he was obsessed with the idea that everybody would presume that he was gay. He therefore felt the need to continually pepper his conversation with sexual banter to demonstrate just what a clean knobbed heterosexual he was.

'Hi Carre, it's Toole. Still getting plenty?'

'Christ, *unbelievable*, I mean just *unbelievable*. I am getting so much pussy at the moment. I don't know what it is, but really, *unbelievable* . . .' Carre talked without moving his lips, in what he believed was a languid, public school drawl. An accent that only Prince Charles can carry off, and even he, only just . . .

'I mean, honestly, I don't think there are any poofs left in the firm these days. We all get *so much pussy*! especially me.'

'Glad to hear it, bud. Hey listen, could you do something for me?'

'Maybe. Thought you Yanks could pull your own birds,' said Carre in a manner calculated to imply the guarded response of a cool, keen brain; but in fact implying, and implying clearly, that he was a fatuous git. Except in wartime, working for the secret service must be a particularly soul destroying occupation. It is such a useless job. You can never know if you've got anything right; and even if you did you're not allowed to tell anyone. This is probably why secret civil servants have always invented fantasy lives for themselves; because their real ones are so dull. Carre hadn't even done this with any flair. After all, pretending to get laid a lot is scarcely an original pose. The other thing he did was to sit in clubs full of other young men pretending to be old, saying things like, 'Listen, if Hitler had gone to Eton he'd have made a bloody good minister of agriculture.'

Toole was aware of what a git Carre was, but Carre, being a

slime and a toady, knew things, so he was the quickest way to laying Chrissy's story to rest.

'Listen,' said Toole, 'someone's turned up a shot that I reckon is as long as they come, but I promised her I'd run it past your people. She has a major money conspiracy theory going round the death of a hack on the *Financial Telegraph*, called Linda Reeve. My source is convinced the girl was murdered because she was on the tail of some fat cats.'

'What's your source's name and what's her theory?' Carre blurted out. Had he really been the cool hand he liked to think he was, he would have affected disinterest. Toole was very surprised indeed, clearly he had hit something.

'Oh Christ, some mashed potatoes about corporate Armageddon,' he mumbled cheerfully and evasively. 'What about the Reeve girl?'

'No, what about your source, who is it?' Carrè insisted.

Toole was astonished. Obviously there was a case to answer to after all, at the very least about Linda Reeve's death. He reminded himself to apologize to Chrissy.

'Never you mind about my source. What's going on, Carre?'

'Nothing that I know of,' Carre said, finally managing to introduce a casual note into his voice. 'You know me, always interested in totty . . . I recall the case. The girl was killed and the police asked us to look at it. It was a very professional burglary you see, they were surprised that whoever did it murdered the girl . . .'

'Surely that would have gone to Special Branch . . . if that. More like local CID I'd have thought.' Toole, of course, did not believe Carre. There was one rule above all others in espionage: the cops hated the spies. Cops never took kindly to getting their investigations taken away from them and would certainly never have voluntarily handed over a murder to MI5 – no matter how suspicious.

'Well, for some reason or other they gave it to us,' Carre said, unconvincingly. 'We drew a blank. I just wondered if you had anything, that was all.'

Toole could get nothing further out of Carre, who started trying to talk about totty again. When Toole put the phone down he was at a complete loss about what to do. He had this list of vaguely suspicious, but entirely legal, financial transactions, and a girl with an utterly absurd theory about corporate global manipulation. He had been all set to forget about the whole thing after one call, and now the Brit had as good as confirmed the basis of Chrissy's theory; i.e. that Linda Reeve's death was suspicious. That gave a tiny touch of credibility to the rest of Chrissy's wild thinking. And what were the British doing? Certainly they knew something about this journalist's death. Poor Toole was now as confused as Chrissy. He too shared with her the same pangs of fear.

Not for long though, as it turned out, because within two hours Toole was dead. His nemesis had appeared in the shape of the head of the CIA West European operation. A very big fish indeed, he had never come to see Toole before and when he entered – without knocking – Toole sprang respectfully to his feet.

'Just been talking to London, Toole. You've stumbled on a big one. This Linda Reeve business, how did you get onto it?'

Toole explained about Chrissy Kelly; hoping like hell that he had not trodden on any major leaguer's toes.

'And that's all?' the big man asked, and was assured that it was. Then he pulled the gun with the silencer, bade Toole raise his hands, put the gun to Toole's mouth, shot him and placed the gun in Toole's lifeless hands – Toole had wondered when his boss entered the room why he was wearing gloves.

Nobody knew why Toole had killed himself. The body had been discovered by the head of the West European operation, who had gone over to question Toole about unauthorised conversations with dubious British agents who were known to boast openly about indiscreet sexual adventures. Maybe, people speculated, that was why Toole killed himself ... Lacking any real motivating force in their lives, sex was a spur that secret service types always found tempting to fix on to. People whispered about Toole, pointing out that he had killed himself after talking to a man called Carre at MI5 – which everyone knew had been a den of queers since 1946. What's more, it seemed that this Carre was fixated by demeaning and smutty talk about women – which CIA analysts claimed was probably a denial of his deeper and very different desires. Poor old Carre, the most terrible thing he could imagine happened: his CIA file got marked down as possible subversive homosexual.

Actually Toole died because both Carre and the big American Head of West European operations worked for Stark; although they had no idea of the real nature of their employment. They both presumed that they were simply involved in industrial espionage. Very rich men gave them orders and they carried them out. Carre had been instructed to keep an eye on the Reeve murder – in fact he had recruited a fellow who did it. Hence, he reported his conversation with Toole to Professor Durf's people. They, in turn, asked their top CIA insider to find out what Toole knew, and then kill him. That was it. Five grand to Carre, a hundred grand to the American; money well spent, and the two men returned to their day jobs. Chrissy's address was then faxed to a reliable New York operative.

# ON THE RUN

During the few short hours that this was going on, Chrissy had continued to chew over any bit of information about financial dealings that she could get her hands on. There wasn't much because the depression was biting deeper and deeper. It had taken grip with astonishing speed. The world seemed to have just shrugged its shoulders and admitted defeat. Maybe it was the weather. One article did catch Chrissy's eye. It told how the lucky country was attempting to shrug off the slump more quickly than anyone. Apparently, that brave and individualistic trouble-shooter, Silvester Moorcock, was not taking financial stagnation lying down. Chrissy jumped as she read Sly's name . . . The article informed her that he had created a boom town in Western Australia by staggering everyone and starting the construction of a huge leisure complex in the desert. Further to this, it had just emerged that he had gone into co-operation with fellow Aussie Ocker Tyron, who was handling the shipping in of the enormous quantity of material and equipment required to build such a massive scheme from scratch.

Chrissy wondered . . .

Obviously no way were the world's financiers going to unite to build a Kangaroo theme park. And, of course, the amount of money that had been syphoned out of the system, both before and during the crash, would have built Disneyland on the Moon . . . but it was something. It was the only significant financial activity to emerge since the crash and it involved at least two of the figures on Linda's original list . . . She was nervous about bothering Toole again, especially with something even less concrete than what she had already given him, but she had to do something with her time. She had given up everything to pursue this investigation. And Toole had said that he would make a call for her . . .

She picked up the phone. It was a Donald Duck shaped phone which Chrissy had bought because, since all news is bad news, she figured she might as well get it from a cheery source. Cheering up this call was going to need more than a plastic duck . . .

'Toole's dead,' said Donald, smiling hugely under his little sailor's hat. The C I A had seen no reason for secrecy and hence informed Chrissy that Toole was dead, having taken his own life. It happened quite a lot in his business.

Chrissy was utterly terrified. She had been speaking to Toole only a few hours previously, there was absolutely no way on earth that he was suicidal. He must have met the same fate that Linda had. But, so quickly. Chrissy could not believe it; they had done it so quickly.

Clearly she had to get away immediately, far away. But where? How? It is difficult to formulate a plan when, all of a sudden, you realize that within minutes somebody may try to kill you. She tried to think as she ran about her apartment stuffing passport and credit cards into a bag; a few clothes, her notes. Her eyes fell on the newspaper she had been reading. West Australia was the single remaining avenue of investigation that remained to Chrissy; it was a long shot but she had to go somewhere. There was a ring at the door. Chrissy froze. It could be nothing; on the other hand, it could be her executioner.

Chrissy's apartment was on the third floor, as she rushed down the fire escape she could hear the sound of her front door being smashed down. There was a cab rank at the corner of the street. Chrissy jumped in the first one.

'J F K airport,' she said.

'Yeah, yeah. Everybody wants to go to the airport,' said the cabby. 'No one stays home no more. Mind you, in this neighbourhood, who can blame them? Blacks, spicks, I ain't prejudiced, no way, but they're so dirty, and the mugging and all . . .'

Even in her desperate state Chrissy realized that she was faced with the classic cab dilemma: do you risk the

253

unpleasantness of telling the guy to stuff it? or do you bite your lip and make non-committal grunts. Normally Chrissy, like most people, would not have had the energy to speak up but she was in a reckless mood. 'Listen, mister,' she said, 'I'm Jewish myself so just can the racist shit, OK?'

'You're so right, Lady,' the cabbie replied. 'The Jews are the worst, Christ, they should have stayed in Israel. Maybe Hitler had the right idea. Like I say, I ain't prejudiced, but I do hate Jews.'

Chrissy gave up and tried to plan her escape.

She had just about enough cash for the cab. After that, plastic was her only currency and so it would not be possible to travel under a false name. Chrissy was already beginning to imagine her adversaries as totally omniscient, godlike in their power and penetration – which of course they were. She would have to use her American Diners Card though and hope that it would not be traced, otherwise she would certainly share Linda's and Toole's fate.

How alone she felt in that cab on the way to JFK. She knew something; and she knew nothing, and the driver was a bastard. She had no one to turn to, and even if she had, she would not have done so since contact with her appeared to be the kiss of death. That was the real isolation, she was on the run and as long as she remained alive she would not be able to contact family or friends. She had the plague, the black spot, she was a leper and an untouchable.

## WAITING AND WONDERING

She got into the airport without incident or at least without being killed, because of course her present situation was one extended incident. Having stood in a Stars and Stripes Airline queue she got to a tickets and inquiries person just as she realized that she didn't really know where she wanted to go. She presumed, correctly, that Bullens Creek would not be a destination covered by an international airline.

'Yes, how may I help you, my name is Sandy, thank you for

flying with Stars and Stripes, we will be pleased to assist you in any way we can, have a nice day.' The girl in the uniform smiled so wide it was demonic; the parched over-tanned skin, the bones sticking out of the half-starved face, and the smile, a row of gleaming tombstone teeth in a blood red mouth. To Chrissy, struggling to contain her terror, the Stars and Stripes lady was like death itself; a skull in a pretty little uniform. In actual effect she was just a quite good looking woman of thirty-eight, making the major mistake of trying to look like a very good looking woman of twenty-one.

'Pardon,' stammered Chrissy.

The Stars and Stripes lady gave her the shorter version of official Stars and Stripes consumer friendly approach. 'My name is Sandy, how may I help you?'

Chrissy's mind was blank.

'Uhm . . . Oh God . . . Sandy, have you ever heard of a place called Bullens Creek?'

'Oh, now, yes I do recall, I'm sure I do . . .'

'Great, one ticket please, one way,' said Chrissy, relief flooding over her.

'Well, I believe it's in Texas, now you would want our domestic –'

'It's somewhere in Western Australia!' shouted Chrissy, expecting, every second, a man in a slouch hat to come and shoot her. 'I want to go somewhere in Western Australia.'

'Well I'm sorry, Madam,' said Sandy, switching to the official Stars and Stripes 'now I hope you're not going to cause a scene' voice. 'But you'll have to be a little more specific than that.'

Chrissy's mind was a blank.

'Listen, I've forgotten. What's the capital of Western Australia? Come on, that's where I want to go.'

'Madam, I'm not at all sure you know where you want to go.' The voice was now pure 'if you're a nut I'm calling a cop'.

'Perth!!' blurted Chrissy, with blessed relief. 'I want a ticket to Perth.'

*

255

As it turned out, Stars and Stripes only covered the eastern states of Australia and Chrissy was forced to join another queue at the National Australia desk.

She discovered that the first available flight was still eighteen hours away. On inquiry she also discovered that it was unlikely to be full. This was important. She wanted to buy the ticket at the last possible minute, eighteen hours would give them plenty of time to trace her credit card transaction and stop her boarding the plane. The same logic meant that she had to presume that they would be waiting for her at the other end, but Chrissy could only take things one step at a time.

She bought a hat and some dark glasses and sat for fifteen and a half terrible hours in a coffee bar, eating the occasional Danish pastry – which is catering speak for a lump of dough and a blob of sugar and is about as Danish as Tandoori chicken.

Chrissy hoped that they had not thought to check out the cab drivers.

## A BIT OF LUCK

'Smallish, dark complexion, in a hurry?' Durf's thug was asking Chrissy's ex-driver.

'Hey, hey, hey, what is this, the third degree?' the driver replied. 'Sure I picked up a dame, but I just drive them, OK? I don't feel the need to commit them to memory.'

'Come on! It's only been an hour, think! Was it a Jewish woman?' the thug added.

'No way, pal, you got the wrong cab, the dame *hated* Jews. She told me.'

## THEORIZING

As Chrissy sat, she pondered again, as she had done so often before, what could possibly be the cause of the unholy alliance that she was now quite certain she had uncovered. The swift dispatch of Toole proved to her beyond all doubt that she was on to something very big indeed.

What were they up to? And whatever it was, were they doing it at Bullens Creek? And even if they were and she discovered it, what could she do? Chrissy was quite certain that she would be dead very soon whatever happened.

There were lots of policemen about. How she longed to fling herself on the protection of one, but protection from what? A dinner party in Los Angeles months before? Maybe another one in Singapore? Linda died in a burglary, Toole killed himself. The best she could hope for would be to be locked up as a lunatic. Besides, she had no reason to believe that she could trust the police, her adversaries' tentacles seemed to be everywhere, her C I A liaison had lasted a matter of hours.

No, there was no doubt about it, she was alone, alone and mystified; starting at shadows and expecting every waitress to stab her with a poisoned plastic fork.

Chrissy tried to hypothesize what advantages the world's biggest producers could gain by starting some kind of war. It felt distinctly foolish even to be considering the possibility, but what else could she work on?

Collecting her thoughts, Chrissy made a concerted effort to dedramatize the situation; to come up with a slightly less catastrophic theory to fit the information that she had. After all, the murders meant nothing, people killed for money, it didn't mean that they were trying to change world history.

Putting aside the strange purchases that some of the people who had been at the L A dinner party had made since the crash, it seemed possible to Chrissy that they might be trying to set up some kind of illegal investment bank to buy out or out-produce competition and create some kind of hybrid giant multinational; a world super-company without a nationality. If this were the case, secrecy would obviously be essential because it would, of course, ride rough-shod over trade and monopoly legislation worldwide. Besides this, it would take the competition out of capitalism; it would be a kind of communism for billionaires. Try as she might, Chrissy could not bring herself to see much in this theory. And there was the rocket fuel and the guidance systems ... Australia ... were they going to hold the Japanese to ransom? Blow them up? The Japanese dominated so completely in almost all the new industries, their removal would be a huge new profit stimulus to everyone else. But she knew there were Japanese business-men at the Los Angeles dinner ... Of course that didn't necessarily matter, capital knew no patriotism; that was for workers, to keep them working. Chrissy had lost count of the number of millionaires who lived in tax exile, or had even changed citizenship in order to get over local investment laws. That famous citizen of the world, Rupert Murdoch − a man who owns newspapers that preach arch patriotic xenophobia in their individual countries − had taken US citizenship with the drop of a hat in order to penetrate the US media.

Chrissy's head was spinning, she could no longer get bombs off her mind. Maybe it was the apocalyptic nature of the newspapers she bought in her long long wait. The French power station disaster dominated for the day but the sea-level thing was still big news. It was getting higher and what's more, the floating scum slick had reappeared. That one wasn't going away either, the record high temperatures of the pre-vious Northern summer had wiped out half the US cereal crop and now it looked like European agriculture was going to be contaminated as far as the wheat bowl in the Ukraine for years to come. What arable land remained in the world was going to have to be farmed more intensely; which would mean more chemical fertilizers; which meant more nutrients getting swept into the sea, thus feeding the microscopic algae, who multiply into the floating glob and suffocate the sea. There was a huge picture in one of the papers of the mid-Atlantic, and poking out of the slime that covered it were the fins and tails and noses of a huge school of dead dolphins. The caption noted that under the slime were literally millions of dead fish and various sea creatures.

It being such a long wait, Chrissy finally got around to

buying the English papers that were stocked at the airport. She was relieved to discover that The Princess of Wales had been shopping and that lovely Mandy, seventeen, thought feminists were silly killjoys and she was flattered if men admired her body.

Contemplating the accumulating natural disasters, Chrissy again found herself wondering whether the sick old world would last long enough for whoever it was, to do whatever it was, they were going to do. But that was silly. 'They' would think of something and the world would be OK – 'they' of course were scientists. At that moment, all over the world, scientists were waking up and wondering what they were going to do. They were looking at a snowball. It seemed like only yesterday that they had held that snowball in their fists; they could crush it, shape it, control it. They turned away for a minute and suddenly the fucker was the size of a house, hurtling towards them, too big to hold and too big to control.

But Chrissy herself had more pressing problems to occupy her mind as the hours crawled by in the coffee lounge at JFK. Maybe they would try to hold the world to ransom; maybe Slampacker was going to demand of the world that they either ate more of his Chicken Slammers or he would nuke them?

What with trying to study every approaching face to see if it looked like an assassin, by the time Chrissy got up from the hard plastic chair to finally go and buy her ticket, her head hurt almost as much as her backside.

# BACK IN BULLENS

As Chrissy sat, scared out of her wits, high up in the upper atmosphere, Zimmerman was also preparing to make the trip to Bullens Creek airport. He had to pick up his delivery of comics. Zimmerman was a total comic nut, and he had expended quite a large portion of his meagre resources ensuring that his regular supply followed him up to Bullens.

'Get my comic books tomorrow, I love it when I get my books,' he said as they sat around at the Culboons' house the afternoon after they got back from their exciting trip out to Moorcock's fence.

'Zimm,' said Rachel in disbelief, 'you've just done a whole Superman thing yourself, you took care of those guys as if it was a film, and you're thinking about your comics!'

'That's the whole point, Rachel,' replied Zimmerman. 'I can forget things with my comic books, you know, relax. Kind of lose myself in them, you know?'

The others understood fully. Zimm was, in many ways, a wonderful person, but he was also definitely weird, weird and intimidating. The others sometimes found it rather disconcerting just being around Zimmerman. He actually had to live with himself; it was scarcely surprising that he occasionally wanted to lose himself.

'I dig my comics,' Zimmerman continued. Like all adult comic readers he felt the need to do a big number about it not being childish. 'There's a lot more in them than you think, right? They're really wry, you know, cynical. Like, man, you know, the Phantom and Judge Dread are kind of philosophers.'

Zimm was very big for the whole sub-gothic justice fantasy

260

thing. He played a nationwide game, favoured by hippies and also science students who didn't like rugby, called Dungeons and Dragons. In the game you go through various semi-guided adventures, playing a character that you have invented yourself. Most of the farties who played the game assumed immensely macho characters calling themselves things like Wotan Skulcrusher, Spearman the Axe Bringer and Goblin Trollthrash. They imagined themselves as Thor-like figures, straight out of Tolkien. Zimm's character, on the other hand, was a tiny stooping old wizard; a gentle, peaceful wizard who knew nothing of pain or death; a wizard whose greatest joy was to invent ever more beautiful types of flowers for the children to pick – but a wizard who happened to have an enormous dick and a scrotum that he had to drag behind him on a trolley.

Everybody got their own thing out of the game.

Anyway, on the subject of his comics, Zimmerman was adamant: 'Whatever we do next it will have to be when I get back from the airport man. I've got to have my comics, you know?'

'Well, take your time, Zimmerman mate,' Mr Culboon commented drily. 'I can't see us coming up with our next move for a while. I mean, what the hell do we do?'

Rachel was very wound up, as was CD. Getting shot at in the darkness was a new experience for them both. The Culboons were more relaxed, it had happened to them before, although not in quite a while. For Zimm, of course, it was like old times, in fact for years he hadn't been able to sleep at night unless Walter popped his head around the door occasionally and shouted 'bang'. Walter himself, like CD and Rachel, had never experienced being shot at but he remarked afterwards that he had been surprised at how lacking in heaviness the whole situation had been. Zimmerman assured him that it was worse when you got hit.

Rachel's frustration was growing.

'We've certainly got to do *something*,' she exploded. 'I mean, Christ, if we needed proof that something was going

261

on, we've got it. You don't guard innocent projects with gunmen. What is that bastard Moorcock up to?'

'*Those* bastards, Tyron's in on this too remember,' said CD, secretly wanting to remind Rachel that it was his detective work that had brought them this far.

'And we don't know who else besides.'

'Oh, man, like it's obvious like, what we've got to do, you know?' said Walter in what, for him, was an urgent manner.

It was like a snail trying to dial 999.

'Either one, or all of us people, has got to get over that wire and take a look, you know? But seeing as some of us are not exactly built like commandoes, maybe just Zimmerman should go.'

'I'm bloody going,' said Rachel, 'this is where it starts to get exciting.'

This was too much for Mrs Culboon, who shrieked good-naturedly. 'Oh, darling, if you get excited being shot at and beaten up, just come and live with us Abs for a while, love.'

'Whatever we do, we should leave it at least forty-eight hours,' said Zimm. 'They're sure to be on their guard for a while, but after that I reckon they'll become cool and think we were just a casual hassle.'

Walter looked at Zimm with awe and affection. 'Man, you are becoming so straight and together that I will have to buy you a tie and get you a job in a bank,' he said.

## SURVIVAL OF THE STRAIGHTEST

Walter was right, they had all noticed it. Zimmerman was becoming very together indeed. Certainly he did it in his own very untogether way but, none the less, he was a changed man.

Zimmerman had a theory about staying alive and being alive. He had developed his theory during combat and it was a theory shared by many of his colleagues. Life for a soldier in any war is pretty gruesome to say the least; in Vietnam it was worse because no one in the Australian or US Armies had the faintest idea for what or for whom they were fighting. Whereas their opponents knew exactly what they were fighting for; their country and their families, and had been doing so for thirty years. Faced with this unpleasant imbalance in job motivation, the best thing any allied soldier could do really was to try and relax about it. Unfortunately, if you happen to be spending month after month sat in a sweltering swamp, getting eaten alive by insects and shot to bits by highly motivated and extremely skilled guerilla soldiers, relaxing is easier said than done. One of the quickest and easiest ways to get around this problem was to escape the real world in a false, drug induced reality: i.e., get out of your brain.

Unfortunately, soldiers who are staring at the trees claiming that the colours are dancing and that Jesus is a can of corned beef, don't tend to live very long. Saying 'hey man you're beautiful' at approaching Vietcong cut no ice with them at all, they shot you whether you found them attractive or not. Hence it was absolutely essential to be ready to be straight, or at least functional, when there was danger about. Zimmerman learnt to take his recreation when it was safe to do so and to put up with reality when he needed to be able to rely on himself.

Now although Zimm was never again to be the chemical dustbin he had been when he truly did live in hell (in fact after Vietnam he had given up everything but the odd toot on a bong), the basis of his theory had stayed with Zimmerman ever since. Life was mainly a bummer, so it was best to keep your head somewhere else; invent your own more palatable reality. For Zimm this needed to be nothing more complex than a glass of home-brew, a little grass and a good comic. It didn't matter how often he had read it.

None the less, he never forgot what he had learnt in war: the time to get it together was when there was trouble. Now there was clearly trouble and Zimmerman had returned to earth to meet it.

# NO CHOICE

'Listen,' said CD, who was getting nervous. He didn't really like the idea of heroics but if Rachel was going, he was going. 'Maybe we should do some research in the town, ask the workers, that sort of thing?'

'I tried all morning, man,' answered Walter. 'Like, most of them stay behind the wire, half of them don't even speak English and they're all paid serious money, man, you know, top whack. You ask them once, they say they're building a hotel; you ask them twice, they tell you to fuck off.'

It was clear to all of them that the only way they were going to find out anything more about the great mystery that they had stumbled upon, was to take another look.

CD wished he'd fallen in love with a coward.

# HUNTED

As Chrissy's National Australian jumbo began its descent into Perth International, she knew for sure that they would be waiting for her, having doubtless traced her destination through her use of a credit card. Chrissy knew also that if she walked out into them they would kill her. And yet, somehow, she had to get past them and over to the internal airport to pick up and pay for her ticket to Bullens, which she had reserved in a false name at J F K.

She presumed that she was safe enough through passport control and that the danger would appear after customs. She could not lose her passport because they would simply turn her around and put her on a plane back to the U S A. Chrissy thanked her lucky stars that as a journo she travelled constantly and had an Australian multiple entrance visa in her passport that was good for another year. But it was no good being allowed in so that they could carry her straight out again in a box. She needed a plan. Luckily for Chrissy, she was a journo, and journos are born schemers and natural liars.

After some thought she got up and walked down the aisle. She asked everybody the same thing:

'Excuse me, I have a salt and sugar deficiency, if you've finished would you mind awfully . . .?'

It was such a strange request that people just concurred instantly and handed over the little plastic envelopes. Then Chrissy disappeared to the toilet. She did not re-emerge until the stewardess knocked on the door to inform her that the plane was landing.

After clearing passport control, Chrissy prepared herself carefully to go through customs. She put on her dark glasses, she wet her brow, and she lit up a cigarette . . . then she ran through green. If the plan had failed she intended to trip and allow the bag to burst open, she had already opened it and held it closed with her fingers. As it happened, there was no need because, as she'd hoped, the sight of a sweating, smoking girl trying to run through green with fear in her eyes, fear which of course was very real, was enough to make a young customs officer take a punt on her.

Of course, when she opened her bag and he idly sifted through it, he thought all his Christmasses had come at once because there was the salt and the sugar taped up in a sheet of clear plastic that had once been a bath hat.

The discreet looking murderer stood waiting, as person after person emerged from the US flight, many being immediately and noisily scooped up by tearful families. He could not see Chrissy. He waited and waited, but he could not see her. He waited until long after another flight had flooded the arrivals hall with still more happy huggers, and still there was no Chrissy.

## SALT RUNNING

This, of course, was because she was in a customs lock-up.

'What's this,' they had asked.

'Salt and sugar,' she replied. The last thing she wanted was to be delayed for ever for deceiving the police. She wanted a nice two or three hours while they tried to figure her out.

'Why's it wrapped up like drugs?'

'Is it? That's the way I like my salt and sugar.'

'Mixed up?'

'You never heard of sweet and sour?'

The customs people were a little surprised at her coolness so, instead of whisking her away, they had a look at the package that the young officer had plucked so triumphantly from Chrissy's bag.

'It's salt and sugar,' said the lad.

266

'Get the Prof' to have a look at it, every grain,' said his boss.

After about an hour they decided that what they had found was salt and sugar.

'All right, Miss, what's your game? Trying to make it look like you had a bagful of smack, are you a sicko or what?' The officer was exasperated and disappointed; he didn't like Chrissy at all; he didn't understand her, but he knew that he didn't like her.

'Listen, Buster!' snapped Chrissy, who was beginning to feel that it was time to leave. 'This is Australia, right, not the Soviet Union. So, I got a bagful of condiments? What is that, a federal case? You saying you can't bring salt into this country any more? Is that it? Get this, Mister, if you're so damn paranoid you see drugs wherever you look that's your problem, OK? See an analyst, personally I'm outta here.'

'No you aren't, Miss, you aren't out of here by a long shot.' The officer was very puzzled. Puzzled and annoyed. He could see only two explanations for the taped up plastic bag they had found. Either this woman was a weirdo, or he was being subjected to an incredibly elaborate double bluff. The latter was certainly possible. Any drug-runner ran the risk of being stopped and searched by customs, in which case, obviously there was a good chance their goods would be discovered. Perhaps this woman had conceived the audacious plan of leaving something so confusing on display that by the time it had been fully investigated, and found to be perplexingly innocent, no one would think of searching further.

'Fine toothcomb job, boys,' he spat the words at Chrissy. 'Unpick every fucking stitch in her jumper. Wanda, bung her on the slab.'


## CLEAN GLOVES AND WARM TONGS

And so it was that poor Chrissy took a short break out from being chased across the world by shadowy murderers, in order to have an Australian customs officer stuff a long probe up her important little places. No one is at their freshest after a

267

twenty-hour flight, especially in the terrifying circumstances that Chrissy had endured, so the job wasn't much fun for Wanda either. But she was a philosophical woman and had resigned herself to making the best of what had definitely turned out to be a slightly less glamorous job than she had expected. Probing the bottoms of hippies and wicked old grannies was not absorbing detective work, but she put a brave face on it.

'Togs off,' she shouted in a forced jolly manner, like a games mistress on a cold morning pretending she enjoys her job.

'Laddered your panty hose, dear? Yes, I know,' she said, answering her own question. 'I'm a socks girl myself, put my thumb through just one too many gussets I'm afraid.'

Wanda was a strongly innocent choice of person for the job of extracting deadly substances from the internal body cavities of international villains. On the other hand, she would have been a difficult person to bribe.

'Oh I do envy you skinny girls, lucky things. Honestly, if I haven't got a couple of girders in the old boulder holders, I'm polishing my shoes, honestly I am. . . . Come on, dear, up on the slab, the cat's been on the bum bit, so that should be warm enough anyway. Now then, legs in the stirrups.'

Wanda was not rough at the job but a strip search is still an unpleasant and undignified palaver, made even more frustrating for Chrissy by the fact that she had gone through the same thing with her gyno' only a couple of weeks before. Her distaste must have shown and it hurt Wanda a little. After all, in her job, maintaining a sense of professional pride is pretty much all you've got to hang on to.

'Clean gloves and warm tongs,' she would always tell the new girls, 'even an international trader in death deserves that.'

'Cheer up now, Christine – hope you don't mind if I use first names. I always think it's a bit silly to try and be formal with a person when you've got your hands stuffed where the sun don't shine, eh? So, smile-up girl, smile-up, soon be over, eh?'

But Chrissy could not smile up, she just happened to be one of those strange people who absolutely hate lying on their backs with their legs strapped in the air, and some total stranger peering up their fanny. Some people just have these strange little prejudices.

Finally it was over and Chrissy bade Wanda goodbye. Unlike the officer who had ordered the search, Wanda was very pleased that Chrissy was clean. She always found it so embarrassing when she drew out some horrid damp package, like a magician producing a rabbit from a hat, and being forced to inform some spread-eagled, naked old sad act that they would shortly be starting five to ten in the slammer.

As Chrissy took her leave she felt some comment was in order – their relationship though brief had been intimate.

'Well, goodbye, Wanda,' she said, and then after a moment's hesitation, 'for what it's worth, I think you do a bloody rotten job very well indeed.'

Wanda was very touched. Chrissy was the very, very first satisfied customer she had ever had. Her day was definitely made.

'Thanks old stick,' she said and marched off to water her plants.

## TURNING TO CRIME

Chrissy was let out of the Customs office without a stain on her character which was more than could be said for her togs, as Wanda would have called them. She had now been on the run, in abject terror, for about forty hours and was getting a bit whiffy. But she was still alive and what's more, she was not required to go back the way she had come and go out through the green channel. As she was unceremoniously ejected through a small door about a hundred metres along the terminal floor, she allowed herself a quick glance towards the arrivals point . . . Sure enough, there was a large, impatient looking man in an anorak, despite the heat, standing forlornly hoping that he would be able to kill someone off the next flight.

She took a taxi to Perth Internal terminal. Australia being such a huge place, most internal flights are still trans-continental, and hence they get their own airport. Chrissy walked as calmly as she could up to the Southern Cross Airline desk and inquired after the ticket to Bullens Creek that she had reserved for a friend under the name of Rob-bins.

'Why certainly, I'll just see if I can help you in that way, my name is Charlene and I'll be pleased to offer any assist-ance, thank you for choosing Southern Cross as your internal carrier.' Charlene was an Australian girl, but the American com-munication disease is infectious.

'Why yes, here is the ticket, now if I can just take a credit card imprint.' Chrissy handed over her card.

But, during Chrissy's long flight, some unseen hand had been at work and Charlene was embarrassed to have to inform Chrissy that the computer had blocked her card. What's more, Charlene regretted to have to inform Chrissy that she had been requested to inform American Diners of the time and location of the attempted transaction . . .

Chrissy mumbled that it was the third time this week and she had been assured that the mix-up had been dealt with and disappeared into the crowd. Chrissy had to think quickly, which in a way was lucky because had she had more time to ponder, she would surely have despaired at the hopelessness of her position. She was being hounded by the most powerful people in the world; people who knew, and controlled, every-thing.

Supposing she did get to Bullens Creek? And what if the secret did lie there? What would she do? She was going to be killed very shortly anyway, there was not a lot of point in run-ning.

However, Chrissy had made a plan, a plan to get to Bullens Creek and for want of anything better to do, she determined to stick to it. And so, imbued with the fatalism of somebody who basically considers herself as good as dead, she decided to steal somebody's wallet.

This decision required a lot of courage. Because, even in her perilous position, the thought of being caught as a common thief and marched away in shame through a crowd of embarrassed people still held a real dread for her.

But, in fact, that scenario was an unlikely one because Chrissy came up with a brilliant idea. This was partly because fear lends wings to the imagination, and partly because the lack of individualism which the modern world of global finance imposes on us is not confined to the horrors of Slampacker burgers. The rich are equally susceptible to being told who they are.

## BADGE OF RANK

Chrissy's plan formed the moment she saw the contents of the rich lady's bag, carelessly placed on the floor beside her as she sat reading the sort of novel that would never have been invented if it wasn't for the Wright Brothers. Inside the bag was a Cartige card wallet. There could be no mistake about that, the distinctive dyed grey crocodile skin with pink edges, the gold-plated corner strengtheners. This was the Cartige logo and identity, jealously protected in courts across the world.

Why this jealousy? The reason is that the wallet was no more attractive than a wallet costing a tenth as much, this is why the distinctive livery is so important. That livery, protected in court from imitation, guarantees that anything carrying it costs a hell of a lot.

These identification uniform 'accessories' are literally nothing more than a personal advert proclaiming one's wealth. A small key-ring, or bill clip carrying the logo of a perfume company, can cost easily two hundred pounds. There seems to be no reason for this inflation, other than that it represents an international visual snob code. It would be cheaper, and no less ostentatious, to simply stamp one's income on one's forehead. At least that had been the gist of Chrissy's thoughts the previous Christmas, when Farty Frank, a commodity broker of her acquaintance, had given her a Cartige card wallet in the obvious hope that she would be impressed.

'It's genuine Cartige, you know,' he had said; meaning that whatever its genuine aesthetic value and whatever its genuine practical value, it certainly genuinely cost a lot.

Chrissy did not really like carrying a financial badge of rank but it was certainly a very nice looking wallet, worth at least thirty of the three hundred bucks it had cost, and so, despite brushing off Farty Frank pretty sharpish, she had carried her cards in the Cartige wallet ever since. In honour of his memory, Farty Frank got a starring role in the scheme that his gift made possible.

## THE HIT

'Frank!!' Chrissy shouted, 'Frank, Frank, I'm here,' she scuttled across the terminal as the five Franks in the crowded room turned their heads. Chrissy pushed her way through the people, making as much noise as she possibly could. 'Wait, Wait, I'm here!!!'

This time the carefully pre-opened bag was required, and worked perfectly. It was almost empty, but what contents there were scattered over and into the rich lady's gaping bag. Chrissy played it half-apologetic, half furious. After all the mythical Frank was disappearing and the lady's bag had been in a gangway.

She had to get down first and, as deftly as she could, whipped the lady's wallet, overcoming a momentary paranoia that she was in fact stealing back her own one. Obviously and instantly the rich lady's suspicions were aroused.

'Hey, get your hands out of my bag will ya!'

Chrissy instantly backed off.

'OK, OK, sorry, but I'm in the process of missing my fiancé in from Detroit. It's just the lipstick, the gold compact and the address book . . .'

The rich lady had now assured herself that a Cartige wallet was still in her bag and happily handed over the other items, pleased to meet another American.

'The men you gotta chase are the only ones worth having, dear, go for it.'

Chrissy thanked her and rushed off with a surge of confidence. Not only had she effected rather a neat lift, but also she had covered herself. If the lady discovered the switch, Chrissy could, of course, claim that it had been a genuine mix-up, and take back her own cards with feigned relief. Her only chance of discovery would be if she was caught using the cards and she intended to get that obstacle out of the way immediately.

Watching the rich woman carefully from across the terminal, Chrissy allowed herself only five practises at the signature on the back of the American Diners card. Luckily it was an erratic scrawl which Chrissy, being a journalist, had no trouble at all in emulating.

No more than three minutes after the theft, Chrissy presented herself back at the Southern Cross desk, being careful to choose a different queue to the one Charlene stood at the front of.

Having paid for the ticket, Chrissy returned to the rich woman and explained the mix-up. Not only was Chrissy an honest person who did not wish upon anyone the hassle of having to cancel all their cards, but also she did not need the police after her as well. Obviously the ticket to Bullens would eventually show up on the rich woman's statement but she did not look like the sort of person who kept their transparents and checked them off each month. On her first shot Chrissy had committed the perfect crime.

The rich lady laughed at the confusion.

'Well now, these darn Cart-ee-*jay* things are meant to be so exclusive and here they are falling over each other. Thank you, dear.'

Chrissy was about to leave.

'By the way, did you catch Frank?'

'Frank?'

'That's right, dear,' the lady laughed, 'love 'em and forget 'em. I have three times.'

## LUCK RUNNING OUT

The flight left forty minutes later and Chrissy got on it without mishap. She ordered a beer and tried to collect her thoughts.

She had to presume that despite having slipped past the thug at customs, her adversaries must now know that she was in Australia because Charlene would have reported her trying to use her credit card. On the other hand, she had actually bought her ticket to Bullens Creek with a different card, so with any luck they would take a while to find out where she had gone to after leaving Charlene.

This time though, luck was against her. The poor stooge who had so unsuccessfully staked out the international arrivals had rushed straight over to internal the moment he got the word and was now interviewing Charlene.

'She wanted to pick up a ticket to Bullens Creek, but of course I wouldn't give it to her. If my computer says "hold" I hold.'

Having learnt that a plane for Bullens had just left and that yes, a woman closely resembling his sister had been on it, the stooge rang his boss. That boss then rang his boss, and very quickly the message reached Durf's inner team.

Durf's inner team nearly shat themselves. How on earth could this woman, Christine Kelly, have worked it out! She was going to Bullens Creek, the very epicentre of everything. It was shocking how close they had come to a total breach of security. One thing was certain, this time Chrissy was going to be met at the airport.

# AIRPORT RESCUE

## RECEPTION COMMITTEE

The incoming Southern Cross flight from Perth was going to be a little late and so Zimmerman had nothing to do but hang out in the sweaty, humid, horrible arrivals shed until his comics arrived.

Bullens Creek strip had changed beyond recognition since the day that Sly had first flown in and given his speech. The old arrivals and departures hut was now just a store room. To replace it, a large pre-fabricated building had been thrown up and beside it, a car park full of ex-military air traffic control equipment. This sleepy little place that had once received two flights a day, was now taking eight an hour – almost all freight – and that number was scheduled to double within a month. They had extended the original runway and were building three more much larger ones. Being in the middle of the desert there was no space problem, and already Bullens Creek airport was beginning to resemble a thriving little metropolis all of its own.

None the less, despite the crowds and the hustle and bustle in the huge shed, Zimmerman spotted the four men in sports jackets immediately. 'Pigs or gooks,' he thought to himself without much interest.

It was the overplayed casualness of the unpleasant looking little group that was so transparent to Zimmerman. No collection of people who are all waiting for the same thing are capable of holding a natural conversation. Even if the thing they are waiting for is only a taxi. No matter how communicative an evening has been, no matter how smoothly

275

the conversation has flowed, once both parties know that there could be a taxi at the door any minute, the conversation inevitably becomes stilted. And it is the same when you are waiting for women you have been told to take alive at all costs. Of course, Zimmerman did not know that that was what they were waiting for, but he knew they were waiting for something, and he presumed that whatever it was they were up to no good.

However, Zimmerman decided to ignore them. After all, he and his companions were onto something very big and the last thing he wanted to do was start drawing attention to himself. The men were probably waiting for an atom bomb or something to take behind the wire; but there was nothing that Zimmerman could do about it for the time being. Anyway, Zimmerman decided, if he was going to get shot at some point, which he reckoned was a pretty fair bet, he wanted to have a read of what happened to the Phantom and Judge Dread first.

To die with an easy mind is one thing; to die in the knowledge that the Phantom is still bound to the croc' with live snakes and the Judge appears to have inexplicably turned his back upon justice and made a pact with evil, is another.

## FORSAKEN

As with all flights, when the Perth plane came in, the people got off first. Zimmerman knew that it would be at least ten minutes before the baggage and freight would be taken off and that he would have to wait. He was interested to see that the four men stirred restlessly though. So, it was a person they were waiting for, Zimm deduced. Reception committee or execution squad? Zimm guessed, by the look of them and the bulges in their shoulders, that someone was in for a nasty touch-down.

People began to flow through the arrivals door. The thugs soon spotted their quarry, they moved as one man. The quarry, a woman, spotted them a moment later. There was clearly nothing that she could do. Zimm watched her, his blood quickening. She had a nice face but it was dull with terror. She seemed to be visibly sagging with exhaustion and the desperation of her condition. For Zimm, whose regular prescriptions from Doctor Goodtime had got him into the habit of visualizing things that were not there, she seemed to be disintegrating before his very eyes. It was as if her will to live was physically dripping out of her and collecting in a puddle at her feet.

Zimm felt absolutely awful. He had been a cornered animal himself and he knew that facing a gang of murderous foes, by whom you were totally outnumbered, was absolutely horrid. As the four goons surrounded her, Zimm knew that the Phantom would not have hesitated. He knew that the Phantom would, regardless of personal risk and the natural reluctance one feels to making a scene in a crowded airport, have *done* something. Dodging bullets and armed only with a luggage trolley and stand-up ashtray the Phantom would have sorted it out. Even the fact that he was at present in Central Africa tied to a croc' with live snakes would not have stopped him saving that girl. Zimmerman longed to get stuck in.

It was not fear that held him back – although taking on four armed thugs was fairly high on Zimmerman's list of things he didn't like doing – it was the wider situation. This new, together, danger tackling Zimmerman could see that he was involved in something potentially much bigger than the fate of just one person, no matter how nice a face she had. He mustn't compromise his Eco-mission . . . None of the others would get over the wire without him, and he would be no good dead, or in jail.

Oh well, he would have to leave the poor girl to her fate. Zimmerman knew that his treasured super-hero comics were going to make hollow reading after he had failed to save a damsel in distress.

# TERMINAL TERMINA?

'Don't make any sudden moves or noises, Ms Kelly,' said the lead thug. 'From what you already know of us, I presume that you can guess that we own this town. There is no one here to help you.'

Chrissy knew that he was right, suddenly she nearly fainted with exhaustion. The flight from her apartment with the door being smashed behind her seemed a century away; and now it was over, she was caught and was going to die, probably never even knowing what it had all been about.

'OK, kill me,' she said quietly.

'Please don't be so silly and melodramatic, Ms Kelly?' the thug said with the same smile as if he were greeting an old friend. 'We want you to come with us, that is all, to answer a few questions.'

Of course, reasoned Chrissy, they would need to know if she had told anyone of her suspicions besides Toole; if she had left any notes. Oh well, she was going to stay alive an hour or two longer. It didn't matter, she felt dead.

'Come along, then, Christine, we will show you to your car.' The four men closed around her. She stepped out of the puddle of her will to live and surrendered to her captors. As they led her out she began to weep quietly and copiously.


# A KNIGHT IN SHINY TROUSERS

It was not the spirit of the Phantom that forced Zimmerman to act, although he didn't take much persuasion. He decided to intervene on the girl's behalf because as the men turned around to lead her out he recognized one of the men they had encountered at the wire two nights previously. Not the one whose arm he had broken, the other one. This was proof that whoever the girl was, she was an enemy of whatever it was that lay behind the wire; possibly a much better informed enemy than Zimm and his companions were. Maybe she could shed light in the darkness. Anyway, it did not matter, he now knew she was definitely a comrade in arms and therefore Zimm could not desert her. That was one of the rules of war; you looked out for your brothers, or, in this case, sister.

Still, tough situation.

There were four of them, obviously armed and, Zimm had no doubt, virtually immune from prosecution in this little town that had become an outpost of the Moorcock empire. Besides this, he guessed their transport would be waiting just outside in the car park and once they were in that they were out of Zimmerman's reach.

Pausing only to grab his comics, which fortuitously slipped onto the carousel at that moment, Zimmerman sprinted out to the car park in order to get ahead of them. Four men surrounding a prisoner move fairly slowly and Zimmerman, of course, moved extremely quickly, and so he was out in the car park before Chrissy's tears had even begun to flow.

Anyone looking at him, knowing his intentions, would have thought Zimmerman a strange sort of saviour in his ancient shiny loon pants and his sweaty singlet. Which just goes to show that you should never judge a book by its cover or, for that matter, a knight by his trousers. After all, Superman wears red knickers, blue tights and knee-high booties.

## MEANWHILE EVERYBODY WAS GETTING CANCER

CD had accompanied Zimmerman to the airport but had elected to stay in the car. It was a beautiful day, the top was down and he was happy to soak up the rays rather than hang around in a crowded non-air-conditioned shed. Had he known a little more about the state of the ozone layer he might have felt a little differently and bolted for the shade, no matter how hot and sweaty it was.

Oh sure, CD, like everybody in the world, especially Australians, was aware that the layer was under pressure and that without it the sun might give you skin cancer. But it was so difficult to believe it. The sun looked the same as it had always done; it felt just as good; it had the same revitalizing powers it had always had and it still made all the girls look mega-sauce.

The problem with the ozone layer is it is such a tiny, thin, gossamer layer, like a sheet of very soft loo paper. The difference being that with loo paper, one notices its absence immediately, because you're staggering about with your trousers around your ankles looking for an old magazine to use instead. With the ozone layer you don't even notice it's gone. Not, that is, until they're hacking the malignant melanomas off you.

## ZIMM PICKS UP A GIRL

So CD sat in the car, in the car park, contentedly having his skin cells turned cancerous by the photo-power of the sun, wondering why Zimmerman, who was normally so cool and laid back; who normally motivated himself about the place in a manner that CD felt was rather reminiscent of his own street-cool lope (it wasn't), was sprinting towards him at such an astonishing speed. He was about to comment, but Zimmerman's manner cut him sort.

'Listen, get the engine running, and put it in gear, I've got to get a girl, OK, man? Now, once she's in the wheels, burn man, burn OK? Don't look back, don't stop on red, don't pick up hitch-hikers. Get her home, then dump the wheels. Dig?'

CD was about to protest, he understood Zimmerman's sexual frustrations, he sympathized with it, after all, he was not exactly getting any action himself, but he could not be part of abduction, no way. Zimmerman would simply have to take more cold showers.

Unfortunately CD was not in a position to say anything because Zimm was sprinting back towards the terminal building.

CD turned on the engine and put the car into first. Despite his reservations one's tendency with Zimmerman – especially this new, dynamic and, being honest, violent Zimmerman — was to do what he said.

Zimm arrived back just as the little party of thugs was emerging from the shed with their prey, in fact he nearly blundered into them. Under the circumstances there was little he could do other than confront them right there and then.

'Excuse me, Miss, but do you want to go with these men?' he said.

Chrissy did not reply, she already had Toole's death on her conscience, she did not want another. The leader of the group pushed Zimm and he took a step back.

'She's crying because she's glad to be home. Now piss off.'

'Shit man, if you cry like that coming to a dump like Bullens, you have low expectations in life, real low expectations,' said Zimm, sizing up the opposition. 'Imagine if she ever got to Disneyland, her head would just totally explode.'

The fellow in charge was about to punch Zimm out of the way when one of his companions spoke up.

'Mr Rourke, this is the bastard who broke Pete's arm, I think maybe we should take him too.'

'This guy did it?' said Mr Rourke. 'Now you said the man who did Pete was the hardest fellah you ever did encounter. Fact is, I reckon you said there was six of him. Now are you trying to tell me that this little scruffy piece of hippy shit here took you and Pete to the cleaners?'

Pete's hapless companion was spared further embarrassment because at this point Zimm reckoned that the four blokes were about as distracted as they were ever going to be. He drove his fist full into the face of Mr Rourke, knuckling his eyes and breaking his nose. Following through in fact, almost as part of the same movement, he brought up his right boot between the other front man's legs. He used all of his considerable force, wishing to be absolutely sure that with his first two blows he would halve the odds properly. In fact, he probably overdid it, cracking the man's pelvic bone, but it was a long time since Zimm had had bollocks himself and he had forgotten just how little force is required to be effective.

Nit-picking aside, Zimmerman was doing extremely well; the fight had been in progress for only just one second, and his second victim was already crumpling up. Chrissy was now guarded only from behind. Zimm pulled her forward.

'Across the car park,' he spoke urgently but without alarm, 'Red '66 F C Holden . . .'

He pushed her behind him and hurled himself at the other two guards, crashing both to the ground, one with each hand.

'Go!' he shouted, thanking heaven that Rachel had had the foresight to own a highly distinctive car.

As a journo, Chrissy had long since learnt to take her luck where she found it. She ran into the car park and glanced around wildly. Holden is the indigenous Australian car manufacturer and, being an American, Chrissy had no idea what the classic '66 FC looked like. On the other hand, there was clearly only one old car hanging out in that boom town car park. What's more, it was red, its engine was running and there was a strange, funny little man in sunglasses waving at her.

CD had watched the whole incident with fear and awe. Zimmerman had definitely been hiding his light under a bushel, and a ten foot, lead-lined concrete bushel at that. Zimm's despatch of the front two guys had been awesome. CD now understood that Zimmerman's motives must be honourable and that he wished CD to help him save a person in distress. He shouted and waved, and whilst Zimmerman wrestled with the two remaining thugs, Chrissy rushed across the car park and jumped in beside CD.

Pausing only to momentarily slightly adjust his shades and say, 'Hi, I'm CD and I will be your driver on this trip,' he headed for the exit at speed. He had never been involved in anything remotely as exciting as this before and he grabbed his opportunity to get the pose just right.

'Who the hell was that guy?' asked Chrissy, who was a pretty cool customer herself and had already regained her composure. 'Oh him,' said CD casually, 'yeah, he's one of the team.' It was magnificent posing. But then CD blew it by saying, 'and me, I am as well and what's more, he's my mate, yeah really, he's my mate, I know him.'

# WORLD OPPOSITION TO
# STARK UNITES

Everybody was beginning to be really scared now.

Zimmerman had still not returned. It had been two and a half hours since CD had sneaked Chrissy back to the Culboons' place, having first left the Holden well out of town. That meant a good four hours since the incident at the airport, and Zimmerman had not returned. What's more, the long wait had left plenty of time for Chrissy to explain her recent history. A history of murder; a history that included things like the CIA; a history that hinted at unseen and incomprehensibly colossal power – no wonder they were worried. Walter considered suggesting that they all try to centre themselves, in order to avoid becoming uptight. Unfortunately, under the circumstances, uptightness would only have been avoided by a full frontal lobotomy.

CD had enjoyed it at first. 'This is Chrissy,' he had announced dramatically. 'Zimmerman and I rescued her at the airport. One of the guys who was at the wire last night and three others were trying to take her away.'

The Culboons were hospitable souls and Chrissy was soon sat on the sofa with a beer and a vegamite sandwich. Walter asked her what the problem had been at the airport.

'They were going to kill me,' said Chrissy, with firm conviction. 'They had tracked me from the States, and they were going to kill me.'

'Are you sure man?' asked Walter. 'I mean, that is a very heavy presumption, "kill" is a kind of terminal word, you know? Maybe they were just going to scare you a bit.'

'They were definitely going to kill me,' replied Chrissy.

'Why?' asked Rachel spotting the most fruitful line of questioning.

'Because they think I know something about what they're up to.'

'And do you?' asked Rachel, anxious not to let Walter start.

'No,' Chrissy said and then added, 'do you?'

'Do we what?' asked Rachel.

'Know anything about what they're up to.'

'What who are up to?'

'I don't know.'

There was a pause as everyone realized that the situation was getting confusing.

'Now look here,' Mrs Culboon said, making everybody look. 'It seems that this lady has had trouble with the same bastards as shot at us last night. Now I don't know what that means in the city, but out here in the country it means you got a mate till proved otherwise. So, if Mr Culboon would be so good as to pay another visit to the refrigerator, perhaps we can exchange notes. Yes, I reckon that's about what we should do.'

They all had a beer and Walter explained to Chrissy the scant details of their progress to Bullens Creek.

'What you have to dig here, Chrissy, is that we are like environment orientated, you know? Like, we stand up for the earth, so when we found out that major fat cat bread-heads were forcing people off their land for no apparent reason –'

'By whom you mean Silvester Moorcock and Ocker Tyron, is that right?'

'Dig! Nail on the head time, right,' said Walter, amazed. 'Wow, that is uncanny man, I mean that is *weird!* Did you do that with telepathy or what? Is it a ley line thing? Like, how did you know that those two cats were doing stuff out here?'

'I read it in the newspaper,' replied Chrissy.

Walter was even more impressed.

'Man that is so *together!* That is *clear thinking* lady! Why didn't we think of that?'

'Well it's only become financial news in the last few days,' said Chrissy. 'This damn crash and depression thing has made any development into a story. Especially when it's a leisure complex. I guess you people have been onto this for longer than that?'

'True enough,' said Walter. 'I mean when our man CD here sussed the connection and we became hip to just how much trouble these dudes were going to, just in order to get hold of a bit of territory that weren't worth shit. Like, we thought we'd have a look . . .'

Rachel decided to take over at this point because, as always, it looked like it was going to take Walter a long time to say anything. She explained to Chrissy about the Nazi attack that had made them suspicious; about Aristos, and Moorcock denying his involvement with Tyron. She explained everything they knew, which was, of course, almost nothing, except that they had smelt rocket fuel and that security was strangely too tight for a hotel complex.

In return Chrissy explained the long and terrifying sequence of events that had led her to Bullens Creek airport and near death.

When she had finished there was near stunned silence. Even Mrs Culboon was lost for words, for a moment. Then inevitably she laughed.

'Well, Jes-us this is rich don't you think, Mr Culboon! Here's us thinking we're uncovering a bit of illegal mining or something and it turns out there is a full-on global conspiracy going on right where we used to shower and shit.'

It never crossed any of their minds to doubt the seriousness of Chrissy's conclusions, they accepted absolutely that Linda and Toole had been murdered and that only Zimmerman had saved Chrissy from the same fate. And where was Zimmerman?

# PRISONER OF STARK

Where Zimmerman was, was tied to a chair in a Portacabin on the Stark construction site. He faced both Sly and Tyron, neither of whom appeared inclined to be friendly. They had been extremely badly shaken by Zimm's little party at the airport, especially when, after a telephone consultation with Durf, they realized that they had lost the journalist. A journalist who had already tried to alert the CIA to their activities and who knew all about the murder of Linda Reeve.

'Temporarily lost,' asserted Ocker Tyron, who was pacing about the room in the manner made popular by British actors playing Nazi officers in fifties films.

Tyron and Sly had not been having an easy morning in the first place. They had been in the middle of a fairly epic row when security had come through with the bad news.

## THE PROBLEMS AND THE ETHICS OF PREPARING FOR DOMESDAY

'Listen, Tyron, you're talking and acting like the stupid big-headed wanker that you are,' Sly had snapped, making, it has to be said, very little effort at a conciliatory manner.

'Rome wasn't built in a day and a whole new world wasn't either,' he continued. 'I am preparing the site as quickly as is humanly possible and your coming up here and throwing your weight around is not going to speed anything up.'

But Tyron had his own problems, certainly enough of them to make anyone act like a stupid big-headed wanker, even if they were not naturally predisposed to do so, which Tyron was.

'You want to know what I've got in my garage, Moorcock?' he shouted. 'I'll tell you. I've got seven enormous boxes which contain the components of a processing plant that will extract water from perma-frost to a geo-depth of one kilometre. There is no room for my fucking cars . . .'

Sly could not believe it, he had hundreds of men working around the clock on a construction project the speed and size of which defied imagination – and this idiot was talking about cars!

'Listen, I have stuff to do, OK?' Sly said. 'If you want to talk junk, go to one of your stupid mother's dumb jumble sales.'

Tyron's lid came off, he was not about to have his mother's name taken in vain by anyone.

'You leave my mother out of this or I'll bust your fucking head, Moorcock,' he said in his best boardroom manner.

'Sure, I'll leave her out of it,' said Sly, adding viciously, 'after all, that's what you'll be doing when the shit hits the fan. Isn't that right? Bye bye Mumsy.'

Sly had hit a very major nerve. Like all members of the Stark consortium, Sly included, Tyron had spent not a little time in the past few months pondering the subject of life and death; and more importantly on whom should he confer the former and to whom should he leave the latter. One thing was for sure, as Sly had shrewdly guessed, Mumsy was fucked. Tyron declined to discuss his mother further and returned to the subject of his garage.

'Listen I'm here to discuss distribution, or more importantly, the lack of it. The reason my garage contains a space-age artesian well, is because I have managed to completely cover a four hundred acre site with stuff that you are supposed to be taking delivery of and installing! I have a two hundred grand Ferrari standing in the street for Christ's sake! The birds are crapping on a two hundred grand Ferrari! My wife has to park by the public pavement. You have got my wife walking the streets, Moorcock!'

Before Sly had a moment to argue that the Domesday Group's predictions were now so fore-shortened and the demands of Stark so urgent that he was being asked to perform a near impossible task, the phone rang and they were informed of the screw up at the airport. They had lost the girl, but had captured her rescuer and had him held in the Security cabin.

Sly had hoped to lose Tyron before trying to deal with this new crisis, but to no avail. Tyron had nothing to do and was a born interferer; he was one of those people who are incapable of believing that anyone else could possibly do anything as well as he. Had he visited Van Gogh in his studio Tyron would have simply itched to grab the brush and say, 'Oh for God's sake let *me* do it'. One of the reasons Tyron had had no kids was that he could not believe that something which he so manifestly could not do was worth doing.

And so they both boarded a helicopter for the short flight across the construction site in order to go and interview their captive. Actually they could have driven the distance more conveniently but years of incredible riches had led them both to always instinctively take the most expensive option in any situation.

## TRAPPED IN THE LION'S PORTACABIN

On entering the room they dismissed the guards who had been standing nervously around a severely trussed and bound Zimmerman ever since his arrival. The guards hadn't known who he was, or what he wanted, but they knew him to be dangerous. He had, after all, hospitalized three of their colleagues (if you included Pete with the broken arm) and it had taken the armed intervention of the Bullens Creek Police to bring him in. This long-hair with the slightly greying beard was the hardest case that any of the cocky little security figures had ever come across and when Sly summarily dismissed them they were more than happy to get him off their hands.

'Out! All of you. The Colonel will keep an eye on the prisoner,' Sly shouted – not because he was a natural shouter, he wasn't really, but they were, after all in the middle of an enormous building site cushioned from it only by a flimsy Portacabin. The noise was fairly horrendous.

'Colonel' Du Pont was the head of on-site security. His rank was self-conferred and was a commission in the world army of arrogant macho pricks. He was an unpleasant, officious bully of a man. He had taken up bullying as a profession partly because of his nose – it was a whopper, made gross by the pitted scars of countless failed experiments in plastic surgery. The terrible complex of impotent, bitter rage that his conk gave him had made Du Pont take up bullying for a living.

He had a large staff of lesser thugs – with lesser noses – but he was the only goon to have been indoctrinated into Stark. The brave new future that Stark would create was to be self-regulating. The last thing those involved wanted was anyone bringing along a private army.

Du Pont stood behind Zimmerman whilst Sly addressed him and Tyron paced about.

Zimmerman was gashed, bruised and bound but he did not in any way cut a sad figure. There was a latent strength and dignity about this cornered animal that made him appear like a rather noble early Christian martyr or something similar – until he opened his mouth that is.

'Oh man, I mean, what is the point, for sure, you know, I mean what *is* the point right? Like, all this tying up stuff and bashing in the face scene is a very long way from being cool, you dig? I mean, sure I know I totalled a couple of your guys and like, I'm sorry, but you know? I mean they were hassling the chick right? Like four goons hassling a chick is –'

'Shut the fuck up, you stupid fool,' barked Sly, who was very disturbed indeed to find that the mysterious hippy was the same one who had eaten his burger at Facefull's revolting restaurant. Was there some kind of shadowy conspiracy on their tail? Hippies? Financial journalists? Beautiful girls, what the hell was going on?

290

'Who sent you? Who pays you? Who are you and how long have you been working with that girl you saved?' said Sly, trying not to appear scared in front of Tyron.

Zimmerman saw no reason or profit in lying.

'I just met the chick at the airport, right. I don't work for anyone, no one pays me, I'm just a concerned dude, right? You know, social responsibility, dig?'

In fact neither Sly nor Tyron dug very clearly. Of course they both knew the term 'social responsibility' but it held very little meaning for either of them.

'It's like we told you at that chicken shit burger disaster area,' continued Zimmerman; who despite his disadvantaged position, still felt that the onus of explanation lay with him.

'We're green terrorists. Ever since we heard you sicking those Nazis on our Ab' friends, we've been wondering what goes down.'

Sly shot an angry glance at Tyron, who came as close as he was capable to coming of blushing – which wasn't very close.

'What *does* go down here, by the way?' asked Zimmerman curiously.

'Like I told you, you interfering bastard, we're building hotels. Now where are your –' Sly was nervous and angry, but not half as much as he was about to become.

'Oh come *on* man, I mean like, for sure, you know? I mean, do I look like I've had my brains removed man? Do I look like some kind of space case, lobotomized air-head man?' Zimmerman asked.

It was a stupid question.

'Yes,' interjected Tyron. 'Now what do you know?'

'I know you ain't building nothing but trouble here, man, big trouble. Like you got it all pretty covered man but the chopper your goons brought me from Bullens in was close to the ground, like real low man. Man, I was with the fighting forty-third in 'Nam for five years. I know a launch site when I see one, and I seen a big one man! One mother-of-a-fucking enormous launch site. Silos, towers, you got it all! That's the first time I ever heard of a hotel with enough fire-power to take out the whole of South-East Asia.'

Sly and Tyron stared at the apparition in the chair as if their nemesis had just risen up out of the floor and stuffed a pie in their face. Sly nearly shot him dead there and then.

Of course Zimmerman was aware that by exposing so much of what he knew and what he had guessed, he was basically asking to be killed. But he reasoned correctly that whatever it was they were planning, he was in far too deep for them to trust him alive anyway. Therefore his best bet was to make himself appear dangerous. That way, they would be all the more anxious to find his companions and hence be forced to keep him alive to help them.

'Where are the others, the ones who were with you last night on the wire?' Sly asked, confirming Zimmerman's theory.

'There were no others, man,' he replied, 'your goons were so shit scared, I reckon they just must have multiplied me up a few times.'

'Don't crap me, mate!' Sly shouted, making each word sound like an individual and very special threat. 'Or I'll have your bollocks,' he added, making, in Zimmerman's case, no threat at all.

'I doubt it, man,' said Zimm, 'you'd have to go back to 'Nam for a start and then you'd have to find the right tree, OK? Which would be incredibly difficult, and even then man, like even if you did all that, I really don't think they'll still be there.'

Sly didn't follow any of this and so decided to get back to the interrogation. 'There were four of you at the restaurant; you, the other hippy, the pratt in shades and a girl. The one who came prying around, asking questions.'

Tyron stared at Sly angrily.

'Questions?' he barked, 'I thought you said that nobody had been asking questions? I specifically asked you if anybody had been asking questions and you said that nobody had . . .'

'Yeah, well, if you hadn't got your useless pig of a brother to drag in a bunch of incompetent Nazis then nobody would have been asking any questions in the first place, would they?'

'That's not the point, Moorcock. I specifically asked you –'

'Guys, guys, guys, guys, guys, guys, *guys*,' Zimmerman pleaded. 'You know, you two really have to talk this thing out. You have a definite confrontation problem. You need to discuss your frustrations about each other honestly in the presence of a disinterested third party. But excuse me if I don't volunteer. Like, these ropes are cutting into me so can we maybe put the family row on ice for a while, right? You know?'

Tyron strode across the room and punched the defenceless Zimmerman in the face.

'Tell us where your friends are right now!'

'Leave that kind of thing out of it, all right Tyron. We're not savages,' Sly admonished.

'Maybe we are, maybe we aren't,' Tyron replied, nursing his grazed knuckles. 'But this is a fight for survival, either way; the law of the jungle, and it seems that there are people out there who may know plenty. We need to find out who they are.'

'Well I ain't going to tell you, man! Like you know, I'm a peaceable soul but I don't reckon I'd tell you fellahs if your car was on fire. So fuck off!' Clearly lines were being drawn in this discussion and Tyron and Zimmerman stood pretty resolutely on different sides. Tyron was about to hit Zimmerman again. Sly asked him to step outside for a moment.

## SUCCESS BY A NOSE

Zimmerman was left alone with Colonel Du Pont.

'My name is Colonel Du Pont,' said Colonel Du Pont, who was also acting like a Nazi officer in a film. 'Now you will please tell me the names and whereabouts of your fellow conspirators. Or . . .' and there was a tiny pause for maximum effect – which was minimal effect on Zimmerman because anyone who had spent fifteen years living with Walter was used to pauses. 'Or . . . I shall be obliged to inflict upon you pain beyond belief. Beyond your wildest dreams . . .'

Whether or not Du Pont would have been capable of this is a moot point. After all, a man who has seen his own testicles hanging from a tree knows a fair bit about pain. Plus, somebody who had done as many different and dangerous drugs as Zimmerman would, in his time, have had some pretty wild dreams.

Anyway, Zimm was left with no time to debate this point with Du Pont, because unexpectedly a plan of action presented itself.

Du Pont had been making a pretty major issue out of strutting and posturing in front of Zimmerman. This was because recently most of his time had been spent working out guard rosters and he was relishing the chance to pretend that he really was in the Gestapo. To this end, at the end of his little promise about pain, Du Pont had thrust his face to within an inch of the bound Zimmerman's. He did this because he felt it was intimidating and impressive. It gave him the opportunity to spit his words directly into Zimm's face, and hence gain for them the maximum effect.

This had been his mistake, for in a sudden and wholly surprising move (to both of them) Zimm had pushed his own face forward and grabbed Du Pont's substantial nose firmly between his teeth. Understandably Du Pont was rather shocked, momentarily too shocked to utter, a fact which gave Zimmerman a chance to speak (with difficulty) a few well chosen words.

'Listen, creep mother-fucker!' he spoke up Du Pont's nose. 'I'm gonna bite it off I swear. I truly swear by the Lord I'll bite it off if you squeak man, if you squeak at all.'

Zimmerman was not an easy man to follow at the best of times, and speaking with a nose in his mouth obviously did not make his speech patterns any clearer. However, Du Pont could not help but be impressed by the extremely threatening tone Zimm was employing.

'I swear I will bite it off if you squeak man!' Zimm reiterated. To demonstrate his point he bit hard and Du Pont could feel the skin break and the bone and cartilage creak. It may not seem the most awesome threat in the world, 'don't move or I'll bite your nose off', but in fact, if one thinks about it, as Du Pont was being forced to do, it's actually a pretty heavy deal. The pain and disfigurement would be considerable to say the least.

Du Pont made an effort, he was after all a security officer. His hand moved to the pistol hanging at his side. Instantly Zimmerman twisted his head right down to the left, nearly breaking Du Pont's neck but keeping an ever firmer grip on his honker.

'Don't fuck with me, man,' Zimmerman spat and Du Pont could feel Zimm's saliva running down over his upper lip, adding nausea to the list of Du Pont's ailments. 'Now don't *fuck* with me!' mad Zimm repeated. And with horrible force spun his head from his left shoulder right over to his right shoulder, and then back again, taking Du Pont's nose, head and indeed whole body with him. Inevitably the nose broke and Du Pont nearly fainted with pain. Zimm spoke quickly.

'It's broke but you still got it! Man, you make a squeak I swear I'll be crapping it out with what's left of my breakfast! Now you untie me, man, you untie me or else I'll bite off your nose and suck out your eyes!!!'

Mad Zimmerman was an intimidating force indeed when he was being mad. In fact what with Zimm's unusual speech impediment, and the considerable noise coming from the building site, Du Pont was not really following the finer points of Zimm's monologue. But it was quite clear to him what Zimm must want, and how best to end the terrible pain.

Du Pont's salt tears ran into Zimm's mouth as Du Pont reached behind Zimm in a strange embrace and fumbled blindly with the knots. They came away and Zimmerman's arms were free. He took Du Pont's gun and released his nose, spitting as he did it and grabbing a quick gargle from the jug on the table – these are, after all, paranoid times.

Then with one deft little chop of his hand he knocked Du Pont unconscious and headed for the window, pausing only to pick up the Judge Dread and Phantom comics that had been left on the desk by the guards who brought him from the airport.

# DAVID AND GOLIATH

The old biblical story of David and Goliath, in which we are reliably informed a plucky young lad bested a great big bully, is a story fraught with moral contradictions. The principal contradiction being that David only achieved his famous victory by means of superior weapons technology. His use of a sling shot (an early version of the Stinger, the Exocet and the Cruise) allowed him to floor Goliath before the big fellow even got close. The moral weight traditionally ascribed to David's victory establishes a fairly dangerous precedent. For instance, when a mere handful of British Empire troops were able to slaughter thousands of their spear-carrying opponents by means of the Gatling Gun, was it a David and Goliath situation? When a few hundred USAF flyers attempted to 'bomb Cambodia back into the Stone Age' were they plucky little Davids using wit and cunning to overcome the Goliath that was the population of Cambodia? In fact Goliath was no Goliath at all but a pathetic, muscle-bound Neanderthal throwback. An elephant charging a bazooka.

Now *if* in that bible story, David, a small boy in a loincloth – which is the biblical version of wandering around in your underpants – had been facing a Goliath who was a multi-headed, multinational monster, richer and more powerful than any other force on earth. A monster bent on committing craven and wicked acts in the final seconds before the domesday clock strikes twelve and the dark midnight of ecological oblivion cloaks all life on earth. If that had been what David had been up against, the trick with the sling shot might have cut a little more ice.

# DAVID

As Zimmerman hopped it out of the window, his friends, old and new, were hopping it out of the Culboons' place. It was beginning to seem to Chrissy as if she had been scampering about in terror all her life.

They had decided that after Zimm had been missing for five hours, they would take a calculated risk. They would ring the police.

'After all,' Rachel had said, 'maybe he just got busted, I mean arrested . . .' Even in this moment of crisis Rachel fiercely resisted the slow, insidious encroachment that Walter's language was making on her brain. 'It would have been a pretty serious disturbance up at the airport. Perhaps he's just sitting in a cell waiting to get done for disturbing the peace.'

'Listen, Rachel, I'm telling you,' insisted Chrissy, 'the guys Zimmerman was mixing it with run the world. When they have a problem they are not going to call the local cops.'

'Maybe he's in hospital,' suggested CD.

'Sure. Propped up in bed with a bunch of flowers signed love from the world's billionaires,' said Chrissy to Mrs Culboon's laughter. 'They've got him, I'm telling you, they've got him.'

'Well, if they have got him,' said Mr Culboon, sucking on his pipe, 'they're going to be coming after us pretty soon. I reckon Zimm won't tell them nothing but we can't lie low for ever.'

'They know us blacks were involved,' added Mrs Culboon. 'Why there ain't no more than fifty of us in the town, won't take them long to get here.'

'Exactly,' said Mr Culboon, 'we have to fuck off mates. Somewhere to think.' It was at this point that they decided to ring the police.

'I mean, man, if they're going to get on us anyway, we might as well at least check that nobody knows where he is,' said Walter. 'You know he could be dead or dying or . . . or maybe he just had a little victory celebration after the fight and got done for tooting on a doobie.'

Unfortunately Chrissy was right. The police denied all knowledge of the airport incident, which meant for sure that Zimm was being held by the shadowy mega-corporation. Also it meant that the police were bought . . . 'And it means that that call you've just made, Mr Culboon,' said Chrissy, 'is being traced as we speak.'

'OK let's split,' said Walter.

And so it was that the entire world opposition to the Stark Consortium was splitting at once. Zimmerman was climbing out of the window of Du Pont's office. Rachel, CD, Walter, the Culboons and Chrissy were running out of the back door of the Culboons' house. They loaded up the old station wagon with what food they could, also some spare clothes and the guns and grenades that Zimmerman had taken from the guards at the perimeter fence, and drove out of town.

## GOLIATH

Tyron and Sly stood in the burning sun on the steps of Du Pont's Portacabin, shouting to make themselves heard above the noise. Although as it happens they probably would have both been shouting anyway because they were so furious with each other.

Sly strongly objected to Tyron's interfering and his casual violence. Tyron objected to what he saw as a lack of urgency in Sly's manner. After all, there appeared to be a situation developing where it was possible that a carefully orchestrated plan of infiltration was being carried out against them. Who could tell how far it had got already.

'We have absolutely no idea how big this thing is,' Tyron yelled, 'maybe it's the Russians! Those Kremlin Ayotollahs would give their balls for a piece of what we have going here!'

'For God's sake, Tyron, don't be such a dickhead!' Sly shouted back. All around them the roar of Stark's ghastly creation seemed to swell to match their mood. 'We've run a full background make on the KGB, the OKVD, the ABC and XY fucking Z for all I know!' Sly continued. 'Nothing. Nobody, has a hint of what's going on here. We have an eye in every intelligence agency there is. We pay for half of them for Christ's sake! Durf's on the case, he says there isn't a major criminal, government or military establishment that we aren't monitoring. We are too big to touch.'

'So who's running Rambo in there?' Tyron jerked his thumb towards the door of the Portacabin.

'No one's running him! I'm telling you, Tyron. I've met them, they're kids and ageing hippies; greenies. They have not got the faintest idea what's going on. They're just troublemakers taking a long punt on a short idea because of your stupid Nazi pogrom. Even this journalist from the States doesn't know what she's discovered. We have that from the report on what she told Toole. There is absolutely no reason to panic, and certainly no reason to go around slapping hippies.'

'Know nothing!' shouted Tyron, 'know nothing!! Christ that damn hippy I just slapped had identified the world's six biggest rocket silos! How much does he have to know?'

'Yes, well he's in our hands isn't he? All we have to do is to try to persuade him to tell us where his friends are and then we'll have all of them, won't we? And let's try to do it peacefully, eh?'

They re-entered the office to find Du Pont's prostrate form stretched out on the floor looking like the victim of some terrible sexual liaison . . .

'Oh man, we went all the way, just about bit off each other's noses and everything.'

Whatever had happened, the prisoner was gone.

## COUNCIL OF WAR

The little EcoAction team got out of the Culboon's nice new house about ten minutes ahead of the horrible criminal squad who broke in and took the place to pieces, finding nothing but a note left by Mrs Culboon saying:

Dear Bad Fellahs, fuck you. PS could you leave the back door slightly ajar for the cat.

As it happened, by the time the leader of the search squad was presented with this note by a subordinate, the back door had already been reduced to match-wood.

Mr and Mrs Culboon knew a little place that they called their holiday home. It was about thirty kilometres in the opposite direction from the construction site; a tiny cave squeezed into the side of one of the piss-poor little hills that ringed the Bullens Creek area.

Quite a few Aboriginals, especially country ones, set a great deal of store by meditation, or dreaming, or just sitting staring into space, depending on individual mood, and the little cave in the hills was where the Culboons did their bit of drifting.

'Reckon we've sat here dreaming and peaceful many a time, haven't we, Mr Culboon?' said Mrs Culboon.

'Reckon so,' replied her husband with a tinge of sadness.

'It'll make a nice change to sit here shitting ourselves in terror instead,' she shrieked, and everybody laughed with her.

'OK, you know, man,' said Walter calling things to order. 'It is time to assemble our thoughts; it is time to get it together man; it is time to make some kind of plan, dig?'

Of course they all dug very well.

'The problem as I see it, you know? Right? Is that it is comparatively easy to dig the plan that we have to make a plan. It is less simple to dig the actual plan. I mean in order to do that, we have to *have* a plan, which we don't. Dig?'

'Of course we don't,' said Rachel, 'but we haven't had a plan from the beginning, have we? We've just followed our noses. And that's all we can do now. It's obvious that we have to help Zimmerman. We have to find a way through that wire and help him.'

'I'm really sorry to be so negative,' Chrissy replied, 'but from my experience of these people, my guardian angel will be beyond hope by now. The guys he took on are more than a police force, or an army, or a government even. They're money, dirty money, they are everything and they own everything, and that, I'm afraid, includes Mr Zimmerman.'

'They don't own Zimmerman, lady,' said Walter. 'He's not a part of their world, he doesn't even live on it. He got in a space rocket and left the minute he got back from 'Nam.'

'Anyway,' Rachel asked slightly resentfully, 'what do you suggest we do then?'

Rachel could not avoid thinking that things hadn't been so bleak before Chrissy had turned up.

'I don't know,' said Chrissy. 'I just don't know. We still don't have a clue of what it is we're really up against. Even if there was someone in authority that we could trust, we actually have nothing whatsoever to tell them. I suppose you're right, Rachel, we will have to go in. On the million to one chance that instead of getting our butts shot off, we discover what they are up to.'

'Hey, Chrissy, you should curb it with the blind optimism,' CD said. 'We don't want to jinx ourselves.'

Mrs Culboon, of course, laughed. Nobody else did much.

'Well, you know, I guess we should not, like, *all* get down on it, right?' said Walter. 'Because, like, if Chrissy is right and whoever goes over that fence comes out dead, I for one would like to think that maybe somebody was left around to like try and tell the tale, and also feed the Culboons' cat. I'm serious you know? I see no reason why like the cat should have to collect the bummer that we have walked into.'

'If somebody's going to try and eventually alert some form of authority,' said Rachel, 'it should be Chrissy. She's got a real job and credit cards and everything. What are the rest of us? Just a bunch of no-goods. Chrissy should stay.'

Chrissy had, in the previous forty-eight hours, lied and robbed her way across the world, in the process of cheating death many times. Suddenly she felt very tired.

'Sounds good to me,' she said. 'I ain't the volunteering kind.'

'That's right,' said Mrs Culboon, 'Chrissy's taken most of the shit so far, and she's best qualified to speak up for our corpses. She should stay here. I guess she's used up a heap of luck, what with stealing and pretending to smuggle drugs.' Mrs Culboon laughed. She had greatly enjoyed Chrissy's account of her adventures, told during the futile wait for Zimmerman.

'I think Mr and Mrs Culboon should stay too, you know?' Walter said. 'Mr Culboon's head man of a community. A lot of liberal politico's dig that sort of thing and they're the only ones who are going to listen to anything as weird as what we've got.'

'*Mr* Culboon's head man, I'm not,' said Mrs Culboon. 'I'm sticking with you, Walter. Shit, I want to know what the hell they're doing to our old homestead.'

And so it was decided. Walter, Rachel, CD and Mrs Culboon would try to get inside the wire with the twin aims of trying to find Zimmerman, and of trying to find out what was going on. Meanwhile, Chrissy and Mr Culboon would remain holed up at the holiday home.

Mr Culboon went to the back of the station-wagon and unloaded the guns. 'You know how to use these things?' he asked the four newly commissioned commandos. 'Because I've shot various rifles in my time,' he continued and, shouldering one of the semi-automatic rifles, loosed off a couple of rounds. He was knocked off his feet by the kick-back.

'Yes, just as I thought,' he said. 'It's much the same but you have to hold it a bit more firmly.'

## TAKING COVER

The years slipped away from Zimmerman. It was the early seventies again and he was just the same as he had been then, except of course that he didn't grow his bollocks back. But, apart from that, he was the same: a cunning, ruthless, hunted man, scared and exhilarated at the same time. He lay on the roof of the Portacabin, prostrate along the guttering, listening to the furious altercation below him.

'We should have shot the bastard!!' yelled Tyron. 'We should certainly shoot you!' he added, glaring at the unfortunate Du Pont who looked a sorry sight with his huge conk turned almost sideways.

'I just hope it rains Du Pont,' Tyron continued, 'because the way the guy left that trunk of yours, you're going to drown.'

'Leave him alone. Do you want to have to indoctrine a new security chief into Stark? What happened to Du Pont could have happened to anyone.' Even Du Pont, who was grateful for Sly's spirited defence, had to privately concede that this was pushing it a bit. The chances of getting your nose half bitten off by a securely bound hippy seemed pretty slim.

'Look, he can't have gone far,' declared Sly nervously, 'and he can't get out of the compound. The whole thing's covered by cameras, and it's open country all the way to the wire. We've got fifteen choppers for Christ sake, he can't move.'

Zimmerman had actually already presumed all this for himself, which of course was why he hadn't attempted to move. It was fairly audacious of him to stay on top of the Portacabin, but a calculated risk. A favourite method of hiding in the jungle had simply been to stand stock still and pretend to be a tree. Any searcher will look under hedges and behind rocks; few will study the open spaces very carefully, or, for that matter, the roofs of the prisons from which a person is supposed to be fleeing for his or her life. This was the reason that Zimmerman elected to stay where he was.

'Du Pont,' snapped Sly, 'I want every man on this, and I want more brought in. At the moment he is a maximum of half a kilometre away; a minimum of a few yards.'

Zimmerman went slightly cold. This bastard was a bit too clever for his liking.

'Get on it, take the place apart, fanning out from around this Portacabin,' Sly continued. And Zimmerman hoped that Du Pont would not take this to mean upwards as well as outwards.

If he survived the next fifteen minutes, Zimmerman reckoned he was safe. He then resolved to stay exactly where he was for quite a while, long enough for them to become worried and confused. Long enough for them to begin to wonder whether he had got out after all.

Fifteen minutes later Du Pont, Tyron and Sly were gone. Zimmerman smiled to himself. He was in the shadow of the heating flue and considered it extremely unlikely that he would be spotted from the air. He was pretty safe for the time being. He curled up in the gutter with his *Phantom* comic. He had plenty of time and he intended to luxuriate over every page; digging all of the pictures in detail. Quite often there were little jokes and bits of drama in the drawings that it was easy to miss if you skimmed through. What's more, after the Phantom, he also had two new *Judge Dreads*, he reckoned it could be a pretty good day. All he hoped was that CD had got the woman away and that they all had the sense to stay put.


## THE BRIGHT LIGHTS OF A DARK INTENT

Zimmerman of course hoped in vain. For as the sun set, in all its blazing desert glory, and as the billions of volts of Moorcock lighting came on, almost eclipsing it, the little EcoAction commando unit moved out.

The first major clash of the titans was at hand, for the two armies were approaching each other. Du Pont's men, dogs, trucks and helicopters were heading for the wire from within, spreading ever outwards, looking for Zimmerman.

Meanwhile, from the opposite direction, outside the wire, the resistance forces were rushing to their fate; a huge peace freak, a lovesick dickhead, a born again environmentalist and a middle-aged woman with a degree in sarcasm. The last of these was driving and she was having some difficulty, because they had elected to travel without lights in an effort to sneak up on their quarry.

'That'll fox 'em right enough,' said Mrs Culboon, pursuing

her preferred line of humour. 'If we turn the lights off they'll *never* see us. After all, they only rule the world.'

Progress was being rendered more than unusually difficult by the weaving, flickering lights on the horizon. The distant sky was a blaze of eerie, unnatural colour. This turned the pitted, wind shaped desert floor into a mass of treacherous shadows, any one of which could be deep enough to snap a twenty-five-year-old axle. Even more disconcerting was that occasionally one of the shadows turned out to weigh ten stone and be capable of jumping sixteen feet. It was a tense situation, Rachel's car was a soft top and they had visions of being joined from above by a kangaroo.

'There just isn't room back here,' CD said, 'it will have to sit in the front on your lap, Walter.'

They abandoned the car about a kilometre from the perimeter wire and, carrying their guns and a set of wire clippers, began to slowly approach the scene of what they realized could be their destruction. They recalled all too vividly the trigger-happy encounter on their previous visit to the wire. This time there would be no Zimmerman to miraculously save them. In fact, it seemed, there was a good chance that Zimmerman was already dead. The things they had learnt from the new comrade, Chrissy, had been shocking and fearful. Billionaires plotting together; ruthlessly slaughtering anyone who got on their trail. They crept up to the brightly lit wire with an almost fatalistic detachment.

'Oh *man*!' whispered Walter, pointing. 'Closed circuit TV in the desert! These people are unnecessarily paranoid.'

He had spotted a camera mounted high on a pole. It was turning slowly towards them. That was it, he, CD and Rachel thought. The moment it focussed on them the game was up.

'The thing probably has a death ray fitted as standard,' Walter whined.

Mrs Culboon raised the night-sighted rifle that she was carrying and destroyed the camera with a single shot. There was a surprised silence — silence that is, apart from the humming din emanating from the centre of the construction site.

'Well done, Mrs Culboon,' said CD after a pause, 'I was thinking of doing that myself.'

'Hey, Mrs Culboon, I was never hip to the fact that you could shoot,' said Walter, excited and impressed.

'Mr Culboon hates the fact that I can out shoot him every time so I try not to rub it in,' Mrs Culboon laughed modestly. And there was momentary elation at their minor victory until Rachel reintroduced a touch of realism.

'I reckon pretty soon somebody will be beginning to wonder why a screen's gone dark and start thinking about looking into it,' she reminded everybody. 'So I think we should make the most of our small advantage.'

'Dig,' said Walter.

They cut the wire, which was not electrified. This had been a deliberate decision on Sly's part, the last thing he wanted was a load of barbecued kangaroos drawing the unwelcome attention of animal lovers.

For a moment the scared little group stood on the outside, staring at the hole that they had made. Then, with hearts beating nineteen-to-the-dozen, and bowels struggling to maintain some semblance of control over the situation, they climbed through.

At first they had it very easy. They walked for an hour, covering maybe four kilometres and did not see one truck, one guard or one helicopter. Of course they didn't realize it but this was because the security people were not worrying about intruders that night. In fact, nobody had even noticed the dead camera that Mrs Culboon had destroyed. They were all looking for Zimmerman, every single one of them. The four intrepid Eco-commandos had not yet reached the exapanding area covered by the search, but they soon would.

'Well, you know, man,' said Walter, lazily rolling a cigarette as he sauntered along, his hunched lope growing looser and more relaxed with every step. 'I guess maybe the chick Chrissy has lived too long in the US of A. I guess maybe, like a few Yankees I've met, her paranoia dial is set to double ape-shit. I make this observation because we have been strolling in the lion's den so to speak for the space of five whole cigarettes now and, as I hope you have noticed, we are by no means dead.'

'Yeah,' added CD. 'You know, if I'd known that terrorist infiltration was going to be as easy as this I would have taken it up long ago. Don't you think, Rachel, I mean, we could have skipped all those peace bazaars and stuff and just strolled into the White House and kidnapped the President.'

'Listen you two idiots,' Rachel snapped, causing CD to shiver with frustrated urgings. Such was his monumental desire for a passionate encounter with Rachel that CD relished any display of emotion towards him on her part, even when it was derogatory. He would have got a hard on if she'd tattooed 'what a wanker' on his forehead while he was asleep.

'I love it when you're bitching,' he observed irritatingly.

'Colin *please* try to be less pathetic,' said Rachel, causing tense little sparks of suppressed sauciness to pitter patter up and down CD's trousers. 'You're both being pathetic,' she continued. 'We haven't done anything yet, we haven't found anything out, we haven't rescued Zimmerman, in fact we haven't started. Still being alive is the absolute minimum we could have achieved. So don't be so bloody smug.'

'Ha ha, I reckon Rachel told you boys,' said Mrs Culboon, and even with the ever present industrial roar in the distance her voice could still shatter granite. 'Here's you two congratulating yourselves like we've saved the world and all we've done is take a walk under the stars.'

'All I'm saying, man, is that maybe the people we're up against are not such a terminal bummer as we had imagined, dig? All I'm saying,' insisted Walter, 'is that maybe these people aren't as big as they'd like to think they are, maybe they ain't so tough and all powerful, and maybe we're a match for them. Is that so dumb?'

And Walter's question was answered because shortly after he had made this monumentally optimistic observation, they came to the edge of a small ridge in the land and the full and majestic scale of their opponent was revealed to them in all its roaring, burning, terrible beauty.

They had been climbing very gently since crossing the wire and were now crossing the little undulating hills which had once ringed the Culboons' quiet, dingy existence and now ringed the central axis of the Stark conspiracy. From where they now stood, the desert floor swept down into a very shallow valley, a valley which was in fact really little more than a dip in the vast, flat desert.

In the middle of this place, a place of ancient peace; a place which had slept almost undisturbed since the waters of prehistory subsided: a place untouched by human hand, save for those few souls who had scratched out a meagre living on its barren surface. In the midst of all this, boring deep and spreading wide, lay the Stark construction site. Hissing, steaming and glaring into the still desert night.

It wasn't that the area covered was particularly huge, it was more the intensity of the activity that struck the little group of conspirators dumb. Stretched out below them were six burning bright areas of weaving lights and towering cranes – or at least they seemed like cranes, perhaps they were towers of some kind. These hellish patches on the desert floor were arranged not in a circle but in an asymmetric, almost haphazard way, like great fluorescent lilies spread across a pond. From each of these six places came constant blasts and explosions; first an eerie silent flash and then, moments later, a dull crump that could be felt deep in the belly. The exploding lilies were connected by snakes of orange light, along which travelled other lights, some white, some red. Above it all hovered helicopters throwing their own beams downwards in a seemingly futile effort to add to the orgy of illumination. All light soon blended and was lost in the great and terrible glow. A glow that had a strange, translucent quality, induced by the clouds of dust and steam that were constantly being thrust upwards into the shuddering air.

It was like Hell's kitchen on the day that all seven deadly sins had come to dinner and the Devil was trying to do a complex Taiwanese banquet that he'd never attempted before. In silence they began to descend down the long, shallow, featureless slope. It took a lot to shut up CD and Mrs Culboon, but for once neither of them had anything to say. They were all thinking much the same thing; which was that any group of people who could organize the Devil's kitchen that they were now approaching, could probably handle four ecologically concerned individuals.

'Still think that Chrissy's paranoid, Walter?' said Rachel.

A moment later the little group finally met up with the outer limits of the expanding search for Zimmerman. The phoney war was over. It all seemed to happen at once. Above the general roar, the gutteral rat-a-tat-tat of a helicopter emerged as a single and definitive sound; and it was getting louder. Soon they could see it, in the distance, its search-lights scanning the ground below.

'Take cover!!' snapped Rachel.

'Where?' replied Walter, and he had a point.


## THE GREAT SANDY DESERT

The Great Sandy Desert of Western Australia is not known for its prominent features. If it were, perhaps it might have had a slightly more interesting name. It might have been called 'The great, sandy and with lots of interesting little nooks and crannies and rocks and caves and great places to hide in Desert.'

But it wasn't called that because there are virtually no nooks, crannies, rocks or caves. All there is, across 99 per cent of its surface, is space and sand. It is a great and sandy desert. Never was a place more aptly named.


## BATTLE AND CAPTURE

The four frightened fugitives stared around them looking for somewhere to hide and there was nowhere. Or at least there was nowhere that they could see. Had Zimmerman been with them he would have calmly told them to crouch stock still and think like a bush, or lie flat along one of the tiny creases of land caused by the soft desert wind.

'Stillness is the essence of camouflage,' he would have told them, 'it is very difficult to pick out something that doesn't move.'

That is what Zimmerman would have told them had he been there, but of course he wasn't. And so his four friends ran around in circles flapping their arms in panic shouting, 'What the fuck are we going to do!! What the fuck are we going to do!!'

There was literally nowhere to run to. The chopper was approaching fast, making great sweeping arcs with its horrifyingly powerful search-light, covering hundreds of square metres of flat, featureless terrain and subjecting it to careful scrutiny.

Suddenly, for the four terrified commandos on the ground, it was day, bright bright day as they were swathed in the harsh light. Their shadows stretched out like deep black ditches behind them. They stared, blinking into the beam, frozen into momentary petrification. Four skittles waiting to be knocked down.

Then CD had a thought.

'Scatter! I'm going to take out the light!!' he shouted, and raising the automatic weapon to his shoulder, squeezed the trigger.

Considering that CD had never fired any form of gun before, and that he was starting out on a state-of-the-art machine gun that could have cut the front off a house, it wasn't a bad effort. He missed the light but he was very close. As it happened, he hit the fuel tank, causing the helicopter to burst into a horrifyingly brilliant fireball.

The machines that Stark employed were police-designed craft, hence they were not armoured. Contrary to what cop shows would have us believe, most police helicopters are used for traffic surveillance and it takes a pretty vicious contra-flow system to provoke the average motorist to dig out an automatic rifle.

The instant inferno hung in the air with its spinning blades hurling burning debris into the night. Strangely, and rather eerily, the search-light which emanated from the helicopter's nose cone, remained on, although it no longer bobbed and weaved about. For a little while nothing further happened. The helicopter burnt in the sky and the four figures on the ground remained motionless, transfixed by what they had done, still casting their long black shadows in the light that shone from the dead aircraft. Then it crashed to the ground with the sort of noise that only a burning helicopter crashing into the ground can make, and gloom descended once more.

Still the four of them did not move. They just stood, trying to get their heads around the enormity of developments. The stakes had suddenly got a very great deal higher. Now they were killers, murderers. CD was vaguely surprised to note that the old cliché that 'it didn't seem real' was true. It didn't.

'You should have let me do it, CD,' said Mrs Culboon. 'I'm the one who can shoot, remember?'

'I forgot,' said CD lamely.

'You had to do something,' said Rachel, her voice hard. 'It was us or them.'

'We *hope* it was us or them,' corrected Walter. 'Man, all I can say is that this whole situation had better be as serious as the paranoid Yank chick says it is, because if that chopper was just patrolling a building site we're going to prison for ever.'

The terrible thing that had happened seemed to have driven the memory of their recent and stunning sight of the construction site from his mind.

'Oh come *on*,' shouted Rachel, 'we *know* it's serious, for God's sake, Walter, they were shooting at *you* the other night with these very guns. They've taken Zimmerman and the police claim there wasn't even a fight at the airport. And anyway Walter, what the fuck is that!! A retirement village!' She pointed down towards the site. Now that the burning helicopter had ceased to light up the sky, the construction site had regained something of its awesome brilliance.

'Chrissy has *got* to be right,' Rachel urged. 'Something

utterly terrible is going on and CD was absolutely right to do what he did.'

'Well, right or wrong, we're in the shit now,' said Mrs Culboon, 'so I say we press on as fast as we can and get away from that cemetery over there.' She pointed at the wreck of the helicopter and CD wished that she had chosen a different phrase. He did not know how many people it took to crew a small helicopter, but however many it was, that was how many people he had killed.

They began to run; Mrs Culboon, as the slowest, setting the pace. They ran towards the glow of the building site, each pondering their own confused thoughts. They did not know what they were running towards, what they would find, or what they would do when they found it. They were just running away from a burning helicopter full of dead men.

As it happened, what they were running towards was, in their case, even worse than a burning helicopter full of dead men; it was a not burning helicopter full of live men. Men who did not take kindly to the sort of shock that CD had just given them. On the whole, people take jobs in private security firms in order to throw their weight about, not in order to get shot out of the sky.

After a minute CD, Rachel, Walter and Mrs Culboon stopped running. They could hear the helicopter coming, they could see the headlamps of the trucks and jeeps which were also hurtling across the sand towards them. There was absolutely nowhere to hide.

Mrs Culboon cocked her rifle.

'Oh man,' said Walter wearily, 'I think we've done enough of that, you know? I mean, we are in a no-win situation here, you dig? Like, they are going to get us for definite, no way can we fight them all so I think maybe it would be wrong to just kill people for no reason, even if they are the bastards who are after us.'

As it happened Mrs Culboon had not really wanted to fight. She was just thinking of trying to defend her friends; acting instinctively that was all. None of them wanted to fight, they all wanted to go home to their mothers and be tucked up in bed with warm milk and vegamite soldiers. But they couldn't, they would have to face the music.

'Drop the weapons,' a voice barked.

They dropped them and with a fair degree of unnecessary force, were bound and thrown in the back of a truck.

Mrs Culboon and Walter lived on the fringes of society, this was not for either of them their first experience of brutality and danger. They didn't like it but they recognized it. For CD and Rachel, it was unknown territory, and hence utterly terrifying. All people who live in well-ordered societies harbour a secret dread of what would happen if order was removed. If suddenly they found themselves in a brutal human jungle without the protection of the social rules on which we all rely. It was happening to CD and Rachel. It seemed to them, lying face down in the back of a three ton lorry, that they were beyond action and beyond help.

CD would have given anything to see a copper. It wouldn't have mattered how young or arrogant; seventeen-years-old and a face like a plate of rhubarb and custard, CD wouldn't have minded. But there's never one there when you want one.

# IMPRISONMENT AND INTERROGATION

## THE CENTRE OF CREATION

Sly and Tyron were in the project control building when they got the news regarding the capture of four intruders. At first Sly thought that this might wrap the problem up. If necessary they would simply hold the fugitives until after Domesday.

Unfortunately, he quickly discovered, to his extreme frustration, the original fugitive, the highly dangerous nose-biting hippy had not been recaptured.

For the first time Sly began to feel a twinge of doubt about the whole bloody business in which he was involved. These little human intrusions on their vast and inhuman project made him vaguely aware of how small he was himself. That, coupled with the continuing and irritating presence of Ocker Tyron, a genuinely small man, despite his size, made Sly feel uncomfortably impotent in the midst of all his power.

The project control building was a depressing place in which to experience doubt and humility, containing, as it did, an awe inspiring array of high-tech equipment, most of which was going blip blip blip in what seemed to Sly to be an unnecessarily irritating manner. The stuff had been assembled by Nagasyu at various collation points all over the Far East and so efficient had his administration been that when all the gear arrived, there was little more to do than to plug it in. Incredibly it had even had a plug on it.

The whole thing certainly looked cool; a quarter of an acre

of chrome, plastic, glass and brushed stainless steel, all
bleeping, spinning and flashing. Almost as complex as the
dashboard on a BMW. Yard after yard of console covered in
monitors and buttons, walls of tapes, sometimes spinning one
way, then, no doubt for some reason, spinning another. It was
an exhilarating and terrifying sight. And so it should have
been. There was, after all, only slightly less equipment in the
room than it takes to record a Pink Floyd album.

Twenty-five or so white-coated technicians bustled about
flicking switches and looking intelligent. Tyron had been
impressed, despite himself.

'Now all it needs is something to shoot,' he had said.

'What's your hurry, mate! Anyone would think you're
looking forward to this bloody awful thing . . . this . . .' Sly
searched for a word, '. . . Apocalypse. Christ Almighty,
let's enjoy what time is left.'

'I just don't want any fuck-ups when the time is right,
we're only going to get one chance at this, Moorcock, one
chance at life or death, right! I want us to be ready.'

In fact in a strange way Ocker Tyron was looking forward
to it. Utterly horrible though the prospect was, its hugeness
still gave him a strange exhilaration. He had had the power of
life and death over virtually everybody in his life for so many
years that Tyron was definitely a hard man to thrill. Stark,
however, made his very trousers tingle. Despite its irreversible
horror, Tyron still felt a pretty considerable buzz at the
prospect of playing God, even if it was a multi-headed
corporate God. He relished the prospect of being one of the
chosen ones, one of those chosen to survive. Besides this,
there was the eerie potency he felt about his part in choosing
who should die. In a way it's not surprising he was a little
excited, it is quite something to be a father of creation. Only
God had made a world before.

## MINOR IRRITATIONS

Tyron's delicious little fantasies were cut short when one of

316

Du Pont's security men entered and announced the capture of the prisoners. Suddenly Sly found himself wondering about the girl.

'Look, Ocker,' said Sly. 'I can handle this, all right? Why don't you just sod off back to Perth, eh? It's just a minor irritation, some hippies who think we're destroying precious natural flora. I'll talk to them.'

The security man knew he had a chance to make a big impact and he grabbed it.

'They shot down a helicopter,' he said.

There was a pretty stunned silence, apart from all the blipping going on that is.

'Shot *down* a fucking *helicopter*!' said Tyron incredulously. 'What the hell is going on? Christ first a guy disarms our security chief with his teeth, then one of our choppers get shot down.'

'Look, will you cool it, Tyron,' said Sly, not really knowing what to say. 'We have to think.'

'Too fucking right, mate!' Someone's found out what we're up to and they want in. This is only the beginning.' Tyron was pretty badly shaken. It always gives a person cause for thought when he's just been having a God fantasy and somebody shoots down his helicopter.

'Don't be stupid,' Sly replied. 'These people are just dumb meddlers. It's an ecological thing, we know that from the hippy who bit Du Pont.' Sly was still thinking about the girl. 'Mind you, they certainly know how to meddle . . . We won't tell Durf about this, or the others, it's not necessary. I intend to deal with this situation right now.'

## FANCYING THE ENEMY

Sly could not kid himself, he was pleased to see her. There was no doubt about it. As he walked towards the room where the captives were being kept he had been hoping that she would be there and when it turned out that she was, he was pleased.

317

This was an entirely new experience for Sly. Occasionally in the past he had developed 'things' about girls, but never on so short an acquaintance and certainly never with such immediate force. After all, he knew nothing about the girl apart from the fact that she seemed to be firmly against absolutely everything that he stood for. There was no getting round it though, he was pleased to see her. She seemed even more pretty than when they had met in his office. Action and adventure had lent a highly attractive flush to her cheek and her eyes sparkled with defiance and fear. She was also firmly tied to a chair, which was something that normally took Sly ages to persuade his girlfriends to put up with.

## QUESTION AND ANSWER

Sly pulled himself together. This was a time for masterly self-assurance. He stood before the sorry gang of renegades and addressed them with what he hoped would be an icy and intimidating tone.

'What in the name of fuck do you think you're doing?' he blurted.

Walter looked at him defiantly.

'Trying to find out what you're up to, man,' he said. 'Just like last time, you know, like, still trying to suss out what goes down.'

'What goes *down*, you filthy bastard,' shouted Tyron, 'is one of *my* helicopters!!'

Sly tried to calm himself. They couldn't both stand there screaming at a bunch of hippies. It was so unreal. Here he was, a colossus in the world of power and money and he was standing shouting and screaming at a Carlton drop-out. That's the trouble with spending all your time on the twenty fifth floor, when you come down there's a hell of a bump.

'Why are you so interested in what I'm doing?' he asked.

'We, we won't know that until we find out what it is, will we man?' replied Walter. 'But we have a pretty good idea that whatever it is, it's heavy. Now where's my man Zimmerman?

If you've harmed him I swear . . . I swear, I'll lay some *very* bad Karma on your head. Dig?'

Walter's three comrades felt slightly embarrassed at this. Having Walter lay some very bad Karma on your head sounded something akin to being savaged by Bambi.

Sly did not even realize that he had been threatened.

'Who are you talking about?' he asked.

'My man Zimmerman, a kind of hippy dude, he ate your hamburger at Facefulls.'

Sly was about to add that since then he had eaten his security chief's nose as well, but he decided to be more circumspect. 'We have him safe, don't trouble about that,' Sly lied.

'You'd better start worrying about yourselves,' Tyron chipped in. 'Now what the fuck do you know? All of it, everything. What do you know and where's the Yank bitch? Come on, out with it. Now!!'

There was a sullen silence.

Tyron grabbed a gun from one of the guards and pointed it at them. Sly tensed up and watched Tyron carefully.

'You answer me right now or you're dead, you hear,' Tyron barked. 'I don't suppose there'll be anybody much mourning any of you, we'll just leave you for the dingos. Now come on, answer me.'

Walter's reply was a shrewd one.

'You ain't going to shoot us man. No way,' he said. 'Because you don't know what we know and . . . and . . . you don't know what the Yank chick knows. And you don't know who we've told . . . and you don't know, uhm . . .' Walter seemed about to flag, but then he got his second wind, he always did love to bullshit, '. . . and you don't know how many of us are out there. Yeah, that's right, you have no idea of the hugeness of our network, yeah, you have no concept of its almost cosmic enormity. You don't know how many heavily armed and totally dedicated hippies are out there just waiting to come in here and . . . and . . .' endless late nights watching American cop shows came to his aid, '. . . come in here and cream your arse, yeah, that's it, cream your arse . . . and uhm . . . expose all the things that we know to the world.' He finished and then added 'man' as a kind of full stop.

It was a good performance. CD nearly spoilt it by applauding. Luckily his hands were tied behind his back. Unfortunately for Walter, Sly was not stupid, he simply smiled and said, 'Oh yeah, if you're all so heavily armed mate, how come you came in carrying only the guns you pinched off us in the first place?'

There was a pause.

'Uhm . . . irony, man,' said Walter. 'Yeah, that's it, we have a keen sense of irony.'

'These people don't know shit,' said Sly, 'they're shooting in the dark.'

'And bringing down helicopters,' added Du Pont, who saw no reason why he should be the only person to feel a dickhead that day.

Tyron was not satisfied with Sly's confidence.

'I agree there's no way they can know much,' he said, 'but we have to find out what little it is. Besides that, we've got to find the American girl. Du Pont, can you make them talk?'

'Of course I can make them talk,' said Du Pont and his tone was not pleasant, especially if you happened to be his prisoner.

'Now, what the hell do you two think you're talking about?' Sly shouted. In a way he was going through a similar learning process to that which CD and the others were going through. They had never been involved in gun battles before and he had never heard colleagues casually hint at torturing total strangers. It was being brought home to all of them just how high the stakes were getting.

'What I am talking about,' Tyron shouted back, 'is the Stark project and the countless billions that we have all invested in our future. I have no intention of letting a few adventurous idiots like this ruin everything. Ruin the biggest thing in the world . . .'

There was a moment's embarrassed silence as everybody

realized that Tyron had been about to reveal all. He turned to the four captives. 'Now you can either tell us peaceably what you know, or Colonel Du Pont here can force it out of you. What do you know?'

'We don't know shit, man. But you sure are making it all sound interesting,' said Walter. 'Why don't you tell us?'

'Right, Du Pont, which will be easiest?' said Tyron.

'The kid in glasses maybe, or the girl,' he replied.

'No!' barked Sly.

Mrs Culboon decided to have her say. 'Listen! My friend's telling the truth, we don't know nothing about your big stuff and your damn future. We're here because I got beaten up on my own land by racists and that's all we know. And if you don't tell us no more, then we'll still know nothing, and you can let us go.'

'That's right,' said Sly and Rachel thought he was acting extremely reasonably considering that they had shot down his helicopter.

'Like fuck they don't know anything,' asserted Tyron, heating up. 'They have to know where the Yank is, maybe even where this hippy Zimmerman fellah got to.'

'Oh yeah? Thought you said you had him safe,' taunted CD.

Tyron turned towards him with a look like granite. 'Get on with it, Du Pont,' he said.

'Stay exactly where you are Du Pont,' Sly countered. 'Tyron, can we have a private word please?'

He ushered Tyron out of the room leaving Du Pont to guard the prisoners. Despite the fact that this time he had four guards with him, Du Pont was careful to keep his nose out of reach.

## ORIGINAL SIN

Outside the room there was yet another tense altercation between Sly and Tyron.

'For God's sake, Tyron, you were about to have those people tortured!' said a rather disturbed Sly.

'I still am, mate, if it's necessary,' Tyron replied.

And of course Sly could see his point. They had no way of knowing what these irritating people knew, and who, if anyone, they had told it to. Besides this there was the much bigger problem of the American journalist still being at large, they really did need to find her. On the other hand to discard any civilized behaviour so quickly, right at the very beginning of the great plan, did not bode at all well for the future. After all, the whole point of the Stark project was to reshape civilization and give it a new start; a fresh chance. Stark was to be a phoenix rising out of the dead ashes of a failed and disgraced civilization. If they started this way, they were bound to fail again. It was almost as if Sly was looking the Original Sin in the eye.

## LOVE FINDS A WAY

Of course, Sly did not consider all these thoughts so coherently in the few seconds that elapsed before he replied to Tyron. Mainly he was thinking about Rachel. His natural repugnance to Tyron's casual acceptance of brutality as a viable course of action was multiplied *ad infinitum* by the thought that he intended to practise it upon the girl Rachel. He really did seem to have gone soft on her.

'Listen,' Sly replied, 'I agree that the situation is touchy. But don't forget that nothing we're doing here is actually illegal. Totally shithouse morals-wise, perhaps, but not actually illegal. They can't possibly have anything on us yet and if the American does try to make a move, well, let's face it, we've got her. We control the police, the phones, the transport, the credit. We control everything.'

'Yes I know, but they've still got this far,' replied Tyron.

'Look, just give me a day or two to sort this situation out my way, all right? Leave them alone for the time being, eh? I mean, the minute anyone makes a move anywhere in the world, let alone in Bullens Creek, Durf will know. So what's the problem? Let me talk to them, I'll find out what they've got and it will be nothing.'

Sly had already decided on the course of action he must take.

He and Tyron re-entered the room.

'Don't worry,' Sly said. 'We're not going to hurt you. I will simply be questioning you one at a time. You first.' He pointed at Rachel and motioned a guard to untie her and lead her out.

It nearly broke CD's heart to see Rachel thus contemptuously ordered about. Luckily he was securely bound and so was not forced to try and do something about it. Better a broken heart than a broken neck.

# THE SWORD OF DAMOCLĒS

While CD's heart was breaking in northern WA, not too far away, just off the coast, near a place called Shark Bay, something else was breaking, something that was going to make a broken heart seem small beer and even a broken neck a minor inconvenience.

## SHARK BAY

The early Aussies, as was their unerring habit, had named Shark Bay after the sharks which were the bay's most prominent feature; apart from water of course. Undeniably the most prominent feature of all in the bay was water and so for a while there was a strong movement amongst those tough, hard bitten and laconic men and women, to call it 'Waterlogged Bay'.

The more sophisticated souls countered that if you started calling bays 'Waterlogged Bay' because they were waterlogged, then all bays would have the same name and it would be impossible to tell the buggers apart. And they got called a bunch of poofs for their pains.

'If you can have a Great Sandy Desert, a Snowy Mountains and a Southern Sea, you can have a Waterlogged Bay,' the laconics claimed.

'But there's only *one* of those things,' pleaded the more sophisticated souls, 'there are loads of bays.'

In the end, the logic of this statement had been grudgingly accepted and so it was decided to name the bay after its most prominent feature apart from water.

Somebody suggested that the fact that it was a bay was a

pretty major feature, but 'BAY BAY' had been rejected as sounding too childish. 'Horizon BAY' had been considered for a while, it was a pretty name, but was eventually thought to have the same problem as 'water'; i.e., that it could describe any bay (as could 'wave' and 'tide').

Eventually, after a fellow called Jim had come home from a fishing trip minus a leg, having been gored by a shark, it had been decided to call the bay 'Shark Bay' and to call Jim, 'One-Legged Jim'. There had been a small group of poetic, erudite individuals who had lobbied hard for 'Bay of the Bitten Jim' but they were told to fuck off back to Sydney where their type were tolerated.

And so Shark Bay it became, because there were sharks in it.

Not everyone was happy of course. One-Legged Jim, for instance, was monumentally pissed off, but this wasn't because of the name business. He was unhappy because he had been horribly mutilated and now he only had one leg. Jim's pragmatic, no bullshit attitude to life was much admired by all.

Some of the citizens of Carnarvorn, the town on the northern tip of the bay, had wanted to call it Carnarvorn Bay and wandered around for weeks muttering under their breath that there were sharks in every bloody bay in Australia. None the less, Shark Bay it had stayed for a hundred and fifty years until the the thread broke on the Sword of Damoclēs and rendered life for a shark in Shark Bay utterly impossible.

## THE SWORD

As the Domesday Group had constantly made clear to Stark over the years the ecological cause and effect syndromes which they had isolated as The Swords of Damoclēs were very different indeed from those which were categorized under the Avalanche Effect.

The actual story of Damoclēs and his monarch Dionysius is of no relevance here, except, that is, for the punch line, which left Damoclēs sitting at dinner beneath a naked sword suspended from the ceiling by a single thread. The moral of the legend being that a person's situation in life is always chancy. Another moral might have been that if you find yourself at dinner with a sword hanging over your head, move seats.

And that was exactly the point made by the Domesday Group. Ecologically, the difference between avalanches and Swords of Damoclēs was that with avalanches you didn't know about them until they fell on you; but Swords of Damoclēs were slightly less serious because the danger was there for all to see, and hence it was possible to do something about it. A typical example of the Swords that Domesday regularly put before Stark were the so called Leper Ships; ships so loaded with appallingly toxic chemicals that no country would let them enter their ports. Alone and virtually stateless, they roam the seas searching for a place to disgorge their vile load.

'One of them's going to sink one of these days,' the Domesday Group would say.

At Shark Bay the thread broke.

## THE *ATARIA C42*

If Captain Robertson on his North Sea shit sludger thought he had a tough job, he should have tried carting the real crap around like poor old Captain Popplewell had to.

Captain Popplewell, the master of the Liberian registered *Ataria C42*, had three years of hell then died. It started when his ship was chartered by a company called Dispo Holdings, who wished him to ship a few barrels of ash and sludge to a toxic-waste disposal company in Britain – a country with a world reputation for taking on other peoples' shit. Whilst at sea a scandal burst revealing the true nature of the load which turned out to be a horrifying cocktail of chemical and heavy metal poisons. A mix of aluminium, arsenic, barium, cadmium, lead and mercury, so potent that no port in the world would take it.

326

At first Captain Popplewell was instructed to do what so many others had done before when faced with a cargo that cannot be offloaded. He was told to dump it in the Third World. For years, contrary to every legal and moral objection, Africa has been used as a dustbin for the impossibly toxic residue of the life-styles of the West.

Unfortunately for the *Ataria C42*, her cargo had become somewhat notorious and environmental activists were on to her – hence even Third World ports were barred to the ship. It was bitter gall indeed for Captain Popplewell to see other Leper Ships successfully slipping in and dumping their terrible loads and having wild leper ship parties, whilst he was forced to skulk about in mid-ocean like the pariah he was. Of course, he and the ship's owners turned to the company that had chartered them, but, as happens too often in these situations, they had gone into liquidation. In fact Dispo Holdings might be said to have pulled off a brilliant business coup in the same way that Sly did by destroying healthy businesses with his corporate raids. Dispo had accepted a contract to dispose of large quantities of appallingly toxic waste. They had performed their duties by chartering a ship and putting the waste on the ship. When it proved impossible for the ship to find anywhere to sail to, Dispo had gone into liquidation. Brilliant.

Sly's attitude would probably have been that business is a tough game; dog-eat-dog, and you had to admire their audacity.

## THE FIRST OF MANY

During the three years that the *Ataria C42* drifted about, occasionally being allowed to take on more fuel or food, the seas became crowded with lepers. Slowly, as people began to wake up to the appalling danger of this stuff, fewer and fewer were prepared to even consider trying to deal with it. Unfortunately, the poisons still got made and so more and more ships found themselves floating about, sitting on enough poison to wipe out an ocean. These were the Swords of Damoclēs.

Just as CD was crying over Rachel, crying over the sort of small, human things that make life worth living, the sword fell for the *Ataria C42*. In a terrible storm just west of Shark Bay, the ship ruptured and fifty-five thousand gallons of the choicest contents of Pandora's Box flowed into the Indian Ocean, and hence into all the seas of the world.

# RACHEL AND SLY

'Why are you doing this?' Sly asked bluntly, once he and Rachel were installed in the lounge room of his private quarters and he had poured out a couple of gin and tonics.

'Doing what?' replied Rachel, wondering hard how to play the situation.

'Pursuing me and my business. Don't you have anything better to do?' he asked.

'We're concerned citizens. You're the sort of person who will have bribed and bought out all the usual restraining influences so it's up to people like us to keep an eye on you,' Rachel replied.

'And what is it that you think I'm doing that is so very wrong?' asked Sly.

'Well, shipping in high-grade missile fuel disguised as petrol, for a start.' Rachel was gratified to note that Sly was extremely taken aback by this bald statement. She realized that in making it she had removed a card from her sleeve and placed it on the table, but there seemed little point in concealing her knowledge. After all, he could not tell from it what else she knew. Rachel felt that Walter had been right, if inept, in his efforts to convince Moorcock that he was up against a formidable force. Rachel did not know whether her life was in danger or not, but she thought that if it was, Moorcock would be less likely to do away with her if it seemed likely that there would be others to follow on and avenge her.

'What do you know about the rocket fuel?' asked Sly.

'I don't intend to answer any more of your questions. Let me and my friends go, or you'll be sorry.'

Rachel was well aware that this statement had a credibility

reading of zero but she didn't have anything else to say. She had absolutely no idea of how to handle the situation for the best and so had decided to shut up. She needn't have worried, Sly was going to be doing most of the talking. For a moment he sat staring at her across the room. She was sitting cross legged on the sofa, holding her glass defensively, like a shield. She looked great.

Sly was preparing to throw caution to the wind.


## CRUSH

Not everybody falls in love as impulsively as Sly had done. For some, love grows; it slowly dawns on them. One day they might think 'mmm nice bum' and leave it at that. Later, perhaps at the office party, whilst casually chatting, they discover a mutual interest in religious music. After that, dinner and a movie just seem like a logical step . . .

'No way is it serious, I don't even know if we get on, actually.'

A massively disappointing first shag serves to cement a mutual sympathy and finally, about a decade later, comes the, 'You know, I don't know, but I think I might be in love with you, what do you think? Or is that stupid, I mean, if it is, forget it?'

But not everybody is so cautious.

Once, whilst driving along a country highway late at night, Sly had caught a seven foot Red Kangaroo in his head-lights and, seconds later, had slammed into it full across the 'roo bars at a highly illegal hundred and forty kilometres. This is how some people fall in love. Sly had always wondered how the 'roo must have felt. Now he knew.

The reason so many 'roos get spread across bonnets is because they have an instinctive fascination for light sources. Unfortunately for them, when they get caught in head-lamps, they stop dead still and stare straight into the light; oblivious of the consequences; entirely captured by the magic of the beams. Sly was just the same, except of course that he didn't

330

have a huge long tail and a pouch with a baby in it. He was mesmerized by Rachel's light.

It can happen. Especially to a man like Sly whose life-style meant that his experience of real people – straight, unaffected people – was minimal. Coupled with all this was the fact that Sly wanted to fall in love. For the first time in his life he was desperate to find someone, and quickly. He fancied Rachel; he thought her different and interesting; she was in the right place at the right time. Sly, a man used to making decisions, decided to fall in love. Of course at the time, Sly would probably have denied that the emotions he was nurturing were anything like that intense. He would have admitted to lust; he might even have conceded an objective interest in her strange personality, but he would not have admitted that he was falling for her.

None the less, he was.

## SMALL TALK

'What did that long-haired guy who talks through a time warp call your group?' Sly asked, breaking the silence.

'EcoAction,' replied Rachel defiantly.

'And what's that supposed to signify then,' Sly asked with a slightly mocking tone.

'It's supposed to signify, *mate*,' said Rachel, bridling at his attitude, 'that if something isn't done soon, the world is going to die, that's what. It will die, you arrogant, smug, complacent . . . rich bastard.' Rachel was, of course, a born again Eco-freak; a convert, and in any system of belief it is the converts who are the real zealots. If there was one thing that Rachel couldn't handle it was people taking the piss out of the stuff she was into.

'You're wrong,' said Sly quietly. 'The earth isn't going to die unless you stop it.'

'Oh yeah well you would say that wouldn't you,' Rachel sneered. 'You've got a vested interest in carrying on fucking it up.'

'You're wrong,' continued Sly, 'because it's going to die anyway. It's virtually dead already, and there is absolutely nothing that you or I or anyone else can do about it. The earth is going to die.'

'Well that's a bit sodding cheerful I must say,' said Rachel, sarcastically. But none the less she was shaken by the cold certainty in his voice.

Sly gulped down his gin and tonic, poured himself another, even stiffer, and decided to go for it.

'Rachel,' he said, 'do you know the story of Adam and Eve?'

He stopped himself, realizing that he was about to embark on the most monumentally naff tack he could possibly take. He decided to start again. 'Forget that,' he said. 'Hot isn't it? Let's talk about the greenhouse effect.'

# COMMUNICATION
# BREAKDOWN

By morning Tyron was getting impatient. He had never much liked the idea of waiting for the miraculous Moorcock powers of persuasion to convince the captives to divulge all that they knew. Now Tyron felt that his cynicism had been amply justified since many hours had passed and he had not heard a thing from Sly. He felt, as he did about everything in life, that he would probably do a much better job of interrogation himself. Besides, it was very difficult to sit still and do nothing, it was so bloody hot for a start. The night had brought a little relief but now it was morning again and he felt like he was sitting in a grill pan. It was definitely the worst summer Tyron could remember. The whole world seemed to be having it at once. He'd heard that there was no skiing at all in the USA and you had to be an eagle to try it even in the Alps.

Everything was getting so depressingly hellish. Everything seemed to be stinking and rotten. You couldn't trust the water any more because unseasonal flooding had contaminated the supplies. What's more, there were millions more bugs than usual, probably because of all the rank water that was lying around, steaming up into the clouds and then pissing down again almost immediately in torrential poisoned deluges. It was hot and horrible, and now besides that, Tyron had this smelly crew of blacks and hippies to deal with.

There was still no sign of the fugitive Zimmerman. Tyron was forced to accept the possibility that he was now outside the wire. Even more reason then for discovering where it was that this irritating little group had based themselves and hence where Zimmerman would be heading. Tyron decided to have a go at the prisoners.

## POWERS OF PERSUASION

Mindful of the time honoured techniques of interrogation, where it is considered important to establish both a hard option and a soft option, he decided that his first approach would be to exercise his charm.

Unfortunately, Ocker Tyron possessed all the charm of a job at Kentucky Fried Chicken and so he had little chance of getting very far. Tyron was a shouter. He was under the impression that it was possible to persuade people that you had almost instantaneously become their bosom buddy simply by assuming a kind of rugged, good-humoured *bonhomie*. He had learnt to communicate at the 'Adverts for Furniture Warehouse School of Sincerity'. A place in which the sad figures who own carpet and furniture warehouses, or second-hand TV emporiums are taught to star in their own television adverts. Desperate, desperate men in loud, slightly comical sports jackets, standing superimposed in front of a photograph of their place of business, shouting at the camera, possibly playing on a slight speech impediment, to single them out as individuals.

'Why pay those *fancy* prices!!! Get the family down to BudgetPriceMart! Bring the *kids*. If *you* can find *anything* cheaper, Honest Bob'll *refund ya! OK!!*'

These people are under the impression that a rough and ready display of overblown pig-ignorant philistinism will somehow endear them to the general public as straight talking, good blokes. In fact, everybody wonders why this stupid wanker keeps shouting at them.

Ocker Tyron had himself, in his early days, appeared in one or two of his own ads. He had been trying to shift a warehouse full of dodgy nylon 'fur' coats and had appeared on TV with a bevvy of West Australian lovelies, all wearing the 'fur' coats, and nothing else.

334

'Tyron's bargains,' he had screamed at the camera, at the top of his voice. 'These terrific, low budget, family, fur substitute, luxury style winter warmer, garment, casual wear designer durables are so like the real fox, sable and mink, retailing at thousands of dollars . . . Ha ha, you'll think they're going to bite ya!!!!!'

And then had come the obligatory sting, where Tyron put his arm around a lovely, and there was a taped lion roar, cut to freeze-frame close up of Tyron's honest, comically shocked face.

Tyron's mum ended up giving all the coats to a Methodist mission. But he did not learn his lesson and Tyron still shouted when he was trying to be ingratiating and convincing.

## IRON HAND AND VELVET GLOVE

'Aw, come on guys,' Ocker roared at CD and Walter with a big smile – he ignored Mrs Culboon. 'Just tell us what you know and you can piss off. No hard feelings, wadaya say?' He held a cup of water to CD's lips.

'We don't know anything, mate. We were coming to find out,' he replied, with a fair degree of honesty.

'Now look here,' Tyron continued, 'I reckon you and I see eye to eye. Similar breed, straight talking if you follow me. I guess we're just a couple of OK West Australian blokes. Am I right?'

'Well not really,' CD replied politely. 'I'm British.'

'Well, even better,' said Tyron, delighted. 'You can't get more Aussie than that. After all, the poms were the very first Australians.'

'Ha bloody ha mate,' snorted Mrs Culboon contemptuously.

'A Stone Age fucking culture is not what I call being Australian,' snapped Tyron. 'I call it dumb. Christ you lot had the place for forty thousand years, you never even invented cricket, ha ha ha!' Tyron had more in common with Gordon Gordon than he would have liked to think.

'Listen you,' said Mrs Culboon, 'we don't know nothing and we ain't done nothing, and that's the truth I reckon.'

'You shot down one of my helicopters, Mrs,' said Tyron.

'Look, that was a very heavy trip for us, too, you know,' Walter chipped in with a hint of reproach in his voice. 'Each of us is trying to come to terms with it in their own private space, and I have to say that it would help if you didn't keep dragging it up all the time.'

'Anyway, mate,' added Mrs Culboon, 'I reckon he would have shot us. Oh yes, I reckon he would, that's for sure. What should we have done? Stood there in the light and said come on and shoot us? Ha! I don't reckon so . . .'

'Shut the boong up,' snapped Tyron; and Du Pont stuffed a rag in her mouth.

'Hey listen, man!' protested Walter. 'Like, can we keep the heaviness down, OK? I mean can we just cool the heaviness. You know heaviness never solved anything right, like.'

'Right!' shouted Tyron, giving up on the charm-school effort and making his decision to break his deal with Sly and get rough. 'What do you know? How many more of you are there? And where are Zimmerman and the American journalist?'

His tone was very threatening and there was a sullen silence – from Walter and CD that is. Mrs Culboon was grunting unintelligibly through the rag. Which just goes to show what a small barrier to communication a lack of language can be, because it was quite clear to everyone that Mrs Culboon was saying, 'Get the fuck this rag out of my mouth.'

Tyron was about to turn up the heat on the proceedings considerably when his three hostages were granted a last minute reprieve. A messenger arrived to announce that Professor Durf had arrived and would be obliged if he could see Tyron urgently.

# TO BE OFFERED THE WORLD

In the long hours of the night, whilst Tyron had lain cursing the heat and slapping the bugs, Sly had indoctrinated Rachel into Stark.

It had been a shocker, no doubt about that. Certainly the most surprising thing anybody had ever told her; more astonishing even than her youthful discovery that Daddy had a seed which he put in Mummy's tummy because they loved each other very much.

## VANISHING POINT

First of all Sly had given Rachel a run-down of the apocalyptical doom scenario that he had first been fully made a party to at the dinner in Los Angeles. He explained the theory of the approaching vanishing point. 'The world does not know the half, a quarter even, of the shit it is in, Rachel. All your wildest fears; your conspiracy paranoias; your worst predictions about the state of the world, it's already happened ten times over. Words cannot describe the vandalism that has been perpetrated on this planet.'

Rachel did not know where this could be leading to. The last thing she had expected Sly to be was a green activist. He continued in the same dry tones.

'There are virtually no forests left. There are no longer any effective atmospheric barriers. Soon there will be no polar ice-caps. Coupled with this, every single thing on this planet has been subjected, to a greater or lesser extent, to toxification. It is a fact that nothing on earth can be said to be clean. Not one drop of water, not one gulp of air, not one mouthful of food. It is all irreversibly filthy. Without the forests, deserts will very soon take over the majority of land remaining above sea-level. Which will not be much because once the ice has melted all low lying land will be submerged under a filthy sea.'

Sly always did love to hold the floor and on this occasion he was particularly anxious to make an impression on his audience. He assumed an almost schoolmasterly air, pacing about with his hands behind his back. He near as damn it put on an English accent, which is how the Australian advertising industry implies weightiness. If they want to impress upon people that a particular box of cereals has dignity, they get a pom actor to do the voice-over. Sly was trying to sound weighty.

'The degradation of the soil through salination, chemical imbalance and intense over-farming is set to make almost all agriculture untenable worldwide. When that happens, billions of people are going to turn on each other in starving fury. If it hasn't already died of skin cancer or toxic shock, the human race will commit bloody self-murder . . .'

This was one of Durf's phrases and Sly felt it sounded rather good. He continued, 'This combination of various ecological disasters, any one of which alone could see us off, we call the Vanishing Point and we are satisfied that it will occur within the next two or three years. It is a straw that broke the camel's back situation really. Things will stagger on just about getting by, until one day a crack appears that shatters the entire structure and everything comes tumbling down at once.'

Sly spoke of the end of everything without any great emotion. Of course he had been living with the facts and the figures for many months, but he was still pretty cool about it.

The reason he was so cool was, of course, that he knew that it wasn't *quite* the end of everything.

## WASTED TIME

'Oh come on, this is out of it,' said Rachel, understandably shocked. 'I'm sure something can be done.'

'Something *could* have been done a long time ago but we didn't do it, did we chum?' said Sly.

'Who's we?' asked Rachel, wondering why the hell Sly was going on about ecology. Surely he wasn't hoping that somehow he could persuade her that her principles were futile and hence she should leave whatever evil stuff he was up to alone?

'Well everybody, of course,' said Sly in answer to her question. 'But mainly myself and the other big players. Ever since the first industrial revolution when James Watt boiled a kettle and invented acid rain, or whatever the hell happened, the natural, life-forming parameters of our world have been like an hour glass, getting thinner and thinner. The question being, would we squeeze past the middle and break on through to the other side. Now, if we had acted earlier, when it first got obvious that we were really screwing up home sweet home, then maybe it would have been OK and we could have started looking after the old world and the chances of life on earth might have expanded again. But we didn't do it did we? We opted for instant profit and comfort; beer and skittles at the expense of the whole of future history. Anyway, now the gap in the glass is plugged, it's a vanishing point, there isn't a way through any more.'

'So how can you be sure?' demanded Rachel.

'Rachel, it's happening, now, we don't need to speculate, the facts are all around us. All you have to do is make a little graph of the deterioration in the various life forces; the toxic overload being forced into the air; the food; the very dirt we walk on! Expand the curves just a brief moment into the future and you have complete Eco-breakdown.'

## GUILT AND REDEMPTION

Understandably Rachel was extremely shaken by his conviction, and, of course, rather scared.

'What was that about you and the other big players then?' she asked. 'Who are you?'

'The super-rich; those of us who own the means of production; the people who make everything that fucks everything up. Now listen, don't get me wrong. I ain't absolving the little guys from guilt, they bought the stuff we made, they wanted the stupid little things that we swapped the planet for. Nobody objected. A quick look at the litter on the Carlton beaches makes me pretty doubtful that things would be much different if "the people" had been in control . . . But it's still mainly my fault, mine and my colleagues. I mean, is the man who buys pornography as guilty as the man who makes it and sells it? I reckon not, after all, the poor wanker on the receiving end would not have thought to even want it if it wasn't stuffed under his nose.'

Sly was enjoying getting all this off his chest. He had kept his own counsel for so long that it was an immense relief to talk about it, wallow in his guilt. Especially to Rachel, a greeno who he had developed such a desire for. He was like the adulterer who confesses all to his faithful wife in order to absolve his own guilt; laying it on the least deserving recipient. This was confession and absolution for Sly, he needed it. And, of course, he would pay Rachel back for her patience a billion fold. After all, he had the whole of creation to offer her.

'You know I was once the major backer for the development of a kind of instant French fry in a tube,' Sly said, continuing his strange confession. 'What you did was heated up some oil in a frying pan and pumped the tube into the fat, out came a chemically expanded string of reconstituted potato. *Voila!* No need for deep-fat chip pans and peeling spuds and all that. What's more, it was terrific fun, you could have chips as long or short as you liked them. You could have them in whirls, tie them in knots, write messages with them. As crap products go this one was actually kind of nice.'

'Sounds good, I'd have bought it, once, just to see what it was like,' said Rachel, fascinated to find out what all this was leading to.

'Yeah, a lot of people did. We only put it out in the States but it made a packet. I was real sorry when we had to take it off the market,' said Sly.

Rachel did not ask why he had to take it off the market, reckoning that he was going to tell her anyway, which of course he did.

'Damn thing finally got banned. It was a kind of aerosol, see. The potato mixture was expanded by Chlorofluorocarbons, CFCs, you know the ozone eaters.'

'I'm an environmental commando, Mr Moorcock,' said Rachel, wishing to assert herself but actually sounding pretty dumb, 'Of course I know what a Chlorofluorocarbon is.'

'Yeah well I knew too, right from when I started marketing the stuff. It didn't stop me backing an aerosol that made chips though. What's more, I used every damn bit of political clout I had to lobby the politicos to stop them legislating against CFCs.'

'Well you're a bastard, aren't you?' said Rachel.

'Well, I suppose I am. It didn't seem that way at the time but I suppose I was and I suppose I still am, because I *knew* what that damn can was doing to the sky and yet I still put it on the shelves. People trust things on shelves, they think if there was anything wrong the government would do something. I mean, let's face it, nobody asked for an aerosol that sprayed chips . . .'

Rachel was getting tired now.

'Look, what the hell is going on?' she snapped suddenly, 'what are you doing here? What's all this shit about the end of the world? And what do you want with me? Come on, give me an answer . . . or . . .' There is nothing more demeaning than getting half-way through a threat and realizing that you don't have a punch line.

It was all right though, Sly had one of his own.

## WELCOME TO STARK

'Welcome to the Stark project, Rachel. I've told you that the

341

world is dying. It is, believe me, it really is. But, the vanishing point isn't total. One grain of sand is going to slip through – I and my colleagues are getting out. This construction area is to be the launch site for the Star Arks, a small fleet of rockets that will carry us away and with us everything we need to start again, to build a new world. This, if you like, is the dawn of creation. Genesis.'

Necessarily there was a pause, Sly's statement was not the sort to which there is a stock answer. Eventually Rachel said:

'Well, Darth Vador, this is fascinating, but don't you think it's the sort of fantasy you should have had when you were six?'

'We're going to the moon, Rachel, and from there we will watch the earth die.' Obviously Sly was aware that it was all going to sound a bit far-fetched, so he set about trying to make it convincing. 'It's over twenty years since the Americans landed on the moon, isn't it?' Sly continued. 'Haven't heard much about it since, have we? Not a squeak really. All that huge effort, a whole generation ago, and then nothing. Why do you think that is, Rachel?'

'I'm sure you'll tell me,' said Rachel wearily. It was clear that whatever else this loony intended he wasn't in a mood to let her go.

'We bought it,' said Sly, and Rachel was surprised. Sly was pleased he had finally solicited something other than disbelief or contempt.

'You bought the moon?' she asked.

'Not me,' said Sly, 'I was only fifteen at the time. I've only been a party to the Stark project for a few months. But the then members of the consortium bought it. The US government had stuck a flag in it, just the way the British once stuck a flag in Australia, and like the British the Yanks thought that meant they owned it. Well, there wasn't much they could do with it at the time, the whole project had been a prestige affair anyway, so we made them an offer, and they sold it to us, along with all the research, technology and hardware that had gone into getting to it in the first place.'

Sly could see that he had given Rachel real cause for thought. It had, after all, been a whole generation since the moon shots, and it was true that nobody had been back since.

'The original reasons given were potential mineral research and all that,' Sly continued. 'Which was partly true as well. In those days the super-rich still thought that earth's Vanishing Point could be avoided and that the moon would just become another place to make money. Since then the situation has changed a lot. The importance of a bolthole like the moon has become rather clear.'

'Bolthole!!' exclaimed Rachel. 'Don't be ridiculous, you can't live on the moon. There's no air and . . . and . . . well there's nothing, no food, no . . . Oh God I don't even know why I'm talking to you. The whole thing is just bloody ridiculous.'

'You've got no idea what we can and cannot do, Rachel,' said Sly glaring at her and trying to be tough and commanding. 'The richest people in the world have been working on this for nearly three decades. Think about it, three decades *before* the moon shot they had only just developed a jet engine. What do you think we can achieve so long after?'

'I don't know, but whatever it is it can't possibly be a viable alternative to slogging it out on earth, however bad things get,' protested Rachel, amazed at herself that she was even discussing it.

'I keep telling you!!' said Sly, for the first time slightly losing his cool. 'Don't kid yourself, the earth's illness is not like a normal disease that you just presume one day "they'll" come up with a cure for. There is no cure, it's dying, all our research is conclusive, we *have* to try and get out, however unpleasant or difficult the prospect. Don't you see?'

'No, it's insane, you're mad, this is all ridiculous. I don't even know why I'm talking to you . . .' said Rachel, also losing her cool. Sly pressed on.

'For fifteen years now we have been blasting off the necessary equipment, leaving it floating up in space ready for us to reclaim, should the need arise. The orbit of the moon is

343

one vast warehouse of spinning hardware: 65 per cent of the hundreds of commercial satellite launches that have taken place over the years haven't carried communications satellites at all. They've carried dead weight of hardware, everything from food to frozen sperm. Thousands of tonnes of it has built up and it's all been left, spinning around the earth or the moon, all armed with little booster rockets, waiting for the time when we will fire them down onto the moon's surface. And that time is almost upon us. Come on, I'll show you something,' said Sly.

He grabbed Rachel by the hand, which was the first time they had ever touched, and led her to the door.

# NOAH'S WORKSHOP

It is very difficult to take in something really impressive. This is probably a good thing because if the mind was truly capable of comprehending the magnificence of, say, a great cathedral, or the strangeness of most fish, we would probably all go mad.

Certainly Rachel had considerable trouble getting her head around the creation that Sly was so spaciously showing off for her benefit. She felt as she had used to feel at school when faced with Shakespeare; she knew it was huge stuff and she could sort of see why, but the truth was it still failed to penetrate in a genuinely moving manner.

First Sly showed Rachel one of the biggest holes in the ground she had ever seen, a massive concrete chasm, filled with tiny figures working on things in it.

'I reckon some of those guys must be beginning to think it's a strange kind of hotel they're building,' said Sly. 'Still, fuck 'em, they're getting paid more than they could ever have dreamed of, and they're all foreign anyway. So fuck 'em. I don't guess anyone's going to be over anxious to rock the boat and lose a job like this, especially with the depression we've got going right now. What do you think of it?' said Sly turning to Rachel with a degree of proprietorial pride.

'What is it?' she asked, not really wanting to hear.

'It is one of the six largest launch silos in the world,' said Sly, 'the other five are all within three miles of here . . .'

They stared over the edge together in silence, then Sly mused, 'and the Lord said, make it a fuck of a lot of cubits tall, and a fuck of a lot of cubits wide,' getting biblical for a minute.

They drove in Sly's Jeep to one of many warehouses. Sly

showed her four huge, silvery rolls of a kind of gossamer thin metallic mesh. 'Three hundred and fifty miles of solar cells, woven into a flexible fibre,' Sly said. 'This will be part of the payload of one of the three unmanned launches which will blast simultaneously with the Star Arks . . .'

And even in all the strangeness of her situation, Rachel found herself snapping . . . 'Unstaffed.'

'Yes, sorry, unstaffed. Hopefully our new world won't be a sexist one,' Sly continued in the sort of tone Hitler must have used when he was guaranteeing Czechoslovak neutrality.

'Everything we need is already up there but the consortium has always reserved one final set of launches to allow for improved technology. Obviously, at the last minute we want to take the very best the world has to offer. These solar cells make the ones we sent up five years ago obsolete. They'll provide the power of four nuclear plants, and no chance of pollution you see.'

'That's nice,' said Rachel, for want of anything better.

Sly continued, 'The idea is that with the human launch we establish a kind of camp which will be supplied entirely artificially, from what we take with us on the blast. This is why the silos are so big, there's a lot to take. It'll be a bit cramped, but we'll live in the camp while we concentrate on building a self-sufficient world . . .'

As they walked through the warehouse, Sly felt obliged to confess some doubts. 'It all *sounds* all right. I suppose it might work, it might not. Quite exciting really. These solar sheets will simply be flown up and left spinning in the moon's orbit with the rest of the junk until we are ready to boost them in. The estimate is approximately five years. Everything will stay in orbit until we are ready to bring it in. There's even a micro-film library floating up there. Wonder when we'll need that, not for ages I suppose. Bet it's all Keynes and Adam Smith anyway. That's the trouble with setting off with a bunch of bankers . . . Apparently we're taking with us from earth enough of everything for five years. After that we're on our own. But I'm told our only real job will be to create a viable atmosphere, after that all else will follow on . . .'

'Just create it, eh?' said Rachel.

'Yes, it will be done with plants, photosynthesis, all that biology business, the plants will use the available carbon dioxide and the sunlight to create oxygen. The water comes from under the surface.'

Rachel's mind was reeling, as Sly had intended that it should. He knew how she felt, he had felt exactly the same way when the whole terrible, enormous, cowardly, craven project had been put to him.

'There are seventy-five members in the Consortium,' said Sly, adding casually, 'each can take a partner. Then there is a scientific and work team of fifty who have been indoctrinated into Stark. They will also be allowed a partner, but one who will be required to have some medical or scientific skill. All told, there will be two hundred and fifty individuals in the Arks. A decade from now they will be all that is left of the human race. But we are taking a lot of frozen embryos. I suppose if the water runs out we can always drink them.' This was a joke but not one that Rachel appreciated.

'We're also taking a lot of animal foetuses all frozen in suspended animation. Same principle as Noah really, but a bit more high tech. And obviously we aren't taking the nasties. No cockroaches for instance, although what's the betting a couple of the bastards manage to sneak into the ship.'

They wandered into another warehouse.

'See that,' said Sly, pointing at a box that on opening appeared to contain an ice-making machine. 'That's a kind of filter. It can get the horrid bits out of sweat and piss and all that, so you can drink it again. Apparently a very large percentage of the water that we will require we actually take up in our own bodies, clever eh?'

Rachel believed him. She could not believe that she believed him, but she did.

'You know that if the world finds out that, having made a pretty substantial contribution to the mess we're all in, you're all pissing off, well there's probably going to be a fair degree of protest,' said Rachel.

347

'Yes, we know that,' Sly replied.

'I mean they'll probably all march up here and tear you limb from limb and torch the whole disgusting dump,' Rachel continued.

'I don't think so, Rachel,' said Sly. 'I reckon they'll come up here, all right, but they'll be trying to get on the Arks, mass panic. Billions of people trying to be one of the two hundred and fifty. But if people did find out, I doubt they would believe it, you didn't until you saw it and I'm not about to show it to anybody else. But no one will know. Between us the members of the Stark Group own far too much of all the newspapers and TV and radio stations in the world, Soviets excluded of course, but we just ignore them and they just ignore us. Imagine if the Chairman of the Central Committee of the Politburo or whatever it is, tried to tell the world that good old Tex Slampacker, who has done so much for little children in hospital, was going to fuck off and leave them all to Eco-doom. Nobody would believe him would they?'

Rachel asked the question she'd been meaning to ask for some time.

'Why have you showed me?' she said.

Rachel was not at all a vain person but she had guessed his answer. 'Because, Rachel, I want to take you with me,' Sly said.

## A HELL OF A DATE

Well, of course, Rachel had been propositioned before, she had some small experience of chat-up lines that went beyond a casual 'what about it?' She had been promised meals, asked on holiday, CD had even offered to devote what remained of his life to making her happy. But no one had ever offered to save her from a dying planet. No man had ever asked her to go with him to the moon and stay there. And of course, if what Moorcock said was true, then nobody had ever offered to save her life before. The whole situation was one that would confuse anybody.

'Why me? Haven't you got a girlfriend, a wife?' she asked.

'No,' said Sly. 'I have no one to take and I want to take you.'

'To the moon?'

'To the moon.'

'You do realize,' said Rachel, 'that this is tantamount to asking me to marry you?'

'Of course,' replied Sly.

'And you've known me for about five minutes?' she continued.

'Look,' said Sly, 'I have no one to take, all right, no one I would even dream of considering. I liked you the first moment I saw you, the whole situation's insane anyway. I'm acting on instinct.'

Rachel said she'd think about it.

# TIME RUNS OUT

The next morning Durf arrived and Sly, like Tyron, was asked to kindly join him in the project control room. He brought bad news.

## HANGING ON THE END OF A CHAIN

'Gentlemen, I have received predictions from the Domesday Group which have convinced me that Vanishing Point is upon us. I have alerted principal Stark shareholders to proceed to this location forthwith. Once enough have arrived for us to be quorate, I shall propose immediate departure, suggesting that we deploy the eight day count-down procedure as agreed in Helsinki.'

Sly and Tyron just stared at him. There isn't a lot one can say to a man who has just told you that you are emigrating to the moon in eight days. Perhaps sensing the need for small-talk Durf added, 'Personally I wouldn't eat that crabmeat sandwich.'

Sly and Tyron stared at him again. In fact, they just carried on staring at him since they hadn't stopped from the first time. There was a plate of sandwiches on the desk. They had come with the coffee, Tyron had absentmindedly picked one up.

'I am reliably informed,' said Durf, 'that the long feared TTO has occurred in a food layer stretching from micro-organisms right up to simple animals.'

Eight days? Sandwiches? TTO? Sly, at last, found his feet. 'Durf, what the fuck are you talking about, you patronizing, one-eyed, South African bastard.'

Sly's attitude did not surprise Durf. After all, he was a patronizing, one-eyed, South African bastard.

'What is the long feared T T O and what is the problem with the sandwiches?' asked Sly, deciding that things would probably move faster if he was less confrontational.

'T T O, is Total Toxic Overload and it is the point at which a species becomes so compromised by toxic waste that it becomes a liability to the food chain. Unfortunately, only man is capable of recognizing this problem and isolating the offenders . . .'

Only Durf could have called a polluted microbe an offender.

'If we are told that a tuna has been contaminated with mercury, then we do not eat it. But all other creatures who include tuna in their diet will, of course, continue to eat it, and hence become compromised themselves.'

Durf had the politicians' habit of sanitizing unpleasant things by refusing to describe them properly. Hence 'polluted' became 'compromised' and, no doubt, 'polluted to death' would be 'terminally compromised'.

Durf continued his description of the terminally compromised food chain. 'Each creature is poisoned by its diet and then itself becomes the poisoned diet of a superior creature. In this manner the poisons gather momentum on their way up to the top of the food chain where sits man. Man eats everything from simple crustaceans to highly evolved mammals, hence it is fair to say that we consume the accumulated pollution of all other species.'

The sandwich fell from Tyron's limp grasp. It lay on the floor, poised and vicious, like a scorpion, primed and ready to kill.

'Well, that's great isn't it?' said Tyron.

'Now that the entire base of the food chains have achieved, or will soon achieve, T T O . . .' Durf spoke as if the base of the food chain should get a prize for this, '. . . we can assume that within a single season, all animal food on earth will be poisoned and entirely inedible. This, combined with the

351

world crop failures, which are now a regular feature of our greenhouse summers, means . . .'

'It really is all over,' Sly spoke slowly, like a person just waking up and trying to remember where they are.

'There can be no doubt about it,' said Durf. 'The nuclear pollution in the Northern Hemisphere has forced a far greater reliance on food from southern seas. With the wreck yesterday of the toxic waste ship, *Ataria C42*, off Shark Bay, that source, already massively strained, collapses altogether. There is virtually nothing left to eat on earth. We have polluted all of it. This is why I am calling in the shareholders. With their permission we will start the eight day count-down.'

'Well you've got my permission, let's bugger off while we still can,' said Tyron.

'But the rockets are only just in place,' said Sly. 'We can't possibly be ready?'

'We *have* to be ready, Mr Moorcock,' Durf insisted, 'otherwise we go with what we have. Nagasyu is only a few hours sail from the west coast with the remaining hardware. I have every confidence in him. We *will* achieve what is necessary.'

'And then I suppose we walk on water for an encore,' Sly found Durf's manner irritating, 'although with the shit that's in it these days, we probably could walk on water.'

'It is not a question of miracles, Mr Moorcock, but careful planning. Planning that commenced considerably before your own indoctrination into Stark,' said Durf, who sometimes forgot that he was an employee. 'The only problem that seriously concerns me is that of the American journalist. My men have not so far located her in or around Bullens Creek. I am confident that she knows nothing and has no means of alerting people, even if she had something to say —'

'So what's the problem then?'

'There *is* no problem. It is just that the world is about to realize it is dying. Even the suspicion that there is an escape route might cause the more volatile to investigate. There is no room on Stark for panic-stricken hordes. The chances of information leakage are at present small but then again so are the microbes at the bottom of the food chain and look at the damage they have wrought. It would certainly be preferable if we could locate the American.'

'Locate' of course being Durf-speak for kill.

# POWERS OF PERSUASION

Neither Sly nor Tyron had mentioned to Durf that they held all but one of the journalist's friends who, one presumed, must hold the key to her whereabouts. Sly had kept quiet because he was concerned for Rachel, and Tyron because he was determined to sort the situation out himself. He would make them talk, he would find the American and everything could proceed as planned.

Therefore, while Sly returned to his quarters to tell Rachel that the moment had come and that she'd better decide, Tyron collected Du Pont and returned to his prisoners.

## ADMINISTRATIVE METHODS

The prisoners had now spent nearly an entire night tied up on chairs and were looking pretty bedraggled – which in Walter's case meant exactly the same as usual. However, Tyron was disappointed to discover that their long hours of discomfort had made them no more co-operative. With only eight days left, Tyron determined to dispense with the charm idea altogether and get straight down to business.

He ordered Du Pont to do his stuff.

Du Pont had the guards drag CD, still bound to a chair, into the middle of the room.

'Guys, guys, guys,' said CD, trying to lighten the tone a little. 'Really this is so medieval, surely there is a better way. I mean, we just don't *do* this sort of thing any more.'

'On the contrary,' said Du Pont, who loved saying things like 'on the contrary' to helpless prisoners. It ranked up there with phrases like 'that was very foolish' and 'please do not underestimate me, Mr Bond'. Despite his bandaged nose, Du Pont was feeling particularly tough and hard. 'Torture is more prevalent today as an accepted part of the armoury of the busy administrator than it has ever been,' continued Du Pont.

CD watched in cold horror as Du Pont opened his small suitcase and took from it, amongst other things, a kind of wire sponge, rather like an enormous pan scrubber. CD wondered if he was to be flayed alive with a huge scouring pad.

'I'll tell you a good way of torturing people,' CD babbled. 'Water! It's a sure fire one, water! That's right, the Chinese water torture. What you do is you drip water on a person's head . . . Ugh! It's just horrible! I mean, it drives people into agony and insanity through the sort of maddening in-evitability of it. Why don't you do that one to me? Go on, drip water on my head, phew! I bet I wouldn't be able to take that one.'

But it was a futile effort. CD was relying on the old war movie cliché that the worst tortures are not physical, but ingeniously psychological. Well doubtless you end up with less mess on the carpet, but if one were to ask the average victim whether, given the choice, they would opt to be irritated by water, or have five billion volts shot through their nipples, that person might just choose to learn to live with the splish, splish, splish.

CD was not to be given such an option. It was to be straight physical intimidation for him. He realized he had been wrong with the flaying theory when Du Pont put on thick rubber gloves and attached two jump leads to the wire wool. The leads ran back into a variable transformer, which was, in its turn, plugged into the wall.

'Look, man, please, I mean, you know!' said Walter. He was a hard man but what was going on would have upset a horny sadist in a party mood. 'Look, this is ridiculous, I mean, please.'

'Just tell us where the Yank bitch is,' barked Tyron, using the word 'bitch' in order to enter into the spirit of the occasion.

CD was thinking hard. To disclose the location of the Culboons' holiday home, where Chrissy was waiting, would almost certainly mean her death. On the other hand, he had no illusions as to what his performance would be under torture. He was faced with what must be the classic dilemma in such circumstances. Why not give in immediately? Since the chances are almost certain that you're going to capitulate in the end, should one not simply collapse in the first place and save oneself a great deal of unnecessary unpleasantness.

CD had considered lying of course, saying something along the lines of, 'The Yank bitch is holed up in the old quarry'. But he knew it would be pointless, his interrogators knew that Chrissy was either in or around Bullens Creek. A helicopter could check out any story in less than fifteen minutes, and then no doubt it would be a bigger sponge and longer jump leads.

Du Pont instructed one of the guards to pour a jug of water over CD. The guard had to fill it, because it was the same jug that Zimmerman had gargled with the previous morning as a health precaution after biting into Du Pont's nose.

They soaked CD down, but he was under no illusions that he was to be subjected to Chinese water torture.

## WARTIME MEMORIES

On the roof Zimmerman wondered how long he could afford to give it before he made a move. He did not particularly wish to make a move. He was, after all, pretty heavily outnumbered and a day and a night hiding on top of a roof in the searing greenhouse heat had made him wilt a little. But he would have to do something. Through a tiny crack in the guttering he could see the steel-grey sponge and he recalled the last time he had encountered such a device.

The Vietnam war had been an unpleasant one even considering the high standards of horror set by modern conflicts. Both sides paid scant regard to the Geneva Convention. Zimmerman had himself taken part in Napalming civilians

356

although he had never committed the private cruelties of rape and pillage that were so common. On the other hand, he had himself been subjected to inhuman cruelties by the other side. The Vietcong had caught him on a forward reconnaissance, and had, with the aid of the battery from a crashed US helicopter gunship, subjected him to electric shock treatment in order to discover where the rest of his Yankee unit were. In vain had Zimmerman protested that he was Australian, they were not interested.

Zimmerman had been almost as mad at the time as he later became and so he was able to withstand the torment for the ten minutes he underwent it. That is until a low-level bombing raid mercifully dispersed the party. On the other hand, he was aware that he would not have lasted much longer. It hurt.

## SHOCK TREATMENT

CD's whole body convulsed. Despite the fact that he was tied to a chair, he managed to jump about six feet in the air. He screamed. Walter screamed. Mrs Culboon bit her rag grimly.

The world will never know how much CD could have taken, although he himself later admitted with disarming honesty that as the water dispersed the shock across his whole body, he knew that he could have taken absolutely no more whatsoever. But, before anyone had a chance to find out if this was the case, Zimmerman sailed back in through the window out of which he had made his exit so many hours before.

Everyone was shocked at this sudden apparition. It was Tyron's second shock within a few seconds. He had not really imagined that the disgusting Du Pont would actually start torturing anybody for real. Even Tyron balked a bit at that. He had presumed that the whole purpose of the torture threats had been to scare the prisoners into submission. Oh sure, a punch or two maybe, but not this. Tyron was a businessman, and this wasn't his business. He was quite capable of ordering death and beatings at long distance, and had done so in the case of Linda Reeve, but this close up horror was too near the knuckle by half.

Du Pont had rather shocked himself as it happened, he was just a little git really and for all his bluster he had never had the chance to properly do something like this before. Zimmerman had been surprised too. He never thought Du Pont would do it. He thought, like Tyron, that the whole thing was bluster and intimidation. That was why he had let CD take the first shot, he hadn't believed that it would happen. Of course, now that it had, he was forced to act.

Of course, the person most shocked of all was CD, but that was because he had just had about a million volts up him.

When he heard CD scream, Zimmerman realized that his only allies were speed and surprise, hence the entry had to be good. He flipped over onto his back, gripped the guttering, kicked hard, throwing his legs over his body, off the edge of the roof and swinging down in through the open window.

'Zimm!!' shouted a delighted Walter, 'Oh man . . .' He was about to add that Zimmerman's sudden appearance just had to be one of the very finest trips since the Beatles released 'Pepper', but there simply wasn't time.

'Freeze!' said Zimmerman, brandishing the gun that he had taken from Du Pont.

At least he would have been brandishing it if he hadn't accidentally left it on the roof. All he was actually brandishing at the surprised guards was fingers. Luckily he realized his mistake before anyone else did and he was able to grab the gun of the guard standing nearest. Zimm did not even have to hit him, the guard just let go. This is the sort of effect that you can get if you start a fight by flying in unexpectedly through the window.

'Right,' said Zimmerman, 'I'll start again. Freeze!!'

# CONTEMPLATING
# TREACHERY

### HORROR MOVIES

The previous night, after Rachel had told Sly that she would
think about his unusual chat up line, he had very
considerately left her with what he hoped would be sufficient
evidence to bring her around to his way of thinking.

The evidence was in the form of a video film and it made
your average horror movie look like something intended for
Granny and the wee ones. Any Hollywood producer worth
his salt who had chanced to see Sly's video, would have
quickly realized that all the stuff about monsters exploding
out of people's stomachs and small girls being raped by the
devil, was totally out of the window. Once you've been chilled
and thrilled by the story of the Sandoz Chemical Plant
screwing up the Rhine or the slow death of the Baikal Lake, it
no longer seems particularly worrying that a group of
teenagers on a holiday camp get cut to bits with chainsaws
because they're too stupid not to go down to the old boat
shed.

The Sandoz and Baikal stories were just two of the many
that were touched upon in the videos that Rachel watched
with increasing despair. It opened with the bleak
announcement that it was a top secret preparation to be
viewed by members of the Stark consortium only. Sly was still
in the room when this message came on . . .

'I'm not a member of the Stark consortium,' Rachel protested.

'Once you've watched that you will be,' smiled Sly and left her to it.

The show opened with a smart-alec looking fellow in an eye patch, addressing the camera. Professor Durf announced that the time had come to leave. That the long feared moment of truth was finally upon the Stark consortium.

'I can think of no better illustration to underline the urgency of our situation than to suggest that were God to attempt to take out an insurance policy on the world, he would not be able to afford the premiums.'

This was Durf's little joke. He had decided to kick-off with a gag just to show that, despite things being in a terrible state, he at least could maintain his suave intellectual detachment.

'What an arrogant creep,' thought Rachel.

Durf followed his little gag with a warning against a false sense of security engendered by current political cant.

'Of late, certain politicians have been attempting to play the green card in their grubby scramble for public support. Believe me, such tokenism is entirely cynical. The situation can never be reversed whilst market forces remain superior to political will. The politicians have always left us alone, and they *will* always leave us alone, because we pay the piper, and we call the tune.'

Much of what followed Rachel already knew something about, but the sheer weight of current catastrophe certainly took her by surprise. It could not have been a more unmitigated tale of gloom and impotent despair if it had been written by Dostoyevsky.

It started on a fairly light note, briefly detailing the world's smaller disasters, like the 1986 Sandoz Chemical leak in Switzerland. This minor incident, which at the time was entirely overshadowed by the World Cup, concerned the accidental discharge of thirty tonnes of toxic waste into the Rhine. Of course, thirty tonnes doesn't sound that much – the lead singers of heavy metal bands can sometimes weigh as much as that – but the seriousness of a toxic leak depends entirely on how toxic the leak is. Well, in the case of Sandoz,

the words 'very, very' spring to mind, and then spring out
again as being scarcely adequate. And then spring back again
for the want of a better alternative. Put it this way, if the
universe is very, very, big, then the Sandoz leak was very,
very toxic. That thirty tonnes leaked from one factory, into
one river, swept through France, Germany and Holland and
killed every single living organism in its path.

The catalogue of disaster unfolded before Rachel. She
learnt of the Baikal. Situated in the Soviet Union it is the
world's largest lake. The Russian people harbour a love for it
of huge and mystical proportions, which is rather apt because
the lake is itself of huge and mystical proportions, being a
kilometre and a half deep and containing, according to some,
20 per cent of the world's fresh water. 'Fresh' of course being
a loose description for something that is being filled with shit
and industrial waste.

Everything that Sly had attempted to impress upon Rachel
unfolded before her on the TV. The message was always the
same. The myriad destruction in every single area of the
natural world must soon provoke a total breakdown. The time
had come to bugger off.

Rachel's head was numb. It couldn't have been more numb
if she'd woken up in the middle of the night to discover that
she'd been sleeping on it in an awkward position . . . So this
was the way the world was to end. Not with a bang, not with a
whimper, but with retching nausea as the teeming billions
struggled for their final gulps of food and air before sinking
for ever into the stench, filth, disease and slime that would
certainly be our final environment in the huge rubbish dump
and toilet that we have created out of Paradise.

## LORDS OF CREATION

Professor Durf was speaking again . . .

'As you all know, as principal creators of the world's wealth
– the one human creation, I am happy to say, that remains
untainted and unpolluted – we have known for many years

now that were human activity to continue unchecked it would and must lead to oblivion. We declined to interfere though, believing social engineering to be immoral. We all hoped, of course, that market forces would produce a solution; that ecologically responsible activity would somehow become profitable. As we know, it hasn't and that is just too bad. We had a duty to progress, to make money and create wealth, that was our bounden mission. If the earth had to die in the defence of a free market economy, then it is a noble death.'

Rachel glanced around for a bucket, this man was the human equivalent of sticking two fingers down your neck.

'Now is the time to look to the future,' the televised Durf continued. 'Now is the time to board the "Starks", the Star Arks. It is fitting that you, the world's richest men, should lead the human race to fresh fields and pastures new. For in the time of the first Ark the people worshipped God and hence, Noah, the most pious of men, was chosen to survive the flood and shape the future. In modern times people worship money, Money God in that it has been deified and can clearly be said to rule our lives. Hence, as I say, it is fitting that you, the super-rich, those who have worshipped money with a diligence and conviction far above the faith of lesser men, that you should board the Star Arks and carry our faith to a new civilization beyond the flood, on the moon.'

## A DIFFICULT OFFER TO REFUSE

Clearly Rachel's moral dilemma was a considerable one. Such was the depth of her concentration that she scarcely noticed the thunder in the sky which signalled the arrival of Nagasyu's final deliveries.

On the one hand she was disgusted. It was worse than the time she had inadvertently seen someone pick their nose and eat it. These repulsive people, having made a very large contribution to screwing up the world, now intended to slink off and leave everybody literally in the shit. Rachel would no more wish to associate with this type of human slug than she would voluntarily set up home in a nest of game-show hosts . . . And yet . . . and yet.

One thing was certain, Rachel no longer doubted the Vanishing Point scenario. Everybody was going to die, and die pretty unpleasantly at that. Except of course, not everybody. There was, it seemed, a flight out, and because a man with the hots for her had got a couple of tickets, she was being offered salvation.

She played the situation around and around in her mind. Strangely she was not over-exercised about the imminent end of earth. Despite the fact that she believed in it now, it still seemed like a story. What Rachel was wrestling with was simply the moral dilemma. The choice between a pointless act of suicidal courage and an act of pragmatic self-preservation. It was clear that no useful purpose could be served by her staying and she flattered herself that she deserved to live as much, if not more, than some bimbo that Moorcock might choose to take if she declined to go. The morals of the situation were by no means cut and dried. Rachel was no more guilty than anyone else, it wasn't her fault that we killed the world.

She kept on thinking. Wondering what she would do; wondering where her friends were; wondering what she thought about Sly.

And so the long night wore on, the last night before the Stark count-down began.

In the morning Sly returned from his meeting with Durf and Tyron where he had discovered T T O and the fatal sandwich. It was decision time.

# THE TABLES TURN

## GETTING TIED UP IN KNOTS

Covering his erstwhile captors with one hand, Zimmerman cut his comrades' bindings.

'Man, I've been hanging out on that roof for twenty-four hours,' he remarked, 'I don't recommend that kind of shit to anybody.'

'Zen is the only way to deal with trips like that, Zimmerman,' said Walter. 'I guess you must have found your centre and relaxed into a meditative balance.'

'I killed two lizards and ate them,' replied Zimm.

Walter agreed that this was one way of passing the time and that everybody had to do their own thing.

By now Zimm had released all three prisoners. He dragged a chair into the corner of the room and stood on it, this gave him the optimum available field of fire with which to cover operations while the others used their bindings to tie up Tyron, Du Pont and the guards.

This done, Zimmerman inspected the knots. 'CD, man, this is a double bow,' he protested.

'It's the only one I know Zimm, it works fine on shoes,' said CD who had not really recovered from his interrogation and still looked like you could have run a three bar electric fire off him.

Zimmerman attempted to explain the art of knot tying to CD, taking the two ends of the rope and creating a complicated system of loops and bows. 'This is a knot, man. You have to make a tunnel, then the train goes through the tunnel, right? Then these two ends here are the people OK?

And you put them perpendicular to the train and wind the track round them, right? Then you gather up the slack right, that's the uhm . . .'

'Station buffet?' enquired CD.

'Well, no man, I don't think so, but I guess we can call it that, because actually, rules are just mind control,' said Zimmerman who, it must be remembered, was only lucid when he absolutely had to be. 'You gather up the station buffet . . . stuff it into the train . . . Oh yeah, that's right, it's the *coal*, not the station buffet, it's coal, right . . . you stuff the coal into the train, and pull the train back through the tunnel, man, then you jerk the signal tight and dig, the dude will *never* escape.'

As Zimmerman said this the knot fell apart and the two ends of cord fell to the floor.

'Maybe you forgot the driver, man,' suggested Walter. 'When I was in the boy scouts I remember there was always a driver.'

'You were in the *boy scouts* man!' said Zimmerman, surprised.

'Well, yeah, like for a week,' replied Walter defensively, 'until I discovered it was just fascistic social engineering. Anyway, man, what's your beef? You were a fucking Marine Commando.'

'Oh yeah, Walter, that's right, dwell on the past,' said Zimmerman.

Mrs Culboon tried to restore order. 'I can do knots,' said Mrs Culboon. 'I'll tie them up.'

'Hey, listen lady, I can do knots, right?' said Zimmerman in an offended tone. 'I mean, knots are one of my big things.'

'Ha!' said Mrs Culboon. And even mad Zimmerman had to admit that she had a point.

'Look, be sensible,' protested Tyron, 'you can't possibly get away, it's many miles to the wire, there are guards and cameras everywhere. And even if you did get through, where will you go then? We own Bullens Creek, lock, stock and barrel, and everywhere else for that matter. You're in the middle of a desert, what can you possibly achieve?'

'Oh yeah, that's right, bring us down,' said Walter. 'Make it all sound totally depressing, why don't you? You have a real attitude problem, Mr Tyron. You have to take a more positive trip. It's just a bio–rhythm thing.'

'Listen,' interjected CD. 'I don't care what there is to face out there. While we were in your care, Mr Tyron, I got plugged into the wall and turned into a light bulb. Personally I'll take my chances.'

'They're all tied up good,' said Mrs Culboon.

## FURTHER INTERROGATION

'OK,' said Zimmerman, 'nearly time to go, but first we need a few answers. After all, I reckon that's why we came here in the first place, to find out what's going on . . . So, what is the scene Daddy? What goes down here? Why the rocket fuel? The launch silos? The guns and stuff? Man what *is* this trip?'

There was a sullen silence from Tyron and Du Pont, the guards obviously said nothing because they knew nothing.

'So you ain't going to tell us nothing, then?' continued Zimmerman. Still there was a sullen silence.

'CD would you be so kind as to pass me the electrified wool, please,' said Zimmerman. 'Taking care to hold it by the leads. Dig?'

There was a surprised silence at this turn of events. CD crossed the room and picked up the instrument of torture. It crackled a little and a few tiny sparks flew from it.

Tyron and Du Pont were thinking. Tyron was thinking about guts, honour and not being pushed around. Du Pont was thinking that this was a mad hippy who had recently nearly bitten his nose clean off.

'We're building a colony fleet of rockets to emigrate to the moon because the earth is in rapid and terminal ecological decline,' blurted Du Pont and Tyron gave him a disgusted stare.

The ironic thing was that Du Pont's craven cowardice did him no good at all because obviously nobody believed him.

366

'You sure do have to hand it to these fellahs,' laughed Mrs Culboon, 'when it comes to thinking up really shitty excuses for what they're up to they are the very best. The moon! I reckon that's even better than the story about building a hotel.'

There was general laughter, and then Zimmerman seemed to snap. 'Now let's have the fucking truth!' he screamed making everybody jump at once. 'Right now!' He grabbed the electric sponge from CD and held it so that its edge was a millimetre away from the whimpering Du Pont's face.

'It's own medicine time, man!!' Zimmerman's eyes were wild and fearful. The veins on his hands stood out firm as he gripped the clamps of the jump leads. 'You're gonna *burn* man, you are gonna fucking burn!!!!'

Walter had no cause to love Du Pont, even less so did CD, but they both felt that Zimmerman was becoming somewhat alarming.

'Hey, Zimm baby, this is your man, Walter . . . Listen you have to cool it, you know? I mean, we cannot start torturing people, because like, in many ways that puts us on the same level as them, right? Which kind of begs the question, what are we fighting for?'

'Yeah,' CD chimed in, 'he who sups with the devil should use a long spoon and all that.'

'Give him a tickle with it, the bastard deserves it,' said Mrs Culboon, representing the hawks, so to speak.

Zimmerman just went wild. He screamed that everybody – and he meant everybody – should shut the fuck up. And whilst Walter mumbled something about hurting a guy's feelings, Zimm hurled what was left in the jug of water at the wall, then he dragged the electric wool back and forth across it, in huge sweeps, causing great showers of sparks to burst further from it.

'We have no *time* man!!!!' he shouted, 'We have no time for chicken shit liberals!!!'

Had a psychiatrist popped his head around the door at that moment and taken a peek at Zimmerman, he would have instructed his secretary to cancel all calls for the next decade because he had a big job on.

'We have been shot at! Imprisoned! Sexually abused!' This last one was a surprise to everybody, but Zimmerman was employing the degree of dramatic license traditionally afforded to the psychotically insane. 'My main lady, Mrs Culboon, has been hassled by Hitlerheads,' he continued, pausing only to kick Tyron in the chest so that the chair which he was tied to toppled over backwards. 'And I want to know *why* man!! I want to be hip to what is going *down* here! And *this* dude!!' He flung a fist across Du Pont's face '. . . is going to lay it on me! Man, he is going to divulge the whole vibe, or the lights are gonna dim all over Australia, because he will be soaking up most of the national grid!!'

Zimmerman spat on the wire to make it crackle. 'Now – lay – it – on – me – man!!' And he punctuated each word by sweeping the mesh at arms length in front of a weeping Du Pont, missing him by a hair's breadth – and a thin hair at that, not the thick, coarse, lush kind, but the sort that comes from a person that you always think is going bald, even if they aren't.

Du Pont was, understandably, terrified and also rather confused. All this dig, dude, hip and vibe talk was new to him. He had spent the sixties as an administrator at a Swiss finishing school.

'What does he want?' Du Pont pleaded through his tears.

CD jumped in. 'He wants to know what you're building here, and please tell him quick.'

'I swear you'll fry, man, I swear!!' added Zimmerman unnecessarily.

Du Pont nearly had a heart attack.

'I've told you,' he bawled, his cheeks wet, 'we're building a colony fleet of rockets to emigrate to the moon because the earth is in rapid and terminal ecological decline. It's true, please believe me, it's true.'

'Like fuck it is,' said Zimmerman suddenly calming down and turning off the electricity at the wall. 'But you're a brave bastard, man, that's for sure. I took you to the edge, nothing

368

left to do after that but fry you and I'm no pig. I'll leave that to you.'

The tension in the room relaxed somewhat.

'Well you certainly had me fooled, mate,' said CD, 'I really thought you'd gone completely mad for a minute there.'

'I did go completely mad,' said Zimmerman, 'but I'm completely mad anyway, so it doesn't make any difference.'

'You should have given it to one of them,' said Mrs Culboon, 'now they know you won't do it, none of them will talk and maybe we'll never know.'

'If you want to do it, Mrs Culboon, be my guest,' Zimmerman offered her the jump leads but she declined.

'I ain't the damn loony Vietnam hero,' she said. 'You are, Zimmerman. It's your job to do any electrocuting that needs to be done.'

'Well, I'm not going to. So let's get out of there,' he replied.

'Hang on, hang on, what are we going to do about Rachel,' protested CD. And suddenly CD's mind flooded with horrible fears and suspicions. What the hell had that man Moorcock taken her off for?

# DECISION TIME

Sly knocked on the door of his quarters. He had not seen Rachel since the previous night when he had shown her around the launch site, and left her with the videos to consider his proposal.

She was standing at the window when he entered, watching the intense activity which the impending commencement of departure count-down had made all the more intense.

'Those are the rockets, the Star Arks,' he said, 'we've started preparing them for lift off.'

'Really? I thought you were putting in some new plumbing,' replied Rachel, who may have been seeing too much of Mrs Culboon.

'We're going real soon. Probably in eight days. Apparently the food chains are collapsing, it's Russian Roulette every time you have a sandwich,' said Sly ignoring her sarcasm. 'Better make up your mind, Rachel, there's only going to be one trip. Those who go, will be gone for ever, those who stay will stay for ever. The only difference being that those who go will still be breathing.'

'Breathing bottled air in a tiny cage.' Rachel was trying to protest but knew that she was wavering.

'Don't knock it, I expect it will be welcome enough when that's all there is. Besides,' Sly continued, 'that will only be for a year or two, slowly but surely we shall expand the cage and with that will come a less artificial environment, with oxygen from plants rather than bottles.'

'But you can't just go . . . can you?' Again she felt herself assailed by doubt.

'Well, I'm assured we can,' said Sly, 'I suppose maybe it'll screw up, but as I hope you have now accepted, the alternative is certain death. I know it sounds cowardly, I suppose it is, but at least somebody will be getting out. Would you rather we went out and picked up a couple of hundred hippies and dropouts? Would that be a better, more moral thing to do?'

## WHO DO YOU LOVE?

'Look,' said Rachel, getting down to the main point. 'Why me? I mean a new life on another planet is a lot to offer a girl you hardly know.'

'Who would you take?' asked Sly.

'What do you mean?' replied Rachel.

'Exactly what I say, who would you take?' he continued. 'You're not particularly attached, you have to take someone, or else you'll be all alone in space, so who?'

'Well . . .' said Rachel with hesitation.

'Not so easy, is it? Sure, at first you think that there must be someone. You think, after all, I'm very fond of any number of people. But that's not enough is it? If, despite knowing them well, you're only fond of them and not in love with them, then there's a reason for that. Sides of their personalities that you can avoid on earth, you couldn't get away from when you're drinking out of the same bottle of air. So, for a single, essentially lonely man, there is no clear choice, in fact there is no choice at all, I simply don't know anyone I love enough to take . . . In fact I'll go further, despite being fond of quite a few women, I love them so insufficiently that I *actively* don't want to take them . . .'

'And me?' asked Rachel, seizing the obvious line of questioning like an ace lawyer.

'Well, I don't know that I love you, but I certainly fancy the knickers off you, besides you're a spunky type . . . Now I'm a clear-headed enough bloke, I've fallen for girls before, it could all be over in a week, but you see I don't *know* that, do I? Maybe these feelings will last for ever, that's the difference, you see. With all the other girls that I care anything for at all, I *know* I know that I will never love them. With you I have a chance. That's why I want you to come with me. Until you busted your way into my life, frankly, I had no idea of what I was going to do . . .'

'Well, I must say you certainly have some terrific root lines. Live with me because I might not end up hating you . . .' replied Rachel.

'But that's not what I'm offering, that's not the reason you should come with me. The reason you should come with me is because that way you'll stay alive and what's more, it's the only way . . . Listen I'm not going to try and jump on top of you the moment we blast off . . .'

'Well thanks,' said Rachel, dryly.

'I'm just saying that, well with a bit of understanding, we might be able to build something together . . .'

'Please spare me the hearts and flowers, Mr Moorcock.'

'Look, don't take the piss out of me, girl! Because this is not a piss taking situation! I'm offering you life for Christ's sake.'

'All right, all right!' Rachel snapped, 'you've been living with this for a long time you know. It's still fairly new to me.'

She sat down, stood up, wandered around a bit, trying not to think about her family and the people she knew . . . they were all so far away.

'Well . . .' she said, and looked at Sly for a long time. He was certainly quite tasty. What's more he'd been straight with her about his emotional end of it. He didn't seem quite the bastard he had before. And after all, *somebody* had to survive the Vanishing Point.

'Well . . .' she said again . . .

# BETRAYAL

Sly's conversation with Rachel had taken place whilst Zimmerman had been going mad and threatening Du Pont with electrification.

When Rachel had thought a bit more, she and Sly made their way over to the complex of security cabins. They entered just as Zimmerman and his little party were gingerly emerging from the room containing the bound and furious figures of Tyron, Du Pont and the guards. For a moment the two groups stood at either end of the corridor, very surprised to see each other – CD was ecstatic.

'Rachel!' he shouted, 'you're back, you look fantastic, no really, fantastic. It's OK, don't worry, we've escaped! God you look great.'

'Keep it quiet kid,' said Zimmerman, pointing his gun at Sly. 'Thanks for bringing our comrade back, man, if she's been hurt you're going to suffer for it. You OK, Rachel?'

'Umm, yeah, great,' said Rachel rather nervously. 'Listen, Zimm . . .'

'Then what are we doing hanging about?' replied Zimm, 'we'll just tie-up the fat cat here and we'll all be on our way.'

'Zimm,' said Rachel more firmly. 'It's not going to be like that, I need to talk to you all.'

'Rachel, for Christ's sake, we have to split,' said Walter.

'No really,' said Rachel. 'I need to talk to you.'

Zimmerman gave her a puzzled frown, then he waved his gun towards the open door of an empty room. As quietly as possible, they all hurried in.

'Uhm, Colin,' said Rachel. 'Mrs Culboon, Walter, Zimm.

This is Silvester.' She looked slightly nervous, on edge, all sorts of terrible thoughts entered CD's head . . .

'What have they done to you, Rachel?' he shouted. 'What's he done to you, I swear I'll . . .'

'Oh do shut up, Colin, we don't have much time. I've found out what we wanted to know.'

CD nearly had an apoplexy.

'How! How did you find out, what did he make you do!!'

'Shut *up*, Colin, I'm telling you . . .'

And she went on briefly to outline the things she had learnt. She did the best she could to convince them of the true facts about the earth's condition, explaining that most of the terrible evidence had long been suppressed in order not to interrupt commerce. She described some of the things that she had seen on the video, and some of the things that Sly had told her. She spoke passionately, but of course, they were very sceptical, she had been herself. It is extremely difficult to convince people that their world is in a hopeless condition and virtually dead.

She explained a few of the details of Stark which sounded even more far-fetched. It wasn't until the end of her little speech that she managed to impress on the four sceptical listeners that she at least certainly believed every word that she was saying.

'I'm going,' she said, 'I'm going with Silvester. He offered me a place and I accepted.'

Obviously it was a shock. Walter was the first to speak.

'Man, you have got to be crazy?' he said inadequately. 'With this dude? With this bread-head? What about all your . . . all your *stuff*, man, the things you believe in. I mean the whole Eco-trip . . .'

'It's got nothing to do with the things I believe in,' said Rachel not very convincingly. 'I still believe all the same things . . . this is simply a matter of life and death, that's all. My principles won't be any use to me dead will they! I'm sorry, but if you get the chance you might as well choose life . . . You're going to die . . . I'm telling you, you are, and I think given my opportunity you'd make the same decision . . . Yes you would, you fucking well would. It's easy to say you wouldn't because you don't have the choice to make, but you would . . .'

CD found himself crying.

Sly tried to help her out.

'She's right you know,' he said, 'any one of you would jump at the chance, if you had it. But you haven't, so shut up and listen.'

'I'm not listening to you, you . . . prick!' shouted CD.

'Colin, if that's your attitude, just shut up, all right!' Rachel shouted back. 'And that goes for all of you! Silvester and I have made an understanding. He's my . . . friend. So if that's your attitude, any of you, just insulting him, well screw you! I only came down here because I made releasing you lot a condition.' There were many tears starting in Rachel's eyes.

'We don't need any favours girl,' said Mrs Culboon, 'this fellah's giving you stuff, and he gets what you've got in return, right? Well, there's a word for that kind of woman where I come from, and it isn't a pretty one.'

'All right, you watch your mouth,' shouted Sly, 'right now! You start watching your mouth.'

'You telling me what to do? Ha!' said Mrs Culboon, who loved saying, 'ha'. 'I got a gun this time, Mister, and you ain't. So this is what it feels like to be a boong, OK!'

She poked Sly in the ribs with her rifle. Walter decided it was time to pour oil on troubled waters.

'Hey, come on everybody, be cool. Please can we just be cool? You know it's still a free world, right? even if it is dying. A chick can hang out with whatever dude she pleases and for whatever reason you know man? I think that's in the American Constitution or something. Like what I'm interested in Rachel, is your prior implication that you might be able to help us get out. Is that for real?'

'We don't need any help, Walter, we've being doing just fine on our own,' said CD.

'Oh yeah, kid?' Zimmerman was in a lucid mood, 'well

375

certainly *we've* being doing OK so far, but may I remind you that we are still in the centre of the pig-pen and I reckon two hippies, a middle-aged black woman and a guy who won't take off his sunglasses are not necessarily guaranteed a safe passage out of here.'

CD had not taken off his shades since the mission began, not even at night, possibly this was how he had come to shoot down the helicopter.

'Can you help us get to the wire?' Zimmerman asked Rachel.

'Of course. We'll be gone very soon,' said Rachel. 'There's nothing you can do to stop it and anyway, I can't be involved if you lot are all locked up like animals. I've told Silvester that he has to let you go.'

'I won't go!! I'm staying here, I can't leave Rachel with that . . . that . . .!' About five minutes later CD would think of a magnificent and perfect insult but for the time being his mind was blank. Zimmerman gave him little time to think.

'Shut up, man,' said Zimmerman, 'if we can split, we will split.'

'Stop telling me to shut up,' shouted CD even louder, but it was clear that everybody thought that he should shut up.

'I have security passes here, they should get you through if you're careful,' said Sly.

'Hey, uhm, forgive me if I appear cynical man,' said Walter, 'but, like, why should you do this thing for us?'

'I can't see a problem with letting you lot go,' replied Sly. 'After all, what we're engaged in is not actually illegal. We were always more concerned about the panic that we would spark if what we were up to was known. There's no time left for you to even convince the people of Bullens Creek, let alone anyone else. We own most of the papers, we own most of the TV, we'll be gone in a matter of days. What can you do? Anyway, Rachel wants it –' He looked at Rachel.

'How very fucking touching,' observed CD bitterly.

Rachel tried once more to convince them that she really had no choice. It was difficult of course because it rather meant rubbing in the hopelessness of her friends' own situation. After all, her argument for picking up on Sly's offer was the absolute certainty that the world was dying.

She soon gave up and took her leave without a word, Sly followed her. Zimmerman considered detaining them, but could see no point, they had been given the passes, there was no reason for Moorcock to come after them. Anyway, it was still difficult to see Rachel as one of the enemy.

# FURTHER DIVISIONS

'Mrs Culboon,' said Zimmerman, 'we have to find our way back to the wire where I'm presuming you have wheels. This is your patch, you'd better lead.'

'Hey, it wasn't a rocket launching site when I lived here,' Mrs Culboon protested, 'things have changed.'

And so they had. Already the consequences of the proposed eight-day count-down were being felt, the whole site was alive with thunder and light.

'Well, I know it's tough, Mrs Culboon,' said Zimmerman, 'but you have to try and guide us, we need to get out and to consider this. It's like an incredibly heavy conspiracy that we have uncovered here and we have to consider it very carefully.'

'We have to do something about Rachel,' insisted CD desperately.

'That woman's doing just fine by herself, boy,' said Mrs Culboon. 'You'd better start thinking about your own problems.'

'We can't just leave her!' CD protested. 'I mean he's probably brainwashed her or something.'

'Listen man, I know you are hot for the chick,' said Walter, trying to be soothing, but failing utterly, 'but you have to curb your urgings you know? Like put the lid on the whole passion thing, turn down the sex heat until we have a plan.'

CD bridled.

'It has absolutely nothing to do with a passion/sex heat thing,' said CD sniffily. 'I will have you know, Walter, that my emotions and intentions towards Rachel are entirely honourable.'

'Ha!' barked Mrs Culboon, who could be as irritating as anybody when she wanted to. 'Boy, I reckon your tongue's been hanging out so far for that woman I'm surprised you don't have cleaner shoes.' And she laughed long and loud. Discretion was not a major part of Mrs Culboon's nature and despite the fact that they were trudging through the enemy camp she could not keep her voice down. Luckily people were far too busy to notice.

CD was surprised, he had thought that he'd been discreet about his obsession. Of course, he had confided in the guys, but he could not recall sharing the secrets of his heart with old Mrs Culboon.

'How did you know?' he asked in all innocence.

'Listen son, when a fellah eats up a girl with every look and follows her around the room like his eyeballs were attached to her legs with string,' Mrs Culboon explained, 'I guess he ain't paying a casual interest in her.'

CD blushed to be so transparent. Then Zimmerman lost patience.

'Oh man, I mean, what is the point, no, like for real, you know? What is the point? Like I have to lay some information on you people right? We are in heavy shit here, you know? But are we doing a little hurrying? No way, man! Is there a degree of urgency in our actions? Is there fuck! No like there's just a whole lot of hanging out and chatting about sex, a subject incidentally, right, that *some* of us find like a drag and irrelevant, OK? I mean just what *is* the *point*! I rescue you all from death by electrocution and . . .'

'Zimm, you're getting hung up, man, you have to deal with it . . .' Walter, like Zimmerman, was anxious to move things along. They were, after all, still in the midst of the enemy camp and, despite their security passes, by no means out of danger. He for one had no desire to find himself back in a chair facing the electric wool.

'We really do have to split.'

And so with Mrs Culboon as a very nervous guide, they set off to make their way out of Hell's kitchen. She did think

379

about trying to make a route by the stars but was forced to discard the idea as it was still daylight.

## LEARNER DRIVER

The little EcoAction team were not the only people to be trying to get out of the compound that morning. There was a constant roar as trucks carried off workers whose tasks were now finished. There was much whooping and hollering from the happy ex-employees of Stark as they headed for Bullens Creek airport. They were all suddenly very rich, having received upwards of a year's salary for a couple of months' work. Stark had paid well for fourteen hour days with no questions asked and now they were laying off the workforce, giving them the sort of severance pay normally reserved for loyal employees of fifty years standing.

'Maybe,' suggested Mrs Culboon, 'we should try and hitch a ride out on one of these trucks because even if I can find the route, it's going to be a hell of a walk.'

'I've got a better idea,' said Zimmerman.

A couple of hundred metres or so from where they stood was the source of Zimmerman's idea, a heli-pad, on which stood four helicopters.

'You think we should steal a chopper?' asked CD, momentarily forgetting his misery over Rachel in this new excitement.

'I don't really accept the term "steal",' replied Zimmerman. 'I mean, in the greater scheme of things, like that helicopter is as much ours as it is anybody's.'

'You should have studied law, man,' said Walter. 'You'd blow the average wig-head away.'

Zimmerman began to lead the little group towards the helicopters, strolling casually, as if he was off to the shops.

'Take it easy everyone,' he suggested, 'it is important to be inconspicuous . . . C D, what goes down?'

It looked like CD was going down. He had adopted a sort

of crouched, low lope, dodging about behind parked cars and piles of equipment, scurrying from one thing to another.

'We're trying to steal a helicopter, Zimm,' said CD reprovingly, 'don't you think maybe we should take some cover?'

They were having to shout to make themselves heard, they were close to the heli-pad and one of the machines was ticking over noisily.

'Hey listen, CD, I didn't expect the SAS you know? But you are a definite liability,' shouted Zimmerman. 'Did you take lessons in looking suspicious, or is this a natural talent? I mean if you lope around like that, you might as well hang a sign around your neck saying "I shouldn't be here, please shoot me". The art of camouflage is to blend in, man, be inconspicuous.'

There was a pause.

'What?' shouted CD.

Zimmerman gave up, reflecting that despite the impracticality of CD's approach, it was probably better karma if everybody did their own thing. And anyway, there were no rights and wrongs in life, only different ways of being.

They walked along together, both pursuing entirely contradictory methods of disguise. Zimmerman, strolling with confidence and brazenly nodding greetings at passers by. CD crouched low, dodging about, occasionally jumping behind piles of equipment to emerge moments later glancing furtively over his shoulder with his collar turned up. Zimmerman made a mental note to ask CD why he felt that turning up his collar made a man about to steal a helicopter less easy to spot.

Of course, Zimmerman never did enquire, because for him, making a mental note was about as reliable a memory-jogger as writing condensation in the window.

The four of them strolled onto the pad and a great big man with a leather jacket and a gun asked them who they were. Zimmerman grunted and waved the pass that Sly had given him. This seemed to satisfy his macho challenger, who, if he thought them a pretty strange crew, decided to let it go. Live and let live was the guard's philosophy. He believed that everyone should be different, that was what made the world go around. In fact, under the leather belts and buckles and bullets, he himself was wearing white silk panties. Why should he worry because some bloke doesn't comb his beard, no reason to start a war. Private security attracts all sorts of types. Wearing a crash helmet for a living is, after all, a fairly weird job in itself.

There was an engineer working on the craft that had its engine running. Zimmerman approached him.

'This bird work good?' he asked.

'Sure, just fixed it up myself,' the man replied.

'Good, we're taking it.' Zimmerman did not even need to use his pass. The whole Stark operation had come together so quickly that everyone was a stranger to everyone else. What's more, none of the people employed in security had the faintest idea what it was that they were supposed to be guarding. The helicopter engineer accepted the arrival of the four weird looking strangers with the same fatalism that he greeted his enormous pay packet. He didn't know what it was about, but he certainly wasn't going to start rocking any boats.

They squeezed into the machine. It was a tight fit because it was clearly really only designed to take three, which meant it would have been tight for Walter on his own. CD grimaced, it had been one of these same craft that he had shot at, he could imagine the men screaming and writhing desperately in the tiny space as they burnt to death.

'I must say, Zimmerman,' said Mrs Culboon, sitting in Walter's lap, 'I must say, there doesn't seem much that you can't do mate. All this fighting, and shooting and stuff and now knowing how to fly a helicopter. Yep, I reckon you're a pretty spunky all-rounder and no mistake.'

Having delivered this magnificent compliment she settled herself as comfortably as she could on top of Walter.

'I don't know how to fly a helicopter,' said Zimmerman, waggling the stick and punching buttons.

'Ha ha!' shrieked Mrs Culboon, 'and I reckon you're quite a card with it, ain't that so mates?'

She twisted around, soliciting Walter's agreement for her sentiments, but Walter knew Zimmerman better.

'You say you can't fly this thing man?' he asked nervously as Zimmerman experimented with the levers under his seat.

'I didn't say I couldn't, I just said I didn't know how to,' Zimm replied.

'Oh yeah? Well like, what the fuck is that supposed to mean?' asked Walter, not unreasonably.

'Well, there's a difference you know? Like I might be able to guess.' With that Zimm must have pushed a particularly significant button, or pulled on an unusually sensitive knob, because the whole craft screamed and shuddered and rattled and vibrated so that the poor occupants could scarcely focus on each other. Fortunately it resolutely refused to leave the ground.

'I think maybe the anchor is out or something,' shouted Zimmerman. 'I mean we have plenty of power here, but no rising-up scene, is going down.' The others could not hear him, they could not even hear themselves think. Had they been able to they would probably have heard themselves thinking, 'Get the fuck out of the helicopter'. However, before this idea had a chance to percolate through the shuddering and the noise and penetrate into their rattling brains, an alternative course of action presented itself. The engineer whom Zimmerman had addressed before, came charging out of a nearby hangar to see who was making a purée of his chopper's gear box. He rushed up to Zimmerman's window and began frantically banging on it, jumping up and down, mouthing obscenities and generally employing body language to express distress.

Zimmerman opened the window – probably the only function in the whole helicopter that he was capable of working. He hung his elbow out and turned his head slightly. He looked for all the world like he'd just parked his '57 Chevvy down by the boardwalk and was preparing to eye the chicks, catch some rays and take it nice and easy. The fact he was sitting in the middle of what was beginning to resemble a mini-earthquake, had yet to dent his sang-froid.

'Yeah?' he mouthed at the frantic engineer.

The engineer leaned in through the window and flipped the controls about a bit; here a knob, there a lever. The machine spluttered and the juddering mercifully calmed itself, the noise dropped to something just below ear bleeding, and the vibrations no longer threatened to actually remove teeth.

CD, Walter and Mrs Culboon breathed a sigh of relief. Now it was merely intolerable, before it had been like a disco.

'Don't you know how to fly a chopper, Mister!!' shouted the angry engineer.

'Nope,' confided Zimm with disarming honesty. 'Do you?'

'Well of course I do,' the man screamed, 'but that's not the point. What I want to know is . . .'

He stopped there, not because he had suddenly lost his thirst for knowledge but because Zimmerman was pointing a gun at him.

'Get in,' Zimm said.

'Don't be absurd, look what the hell is going on . . . There isn't any room.'

But a glance at Zimmerman's expression convinced the engineer that it was time to make room. With resignation he squeezed in and sat on Zimmerman's lap.

'Ha ha!' laughed Mrs Culboon, mightily relieved that Zimmerman had relinquished the controls. 'Take us towards Bullens Creek, cab driver, and no racist anecdotes.'

## BIRDS EYE VIEW OF GENESIS

They soared above it all. Above Tyron and Moorcock and the ghastly betrayal in which they were both involved. They soared above Rachel too. CD stared desperately downwards, in the absurd hope that he might be able to spot her amongst all the trucks and construction and scurrying figures. Under normal circumstances, the thrill of his first ever ride in a helicopter would have driven all other considerations from his mind, but this was different. Already he didn't care, he only cared about Rachel, despite the fact that she had betrayed them. Except he could not think of her in those terms, not as a betrayer, as a Judas. He knew that however weak-willed she had shown herself, he would always forgive her. In the midst of these fine emotions, it was bitter gall indeed for CD to know that Rachel almost certainly didn't give a flying bugger whether he forgave her or not.

Mrs Culboon and Walter had no such romantic distractions to block their view of the fascinating scene beneath them. Five rockets were already in place, towering out of their silos and jutting up towards the helicopter. The rockets were supported by the spindly latticework towers that the previous night Walter and Mrs Culboon had taken for cranes. The final rocket was still awaiting installation. It lay on its colossal transport, like a designer biro, silver and white shining in the terrible burning sun. It bore the legend 'Star Ark' and beneath that a stylized representation of the moon. Even at this desperate moment, the grey figures of Stark, whose lives had been ruled by obsessive marketing, had not been able to resist the temptation to imbue their final product with a logo, designer graphics and a corporate image.

With the exception of the final rocket that had not yet been stood on its end, the Stark edifice was pretty much complete. It was an awe-inspiring sight.

'This really is vaguely out of sight,' said Walter.

'Sure is,' said their pilot, 'weirdest hotels I ever saw. Still, I guess the kids will like them and it'll certainly bring a lot of money into the state.'

It's quite difficult for an astonished silence to fall upon a group of people who are bursting out of an over-stuffed and roaring helicopter, especially when the group includes such gregarious individuals as CD and Mrs Culboon. None the less, an astonished silence is what descended in reaction to the pilot's statement.

Walter recovered first.

385

'Uhm, listen, forgive me man, but you do not need to be Dan Dare to work out that those are rockets down there,' he said.

'Rocket shaped hotels,' replied the man.

Silence returned; a silence sufficiently imbued with awe to deaden the tumultuous thwaka thwaka of the blades spinning above them.

'Rocket shaped *hotels*?' inquired Walter.

'Sure,' said the pilot cheerfully, who did not seem to mind being abducted. 'I guess it's some kind of theme park, you know, like Disney. Reckon kids could get pretty excited about sleeping in a rocket. Yeah, it sure will bring a heap of money into the state.'

## A FINE STATE

It is a strange feature of federated countries like the United States or Australia that there is often even more pig ignorant xenophobic tunnel vision regarding the rivalry between states than there is in the area of national patriotism. It is common to hear some brain-dead tub of lard politico, running for office, whose principal argument for being elected is that he was born in the same state as those whom he seeks to lead. The fact that his qualifications for being a leader of men extend no further than the fact that he is human, is less relevant than where his mother happened to drop him.

'Intellectually he may be a vegetable but at least he's a vegetable from Texas' which of course makes him superior to an Einstein figure from any other state.

Likewise, in the field of economics, more can be excused if it can be proved to be of benefit to the state than would be acceptable if it were the business of the entire nation . . .

'Slavery is clearly a grey area and certainly there must be a proper regulating body. None the less, it provides work and more than that *it will bring money into the state*.'

It is this parochial patriotism that explains Sly's early popularity despite his selfish and destructive business practices. He may have been a bastard but he was a *West*

*Australian* bastard. People would have liked to see any of those poofters in Sydney or Melbourne produce an entrepreneur with half his ability to create misery and unhappiness.

## TOUCH-DOWN

None the less, localized xenophobia notwithstanding, it was still a deep shock to all in the helicopter, excluding the pilot of course, to discover that people were still happy to swallow the leisure story.

'Yeah, I heard there'll be planetariums and stuff and weightlessness and everything, I guess the parents'll love it as much as the kids.'

They had crossed the site now and were heading for the wire. Walter seized the opportunity to try a little control experiment.

'Yeah well, that's shit man,' he said, trying to sound sincere, 'there ain't going to be no hotels, and there ain't going to be no money for WA. Those are real rockets man! The world's dying and the fat cats are splitting.'

But of course it was no use, the man just laughed and said that he had guessed that his abductors were weird, but they were really *weird*.

Walter gave up. Zimmerman asked Mrs Culboon to point to where they had left the wheels.

The helicopter put down with a bump and the squashed occupants burst out. As they unloaded the weaponry that they had taken plus that which was in the helicopter, the pilot spoke up rather nervously.

'Hey, listen you people, I want to thank you,' said the pilot, whose name, it turned out, was Eugene.

They were all a bit surprised at this, they had after all abducted him at gunpoint which hardly seemed like grounds for gratitude. None the less, Eugene seemed quite happy. In fact he had been surprisingly cheerful throughout the whole experience.

'It's just that I've never flown before,' Eugene explained.

This was worse than Zimmerman, at least he had admitted that he didn't know how to fly before they took off. Mrs Culboon, Walter, and CD all shouted in their own shocked and individual ways that Eugene had said he could fly.

'I can fly,' protested Eugene, 'and I did didn't I? We're here aren't we? Of course I can fly. But I'm just a mechanic,' he added bitterly.

'*Just* a mechanic, ha!! I'd like to know how long they'd stay in the air without us mechanics. But do we get any thanks? Do we hell . . . Excuse my language Ma'am,' he directed this at Mrs Culboon.

'I don't give a fuck what you say, Eugene,' she replied.

'They just strut around and insult you,' continued Eugene, who had clearly hit a pet subject, 'they say it's not clean enough or it's missing on a cylinder when you *know* that it's as sweet as a nut and it's just that the big-headed twerps can't fly properly. But will they give you a go? *No way* ha! They just –'

'Yeah, OK Eugene, we get it,' said Zimmerman.

'They just tell you it takes training and that you have to have a degree. Oh yeah? Well I've been trained mate, yes, in the school of life, I've got a degree in hard knocks.'

'Yeah, fine, Eugene . . .' Zimmerman interrupted again.

'They always say that we don't have a class thing in this country, but we *do*, we're worse than the pom's. *I* couldn't train as a pilot, oh no, not poncey enough, I had to be a mechanic because *my* dad was only a door-to-door trouser sales-man . . .'

'Eugene! Shut the fuck up!!!' screamed Zimmerman.

'No, but really, I mean, really, you don't have to be a daddy's boy to . . .'

They left him and headed for the car.


'So, what next?' Mrs Culboon asked as she drove them all towards the holiday home. 'I can't think of a single thing we can do.'

'Well all that stuff we discovered,' protested CD, 'the launch silos and everything. I mean it must be illegal . . .'

'Hey man, it's a wicked world you know?' said Walter. 'Like, if a couple of bread-heads want to dig holes, they can.'

'And that's just the point isn't it?' whined Zimmerman. 'The whole system of values is just *so screwed*. Like they bust me for having maybe one tiny toot on a mild and tension relieving doobie for my own personal private use. The world gets protected from me lying on the carpet for twelve hours giggling and then eating fifteen Mars Bars. I get hassled by the pigs for destroying nothing more than what's left of my own brain, man, and you're saying that some freaked out, off-the-planet world domination mind-fuck can launch rockets to the moon and everything is cool?'

'I'm just saying, man, that a dude can dig a hole. OK? I mean –'

'Oh shut up will you fellahs?' said Mrs Culboon. 'First Eugene, now you, going on and on, I'd rather listen to a didgereedoo, and that's saying something.'

They drove on in silence feeling awful about everything.

# COUNCIL OF WAR

Mr Culboon and Chrissy were very relieved to see their friends again. It had been both a wearisome and a frightening wait in the parched desert with the temperature some five degrees hotter than usual. The physical discomfort had been complemented by a fair degree of the mental kind. It is a strange and disconcerting experience to sit in what should have been the still of the desert while Hades appears to be under construction not far away. They were very relieved that whatever happened next, at least the waiting was over. After the initial greetings, Mr Culboon noticed that not the whole party was present.

'Where's Rachel?' he asked.

'She's gone over to them, man, and for kind of a depressing reason,' answered Walter.

'Who is them?' asked Chrissy, eager to discover at last the nature of the beast she had been stalking.

And so between them Walter, CD and Mrs Culboon explained all that they had learnt. Chrissy was completely astonished by their extraordinary story; it far outdistanced any of the possible scenarios that she had conjured up herself to explain what was going on. In comparison to trying to recreate the story of the Ark, the idea of holding the world to nuclear ransom seemed fairly mild.

'You are saying that they are convinced that there is no hope for the world. It really is dying?' asked Chrissy.

'Yeah, and they're splitting man. The rats are leaving the sinking ship,' said Walter.

'Well we have to try and stop them!' Chrissy replied.

'Oh yeah, how?' enquired Walter, 'and also for that matter,

why? Who gives a fuck? Let them go. If I have to die I don't need pigs like that at the funeral.'

'And what about Rachel?' snapped CD who died a little every time he thought of Rachel's decision. 'Is she a pig?'

'She had a chance, she made her choice,' said Walter. 'I have no problem with that. Personally I wouldn't have decided to go. Like, for me, eternity with a bunch of bread-heads would not be a viable option.'

## THE GREEN EYED MONSTER

CD was at the end of his emotional tether, suddenly he found himself so hemmed in by unhappiness that it left him gasping for breath. He lit a cigarette without even trying to look cool. He was too far gone even to manage to construct some romantic fantasy out of the character of betrayed friends. An emotion had burrowed its way into his stomach and his soul, an emotion of such intensity that no matter how many times it washed over him, he remained surprised at its strength. He had become a jealous guy.

On the trip back to the cave, CD had tried to persuade himself that the anger and frustration, and deep deep sickness that he felt to his stomach, were to do with *whom* Rachel had chosen. He told himself that it was the fact that it was Moorcock that really hurt, the fact that she had defected to the very world which she and he had been trying to fight. This, he tried to believe, was the root of his despair, and an understandable and righteous root it would have been.

But it was not the case, this was not why CD felt the way he did. He would have felt the same way if Rachel had opted to go with St Francis of Assisi or the Mahatma Gandhi. CD was not seething over some betrayed principle. He was not sinking into chasmic despair because of the discovery that Rachel had feet of clay. He was in the state he was in through pure, unadulterated jealousy. He was discovering that beyond love, beyond unrequited love, perhaps beyond any other passion known to humanity, deep deep in the depths of the turgid, clinging, swamplike pit of despair that lies dormant, within every soul, lurks jealousy. Jealousy, that most demeaning and debilitating of emotions. Jealousy, which doubles the strength of the love upon which it is based but whilst doubling it, warps and perverts it, demeans it, until it is no longer recognizable as the thing of beauty it once was and nothing is left of love but lies, doubts and bitter self-loathing. Jealous love is no more like true love than Mr Hyde was like Dr Jekyll or a stagnant swamp is like a freshwater lake. CD could not be said to be feeling his best.

## WHAT NEXT?

Still, if CD was feeling down, at least it kept him from dwelling on the imminent death of the earth, which was the cheerful subject that the others were mulling over.

'I still don't believe their story,' said Mr Culboon. 'The world ain't dying. I reckon they're fixing to kill it, I still reckon they're going to nuke the world and make us all slaves.'

'Oh shut up, you old fool,' said Mrs Culboon. 'You weren't there. I heard it from Rachel. They're fixing to go all right and damn soon.'

'Well for God's sake we have to do something then!' shouted Chrissy. 'I mean we're still alive aren't we? The world isn't dead yet is it? What are we going to do?'

'Well, personally I was thinking of selling my pad,' said Walter, 'scoring the best grade shit I can and smoking my way to hell.'

'Nice,' said Zimmerman. But Chrissy did not think so.

'Look, these people must know something, they must know a hell of a lot if they've made the decision they have. Maybe they know something that could help!' Chrissy almost pleaded.

'Listen, Chrissy, it's exactly what they do know that's made them make the decision they have. I mean, these guys have everything, they're not likely to give it up unless they have no choice. I mean that's why Rachel made the decision she did,' said Walter.

Chrissy was astonished at his fatalism but of course she had not heard what he had heard, and she wasn't a hippy . . .

'It *can't* be too late,' she continued. 'Nobody's even tried to stop the rot yet. But I'll tell you something, if the world knew that men like nice old Slampacker's hamburgers were doing this terrible thing, then they might wake up. We might still be able to patch things up on earth. This whole terrible plan could be the very motivation people need to get their act together!'

'I think Chrissy has a point,' said Mrs Culboon, 'and also there's another thing. If that bastard Moorcock is right, and it really is the very end of everything. And what goes up in those rockets really is going to be all that's left of the human race . . . Well I reckon I'd die easier if I thought some decent folks were watching down on us from on high, instead of a bunch of men, selfish, grasping . . .' she was, for once, lost for words '. . . I'll tell you one thing, I bet no black people have tickets on that flight at present.'

But she had struck a chord. CD spoke up, he was anxious that they should decide to do something, he could not stand just sitting around feeling the way he did. His guts were so heavy he felt that he was in danger of sinking into the ground.

'Mrs Culboon's right,' he said, 'I mean if we could stop them, I don't know, get them arrested or something . . . then somebody else could escape instead . . .'

'Like who?' asked Mr Culboon.

'Well, I don't know, they could have a competition. Artists or something, I don't know. . .'

'Man all you'll see is another set of fat cats standing in line,' said Zimmerman cynically. 'Politicians, soldiers, all that shit.'

'I'm telling you, the thing to do is to *stop* the thing altogether,' pleaded Chrissy, '. . . use it as a shrine, a monument, something to galvanize the human race into action . . . Christ even if we all have to go back to living in shacks and being penniless there must be a way to stop the rot.'

'What do you mean, go back?' asked Mrs Culboon, her humour returning.

'Besides that,' added Chrissy, 'if anything is to be done to save the world we may actually need these people.'

'Oh yeah, like a freak needs a drug squad,' said Zimmerman. 'I mean, shit Chrissy, these people have fucked absolutely everything right up. What the hell do we need them for?'

'Look,' said Chrissy, trying to martial her thoughts and not to sound patronizing, 'it is possible, in fact it is pretty likely, that only those who have the power to destroy things so effectively have the power to create . . . The way the world is run, the way things get done, are incredibly complex . . . The means of production are owned by individuals; the raw materials of change are owned by individuals . . .'

'Oh come on man,' interjected Walter, 'don't give me any of that commie shit, like that's all the same trip man you know? Like two sides of the same coin, "if you go carrying pictures of Chairman Mao, you ain't gonna make it with anyone anyhow",' he said, quoting from the classics.

'Listen meat-head,' said Chrissy, whose long wait had not improved her temper, 'it's got nothing to do with commie shit, I'm a Roosevelt Democrat like my daddy before me, OK? I am talking economics,' she continued. 'If these bastards actually think that time is so short for the earth that they're leaving, well then hell, time must be that short, right? . . .'

'Now I reckon we'd better listen to this here Yanky woman, yes I do,' said Mrs Culboon. 'After all, we got to do something that's for sure, and I guess she's thinking a whole lot clearer than the rest of us sun-fried bunch of no hopers. Ain't that right, Mr Culboon?'

'You speak for yourself, woman,' replied Mr Culboon. 'I'm as sharp today as I ever was.'

'Which is sharp as shit I reckon, old man,' replied Mrs Culboon, 'and that's blunt. Go on, Chrissy. What's the plan?'

'I don't have a plan, godammit, I just know,' said Chrissy, 'that these people represent a workable economic structure within which things get done. A structure which, in an emergency, could react quickly. It may be a shithouse structure but it's there, it's in place, it's controlled and it takes orders. Now, if every damn boss in the world high-tails it, there will be complete economic chaos . . .'

'As opposed to what we have now,' interjected Walter, cynically.

'Listen buster,' said Chrissy – who had never said buster before in her life. 'What we have now is a controlled slump, a cycle dip, it just means poor people starve, that's all, it ain't anarchy . . . Now if most of the damn bosses suddenly disappear *at once* it could be months, maybe years, before new chains of command emerge within their empires. There will be power struggles, court-room battles. For a while at least it will be almost impossible to shift money about, utilize assets, mobilize equipment, *make a decision*!! . . . Don't you see? I understand money, nothing will get done! And it's those few months that may mean life or death for the earth. We have to stop them leaving and force them to help save the world.'

'*If* it ain't dead already, lady,' said Zimmerman.

'OK that's it, fuck you,' said Chrissy getting up. 'I don't know about you lazy bastards but back in New York City where I come from we like to put up a fight,' she added, lapsing briefly into parochial xenophobia. 'You don't lie down till you're dead, and even then you bite their damn ankles. I don't know what I'm going to do, but I'm going to do something. See you, hippies, I'm going to save the world. You Culboons coming, CD?'

CD wasn't actually listening but the Culboons were about to agree when Walter interjected.

'Hey hey hey, Lady. You like . . . well . . . you certainly know how to hurt a guy, you know?'

'Yeah,' added Zimmerman. 'Just because we're indulging in a moment's negative vibe does not mean that we are off the team, it's just a ying and yang thing, OK, balance, that's all.'

'So you're prepared to try and do something then?' asked Chrissy rather suspiciously.

'Of course we are, man,' said Walter. 'Hey listen. I have to

395

tell you something. Ego is a bad thing, and pride comes before a fall, but I have to tell you man, that while you have spent your life tapping out shit about bread for the papers, me and Zimm here have saved a couple of two hundred ton whales, right?'

'And what's more, it spoke to us,' added Zimm, 'and told us of its life beneath the deep, within the whale nation.'

'Yeah, well, that was Zimm's interpretation,' said Walter, 'and as such it was valid, but some other people on the team thought they were just going eep eep eeeep.'

The brief schism over, discussion recommenced on the problem at hand.

'OK Chrissy,' said Walter, 'like what do you suggest? These cats have had us hiding out and running every time we so much as breathe. Man they chased you all around the world. You'd be dead right now if it wasn't for crazy Zimm. By the looks of it, they're fixing to split real soon. What do you suggest we do? How in fuck, man, do we stop them blasting off, so's we can like use them and their fat cat bread-head corporation to tell the world that it's dying?'

'I don't know,' said Chrissy quietly.

There was a pause.

# THE RATS GATHER AROUND
# THE LIFE BOAT

The count-down had begun. There were no objections. The consensus was that if the foul deed had to be done, then it would be better if it were done quickly. The terminal, global decline was now visibly apparent everywhere. From the alternately parched and steaming earth, to the gloomy haze of pollution that hung high above them; a haze that made the intense heat dirty and sticky, like wearing a filthy old wool blanket in the blazing sun. The Leper Ships floated on the suffocated sea, the dolphins struggled in the nylon nets. The maple forests withered where they stood, the iguanas felt the rumble of the dozers. The sewage slid out of the sludge ships and the salt bubbled up through the ground. Durf's talk of TTO in the food chain was not really necessary to convince the terrified old men. Each day as their factories belched out poison, they lived in abject fear at the possibility of an avalanche factor developing and scuppering the whole thing. Every day that they hesitated, something could go wrong . . .

Besides the imminent possibility of Stark being thwarted by a natural phenomenon, the other reason for immediate departure was that with everything now ready, things could only go wrong in human terms. Discovery, government intervention, mass rioting, theft, played heavily upon Durf's mind. The majority of the security had been laid off along with the construction workers. Obviously Durf had had no desire for there to be a large group of heavily armed men around, at the point at which it became clear what was going on. The prospect of a couple of hundred gun-toting thugs, trying to force their way onto the absolute last train out of the ghost town, did not attract him. However, it had meant that Durf was forced to take the calculated risk that the last few days the Consortium spent on earth would be comparatively unprotected. Even a mob from Bullens Creek would probably be capable of ruining everything.

The news that Tyron had lost the captives and been discovered hours later trussed and bound along with his security chief, had been a shock. Sly had asserted that there was absolutely nothing these people could do in practical terms (except destroy helicopters). None the less, it was most disquieting.

Anyway, all things considered, no one had debated the fact that it was time to move, and the count-down had begun even before Zimm had commandeered the helicopter.

The far-flung and disparate members of the Stark Conspiracy – people who wielded such huge power and influence on their societies – were simply told to get up, take one piece of hand luggage, collect their partners and leave their entire lives for ever.

## ADAMS AND EVES

Obviously the 'partner' business was fraught with indecision and embarrassment. There were those of course, indeed a surprising number, who had decided to take their spouses.

Since the whole project was a self-financed, self help group, rather than some noble scheme to perpetuate the human race, youth and fertility were not required. The object of the exercise was personal preservation, pure and simple, so people could take whom they liked. Anyway, the future had been taken care of in pre-packed and frozen form. Actually some of the crusty old couples, exhausted by a lifetime of hatred, violence and naked greed were rather looking forward to spending their old age peacefully on the moon, bringing up little test-tube space children.

These were the lucky ones, the people who had been able to

make their decisions early and hence also their preparations; sharing the whole thing with their wives or boyfriends – eight of the conspirators being gay – and in three cases, husbands. There were only three female Stark conspirators – the upper echelons of international capitalism being still very much a male domain. The richest woman in the world, the Queen of Britain, had not been approached. It had been considered that on the whole she was likely to prefer to go down with the ship, and would probably have blown the gaff. Besides, it was one thing Sly selling off his brewing interests to raise his contribution, but alarm bells really would have started ringing if Balmoral had suddenly appeared on the market.

## EVE WITH A STAPLE IN HER STOMACH

For the adulterers the process of departure was not so smooth. Ocker Tyron, for instance, had definitely decided not to take Dixie. Unfortunately he had also raised her suspicions. Obviously she did not suspect that he was about to leave her behind on a dying planet to face ecological oblivion alone. But she did suspect that he might be putting together a little illicit rumpy pumpy – which of course he was.

Tyron was playing a very dark hand; lying to his wife, and lying to the rumpy pumpy. He had not told the *Playboy* centrefold what it was he was taking her to the desert for. He could not trust her discretion. He had merely told her that it was a big adventure and a big surprise. Now she found herself stuck in the middle of a baking desert, with very few amenities indeed, amidst an ever-growing group of people she did not know, most of whom were in late middle-age. Understandably she wanted to know what the big surprise was going to be. But Tyron wasn't there to tell her, he was back in Perth, about to leave his house for the last time, trying to deal with Dixie.

He was trying to grab a toothbrush whilst she was lying on a machine which wobbled her fat about . . .

'It's not right that a girl should have to go so long without her man,' Dixie whined. 'What's going on, Ocker? Come on out with it.'

'Business,' said Ocker, 'now shut your face.'

His mother had followed Ocker into his and Dixie's private bathroom – something which she felt perfectly at ease in doing. She leapt at the chance to have a shot at Dixie.

'If you can't keep a man in the marital home, Dixie,' she spat, 'it's no good complaining to him when he's gone.'

'This isn't a marital home!!' shouted Dixie wobbling away, 'it's a damn old peoples' home!! Run for the exclusive benefit of one resident!! And this is Ocker's and my *private* en suite!'

'I know that, Dixie dear, but he doesn't have private things from his mother. Good Lord, I've seen a lot more than his bathroom in my time.'

Dixie, thighs flapping away, biting her lip with fury, turned to Ocker for support. But he was gone, they heard the door slam . . .

'Ocker!! Ocker!!' shrieked Dixie, jumping off the wobbler and running to the stairs, 'don't you dare just walk out like that . . .' But he was already in the car and could not hear her.

She went downstairs in fury, followed by her mother-in-law. There was a moment's silence. Then she noticed a blank space on Ocker's desk.

'He's taken his picture,' she said slowly, '. . . the picture of his school team, that's his favourite thing . . . He doesn't even let the maid dust it . . . Why would he pack that in an overnight bag?'

Dixie Tyron and old Mrs Tyron looked at each other, for a moment united in shared fear and suspicion.

'Ocker!!' Dixie shrieked, running to the window. But the car was at the end of the drive already. She sank back into her chair.

A picture of her had always stood beside the team picture on Ocker's desk.

'I notice he left your picture,' said Mrs Tyron. Their moment of solidarity shattered.

# FROZEN FOOD ON A
# HOT NIGHT

On day minus eight and day minus seven, Sly found himself with plenty to do. The three remaining rockets had to be erected in their silos, and then all six had to be loaded and made ready for blast off.

Time seemed almost as stodgy and untraversable as the weather in those final, baking days. It was almost as if it had to be waded through, like a swamp. As Sly stood watching the rocket-moving transport crawl along at its top speed of three miles an hour, he felt as if the actual moment was destined to never actually arrive and that they would all be locked in the process of last minute preparation for ever.

'Don't rush it, it's nearly a vintage machine, Mr Moorcock,' Nagasyu had remarked, commenting on the fact that the transporter had been purchased from NASA nearly twenty years earlier and was actually the same rocket-mover that had brought the Apollo moon shot, Saturn V, to its pad. Nagasyu considered this a good omen.

Stark had purchased the thing in the late seventies and held it in storage ever since. They had got it for peanuts because the American love affair with space was over and, with its budgets cut, NASA had no need for such machines. They moved into shuttle research and the concept of a re-usable rocket. Stark, of course, did not have the same problems since they were only taking a one way trip.

# BREAD AND LASAGNE

On the fifth night before the blast off, Sly visited Rachel. They had not seen each other since shortly after leaving Zimmerman et al in the security complex. Rachel had spent her time walking about the site, making an effort to take it all in, talking to whom she could and trying to understand and come to terms with the enormity of the thing that she was involved in.

Now it was evening and Rachel stood alone in the same room that Sly had first brought her to, watching for the fifth to last time as the hazy red furnace that used to be the sun sank through the sweaty, gaseous quagmire that used to be the sky.

Rachel was, by nature, of a fairly buoyant personality, but standing alone amongst strangers, watching the world die, would depress anyone. When Sly strode in she was pleased to see him.

'So, shall we have that dinner then?' he asked.

'What dinner?' Rachel replied.

'The one I asked you to about a century ago.'

Sly was astonished to discover that he was nervous. This was a very new sensation for him. Normally he didn't care enough for the women he found himself alone with to be ill at ease in their presence. What's more, their acquiescence was so utterly guaranteed that there was never any question of fear of rejection. This time things were as different as they could be. He did care what Rachel thought of him and he was by no means certain that she desired him in the same way he did her. He had, after all, persuaded her to hang around with him by telling her that she would die a reeking, steaming, panic-stricken death if she didn't. Many a girl might have responded to a chat-up line like that.

'Don't mind. Why not,' replied Rachel, regarding the dinner.

And so Sly prepared it. Peripheral Stark personnel had been cut to a minimum and there were no cooks or serving staff in those last days. Each cabin had a microwave and a huge stock of frozen food . . .

'Pretty shithouse tucker, I'm afraid,' said Sly, bunging a couple of lasagnes in the oven, 'still guess it's kind of better than what we can expect for the next few years, until the greenhouses get going and the frozen foetuses turn into lamb chops.'

Actually, as far as Rachel was concerned, the food she had eaten since joining Stark had been superb. Compared to toast and vegamite, which was what she normally had for supper, gourmet frozen lasagne was a pretty good feast. She didn't say though, Sly liked to talk and Rachel liked to let him.

'One thing about them,' he said as the oven went ping, 'this stuff was packaged a good three years ago, I own the factory actually. No Total Toxic Overload in this. Christ, Durf's got me so spooked on the food chain business I look at the sell-by date and hope the damn thing's *past* it.'

They drank some wine and ate the lasagne, no bread, the last thing you want to risk before embarking on a trip to the moon is food poisoning . . .

'I guess the shits would be pretty unpleasant if you're stuck in a space-suit,' Sly said, and he laughed.

## MOULDY OLD DOUGH

It wasn't that the grain itself was massively toxic, but the intense heat and humidity (caused by the flooding, caused by the deforestation), had created an atmosphere that had been a perfect breeding environment for all sorts of microscopic organisms. Therefore, what crop had grown in that last, famine-struck summer of Stark, was mouldier than the washing up in a student residence. Unfortunately, because it was all that there was, it still got ground into bread and, what's more, because there was so little of it, the stuff actually doubled in price. Mouldy bread was one of the few healthy items on the stricken stock market . . .

'Get into food,' the arrogant twenty-one-year-olds in bow

ties and pink glasses had said to each other.

'Food is very big right now.'

## TOO GUILTY TO PARTY

As he attacked his lasagne, Sly pondered the contradictions of life.

'Funny to think that I own bakeries that are making bread that I'm too scared to eat, and yet the same stuff is turning in a straight 200 per cent profit and curving skywards. Not that major profit strikes are any use to me now. Still, it's funny,' he was in a philosophical mood.

'Please, Silvester,' said Rachel, 'try not to be such a ruthless pig. I'm trying to persuade myself that I don't dislike you.'

'Well, it *is* weird,' he replied defensively. Sly had not realized he was being a ruthless pig, nor had he been spoken to by a woman this cool in years. Not surprisingly he found it exciting. 'That bakery was my first ever corporate takeover. I only kept the bread bit, sold the rest off and now the bread's poisoned, and more profitable than it's ever been. I call that weird. Don't you call that weird?'

If Rachel was a different experience for Sly, well the opposite was also the case. Rachel had never met a man with so little remorse, so little guilt, he simply did not bother to anguish over the terrible repercussions of his horrible life. This sublime peace of mind was entirely alien to Rachel. Those like her, who aspire to a social conscience, spend their lives consumed with guilt. They can never take full pleasure out of the nice things that come their way because they cannot escape the gnawing conviction that their happiness is *unfair*.

Sly, on the other hand, knew that life isn't fair, and what's more, the bastard didn't seem to mind. It was a new experience for Rachel, who generally hung around with worried liberals like herself, to be talking to someone who could make a statement like the one Sly had made about the bread, without feeling the need to conclude it by adding, 'I mean, God I *know* it's terrible, but I really don't know what I can *do* about it, you know? I mean it's so *difficult*.'

It wasn't that Rachel condoned his callousness, nor did she wish that she could emulate it (not much anyway). It was just strangely refreshing to be talking to a person who had conquered the guilt that oppresses us all. Perhaps this is why rogues are such popular figures of fiction; they have the ability to be bastards and not worry about it – they give us a chance to escape the ever oppressive conscience.

## THE MOON SHINES BRIGHTER

Anyway, for whatever reason, Rachel decided to go to bed with Sly. He was pretty despicable but also exciting, like a Dirty Harry movie. Rachel had always had a penchant for big, strong men. The perfect combination for her would have been new man politics combined with a macho man body. In this case she was prepared to settle for the latter on its own. It had, after all, been quite a long time for Rachel, she was a pretty choosy girl. Also the condoms she carried in her bag were in danger of slipping past their sell-by date. Going without gets frustrating in the end.

The last thing Rachel expected with a man like Sly was that they would have to go through the lengthy and gruelling familiar rigmarole of coffee and more coffee and edging towards each other that precedes most first bonks. But to her amazement, they did.

Sly could not be his usual, forceful, demanding self with Rachel, he found her too confusing, worrying even. Rachel was also inhibited because despite her politics she had never been one for making the first move. It still sounded weird to Rachel, a woman asking a man to go to bed; she knew it shouldn't but it did. Language and convention remain great barriers to enlightenment.

And so, with the earth on the brink of extinction, and the conspiracy of cowardice and betrayal lumbering towards its thunderous climax, Rachel and Sly nervously chatted, drank more coffee, played some music, drank even more coffee and finally got close enough to go for it. It was more like two students at the end of term rather than two conspirators at the end of the world.

Well the moon held no more fears for Sly, suddenly it shone bright and friendly in the sky because now he knew how he wanted to spend his time on it. He wanted to spend his time rooting Rachel. It had been a revelation! Sly hadn't really liked sex up until that point. Now he loved it. Suddenly he felt as if he had been completely wasting his time since his balls dropped. He realized that all the sex he had had in the past had just been elaborate wanking; he had finally discovered the real thing. This was not the case for Rachel of course. She had enjoyed it, certainly, but that was all. Not being obsessed with power and money she had not found it necessary to put in a sixteen-hour day, seven days a week all her life, acquiring things that she could not possibly use, therefore, despite being many years younger than Sly she had found much more time in her life to develop satisfactory relationships.

But Sly was ecstatic; and as he lay there in the dark wondering whether Rachel fancied another bash and if so could he coax a magnificent third erection out of his frankly startled penis, and deciding that he probably could if Rachel helped – he was looking forward to going to the moon.

# SPREADING THE WORD,
# PAYING THE PRICE

Chrissy's plan was to try to drum up sufficient media outrage
in order to force either the authorities or the mob to intervene
against Stark. Clearly she had a major problem in this
situation, and that was that no one was likely to believe her
story in a million years. Chrissy didn't know that she only had
a week in which to act, but she could guess that however long
she had, it wasn't very long.

It had been decided during the Council of War at the
holiday home, that Chrissy would do her best to provoke press
interest and that Mr Culboon and Walter would have a bash
at alerting pressure groups and sympathetic politicos. This
fairly hopeless and frankly embarrassing task was further
complicated by the fact that they believed that the moment
they showed themselves in public they would either be
captured or killed. What's more, they carried the
uncomfortable responsibility that if they did manage to bring
anyone into the situation, they would be putting that person
in great danger too.

However, in the two or three days following the helicopter
flight, it looked as if their consciences at least would remain
clear. They were unlikely to be putting anybody in danger,
because trying to alert total strangers to an utterly fantastic
situation, whilst remaining anonymous, proved beyond any of
their persuasive powers.

Chrissy, Walter and Mr Culboon had travelled back to
Perth in Rachel's Holden.

'I feel that we have a right to requisition our erstwhile

comrade's wheels to the cause. This hog is now a peace tank,'
Walter had said.

It was, however, a peace tank which did not like being
thrashed along red-hot highways by terrified renegades. It
took nearly two days to get back to Perth.

They planned to operate out of telephone boxes, fearing
that if they happened to contact anybody who was in the pay
of Stark, the call could be traced. As it happened, what with
Durf at the launch site and all the conspirators heading
towards it at full speed, the omniscient power of Stark had
been much reduced. But Chrissy did not know this and even
if she had, the experiences of the previous few weeks would
still have led her to be very very careful.

## COMMUNICATION BREAKDOWN

Feeding in money that they could ill afford, Walter tried first.
He phoned the office of the only member of the state
parliament who had been elected on a no nukes platform.

'Listen, uhm, I have to speak to Ms Grant, OK?' Walter
asserted. And, feeling the need to underline the urgency of the
situation he added, 'You have to get the chick on the line,
right now, I mean, like yesterday or the lid comes off. Dig? I
mean the lid comes *off*. And that is off with a double 'F' right?
I am talking the Fucking lid comes off, OK? You seeing
where I'm coming from sister? Well you'd better because
unless you get the main lady blowing in my ear pronto, we
ain't *going* anywhere. I am talking about being *dead* lady.
Dead with a capital 'F' . . .'

Inevitably Walter was asked his business. This rather
surprised him. He had not thought that the groovier type of
politician would go in for all that bureaucracy crap.

'Lady, can we please leave the mind control until we have
the leisure to enjoy it?' he asked. 'You know, just put Big
Brother back in his box. Because what I have to lay on the
boss is very very very heavy. Right? It's something that she
needs to know . . .'

The communication breakdown was unavoidable. Walter could not say who he was, and also he would prefer not to state his business except to Ms Grant personally . . .

Eventually, having been told three times to put it in writing and it would be dealt with he shouted, 'Listen, up at Bullens Creek they're fixing to blast off, man! The earth's dying and they're splitting!' The phone went dead.

After his first attempt, Walter was relegated to selling off his few possessions to acquire dollar bits for the phone. Sadly, Chrissy and Mr Culboon fared no better than he had.

They both tried many times, many different people and did it much more articulately than Walter had done, but the results were the same. Two days went by, Chrissy's finger ached from punching the phone. They seemed to have tried every media outlet and free-thinker in Australia. With no money, no time and no one to turn to, all three realized in a great wave of desperation that the chances of alerting the world were about zero. Walter was just thinking of suggesting that maybe they should try using the small ads and perhaps even put up some cards in newsagents windows, when they got a break.

It wasn't international, it wasn't even national, it was just a local TV news programme going out around Perth, but it was all they had and they had no choice but to go for it. The risks involved were horrible because the company insisted on a personal appearance. They said they could not possibly lend the credibility of their programme to rumour, hearsay and uncorroborated stories. This was most unfortunate because the three conspirators knew that whoever went on the television would be putting their head above the trench in no uncertain manner. None the less, they had to go for it. After all, they, like the world, had nothing to lose.

Mr Culboon and Walter felt that they should all face the music together, but Chrissy was insistent. There was no point them all risking their lives, she would go alone.

'Well, I reckon maybe you're right,' said Mr Culboon, 'you sure got the style Chrissy. I reckon there's plenty out there wouldn't want to listen to some old black fellah whining about his land. And as for Walter . . .' Mr Culboon simply shrugged his shoulders and exhaled.

As Chrissy got into her taxi she could still hear Walter trying to get to the bottom of this gesture.

'So what was with the shrug man . . . I mean maybe I'm being paranoid here, but well, it struck me as being dismissive.'

## DEATH WARRANT

On arrival at the studio, Chrissy was met by a researcher who led her straight to make-up for the ubiquitous 'touch of powder, just to take the shine off'. The show was going out live and it wasn't at all long to air.

'We were *so* pleased that you could come at such short notice,' the researcher, whose name, like many researchers, was Jan, had said over her shoulder as they wound their way through the long corridors adorned with huge glossy photographs of newsreaders, weather men and stuffed cuddly Emus.

'We were well and truly *stuck* for an item when the wombat died, just tearing out our hair. Your story was a gift from heaven.'

Chrissy couldn't help thinking that this was a very strange way to view the profession of journalism, even at a local level, but there was no time to pursue her doubts. After five meaningless dabs with the powder pad they were led into the studio.

A shiny, very tanned man wearing a suit that was both trendy and conservative at the same time, sat reading the news. He looked like a footballer who had been invited to open a disco. Chrissy felt that local newsreaders always looked like footballers who had been invited to open a disco, or, if they were girls, aerobics instructors at a wedding. It was not going to be easy to make this work.

Chrissy was very tense. This was her one chance to make

410

her story public. It *had* to be good. Chrissy was convinced that the only way to construct an even remotely effective last ditch defence of the earth was for those who controlled the financial infra-structure to stay in place, at least for the time being. She had one chance to force a public reaction against Stark, and hence an intervention against the launches. One chance, she would give it all she had, even if she was signing her own death warrant.

As Jan and the floor manager sat her down in the interview chair opposite the tanned man in the footballer suit, Chrissy felt a tremendous sense of purpose; she had a rendezvous with destiny and she intended to pitch her story like no story had ever been pitched before.

The suit and the tan were winding up.

'. . . motorists are strongly advised to avoid that intersection until further notice,' said the newsreader and Chrissy knew by the way camera two swung around to face her that the moment of reckoning had arrived.

'And now it's time to brush away all the doubts and cares because news doesn't have to be all bad, there's always someone about to put a smile on all our faces. Yes, it's time for our Daily Daft Dingo, a look at the sillier side of life. Now we had said yesterday that we were going to bring you William, the wombat who can say 'Western Australia, pure Aussie' but unfortunately William's caught a little cold and won't be with us today. But fear ye not! We have another and even sillier Daft Dingo to chat to, not a wombat, but a lovely lady from the good old US of A . . .'

The bowels of the Daft Dingo, or Chrissy as she was known to her friends, were dissolving beneath her.

'. . . this super silly has a theory, get this, that the new Moorcock Tyron Leisure Centre up at Bullens Creek is, in fact, a rocket launch site. Ha ha. And that the world is so polluted that Sly and Ocker are going to blast off and leave . . . ha ha! As if anyone would ever want to leave WA, the greatest state in the world – the state of excitement. I mean sure, things are a touch hot and stinky right now . . .'

411

Chrissy did her best.

She tried to sound learned and convincing, consumed though she was with anguish and embarrassment, she explained the story of Stark, her confidence which had already been shattered, wilting further with every word she uttered.

Public ridicule is a strange thing; being right makes it no easier to bear.

'But surely, Chrissy,' laughed the interviewer, 'the explanation that it's a space-age theme park would seem a little more likely than the concept of Star Arks . . .?

Chrissy kept trying, and the interviewer kept laughing . . .

'Sure, we realize everything's a little strange at present; the economy, the weather, agriculture . . . but I hardly think a couple of true Aussies like Sly and Tyron are going to run away from their problems, do you?'

Chrissy shouted in her shame, which of course made her look even more of a dickhead than before . . .

'Please stop laughing, godammit, the world is dying. These terrible people are trying to get out while they can,' she pleaded. 'We have to *do* something.'

But the studio laughed, and the viewers laughed. The only people who did not laugh were Durf, who was in the mission control room at Bullens, reaching for the phone, and Dixie and Mrs Tyron who were putting two and two together in stunned disbelief.

## WARRANT PRESENTED

Chrissy ran out of the TV building, burning with frustration and shame, the cruel laughter of the bastard presenter ringing in her ears. She could not get out of the place quick enough, which was a bit of luck for her as it happened because Stark still had claws enough to deal with people who went on TV to blow the gaff.

Two minutes after she left, Durf's henchmen arrived at the studio. Moments later they were taking fresh orders from Durf over the phone.

'Find out from the television company where they are staying . . .'

Chrissy ordered the cabbie to drive around for a while, she wanted to collect her thoughts, come to terms with the failure and humiliation.

'You want to sightsee in an area like this?' said the cabbie. 'The whole place has been ruined by Asians, Vietnamese running drugs and killing each other, boongs getting pissed on the pavement . . .'

Chrissy did not even hear him. It was half an hour before she finally had the cab pull into King Edward the Seventh Empire Terrace, the home of Walter and Zimmerman, where Rachel had first visited them a few months previously. Then it had been dead of night, now it was bright searing sunlight; then it had been silent and peaceful, now the air rang with the harsh cracks of gunfire and the desperate screams of men.

Durf's killers had been trying to hold Walter and Mr Culboon quietly until the girl came back but whether in some desperate effort to warn Chrissy, or simply because they knew that their time was up anyway, they had tried to make a break for it.

Walter moved first, a frenzied, scrambling rush past his captors to the door. Unfortunately for Walter, these men were not quality, they did not know their work. It would have been easy for them to detain Walter but instead they shot him. Moreover, they shot him with machine guns. His huge body was lifted up by the force of it and danced for a moment in the air like a marionette, as he was perforated with bullets. When the endless split seconds of mayhem and smoke were over, Walter fell to the floor approaching extinction at last.

Mr Culboon, seeing how the land lay, charged the window. He almost made it. The thugs were still contemplating the soggy mess, above which the soul of Walter was beginning to hover in peace. Their attention was distracted. Middle-aged as he was, Mr Culboon launched himself through the glass and landed, rolling in the uncleared jungle that surrounded

413

the house; a jungle which was, if anything, thicker and more inpenetrable than when Rachel had encountered it. The weeds and the brambles closed in on Mr Culboon like a net. If Zimm and Walter had a lawnmower about a decade earlier, Mr Culboon might have made it to Chrissy's cab. Instead he fell victim to Walter's lifelong belief in non-interference with the natural environment, which translated loosely as a lifelong hatred of gardening. From Walter's dash to Mr Culboon's ensnarement, was a matter of a few short moments, although time, of course, is a relative and a subjective concept. For Mr Culboon this tiny period represented all the time in the universe. For it was the rest of his life.

Chrissy's car was still approaching, she was staring wildly out of the window. Mr Culboon saw her as he struggled with the tropical brambles and uttered his last words on earth. 'Get out Chrissy, Walter's dead, get the fuck . . .'

As with Walter, the point blank range leant tremendous power to the bursts of fire that tore through poor Mr Culboon. He too was lifted up with the force, but he did not dance in the air, he was immediately jerked down again. Zimm and Walter's garden did not give up so easily and seemed to grip Mr Culboon ever more firmly with each successive burst of fire. Even after his death, Mr Culboon's body still strained to escape into the air, shooting forward, propelled by the bullets, only to be dragged back by the jealous tentacles and twine.

'Get out of here,' screamed Chrissy at the driver. An unnecessary command, since by the time she made it her car was already a block away. Having got thus far, it screeched to a halt.

'Out,' shouted the terrified cab driver.

'But . . .' mumbled the equally terrified Chrissy.

'Just get out. Now, get out, please get out,' the driver was nearly hysterical. Chrissy tried to collect her wits . . .

'You have to take me somewhere where I can hire a car . . . Please.'

But the driver did not hear the 'please'. He had jumped out of the car and rushed around to Chrissy's door. He tore it open and dragged Chrissy out onto the pavement. 'It's nothing to do with me,' he shouted, 'I don't need it, I don't want it, I work hard. Get out, get out, get out.' The driver was blithering, Chrissy was already out; she was spread-eagled on the pavement. He rushed back around the cab, jumped in and drove off, leaving Chrissy sobbing, her head in the gutter.

# LOVE AND WAR

Mrs Culboon and CD were sitting alone in the holiday home when Chrissy returned. There had been nothing for them to do so they had simply had to stay put. Zimmerman, who it seemed had mysterious plans of his own, had brought them some food but then disappeared. That had been two days before and they hadn't seen him since. Not surprisingly they were pleased to see Chrissy when she turned up. She had managed to acquire a hire car on the strength of some hocked earrings. It was now way overdue, but nothing seemed to matter much now anyway.

She told her story.

When it was finished, there was nothing anyone could think of to say. CD was crying, Mrs Culboon sat stoney-faced, Chrissy who had driven non-stop for about sixteen hours in order to bring this terrible news, sat chewing her lip.

How lonely could three people be? In the case of CD, Chrissy and Mrs Culboon, the answer was very. Chrissy was ten thousand miles from her home and friends, Mrs Culboon's husband was dead, CD had lost Rachel to Mr Culboon's murderers, Walter was dead. The scale of their sadness and their defeat was incomprehensible. Set against it, the death of the earth seemed a comparatively simple thing to assimilate. They sat in silence, the noise from Stark had gone now, save for intermittent murmurs. The silence of the grave descended upon them in the sweltering desert. It was as if they all believed that they would simply remain where they sat until they died. Perhaps they would have done had not Zimmerman returned.

They heard the padding first, rhythmic thudding that

managed to sound both hard and soft at the same time, as if somebody wearing a boxing glove was punching the ground very hard. It was getting closer, and sounding stranger and more ominous. It reminded Mrs Culboon of something but she could not remember what. CD wondered about taking up a rifle and putting up some semblance of self-defence, but then he wondered what the point would be, and decided that there wasn't one. Then Mrs Culboon remembered what the noise sounded like, it sounded like a camel. Shortly after which, she heard it snort and decided that it was a camel.

## BATTLE CAMEL

From behind the rocks that formed the cave rode Zimmerman resplendently perched atop a great ship of the desert, like an Australian Lawrence, burnt by the sun, cloaked in white and swathed in weaponry. He made an impressive figure.

'I've been speaking to some of the workers they laid off,' he said, without bothering to greet them. 'The shit is definitely about to hit the fan. We have to make our move.'

'I think we've made enough moves,' Chrissy said dully. 'Walter and Mr Culboon are dead.'

Zimmerman sat on his camel in silence, his expression did not change. It was as if he hadn't heard.

'That's why we have to do something, I reckon,' said Mrs Culboon, her face still like granite and her voice flat as the Great Sandy Desert. 'What move did you have in mind, Zimmerman?'

For a moment Zimmerman continued his silence, then he seemed to return from wherever it was that he had been. 'Gotta fight, I guess,' he said quietly.

'Oh Zimmerman,' Chrissy's voice was so tired and dull. 'How can we fight them?'

'Got to fight them,' he said and the camel snorted. 'Isn't a question of how, we've got to do it.' He still hadn't mentioned the death of his friend.

'Walter's dead,' Chrissy repeated.

'This has nothing to do with Walter, lady,' said Zimmerman. 'He's doing his thing some place else. We fight for whoever's left. That's the way we always did it back when the sharp end was sharp. Remember the dead, sure, but defend the living.'

Something had been bothering CD. At first he couldn't place it, then he remembered. He knew what it was he wanted to ask.

'What's the story with the camel?' he said.

'I found her,' answered Zimm.

'You found a camel? Where have you been, Arabia?'

'They have camels in Oz. They brought them over before they knew about Toyotas,' asserted Zimm without changing his tone. 'Some are wild, some are tame. Walter here was wild, but now she's tame. I had to punch her in the mouth one time but camels don't mind. She's gonna see a heap worse than that before she gets much older.'

'Walter?' asked CD.

'Yeah, her name was Sai Wan after a girl I once knew, but now it's Walter. I can call her Walter Culboon if you'd like that, Mrs Culboon?'

'Not particularly,' said Mrs Culboon, 'although it's a nice thought.'

'Actually I'd like to,' said Zimmerman. 'Mr Culboon was a brother too, you know?'

'OK, whatever.'

Zimmerman sat on the ridge, on top of Walter Culboon the camel. He towered above the other three, almost black against the sun. He was clearly mad. This was why the others could handle the conversation. The world was mad, Zimmerman blended in. If he had been straight he would have been a freak. The world was about to die and Walter and Mr Culboon had gone before and now they had both come back as the same camel, and Zimmerman was sitting on them. Chrissy, who had seen a man shot to pieces and then driven for sixteen hours in temperatures that would have defrosted a frozen elephant in time for supper, felt dizzy.

'Where's my man lay?' asked Mrs Culboon when the silence was finished.

'Yesterday he was in Zimmerman's back garden ...' Chrissy could not bring herself to say 'Walter's as well'. Camels didn't have gardens. 'I guess they must have moved him by now.'

'Hmmph,' said Mrs Culboon. 'Reckon the police are pretty used to getting rid of dead blacks.'

'It's morning now,' said Zimmerman. 'We'll hit 'em an hour before dawn tomorrow.'

'On a camel?' asked CD who was staying closest to reality. Wherever that was. It was a new experience for CD to be the most together member of the team. Maybe Chrissy sensed this, she pulled herself back from the place she was drifting in and blinked the salty sweat out of her eyes.

'Yeah,' she said, 'won't they laugh at the camel?'

'The camel can cover very rough ground at great speed,' said Zimmerman. 'It is incredibly hardy and has a very unfazeable personality.'

If Walter Culboon realized how highly she was being spoken of, she did not show it. She chewed and shuffled about a bit. Perhaps Zimmerman knew what he was talking about, she certainly did not seem fazed.

'It is a stealthy beast,' continued Zimmerman in his quiet drawl, 'with soft, padded feet and is ideal for approaching an enemy in silence.'

Perhaps Zimmerman should have added that she had great timing, for this was the moment that Walter Culboon chose to let rip with an unfeasibly camelish bottom burp that rent the air in twain. It barked its way around the desert for a good eight seconds and rolled down into the little hollow in which the other three were sitting, leaving them knee deep in a primeval fug which made even the air of the summer of Stark seem vaguely alpine. Nobody was cruel enough to say anything, but even Zimmerman could work out what they were thinking.

'Now I know, like, that you're thinking that the farting

419

situation kind of contradicts the stealth and silence thesis,' he said, his voice showing some emotion for the first time since he had appeared. 'But like, I suggest you put yourself in the position of a security guard, right? Who, whilst doing his security guarding thing, hears a camel blowing off in the still of the desert night. Like, does that guard think to himself, oh wow, bummer, the avenging hand of EcoAction is upon me? Or does he think that a camel has blown off . . . or maybe a lonely kangaroo?'

Nobody had the faintest idea what to say to this and so Zimmerman explained his battle plan.

## A MOMENT OF DOUBT

As Zimmerman talked of battle, listing his resources – which consisted of four people, a station wagon, a hire car and a truck; as his companions listened, becoming, in the process, almost as flatulent as Walter Culboon the camel, the fifth night of the count-down approached. On the following morning there would be three days left.

The eight day period had been defined for purely practical reasons. Durf was in a position to trigger the remote launch procedure at any point. The time had been decided upon in order to ensure that all members of the consortium would have time to withdraw from their lives in an orderly fashion, without provoking comment, pick up their partners and make their way to Bullens Creek.

In fact by the fifth night, most of the conspirators had arrived. They were all acutely aware that if they missed this particular bus there would not be another one along in a minute.

Rachel and Sly lay together sweating in the heat. Sly's work was done, there was nothing left to do but root, eat frozen lasagnes and shower about every thirty minutes.

'We could root in the shower and save time,' said Sly through the darkness.

'Save time for what?' Rachel's voice replied.

'We only have three days left.'

This provoked a silence that even Walter Culboon would have felt embarrassed to intrude upon.

'Oh God, Silvester, let's not go,' said Rachel, 'please let's not go. Come back with me to Carlo, we can eat ice-cream at Fernandez.'

'Rachel,' said Sly, and he held her hand, 'I'm saving your life, I'm saving your life because I love you. Don't you want that?'

'Yes I want it,' said Rachel, and she did want it.


## ORDER OF BATTLE

During the previous afternoon, Zimmerman had done a little scouting on Walter Culboon. He had brought back encouraging news.

'Man, things are definitely no longer so tight,' he said. 'I reckon they're fixing to split and they don't want no bully boys around to put two and two together and try to hitch a ride.'

'There's no one left to fight?' asked CD, for whom, it must be remembered, hope sprang eternal.

'Shit man, a whole lot more than we could ever handle,' answered Zimm, 'but at least it ain't no army no more. The security seems to be situated in an outer ring about 15 kilometres from the epicentre,' Zimm continued. Being about to enter combat he had become lucid once again, if, in a rather manic kind of way. 'I reckon they're keeping the thugs away from the business end. They got a truck with a bunch of guys about every seven kilometres in a ring around the base. I got the glasses on Du Pont one time, I sure hope we get that bastard . . . Now,' said Zimm, getting to the point, 'we have to get past this ring to get right in and destroy the rockets, OK?'

'Hey listen, bud,' said Chrissy, 'I may not be General Custer but I guess that I can figure out that we ain't gonna knock 'em out by going back to Perth.'

'*Listen*, soldier!' hissed Zimm. 'This is combat preparation, and in combat preparation you state the obvious because that way everybody knows the *same* obvious, and you'd better pray your brothers and sisters do know the same obvious because when *your* arse is on the line, your cover needs to have his gun pointing in the same direction as you're going.'

'All right already, so make me do some push ups.'

Zimmerman ignored this and continued. 'Obviously they have to have some form of mission control and our job is to get in there and fuck it right up. OK, just fuck it straight to hell, just fuck that mother like the pig that swallowed a hand grenade . . .'

'Zimmerman, please, just tell us what we have to do.' Mrs Culboon paused and then added a second 'please'. She, like the others had accepted that today was not a real day and that her ordinary life was still going on somewhere else. None the less Zimmerman, on full throttle, was taking freak tolerance too far.

Somewhere in the depths of Zimmerman's hat support structure, Mrs Culboon's tone hit a chord. He calmed down.

'I was psyching my head, it's important to psyche my head. Don't you feel that you should psyche your heads?' he asked.

'My head is psyched,' replied Chrissy.

'Me too,' said CD, and it was clear that Mrs Culboon felt the same way.

'OK, cool,' said Zimmerman. 'I'll psyche my head on my own after the briefing. Everyone must do their own thing and find their own astral plane to die in. I like mine angry.'

'Zimm,' said Chrissy, 'tell us what we have to do.'

Reality returned. In as much as their situation would allow it to, that is.

'OK,' said Zimm. 'Now we have to hit the control centre, which means getting past the security ring. Now they have trip-wires and cameras and electronic beams running between the guard concentrations so there is no way we can slip through, like, discreetly. Unless, of course, they aren't looking and listening. What I propose is that you cats attack our chosen guardpost directly from the front, creating a diversion, and while that's going on I'll slip through further up the line and then come around and attack them from behind, OK?'

'How many guards in each of the concentrations, Zimmerman?' asked Chrissy, not wishing to hear the answer.

'Twelve,' he replied, 'but they're lightly armed and we have the element of surprise.'

'We sure are going to surprise them arriving on a camel,' said Mrs Culboon, cracking her first joke since she had heard of the death of her husband. She remained in a daze over the tragedy. Not in as much of a daze as Zimmerman was in about Walter's death, but then Zimm had started out way ahead of Mrs Culboon in the daze stakes. Mrs Culboon was reserving the full burden of her grief for another occasion, should one arise, when she would have the time and the peace to assemble her ruptured emotions and take stock of her loss. For the present she knew that the battle in which Mr Culboon had fallen was far from over, and that it was a time for courage and good humour, not mawkish introspection. Mrs Culboon had seen and felt suffering before. That was why she had cracked the gag about the camel.

'They aren't going to see the camel until it's too late, Mrs Culboon,' said Zimmerman. 'Because of the diversion, right? What you have to do is this. At a specific time . . . you know, a time that is the same for all of us, right? A time, right, that we have all dug together . . .'

'Yes, Zimmerman, at the same time,' said Chrissy.

'You got it soldier, well done,' said Zimmerman. 'At that time, you three hit our chosen troop concentration full on from the front with whatever we've got. Now so relentless will be your withering barrage,' said Zimm, whose words were growing with his stature, 'so pulverizing will be your symphony of death, man, that those cats out there are going to be under the impression that the whole Australian Defence Force has forgotten about the Japs and is coming at them all at once, right?'

The others merely stared.

'And while their attention is diverted with saying things like "oh fuck what are we gonna do" and shitting themselves and stuff like that. But mainly while they are looking outwards at you, I'll cross the wire on Walter Culboon and knock them out from behind. You dig?'

They nodded. Despite the extravagance of Zimm's description there was no doubt his plan appeared feasible. Three people shooting in the dark could certainly make enough noise to distract a company of twelve. After all, Zimmerman only wanted them to get the guards' attention. He was going to kill them, it seemed.

'When they're down,' Zimmerman concluded, 'you come through in the station wagon and we burn for the middle. If we can't crack them, I'll head in on Walter Culboon and try to do it alone.'

## EVE OF BATTLE

They spent the first part of the night before the battle cleaning and checking the weaponry. Zimmerman took them through the reloading and firing procedures of the pistols, the rifles, the automatic weapons and the grenades. There was only one shoulder-held launcher, so this he kept for himself.

Around two, Zimm declared that they knew enough. There is only so much about the science of armour that can be taken in at once, besides which, according to Zimmerman's plan, the other three were only expected to cause a huge distraction and draw the enemy fire. Zimm himself would do the precision killings.

For the hours preceding the strike, each sat alone with his or her thoughts. Occasionally Zimm would stand upon the ridge beside Walter Culboon and stare out towards the field of battle and the target beyond, psyching his head.

'I still can't quite see how it came to this,' said Mrs Culboon, 'the four of us defending the whole world. But I want you all to know that I'm proud to be a part of it, and proud to be alongside you all.'

It was a nice thing to say. For a moment CD wondered why Walter did not say something nice back on behalf of everybody, he normally did that sort of thing very well. Then he remembered that Walter was dead. CD went back to thinking about Rachel and what honeyed words and stirring arguments he might employ to bring her back to them once the battle was won. Who could tell? he thought, hope springing, as always, eternal. Maybe she'd be so ashamed of herself she'd let him sauce her there and then, under the big desert sky, as a penance. Yes! that was it, this was his big chance.

## BATTLE

'OK let's go,' said Zimm in the low, almost hissing murmur that he had adopted ever since he had turned into Clint Eastwood. 'We got just one shot at saving the world.'

The hours of waiting had embittered Mrs Culboon.

'And avenging our dead,' replied Mrs Culboon. 'Most of me is doing this for my husband.'

Each had their ghosts to bury. If any of the combatants fell, they would be in good company. Mr Culboon, Walter, Linda Reeve, Toole . . . Rachel. CD certainly harboured the most searing sense of mission. The others had only lost the dead; he had lost the living. He was going in to save Rachel from a fate worse than death, he would do anything to stop the launch and give her a chance to come to her senses.

They shouldered their arms and whilst Zimmerman mounted Walter Culboon, the other three got into the station wagon. They had decided on using the station wagon only, being shot was going to be bad enough, there was no sense having to pay for a damaged hire car as well.

'Now don't forget,' Zimm said, 'don't try and take 'em, that's my job. Just draw their fire, I'll be coming up behind them.'

The proposed target was very clear, a truck and two search-lights, men hanging around, some making a desultory attempt at being guards, others just crashed out on the ground. There were two camp-fires and a number of lamps run off a little generator by the light of which some of the men were playing cards.

'Well they certainly have gone to a lot of trouble to pick themselves out as targets, haven't they,' said Chrissy.

'It's nearly time,' said CD who had been earnestly studying the luminous dials on his watch.

They began to crawl closer. As they did so, they spread out, to about fifty metres apart. When they started shooting it was essential that the enemy believed themselves to be facing a formidable opponent. Zimm had told them to vary their weapons every few bursts, even to fire with both hands − it didn't matter what at since they were only the diversion.

CD fired first. From somewhere to Mrs Culboon's right she heard the crackle of automatic fire. Almost simultaneously she opened up, as did Chrissy to her left.

'Make it look like they've got a fucking army in front of them,' Zimmerman had said. 'Just party down man, whoop, holler and make it big.'

CD was the best at it, he was throwing grenades vaguely towards where the light had been, shouting at the top of his voice quotes from all the war movies that had got him through so many endless Sunday afternoons.

'Steady there,' he screamed. 'Dress from the right. Up periscope. We're all scared kid. Charge. Take cover. Banzai.'

It is unlikely anybody ever heard him but the explosions he was lobbing certainly had their effect, even if they were falling about sixty yards short. All the lights went out in the security encampment and it began to return fire. They seemed to be doing it in as haphazard a way as EcoAction, and of course they were, because three people make extremely small targets in a great big desert and the guards firmly believed themselves to be facing a much larger enemy.

Once Zimmerman heard the return of fire he figured that they were about as abstracted as they would ever be and spurred Walter Culboon on towards the cameras and electronic sensors of the security perimeter.

# AN ARMY APPROACHES

The battle had been going for less than a minute when Durf made his decision. What could he do? He had no idea what was attacking him, but if it was anything bigger than a handful they were in trouble, and it sounded a lot bigger.

'Whatever you do hold them where they are,' he barked down the phone at the officer in the field. 'A ten thousand dollar bonus to each man; they must not get through.'

A few minutes later Durf was addressing a very shaken final Stark Summit Meeting.

# A MERC' AND A CHEVVY APPROACH

As Zimmmerman and Walter Culboon galloped towards the perimeter he was astonished to be passed by two cars, a Mercedes and a Chevrolet, about a hundred metres to his right. Zimm wondered if this was the long delayed effects of some unwisely taken hallucinogenic. But it couldn't be, he had been straight for donkeys years. Zimm was a pretty laid back guy at times but there was no way his body worked that slowly. As Zimm charged along he decided that the cars must be real but there was no point worrying about them.

# A TRUCK AND THE CAMEL

Zimm galloped across a wide diagonal sweep of desert floor in order to place himself behind the scene of the battle. His friends were still kicking up as much racket as they could but it would clearly not be long before the guards cottoned on to the fact that very little was happening. Speed was of the essence. Zimmerman had to get to the enemy and hit them while they were still confused.

The security guards had retreated to the comparative safety of a sand dune from where they were vaguely popping bullets out towards the source of their discomfort. As Zimm cantered up behind them he heard a commanding voice ring out. A depressingly commanding voice, the last thing Zimm needed in the enemy camp was somebody who knew their job. Unfortunately that was exactly what he had got.

'Hold your fire!!' he shouted raggedly, for his men were scarcely crack troops. He was obeyed.

The result was slightly embarrassing really. A quarter of an hour before when CD, Chrissy and Mrs Culboon had opened fire, their collective mayhem had seemed quite convincing and impressive, coming as it did out of the eerie stillness of the night. Since then the company had been joined by the noise of twelve men firing back and the noise had been terrible. Now that the defenders had stopped shooting and the three Eco-attackers' fire was left to itself again, it no longer sounded impressive, in fact it sounded pathetic. It sounded like exactly what it was, which wasn't much.

The commanding voice rang out again.

'Christ, there's fuck all out there. This ain't no army, it's kids or yobs or something. I want three men, we'll clean 'em up in the armoured truck.'

If the commanding officer had thought to radio his conclusions back to Durf the outcome of the night might have been very different. However, he didn't because he suddenly had other things to think about. This being that his armoured truck was now a blazing fireball and clearly not about to clean up anybody, at least not until they had put it out.

Zimmerman, on hearing the commander's aggravating grasp of the situation, had decided immediately to go onto the offensive. He started his campaign by shooting a shoulder-launched anti-tank shell into the security truck. This, Zimmerman had intended to be only the beginning, unfortunately after this he lost control of events.

## MAN OVER CAMEL

When Zimmerman had first met Walter Culboon, he had based their relationship on a combination of brute force and superior will. Having stalked her at a dried up water-hole (the same one at which her distant ancestor had killed the explorer Bullen), Zimm wrestled her to the ground and punched her in the face. After this Zimmerman had tried to establish some form of psychic bond between them. He had talked long and hard into her ear; he had developed eye contact and applied his small knowledge of hypnotism to the situation. His will had unquestionably triumphed over the camel's and Walter Culboon had decided to do what she was told.

Zimmerman flattered himself that this was because the camel recognized a fellow wild beast when she saw one; another creature who knew the terror of the hunted.

'I'm more camel than I am man, man' Zimm had assured the camel as he twisted its neck upon the ground as one would a steer, 'except for the hump and stuff obviously. But like inside we are the same.'

Actually Walter Culboon had not recognized a soul mate, but she had recognized trouble. Her finely attuned animal survival instincts had alerted her immediately to the fact that she was in the presence of an unstable wild bastard. The fact that he had jumped her from behind, throttled her to the ground, punched her in the face and then appeared to be trying to make friends, did nothing to dampen this impression. This was why she had decided to do what she was told.

The present situation, however, had forced Walter Culboon to revise her decision, the bloke on her back might be an unstable weirdo with a fist like a 'roos tail, but he did not explode in a twenty foot mushroom of burning oil. The truck had, and the camel didn't like it. Gunfire and explosions were out as far as Walter Culboon was concerned and so she decided to run like fuck.

Unfortunately she was facing the wrong way because Zimmerman had been approaching the enemy from behind. He now found himself careering back towards his friends, all his efforts at penetrating Stark in vain.

'Hey listen, I thought we were a team,' protested Zimmerman as they careered across the desert back towards the others. 'At least run the other way Walter Culboon,' he pleaded, 'we have to save the world here.'

But it was no use. Walter Culboon had made up her mind, she wanted out. Obviously when the other three saw Zimm careering towards them out of the dawn on his camel, they stopped firing, therefore, quite suddenly, through the actions of one camel, peace descended again upon the desert. Hearing this, Walter Culboon responded at last to Zimm's frenzied pullings and pleadings and stopped running. By now Zimm was about another hundred metres past Mrs Culboon heading towards the holiday home. He turned Walter Culboon around and headed back to regroup.

In the sand dune the apparition of a wild figure on a camel appearing from nowhere and blowing up their truck had left the security forces in thoughtful and subdued mood.

'Shall I radio back a report, sir?' said the radio operator.

'What, and tell them that we got beaten by a man on a camel? No way. Turn the damn thing off, this needs thinking about.'

# THE END AND THE
# BEGINNING

## RACHEL

All Rachel's plans were completely thrown. The careful
scenario that she had been plotting for almost a week was as
knackered as the ozone layer. They had been awoken shortly
before dawn by the sound of intense gunfire and a series of
explosions out towards the security perimeter. Sly jumped out
of bed, unlocked his desk and brought out a machine pistol.
He put it beside him and began to dress hurriedly. The phone
rang, it was Durf. When they had finished speaking Sly
slammed down the phone, told Rachel that everything was all
right, that he would be back shortly, and rushed out of the
room.

Rachel sat, wondering what on earth could be going on out
at the perimeter; wondering what it meant to her and her
plans, wondering what she was going to do right now.

She did not have long to wonder, for much more quickly
than she had expected Sly rushed back in, breathless and
fantastically excited.

'This is it! This is fucking *it*!! We're leaving early,' he blurted.

'What do you mean?' said Rachel, very scared. 'We can't.
What's going on?'

'Trouble out on the wire,' said Sly pulling out their pre-
packed flight packs. 'Looks like something's coming at us . . .
seem to have a hell of a lot of fire-power too, heard some
vague talk about camels. Those are the new Soviet hand-held

armour piercers. Could be anything from ten men to a bloody army! Durf thinks it's big. Anyway, whether it is or not, we aren't hanging around to find out. There's only five members not arrived yet and it's been decided to leave them . . . This is it, darling! We're going, we are fucking *going*!! Off to a new world. In forty-five minutes we will be in fucking *space*!!'

Sly was breathless with excitement. He was shaking as he took the bags to the door. Who wouldn't have been? The world was an itchy, steaming, rotting pigsty and he was off with his best girl to the pure, cool cleanliness of space. Except he wasn't.

He turned at the doorway to urge Rachel on.

For a moment she felt a terrible regret, not doubt, but real regret. It would, after all, have been a very big adventure.

She had walked across to the desk and snatched up Sly's gun. Now he was looking down it, the elation frozen on his face.

Rachel hated it, she had not wished to confront Sly, she liked him too much for that. Their passion had been a genuine one. Her plan all along had been to wait until the morning of the launch, perhaps even as the ships were loading, before making her move. She had intended to claim a desire for one last private walk upon earth. Then she would have made her way to the mission control room which by then would be functioning on remote, and hence be empty of staff. Once there she had intended to kick it, unplug it, throw chairs at it, basically carry out any method of disabling the controls that sprang to mind at the time. Having done what she could and, presuming that nobody had shot her, Rachel then intended to make her way out into the desert and try to find her friends.

The basis of this plan had formed the moment that Sly had made his proposal. She had seen instantly that here was a chance to transform herself from hunted nuisance to privileged insider; she had known at once that no such opportunity would ever emerge again to stop Stark. And stop it she must, that she knew.

Rachel's instincts had reached the same conclusion as

432

Chrissy's logic. She could guess that if the world was to stand a chance, which surely it must, if only a tiny one, then those in control, those with power and influence, must be forced to take some responsibility for that which they had helped to create. It was obvious to Rachel that the fastest way to motivate the world was to make Stark admit to its vile plans and then be forced to use their colossal resources to help try and deal with the awful situation instead of running away from it. Therefore, from the first moment that she had been indoctrinated into Stark, she had resolved to use the unique position that her sauciness had presented her with to abort the launch.

However, she had not expected to be confronted by Sly, intent on rushing her straight into a ship and she had not expected to feel that she was betraying him.

'What the fuck are you doing, Rachel?' demanded Sly staring at the gun in disbelief.

'Stopping the launch, Silvester. I'm sorry but nobody's leaving. We're going to the mission control room. Lead the way.'

Of course he protested, but she cut him short.

'Shut up! I don't want to hear. I tried to persuade you to give it up, I said let's stay, you and me, but you're such a selfish bastard, you wouldn't do it. We're going to the control room, lead the way.'

Sly was astonished, it was twenty years since anyone had spoken to him in that manner. Actually he was rather hurt. They left the room in silence.


## THE MERC' THE CHEVVY
## AND THE CENTREFOLD

Outside, as Durf and the rest of the technical team began to marshal the bleary-eyed and rather terrified conspirators towards the transports that would take them to their rockets, two cars screamed to a halt in the pre-dawn half-light.

433

Tyron was in the process of trying to persuade his centrefold, whose name was Suki, to put on her flight suit when he saw the cars. Understandably Suki was beginning to wonder what was going on. This did not look like the jolly, supersonic ride she had been promised, it looked like something much more serious . . . When Dixie Tyron got out of the first car, she reckoned she was right . . .

Despite her enormous sunglasses, Dixie seemed to be able to take in the whole scene at once. She spotted Tyron immediately and stormed towards him. Suki was terrified, she was well aware that the position of 'bit on the side' held very few rights or privileges once the wife turned up. Dixie was certainly an intimidating sight, appearing out of the shimmering heat, a cloud of silver-blond hair, tightly bound body thrust forward as if two invisible strings were attached to her nipples and were being wound in by some distant winch. Her blood-red mouth seemed to snarl crimson venom at Suki. It was as if she had eaten one or two of Ocker's playthings already that morning and would be happy to devour a third as an early lunch.

Scuttling after her was Mrs Tyron. She emerged from the second car which had been chasing Dixie all the way from Bullens, waving a birth certificate.

'I'm your mother, Ocker!' she cried. 'I'm your mother . . . sixteen hours of pain . . . I refused all drugs, I wanted to experience your birth in all its beauty . . .'

Dixie pushed Suki roughly out of the way.

'Excuse *me*!' said Suki who had her pride after all.

'Listen, cow, one word! Just *one word*,' said Dixie, pointing a talon that looked like it should have been scooping fluff out of the devil's belly button, 'and the next man fondling your scrawny body will be the police mortician . . .'

Durf tried to interject, he could still hear gunfire out at the perimeter and was desperate to hurry.

'Ladies, please, I must insist –' he got no further.

'You zip up too, Mister,' said Dixie, brandishing a second talon, 'or you'll lose the other eye . . . Hullo Ocker love.' She turned to Ocker with a voice that nearly warped the rockets, 'I think you forgot to tell me that we were going on a trip!'

'Sixteen hours of pain, Ocker, I refused all drugs! Your own mother, Ocker!' Mrs Tyron butted in, 'I must just not have found your note . . . where did you leave it, darling?'

Dixie turned on her mother-in-law in fury.

'Look! For the last time will you bugger off and leave me alone with the man I love, you ancient stinking old cow.'

'Man she loves! Hark at the fat pig,' countered Mrs Tyron. 'I don't notice that young delivery boy who always seems to take two hours to drop off the dry cleaning around here.'

'You damn snake, you skunk, you . . .'

Cow, pig, snake, skunk, it was indeed ironic that Dixie and Mrs Tyron should be trying so hard to get onto the Arks because between them they seemed to represent most of the animal kingdom.

Just as Ocker was feeling that the situation could get no worse, Aristos emerged from his mother's car.

'Hi guys,' he said addressing the assorted millionaires and their partners who were standing about in a rather bemused fashion. 'Ciao Ocker,' he said, turning to Ocker. 'Been trying to get me? Sorry, I've had the girls hold all calls for days, meetings, meetings. Even turned off the carphones. I've got two now, you know, in the same car, different numbers. It's *such* a godsend, don't know how I managed. Hey Ocker,' Aristos had noticed Suki, 'fo-o-xy chick, and how! wow! woof woof!!!'

'Yes, she *is* a pretty thing, Ocker,' said Mrs Tyron with great malice straight at Dixie, 'just your type – slim. Tell us her name, why don't you?'

The etiquette of the situation was not easy for Ocker.

'Uhm yeah, this is . . .'

But Suki saved him the trouble, she had had enough.

'Don't bother, Ocker,' she said, 'when I have affairs, I sort of prefer it when the fellah doesn't bring his whole family along . . . Call me in Sydney.' She turned and walked towards the little red jeep that Ocker had provided for her amusement

435

during the week they had spent in the desert. Ocker watched her fabulous bottom swaying away from him.

'Suki, wait!' he shouted.

'Ocker!!' shouted Dixie and Mrs Tyron in unison, and Ocker's courage deserted him. Even at this moment of destiny, he could not exorcize the lying hypocritical relationships that had been the one constant element in his life for three decades.

Suki got in her car and drove off towards Bullens. It wasn't until about forty minutes later when her rear view mirror suddenly filled with the flame and smoke of burning clouds that Suki realized that she might have had a luckier escape than avoiding being punched by Dixie.

The whole embarrassing scene had only taken a few minutes, but Dixie could see that the people around her were getting restive and that there was a man with an eye patch who was clearly anxious to move things along.

'Right,' said Dixie, icy calm in her eyes. 'Clearly my husband has made a *mistake* uhm . . .'

'Durf, Madam, Professor Durf,' Durf replied.

'But the mistake has gone, and I'm here now,' she put her arm through Tyron's forcefully, 'where are we sitting?'

This was too much for Mrs Tyron who kicked Dixie. Pushing Aristos forward she announced, 'I'm his mother, he's taking his proper family . . .'

Before Tyron could speak, Durf, desperate to get moving, interjected. 'We are having a shortfall of five Stark members, there will be no problem accommodating all of you,' he said.

Tyron could have killed him.

He was heading for the moon to be a part of the phoenix human race, rising out of the polluted ashes of its dead self. However, he was to be accompanied by his wife, his mother and Aris-fucking-stos. Ocker Tyron could scarcely believe this appalling turn of events.

As they awaited their final instructions his family huddled close around him, fearful that he would yet find a way of deserting them. But he had none.

# PRISONER ONCE AGAIN

The site was eerily empty. All non-indoctrinated personnel were either on the perimeter or had been dismissed altogether. The actual conspirators were now milling about at the transporters awaiting the final trip out to the rocket silos which lay a few kilometres further on into the desert. Only Sly and Rachel were at large.

'Please, Rachel, darling . . . uhm, love boat, honey bunch . . . For Christ's sake they'll be gone soon,' he pleaded, 'we'll miss the fucking boat . . . Look we've *got* to go, there's nothing left here on earth but hell . . .'

'Nobody's going anywhere, so shut up. We're going to destroy the control centre,' Rachel replied. 'Your bloody friends can damn well try and save the world not run away from it.'

'But it *can't* be saved,' Sly was desperate now. 'Do you think if I really thought there was a chance I'd be going? God Almighty, Rachel, why the hell would I?'

Even though Rachel was behind him, Sly could feel a moment of tension and doubt descend upon her.

Just then, far away, on the perimeter, Zimmerman blew up the armoured truck. Sly knew that this was as distracted as Rachel was ever likely to get. He had to take his chance. He was fighting for his life, and hers. Besides, he didn't think she'd shoot him.

She didn't. Rachel never knew if she would have done, he was too quick for her. In the split second of distraction following Zimm's blast, Sly swung around and grappled with her for the gun. In an instant, the tables had turned.

'Right, we're going to get in the fucking rocket,' said Sly viciously.

'You maybe. I've told you, I'm not going.'

Sly knew how little time he had. For a whole five minutes he tried to reason with Rachel, again explaining why the whole thing had to happen whether they liked it or not, telling her he loved her, but Rachel was adamant, she would not leave.

437

Then, the final thirty minute count-down started. Zimmerman's blast had also spooked Durf. He tried calling up the perimeter on the radio, but it had gone silent. Durf had no idea what the problem was and he had no wish to wait around to find out. He hit the button that activated the actual launch procedure.

Inside the control room, outside which stood Sly and Rachel, a tape began to turn.

'Attention, attention,' the pre-programmed NASA equipment boomed. 'Clear launch site, final count-down commencing, minus thirty minutes and counting,' continued the long-since recorded voice.

Sly grabbed Rachel roughly.

'Listen you bitch, if you ain't coming you picked a fine time to tell me. So *I'm* telling *you*! You are coming. I'm not going up there alone, without a companion, a woman, how can I? I wouldn't be a man in the moon, I'd be a fucking nothing in the moon! You put me in this position, you're what I've got and I'm taking you now. Move!'

'*I'm not going*,' screamed Rachel through her tears.

'You are! Now move!' replied Sly, brandishing the gun, 'or else I swear I will knock you out and *carry* you onto the fucking rocket. Can't you see girl!! Can't you see! How could I go without you? . . . don't even think about it, you're coming.' Rachel realized that unconscious she would be done for sure. She had to concentrate, there were after all thirty minutes left. Slowly, she turned, and got back into the car for the drive to the assembly point where Sly intended to force her, if necessary, onto the last transport out to the rockets.

## VOICE ACROSS THE SAND

Out on the perimeter Zimm had just managed to tempt Walter Culboon back to where Mrs Culboon crouched in the desert. CD and Chrissy had assembled too. Having seen Zimm's wild and ungainly charge away from the epicentre

438

they all presumed, rightly, that things had fucked up somewhat and that they had got nowhere.

'Don't blame the camel man,' said Zimmerman, 'it's not the camel's fault.'

Just as the others were about to protest that they had no intention of blaming the camel, they saw a truck from another perimeter post approaching; the one that they had been attacking. Clearly their dash for the centre was now completely cut off. What's more, it was obvious to the meanest intelligence that their enemies were not going to take the indignities inflicted upon them lying down.

EcoAction had exposed itself as the weakened force that it was. Now, yet again, it was they who were the hunted.

'We'll have to pull back,' said Zimmerman, 'but I don't think those guys are going to make it easy for us.'

'We can't pull back,' said CD in panic, 'we haven't got Rachel.'

'Listen, man, will you just stop thinking about sex all the time,' shouted Zimm '. . . I find it just totally insensitive. The chick made her choice man. Now listen, this place is blown. We have to move further up the wire. You people make for the station wagon. I'll cover you, then I'll follow on Walter Culboon.'

Walter Culboon could not speak English but she knew a worrying tone of voice when she heard one. More and more her keen camel instincts with their delicate sensitivity to the biorhythms of life were shouting at her, 'You got a looney on your back!! You got a looney on your back! Buck the bastard into a dune and run like fuck.'

Walter Culboon was about to do exactly this when, like everybody else, she was distracted by the voice across the sands.

For just as Zimmerman was giving his orders, and just as the commander of the security unit that had lost its truck was about to commandeer the second truck, with the intention of 'killing the fucking jerk on the camel'. Just as that morning's biggest earth disaster was about to hit the first editions – flash flooding in Bangladesh put three-quarters of the country under water.

Just then, Durf pushed the button and the count-down started. The voice that Sly and Rachel had heard was clear as day across the desert – it was probably heard in Bullens Creek where, no doubt, they thought that the Moorcock leisure park was installing the sound-track for a new ride.

'Attention attention,' the recorded American voice spoke from the sky. 'Clear launch site, final count-down commencing. Minus thirty minutes and counting.'

Everybody turned and looked. Attackers and defenders alike, turned and stared as one person towards the centre of Stark, all forgetting their differences and the battle which they had been fighting in response to this eerie voice.

In the clear light of the morning, ten, maybe fifteen kilometres away, the six rockets pointed upwards from their silos, supported by the spindly towers. It seemed impossible to comprehend, but the voice was referring to the rockets and it was being serious. The jaws of the security guards dropped lower and lower. The rockets had, after all, only been visible for a few days, and of course, being security guards they had seen it as a matter of professional pride that they had never questioned what it was that they were guarding. Now they had no choice . . .

'Count-down has commenced. Final loading must be carried out immediately. Repeat immediately.'

'Jesus,' whispered Zimmerman. 'They're going to blow all six at once. Shit I guess I'm glad we didn't get any closer man. I mean, we would have been *fried* man! Fried, as old Walter would have said, with a capital 'F'. And that's *fucking* fried.'

Zimmerman gave Walter Culboon a friendly pat, which nearly stunned her.

'Man, if Walter Culboon hadn't gone the wrong way I'd have been riding *into* that man, finding out what it feels like to be a meat pie looking at a microwave.'

'Aren't we safe, then?' asked Chrissy more out of abstract interest than anything else.

'I reckon we're probably safe where we are,' said Zimm, 'but, oh boy, when those mothers blow you're going to see a burning cloud roll across the desert like surf from Hades. It's going to look like they dropped the big one right in our laps.'

Everyone, guards, officers, Eco-terrorists, had turned to stare across the desert at Stark. Mrs Culboon had fished out the high-powered field glasses taken from the helicopter ride and had wandered up to the top of the ridge behind which they had been sheltering. She felt no fear at exposing herself in this way. In a matter of seconds, the whole situation had changed. The launch count-down, floating across the desert, had made them all comrades in wonderment.

She steadied the glasses on a rock and peered.

'Christ,' yelled Mrs Culboon, 'I can see the buggers queueing for seats, there's funny kind of trucks taking them out towards the rockets. Jesus, God, Lord, Almighty, there's that bastard Tyron.'

One by one, they all took a look, as the voice counted off the last thirty minutes to the blast. CD was last to get hold of the glasses. By the time he looked most of the passengers were heading for the rockets. There was only one bus left . . . the departure point was almost empty.

Almost empty that is. He could just make out two figures marching in single file – one of them had a gun.

Month in, month out, CD had studied her walk, he had ogled her legs, stared at her every move and posture. He had devoured the shape of her bottom, tortured himself over the tilt and movement of her breasts. He had longed and ached for every part of her, the way she held her head, the tiny bulge of her tummy that only showed with tight skirts and which she hated but which he desperately wanted to sink his face into. With the unique passion of the unrequited, CD had stored up her every little shape, tilt and movement of use in his private fantasies – to conjure up again when he was alone in his bed.

He had pictured her so many times, there was no way he could mistake her now, even over fifteen kilometres with the

441

binoculars shaking with passionate anger. That was Rachel, and what's more, she was being forced onto a rocket. 'The bastard' he screamed, 'that bastard Moorcock is forcing her! Hang on Rachel, I'm coming!!'

He ran for the station wagon . . . Zimmerman saw him and shouted, 'It's too late man!! You won't get half-way there, it's eighteen minutes, you'll fry, you'll burn! CD there is no time!!'

But CD was in the car and away . . .

## A VICTORY FOR HUMANITY

Moments after CD had thrown down the binoculars, Sly and Rachel arrived at the door of the final transport. Durf was in an agony to be off.

'Come *on*, Mr Moorcock,' he protested.

'Get in,' said Sly brandishing the gun.

'No! Never!' said Rachel. 'It's horrible, I won't go!'

'Please, Rachel,' said Sly quietly.

'Look if the girl won't go voluntarily, knock the silly bitch out,' said a sweating Durf.

'You shut your foul mouth, Durf,' shouted Sly, waving the gun, 'or it'll be you that won't be going.'

'But we have to leave *now*,' pleaded Durf. 'We are only sixteen minutes from ignition . . .'

'Rachel, I'll give you the moon!' Sly shouted, turning her towards him, feeling tears start in his eyes – his first tears in decades. 'No girl was ever offered that, please, for God's sake come, I love you.'

'Then stay here with me,' said Rachel quietly, whilst Durf hopped from foot to foot on the step of the transport, desperate to hurry things along, but recognizing also that Sly was armed and in a highly volatile state. Sly no longer even knew Durf was there.

'I can't stay here,' he said, 'everyone's going to die here. A whole race of losers, I can't be a loser . . .'

They stared at each other for a moment. Sly thought of

pleading again, but he knew it would be useless. Perhaps that was the reason he loved her, she was strong.

'Mr Moorcock,' shouted Durf, 'we've got to go! Either get this girl on the transport or I'll drag the silly bitch on!'

Durf made to grab Rachel and Sly grabbed him, banging his head against the door of the transport.

'I told you to keep out of it you bastard, and you'd better or I'll kill you, understand? I'm going to get her on!'

'Then you'd better start running,' said a triumphant Durf.

Rachel had grabbed her chance. She was running for the car. The control bunker was only a minute away, she'd be safe in there – obviously it had been built to withstand the blast. She was presuming that Sly would not shoot her in the back. She was hoping that he would follow her. He did neither.

'Rachel!!' he screamed, raising his gun, but what was the point . . .

'Wait here,' he snapped at Durf.

'If you go after her we will have to leave without you,' said Durf icily, his hand on his gun, blood trickling from his injured head, 'The count-down is irreversible, we have no choice.'

Nor did Sly, he couldn't make himself a loser for a girl, he just couldn't do it.

'Rachel,' he shouted to her as she jumped into the car, 'come back you stupid bitch! You'll all be dead in a year . . . You stupid bitch . . .'

But she drove away and Sly and Durf boarded the transport.

'You should have dragged her on,' said Durf, as they tore towards the rockets. 'Now you'll be alone, you will have to wait for one of the frozen embryos to grow up.'

'Just one more word, Durf,' hissed Sly. 'One more fucking word, and I'll snap your scrawny neck in two.'

Everybody seemed to be threatening Durf that day, he wished people would not be so emotional.

Rachel had not a moment to lose. She raced the car back to

443

the control area, screeched it down the ramp into the underground loading area, jumped out and rushed into the central control room, slamming the lead and concrete doors behind her.

The voice informed her that there were thirteen minutes to go. She considered trying to carry out her plan of destroying the controls, but she had no weapon – where was all the modern furniture? Rachel had presumed the place would be full of glistening steel chairs. The sort of chairs that Sunday supplements inform you are the way furniture is going for the next decade – chairs that ought to come with their own osteopath.

But there were no chairs, just rank upon rank of glistening console going bleep bleep bleep. Rachel would probably not have tried to destroy the place anyway, they were all aboard, she might kill them. Sly was aboard. Rachel collapsed in an orgy of self-recrimination. Because of her lies, Sly would have to face life alone, perhaps for ever more, without a woman. If she had not plotted against him, he would have taken someone, now he was alone. Then again, they were all alone, everyone in the world, just waiting to die.

## CHASE

Something in Walter Culboon's instincts urged her to obey Zimmerman. There was such genuine anguish in his tone as he jumped upon her back that she felt able to take courage and head back towards the scene of her previous terrors.

'Shit man, he won't get half-way there, and then man, bang! Poof! CD is part of the greenhouse effect,' Zimm had shouted as he ran towards Walter Culboon.

They charged off together, heading towards Stark in CD's wake, and nearly ran smack into a little jeep picking its way along in the opposite direction. It was driven by a stunning looking girl and had the name 'Suki' written across the sunstrip.

'Don't worry, Walter Culboon,' said Zimmerman, 'it's only another "woman driving across desert in car" hallucination.

444

I'm having a lot of those today.' Luckily the camel did not think it was a hallucination and swerved to avoid it.

They pressed on after CD. Zimm was armed and ready to fire should the security cordon have tried to stop him, but they had clearly decided that events had got bigger than their brief. Some were staring at the rockets; some were heading towards Bullens in terror. Either way, Zimmerman sailed right through them, as CD had done moments before.

Zimm reckoned he had a chance, CD was not making fantastic headway. The desert floor was extremely uneven and it was not possible to drive quickly, on the other hand he did have a start and Zimm was chasing him on a tired camel.

Over the harsh scrub he thundered in the wake of CD's dust cloud, every step taking them closer to being engulfed in a mega-cloud of burning rocket fuel and white hot fall-out.

CD didn't care, he was hunched manically over the wheel, conscious of only one thing – the need to rescue Rachel.

As the minutes ticked away, Walter Culboon pushed herself to the limit whilst Zimmerman sat astride roaring at CD to stop. 'Why don't you listen you stupid bastard,' he screamed.

The terrible voice of the count-down boomed again across the desert, drowning Zimm's puny efforts, informing all and sundry that they were now eight minutes from ignition, seven . . . now five.

Five minutes to a sextuplet rocket launch and CD was trying to drive into it! Zimm knew that he himself was crazy but he thanked heaven that he wasn't that crazy.

'Stop, you insane arsehole,' he screamed over Walter Culboon's head, as they careered towards oblivion . . .

'Four minutes and fifty seconds,' said the voice.

Then Zimm saw his chance. There was a little hillock ahead, only about ten feet at its peak, but it was the top of a long sand wave that CD would certainly have to traverse if he wanted to head on in.

'I hope the bastard smashes straight into it,' thought Zimm . . . But no, CD's brain was still clear, except of course for the

445

part that was telling him to commit a pointless and suicidal act.

CD turned the car to travel along parallel to the ridge of sand, this gave Zimm his one chance to get ahead.

As the voice informed him that he now had four minutes and forty seconds left to live, Zimm spurred Walter Culboon up to the top of the hillock. He unslung the shoulder-held launcher and attempted to judge the distance between himself and CD, the speed CD was travelling and any likely changes of direction. What he wanted to do was to put a shell in the ground about twenty metres ahead of CD's car. This, Zimm hoped, would stop the car without killing CD, although why he was bothering with the stupid bastard was a mystery to Zimm. His own years of acting like a maniac had not made him any more sympathetic to when other people tried it. There was so little time, Zimm had to force himself to take aim carefully, he knew he would only get the one shot.

Before the smoke had cleared, Zimm had urged Walter Culboon down into it, where, amidst the dust and fumes, they found CD crawling out of the shattered car.

'Dig you stupid dumb pommie bastard,' shouted Zimmerman.

And the voice said, 'four minutes and twenty seconds to ignition.'

'Dig?' asked a dazed CD.

'Dig!' shouted Zimmerman. CD was confused.

'Yeah, uhm, right Zimm, I dig,' he said.

'Dig the ground,' said Zimm, grabbing CD by the neck.

'OK, OK,' spluttered CD, 'I dig the ground, although I don't see what's so great about it.'

'I mean, really dig, actual digging, not the hip word, dig?' shouted Zimm and he frantically started attacking the ground.

'Oh *dig*,' said CD understanding at last.

'Dig,' said Zimm.

Luckily the Culboons' station wagon was equipped with spades, as indeed are many outback station wagons. Zimmerman grabbed a couple.

'I mean man, what is it with you? And what's more, what *is* the point!' moaned Zimm thrusting a spade into CD's hand. 'Like can I just relax and watch the blast? No, not me, not old Zimm, I have to be fucking *in* it!!'

'I'm sorry, Zimm,' said CD.

'Not as sorry as you're going to be if we can't make some cover. You dig a trench for yourself and me, I'll look after Walter Culboon! We stop at minus twenty seconds!!'

CD realized that with the car gone Rachel was now definitely beyond reach and so for three minutes, as the voice counted them towards near certain oblivion, they dug.

Zimmerman was a wild man, he needed to be, trying to make a hole big enough for a camel. But they were at least in a natural hollow with the ridge CD had been trying to drive around between them and the blast. With forty-five seconds to go Zimm stood Walter Culboon, who was wondering what the excitement was about, at the edge of his shallow little trench.

'Sorry, Walter Culboon, but you'll thank me for this . . .'

He chopped the camel in the neck and Walter Culboon fell neatly unconscious into the hole. Even in this moment of extremis, CD could not help noting that being able to lay out a camel with a single blow, really was pretty mega-cool.

Walter Culboon collapsed and in a blur of energy, Zimmerman scraped down debris from the side of the incline on top of her.

'Ignition minus twenty-five seconds and counting,' said the voice.

'OK, get in,' shouted Zimm, and keep your head down, man. It's a shame, we're going to miss the whole scene . . . but I suppose really it's the sort of thing you ought to see stoned anyway.'

They lay down together in the little shallow grave that CD had dug and desperately tried to pull earth in on top of them.

'Leastways they won't have to bury us,' said CD in triumph – he had finally managed to crack a gag during a moment of extreme tension.

'Minus five,' boomed the voice.

'Cover your face, arsehole,' said Zimm.

And as the world seemed to erupt in heat and shuddering noise around him, CD's last thought was to wonder why Zimm should want him to cover his face and arsehole.

## A HELL OF AN EXIT

Back on the perimeter, as they listened to the final count-down, Mrs Culboon and Chrissy took shelter behind some rocks. They could see across their former battleground that those security personnel who had remained were doing like-wise.

It was a hell of an exit.

Six old style space rockets blasting off in close succession. No sooner had one great tidal wave of burning atmosphere rolled across the desert towards them, when another would start, and then another. And out of this thick, bubbling carpet of shimmering orange heat and black black smoke the rockets rose slowly, almost seeming to hang in the air, reminding Mrs Culboon of the helicopter that CD had brought down, making her half expect these rockets to suddenly lose their fragile momentum and come crashing back down to the ground. But they did not, of course. Stark had been preparing for too long to make any mistakes.

And so Stark flew away.

Slowly the rumbling died down, the streaks of flame began to fade in the sky and they were gone.

# HELL ON EARTH AS
# IT IS IN HEAVEN

And so it came to pass that the Stark consortium left the earth in their Star Arks. Escaping just in time as the storm of ecological disintegration gathered to become a catastrophic deluge; a great flood of dust, disease, heat and filthy, poisonous water, rising to engulf the billions who had created it.

As had been predicted, the horrifying legacy of all the years of thoughtless vandalism turned in upon its creators, and upon all other forms of life on earth, for whom ignorance was no defence. Wave after wave of pollution washed across the dead and dying dirt. Warm, thick, heavy toxic rain fell from the muddied, burning skies, the acid in every drop bursting out upon what life remained, sad useless weeds, clinging to the shifting sands of the barren, infertile, salty ground.

The seas, swollen and bloated by waters which had remained frozen since before the birth of humankind, rose up to reclaim the earth that had been theirs before the cold had bound them.

The deserts that for so long had been chained and guarded by the great forests leapt forward claiming all the land that the seas did not seem to want. And everywhere along the changing shorelines of our retreating world, was washed up, with every tide, the filth and waste disgorged by the teeming billions day by day. Sand and pebbles became a memory as the shrinking coast grew mountainous, piled high with the live and festering muck which nobody knew where to put any more.

All these things came to be, just as the scientists who served Stark had said they would. Indeed, all these things had already come to haunt the earth long before the rich and powerful finally took their leave. The seas have been rising, the deserts spreading, the stinking piles of rubbish growing, the poison rain falling and the land drying, since before the members of the Stark Conspiracy were born.

## THE TRUTH DAWNS

After the Stark blast off, the world very quickly learned the facts of what had happened. At first there had been mystification as the news of the launches swept around the world. Then some bright spark at a local Perth TV studio realized that they had a scoop. Suddenly the Daft Dingo became the hottest news on earth. The tape (with the interviewer's derisive comments edited out) was beamed around the globe.

Chrissy's voice was heard everywhere.

'They have a research team called the Domesday Group, who have proved that the world is dying . . .'

'. . . I've seen the evidence, it's true . . . there doesn't seem to be any hope any more . . . but there *must* be, I mean we're not dead yet, are we . . .'

For those who still doubted, the final proof came the next day with the first broadcast from the Stark fleet; a sombre message, explaining the situation, and almost apologizing for leaving.

'We are sorry,' Durf's voice and image bounced off the world's myriad communication satellites, 'but we knew the truth, the Domesday Group had proved it for us. There is no hope. The Stark Consortium is now the human race. We will do our best to make it work this time.'

Panic and fear swept the earth as daily reports of the departed renegades dominated the media. The world's richest and most powerful producers had gone and left the consumers to their fate. Strangely there was little bitterness, or anger, it was all too hot and hopeless for that. People knew that they were all to blame, not one single person was without guilt. The least anyone had done was to stand idly by. The best that could be said of a person was that they had done no more than close their eyes to the cost of the great global party.

People felt that the cynicism of the Stark departure was no greater than the cynicism with which the riches of the earth had been squandered. The world was dying and the world deserved it. This was the shocked fatalistic attitude of the final generation. If those bastards had bought their way out, it didn't matter any more anyway.

## IF ONLY

'If only,' people sighed, 'if only we had *done* something. Acted when we still had time, even just ten years ago,' they said, 'back in the late eighties, the early nineties when there was still time. The signs were all there, why didn't we *do* something.'

But they hadn't, back in '89, '90 and '91, the years when the decisions needed to be taken, nothing had been done. People had listened to the politicians' empty rhetoric at election time but nothing huge, nothing drastic, nothing *real* had actually been done. Too much money was involved, it simply wasn't economical. Nothing had been done and now the reckoning was upon them all.

## PARTY TIME

After the blast CD had tried to say 'is it over, Zimm?' but it is rather difficult to speak when you seem to have eaten about half of the Great Sandy Desert.

Spitting and spluttering dust out of his mouth he rose up to find Zimmerman, sitting on the prostrate form of Walter Culboon, rolling a ciggie.

'We have to wait for Walter Culboon to come around man, I reckon I hit her a little hard,' was Zimmerman's reply.

451

As they waited they saw a car heading out from what had been the launch site. Zimm presumed it was another hallucination and ignored it. For CD, as always, hope sprang eternal, and just this once it was justified in doing so, because it was Rachel.

It is a tribute to CD that the ecstatic relief he found in Rachel's survival, and the discovery that she had remained loyal to the team all along, was only slightly tempered over the next hour or two by the dawning realization that Rachel's experiences had not been sufficiently cathartic to shock her into wanting to sleep with him.

The four of them headed off together, away from the smouldering remnants of Stark, until they found Chrissy and Mrs Culboon. There they said goodbye to Walter Culboon and the remnants of EcoAction (in CD's case, smouldering), headed on back to Bullens Creek. Back to the home that Mr and Mrs Culboon had bought so recently when they had thought their luck was in. Now Mr Culboon was gone and Durf's thugs had smashed most of it up. Anyway the earth was dying. The cat was OK though.

'So what do we do now?' said Chrissy.

'Well, I reckon we should sell the hire car and buy some beer,' said Mrs Culboon.

'I could certainly do with getting a bit pissed,' said Rachel.

'Yeah, but it's not really the time for a party is it?' said CD, thinking of the friends they'd lost and the failure of what they'd tried to do.

'Sure it's the right time,' said Zimmerman, 'it's time to party like there's no tomorrow.'


# HELL

And the pioneers of Stark? Their lives were hell.

It was too much for poor Sly. After only one year, on yet another lonely lonely night, he opened a pressure door and allowed himself to float away to heaven. He was glad that Rachel had not come with him. He would not have wished the world that Stark had created on anyone, let alone someone he loved.

He was not the first to crack, and he would not be the last. The frozen embryos were destined never to be brought to life. The problem was not the conditions, it was not the work they had to do, nor even the food – the problem was the company.

The pioneers of Stark hated each other. They had created Hell in Heaven. They had escaped pollution on earth, only to discover that they had carried with them another pollution, a pollution that they could not escape. The pollution in their own souls.

# GRIDLOCK

As host of *Saturday Live* and *Friday Night Live* Ben Elton has proved himself the most popular and the most controversial comedian to emerge in recent years. As well as his own stand-up routines Ben's numerous writing credits include *The Young Ones*, *Filthy Rich and Catflap*, *Happy Families* and the award-winning *Blackadder*.

# AN OFF-PLANET
# INTRODUCTION

Before beginning this story proper, a story which has its fictional feet very firmly on the ground, it is worth taking a moment to look upwards, high above the teeming masses of rush-hour London where most of this story is set. Above the tired office workers, tired of office working; the tired media lunch-eaters, tired of eating media lunch; the strange cockney philanthropists, who are prepared to offer you not one gold watch, not even two gold watches, but three gold watches for a tenner. Up and away from the deep carpet of burger boxes and homeless people. Up through the dirty air, over the satellite dishes currently receiving fifteen different Italian game shows, some with bikinis. On, up past Nelson, through the flock of pigeons with the telescopic sights on their backsides, past the great crowd of 747s playing aeronautical Russian Roulette on their way to Heathrow. Through the hot, sticky fog of greenhouse gases, sadly no longer through the ozone layer, past the awesomely sophisticated satellite technology currently employed in transmitting fifteen different Italian game shows, some with bikinis. Up up up and out into space, for it is here, in space, that there recently hovered a spaceship.

This spaceship contained a group of television researchers from the Planet Brain in the process of analysing humanity, in order to compile a three-minute comedy item for their top-rated television show, *That's Amazing, Brainians*, which followed the early evening news.

The researchers were pleased, they had noted much which was amusingly amazing, and they assured each other that Earth had provided the easiest bit of researching that they had done in aeons. Brain is populated by beings of immense intelligence and so far it had taken them only a quarter, of a quarter, of a single second to assimilate and comprehend humanity.

All those things which we on Earth believe to be complex and difficult had been simplicity itself to the beings from Brain. The situation in Beirut; what Hamlet's problem was; how to set the timer on a fourteen-day video-recorder – these things were not mysteries to the Brainians. In that quarter, of one quarter, of a single second they had answered it all. Although, in fairness, it must be added that two weeks later, back on Brain, the researchers would discover that they had managed to record a documentary about Tuscany rather than *Dirty Harry* which they really wanted to watch.

But such slight slip-ups aside, the Brainians had humanity taped. They understood the rules of cricket, how the stripes get into the toothpaste and the reason why there is no word in English for the back of the knee. In that quarter, of one quarter, of a single second the research team had answered all the great philosophical questions. They knew whether an object still exists when you are not looking at it (it does); whether there is a God (if you want); and why people eat Kentucky Fried Chicken even though it makes them feel ill (human beings are stupid).

But then, they were stumped. They had encountered one aspect of human activity which astonished and mystified even those hardened researchers. Researchers who thought they had seen every illogicality and lunacy that the universe had to offer. On this very planet they had seen pointless wars and pointless destruction; they had visited the Tate gallery; they had listened to modern jazz; they had read the novels of James Joyce; they had seen ice-creams which claimed to be shaped like faces but were actually shaped like amoeba – and they had understood it all. But this one had thrown them. This one had them scratching their multiple thought podules in a perplexed manner and saying '*akjafgid-kerhs lejhslh hei!*', which translates as 'Bugger me, that's weird!'

The problem was one of transport.

The Brainians could see the long, thin arteries along which the humans travelled. They noted that after sunrise the humans all travelled one way and at sunset they all travelled the other. They could see that progress was slow and congested along these arteries, that there were endless blockages, queues, bottle-necks and delays causing untold frustration and inefficiency. All this they could see quite clearly.

What was not clear to them, was why.

They knew that humanity was stupid, they had only to look at the week's top ten grossing movies to work that out, but *this* was beyond reason. If, as was obvious, space was so restricted, why was it that each single member of this strange life-form insisted on occupying perhaps fifty times its own ground surface area for the entire time it was in motion – or not in motion, as was normally the case?

The super intelligent beings transmitted their data back to the producer of their programme and they received a right earful in reply (which was rather a lot because, although Brainians are only eight inches tall, their ears are the size of wheelbarrows and have to be rolled up like blinds).

'You're mad,' bellowed the producer using his inter-galactic portable phone because, like producers the universe over, he was having lunch.

'You're trying to tell me that they're all going in the *same* direction, travelling to much the *same* destinations and yet they're all *deliberately* impeding

4

the progress of each other by covering six square metres of space with a large, almost completely empty tin box?'

'That's exactly what we're trying to tell you boss.'

'You're drunk,' shouted the producer, and he was so annoyed that the binding on one of his ears snapped and about six square feet of flapping lug-hole flopped into his pasta.

'We're bloody not drunk,' responded the aggrieved researchers. 'They're all stuck down there, beeping and screaming at each other and working themselves into a frenzy, not getting anything done, not producing anything, just stuck.'

'Oh go on then, let's have another bottle of wine,' said the producer, which naturally rather confused the researchers, but in fact the producer hadn't been speaking to them, his last remark was addressed at his lunch companion. Having another bottle of wine is something else which producers do the universe over – except in Los Angeles where people who, ten years ago, took cocaine in their coffee now give you the phone number of Alcoholics Anonymous if you ask for a beer.

Returning to his telephone conversation, the producer allowed himself to be mollified.

'You mean it's really true?' he said. 'A society sufficiently sophisticated to produce the internal combustion engine has not had the sophistication to develop cheap and efficient public transport?'

'Yes boss,' said the researchers, 'it's true. There's

hardly any buses, the trains are hopelessly under-funded, and hence the entire population is stuck in traffic.'

'Well that's amazing,' said the producer.

'Yes boss, it is amazing,' the researchers agreed.

'Get your asses back to Brain,' said the producer, 'we got a show.'

## Chapter One

# THE MAN THEY
# TRIED TO KILL

### LOVELORN EGGHEAD

Geoffrey sat alone in the big open-plan office of the
Institute of Industrial Research where he worked.
He was surrounded by computers and they all
winked and flashed at him, but, despite being
intimately acquainted with every one of them,
Geoffrey neither winked nor flashed back. He
wasn't thinking of computers. He was thinking of a
beautiful girl, and how one day in the not too distant
future, he, Geoffrey, would set that girl free and by
doing so would win her love. He would achieve this
end with his fantastic research development. A
research development so colossal and stupendous it
made Penicillin look positively mouldy.

There was a bottle in front of Geoffrey and he was
allowing himself a small toast, a little celebration,
to mark the imminent realization of all his wildest
dreams. Not all of them obviously, not the one set
in a nunnery where all the novices turned out to be

Dolly Parton for instance, nor the one about the recurring ostrich, but all the ones fit to print. The dreams about success, peer group respect, enormous mountains of serious cash and setting free the most beautiful girl in the world, hence winning her love. If that wasn't worth a sloosh of pop whilst alone in the old research lab, then Geoffrey wasn't the man he thought he was. And Geoffrey certainly was the man he thought he was, because Geoffrey's was a thorough and precise mind and it wasn't the sort of thing he would make a mistake about.

So there he was, warm glow of satisfaction in his gut, love for a good woman in his heart, a little drinkie on the table, and bent over the arm of his chair staring at the carpet and dribbling.

## UNWELCOME VISITORS

There was a buzz from the intercom. Obviously somebody was at the door. Geoffrey was a bit annoyed. He had no wish to be disturbed by anyone, unless of course it was by the girl of his dreams, or possibly Dolly Parton in a wimple, but since these were both rather unlikely, any visitors were unwelcome. Actually Geoffrey had no idea just how unwelcome these visitors would turn out to be. For they were professional killers – which is nearly as bad as having the Jehovah's Witnesses knock on your door.

With difficulty Geoffrey got up, or at least partly

up. He managed to get to his feet but it wasn't what you would call a particularly perpendicular performance. None the less, it was the best Geoffrey could manage under the circumstances. He fixed his eye upon the intercom some thirty yards across the room. A room crowded with obstacles. Getting across it was going to take some concentration. There were computers, printers, swivel chairs, kettles, stuffed Snoopies and amusing stickers proclaiming that you didn't have to be mad to work there but it helped.

These stickers were originally developed by psychologists as a test to enable office managers to determine an employee's utter dullness. If, for instance, the manager is seeking to find a person to whom may safely be entrusted the organization of the coffee-making rota. If he needs a reliable sort who will ensure that a good tin is provided for the sugar so that the office does not end up with a soggy paper bag containing forty-seven congealed brown sugar globules. All the manager has to do is spy out the employees with the sticker on their computer amusingly proclaiming that 'You don't have to be mad to work here but it helps'. That person will be guaranteed dull, dependable and sane as a pair of corduroy trousers.

Geoffrey lurched forward towards the vast expanse of potential croppers that lay between him and the buzzer. His work place was one of those modern open-plan areas where everything is rendered much more frank and relaxed by virtue of there being no nasty walls to divide people or doors to intimidate them. The actual result of course being that everyone develops nervous ticks due to never knowing who's eavesdropping on them and never feeling safe to have a really good bitch.

An added disadvantage of these spaces, especially if you happen to be in the condition that Geoffrey was in, is that plug and telephone sockets stick up out of the floor in the most unexpected places and there are wires everywhere. It was whilst attempting to negotiate a particularly tangled bit of technology that Geoffrey skidded on the bit of pizza that was left over from a leaving bash which had taken place on the previous Friday evening.

## THE LEAVING BASH FROM HELL

Geoffrey lay on the carpet tiles, with his head in a waste-paper bin, quietly cursing. The leaving bash from hell had returned to haunt him.

All leaving bashes are awful. Perhaps not as awful as birthday bashes where one is forced to annoy an entire restaurant by singing *Happy Birthday* whilst a waiter proudly brings forth a mound of whipped cream with a sparkler in it, but pretty bad, none the less – and this leaving bash was worse. The nightmare had started with the card. Geoffrey had barely known Suzy, the lucky recipient of all that office warmth, symbolized, as it was, by a large picture of Snoopy holding a horseshoe. However, he had felt obliged to rack his brains for twenty minutes trying to think of something witty to write. Eventually he had decided on 'I don't know who you are, but very best wishes'. The biro had scarcely come to a standstill when he deeply regretted his decision. Paranoia consumed him, the phrase was too hard, too dismissive. The scrawled sentence Geoffrey had written seemed to dissolve before his eyes and reform into the words, 'Bugger off, nobody'. After all, that was what his message implied wasn't it? In that instant Geoffrey convinced himself that the girl would be very hurt and that the rest of the lab would despise him for messing up their nice card. Already he could feel the icy hand of social ostracism fingering his collar.

In desperation he opened a bracket. Impulsively he wrote, 'Just joking, really, it's been great working with you'. Geoffrey closed the bracket and descended fully and completely into the paranoid zone. Talk about making a bad thing worse! Maybe he should just go have a shit in the poor woman's pending tray! The first joke had been merely tasteless, now he had turned it into pure hate mail. Everything he had written seemed to just deliberately and maliciously draw attention to the fact that he had scarcely ever spoken to the girl and did not care whether she lived or died. Frantically Geoffrey considered a second bracket, a square one, just a simple and affectionate message to repair the

damage of the previous two efforts. Perhaps something along the lines of, 'Actually I want you to be
the mother of my children! . . .' or, 'Listen Suzy,
name your price to forget about the whole thing.'
Fortunately for Geoffrey reason returned to its
throne. He realized that there would not be sufficient brackets in a book of algebra to extricate him
from the tact swamp into which he had dived. He
would simply have to let it go.

Geoffrey firmly closed the card and, with a weak
smile, handed it back to Denise, unofficial social
secretary for the whole building and the girl with the
'mad' sticker on her desk.

Denise, who had about as much tact as the
Wehrmacht, reopened the card and read Geoffrey's
message. 'Oh that's *lovely*,' she said, in a voice that
you could have beaten down and forged into drill
bits. 'I'm *sure* Suzy will see the joke.'

Attending the 'do' itself had been worse than
writing the card. There is a type of white wine which
is produced in continental Europe specifically for
leaving do's in Britain. It is described as 'an elegant,
delicate, fruity dry' which is Euro-plonkspeak for
abrasive and it is made by putting sandpaper and
lemon juice into a blender. Within two sips from his
or her plastic cup the unhappy imbiber's throat
becomes coated in a thick layer of bitter tasting
phlegm which can only be removed with a pan
scrubber. Unless of course you happen to be talking
to the boss, in which case the phlegm will instantly

leap out of the back of your neck and cling desperately to his tie.

This wine also contains a special kind of alcohol that cannot get you happy-drunk but can only get you bored-drunk, which was the state that everybody was in when the 'do' finally wound down at about eight-thirty.

This is an appalling time for an after-work social to end. Up until eight-twenty everyone has spent the entire time making desperate conversation and wishing they were somewhere else. Then suddenly, with no warning, people are sufficiently bored-pissed on plastic cups of warm French expectorant to agree to go on for a curry.

It is a strange factor of this kind of euphorically dull drunkenness ('Oh go on then, sod it, why not? The evening's buggered anyway.') that it lasts for only twenty-five minutes. This is exactly long enough to get trapped in a curry house between two people you have absolutely no desire to talk to, who are on a different table from the person you have vaguely begun to fancy, while you watch one person order three – no better make it four – popadums each, and someone else order a large brandy. All of which you know you are going to have to pay for a fifteenth of, even though you're not particularly hungry and you can't drink any more yourself because you're driving.

All of this had taken place on Friday night, and now it was late Sunday afternoon and the leaving bash from hell was back. Like some evil curse from a darker age it refused to let Geoffrey be. Having caused him untold worry, bored him stupid and cost him over twenty quid, it had now dumped him down with a thud on the carpet tiles and left him with his head in a waste-paper basket, wherein, a polystyrene cup was in the process of pouring half an inch of cold coffee with a fag end in it, up his nose. How much more could one leaving bash do to a man?

## ENGLISH COMPREHENSION

The buzzer was still buzzing, Geoffrey wanted to shout 'All right, hang on, where's the fire, dickheads,' but he was a realist and in his condition he didn't reckon he would be up to making himself understood. If you're going to start being brusque with people, the last thing you want is them looking puzzled and replying, 'You what?' It detracts from your impact.

With some difficulty, Geoffrey extricated his head from the waste-paper bin that the pizza had dumped it in, and continued his uncertain stagger across the room, finally arriving at the intercom buzzer.

On the second attempt Geoffrey managed to press the button . . . 'Yurgh,' he grunted into the microphone. Which translated meant 'Yes, who is it?'. However, since no interpreter was available at the other end, the two killers waiting on the pavement had to make do with 'Yurgh'.

'Uhm yeah,' shouted one of the killers, for the traffic was loud in the street, 'we're looking for Dr Geoffrey Peason. He around?'

'Yes, that's me, come on up,' said Dr Geoffrey Peason – or rather he didn't because he was having a bit of trouble getting his tongue and larynx to cooperate with each other. The sentence had departed from his brain in perfect condition, but by the time it struggled out of the intercom into the street it had become 'Urg-ats-mm-uhmonup'.

The two men in the street did not know what to make of this cryptic message. They couldn't see the condition Geoffrey was in so they just presumed that they were dealing with a foreigner, or perhaps a mental defective.

The more talkative killer began again, employing the accepted method of communication employed by the British whenever they encounter someone who does not appear to understand English. He raised his voice.

All over Europe, each summer, can be seen the sad picture of frustrated, purple-faced Britons screaming in the faces of non-comprehending natives, 'WHERE . . . IS . . . THE . . . PUB-LIC . . . CON-VE-NIENCE'. The curious theory that a strange language can be rendered understandable by increasing the volume at which it is spoken is one of the great mysteries of the British abroad.

In Paris the cause of the commotion is slightly different. Most Parisians do in fact speak some English, but out of pure bloody-minded snobbishness they refuse to do so in the company of the British. When accosted by a desperate, sweaty, confused Brit asking, 'Excuse me, but do you speak English?' the immaculately dressed Parisian will raise a languid eyebrow and enquire, 'Yes, do you speak French?'. It is a little known historical fact that it was this irritating habit which was the principal cause of the Hundred Years War.

Anyway, in an effort to make himself understood, the man in the street raised his voice. Since he had already been shouting to get above the traffic noise the effort caused veins to stand out on his forehead. He accompanied this tonsil-tingling rant with an elaborate pantomime, this being another aspect of the standard British method of getting your message across to foreigners – scream at the top of your voice and wave your arms about in massive but vague physical gesticulations.

This sad display provides mainland Europeans (again, particularly, the French) with endless entertainment. Outside the Georges Pompidou Centre in Paris, there can always be found a cluster of extremely dull mime artists in tights and bowler hats with flowers sticking out of them, miming walking into a high wind. These irritating performances are invariably accompanied by a clutch of Americans, Brits and Japanese delightedly assuring each other that the bowler hatted one indeed looks *exactly* like he's walking into a high wind, or quite anyway. The locals of course, know that far more fun can be had watching a British tourist attempt to mime 'Can you direct me to the Museum of Contemporary Sculpture please?' and what's more he won't shove his bowler hat under your nose at the end of it.

## JUDGING A BOOK BY ITS COVER

So there they were, the two men on the pavement, one of them roaring at the intercom and miming wildly. Geoffrey, deciding that actions speak louder than words, even words as loud as the ones making the intercom shudder, pressed the lock transmission button, thus providing the first clear message of the whole communication.

After the obligatory electronic lock dance, in which a person and door push against each other to the tune of a buzzer going on and off, the door swung open and the men stumbled in.

They took the lift to the floor marked 'Transport, Fuel and Engine Research' and emerged from it to find Dr Geoffrey Peason waiting for them. Geoffrey held out a shaking hand and tried to greet them cordially but he wasn't really up to it and the two men clearly weren't very impressed with him. However, at first they made at least a pretence at the easy good manners which killers are wont to adopt before unmasking themselves as the angel of death.

They enquired again after Dr Geoffrey Peason stating that they had business with him regarding his recent application for a patent. Dr Peason, also attempting easy good manners but blowing it by dribbling a bit, again replied that he was the said Peason, Doctor of Physics and patent applicant, and what could he do for them? Unfortunately Geoffrey still was not making himself very clearly understood and the visitors' tone became impatient.

'Now listen Sonny, we haven't got a lot of time to waste, so you pull yourself together, all right? And tell us where Peason is.'

Geoffrey was suddenly very tired. He hated being patronized and he hated being dismissed as of no importance. It was always happening to him. He turned his back on the men and staggered back to his chair. Plonking himself down rather heavily he knocked his bottle onto the floor.

'Bollocks,' he said, or rather 'Burgles', an exclamation which he accompanied with an impulsive looking gesture of despair.

Faced with this incoherent hurdle to their enquiries the two men's tone became markedly more intimidating.

'Where's Peason?' the talkative one barked. 'This is where he works isn't it? Our information is that he's always here Sundays.'

Again Doctor Peason tried to explain that he was the man they sought, but the men just did not have

18

the patience to listen to him. They had been briefed to pay a visit on a brilliant scientist and inventor. A man who had invented something quite brilliant and scientific. Confronted by this slurring, unpleasant, uncoordinated young man in a leather jacket and torn jeans, they assumed that the doctor was out. However, since the dribbling rocker was clearly their only available source of information they had no choice but to continue their clumsy enquiries.

Advancing towards Geoffrey one of the men slipped on the pizza.

'I just did that,' said Geoffrey trying once more to be friendly, but still failing completely to make himself understood.

'Don't laugh at me you disgusting little git,' barked the man. He grabbed Geoffrey's cap from Geoffrey's head. Geoffrey was wearing a cap he particularly liked, it was a comedy cap. It had a stuffed arm holding a hammer emerging out of it which appeared to be beating the wearer on his own head. The man wiped the pizza from his shoe with Geoffrey's hat.

Geoffrey may have been having more trouble than usual making himself understood that day but this last gesture confirmed an understanding that had been dawning on him for some time: that he was in the presence of a couple of potentially very dangerous people.

Pizza-shoe roughly crammed the hat back on Geoffrey's head.

'Where's the Doc zit face?' he demanded.

Geoffrey gulped.

'He can't tell you nothing, can he,' said the other, speaking for the first time.

'Look at the state he's in. Let's search the building.'

And with that Geoffrey's interrogators stalked from the room, leaving Geoffrey rather shaken by his unpleasant encounter. Not as shaken as he would have been if he had realized that, had he not been a spastic, he would have been murdered. But none the less, pretty shaken.

Being a spastic had not done Geoffrey a lot of favours in his life. In fact it could be said to have been a total and utter drag from start to finish. However, in that brief moment, being a spastic had actually made up for quite a number of its short-comings as a physical condition. It had unquestion-ably saved Geoffrey's life, because if Geoffrey had not been a spastic, or CP sufferer as some people call it, the two thugs would certainly have killed him.

This is not to say that they refrained from such a course of action out of any sense of sympathy; they did not say to themselves, 'Oh look, hell, the poor bugger's been knocking glasses off tables all his life and probably never been able to masturbate prop-erly. Let's give him a break, eh?' No, the two thugs in question were far too hard of heart for that. It was simply that it never occurred to them that the strange, guttural sounding, twitchy chap sat before them could be the brilliant scientist and inventor whom they had been ordered to murder. But he was.

People with disabilities are very used to being looked through, over, and around. Judged by their covers so to speak. They no longer find it surprising when it is presumed that they have little or no potential and nothing to add to a conversation (other than a conversation on the subject of disability). This is not to say that it gets any easier to put up with, spending one's entire life being underestimated never ceases to be anything other than a horrendous strain, but people with disabilities certainly recognize the attitude. Geoffrey did, he was always being either ignored or patronized and on this occasion he was extremely fortunate that it was the case.

## Chapter Two

# WHAT IS
# IN A NAME?

There is a debate surrounding the word 'spastic'. This concerns its appropriation, by those who do not suffer from cerebral palsy, as a term of contempt. There can scarcely be any able-bodied person who has not used, or at least failed to confront the use of the word 'spastic' as an insult.

It is normally a youthful insult, particularly beloved of small farty boys ('Cripes spew face, you're such a spastic'), but it resonates throughout the population. We all know that to call someone a 'spastic' means that they are stupid, worthless and beneath contempt. Hence the debate for those who actually *are* spastics about what to do with such a tainted term. It's their word, it describes a condition from which they suffer, but it has been stolen, and the question is, do they want it back? Being as how the word spastic has come to imply an all-encompassing and extremely negative summation of a person's abilities and personality, is the word any longer of any real relevance to those who suffer from cerebral palsy? Has the very word itself not become yet another cross that people with this condition are fated to bear?

Some say yes. Some say that the word has been debased beyond redemption. Some say that it must be discarded as a lost cause, and that a new, untainted word or phrase must be found. They suggest 'CP sufferer' for instance, a phrase which certainly has the advantage of clearly only describing an aspect of a person, and not appearing to sum up their entire personality. On the other hand, there are those who insist that the word 'spastic' must be reclaimed. It must be wrested from the mouths of thoughtless little boys and restored to its true meaning. These people look to a day when they will be able to say 'I am a spastic' or 'my daughter is a spastic' without it sounding a bit like a gag.

Geoffrey was of the latter faith. Ever since he had first understood the nature of his severe disability, he had laboured to escape from the social stigma that such a condition engenders. He knew he could not escape from its physical limitations but he could definitely try and stop people thinking that he was a thick, useless, embarrassment.

His method, not one that would work for everyone, had been to take the linguistic battle to the aggressor. He proclaimed himself a 'spasmo'. He had had the words 'Geoffrey Spasmo: Satan's Hell

Dog' written in studs on his first leather jacket and worn it to school. Geoffrey, who always found walking quite difficult, had in his youth sometimes been pushed around in a wheelchair. To his mother's intense embarrassment he had the word 'spasmobile' beautifully inscribed on the back. He had done it in the same lettering as the famous Triumph motorbike company logo, and it looked very cool.

It was at this time, during his wild youth, that Geoffrey had attempted to set up the first wheelchair chapter of the British Hell's Angels. The Angels, who have a highly developed outcast mentality themselves, were quite sympathetic, but Geoffrey dropped the notion when it was explained that besides kissing the arse of a dead chicken, he would be required to piss on his jeans and wear them forever.

Geoffrey's aggressive confrontation of other people's attitudes to his condition upset and annoyed some people. His parents had been terribly upset when he had wanted to officially change his name from Peason to Spasmo, so he hadn't done it. Other spastics, or CP sufferers, were also ambivalent about it, some considered that it played into the hands of the enemy, and Geoffrey conceded that this was possible. However Geoffrey wasn't doing it on behalf of the whole spastic community. He was doing it for himself, to create his own style and his own identity. He was Geoffrey Spasmo. Even now, as an eminent physicist, his leather jacket still spelt it out in studs. His shades, his Sex Pistols T-shirt and torn jeans still spoke of the time in the mid-seventies when he had emerged from his shell and begun his personal rebellion. Geoffrey's had been the only wheelchair to make it to the front of a gig on the Clash's *White Riot Tour* in '77. His Dad had to hose it down to get all the gob off afterwards.

# MAN ON THE RUN

## THIEF

In another part of London Sam Turk sat alone in his office. Sam had no physical disabilities, unless you counted a copious beer gut, but he did have a seriously retarded soul. It was this moral deficiency that had led him to unleash the killers on Geoffrey.

Sam was not naturally a killer, it was circumstance which had made him deadly. Circumstance in the form of a great sheaf of diagrams and computer printouts which lay before him in his office. The diagrams were complex, and Sam was a good enough engineer to realize that to fully understand their subtle intricacies would take months, perhaps years. However, even a superficial perusal had been enough to convince Sam that what lay before him was a revolution, a revolution that would change the world.

Sam's mind reeled at the almost limitless potential of what had fallen into his possession. Limitless is a word that comes more easily to a copywriter than an engineer, but Sam knew that on this occasion it was apt. Fame, power and wealth without boundary of constraint were his for the taking. First, however, Doctor Geoffrey Peason would have to die.

## MISTAKEN IDENTITY

Dr Geoffrey Peason was considering his position, a broken lemonade bottle at his feet and two extremely aggressive looking thugs wandering around the building.

Geoffrey was, of course, unaware that these two men wished to kill him, on the other hand it was pretty clear that they were not intending to give him a great big French kiss and a little box of choccies either. Their attitude had been distinctly aggressive. Geoffrey was reluctantly forced to conclude that the two men had intended to do him no good; possibly the beating up, robbing and leaving for dead type of no good. Geoffrey did not know how he had come to annoy them or what they could want. In fact he was quite certain that the whole thing was a mistake and that they were after an entirely different Geoffrey Peason. Possibly Geoffrey 'chainsaw' Peason who had managed to cross some shadowy 'Mr Big' on some matters of drugs, whores and unpaid gambling debts. Now, however, Geoffrey realized was not the time to sort the matter out. Now was the time to clear off and have a bit of a think, what's more speed was of the essence. It was Sunday and the research facility offices, the labs and the little tea making areas were empty. It would not take long for the two thugs to discover this. Then perhaps they might put two and two together and work out that 'dribble lips' in the computer room might just be the person they thought they were looking for. Actually Geoffrey thought that this was fairly unlikely because, as he well knew, changing the first impressions that people form of those with disabilities was well nigh impossible. As far as the able-bodied community was concerned, if you twitched, and spoke with difficulty, you were a retard. People say that first impressions are so important, for people with disabilities they are a ten foot wall to climb. Which, if you happen to be a quadriplegic, is a bloody difficult thing to do.

None the less, on the off-chance that one of the thugs might be sufficiently enlightened to make the chasmic mental leap required to realize that a spastic might also be a brilliant physicist, Geoffrey thought it wise to get out.

## POPULAR DEMOCRACY

Geoffrey scurried out onto the Cromwell Road, which was where he worked, and started looking for a cab. Normally they were pretty frequent around Kensington but on this occasion there were of course none to be seen. Geoffrey waited, nervously glancing back at the door of his office, caught in the classic cab dilemma, should he start walking and look for one? or should he stay put and look for one? Geoffrey agonized. If he started walking what was the betting that ten would arrive where he presently stood. On the other hand, perhaps the same ten were at that moment hiding around the very next corner. This dilemma is in fact a principal cause of urban pedestrian fatalities, because people will sometimes throw themselves under a bus rather than make a decision.

On this occasion however, Geoffrey managed to pull himself together and had just decided that he would be better off getting away from the two thugs even if it meant walking, which was something that he found quite difficult, when a cab pulled up. Unfortunately, as Geoffrey got into it, the two thugs having tired of their search, emerged from the office. They had not yet freed their minds sufficiently to realize that Geoffrey was Dr Peason, but they had decided to interrogate him further, and on finding him gone from the office had begun to wonder whether their bird had flown.

'There he is, the little bastard,' they cried unkindly, as Geoffrey's cab pulled away and they ran for their car.

'West Hampstead,' stuttered Geoffrey, 'and step on it' – a phrase he had never imagined anybody actually used.

Unfortunately, in London, stepping on it is a very rare achievement (as opposed to stepping *in* it, which is almost impossible to avoid). London is, of course, the capital traffic jam of the UK and even though it was a Sunday the streets were still very busy. Unusually so in fact, and as Geoffrey's cab drove up Queens Gate things became positively teeming. A great colourful mass of people streamed down both pavements heading away from the park. Some braver souls were even venturing to colonize those parts of her Majesty's highways reserved exclusively for cars. Geoffrey was taken aback for a moment, as one aggressive youth pointedly lingered in the act of crossing the road, thus causing the cab to stop, and the cabby and the youth to engage in a brief exchange of views conducted wholly in Chaucerian vernacular.

'Funny thing innit?' the cabbie opined to Geoffrey after the youth had flicked his last V sign. 'Here's this lot all wanting to protest about road building plans. So how'd they go about it? Create a bleeding traffic jam, that's what. I mean that's like screwing for virginity isn't it? If ever there was an argument for building roads, it's a traffic jam. I mean, a traffic jam shows the road's inadequate doesn't it? London needs more roads, there's just no arguing with that.'

Despite this predicament Geoffrey took a moment to go through one of two stock emotions people reserve for when they are sitting in the back of cabs.

Not the one about being convinced that the driver is taking you on an eight mile detour which will cost two hundred pounds, but the one about totally disagreeing with some horrendous prejudices that the cabbie has glibly spouted but not having the moral fibre to take him on. Geoffrey did not think that London needed more roads and heartily agreed with the principles of the rally which had been called to make this point.

It was widely believed that the government had a massive hidden agenda on road building. Nothing was known for certain, but then again nothing is ever known for certain about the actions of the British Government. Whitehall makes a positive fetish out of secrecy. Many a fresh young Civil Servant has had their first day ruined because no one will tell them where the toilets are. None the less, despite the absence of any real proof, there was a growing conviction amongst environmentalists and public transport unions that large sections of Britain were in danger of being submerged beneath concrete.

Of course, the government strenuously denied it. Indeed it went so far as to employ its most open and accountable means of communication; the private, off-the-record briefing. In these private, off-the-record briefings, a senior Civil Servant (in this case Ingmar Bresslaw, Chief Permanent Occasional Over Under Secretary to the Cabinet Office) hands out a private, off-the-record statement, with which the Prime Minister is in no way associated but which he none the less expects to see in the following day's national newspapers.

The private, off-the-record statement which Ingmar Bresslaw handed out, of course, completely dismissed environmental fears regarding road building, but none the less spoke suspiciously in terms of reviewing the 'infra structure', reconsidering the 'road to rail relationship' and 'seeking always to protect the inalienable rights of the private motorist'.

It was this rather inconsistent statement that had provoked the protest in which Geoffrey found himself caught up. A protest which, under normal circumstances, he would gladly have joined. Geoffrey, like many people with disabilities, was dependent on public transport and did not relish the prospect of having to hobble half a mile along a six-lane suburban motorway to get to the footbridge (and frog-tunnel) so that he could cross over, in order to hobble the half mile back down the other side, to get to the bus stop. However, sympathetic though he might be, for the time being Geoffrey had more pressing matters to contend with. His cab was still stationary, behind it was a lorry, behind that, Geoffrey guessed, lurked his pursuers.

'I've changed my mind,' Geoffrey said. 'How much do you reckon to Harlow, Essex?'

'In this traffic,' said the cabbie, wincing as if in pain, "s'gotta be twenty notes hasn't it?'

'Fine,' said Geoffrey, handing over the money. 'I want you to deliver this hat to Harlow Town Hall,' and, having perched his comedy hat on the back shelf of the cab, Geoffrey slipped out of the door and into the crowded street. Geoffrey was a small man, he sat low in a cab, he felt fairly confident that from behind, it would appear as if he was still in his seat with his hat being the only part of him that was visible.

Geoffrey was soon deep in the crowd, jerking his way past the numerous vans dispensing salmonella in a bun. He passed the inspiring and beautiful trade union banners depicting tools that nobody used any more and solidarity that nobody felt any more. He passed the punky-looking kids surrounded by photo-journalists trying to persuade them to throw bricks. He passed London's community policeman, with his big community smile. The same kindly chap produced by Scotland Yard for all such events, who every year at the Notting Hill Carnival got his picture in the papers, dancing with a black woman who was wearing his helmet. Then there were the coachloads of non-community policemen hiding in the side streets. Confronting these, snarling and spitting at them all the while, were the inevitable knots of anarcho/punk/hippy/skinhead arseholes, hoping to provoke a confrontation so that the police would overreact, there would be a riot and they could nick a TV from Rumbelows.

Every cliché of liberal dissent was milling around

Hyde Park that day and Geoffrey felt the inevitable sinking feeling that anyone who has ever attended a protest march feels. That niggling voice in the back of the mind that says 'Do we all look like a bunch of utter gits?'

Rallies are a very double-edged sword. On the one hand, they can serve as a powerful demonstration of popular feeling, on the other, they can simply make everyone look a bit pathetic, it's a thin line. Some types of protestor are entirely counter-productive. Worse even than the middle-class pseudo-punk demanding class war, is the over-excited student who insists on leading chants that nobody wants to join in with.

'Digby Digby Digby,' Farty would scream, invoking the name of Digby Parkhurst the Minister for Transport and principal hate figure of the rally. 'Out out out,' a few loyal comrades would shout in weary reply. 'Digby Digby Digby,' Farty repeats in his hoarse yell, clearly feeling the need for further elaboration. Again, a now diminishing gang reply, 'Out out out.' 'Digby,' bellows Farty, honing down his debating style somewhat. 'Out,' comes the equally succinct reply. 'Digby,' repeats Farty, pressing the point. 'Out,' reiterate his pals, as all around them gnash their teeth. Finally, just to make his position absolutely clear on the subject of Digby, Farty returns to the original rhythm, shouting 'Digby Digby Digby,' and the gang again rewards him with three rousing 'Outs'.

That is the chant as heard on many a march in the last few years. It always emerges at some point – presuming the hate figure in question has been considerate enough to have a two syllable name, 'Theophilus Theophilus Theophilus,' not having quite the same rabble rousing feel. The problem with the chant is that most 'outers' go along with it only out of a sense of duty and to avoid being embarrassed on Farty's behalf, in the way that an audience will murmur at a joke they find unfunny, just to get through the embarrassing silence. They go along with the chant but they feel pretty stupid doing it, and thank God when they get to the final 'Out out out' and can return to silent anonymity.

Unfortunately, what inevitably happens is that Farty, emboldened and intoxicated with his new roll as cheerleader, rabble rouser and street-fighting man, tries to go for the whole thing again. This condemns it to an inevitable and eggy petering out which renders the entire exercise so limp as to actually work against its intention. At the end of the chant, any non-aligned observers would definitely be left with the impression that Digby, far from being 'out out out', was more entrenched than ever.

## NOT QUITE JERUSALEM

'Oh God,' thought Geoffrey, 'please, please don't let anybody strike up "Here we go".'

'Here we go' is a football chant performed

vaguely to a fairground barrel organ tune which, during the Miners' Strike of 1984, did useful service warming people up on 5 a.m. picket lines. Since then, however, it has been adopted as a kind of catch-all anthem of protest and has been heard near missile bases, outside hospitals in danger of closure, inside town halls where new cuts were being announced and at the end of Labour Party meetings. Indeed such a contribution did this chant make to the cultural backdrop of protest in Britain in the eighties that it is worth recording its lyric in full, that posterity might not forget the depth and subtlety of its message. The text runs like this:

Here we go, here we go, here we go,
Here we go, here we go, here we go-oh.
Here we go, here we go, here we go,
Here we go-oh, here we go.
(Repeat until your cause is lost.)

Where we were going is not touched upon, why we might want to go there is also left to the imagination, the one salient point is that we are off. Sadly, never was a lyric more apt. 'Here we go' would be sung, and pits, jobs, services etc., duly went.

Compare this turgid, lifeless effort with 'Jerusalem', or 'We Shall Overcome' and it is possible to see what a momentous own-goal in public relations this chant was. Mindless as 'Oompah oompah stick

it up your jumper,' but without the biting wit. So
mindless is it in fact that the only possible explanation for its continuing emergence year after year at
every possible protest event, is that it is the result of
infiltration by *agents provocateurs*. Just at the point
at which the audience at a protest are at their most
emotionally and intellectually moved, a right wing
infiltrator in a bobble hat will ruin it by striking up
'Here we go'. It works every time. The hall groans
inwardly, but none the less joins in under the
mistaken impression that not to do so would give the
appearance that the event has no unity, soul or
fervour. The impression actually given is that the
event is made up of a bunch of parrots without an
original thought between them.

## MESS: THE ULTIMATE SOLUTION

Geoffrey got on the tube at Marble Arch and, by
coincidence, arrived home at almost exactly the
same time that a bemused cabby found himself
standing on the steps of a firmly locked Harlow
Town Hall, holding a comedy hat, whilst behind
him two furious thugs stared into an empty cab.

Geoffrey let himself into his ground floor maisonette and began to pick his way carefully through
the mess. Any stranger opening the door of Geoffrey's place would have presumed that Geoffrey had
just been burgled by a hyperactive burglar who had
taken a line or two of speed to get him into a good

37

burgling mood. The place was a mess. It could not have been in more of a mess if it had been occupied by a fifteen-year-old girl who had decided to rebel against the bourgeois mentality of her parents because neither they, nor indeed anyone else in the world, understood her.

In choosing to live in a manner that would cause a punk sewer-rat to raise a dubious eyebrow, Geoffrey was unlike many other people with disabilities, who treasure order. Because simple functions are more difficult for them it is important to them to know where everything is and to make sure that wherever that is, is the most convenient place. If you are in a wheelchair for instance and want to read your book, it is obviously less hassle to know where the book is and also to have a clear, uncluttered path to reach it.

Geoffrey was not in a wheelchair, but he did move in a vaguely unpredictable way, which meant he often knocked things over. He really only became truly aware of the mayhem this can cause when he left home to go to university. Like every other new student Geoffrey discovered, to his astonishment, that clean socks do not organically form inside drawers and that mugs left around the house do not magically bathe themselves thoroughly and then levitate back onto a hook – they go mouldy. Geoffrey, like many an eighteen-year-old before and since, was forced to realize just how many of the true facts of life his mother had been keeping from him.

Facts like, sheets go yellow if you don't wash them, the rims of toilets become encrusted with dust and pubic hairs if you don't wipe them, meals do not grow on the table and, in Geoffrey's particular case, if you don't pick things up, everything you own eventually ends up on the floor. Geoffrey struggled against this problem for many years, just as his mother had done before him, endlessly picking things up in order to knock them over again. Until one day the futility of it all suddenly dawned upon him. He felt like a philosopher contemplating war, or a British gymnast contemplating the Olympics. He realized that there was no point. He realized that the solution to knocking things over, was simply never to pick anything up, thereby depriving himself of ammunition. From that day on, Geoffrey allowed the bulk of his worldly goods to remain on the floor.

Geoffrey was of course lucky, he had a wonderful cleaner who, after initial reluctance, had agreed to apply Geoffrey's method. The rule was very simple, she cleaned up anything wet, and left anything dry. Geoffrey never cooked, either eating out or having pizza delivered, so the system worked pretty well.

## ROBO CUP

Geoffrey's passion was mechanics and, in particular, robotics. Perhaps because his own motor mechanism was so faulty he took a peculiar delight in clever and smooth-running machinery. His little maisonette was filled with fantastically complicated electronic gadgetry; a mass of bits of mechanical arms, half-finished vacuum cleaners that were supposed to do the hoovering by themselves, concertinaed platforms designed for lifting heavy objects. Geoffrey had work to do on most of his gadgets. At present the lifting platform was a touch enthusiastic. It lay almost flat on the floor and was designed to lift a wheelchair up a step for instance, or simply raise a heavy suitcase. Unfortunately such heavy-duty hydraulics are rather expensive, so Geoffrey was experimenting with pistons loaded with small explosive charges. Geoffrey would have been the first to confess that he was having trouble getting the pressure right, also the balance. In fact on the last attempt the suitcase had been catapulted out of the window and into the front garden. Geoffrey was grateful he hadn't tried it on a person in a wheelchair.

Geoffrey sat down, not unnaturally, still ruminating over the threatening manner of his two interrogators. He decided to have a glass of wine to facilitate thought. Sitting in his chair, he took up a little remote control device with switches and a joystick; Geoffrey's cerebral palsy was not as severe as for some and he had one fully working hand. He flipped a switch which activated his new mechanical corkscrew. Geoffrey liked his drop of sauce of an evening, and getting bottles open was a major drag for him, so he had invented a mechanical arm with a needle on the end, a needle attached to a canister of compressed air. The idea was that the radio-operated arm manoeuvred the needle over the cork and then plunged it down into the bottle, the downward movement causing the air to flow from the canister into the bottle, thus forcing the cork out. The machine was on the sideboard next to his booze stash. From his armchair on the other side of the room Geoffrey positioned the needle and sent the arm plunging down, there was a hiss of compressed air, but sadly the cork was a stiff one, the bottle gave out before it did, exploding with a loud bang and sending broken glass and Rioja everywhere.

Geoffrey was used to failure, he could not possibly afford the equipment required to make his equipment foolproof. He decided to have a cup of coffee instead. There was a pot all brewed in the coffee-maker. The pot was attached to an extendable robotic arm. Geoffrey's mug was where it always was, on the arm of his chair, he did not take milk or sugar so it was never washed. With a twiddle of the remote Geoffrey began to manoeuvre the coffee pot through the air towards him. When it was positioned perfectly, he twiddled again and the pot tilted. It was a triumph, a brimming cup of scalding coffee without leaving his seat. Geoffrey sent the pot flying home, put in his straw and head jerking a little, took a careful sip. Relaxing, perhaps for the first time since the intercom had gone off in his office, Geoffrey continued to muse on that afternoon's disturbing encounter. For a moment he toyed with the idea of reporting it to the police, but then, what was there to report? Two men had enquired after him at his place of work. Certainly they had been unpleasant, but that isn't a crime. If it was, the courts would be packed with television astrologists and BMW drivers. Burglary is, however, a crime, and it was as he sat pondering that Geoffrey first noticed that he had been burgled. As has been pointed out, Geoffrey's place always looked as if it had been burgled, which is why it took him so long to realize.

It was not a bad burglary as far as Geoffrey could see. In fact, when he considered some of the horror stories he had heard, he reckoned he had got off fairly lightly. The burglars had been a thoughtful and professional bunch. They had refrained from having a crap on the coffee table or masturbating into Geoffrey's underwear drawer. In fact all they seemed to have taken was his television.

Geoffrey steeled himself to make the phone call, he hated ringing up people he did not know.

'Hello police? I've been burgled,' said Geoffrey, adding, as he always did, 'and I talk this way because I'm a spastic.'

# GOING TO
# THE PARTY

## OFFICIAL BOOZE UP

Whilst Geoffrey was being pursued by murderers and discovering the theft of his television, Sam Turk, the man responsible for this mystifying harrassment, was in the back of a luxury car on his way to Brighton. Starting on the morrow, Brighton was to play host to a Party Political Conference, or Party Political Piss-up as the more honest politician would concede.

There is a similar institution in the world of marketing, it is called a 'sales conference' which, despite its business-like title, is a corporate institution whereby the staff get the opportunity to become legless at the company's expense and the sales reps have a chance to try and shag the secretaries. Of course this is denied absolutely when the Inland Revenue queries the drinks bill. Then much corporate gobbledegook is spouted concerning 'late night policy sessions', 'target dinners' and 'strike-unit damage control briefings'. None the less, the sales conference is a piss-up. And why not? It is a small reward, a chance to get out of the Ford Sierra and into the bar; to get away from the typewriter and into a little black cocktail number. It forges *esprit de corps*. The Japanese have their company songs and exercise sessions; the British have their eleven pints of lager and at 3 a.m. attempt to break into the hotel swimming pool. People need a chance to express themselves.

Party Conferences are the political world's equivalent of these fine corporate institutions. The only difference being that they last a week and provide an excellent opportunity for behind the scenes wheeler-dealing. This was why Sam Turk was going to Brighton.

## KILLER ON THE LOOSE

Sam was not a politician, not in the elected sense anyway. But he certainly dealt in power. He was a carmaker.

He worked for Global Motors, a US based multi-national auto manufacturing company, and he had come to London the previous year with the declared intention of kicking some English bottoms at Global Motors UK. The British motor industry, as Sam well knew, was still residing in the 1920s which, considering the US motor industry had made it as far as the 1950s, meant that Sam had a lot of work to do. The Japanese motor industry is, of course, in the 1990s. It was Global Motors' secret target that by the year 2015, they would be in the 1990s too.

For the moment however cars were not on Sam's mind, but killing was. In his briefcase lay hidden the most exciting designs that he had ever come across. However, in order for Sam to realize their full potential, he needed their creator dead.

'D'yah knock out the professor guy?' Sam asked Springer, his loyal Lieutenant of many years.

Springer winced a little at this abrupt enquiry. He had not enjoyed the task of organizing a murder one little bit. In fact he had for the first time in all his loyal service attempted to defy Sam. It was only after Sam had reluctantly shared the momentous secrets of the plans with him that Springer had steeled himself to the task. It was immediately clear to Springer that the good of the company, indeed the good of the entire economy of the United States, might be at stake.

'I guess he must have bought the farm by now,' Springer replied. He had served in Korea and loved to talk like a soldier.

Sam nodded with grim satisfaction, none the less, he could not help but feel a pang of something. One wouldn't go so far as to say it was actual remorse, but it was definitely regret. Sam had led a pretty rough life in the paranoid world of the US motor industry and he had done wicked and unpleasant things. But he had never before had anybody killed.

'I can't help feeling that bumping the guy off was wrong,' he said.

Springer was surprised, it was most unusual for his boss to be tormented by doubt.

'I can get the driver to haul ass to a church boss. It might be best to let a priest handle this,' he said sympathetically.

'I ain't talking morally wrong,' said Sam. 'We had a serious situation, and we made a move. That's business, that's what I'm paid to do, my conscience is clear. But was it the *right* move I ask myself? Death *is* kind of radical. I still can't believe we couldn'a bought the damn thing off the little fuck'n' brain box.'

'I'm telling you Sir, there's no way he would have sold,' said Springer. 'We ran a full background make on the guy, major reconnaissance. He's a public transport nut, he hates private cars, reckons we should all be sat behind each other on stinking buses, picking the chewing gum off our pants.'

'Mother of God ain't people sick?' said Sam in disgust. 'The guy's probably into free love too.'

'I guess he would be at that,' Springer agreed.

'You want someone like that having the right to ball your old lady?' Sam was working himself up into a fine state of self-justification. 'Smoking his pot and corrupting college kids? He got what was his. We did the world a favour.'

'We had to do it, Sir,' Springer affirmed. 'His invention in the wrong hands could take out our entire operation. They'd be sending Global Motors home in a body bag.'

This last analogy was sufficiently ghoulish to re-concentrate the minds of the two men on the human cost of their business decisions. They lapsed into a brief silence.

'Yeah,' said Sam eventually. 'The little commie sure had it coming.'

## DELAYS

The knock-on effects of the protest rally which had impeded Geoffrey's escape continued to paralyse part of London. Traffic jams are strange things, they resonate. As when a stone is dropped in a pond, the matter does not end with the initial plop. Six feet away some frog on a lily gets a series of rhythmic ripples up the back flap and hops off going *ribbit* and looking for something semi-aquatic to shag. It is the same with traffic. It's quite possible for a person to miss a train at Waterloo because half an hour previously a one-driver bus on the Strand was confronted with someone who didn't speak English, only had a twenty pound note and wanted to be taken somewhere that provided traditional English scenes, haddock and tea-time. Traffic jams never actually end, they merely expand and contract, merging into one another, endlessly connected by frustration and grinding synchromesh. There is a little bit of the very first traffic jam in every one that has happened since.

Sam was caught up in the ripple effect. His car, like his industry, was at a standstill and he was getting impatient.

'Jeez,' he barked, lowering the electric window which separated him from the driver. 'I never seen the city this bad. It's Sunday goddamit, doesn't anyone in this damn country worship the lord any more? What the hell's going on?' The driver explained that the traffic was particularly bad that day because there had been a huge protest rally in Hyde Park and the effects had fanned out across the city.

'A *protest* rally? What, like a hippy thing?' gasped Sam in astonishment. 'I don't believe this fucking country! It's like it never left the middle ages! A *protest* rally! What's there to protest about, there ain't no war or anything? Sometimes I just want to throw in the towel. The whole of Eastern Europe comes to its senses and kids in the West are still shouting about Ho Chi Minh.'

The driver explained to Sam that the protest was to do with the suspected new road plans for London and the South-East of England. Sam knew all about these plans. In his capacity as boss of Global Motors UK he was on very close acquaintance with Digby Parkhurst, the Minister for Transport and whole-heartedly supported his policies. This was something which Digby took great pleasure in. It did not occur to Digby that it was perhaps a little unhealthy for a person whose function was to represent the best interests of the people in the area of transport, to be quite so close to one of the country's largest car manufacturers.

Sam was delighted.

'A protest about the road plans! Well that's great,' he cried. 'That is my kind of protest. What is it, they don't think it's radical enough? I told that stupid son of a bitch Parkhurst that nobody gives a damn about Nelson's column.'

The driver was forced to disillusion Sam as to the political slant of the march. '*Objecting* to roads!' said Sam in astonishment. 'But that's crazy! What are they gonna object to next? Food? Don't they want to be able to get from A to B!'

'I think that they're concerned that there should still be an A to come from and a B to go to Sir,' replied the driver who cherished his individualism.

'What did he say?' enquired Sam who, as was his wont, had only been asking a rhetorical question.

'I think he said that he'd better button his lip or get fired,' said Springer, raising the sound-proofed electric window again.

Sam looked sadly out at the rag-bag of protestors making their way home. 'I don't know,' he said wearily. 'People. You try to make a better world for them, and what do they do? Throw ball-bearings under police horses.'

It was while Sam was having this philosophical ponder on the ingratitude of 'the little fellow' that

Springer's personal phone rang.

'This is it Boss. News from the dead professor,' said Springer.

'You got hit-men calling you here? In *my* car!' replied an astonished Sam.

'Relax,' said Springer. 'This is a brand new portable phone, after this call I chuck it in a river.' He answered the phone.

'What's he say? What's he say?' Sam demanded impatiently.

Springer's face had fallen.

'He says the Gerbil is still twitching.'

'And why did he say that?' asked Sam, not unreasonably.

'Because the guy ain't dead yet. They missed him,' Springer admitted.

Sam grabbed the phone in a fury.

'Now listen here, you lazy, Limey fruit!' he shouted. 'When I employ tradesmen I expect them to get the job done and get outa my face, not to ring my car to say some hampster is still doing the rumba. What you doin' you English fuck? Taking a *tea-break*? On a frigging *strike*? Jesus Christ, what is it with you English? You can't make cars, you can't kill people, how the hell d'you ever get yourselves an empire? I'll tell you how, you got the *Scots* to do it for you! That's how.'

'*Pardonez moi, monsieur*,' said the impeccably polite French voice of the contract killer on the end of the line. 'I am Anatole Chiraud of Euro Despatch and I can assure you that the gerbil which you require to be sedated has only been briefly mislaid. The contract will be completed as soon as possible.'

The line went dead, leaving Sam frustrated and bemused.

'A French hit-man?' said Sam. 'What is he going to do, breathe on the guy?'

## CONCRETE AND STEEL

Digby Parkhurst, the Minister for Transport, friend of Sam Turk and the man at whose image the students had spent the afternoon chanting 'Out out out', was preparing for his departure to the conference at Brighton. He was a little sad because he was going to have to leave his beloved models behind him. They were beautiful models, mounted on trestle tables all through his department, and he loved to touch them. He loved to feel the long, grey ribbons and stick his fingers in the tiny little tunnels. The models were of bits of the British Isles, although a native of those same islands would have been hard put to recognize them as such. Hills had been removed, villages relocated, lochs drained, and in their place were roads – long, empty, beautiful roads.

Well not quite empty, here and there on the larger scale models the architect had placed a tiny model of a car. Just one, and a lovely looking car at that. One could imagine it carrying a family off to have a picnic. Perhaps the family were planning to have the picnic under one of the little trees that the architect had thoughtfully placed on the beautiful models.

## THE CATERPILLAR AND THE BUTTERFLY

The architectural model is like the sluggish, hairy caterpillar that turns into the beautiful butterfly. Unfortunately, it happens in reverse. Take a stroll round something large and concrete in any neighbourhood, and then, with the image still in mind, rush round to the planning department of the local council and demand to see the original model and drawings. It will be a strange experience. For, although the dimensions of the building you have rushed from, and the model you are shown, will be the same and the colours similar, none the less the two images will *bear no resemblance to each other whatsoever*.

The transformation between fiction and reality is as stark as that which drunk strangers, who screw each other after parties, go through during the night. How beautiful they had appeared in each other's eyes after a bottle or two of Spanish, but reality must be faced in the morning. Any little boy who has been entranced by the picture on the front of a soldier-kit box, the brave GI with gun blazing, will be familiar with the architects' trick. He will know the disappointment of Christmas morning when the box turns out to contain a squashed plastic hat and a gun that does not even go 'click'. Just as residents (and no doubt the architects themselves) know disappointment at the appearance of great rust streaks down the concrete walls and puddles of piss in the lifts.

It is not always the fault of the architect, planners give them impossible briefs and inadequate budgets, but they might make their failures more easy to bear if on the original models, instead of lots of pretty little trees and a tiny motor car, they placed models of hundreds of cars, three dead trees, a little discarded supermarket trolly, some model dog turds and plenty of damp.

## KING OF THE ROAD

Digby wandered like a dreamer from one pristine model to another, touching them gently, stroking their contours. In this exquisite private moment he even knelt down and pressed his cheek against the cool surface of a miniature flyover. As he stood up, a faraway look crossed his features. He could see clearly in his mind's eye, a sunny day, a crowd of dignitaries standing on the spotless concrete, a long, blue ribbon of delicate silk stretched across the ten proud lanes, he himself sternly holding the golden scissors. Digby's eyes grew misty. 'I, Digby Parkhurst, Her Britannic Majesty's Minister for Transport, do hereby declare the UK orbital ring road open.'

It was a delicious dream, to be immortal, to be set in concrete. One of Digby's recurrent fantasies was that he would be remembered as 'King Of The Road', that school-children would be taught of his great achievements . . .

'And this infrastructure,' Digby said to himself, assuming the personality of mythical teacher of the future, 'was set in place by Digby The Road Builder. Yes class, Digby Parkhurst, the King of the Road.'

## Chapter Five

# FIRST BLOOD

## WICKED WORLD, SIR

As Sam Turk angrily slammed the phone down on the French hit-men, the object of his concern was still very much alive and the reason that the Gerbil could not be sedated was that the Gerbil was, at present, in the company of the Police. This is a state of affairs likely to impede any murder. One of the first things they impress upon rookie hit-men during their hit-man basic training is, that if you are contemplating perpetrating a homicide, it is advisable to avoid doing so whilst there are uniformed bobbies present.

Unfortunately for Geoffrey, his protector was on the point of departure. 'We'll be in touch if need be, Sir,' said the copper, having looked at the forced window-pane and noted the absence of a television.

'Is that it?' said Geoffrey astonished.

He had perhaps not expected an immediate arrest but he wouldn't have minded some small indication that an arrest might one day be within the bounds of possibility. Geoffrey could not help feeling that he would have got more investigative vigour and commitment to law and order if he had called in the Brownies.

'That's it for the moment, Sir,' said the policeman.

'But this is absurd,' Geoffrey stammered, struggling to keep his speech comprehensible. 'Where are the blood-hounds? The lines of dungareed cadets beating the undergrowth? Surely you'll need a sample of my semen so that you can rule me out when you start the genetic fingerprinting?'

Detective Constable Collingwood smiled his weary smile. He was used to outraged householders demanding action. It always comes as a great shock to people, perhaps second only to that of the actual burglary, to realize that there is virtually nothing the police can do about it.

A population raised in the comforting company of *Dixon of Dock Green*, fondly imagine that the police have sufficient resources to do their job properly. George Dixon was a policeman who was not only happy to investigate minor crimes but also found the time to deliver lengthy philosophical monologues on the nature of the villainy he encountered. Sadly, the real police force, in the real world, were long ago forced to recognize that their chances of keeping up with the thousands of burglaries committed each week are non-existent.

'This mean city's a bubbling cauldron of sleaze and crime,' said DC Collingwood, who enjoyed the occasional Batman comic. 'Our job's to keep the lid on, Sir. I have to ask myself what is more important: your telly, or some slime-ball pushing crack onto a teenage girl to get her hooked and turn her into a piece of filthy human wreckage, so that she can be lured onto the game?'

Put that way Geoffrey began to feel a bit guilty about having called the police at all. The last thing he wanted was to be the cause of a teenage girl becoming a piece of human wreckage. Geoffrey had been about to mention the two men who had visited him that afternoon but he decided to forget it.

'As I say, Sir,' continued Collingwood, 'we'll call you if we find anything out,' but he knew that there was no chance. Much as they would like to, the police don't investigate burglaries any more. They write them down in a big book and then, at the end of each police year, they take the big book to their annual conference, show it to the Home Secretary and ask for more money, which they get, but only if they promise to spend it on riot gear.

Of course, if the young detective had had any idea as to where Geoffrey's small burglary was going to lead; if, for a moment, he could have seen into the future and caught a fleeting glimpse of the mayhem and destruction that would eventually stem from this one tiny entry in the big police burglary book; if DC Collingwood had glanced into a convenient crystal ball and seen the murder, mayhem and environmental catastrophe that lay at the end of the chain, which began with the theft of Geoffrey's telly – he would have had a look round for some fingerprints and stuff, he would have got down on his knees with some tweezers and started putting bits of fluff and fag ash into envelopes, he would probably have accepted Geoffrey's kind offer of some semen. But Constable Collingwood didn't know, so he went on his way. Leaving Geoffrey feeling rather rotten and depressed.

But Geoffrey's time of trouble had only just begun. He was destined, in a very short while, to feel a great deal more rotten and depressed. It was only, in fact, to be a matter of minutes before Geoffrey would be looking back on that vague sensation of feeling rotten and depressed as a positive high point of his day. He had not, as of yet, made any real and concrete connection between the theft of his television, and his unpleasant experience with the two thugs at the lab. But he was about to.

## ROBO CUP 2

Finishing his coffee, Geoffrey got up and wandered into his study. It was only then that Geoffrey noticed that the hard disc drive had been removed from underneath his computer. He had not noticed before, because the computer itself, which was by far the more valuable item, had not been stolen, neither had an extremely expensive laser printer borrowed from the lab. Only his hard disc had disappeared and also, he now noticed, all the back-up floppy discs as well.

Why on Earth would any burglar wish to steal discs?

Geoffrey came to the rather worrying conclusion that they were after his research. The television had been either mere opportunism, or a blind to cover up the true purpose of the burglary. Geoffrey now understood that the two fellows he had encountered at the office were not acting under any misapprehension. They had mentioned Geoffrey's patent application, and now, on the same day, all his work, all his electronic files had been stolen. The conclusion was dawning on Geoffrey that somebody did not like his invention, and in fact, disliked it enough to steal it, and send thugs after its inventor. Geoffrey thanked his lucky stars that he had already submitted the project to the patents office. Whoever it was who had stolen his work would not be able to suppress his brilliant invention simply by pinching it.

Geoffrey returned to his armchair pondering his predicament. Should he tell the police about the threatening men? about the theft of his work? He supposed so, but it was a tiring prospect. Long and bitter experience had taught him that it was extremely difficult for spastics to get themselves taken seriously. People often didn't even want to talk to them, let alone hear about their problems. The first thing to do, Geoffrey felt, was to get away from his house. Clearly something was very wrong and he needed peace to consider it. He had just decided to go and spend the night at a friend's place when he heard the unmistakable sound of his front door being kicked down.

Geoffrey's life had demanded from him a peculiar courage and strength: but it had not prepared him for having violent thugs kick down his front door – and he was shit scared. Years of being demeaned and patronized had caused Geoffrey to develop a very thick skin, but he knew it was not thick enough to withstand physical assault. Geoffrey shrank into his chair as he heard the sound of heavy feet in the corridor and, before he knew it, his two companions of earlier in the day were standing before him. Geoffrey could not believe his stupidity for hanging around in his house. Obviously, if they knew his work place, they would know his home. He could have kicked himself. As it happens, he was kicking himself because the tension of the situation had caused him to lose a degree of control over his lower limbs.

'Stop fucking twitching,' said a thug, disgust in his voice.

'He can't, can he? Look at him,' said the other, adding 'makes you wanna puke dunnit' thus dispelling any suspicion that his rough exterior might disguise a sympathetic soul.

'So you're the bleeding egghead then?' continued the thug (whose name was Frank). 'Who'd of bleeding thought it?'

'He looks like a total spastic, dun' 'e?' said the other.

'I am,' said Geoffrey, trying to keep his head still.

'Shut your face you mongol,' barked Frank. 'We've wasted a whole bleeding afternoon looking for you. We followed that taxi all the way to Harlow.'

'Let's kill the pathetic little bastard and piss off,' said his colleague (whose name was Gary) as he produced a gun.

Geoffrey was slightly stunned. He had no idea that the stakes were quite so high. It appeared that these men were actually going to kill him.

'Probably doing you a favour, eh, Professor? Put you out of your misery, eh? Jesus, look at the state of it, eh?'

In truth, Geoffrey was in rather a state. Small and twisted in his armchair, he was jerking and dribbling and his voice was not working.

'Och och och,' he grunted for no apparent reason. Adding, 'uuuurrrrgh.' In fact, Geoffrey was pleading for his life, but this was somewhat lost in the translation.

'Come on, Frank, kill it and shut it up,' urged Gary unkindly. 'Makes me sick that noise does.'

Geoffrey had always been aware that many people found him distasteful, that their stomachs weakened at his twitches and grunts and they longed to be away from him – but no one had ever been so up front about it before. On another occasion, following his policy of confronting his Cerebral Palsy head on, Geoffrey might have applauded such honesty. However, on this occasion, he was too scared to applaud anything.

'Can't kill him, can we?' said Frank to Geoffrey's intense relief. 'Not until we've tortured him,' he added, which somewhat mitigated Geoffrey's enthusiasm.

'It won't need torturing mate,' said Gary the death enthusiast. 'Look at it. It's shitting itself,' an observation which was not far from the truth. Gary crossed the room and, sweeping away the broken glass from the exploded wine bottle, perched himself against the sideboard. He addressed Geoffrey with exaggerated slowness, as if talking to an idiot . . . 'Here Spaso,' he said. 'Have you got any other work stuff stashed away, besides what we nicked before . . . Dribble for yes, twitch for no . . . ha ha ha.'

Geoffrey was not in a position to answer, every ounce of his concentration was pinpointed on his good hand. It lay underneath his twitching body and in it was the remote control. Very slowly, and with all the dexterity gained through years of doing the work of ten, Geoffrey's five good fingers were gently teasing the tiny joystick.

With his chin, seemingly, attached to his collar

bone and his small body rigid and jerking, rattling about in the stiff leather of his jacket, Geoffrey did not look dangerous. But he was.

The laughing man's bottom was perched next to the wine bottles, Geoffrey could see the big fold of flesh from the sideway's view that his tilted head allowed him. The man was still laughing at his brilliant dribble gag as the little hydraulic arm that Geoffrey had made, silently came to life and hovered across the sideboard. The needle came to a halt above the fold of Gary's plump backside, squashed as it was against the polished wood.

Geoffrey flipped a switch, the shaft of steel plunged downwards and Gary's cruel laughter turned to a scream as the vicious needle buried itself in his flesh. The needle hissed like a snake and the man fell dying on to the floor. As luck would have it, the snake had found an artery, and ten cubic centimetres of compressed air had been pumped, at high pressure, into Gary's blood stream.

Frank spun round, astonished.

'Jesus Gazzer, this is no time to have a bleeding heart attack.'

Even at this moment, Frank could not get over his prejudices. He still could not quite believe that the small, twisted wreck in the armchair could have had anything to do with the besting of his tough, able-bodied colleague. Then Frank saw the jointed robotic arm hanging over the edge of the dresser. He saw its one finger, a long thin spike, crimson with blood, pointing down at the dying man. A stern, accusing finger calling Gary to book for his life of sin. Frank looked from the needle to Geoffrey; then at his now dead colleague – and he began to wonder.

'Did you do that, you little bastard?' he shouted at Geoffrey. 'You're supposed to be some sort of bleeding professor, ain't ya?'

Frank had drawn his gun and his face spelt murder. But Geoffrey wasn't looking at Frank's face, he was looking over Frank's shoulder to the space behind, where a pot of scalding coffee was slowly crossing the room on a long arm.

'All right mate, that is it. You are dead, you hear? I don't care whether we've got all your research stuff or not, you ain't going to be telling anyone about it because you are bleeding dead.'

Frank held up his pistol, and for the first time in his life Geoffrey found himself staring down the barrel of a gun. Except he wasn't really staring down it, his eyes were fixed on the space above his assailant's head. Could the arm reach high enough? Fortunately, it had also been designed for getting things down from the top of wardrobes.

As the man cocked his pistol the coffee pot appeared from behind him and levitated upwards until it hovered above his head. Geoffrey had literally only seconds in which to act, but, to his lasting credit, he found the time to be cool. Making a huge effort to gain control of his voice he enquired . . .

'Do you take sugar?'

Without waiting for a reply Geoffrey again hit the button on his remote, and a pint of boiling coffee descended on Frank. Fortunately, Frank did not fire, instead he screamed in agony and began to hop about. Geoffrey's plan, as far as he had one, was at this point to try to get to the door, praying he would have time to stumble out before Frank recovered sufficiently to kill him. However, as Frank hopped about, fate hopped in beside Geoffrey and offered him an altogether more satisfactory course of action. Frank's agonized jumps had landed him bang on top of the explosive lifting platform. Geoffrey had intended the platform to be used for purposes such as getting wheelchairs into buses, or the paralysed into bed, but he had no objection to it being employed to fight murderers. It was the work of a moment for Geoffrey to hit his remote for a third time. There was an explosion and the unfortunate Frank sailed out of the window – following exactly the same trajectory that Geoffrey's suitcase had done on the previous occasion. He landed head first in a flower-bed and broke his neck.

## THE SMALL MIND OF THE LAW

Detective Constable Collingwood was absolutely delighted.

'I rather think this bears out the point I made

earlier, Sir,' he had said proudly, 'regarding the fact that this city is a murky melting-pot of sleaze and crime. I mean there you were, not an hour ago, with nothing more to complain about than a pilfered telly, and now you've got a couple of raving deadies on your doorstep. Welcome to life at the sharp end, Sir.'

'Shut up, Collingwood,' said the Superintendent having finished his inspection of Geoffrey's corkscrew. 'All right, Doctor Peason. Let's have this story again, shall we?'

For a long time it had proved impossible to make the police believe that Geoffrey had despatched the two thugs alone. However, after he had painstakingly demonstrated the process by which he had achieved his victory they scratched their heads in awe.

'Well it's a neat bit of work, Sir. A very neat bit,' said the Superintendent. 'Especially considering as how you're a, well a . . .'

'Spasmo,' prompted Geoffrey.

'Yes, that's right,' the policeman replied. 'A disabled gentleman. I mean these two are well known to us. And very hard cases they are too. I wouldn't have wanted to face them if I had a shotgun. You done 'em with a bottle opener and a pot of coffee.'

'I think me being a spastic put them off guard,' said Geoffrey modestly.

'Yes, well, we could do with a few more like you on

the force,' the Superintendent replied. But he didn't really mean it. Impressed though he was, he would never have trusted a spastic with the famous tit helmet.

'I reckon the papers will go wild for this one when they hear,' DC Collingwood interjected.

'I'd really rather they didn't hear,' said Geoffrey. 'I mean if somebody wants me dead, the lower a profile I keep the better, don't you think?'

'Oh I don't think it's you they wanted dead, Sir,' said the Super with an annoying tone.

Geoffrey enquired, as clearly as he could, if the copper would like to suggest an alternative interpretation as to why the two men had broken into his house and pointed pistols at him.

'I think it was probably some sort of mistake. After all Sir, why would anybody want you dead? You're a . . . disabled gentleman. Either way I'm sure we'll sort it all out once we get down the station.'

And leaving Geoffrey's flat filled with pathologists and photographers and men with bits of chalk, whose job it was to draw lines round dead bodies, Geoffrey was trooped off to the police station – at present two nil up against the forces of darkness.

## ASK NOT FOR WHOM THE BELL TOLLS

As Geoffrey and the two police officers emerged from his front door, the London night was, as usual, filled with the ringing and wailing of various alarms.

'Listen to that, Sir,' commented DC Collingwood. 'Like I said, this mean city is a seething, writhing, bubbling hotbed of a satanic melting-pot. Your two raving deadies are just part of the Devil's mosaic.'

In fact the Detective Constable was the only person to pay any attention to the alarm bells (except of course the thousands of people with pillows wrapped round their heads screaming 'Turn them off! *Please* turn them off!' into the darkness of their bedrooms). Everyone always ignores alarm bells, which is a shame, because if they didn't Sam Turk might not have found it quite so easy to burgle the Office of Patents and hence he would have had no cause to attempt to have Geoffrey murdered. A little social responsibility can go a long way.

## Chapter Six

# *PARTY BUSINESS*

## CHIEF EXECUTIVE

Digby Parkhurst, the Minister for Transport, prided himself on being a quiet, well-ordered, law-abiding citizen. Hence he would have been astonished to learn that through his unprofessional relations with Sam Turk he was the man who had unwittingly set in motion the events which led up to the deaths of Frank and Gary, the alarm bell ringing at the Office of Patents and Geoffrey being forced from his home.

At present though, blissfully ignorant of the mayhem he had unleashed, the Minister was stuck in the same traffic jam that had caught both Geoffrey and Sam Turk – the one caused by the anti-road protest. It was lucky for the Minister that his car had darkened windows, for had he been recognized by the crowds milling about along the road, he might have been lynched. Fortunately, the leather-lined opulence of his Ministerial limo offered all the privacy Digby required, for it was a spanking new Panther 'Chief Executive'.

The Chief Executive was the first car to come out of the Panther Motor Company since the Japanese had bought a majority shareholding in it – a deal which Digby had himself orchestrated. It was a wonderful machine. A fitting flagship for a great new partnership, a partnership which, as Digby had said at the time, built on the strengths of both nations. And of course it did; the Japanese contributing the technology, the design, the materials and the money; the British contributing the prestige name.

Names are very important in cars. Panther had agonized for months over the name 'Chief Executive'. It was most frustrating, all the really superior names had been done. Ambassador, Statesman, Senator . . .

'Come on, what are you paid for,' the chief executive at Panther had shouted at his hapless creative people. 'We need a power name, a smug name. We're losing our traditional predominance in the arrogant git end of the car buying market. I want a name that says "up yours" to every two-year-old family saloon on the road! I want a name that says "kiss my arse pauper!" to anything under three litres. I want a name that says that the chap in our car has four houses, five directorates, a six-figure income and a pork bayonet that measures seven inches in repose. All right? I want a name that is *well hung.*'

'The Presidential,' one creative person suggested.

'Sounds like a hotel suite,' barked the Chief Executive. 'The chap *sleeps* in the Presidential, the chap does not drive the Presidential. You're fired.'

'How about, The General Secretary of the Communist party of the Soviet Union?' another creative person offered timidly.

'Hmm,' the Chief Executive pondered. 'The Panther General Secretary of the Communist Party of the Soviet Union. It certainly has power.' But then he rejected the idea. 'No, the Soviet Union is falling to bits, our cars fall to bits anyway, we do not need to draw attention to the fact. You're fired as well, clear your desk and get out.'

'I know,' said a youthful enthusiast, taking an insane risk with his career prospects, 'Why don't we name it after you, Sir.'

'The Panther Kevin?' replied the Chief Executive. And there was a lengthy pause whilst the youthful enthusiast reflected that redundancy would at least give him time to lag the roof . . .

'Not bad, not bad at all.'

'Actually I meant "Chief Executive", Sir,' corrected the enthusiast. And so it was that the latest over-priced, personal wealth advertisement on the road came to be called the 'Chief Executive' (Kevin Class).

## THE PARTY SPIRIT

So there was Digby, stuck in traffic in his Chief Executive, on his way to Brighton for his party's annual conference. The jam was likely to make him late, he hadn't planned for traffic (which would make it the only event in Digby's entire week at conference that wasn't planned, for the conference was to be so meticulously choreographed it would make a New Kids on the Block dance routine look like a spontaneous, free-spirited improvization).

(*Author's note*: As it is to be hoped that this book will have a shelf-life longer than a fortnight and will hence be around long after the New Kids on the Block's flame has dimmed and their ten testicles have descended, the reader is kindly requested to substitute whatever pimply teen sensation is currently charging a million quid for a tour programme, a crap T-shirt and about forty-five minutes of synchronized miming.)

There was a time when the three main British Political Party Conferences were very different. The Liberals were courteous and rather worried, Labour were rude and quarrelsome, and the Conservatives were positively robotic in their ruthless insistence on the serflike tugging of the forelock and towing of the party line. Sadly, as the years go by, all three parties are tending more towards the Tory version. A mindless, gung-ho jamboree being considered rather safer than a debate. Millions and millions of pounds are spent on elaborate security precautions. Delegates are continually being felt-up by members of the Constabulary. Ostensibly, all this compulsory groping is concerned with terrorism: the truth is that it is to prevent any delegate bringing an opinion into the building. The other reason is of course that some MPs rather like being felt-up by the constabulary.

The reason for this desperate desire to be bland is one of the great misnomers of modern political life – Party unity. It has become a cornerstone of British political thinking that the single and greatest ideal for any political party to aspire to is that of unity. We got the idea from Stalin. No conference can look to a higher goal than to maintain throughout the week an impression of complete harmony and bland acceptance of the party line. A conference that forgets itself so far as to allow discussion and differences of opinions is deemed to have been marred by rows, open revolt and damaging splits. The ultimate conference delegate would be a person who has no face and ten sets of hands to clap with.

## POLITICIANS' GAGS

Anyway, Digby was nervously running over the rest of the speech he intended to give the following afternoon. There was, as has been said, no need for him to be nervous because he would probably have had to bugger a dog live on stage to fail to get an ovation. Even in that event, party loyalty would probably have held.

'I thought it a considered and statesmanlike speech,' the delegates would say to the news crews, as they left the hall . . . 'Perhaps slightly over long, I would probably have cut the bit where he buggered the dog.'

Perhaps Digby was nervous because he intended to speak on his very favourite subject. A subject much beloved of all transport ministers; the subject of freedom . . .

'I hardly think,' . . . the Minister muttered to himself, practising the toadyish sneer for which he was justly loathed by all right thinking people, and adored by conference delegates . . .

'I hardly think, *thnn thnn*,' he carried on muttering to himself, adding the little rhythmic nasal wheeze with which he habitually prefixed what he considered to be a humorous observation.

'I hardly think, *thnn thnn*, that the British public will be prepared to exchange the personal freedom that their motor cars invest them with, for a, *thnn thnn thnn*, donkey and trap.'

It was not, perhaps, a classic gag, in fact it was something in the nature of a turkey. A gag unlikely to qualify for entrance into even the meanest of Christmas crackers – the sort that contain a three centimetre high blue plastic Indian Chief that won't stand up.

Digby may have been aware that he was opening

his speech with a gag that would be unlikely to find favour, even with the studio audience of a television sitcom – a demographic group that has been known to laugh at an unoccupied sofa. If he knew, he certainly didn't care, because the jokes in Digby's speeches always went well. The fact that most of these said gags would, under normal circumstances, be unlikely to raise a laugh from a pill-popping hyena was irrelevant. For Digby was a politician and, as such, was not subject to the rigorous critical standards of humour by which the rest of us are judged.

With one or two rare exceptions, the average politician would not recognize a decent joke if they encountered it wearing a red nose, while sidling towards a banana skin and reciting the *Monty Python* parrot sketch. As a purveyor of turgid, swamplike non-humour the average politician is second only to game-show hosts and headmasters. And yet strangely, like headmasters, they are never brought to book.

The media collude in the fiction that those who hold over us the power of life, death and the new dog licence legislation, are possessed of great wit. They describe a speech which contains three snide little put-downs against the opposition as 'peppered with wry humour'. They use the term 'memorable' to sum up phrases which everyone has already forgotten. The reason for the perpetration of this flattering deceit is quite simple. It is in order to prevent revolution. If people were ever to realize just how mediocre the minds of most of those who govern us are, come the next by-election, we'd all vote for the joke candidate with a silly name, top hat and yellow tights who stands at the back and grins when the count is read out.

## MISTAKEN IDENTITY

The conference would not be officially starting until the following day but Digby was in a rush because that evening he was to be a guest of honour at a dinner and booze-up organized by Global Motors to mark the occasion of the launch of their latest car. This was of course the real business of the conference. Elsewhere in town the Minister for Defence would be being entertained by arms dealers, and the Health Minister would be dining with drugs companies.

Digby booked into his hotel in a rush, something he hated doing. Normally he liked to luxuriate over it, checking out all the little treats in his room, the individually wrapped soaps, the tiny shampoo bottles, the sachets marked 'shoe shine' which contain a strangely impregnated tissue which leaves shoes entirely unaffected but makes your fingers unbearably whiffy right through dinner. Digby never tired of these small luxuries and would always pocket the soaps and take them home with him. He had a big wicker basket full of them in his bathroom.

However, on this evening there was no time to relax. Digby just shoved on a bow-tie and rushed off to the Global Motors reception where Sam Turk was waiting to greet him.

Sam had been told by Springer that the Minister was at the door and had hurried out into the foyer.

'Minister, Minister,' he said, rushing up and shaking the hand of the smug, obsequious looking fellow in the bow-tie.

'That's the head waiter boss,' Springer whispered urgently under his breath. 'Parkhurst's behind him.'

Sam never missed a beat. He looked about the room with a serious expression on his face and then gave the head waiter an American hundred dollar bill. 'Nice work, thanks bud,' he said, and, passing the waiter, he approached Digby who was on the point of being deeply offended.

'Simple security measure Minister, we do it for the President. Throw in a decoy and see if he gets shot. Today the guy was lucky,' said Sam. 'I know your cops are good, but frankly Minister, you're too important for me not to care.'

Of course Sam had met Digby on a number of previous occasions but Digby, like most cabinet ministers, did not really have a proper face. Even his mother had trouble recognizing him. In the early days of his career he would leave for work in the morning and say, 'Bye Mum,' and his mother would say, 'Who the hell are you?' Then Digby would say, 'I'm the Junior Under Sub Deputy Minister for

Fisheries Mum,' and she would say, 'Oh'.

Sam ushered Digby towards a glass of champagne.

'Well Minister this really is an honour, yes it is Sir. A heck of an honour.' Of course Sam actually considered Digby to be a pretty pathetic figure, but Digby's job involved the annual expenditure of fifteen billion pounds of public money. That was a figure Sam thought worthy of respect. He would have been honoured to meet a cockroach with a turd in its pocket if it had fifteen billion a year to spend.

'I am afraid you've just missed the video, Minister, but it was really something,' continued Sam. 'Yes Sir, it sure was something.'

Prior to Digby's arrival the guests at Sam's little soirée had been watching an obscene video. A really nasty one; a disgusting piece of exploitative filth, featuring human degradation and child abuse. It was the television advert that was to launch the new Global car on the market.

## OBSCENE VIDEO

The star of the advert was a child. Not the sort of child any real parent would recognize. Not a child born on planet Earth. No, this child hailed from Olympus, she was a child of the Gods. So petite, so vulnerable, so clean and pretty, she just made you want to gather her up in all her pink and golden fluffiness, dump her in a bathful of mud, slip her twenty Benson and Hedges and send her off for an afternoon shoplifting.

'I like the kid,' Sam had said. 'Cute.'

Cute indeed. This little angel made Cabbage Patch dolls look like they had been sculpted by a stern-minded socialistic realist in a bad mood. If Barbie had escaped from the toy box and shagged her plastic boyfriend Ken behind a Fisher Price garage, and had so far forgotten herself as to forsake the principles of safe sex, the child that might have been produced could well have grown up to become the gruesomely cutesome little girl in Sam Turk's car advert. She was perfectly calculated to make every parent in the country wonder why they themselves had given birth to the dirt monster. And there, in the video, she stood, innocent and utterly vulnerable on a tough city pavement whilst her father, a lean, finely chiselled, confident man, locked the fortresslike front door of their apartment building.

It was important that this super-yuppy and his Cabbage Patch daughter lived in an apartment, as opposed to a flat. Despite being British actors, playing British characters in a British advert for a British car (which is officially defined as a car in which a minimum of the ashtrays and seat covers are fitted by British workers), the story was none the less set in New York.

The reason for this was because the director

wished to create an atmosphere of gritty realism, and New York will always seem more real than anything Britain has to offer. It is strange that, although the majority of British people have never seen a skate-boarding body-popper, an exploding fire-hydrant, or anybody dunk a doughnut, these things seem infinitely more immediate and happening images than that jar of Horlicks which has stood in the cupboard for forty years.

'New York is good,' Sam had said. Despite the fact that the new car would spend its life stuck in traffic between Redditch and Wolverhampton, Sam was concerned that it should have a global profile.

On the screen, the little girl's face, surrounded by golden curls, is a study of nervous fear. This was hardly surprising, as she appeared to live in the middle of an urban nightmare – leaves blow across the dirty flagstones in a sinister and forbidding manner, lights are on red, abandoned cars burn. A black man with no shoes sprays a wall, he is muttering to himself, probably having a quiet rap, prior to spinning round on his head. We can't tell because the sound track to the video is Italian opera, the reason for this was to make it clear to the meanest intelligence that the anonymous little hatchback in question has class.

The little girl continues her nervous perusal of the tough world she will inherit. An old man with a beard and the face of a philosopher sleeps in a cardboard box.

All cardboard box dwellers shot by groovy film-makers have the faces of philosophers – which is a good thing because, living in a cardboard box in the middle of an urban nightmare, you'd need to be a bit of a philosopher.

In front of the old philosopher a cop busts a hooker, we know she is a hooker because she is sensationally sexy.

In the video tape world, just as all tramps are philosophers, all hookers are gorgeous. Of course, in the real world, street-walkers (who are the poorest type of prostitutes) do not tend to look as if they've walked straight off a Pirelli calendar. Their sad, dispirited appearance tends to provoke either sym-pathy or disgust from most people, rather than lust. However, in the movies, from Louise Brooks as *Lulu*, to Julia Roberts as *Pretty Woman*, we are taught to recognize street-walking whores by watch-ing out for the wittiest, prettiest, most flawlessly beautiful girl in view. She'll be the one risking her life getting into cars with drunk strangers and having to try and get a condom onto him with her mouth, while pretending to give him a blow-job because he doesn't want to use one and he might have AIDS.

'I like the hooker,' Sam had said. Great legs, real class.

The doll-like little girl continues to stare. She is such a beautiful little girl, with such sensitivity and intelligence that by the look of her she is in real danger of growing up to be a prostitute . . .

Daddy has finished sternly locking the doors of his fortress and with swift, strong movements he gathers up the bewildered child and places her safely in the Ghia (leaky sun roof) edition of a new, but utterly nondescript hatchback car. The door of the car slams behind the little girl and the gritty, grainy world of hookers, bare feet and graffiti is locked out.

So far the video has run for six and a half seconds.

'It's a little laboured,' said Sam, 'needs a tighter edit.' Daddy too is nervous and tense. And well he might be of course, considering that every possible cliché of urban decay seems to have elected to come and live on his street. However, we discover that this is not the reason for his discomfort. The fact is that his wife is about to have a child and, Daddy, being a thoroughly modern man, who cares, is anxious that he and the little girl should be present at this happy event.

Why, if he cares that much, Daddy has decided to leave his hospital dash to the very last pico-second, is not explained. Although, considering the man's entire relationship with the woman is based on a previous ad, in which he knocked on her door to ask to borrow some instant coffee, she's actually quite fortunate he remembers who she is.

The key turns and the engine jumps into life. With a flurry of sinister leaves and a knowing glance from the philosophical tramp (No doubt thinking to himself, 'At last, the meaning of life: a boring hatchback and a plastic daughter.') the car is away, whisking Chiselled Man and Cabbage Patch off through streets that are no longer in New York, but appear to have been lifted out of somewhere in Eastern Europe during the cold war.

'Good, I like Eastern Europe, it sells,' said Sam, adding, 'Tell them to turn up the opera, and see if they got any shots where we see more of the hooker's tits.'

The car screeches on through the misty night. Occasionally it is forced to brake on wet surfaces in order to let a flock of geese be herded across the road. Herded incidentally, by an old peasant, who by the look of him, could certainly have given the man in the cardboard box a run for his money in the philosophical stakes. If the two of them ever met they could probably crack the riddle of the universe between them.

Eventually Chiselled Man and Cabbage Patch end up at a private hospital where Mummy, who has a sensible bob hair cut and is not as sexy as a prostitute but makes up for her lack of raunchiness by being drenched in the honest sweat of her womanly duty, presents Chiselled Man with a new baby. (Well, she doesn't do it, the nurse does.) Mum just gives Chiselled Man a tired but adoring smile.

'Good,' said Sam. 'I'm glad the guy missed it. Never met a man yet who really went for all the mess and the slop.'

The scene then cuts to the next morning. Which was quite a good thing, because no doubt two seconds after the smile Mummy screamed at Daddy, 'Where the hell have you been! It's all very well coming in now all shaved and chiselled. Where were you when all the "Oh God it hurts, give me some drugs, push push push" was going on, and there was afterbirth everywhere?'

That bit of uncomfortable realism being avoided, the following morning Daddy pops Cabbage Patch, the sweating madonna (now dried off but still not sexy; proud certainly; vulnerable of course; doting; caring and ex-tremely sensible – but not sexy), plus the new sprog into the hatchback and drives off straight into what appears to be the location for a butter advert. There is a final caption . . . 'You can trust Global Motors with your most precious cargo of all.'

'Makes me want to puke,' Sam had said on first viewing. 'It's perfect.'

## THE MOST PRECIOUS CARGO OF ALL

So why then was this an obscene video? It was offensive perhaps, tasteless, certainly, but why obscene? Because the men at Global Motors (a fictitious car manufacturer invented for the purpo-ses of this book) had spent the previous twenty years actively campaigning against unleaded petrol and catalytic converters. This hypocritical bunch of low-life, had sat there congratulating themselves on their new advert which stressed family values and the protection of kids, and yet they had all been directly and personally involved in rotting the brains of countless children.

These wicked ogres had, of their own choice, brought about the production of an incalculable tonnage of appalling pollutants, every ounce of which directly affected the well-being of each and every child on the planet. They could not even claim ignorance of the facts, these wicked giants in their evil castle. In the United States, where Global Motors, like all car manufacturers, had been forced by legislation to fit the available safety equipment, children had been partially protected since the early seventies. In Britain however, and much of the rest of the world, unshackled by inconvenient legislation, Global Motors, like most other car makers, had elected to carry on damaging, and probably murdering, children. Perhaps not as perfect looking as the one in their advert, but children just the same.

The executives at Global Motors could scarcely have behaved more wickedly if they had prefixed their horrendous corporate decisions with the words 'fee fi fo fum'.

## EUROSPEAK

The video had gone down terribly well. Everyone was congratulating the director, a fifteen-year-old

Dutchman with a pony tail and a crumpled linen suit. Everyone was assuring Sam that the car would no doubt be a huge success, but they knew that it wouldn't be, just as Sam himself knew and had already written the car off in his mind. The problem was the name. The new car was to be called the Global Crappee.

A car may stand or fall upon its name. If the Ford Thunderbird had been called the Ford Fluffy, one wonders whether it would ever have become quite the legend it is today. Had the E-type Jag been unwisely named the P-type Jag, surely it would have experienced greater sales resistance. If the tiny, girlie, Fiat Panda had been named the Fiat Cockroach, it seems unlikely that Penelope would have wanted one for her eighteenth. There are good car names and not-so-good car names. Calling a car the Crappee is marketing suicide.

It had come about through the noblest of motives. Global Motors UK, like most companies in Britain, were pursuing a Euro perspective. They sought to sell their cars in the shiny new Euro market. To this end, Global Motors had opened Euro offices and taken on Euro staff. They had concluded a massive, mutually supportive Euro deal with the Italian car giant Bianco and they had offered ludicrous salaries in order to poach an entire marketing team from the hugely successful Sportif of France. Global Motors' new hatchback was to be a Euro car down to the underseal. It was to have Euro styling, Euro engineering and a Euro name, the Crappee.

The Global Crappee. The French market research had reacted favourably, the Italians were enthusiastic, even the Germans seemed interested, although they would have preferred Krappy. However, the British, who still made up about ninety per cent of Global UK's market were unlikely to be impressed.

'How the hell did it happen?' Sam had spluttered when he first found out. 'Why didn't somebody notice?'

The reason nobody noticed was that the brief, right from the beginning, had been to let the Europeans get on with it. *No xenophobic interference* had been the order. Sam himself had set the tone.

'I don't want any limey bullshit about who won the war,' he had said. 'The US Battle of Britain up your polite British butts. The facts are, our European colleagues sell more cars in a week than Global Motors UK sell in a month. They are our friends and our brothers, even if they are a bunch of Wops. We need to absorb a little of their culture, their ambiance, and above all, their cash. So leave the foreign bastards alone and let them get on with it.'

That had been Sam's attitude only a year or so before when he had arrived from Detroit, but now, faced with an entire new model range called Crappee, he had changed his tune. His cringing minions attempted to defend themselves . . .

'It seemed so right,' they spluttered . . . 'The

Germans wanted something hard, something resonant of engineering. They suggested Krupp after the great arms manufacturer. But the Italian guys were looking for something light-hearted, something fun. Their suggestion was Caprice. The French reckoned everybody would be doing that. They wanted something multi-cultural, something ethnic, something cool. Their people suggested the Global Rapper . . . And, well, we all felt that Crappee combined all the elements suggested; being resonant of engineering, holiday fun and ethnic culture.'

'And shit,' said Sam.

# APPLYING PRESSURE

## THE GERBIL IN THE CAGE

All that had happened months before, but even then, the ads had been made, the styling completed and brochures gone out. Sam had been unable to stop the Euro decision. Now it was history. Besides, he no longer cared, he had bigger things on his mind. He had things on his mind so big that he was in danger of having to buy a larger hat, which was why he was trying to kill Geoffrey Spasmo.

The Crappee launch was in full swing, and whilst Digby Parkhurst buried his happy, shiny face in the champagne and dippy things, Sam snatched a hurried conversation with Springer.

'He dead yet?' demanded Sam.

'The gerbil's state of being is at present undetermined,' replied Springer slightly reprovingly. He felt that if you were going to go to the trouble of setting up a really great code like calling your murder victim a gerbil, you should try and stick to it.

'At present undetermined? Kind of enigmatic this "gerbil" ain't he?' mused Sam through gritted teeth. 'How come?'

Sam's knuckles were whitening around his glass as he struggled to contain his temper.

'I'm afraid I can't explain that, Sir,' said Springer, eyeing his exits. 'Euro Despatch have at present lost contact with their operatives.'

Sam's glass cracked under the pressure.

'You mean they fucked up?' he said menacingly.

'We certainly have to accept the possibility that there has been a degree of up fucking,' replied Springer very nervously. He hated it when Sam got glass-crushing mad – the next move tended to involve Sam reaching for something softer to crush.

Just as Springer was deftly acquiring an empty plate with which to protect the front of his trousers, Geoffrey Spasmo, the gerbil causing all the fuss, was still helping the police with their enquiries. Enquiries rendered more difficult, of course, by Geoffrey's communication problems. It wasn't that the Superintendent could not understand Geoffrey, with a little effort he could follow every word, it was just that he found it very difficult to bring himself to believe that anyone who sounded so thick could possibly have invented anything worth murdering for.

'You say that the hard disc containing your research material had been removed from your computer prior to the assault,' said the policeman.

'Yes,' jerked Geoffrey wearily.

'And you believe that the people who pinched your hard disc, and, I might add, your telly, were the same people who set the thugs on you?'

'Maybe,' said Geoffrey.

'But you have no idea who these people might be?' asked the policeman.

'No,' said Geoffrey.

'Or how they might have come to know about your invention?'

'No, as I've said about five billion times, I was keeping it a total secret from everyone until I got the patent, which I am in the process of doing.'

'And the invention concerns?' asked the policeman.

'It's a secret,' replied Geoffrey. 'That's the whole point.'

Eventually the police let Geoffrey go pending further enquiries. He had acted in self-defence so there were no charges. Obviously he could not return home for the present so the police offered him a hotel room.

'You'll be quite safe there,' they said confidently, mainly because they still did not really believe that Geoffrey had been the real target of the assault, mystery inventions not being high up on their list of credible motives.

Geoffrey declined the hotel room, he had other ideas. Late as it was he would go to see his good friend Deborah. He regretted having to place her in possible danger but he thought it unlikely that anybody after him would know of Deborah. Their friendship was a very private one and the thugs had not even known that Geoffrey was a spastic. Either way, he had to risk it. Geoffrey was convinced that, for reasons connected with his research, he had become the target of a murderous conspiracy, and since clearly the police were not at present intending to take him seriously, he felt he would be safer on his own. Giving the Superintendent his parents' address and refusing the offer of a lift in a squad car (even though he would have liked to have a go in one), Geoffrey took a taxi into the night.

Geoffrey believed that the only copy of his brilliant invention that lay outside criminal hands was with the patents office and he would not rest until he had secured a copy. He was destined for a very tiring time because, on the matter of the plans at least, Sam Turk was ahead of him.

## THE LOBBY THROUGH THE LOBBY

'Find him and kill him,' said Sam to Springer before turning his attention back to the Minister.

Sam, although he was embarking on a plot of cosmic proportions, remained a dedicated, professional, car man. He knew that Digby Parkhurst was preparing a massive road building plan and this was something that, of course, must be encouraged. Digby had allowed himself to be cornered by the press and Sam waited courteously whilst the Minister almost dribbled with slightly tipsy self-importance.

'I think the Crappee is an absolutely super looking machine,' Digby gushed, 'and believe me, the people at Environment are delighted that Sam Turk here has made sure that all his people at Global Motors are committed to producing such a thoroughly green car.'

Digby had in his hand the press-pack which assured the public that the Crappee offered catalytic converters as optional extras on the top-of-the-range models and that, as always, Global Motors were striving towards ever greater fuel efficiency. Two promises which made the Global Crappee about as thoroughly green as an overipe tomato floating in a pot of strawberry jam against a particularly fine sunset. The production of a single private car consumes the sort of natural resources which could keep a famine threatened village in the Third World going for months. This, combined with the incalculable cost of the road it will require and the fuel it will consume, turns each car into an environmental hand grenade. Certainly we need cars. Certainly catalytic converters are very good things, but to imagine that fitting one will make a car environmentally friendly . . .? You might as well fit one to a bucket of napalm.

Sam extracted Digby from the mêlée of press . . .

'Any hints on the content of tomorrow's transport

speech, Minister?' they shouted.

'Wait and see, watch and learn,' said Digby, hoping nobody would notice that he was getting a little erection about how important he was.

'Perhaps you would like to come with me Minister,' said Sam Turk. 'It is a little crowded in here, isn't it? We have an executive dining area, perhaps . . .?'

Digby, who liked nothing better than being pampered by rich and powerful people, allowed himself to be led into a side-room. Besides, he had his own reasons for wanting to get Sam Turk to one side.

Sam led Digby through into a luxuriously appointed little room full of luxuriously appointed people.

'I'm sure there are no new faces here, Minister . . . Peter Logan, of Tar and Grit Road Construction, Jamie Saunders, the concrete man . . .'

There were oil people, tyre people, road haulage people, motoring associations people. All people well known to Digby, all good friends – good friends who had preyed upon his predecessors for generations.

For Digby was in the presence of the road lobby. A shadowy, unofficial alliance, difficult to define, difficult to pin down, but none the less one of the most powerful groups of people in the country. These people wanted one thing out of life, and one thing only – they wanted more roads.

They said that they wanted them to relieve congestion, to free the motorist, to make the nation more efficient. That's why they *said* they wanted them. But actually they wanted them so that they could sell more tar, more concrete, more rubber, more oil and, above all, more cars.

Private individuals make cars and pump oil, only governments can commission roads. Without roads all the people in the room surrounding Digby were finished. Their businesses, their whole industries meant nothing without roads. That was why they loved Digby so much – he commissioned the roads.

Vain, pompous, little Digby was an easy target for these clever, powerful men of the road lobby. They toadied him gruesomely. They made him feel so important, with their specious arguments regarding the massive human good that would flow from a six-mile extension of the M6 and their firm assertions that nothing less than the end of civilization would be the inevitable consequence if an extra lane were not added to the M25.

'And all these things Minister, these *world moulding* decisions,' Britain's biggest concrete mixer would say, his honeyed words massaging Digby's crotch.

'Are in your masterful hands Minister,' a man who owned three hundred car showrooms would add, his tongue extending three feet across a tray of nibbles to tease Digby's ear.

'Quite simply the choice between *freedom*, or a *new Dark Age*, is yours Minister,' the road haulers and the oil people would add, gently unzipping Digby's fly and delicately cupping his ripe plums in their hands.

'For the good of Britain,' chimed the whole gang, their heads full of millions as they went down on Digby . . . 'Build more roads.'

## THE WORM TURNS

Normally Digby would have happily listened to this stuff until his trousers burst, but tonight there was something on his mind. Something that actually made the farty little minister assert himself.

'Later, gentlemen,' he said. Then, in a low voice, he snapped at Sam, 'I want a damn word with you Sam, and I damn well want it damn now, damn it.' Digby was better at saying *thnn thnn* than he was at swearing.

Sam thought, 'Oh Christ, what's got up the little shit's nose now?' But he said, 'Of course, Minister, is there a problem?'

They retired to a cosy corner.

'Listen, Sam, yesterday I had a very worrying call from the people at Patents. They say that damned invention I tipped you off about has damned well been pinched, damn it.'

'No!' said Sam, incredulously.

'Damn yes, and I don't like it, Sam! Damn it, these are *civil servants*, they're very vulnerable, they have the honours list to worry about and the subsidized canteen. They're hopping mad Sam. They don't believe it's a coincidence and frankly nor do I!'

'Minister,' protested Sam, 'Surely you're not suggesting that I . . .? That Global Motors . . .?'

'Oh come on, Sam! I'm sure you don't think I'm a fool,' snapped the Minister, who may have been sure, but he was certainly wrong . . . His voice dropped to an angry whisper. 'The patents people tell me about developments of interest and I tell you, I have no problem with that. We're all in the business of getting Britain moving. God knows we all want the best for Britain.'

'Well, of course, Minister,' Sam interrupted piously.

'But that doesn't stretch to burgling Her Majesty's property!' said Digby.

Sam was surprised. The Minister was actually being quite assertive. He had been so used to Digby's slimey mediocrity, he had never thought he would have to placate him. Sam remembered that even shit got stubborn when you were trying to scrape it off your shoes.

Sam, of course, continued to deny any knowledge of the break-in but it was a difficult process. Not because Digby was at all astute, but because it was bloody obvious that Sam must have organized the theft, or at least known the person who did, because he was the only person to whom Digby had passed the information about Geoffrey's invention.

Digby was having a wonderful time, slooshing top-notch plonk and being all stern and statesman-like. There he was, farty, inadequate Digby Parkhurst, who had been known at school as Shitsby Zitburst, dressing down Sam Turk the President of Global Motors UK, a two-fisted, big-bellied son of a gun. How Digby wished the teenage bullies of his unhappy school days, who used to give him Chinese burns and stuff radishes up his bottom, could see him now.

'Really Mr Turk, I'm afraid I shall have to consider very carefully the courtesies that the Department for Transport grants to the motor industry,' said Digby pompously, 'if they are to be abused in such a way.'

'Oh come now, Minister,' said Sam.

'Please do not adopt that tone with me Turk. May I remind you that I am a Minister of the Crown and not accustomed to being trifled with.' Digby slurped at his champagne. 'Perhaps, *thnn thnn thnn*, you think that Her Majesty's Government exists for your convenience.'

'Not at all Minister,' protested Sam, who wasn't even listening. He understood petty officials like Digby Parkhurst and was more than happy to let him have his moment of self-importance. That way he would get it out of his system and forget about it.

Digby, imagining himself to be having the most tremendous effect, happily accepted more champagne. There were flecks of filo pastry round his mouth and his fingers shone with grease.

'I am afraid I am going to have to consider this matter very carefully indeed. I am forced to ask myself whether the road lobby has achieved a sufficient maturity to justify its special relationship with Her Majesty's Government.'

'You're absolutely right, Minister,' said Sam absently, whilst casting an appreciative eye over the girl serving the drinks and wishing he was not such a staunch Catholic.

'Yes, I should imagine you are wishing you were somewhere else right now, aren't you Turk?' said Digby imagining Sam to be quivering in his boots.

'Well, to tell you the truth, I was, Minister,' answered Sam imagining the waitress quivering in hers.

'I'm glad you understood the seriousness of the situation. I have not decided what course of action I shall take but I commend you to consider what I have said most carefully.'

Of course, as Sam well knew, Digby had absolutely no intention of taking any course of action at all – but what fun he was having.

'Yes, Minister, certainly. I shall consider it most carefully,' said Sam, who had already forgotten everything the Minister had said.

'We shall discuss it again after my speech tomorrow,' said Digby. And draining a final champagne, he bid the road lobby goodnight and staggered drunkenly off to bed, imagining himself to be one hell of a fellow and actually being a git in a bow-tie.

## END OF THE LINE

In another part of the hotel, a small forlorn group of men and women waited for Digby. They too had champagne to offer, although not quite such a decent vintage; they too had choice nibbles, although theirs were potted meat, not salmon.

'I don't think he's coming,' said one.

'He never does,' said another.

The forlorn group of people were the Chairman and senior management of Britain's railways.

Every year, at conference time, they mounted a sad little soirée for the Minister in order to put the arguments of the rail lobby. And every year the Minister did not come and the soirée got smaller and more depressed, like the railways themselves.

'Pretty soon we shall be having the rail lobby in the hotel lobby,' murmured the company gagsmith – but nobody was laughing.

The old man sighed.

'Well gentlemen, ladies. We did our best, we did everything they asked of us . . .,' And indeed they had. During the eighties the government had asked the railways to slicken up their act, to get modern, get groovy, get nasty – and the old man and his team had done it.

They were aware that the lucrative business traveller was ignoring the railways. Why was this? they asked. Was it because the railways were a crap, underfunded service? No, it seemed not. The problem, apparently, was simply one of snobbery. Top people, it was decreed, did not like travelling with scumbags. Britain used to have three classes on the railways, she would do so again! The old man and his team would reintroduce third class. Unfortunately the word 'third' is not a modern word; it is not a word that would much impress the Europeans; it is not a word that wins elections.

The solution of course was marketing. Marketing – that great decade-sized red herring which entirely replaced reality during the eighties. A first class seat would stay a first class seat; that, it seemed, offended none. But the second class seat disappeared, re-emerging bright and new as a 'full standard fare' incorporating the new *Silver* service (a free instant coffee). Finally, third class was revived after an absence of forty-five years, but it was not called third class, it was reborn as a Super Saver.

So there you had it, First, Standard (with free coffee) and Super Saver. First, second and third. The business traveller could now be as isolated as he was in his car, and no bollards or contra flows. It hadn't worked of course, no amount of marketing can modernize lines and put new rolling stock on them.

'I should have fought,' the old man said sadly.

'Why didn't I fight like a tiger?' he mumbled into his booze.

'Because you're a cowardly old git and you wanted to get knighted,' thought his team – but they didn't say it.

'I should have told them to stuff their restructuring up their collective bum holes,' continued the old man. 'You can't run a railway without government money. They understand that in Europe. The garlic-gorgers know it; the sausage-suckers know it; even the pasta-pukers are beginning to suspect – why can't the British work it out? The savings come later. Oh well, it's too late now.'

'Too late, Sir!' gasped the old man's team who thought more creatively than they spoke.

'Yes, I'm afraid this is my last lobby,' said the old man. 'Earlier today I spoke with Ingmar Bresslaw.'

'Ingmar Bresslaw!' gasped the old man's team, taking on the role of the Greek chorus at the tragedy.

And well they might have done, for Ingmar Bresslaw was the government's chief hatchet man. The most terrifying man in Whitehall. It was he who had been chosen to lie to the press about Digby's road building plans; and it was he who had carried the news to the Chairman of Britain's Railways that his industry was doomed.

'Ingmar Bresslaw informed me that tomorrow he will instruct the Minister for Transport to announce the formation of the BritTrak Consortium. Of course, I shall resign.'

'The BritTrak Consortium?' replied the team, still practising their echo effect.

'Yes, the BritTrak Consortium. What's more, ladies and gentlemen, it is my sad duty to inform you that there is no "c" in "trak" . . . Is nothing sacred to these despicable people?' the old man anguished. 'They reduce Britain to a single syllable and the word 'track' to four letters. What will they do to the railways themselves?'

The room fell silent. Well actually the room did not fall silent. The room went on playing the string arrangements of Simon and Garfunkel's greatest hits which it had been playing all along. The people in the room fell silent. They knew that what the old man feared had already come to pass. During the love affair with tarmac most industrial nations had neglected their trams and trains, and now, with eco armageddon looming, and oil producing nations holding the world to ransom, rail was needed again but was in no state to fulfil that need. In Britain, it seemed, the process of disintegration was not over yet.

Sandy Mackay, the youngest rail person, spoke up.

'What will the BritTrak Consortium do, Sir?'

The old man took a deep breath.

'It will reduce the rail network to a single high-profit track, running from the City to a decent little pub in Chobham.'

Sandy was a rail enthusiast. He had wanted to be an engine driver when he was six years old, and he still wanted to be one. His love for trains was wild and huge. He knew what it was that made people stand on the end of station platforms in anoraks, insanely taking down a series of meaningless numbers – it was the beauty of trains. He understood the man who spent thirty-six hours of every weekend in his attic watching Hornby models trundle through tiny tunnels while his wife took lovers in the living-room. It was the speed, the power, the romance of rail. And now it seemed that Digby Parkhurst had been instructed to finally destroy that romance forever.

Sandy decided to act.

## BIG BEARD

Deep deep down in the bowels of the hotel, where the ancient, groaning heating system shuddered and hissed and made sounds which wandered round the pipes, giving the impression that a ghost was being sick in the radiator, there stood one man alone. Deep down in the forgotten underworld of an English hotel, with the great piles of moulding leaflets from failed 50s advertising campaigns (Isn't sunshine all the nicer for not having too much of it?) stood one solitary fellow with a bottle of rum in his hand. He was a huge, wild looking man with great gnarled fists and great gnarled arms. Everything about him was gnarled – the story of how his inside thighs came to be gnarled delighted the lads at the Frog and Gherkin every time he told it.

The man was clearly mad. His wild eyes sparkling over his huge beard. A beard which gave him the appearance of a man who was trying to swallow an Old English Sheepdog and not getting very far; a great tousled mass of steel-grey hair which was a sort of Bermuda triangle for combs and brushes. A great, strong, noble looking man, with a fearful, savage dignity – but mad. That's what they said.

'Old Big Beard,' the hotel porters said, 'bloody mad.'

And they were right, but not mad as in insane, mad as in angry. Old Big Beard was angry as a man with no head who gets a collection of balaclava helmets for Christmas.

'He hasn't come!' Big Beard roared in a voice so filled with passion that even the boiler stopped gurgling and listened.

'Another year goes by! and still he hasn't come!'

This was the annual conference soirée of the canal lobby.

'Hear me! Hear me!' thundered Big Beard, pulling mightily at his bottle and grabbing up thirty or forty cheesy nibbles in his hamlike fist. 'Britain has hundreds and hundreds of miles of canals! Dug with sweat and blood and . . . and . . . shovels,' he continued, slipping from his oratory peak for a moment. 'Dug two centuries ago, to transport goods

about the country. Today, we carry coal by road!!!'
Tears stood in the huge man's eyes. 'Are we mad!
A hundred million years coal lay still in the Earth!
and we take it on its last journey at seventy miles
an hour! Burning oil all the while! Choking the sky!
Scarring the land! Squashing the hedgehogs!' The
tears began to dive out of the old beardy's eyes,
making elaborate somersaults and pirouettes as
they fell and bounced off his oilskin coat – just to
make their point absolutely clear.

Behind Big Beard, mostly obscured by his huge
gnarled tummy, was a map of the British Isles. A
map which nobody but Big Beard ever saw. On it
were marked the canals of Britain and on each
canal was drawn a chain of barges covering its
entire length.

The point was, that although the very first barge
at the front of the queue might take weeks to reach
its destination, from that point on, if the chain were
not broken, barges might arrive every fifteen
minutes. This clearly would not do for perishable
products, but for coal, concrete, brick, wood . . .

'Imagine it,' the visionary screamed, 'a great,
noble shire-horse, running on high octane grass and
bramble, slowly plodding along, pulling perhaps
thirty barges! No fuel consumption, no pollution,
except the kind you can put on your roses . . . !'

'Listen to me! Listen to me!'

Of course there would be pretty considerable
practical problems, you certainly could not get that

volume of traffic through locks as they are currently designed. But then there are considerable practical problems to building motorways, and that never stopped anyone. Anyway, Big Beard was an idealist. He knew nothing of practical problems, mainly because nobody had ever bothered to discuss them with him.

Big Beard took another great sorrowful pull on his bottle and loosened his bow-tie. He fell over. The canal lobby soirée was over for another year.

## Chapter Eight

# NIGHT MOVES

### SET-UP

'What are you doing Sandy?' said the young rail enthusiast's wife, sleepily.

She had gone to bed early claiming that she couldn't stand all the bullshit. She was right, there was a lot of bullshit, but Sandy's wife would have detected bullshit in a house brick, as long as it had been a London house brick. For she was a Liverpudlian, a Liverpudlian graphic design graduate who now lived in London and she had decided that London was entirely populated by bullshitters. Many arty London-based Liverpudlians share with arty London-based Glaswegians the deep-seated conviction that they, despite being artists and film makers quaffing champagne in the same bars as the native artists and film makers, somehow retain an honest earthiness and cynical sense of humour that is their birthright. The longer they live in London, the more convinced they become that nobody in that city is capable of communicating honestly. Whereas back home, a fishwife might be found sitting in a pub with a clothes designer and an ex-murderer discussing architecture. This is of course bollocks. All cities have an equal amount of bullshit, and an equal amount of honesty – and anyone who claims differently is bullshitting.

Anyway, Mrs Mackay was half asleep and she wanted to know what her husband Sandy was doing.

'Nothing,' he said. But he wasn't; he was doing something.

Sandy had spent the past hour trying to find a prostitute. It was his intention to either compromise or blackmail Digby Parkhurst out of announcing BritTrak on the morrow.

Digby was in his late thirties, and still single, but he was known throughout the party for his flirty ways with girls and his frequent, unpleasant and intimidating sexual allusions towards those women over whom he held power. Sandy reckoned that all this indicated, that underneath Digby was probably a sad, frustrated, little git. Also Sandy had seen Digby stagger to bed and knew him to be drunker than an eighteenth birthday party. If ever there was a time to get him, that time was now. At least that was what Sandy reckoned, but then again, he was completely pissed as well.

However, finding prostitutes is not really very easy in nice English towns, or probably anywhere for that matter. As the Global Crappee advert showed, the masturbating fantasies of video directors give the impression that gorgeous prostitutes are standing on every street corner, but of course they are not. Sandy had no idea where to look for one and after a nasty mistake with a late night doughnut maker had retired to his room rather than be done for kerb crawling.

But the defence of Britain's greatest public transport system was not over yet. Sandy had a different plan, an even drunker one. He was a slim fellow, with large eyes and fine bones, and he was desperate.

'Nothing at all, darling. Go back to sleep,' he said, stealing a pair of stockings from her bag.

'I have to pop down and do a bit more business.'

'Bloody bullshitters,' she replied through her sleep.

To Sandy's great good fortune his wife had purchased a wig that day, to wear at the end of conference ball. He took it.

'Quite important people actually,' he said . . . 'Think I'd better have a shave,' and rolling up his trouser legs Sandy disappeared into the bathroom.

## I HEAR YOU KNOCKING

Deborah could not sleep. It was one of those aggravating occasions when one is too tired to sleep. Having had a busy day, she had arrived home pretty exhausted and gone to bed early convinced she would be asleep in five minutes. And here she was, two and a half hours later, wide awake, listening to noises. It was one of those nights when for no particular reason a person feels more scared than usual. Anybody living on their own is going to feel nervous every now and then, particularly a woman, but tonight Deborah had it worse.

Every creak and rustle seemed imbued with murderous intent. The shadows of the trees thrown against her curtain by the street lights turned into a steady stream of mad axe murderers strolling past her window. It was almost as if the All England Federation of Mad Axe Murderers had elected to have their annual convention in Deborah's front garden.

The wind whispered under her front door, and the wind had a very sick sense of humour that night. What other reason could there be for it whispering 'Deborah I'm going to get you. You can't run Deborah, you can't run.' Unless of course it wasn't the wind at all, but an asthmatic sex fiend stretched out on her doormat getting his kicks. To Deborah's restless ear that whispering was beginning to sound more and more like the dickhead who used to ring her up before she got Telecom to put an intercept on her calls. Had he come to get her? Deborah longed to shout 'Piss off dickhead' but it was probably only the wind.

The fridge was particularly talkative that night,

it moaned and it burped, it burped and it moaned. It stopped moaning and burping, waited until Deborah's eyes began to become heavy, and then with a great moan and a burp started moaning and burping again. Eventually Deborah began to wonder whether this relentless cacophony of sound was the fridge at all. Maybe it was one of the mad axemen in the garden. Perhaps an unhappy one with a digestive problem had stepped over the asthmatic sex fiend, crept into the house and was standing in her kitchen by a silent fridge having his pre-murder moan and burp.

When the door bell rang Deborah's heart nearly stopped. Was it the axemen? Was it the neighbours complaining about the axemen? No way was she getting up to find out. Gingerly she reached for the radio that Geoffrey had made for her and tuned into the frequency of her door intercom.

'Hello,' she said, trying to sound like a heavyweight boxer with a gun. Deborah listened then smiled with relief, she would know that guttural stutter anywhere. The relief turned almost instantly to anger.

'Geoffrey,' she snapped into the radio. 'What the hell are you playing at? I thought someone was trying to kill me.'

'Someone is trying to kill *me*,' Geoffrey spoke into the intercom, rather enjoying saying such a momentous and cool thing. Unfortunately the impact was wasted because Deborah, who normally understood at least ninety per cent of what Geoffrey said, was too fazed to follow him.

'God knows what you want, but you'd better come in.' She pressed the button and the ingenious radio wave that Geoffrey had created opened the door for him. Deborah remained in bed whilst, with great care, Geoffrey made some coffee and brought it through into her room, then spilt it.

'OK, duvet head,' said Deborah sternly. 'What's the big idea busting in in the middle of the night? If you've come round here trying to get in my pants again I'm going to be real mad, OK, doughnut brain? I mean, ringing your mom, type mad, Geoffrey! and you know she hates it when you get horny.'

## DEBORAH

Deborah was a citizen of the US. She used to refer to herself as an American, until she got trapped in a bar by a Canadian and a Peruvian who spent two mind-numbingly boring hours explaining to her that America is a continent not a country.

She was twenty-one years old and had been in Britain for three years studying, but the spirit of New York still seemed to hang about her. At any moment you expected her to say 'All right already'. Having had an English grandmother she had come to Britain to escape an over-protective Jewish family circle. Her parents were not rich but they had agreed to help her through her four-year course in textiles.

'You need to travel three thousand miles to learn how to make trousers and blouses?' her Poppa had complained. 'Trousers and blouses you can make in New York and live with your family. Is there a problem with New York I would like to know? Did we all suddenly get body odour?'

'Poppa there's nothing wrong with New York, if you discount the fact that a person can get shot putting out the garbage, and then the city can't even afford to pick up the garbage, so a person dies for nothing and rats move into the neighbourhood hanging around the trash cans taking steroids,' explained Deborah. 'I love New York. It's you and Momma I can't stand.'

'Hear her, Poppa, hear her!' Momma had wailed. 'Deborah listen to me. You turn your back on your family, and you desert your whole people, and your God. Nobody likes a Jew, family is all we got, read a history book.'

'Momma, I'm going to England, not joining the Nazi party,' Deborah had protested. She knew it would be OK, there was nothing her family liked more than a drama. If Deborah had not announced that she wanted to go to Britain her mother would have wailed about Deborah's neckline.

'Maybe you should hang them out of the window,' Momma would protest at anything saucier than a turtle-neck. 'I hear there are still people on Staten

Island who haven't seen your bosom.'

'Momma, I have tits,' Deborah would explain wearily. 'OK, I'm sorry, but they're stuck to the front of me. If I could keep them in a handbag I would.'

'So now it's OK to swear in front of your mother?'

Gradually, over supper that evening Deborah's parents came round to the idea of her studying abroad.

'I suppose New York *is* getting kind of dangerous,' conceded Deborah's mother.

'Kind of dangerous, she says!' said Poppa. 'Like Hitler was a little temperamental. Dangerous? I should go to work in a tank! Drugs, crack, bullets flying everywhere, nobody knows who'll catch a stray next. Last week, Gosha, the watch repair fellow, he was shot in his *own apartment*. Am I still living in America when a man isn't safe in his *own apartment*?'

'Poppa, Mr Gosha shot himself,' said Deborah. 'Crack didn't kill the guy, quartz did. He gave up the struggle when they started giving away watches inside cereal boxes.'

And so the conversation moved onto other topics, and Deborah was allowed to go to London. She was later to reflect on the irony of her parents supporting the trip partly on the grounds of New York's reputation for violence. For the night she let her friend Geoffrey into her home to seek sanctuary, she was letting in more violence than she would have got if she'd skipped London and joined the marines.

## SANCTUARY

Geoffrey strenuously denied the accusation that his intrusion of Deborah's privacy was in anyway carnally motivated.

'Deborah,' protested Geoffrey. 'My motives are pure as the driven snow.'

'Oh yeah?' she replied, 'well I've seen snow in London. They mix it with gasoline and dog shit and pile it up in the gutter.'

Deborah was justified in being a little suspicious. Geoffrey had never attempted to disguise the fact that he craved her, and she had on numerous occasions had to dampen his ardour. It was not unreasonable of her to suspect that this was one of them.

'Pitch me Geoffrey, and it had better be good,' she said.

'Deborah,' Geoffrey replied. 'I'm in trouble, the twilight zone is here. Two men came to my house tonight and tried to kill me. But luckily I managed to kill them first.'

Deborah was flabbergasted.

'That is pathetic Geoffrey,' she said. 'Linda Lovelace wouldn't swallow that story, and she'd swallow anything. If you're going to invade a chick's privacy in the middle of the night you're going to have to do better than that. Go home and take less drugs.'

'No really, Deborah,' stammered Geoffrey. 'It's true.'

And pausing only to knock the glass of water off Deborah's bedside table, Geoffrey explained the events of the day.

## I HEAR YOU KNOCKING TOO

Digby Parkhurst was having a restless night as well.

The booze and the comprehensive way he had put down the mighty Sam Turk had put a right ruddy firework in his jocks. He was restless and randy. Digby knew that elsewhere in the hotel, other, more important ministers were holding court and probably having an amazing time, but nobody had invited him.

He kicked round his room, wishing he hadn't left the road lobby soirée. They would probably still be drinking, probably having a really great time without him. Could he go back? Of course he bloody could, he was the Minister for Transport, he could do what he liked. But even dull stupid Digby knew that it would look a bit pathetic to sidle back now after his magnificent exit. Besides he might run into those dreadful railway people.

Digby realized he had shot his bolt. He dug a scotch out of his mini-bar and was vaguely wondering about whether he could be bothered to haul off his shreddies and have a bit of a twang on the old one-string bass, when there was a knock at the door.

So they weren't ignoring him after all! It was probably Sam and some of the guys from the road lobby come to crawl a bit more. Perhaps it would be a couple of his cabinet colleagues looking for a bit of a lads booze up. Digby opened the door with a big smile.

'I'm awfully sorry to bother you, but I can't find my room. Do you think I might come in and use your phone?' said the tall, slender figure with the tight dress, the flaming red hair and the husky voice.

Digby stared at Sandy. Sandy stared back. They were both very drunk, both for a moment lost in their own thoughts. After a few seconds Sandy felt the onus remained with him to continue the conversation.

'Oh I see you've broken the seal on your mini-bar, I'm gasping for a snort,' he said. Trying to say it through a sexy pout.

Digby, who appeared to have been struck completely dumb, came back to life.

'How did you know? Who else knows? Who the hell put you up to it?' His voice shook with guilt and fear.

Sandy had not really expected this, and did not know what to say next. So he said 'Uhm' and left it at that.

'Get in here now,' said Digby, realizing that his worst nightmare was now reality, and trying desperately to sober up.

'All right, sonny, you tell me, and you tell me now, who put you up to this. If you hold back I swear I shall turn you over to the police as a dirty little blackmailing whore, and hang the consequences.'

'Sonny?' said Sandy rather disappointed.

'Yes, sonny, now answer my question.'

'So you know I'm a bloke then?' continued Sandy, his voice returning to its natural brogue.

'Oh God, a bloody Scot.' Digby was a very worried man. 'I knew they'd get me. Is this because I'm planning to put a road through the courtyard at Edinburgh Castle?'

Sandy did not know what to do. His drunken plan had been to smite Digby with his girlish charms, get a tape recording of Digby propositioning him and then clear out before Digby had a chance to find the sausage. His instant unmasking as a gonad-packing, tackle-swinging member of the male sex had rather blown that out. Suddenly Sandy decided he had had enough.

'Sorry, wrong room,' he said and made to go.

'No you bloody don't!' said Digby, jumping up to stop him. 'Not before you tell me who the hell sent you and who the hell knows I'm bloody gay.'

For Sandy at least, those words seemed to fill the room with music, beautiful music, played on train whistles. He smiled a huge smile. He slipped a hand in his wife's handbag to ensure the tape was running.

In some ways Digby was a victim of his own

cowardice. His unquestioning acceptance that his
sexuality must always remain a dreaded secret was
the very reason that the revelation was so terrible
now. It is true, that such are the prejudices of British
society that, had he confronted it from the beginning, he might not have risen to the cabinet – but
he might have done, and he certainly would not
have lived a life of career paranoia and seedy
intrigue. And now he was knackered anyway, his
carefully cultivated jack-the-lad image making the
truth about him all the more sensational.

'Come on, who's after me? Who knows I'm a gay
transvestite! I only ever do it in Amsterdam . . .'
Suddenly light dawned for Digby. Amsterdam! His
last three trips to the Continent had been as a guest
of the road lobby. They took him to motor shows,
they took him to oil refineries . . . They left him
alone in the evening. God, was this Turk's way of
warning him not to dress him down in public? Was
Turk warning him, in none too subtle a fashion,
that he would burgle as many government depart-
ments as he pleased? How could Digby have been
so foolish as to quarrel with a man like Turk?

'Listen,' said Digby, 'tell Turk, I understand and
I'm sorry. Tell him he can pinch every patent in
London if he likes, I'll stand by him. Tell him I'm
very, very sorry and he won't need to warn me
again. Do you understand?'

The years fell away from Digby. The arrogance
of office evaporated. He knew he was still what he

always had been, a sad scared little farty. Once again he was poor old Shitsby Zitburst pleading with the school bullies.

'Do you understand?' he said again. 'Tell Turk to call it off.'

'Yes, I understand,' said Sandy, who did not understand at all.

'You can go then.'

Sandy got up.

'OK then. It's been very nice.' He was about to leave, but he turned back to Digby once more. 'Just do me one favour will you Diggy? Remember this handbag, will you?' Sandy held up the handbag, and then left without another word.

Leaving a subdued and thoughtful Digby, Sandy staggered away, suddenly realizing how blotto he was. As he entered the lift a maid was coming out of it to collect the breakfast orders. Feeling rather exposed, Sandy confronted the situation with Scottish bravado.

'A bonny evening to you, sweet lassie,' he said.

'Good evening, Madam,' said the girl in a small embarrassed voice. Sandy felt pleased. So his disguise had at least worked on someone. Leaving the lift on his floor he crept back to his room and tried to get undressed without waking his wife up. He failed.

'Will you look at you,' she said. 'You've been living in London too long.'

## SCUM ON THE BEACH

With the departure of the Minister the road lobby
had soon broken up and Sam left the hotel to take
a quiet stroll along the promenade and down onto
the beach. He loved the sea at night, even in a town.
At night you could forget all the crap that was in it
and see it as men had seen it when they first set sail
for the New World – shining and mysterious. It was
a clear night and Sam turned his head to the stars.
Despite the lights on the pier, quite a number were
visible and Sam was just contemplating that he
would probably soon be able to just about afford
one, when Springer scuttled up beside him.

'Boy oh boy,' he panted, 'that wasn't too comfort-
able with Parkhurst there, for a minute.'

Sam kept looking up at his star.

'Who gives a fuck what Parkhurst thinks?'

'Well I was just thinking . . . What with the . . .'
but Sam cut Springer short.

'I do hope you're not going to be stupid enough to
mention our little project Springer.'

'Well, no, of course not. But I mean, when it
comes on line . . . when we start building the
thing . . .'

'Building the thing?' asked Sam.

'Yeah . . .' answered Springer, hesitantly. 'Building the thing.'

Sam looked at Springer quizzically.

'Listen, Springer,' he said, 'Digby Parkhurst is a low-life little cockroach. We kiss his ass while he's a Minister so he builds us roads. That's it, that's all. He has nothing to do with our future plans.'

'But . . . but he slipped us the . . .' protested Springer.

'Exactly, Springer. He gave us the information. So what's he going to say? That he tipped us off to make a robbery? Then he's an accessory and no one will believe he didn't take a piece. Besides, like I said to Parkhurst, we haven't stolen anything. Do you see any stolen property? I don't. What have we got to do with anything?'

'Yes, but when we start to build it, well then it has to come out doesn't it?' Springer persevered.

Again Sam looked at Springer quizzically.

'You just haven't thought this through at all have you son?' he said.

## Chapter Nine

# *BLACKMAIL, THEFT AND DIRTY PHONE CALLS*

## THE POWER BEHIND THE THRONE

Digby woke up the following morning with a monumental hangover, but apart from that he didn't feel too bad. On reviewing the incident of the previous night he reckoned he had got off pretty lightly. Turk and the road lobby had only warned him of their knowledge, as long as he played ball and was a good boy they would have no reason to use it against him.

Besides, Digby had even scarier things to consider. He had been summoned to attend an early breakfast with Ingmar Bresslaw, the Prime Minister's eyes, ears and Doc Martin boots. Digby knew that, despite being a non-elected Civil Servant, Ingmar Bresslaw had more influence on national policy than the whole of Her Majesty's Loyal Opposition, every protest march and petition ever organized plus the European Court of Human Rights, put together.

On his way to the dining-room, preparing himself to genuflect before the great man, Digby encountered Sam Turk. Digby saw his opportunity to establish his puppylike loyalty to the road lobby beyond doubt.

'Uhm . . . Mr Turk,' said Digby nervously.

'Yes, Minister,' replied Turk, expecting a resumption of the ticking-off he had received the previous night.

'I just wanted to say . . . Sam, that you're the boss, OK? I know that Ministers for Transport may come and Ministers for Transport may go, but car builders, well, they stay forever . . . I know that now, it was stupid of me to forget it, and well . . . I'm sorry.'

Sam was mystified at Digby's change of attitude, but he was a man who took his good fortune where he found it.

'Yes, well, what you say is very true, Minister. And I guess if we have to liberate the odd patent for the good of Britain, what the hell, eh? It's only ethics for Christ's sake.'

'Exactly, Sam, exactly. It is, as you so very rightly say, only ethics,' replied Digby. 'And if I come across any myself, rest assured I'll slip them in my pocket for you . . . Patents that is, ha ha, not ethics, good Lord, you wouldn't be needing them . . . I mean . . . Well anyway, ha ha *thnn thnn* . . . Oh and by the way, that working paper the Road Federation presented, the one about turning all of

London parks into car parks, I've been thinking about that one hard, do memo me.'

'I will Minister, I will and good luck with your speech,' said Sam Turk.

'Well that's very kind Sam . . . and, I can forget about uhm . . . last night's little Scottish visitation can I?' said Digby.

'Why sure Minister, you can forget about whatever you please.' Sam had not the faintest idea what Digby was talking about and only the very slightest interest.

Digby, believing he had set matters straight with Sam, went into the dining-room for his breakfast with Ingmar Bresslaw.

'Good morning Ingmar,' he said. Ingmar Bresslaw did not even look up from his bacon, which he was viewing with utter contempt.

'They only ever do it on one side!' he growled in fury.

'What was that Ingmar?' enquired Digby.

'Without doubt the three most misleading words in the English language are "Great British Breakfast". It is a global bloody con and it should be exposed! Us boasting about our breakfasts? It's like the Russians boasting about their cars! We do worse breakfasts than any other nation in the world! The bloody Australians do better breakfasts than us and do you know why Minister?'

Ingmar did Digby the courtesy of addressing him as Minister, but only in the manner that an all powerful, regimental sergeant major might call a nineteen-year-old subaltern 'Sir'.

'Uhm not really, no Ingmar, no I don't,' a nervous Digby replied, desperately wondering what the answer was that Ingmar wanted to hear, and conscious that Ingmar could swat Ministers like flies.

'Because we only grill the bacon on one bloody side!!!' Ingmar said in a voice taut with emotion. 'From a transport café to a four star hotel it is considered enough that the bacon *looks* done. If it looks done the work shy bastard in the kitchen reckons it *is* done and he's off the hook. Is a car finished without the engine? It *looks* finished. Is a man dressed without his underpants? He *looks* dressed. So why is it considered acceptable to grill the bacon only on *one* bloody side!!! I like my bacon *crispy*, damn their bloody eyes!'

'Uhm . . . perhaps you should send it back.' Digby was taking a big risk offering an opinion, but he was at a loss as to what to say.

'Don't be an arse, Minister! Send it back and have some pimply school-leaver in a big white hat phlegm up on it out of spite?' Ingmar pushed his breakfast away and called a waitress. 'Bring me a large, single malt whisky, any bloody brand, and four soluble aspirin. Right then,' he continued after the girl had gone, 'what do you want?'

'I'm sorry?' Digby, somewhat taken aback by this abrupt enquiry.

'Come on, come on, come on Minister, I'm a busy man, what do you want?'

Of course Digby did not like being addressed in this fashion by a Civil Servant, but he was as likely to object as to slam his tackle in the waffle iron which had just been placed at his elbow. Ingmar Bresslaw's power was awesome and he wielded it with the scruples of a bed bug. He was the Prime Minister's hit-man, the toughest thug in Whitehall, and Ingmar's dark shadow in your door spelt terror to any member of the government. What's more, the higher you got, the more terrifying he became, because it was his job to make sure that no one ever got close enough to challenge his boss.

However, Digby could not help but feel rather put out and honour bound to stand up for himself.

'Uhm I'm awfully sorry Ingmar. I mean really, sorry, but it was you who summoned me surely?' he said meekly taking a piece of toast.

'Was it? Oh yes. Don't bother buttering that toast, I haven't much to say,' replied Ingmar.

Digby had just stuck his knife into a curl of butter. His arm was stretched across the table holding the knife. He did not know what to do for the best. Withdraw the knife, in which case the curl of butter might come away with it and Ingmar might imagine that he was being disobeyed, or else lay down the knife in the butter where it was, which would be sloven table manners and Ingmar might feel that insufficient respect was being shown. In the end, Digby remained frozen, conducting his short interview with Ingmar Bresslaw arm outstretched across the table with his knife into the butter. Bresslaw did not notice as he did not bother to look at Digby.

'Right Minister,' he growled, his great wet boozy eyes still staring glumly down at the bacon. 'Your speech to conference, all prepared?'

'Oh yes Ingmar, I'm very pleased with it,' replied Digby.

'I didn't ask how you felt about it, I asked if it was bloody well prepared,' snapped Ingmar Bresslaw. 'You haven't messed about with it? Changed anything since we wrote it for you?'

'Well . . . I did add a joke,' confessed Digby.

'Ye Gods, Saints preserve us, a joke! What bloody joke?'

'Well . . . it's about a donkey . . .' said Digby, his arm beginning to quiver with the strain.

'Well if it's the one I've heard about the donkey, your resignation will be requested mid-speech,' said Ingmar. 'Not that I care. The point is, just make sure you don't get carried away and add anything of substance that hasn't been agreed, all right? Above all, don't mention the road plans, they're political dynamite, all right? The BritTrak stuff is quite a hot enough potato for one conference. That damn anti-road rally yesterday shows people suspect a pretty radical plan, but, as you well know, they don't know the half of it. So it's damned important how we present ourselves on this one. A silly move now would kick up a stink we couldn't handle and ruin the most important bit of legislation since we sold the NHS to American Express.'

Despite the pain in his arm, Digby swelled with pride. He knew his road projects were big stuff but to have the mighty Ingmar Bresslaw speak so seriously about them was a high commendation indeed.

'So have you got that?' said Ingmar. 'Talk rail. Keep off your bloody roads. All right. Goodbye, Minister.'

'Goodbye, Ingmar,' said Digby, and he got up and left. To avoid further embarrassment he took the butter knife plus the bit of butter with him.

## A WARNING IGNORED

Outside the hotel the rail lobby finally got their moment with Digby, they converged on him one step ahead of the press. They were pathetic, like beggars, they knew the Minister would give them nothing and they harried him in a defeated, dispirited fashion. Except Sandy, Sandy lobbied with cool, confident simplicity. Wearing a neat suit and dark glasses he pushed his way through the throng and confronted Digby head on.

'Minister,' he said firmly. 'I am going to say this only once so you had better listen. In your speech today, *don't* announce the formation of BritTrak.'

'Another bloody Scot,' thought Digby to himself, ignoring Sandy and getting into the limo. 'They're all train mad, it comes from living so bloody far from anywhere decent, that's what it is.'

## CROSSED LINES

Despite the fact that he had been up late telling Deborah his story (and making rather a meal of it, it might be added), Geoffrey was up bright and early on Monday morning. And just as Digby was dealing with the train lobby in Brighton, Geoffrey was getting ready to phone the Office of Patents in order to get back the designs of his brilliant invention.

As has been said, the telephone was one of the great banes of Geoffrey's life. Communication is rendered infinitely more difficult when you cannot see the person to whom you are speaking and Geoffrey had to be on particularly good form to make himself understood. On this morning, what with the excitement, the loss of sleep and everything else, he wasn't.

'*Urgh, urgh,*' he said into the receiver on hearing that he was connected.

'Aaaargh! We've got a sicko!' screamed Dolores.

The Whitehall department Geoffrey was phoning, despite being the repository for the very latest inventions, was itself last fully refitted just after the war and it still boasted a nice old-fashioned exchange staffed by nice old-fashioned girls.

131

'I dunno,' she explained to her anxious colleagues' enquiries, 'he just sort of went *urgh, urgh*.'

'Dirty bastard,' chimed Maureen, 'probably gets his filthy kicks going urgh urgh. You shouldn't have screamed Dolores, that's what they like. It makes 'em all excited to hear a girl scream.'

'I couldn't help it,' claimed Dolores. 'He went urgh.'

'Yes, well, you have to be strong Dolores,' asserted Maureen. 'You owe it to other women.'

The phone rang again. Maureen answered it. 'Hello Whitehall Office of Patents.'

'*Urgh, urgh, urgh.*'

'Aaaargh!' screamed Maureen, slamming the phone down. 'It's that *urgh – er*.'

'I thought you said don't scream,' complained Dolores. 'That wasn't very strong. Coo, I'll bet he's excited now. I'll bet he's as excited as anything. I'll bet he's rolling round on the floor rubbing himself with a washing-up glove and going *urgh*. You've gratified him Maureen, that's what you've done, you've given him gratification.'

'Oh shut up, Dolores,' said Maureen.

Geoffrey summoned up all his concentration and dialled again. But this time the girls were ready for him. Maureen possessed a rape alarm and they had sworn that the very next time anyone went *urgh* at them, they would let him have it.

'*Urgh*,' said Geoffrey and an ear shattering shriek shot out of the phone, into his ear, through his brain, out of the other ear and ricocheted against a couple of walls before finally dying down in the goldfish bowl, giving Deborah's goldfish, Jaws, a nasty turn.

Geoffrey decided he would have to wake Deborah and ask for her help. Being a student, Deborah was able, to a certain extent, to make her own timetable. Her timetable this morning had been to try and get some extra sleep, since she had got so little in the night, what with visions of imaginary burping axe murderers, followed by Geoffrey's tale of the real thing.

Deborah snapped into a bleary consciousness.

'What! Where! Don't sit on the Kiwi fruit!' she said, with one of those curious lapses of logic that sleeping or half-awake people specialize in when attempting conversation. Her eyes focused on Geoffrey who had brought her a cuppa, and was endeavouring to keep it steady.

'Geoffrey! It ain't five minutes since I finally prised you off the end of my bed, now you're back. What is it, a charity thing? You get sponsored for how much you can annoy me?'

'Sorry,' he replied. 'I brought you a cup of tea.'

'What's going on? Are Murder Incorporated here? Is it curtains for us, Bugsy?'

Geoffrey explained that there was no immediate danger, and Deborah enquired, far from soothingly, why then, he had woken her up after only a couple of hours' sleep, further adding that perhaps Geoffrey would like to take a hike and not return unless either the assassins or Elvis turned up.

'You have to ring the Patents Office,' said Geoffrey proffering her the extension phone. 'I've tried but they think I'm a raving sex beast.'

'Hmm,' said Deborah, 'they may have a point. Get your eyes off my front, Meathead.'

## OH WHAT A NIGHT

'Get your eyes off my front, Meathead' was, as might be imagined, the phrase which Deborah used when she caught Geoffrey ogling, which was often. Deborah was as pretty as a picture, and what's more, a picture of something very pretty, and Geoffrey was so hot for her you could have boiled an egg in his Y fronts. Of course Geoffrey was hot for a lot of girls and Deborah often had to admonish him on behalf of a stranger they happened to pass. 'It's all very well taking a discreet glance,' she would say, 'but allowing your eyes to extend three feet on little springs and steam to shoot out of your earholes was a bit obvious.' Thoughts of sex play an enormous part in the make up of any individual, and for young men it is close to an obsession. Geoffrey was a young man and, being, as he was, at a disadvantage when it came to asking out girls, his obsession was a nightmare. Geoffrey, quite simply spent his entire life absolutely gasping for a fuck.

Obviously having a disability, even a severe one, is in no way necessarily an obstacle to leading a fulfilling sex life, but Geoffrey had never been lucky that way. In fact he had only ever had-it-off once, and that had been the result of a triumph of organization and bucking the system. It was when he was seventeen and living for a while at a special needs boarding school. There had been seven boys living in Geoffrey's dorm, all in their teens, and, as might be expected, all hornier than the brass section of the London Philharmonic.

They did not have the outlets that other young lads had, something as simple as masturbation was difficult for most of them. This problem consumed Geoffrey. His soul burned with a righteous fury over the injustice of it all. For teenage boys to be denied the chance to have a quick one off-the-wrist seemed too cruel even for one who had faced many deprivations in his short life. Something would have to be done.

Geoffrey Spasmo conceived a wicked, wicked plan. Under his direction, the entire dorm scrimped and saved for months and months and one dark and naughty night Geoffrey dug out his prized possession, a tatty copy of Penthouse, and skipping all his usual favourite pages, Cheryl, Janine, Wanda, he chose a number from the classified ads at the back.

The whole thing was a triumph. A very nice young woman arrived in a taxi, which Geoffrey met at the end of the school drive. At first she was reluctant but it would have taken a harder heart than hers to deny the longing in Geoffrey's eyes. They sneaked up to the dorm, which was now so highly charged that if the window hadn't been open the entire room would have short circuited itself, and the girl, who according to the back of Penthouse was called Suki, got straight down to it. Providing six professional hand jobs in succession, the whole thing took about a minute and a quarter.

'I have to tell you boys,' whispered Suki, 'that this is very easy money for me. I mean I only have to touch them and they go off.'

Finally it was Geoffrey's turn, and Suki was in a magnanimous mood. These young clients were considerably less demanding than blokes in airport hotels who wanted to do it in the wardrobe, then talk about their wives.

'All right Geoffrey,' she said. 'How about unloading your cherry? Reckon you're up to it?'

Geoffrey wasn't sure but it would have taken a tactical nuclear strike to stop him trying. Fortunately for him, Suki was a natural born therapist.

## A THEFT DISCOVERED

But that had been long ago, and there had been many years of frustration since then. Whilst at university he had thought about paying for it a second time, but it really wasn't what he wanted. That first time had been a personal triumph, a great adventure. As an adult it would just rub in his inability to take a woman to bed without paying her.

Which was why, even though he was being sought by an anonymous murderer, Geoffrey could not resist a glance at Deborah's bosom as she took the phone from him, and her nightie afforded him a tantalizing glimpse. However, having been suitably admonished, Geoffrey averted his gaze and gave Deborah the number.

'Why so urgent?' said Deborah wearily. 'I mean OK, so somebody's stolen your invention from the lab. But I mean, hey, come on, they're not exactly going to have got it out of the Patents Office are they?'

But Deborah and Geoffrey were in for a shock.

'I'm sorry, but I have no record of any patent submission from any Geoffrey Peason. In fact, I have no record of that name at all,' the voice said and the voice was not lying, for the cover-up had happened way above the voice's head.

On the Saturday morning, when Deirdre Whelk, the Civil Servant responsible, had discovered exactly which patent application had been stolen, she had stormed straight over to see the Minister in a fury. 'Doing a Deirdre' as her minions called it, and her minions knew to keep well out of the way. Something Digby Parkhurst was not in a position to do, since Deirdre was standing four square before his desk, fixing him with an eye that could have cut diamonds, and what's more, diamonds that were still buried half a mile deep in the granite of the Kimberley.

'Now look here, Minister,' she snapped. 'I understand that your transport people need to keep up with design developments, which is why I have been prepared in the past to allow you a look at certain items of interest which my department finds itself in possession of. But my God, they're for your eyes only!'

'Of course, Deirdre, of course they are, and only I ever see them,' Digby lied.

'Minister, the bloody thing has been stolen. Did you steal it?' Deirdre asked.

'Don't be absurd, Deirdre,' replied Digby, trying to sound statesmanlike, but actually sounding gitmanlike. 'Her Majesty's Ministers do not indulge in felonies, we . . .'

'Oh no?' interrupted Deirdre. 'How would you describe handing on government secrets?'

'Deirdre, you're being pompous,' said Digby, being massively pompous. 'Government secrets? A paltry patent?'

'The Office of Patents is a branch of government,' snapped Deirdre. 'Its secrets are a branch of government. I have broken the law, you have broken the law and whatever sordid oil baron you snitched to has broken into my department! Now for my own sake, and for my own sake only, I am going to screw the lid down on this, Minister. But you,

Minister, are a very stupid man.'

Deirdre stormed out of Digby's office and got to work on a cover up. The result being that when Deborah put the phone down to face Geoffrey she had to inform him that his invention had completely disappeared.

Geoffrey was truly stunned. The disaster befalling him was huge. First they had tried to kill him, now they had stolen both copies of his life's work, and he did not know who they were, or why they were attacking him. Geoffrey sat on Deborah's bed, trying to think what he should do.

'OK, Geoffrey, so give me the juice. What is this crazy invention?' asked Deborah, hauling herself up into a sitting position by means of the bar that was suspended above her head. 'You've always made a secret out of it like it was the recipe for coke. What could be so special? Have you discovered the secret of alchemy?'

'I did it for you Deborah,' said Geoffrey. 'It's an engine, and I designed it for you.'

'An engine?' enquired Deborah. 'That's nice, thanks. You mean like in a car?'

'Yes, exactly like in a car, except it doesn't use petrol. It's powered by hydrogen,' said Geoffrey and adding rather unnecessarily, 'it's a hydrogen engine.'

'Don't be stupid Geoffrey,' said Deborah. 'You can't run an engine on hydrogen.'

'You can run an engine on anything that is a

source of power, Deborah,' snapped Geoffrey. He did not normally snap at Deborah, in fact, even if he had wanted to he probably would not have had the guts, but he was in something of a turmoil. 'Anything at all, oil, electricity, coal, legs . . .'

'Some legs,' said Deborah. 'Mine couldn't power an electric toothbrush.' It had been almost three years since the arsehole in the Global Moritz had tried to rush the pelican crossing on yellow, but understandably she was still a little bitter.

'Yes, some legs,' admitted Geoffrey. 'But you can run an engine on any source of power. The only question is, how efficient is it? I wanted to make a clean engine, a light engine, an engine that could make you truly mobile Deborah. One where the fuel weighed very little but delivered an immense amount of power. When I first met you, I wanted to make an engine that would turn your wheelchair into a Thunderbird. I wanted to make you able to dance and fly. You were the inspiration Deborah, you concentrated my mind. You made me want to build an engine!'

'I have that effect on all the guys,' said Deborah.

*Chapter Ten*

# *BOY MEETS GIRL. BOY ANNOYS GIRL. BOY STANDS NOT A HOPE IN HELL WITH GIRL.*

## DECLARATION OF INDEPENDENCE

Since Deborah's friendship with Geoffrey was shortly to lead her into the most mortal danger it is worth taking a moment to discover how it was that they came to meet at all. It had happened some three years previously on the London Underground. Well not actually on the underground, but at the wall of ticket barriers that the authorities began to erect shortly after the King's Cross Fire, in the apparent hope that next time nobody at all would get out.

Early in the time of Deborah's burden, before she became cripwise to the system of apartheid under which she would be spending the rest of her life, she had attempted to take a tube. Later of course Deborah was to realize that she was as disbarred from such simple public activities as were black South Africans from municipal swimming pools in South Africa. Later of course, Deborah would come to realize that the only thing missing from doorways, steps, lifts, escalators, curbs etc., in London, were neat signs saying **ACHTUNG! No Disabled People Allowed**. However, this was in the springtime of her trouble. The Global Moritz was still a recent memory and Deborah was determined to stay in Britain, continue her education and square up to the slings and arrows of outrageous bastards.

Of course her parents had begged her to return to New York.

'What, you hate your Momma so much you won't let her look after you?'

'Momma,' Deborah had said, 'if I come to you now I'll never get out again. You'll glue yourself to my wheelchair and force soup down my throat for forty-five years till you die, and then I'll starve. Now is the time I have to learn to live my own life.'

'You don't *like* my soup?' said Momma.

## FIRE HAZARD

And so Deborah had stayed in London and, on that fateful day when she met Geoffrey, found herself stuck at the ticket barrier at South Kensington station with a weary looking London Underground person approaching her. Deborah was very quickly realizing how naïve she had been in assuming that, with enough determination, she could roll where she wanted to roll. An enormous revelation was about to be demonstrated to her. A life-time sized truth was looming up at her wearing the uniform of London Regional Transport. Deborah, who before her encounter with the Global Moritz had been a young woman, was now a fire hazard. She had passed through a physical transformation. A transformation even more dramatic than that undergone by female stars in the US who, on reaching the age of forty-five, disappear for a month and re-emerge aged thirty, talking about feminism and being careful not to sneeze too hard in case they implode. Deborah's transformation had been greater even than this. For Deborah, once a warm and vibrant human being, exuding personality and soul, had become, a fire hazard. Fire hazard, and specifically fire hazard. Not obstruction, embarrassment or damn nuisance, but fire hazard.

The reason Deborah was so specifically a fire hazard was that in those two little words, the able-bodied community let itself off the hook. It would of course be churlish to deny someone access to a theatre or pub because their chair would be difficult to get up a flight of steps, or because they occupy more space than walking customers and are hence less profitable. On the other hand, to deny someone access because they are a fire hazard – well, there is a sensible and public spirited action. There is a fast route to the moral high-ground if ever there was one.

'Nobody likes it, love, but there you go.'

Should Deborah, or anyone similarly afflicted be

so selfish as to complain about their effective ostracism from social and cultural life, what would she be doing but wishing pain and death upon the able-bodied community. And let us face it, it is not their fault that she is in a wheelchair.

'It's the possibility of a panic that worries us,' people would patiently explain to Deborah. 'You have to ask yourself what your situation would be in the case of a rush and a stampede.'

Very occasionally Deborah attempted to argue her corner, pointless though she knew it to be.

'Listen, bud,' she had said, as politely as she could manage, to the slightly punky young man who was refusing to sell her a ticket to a play to be performed in the upstairs room of a pub . . . 'It is Saturday afternoon OK? and I have just negotiated the entire length of Oxford Street. I have dealt with it all; the tone deaf dickwit playing two of the three chords of "Blowin' in the wind", who kindly had his guitar case full of five pence bits spread across half the pavement . . .'

'Yeah, all right but . . .' interjected the young man, slightly offended. He did a bit of busking himself and often did a Dylan number or two, after all you had to cover the classics didn't you? However, Deborah was in no mood to be interrupted by a hippy, especially one who thought that having short, spiked hair meant he wasn't a hippy.

'I have got round ten broken paving stones that the council kindly put there to trip up blind people and snag wheelchairs. I have avoided the one-and-a-half million tourists standing in groups wondering how they just managed to pay five pounds for a can of coke.'

The punky hippy tried to interject, but failed.

'I have circumnavigated the thousands of thugs from the city in pretend Armani suits who can't see you because they're talking into their portable phones. So they bash you in the knees with their stupid brief-cases, with the reinforced steel corners, that are absolutely essential to protect the bag of crisps and a copy of Penthouse, which is all they have inside the case.'

The punky hippy was amazed, this woman did not seem to require oxygen.

'I have detoured round the gangs of bored youths who hang around waiting for their balls to drop, outside each and every one of the identical fast food outlets offering identical crap in a bap and Tennessee Fried Dog; the crocodile of French schoolgirls with their beautiful Benetton jumpers tied round their waists, just at a nice level to get caught in my face; the endless men who stop dead directly in front of me to turn round and look at the French schoolgirl's asses; the road works; the bollards; the steaming piles of plastic bin liners; the taxis taking a little-known short cut along the pavement; the bloke who stands around with a sandwich-board saying eat less meat and protein; and the strange bearded tramp waving his arms around and screaming fuck off at everybody. All these things I have dealt with today, in a frigging wheelchair, bud. I think I could just about handle twenty-five assorted teachers and social workers making for the door of an upstairs room in a pub!'

'Hey,' said the punky hippy. 'Don't you ever have to breathe?'

'It's called circular breathing,' replied Deborah. 'The Australian Aboriginals developed it to play their didgeridoos, it means that they can keep blowing for ever. All New York Jewish girls are taught it, that's how we get to marry such rich men.'

The punky hippy was embarrassed. People in wheelchairs weren't supposed to crack dirty jokes. The idea of Deborah making gags about blow jobs embarrassed him . . . after all, he thought, could she? Would she still want to? People in wheelchairs are de-sexed by society, which is why they all have to use the same toilet.

## BARRIER

So there she was, at the ticket barrier at South Kensington tube station, asking if she could be allowed through the gate reserved for those with luggage as her chair would not fit through the automatic barrier.

'I can let you through here love,' the man had said, 'of course I can.'

'Good,' answered Deborah.

'But what about the steps, eh? The steps down onto the platform, eh? Sorry love, but what about the steps?'

South Kensington is partly a ground-level station and the platform for the District and Circle lines are reached by a flight of steps. Deborah enquired whether there was a lift and was informed that not only was there not one, but this was exactly the sort of thing that she should have found out before setting out on her journey. London Regional Transport could not be expected to deal with this sort of problem at the drop of a hat. It seemed like a fairish point, but not when you consider the number of people in wheelchairs in London. The reason why requests like Deborah's were so rare is that most wheelchair users know the score and don't even bother to ask. In fact, if Deborah had phoned in advance she would merely have saved herself the trouble of going to the station at all, because there was no lift and no staff available to carry the chair anyway. And where was she going? Piccadilly? Well she might as well try to get to the Moon. There were the escalators at this end, the escalators at that end, the corridors, the steps, the crowds. It turned out, that in order for a person in a wheelchair to travel by tube they must arrange in advance to be met and helped by London Transport staff at both ends, and only travel at certain times, and only to and from stations where facilities are available.

Deborah realized that she was not going to be

allowed through, and resolved to turn away, vowing then, as she was to vow a thousand times a week for the rest of her life, not to consume her precious energy on anger and frustration. She could not allow herself the luxury that most people indulge in, of letting off steam by having a raving good whinge.

Who can honestly say that they have never been consumed by that intense annoyance, never felt that burning but wrenching tension and anger at life's petty frustrations. A barman repeatedly ignoring you; a screw head that has for some reason been made out of soft putty instead of steel; a traffic light which has a thing about the colour red – such tiny irritations make one ready to kill. What, then, would be the inner fury felt by a person who has lost the use of certain limbs? How terrible would be the endless turmoil to the stomach that simple inanimate objects and petty bureaucracy will engender? If that fury were given expression, the person in question would die of exhaustion within a week. Deborah was no mystic, but, since her encounter with the car, she had learnt to keep control of her Karma.

## CREATING A SCENE

So, with a weary sigh, Deborah nailed a lid down on the fury bubbling up in her guts, and with a left-hand shove started the skilful process of extricating herself. Unfortunately, she now discovered that during her brief negotiations with officialdom, she had become the cork in a crowded bottleneck of people with suitcases and their own problems.

Deborah wanted the floor to open up and swallow her, and not just because this would have been a convenient way of getting down to the tube trains. She had never been fond of scenes and had already discovered that her new circumstances made her a natural centre of attention. In fact she sometimes felt that she was condemned to be either totally ignored or the object of all eyes and asked to choose between the lesser of these evils. Like most people, she would certainly have chosen the former. Since her encounter with the Moritz she had constantly been attracting people's notice; holding them up when trying to get through doors or into lifts; getting in their way when they wanted to carry drinks across the pub floor; being stared at by hundreds of people as she and her chair were manhandled into a concert. She hated every one of these little starring roles of life, just as she hated the one in which she was caught up at the tube station.

Deborah's reactions to all of this were no different to anyone else's. Who wants to be an inconvenience? Who wants to be in the way? Everybody knows the feeling of social villainy one experiences on getting out a cheque-book at a supermarket cash till and holding people up while you write it out. We have all felt the howling wind of that great communal sigh which emanates from the queue behind you.

You can almost hear them all thinking, 'He could at least have filled the name of the shop out while she was weighing his carrots.'

Well that was how Deborah was feeling now, except ten times more. She knew what they were all thinking behind her, it did not take much imagination. 'I wish this bitch would get the fuck out of the way.'

It was at this point that Geoffrey Spasmo made his appearance. Pushing through the small crowd, he lurched up to the London Underground person, and, concentrating hard so as to make himself clear, said in a loud voice:

'This is body fascism! You as a black man should understand what it feels like to be discriminated against.'

The London Underground man was indeed black and he did understand what it felt like to be discriminated against. Unfortunately, he didn't understand Geoffrey, the subtler aspects of Geoffrey's argument were rather lost in his guttural delivery. You had to listen carefully to understand Geoffrey, especially when he was shouting and excited. The only word that the London Underground man made out was 'black' and taking into account the confrontational attitude that Geoffrey was adopting, he not unnaturally presumed that race was central to Geoffrey's point. Which in a way it was but not in the way the London Underground man, whose name was Terry, presumed.

'Listen, mate, all right?' said Terry, pretty angrily. 'Don't come it with me, all right? If you come it with me, you're not going to be in a position to come it with no one else for a long time, right? You know what I mean mate, or what?' Terry did not give Geoffrey time to reply to this last enquiry, for he immediately expanded on this theme, producing, by a remarkable coincidence, an identical argument to the one which Geoffrey had been trying to put across himself.

'I mean you're a spastic, right? What are you doing with that racist shit? Don't you get your own discrimination, or what, I mean, *or what?*'

'That's what I'm saying!' said Geoffrey speaking slowly, and this time Terry understood. 'You should let this lady go on the tube.'

'I can't, can I, fuckwit?' replied the aggrieved Terry. 'What am I? Captain Kirk? Do you think I've got a transporter, or what?'

'In that case,' said Geoffrey, 'I think you should join me in some form of protest. In fact, I think everybody in the queue should. I think we should all sit down so that we can stand up for universal public access.'

Deborah could see that the only crowd cooperation likely to take place in the next few minutes would be Geoffrey's lynching.

'Forget it, pal,' she said. 'You can't get people to stand up for themselves, let alone anyone else. As far as they're concerned we're just a couple of crips holding up their day.'

'But that's the exact attitude we have to fight,' stuttered Geoffrey.

Deborah was beginning to warm to this insanely deluded young man. For one thing, she was grateful that she was no longer the only inconvenient, disabled person irritating a crowd of people. On the other hand, she, unlike her champion it seemed, still lived on the planet Earth.

'*You* fight it,' replied Deborah. 'I have enough problems fighting this chair.' At which point she reversed hard into a big suitcase directly behind her which had been slowly pushing her towards the barrier.

'Well excuse *me*!' said someone who wanted to get to Heathrow.

'Sit on it!' said Deborah, offering a vertical forefinger. She was angry, and tired, and completely stuck.

'You won't get anywhere feeling sorry for yourself,' said the Heathrow traveller, and all the other pushers and shovers turned away. They personally would be too embarrassed to *talk* to a cripple, let alone argue with one.

With a huge effort, Deborah managed to extricate herself from the mêlée and effect a partial escape.

'You mustn't fight the chair,' shouted Geoffrey, leaving Terry to get on with his day and scuttling after Deborah, 'it's part of you.'

Some explanation is required here.

Did Geoffrey leap to the defence of every person with disabilities whom he encountered? Did he run after everyone in a wheelchair trying to engender in them a positive attitude to their condition? No, had he done so there would have been no time for him to gain his Ph.D. in physics. The fact was, that from the first moment he saw her, Geoffrey was smitten by Deborah. This, obviously, was not because Deborah, like Geoffrey, suffered from a disability. A person's sexuality is not governed by their own physical condition but by that which they find attractive in others. When we see pictures in the colour supps of some half-dead, prunelike Hollywood mogul escorting a twenty-year-old blonde bombshell about the place, we do not say, 'Oh I thought he would have gone for somebody more half-dead and prunelike.'

Geoffrey fancied Deborah for the obvious reason that she was very beautiful. Lots of men fancied her and she had had a number of boyfriends. Of course, occasionally, her disability did confuse things, she had to watch out for the weirdos. Deborah soon recognized that there were some guys who got all mushy and romantic over what they saw as her helpless condition.

'You want to protect something? Get a job with Securicor,' Deborah had said to one misty-eyed suitor who had informed her that he wanted to build a nest for her to snuggle up in. There had also been one man who Deborah strongly suspected was actually turned on specifically by her immobility.

'I ain't being no new experience for some jerk who's into bondage,' she had told him. 'Go stick it in a slot machine,' and he had burst into tears.

Like most people her age, Deborah struck up relationships for the fun of it and had no interest in a long-term thing. Geoffrey, who would gladly have married her, had never got so much as a snog. This did not greatly surprise Geoffrey, as he was realistic and did not consider himself the world's most romantic catch.

## A SERIOUS SITUATION

This first, tube-side, encounter had taken place three years previously. Little had changed since then: Geoffrey still loved Deborah and wanted her sauce, Deborah had come to love Geoffrey but definitely did not want his. One thing had changed of course, and changed very suddenly. They were now both in deep trouble.

Geoffrey was very silent after the phone call to the Office of Patents and it was not his Cerebral Palsy that was making him shake.

'Geoffrey, tell me what's going on?' asked Deborah.

His thoughts were far away. 'I was so concerned with building it for you, I never really considered how important it could be to everyone else. I was a bit of a dickhead I'm afraid Deborah, after all, it's obvious, it will change everything.'

'What are you gurgling about?' asked Deborah testily.

'Everything Deborah. The entire economy of the Earth, the political map, the military map. Everything.'

'Crap,' said Deborah, expressing her scepticism.

'Deborah, I've invented an engine that runs on hydrogen,' insisted Geoffrey. 'An engine which runs on hydrogen is an engine that *does not run on oil*. It could change the world!'

'So how come nobody invented it before?' said Deborah. 'Hydrogen isn't new.'

'People have been inventing hydrogen engines for years,' said Geoffrey, 'and biomass engines, and electric engines. The problem has always been that all of these methods carry much less energy density than petrol, hence less power. People *like* power. Most cars crawl along at fifteen miles an hour, but the drivers want the *potential* to be able to do a hundred. That's why engines using cleaner fuels have never been adopted.'

'And you've made your hydrogen dense have you?' enquired Deborah.

'Well, not dense, just more efficient, Deborah. I have invented a colossal thing. It costs nothing to run . . . it's environmentally harmless.'

'And then it turns into a pizza and you can eat it,' said Deborah. 'Come on Geoffrey, I know you've got a brain that gets stuck in doorways but . . .'

'I tell you it costs nothing to run, and it's environmentally harmless,' said Geoffrey, firmly. 'That's why they've stolen it; that's why they tried to kill me – it's too bloody good. The hydrogen is produced by the electrolysis of water . . .'

This sounded vaguely convincing to Deborah, she could dimly remember something from school about anodes and cathodes.

'And the beauty of it,' continued Geoffrey, 'is that it burns cleanly. All it produces is water. Not tetraethyl lead; not carbon monoxide; not nitrogen oxides – just water. It's a potential revolution as big as steam or oil itself!'

'But they've got it, whoever *they* are,' Deborah reminded him.

'Yes, they've got it,' Geoffrey conceded, 'and they're trying to kill me. God knows why. Why not offer to buy it off me, that's the way things are normally done isn't it?'

'I guess they must be nuts. But the point is, what are we going to do?' said Deborah.

'Well I think I'm safe here,' said Geoffrey, reasoning that it would be unlikely that his hunters would connect him to Deborah. No one at work knew anything about his private life. His colleagues had long ago given up even the pretence of making any effort to understand him. They were perfectly pleasant and friendly but they had their own lives to lead.

'Listen, they want you dead because you are a living copy of your invention,' said Deborah. 'Having robbed your work place, and your home, they presume that they hold all the hard copies, so all they have to do is kill you and it's theirs. But they blew it didn't they? So it's simple. Just write out some more copies of the secret and hand them round, give one to the police, put one in the bank, take out an ad in the paper. Once they realize what you've done, they'll also realize that there isn't any point in killing you any more because the secret is beyond their control anyway. They've shot their bolt Geoffrey; they've let you get away. Even if they find you again it will be too late.'

'Not if they find me within the next three months Deborah,' said Geoffrey morosely. 'Because that's my estimate of the minimum amount of time it would take to recreate the plans in any comprehensible manner, and that's if I can get hold of a computer.'

'Three months!' exclaimed Deborah.

For a moment, the seriousness of the engine situation was overshadowed by the seriousness of the having-somebody-crashed-on-your-sofa-for-three-months situation.

'Here's a pencil,' she said, 'I want you out in two and a half.'

157

# DÉBÂCLE

## YOUNG DIGBY

Digby strode towards the podium, calm and confident, he was feeling good. The shock of the previous night was like a dream now, he was back in his element, wrapped in the warm cocoon of his party, and, as long as he avoided offending any major industrialists, he could remain there forever. They had given him a great slot for his speech, just after lunch. Everybody would be mellow and he had plenty of time to get it all on camera before the dreadful '*Play School* turn off' when the television stations ended their live coverage in order to do the kids' programmes.

'The Minister is no stranger to the platform,' said the BBC's political correspondent lovingly into his microphone . . . 'Old conference hands will perhaps recall his first appearance at the famous Blue Podium, when, as a plucky fifteen-year-old, he won many a heart on the floor with a little youthful commonsense. If memory serves, young Master Parkhurst even made one or two of the party grandees sit up and listen.'

The correspondent was referring to a particularly revolting occasion which had happened some twenty or so years previously, when, for a brief moment, Digby had found himself enveloped in the warm glow of uncritical press attention. It was one of those nauseating incidents which crop up periodically, when a youngster is deemed to have spoken with a simple clarity and insight that grown-ups, living in the complex world, had lost sight of.

'I just think,' young Digby Parkhurst (aka Shitsby Zitburst) had said, to a smiling and indulgent conference, 'that it's about time the unions pulled themselves together (warm applause). After all, we're all British aren't we, and I don't think that the men who fell in two World Wars would think very much of these strikes. My father works very hard and has never been on strike. It took him six years to pay for our car, and I'm extremely proud of that.'

Young Digby had been president of his school debating society. He had written an essay entitled 'England or Anarchy?' which had been published in a local newspaper, and, as a result, he had been invited to conference as a 'youth delegate'. The reason that this invitation had been made was that, at the time, the concern in Digby's party was that they had become out of date and were considered unfashionable amongst the young. Searching about for a solution to this problem the party grandees had decided that the appearance of fifteen-year-old Shitsby, school blazer tightly buttoned, hair parted and flattened, a soup stain growing slowly on his upper lip, would make them hip. This was a miscalculation, but conference loved it.

'When I'm set an essay at school *thnn thnn*,' young Master Parkhurst had said, 'I certainly do not go on strike! I jolly well write that essay, for I know that is the only way that the job will get done!' Loud cheers.

## THNN THNN THNN

And again Digby was at the podium facing an expectant conference crowd. Rumour had got about that there was to be an actual policy announcement during the Transport speech, and actual policy was always a treat at conference.

'The Minister is playing to a packed house,' said the BBC correspondent. 'We are all certainly expecting something pretty significant. The rumour is *rail*. It is very unlikely to be roads with the depth of popular feeling on the subject at the moment. We shall simply have to wait and see, but it is certainly going to be a highly significant speech.'

Actually the correspondent knew exactly what was in the speech because Ingmar Bresslaw had given him a full text earlier so that he could write

his copy in advance and meet his afternoon dead-
lines.

'Yes,' he gushed, 'I feel confident that the
Minister has some fairly spectacular policy changes
to set before us.'

He knew it, the hall knew it, and Digby knew it,
but Digby wasn't going to rush things. He was going
to luxuriate in every moment of the build up, the
audience would have to wait three-quarters of an
hour for the big BritTrak moment. In the meantime,
Digby regailed them with his uninspiring succession
of humourless platitudes to which the hall responded
with their uninspired repertoire of Pavlovian
responses. They clapped joyfully, they nodded
thoughtfully, they mumbled 'hear hear' sagely and
scratched their bums and thought about the bar.
Digby loved every minute of it. He positively
glowed; the immaculate Brylcreamed hair, the shiny
cheeks, the fat wet lips. He almost seemed to be
glowing from within. It was as if he'd sat down hard
on a thousand watt light bulb.

The Donkey gag went down a storm.

'A donkey and trap!' they repeated to each other.
'So that was what those Luddite environmentalists
proposed! Ha!' They sniggered and grinned and
clapped and leant over to inform each other that
Digby was on terrific form. Oh yes, they all agreed,
he might even, one day, be in line for the top job
if he managed to avoid screwing his secretary
and didn't get caught drunk driving or making

multiple share applications.

Oh, how Digby was loving himself. The weight of all those years of toadying and being a despised little farty was lifting from his shoulders. If, as Kissinger claimed, power is an aphrodisiac then at that moment Digby could have coaxed an orgasm out of a concrete elephant.

'I hardly think,' he said again. 'I hardly think,' was Digby's absolute favourite phrase and probably the most accurate thing he would say in his entire political life. Digby *did* hardly think, but that wasn't how he meant it. To Digby, the phrase was a three word sneer, always delivered with a tiny laugh.

'*Thnn thnn* (tiny laugh), I hardly think . . .'

Whenever an audience heard that scintillating rhetorical combination they hugged themselves, for they knew that they were in line for a searing bit of ministerial wit. They knew that Digby was ready to sock it to 'em. And he was. He squared up and shot his big gag straight through the transparent autocue.

'*Thnn thnn* (tiny laugh), I hardly think that even the *looniest* environmentalist could be so *green* . . .'

Digby paused, it was his fantastic green/naïve pun. His people assured him it would be a major woof and they had coached him meticulously to pause at this point so as not to spoil it. But there was no laugh. Digby was in that terrible place which comedians fear most of all – the gag swamp.

He hit it again.

'*Ahem, thnn thnn* (larger laugh) could be so *very green.*'

Still nothing, the murky waters were closing over him.

'*Ahhhhhm, thnn thnn thnn thnn* (huge laugh, drum roll, drop trousers and sing *Mammie*) could be so green. By which I, of course, mean *naïve.*'

That was it, he'd got 'em. Digby was enveloped in that comforting cloud of boozy, cigary, lunch-laden whiff that indicates that a thousand conference delegates have got the joke.

'. . . So green and naïve, as to question the inalienable right of every man and woman to own a motor car, if they so wish.'

## SOME MOTORISTS ARE MORE EQUAL THAN OTHERS

There are at present about five hundred million trucks and cars in the world and the Earth is literally staggering under the strain of them. Yet, in fact, only a small part of the world has yet been car colonized. Almost all of the five hundred million cars and trucks are located in the Westernized, developed world, eighty one per cent in fact.

It was lucky for Digby that the three or four billion inhabitants of China, the Soviet Union, India and South America did not turn up that afternoon at the conference and, having had their food bowls thoroughly searched, come into the hall to claim their inalienable rights. Should those populations ever achieve the levels of car ownership prevalent in the West it would undoubtedly and, as a matter of simple fact, destroy the planet. Hence, what Digby really meant was the inalienable right of every man and woman in Europe, North America and Japan to own a car if they so wish.

Fortunately for Digby his audience did not question this point. They were still explaining the green pun to each other.

Having established so eloquently the inalienable right of a person to own a car, Digby went on to argue his rights as a free born Briton to use it with the minimum of restriction.

'What is the point of a chap having the inalienable right to own a car,' he said, 'if he is not entitled to drive it where he pleases.'

This is a very worrying thought because the fastest growing area of the motor industry is that of four-wheel drive. With massively improved engineering, millions of cars now have an off-road capability. Are they to be allowed to use it? After all, the confines of a narrow road restrict a person's freedom. If a fellow is capable of nipping across a field surely it is his inalienable right to do so? If not, why build in the capability in the first place? Such an idea would not be inconsistent with present thinking. A transport policy which is prepared to happily allow a million cars into a city that physically only has room for half that number, despite the general suffering of all concerned, will eventually get round to allowing the owners of fun-top jeeps to chuck wheelies in Kew Gardens.

## TROUBLE IN THE PIPELINE

'The private motor car is a cornerstone of our very civilization,' Digby opined. 'It is, I think, our greatest triumph.'

Triumphs of civilization cut both ways of course. Perhaps the greatest triumph of Roman civilization was the plumbing. The élite of Rome gloried in it and quickly came to ask themselves how they could ever have lived without it. The water pipes satisfied their thirst and washed away their whiffies. Unfortunately for the élite of Rome, these pipes were all made of lead and it is a fair historical supposition to make that within a few short generations the once all-conquering élite of Rome were dafter than a pair of one-legged trousers. This is why they started acting so strangely and became such easy prey for savage marauders. These savage marauders had no plumbing and hence, although extremely smelly, were not dribbling, fiddling and making horses into senators when it came to a world historical shift in the balance of power.

In fairness to the élite of Ancient Rome, they were unaware of the nastier properties of lead and when Caligula started chewing his toga and claiming to be a teapot they of course didn't think to blame the plumbing. We, on the other hand, suffer no delusions as to the catastrophic consequences of failing to address the crisis of the car. The car population is expanding faster than the human one. By the year 2030 there will be a billion of them. This is unlikely to result in the appearance of smelly marauders but the social and environmental consequences will make smelly marauders seem like welcome house guests. On the other hand, as Digby often pointed out, people need their cars, so what could he do?

## A VERY PUBLIC SOLUTION

The solution of course is fantastically simple. There is a solution that would put a stop to the jams, clean up the air, massively reduce the human carnage, *and probably without even having to restrict anyone's car ownership*. The solution is public transport. But it would have to be public transport so good that most people would not dream of going to the expense of using their cars for mundane things like going to work. There would have to be tubes every minute and buses everywhere. Clean transport, safe transport with nice conductors and no chewing gum on the seats. It would have to be free if necessary, and the money saved by unchaining the cities would pay for it in time.

That is the solution; not toll roads, not private clamping firms, but public transport. Unfortunately

Digby's public transport policy was rather different, as he was about to show as he finally arrived at the crux of his speech, it concerned the railways.

' . . . And now, I come, if I may, to the subject of, *thnn thnn thnn*, Rail Transport.'

The audience shifted expectantly in their seats. This was it, the moment of excitement was approaching, they flexed their fingers and cleared their throats, ready to clap and cheer.

'Rail Transport,' Digby repeated, and he almost seemed to spit the words out. He could feel the hall go tense, it was as if the demon king had leapt up beside Digby on the platform. The faceless ones knew the villain had been introduced and they wanted to hiss and boo.

With the exception of a few sad, tired old boys at the back of the hall, the audience hated trains. Not because they were sometimes late, nor because they are often a bit dirty and the buffet runs out of everything except KitKats five minutes after leaving the first station. No, these apostles of a new morality hated trains because you can't *own* them and if you can't *own* something then how can it be worth having? That is the problem with public transport. The individual cannot own a train or a bus, they can only borrow it for the journey they want to make and at the end of it they have to give it back, and, horror of horrors, let somebody else use it. People have to share trains and also they have to pay for them, even when they are not using them themselves. The people that Digby was addressing did not want to share anything. They did not want to share health care, they did not want to share leisure amenities and they did not want to share transport.

'Trains!' shouted Digby, 'are an anachronism,' which, to give him his due was an extremely brave word to attempt in front of a thousand people and four channels of television.

'Contrast them if you will with the private motor car which is a gazelle. What do these great hulking dinosaurs have to offer us? Freedom of movement? no. Personal security and privacy? luxury, comfort and a status symbol of which the whole family can be proud? no. They offer us a form of transport where people are packed in like sardines, which is confined to narrow lines and is in danger of grinding to a halt at any moment at the behest of some horny-handed trade unionist. Let me tell you what this government intends to do with trains!' Digby thundered.

'Let me explain how we shall serve this cumbersome out-moded institution.' The audience strained forward, Digby was coming to that rare thing at a political conference, the announcement of a policy. They all knew what it was, and they could not wait. The Minister, *their* Minister was going to announce the destruction of the railways and they would give him a monumental ovation.

'What, you ask me, will the government do with

the railways?' shouted Digby, eyes wild now. Yes, yes, yes, they did ask him that, that was what they wanted to know.

'What this government intends to do with the railways . . .' said Digby, rising to a frothing, spitting, fist-thumbing crescendo, 'is . . .!!!!'

Digby froze. For a long moment the audience believed it was a dramatic pause. Then, by the look on his face, they thought he had got so excited about dismantling one of the country's greatest assets that he had had a heart attack. 'Good way to go' some of them thought.

Then they realized that he had gone mad, because Digby's next word was . . .

'Nothing.'

## A CHANGE OF PLAN

Sandy sat down again. People had been concentrating so much on the Minister's speech that they had hardly noticed the young man in the middle of the fourth row getting quietly to his feet to hold up a handbag. Out of the bag he took a red wig and a tape recorder. He held them for a moment, and then sat down.

Digby had got the message. He remembered the confessions of the previous night, and he remembered the young man who had confronted him outside his hotel. Above all, he knew that he could not announce the setting up of BritTrak. So there he stood, facing one thousand completely mystified and increasingly resentful delegates.

Where was the promised crescendo they asked themselves? Where was the rousing bit of policy that would bring them to their feet? This was what they attended conference for, or at least why they bothered to turn up for the speeches. They had done their bit by laughing at his jokes, where was the crescendo?

Digby was thinking desperately. He knew what they expected of him, but he did not know how to deliver. The whole of the rest of his speech concerned BritTrak and on that he knew he must be silent. He could see the young Scot sitting quietly in the fourth row, gently stroking a handbag. How alone Digby felt up there, how terribly exposed. He *had* to say something.

As the seconds ticked by he wracked his brains desperately. He was Minister for Transport, there must be something he could rouse them with . . . Bollards would not excite them, he doubted if zebra crossings would get them going . . . A thousand pairs of eyes were on him. The cameras of the nation turned. Digby could almost hear the commentators licking their lips.

It was an appalling moment. Complete public humiliation in front of the entire nation is a prospect likely to make a man reckless, desperate even. So it was with Digby. Into his mind drifted a vision; a vision of great beauty; one that would excite and enthrall as no dull railway policy ever could – it was the vision of a man stroking the model of a motorway flyover. And, suddenly, with the eyes of the world upon him, Digby threw caution to the winds and madness overtook him.

'What are we going to do?' he cried, breaking a silence that had lasted an eternity. 'I shall tell you what we are going to do. We are going to build roads! We are going to build roads, roads and then more roads! We are going to build roads to tunnel under roads, roads to fly over roads, roads to fly over roads flying over roads. Roads, roads, roads, roads, roads!!'

Digby could get no further. The conference was cheering and shouting, some even took up the chant, 'roads, roads, roads, roads . . .' In the television and press galleries the scribblers and wafflers went wild. This was news. This was controversial. This would split the country, it might even split the party. On the platform it was quite easy to see that there would be a split in the party, but only a small one, with Digby on one side and everybody else on the other. But that was something which Digby would face later. For the moment he was fired with evangelical fervour.

'I have plans,' he shouted. 'I have plans to make every city in Britain ten times more accessible to traffic, twenty times. Where will we put the cars you ask?' They weren't asking, they were too excited, but Digby was going to tell them anyway. 'In the parks, that's where. They're called parks aren't they? Let them live up to their name.' This also received a huge cheer, although one or two milder souls did begin to wonder. Certainly Ingmar Bresslaw wondered, as did the Prime Minister. They could see their carefully calculated plans disappearing in a wave of public protest. Digby, on the other hand, was completely intoxicated with the response he was receiving.

'Once the Channel Tunnel is fully working, people in the City, north of the Thames, are going to need ready access to that tunnel and the European Currency Units beyond. But they won't get it will they? And why not? Because South London's in the way that's why! Well not for long! I'm going to pave Brixton! I'm going to tarmac Wandsworth! I'm going to concrete Clapham! Every city centre in Britain is paralysed because you can't get your car into the shops, so what am I going to do? Shall I tell you what I am going to do? I shall knock down the shops that's what. Then I shall build huge multi-storey car-parks and put the shops on top of them.'

## COMEUPPANCE

Digby received a wonderful ovation, and, feeling rather naughty but fully justified by the response he had received, he returned to his seat on the platform. Except he didn't because there was no seat to return to – it was gone. The place was still there, between the Ministers for Housing and Health, but the chair had been removed.

'I say, have you seen my chair?' said Digby to the Minister for Housing.

Perhaps it was the noise of Digby's ovation, but the Minister for Housing did not seem to hear . . . 'My chair, have you seen it at all?' Digby shouted at the Minister for Health, but again he received no reply. Neither of his colleagues even looked at him, it was as if he was not even there.

Digby had no other choice but to leave the platform, he could not very well hang about like the last turkey in the shop. He gathered up his papers and walked with brisk dignity towards the steps that led down from the platform. He attempted in his manner to appear that he had other more urgent business to attend to and could not afford to sit about all day. Whatever impression Digby was trying to give, the one he actually gave was one of a bumbling loser . . .

He did not notice how he came to trip up, it might have been a ruck in the carpet, it might possibly have been an outstretched foot, but there he was, face planted in one of the tasteful potted plants that had been placed about the stage as the central initiative of the party's green policy.

Digby's ovation was over and the Chairperson was moving onto other business as Digby struggled to his feet grinning weakly. He reached for his briefcase. Digby distinctly remembered shutting the clips, but they were open now, and, as he picked up the case, his papers, along with a Mars bar, a little pack of tissues and a biography of Joan Crawford, flew about the platform. The Chairperson ignored the kefuffle Digby was making as he scrabbled about on the floor in front of a thousand delegates. Indeed, everybody on the platform ignored him, for Digby was now a non-person. The party's revenge for boat-rocking is swift and terrible. Without a word being said, all of Digby's colleagues knew that the oily little shit, Parkhurst, was no longer 'a member of the club.' He had opted for the wilderness and he was to be treated as a pariah.

As Digby struggled to retrieve his Mars bar, he felt a painful kick in the behind. Nobody saw it happen, the Minister for Health who delivered the blow had, like the rest of the cabinet, been to a good school and was hence highly skilled in the secret art of kicking an oik without authority being aware of it.

Digby got to his feet, his half closed briefcase under his arm, and managed to leave the platform without further incident. At the bottom of the steps Ingmar Bresslaw was waiting in terrifying silence. Ingmar's large, boozy face was red with rage. He nodded towards a small interview room just off the main hall. As Digby scuttled towards it, he began to consider for the first time just how serious his situation might be. In the heat of the moment, with a thousand delegates, first staring at him in disbelief, and then cheering him to the rafters, the size of his crime had genuinely eluded Digby. One look at Bresslaw's twitching, whiskyfied face had put him right.

'You stupid little shit,' said the Prime Minister's top henchman as he closed the door on Digby's condemned cell. 'Do you really think you can steam-roller us?'

'No really, Ingmar, it's not like that,' pleaded Digby. You see, I uhm . . . I lost my notes about BritTrak so I . . . I just filled in with a bit of harmless waffle about roads . . . Went rather well I thought.'

'Harmless waffle! You ruddy fool.' Ingmar's big bushy eyebrows quivered with indignation like two chilly black mice. Digby thought he could actually see blood vessels bursting on the man's nose as he spoke. 'That roads policy is absolute political dynamite. Half of our own party are going to be bloody uneasy about it.'

'But they . . .' Digby tried to protest.

'Cheered?' barked Ingmar Bresslaw. 'Is that what you were going to say? Cheered? Of course they cheered! This is a party conference you ruddy arse! They're supposed to bloody cheer. But wait till they start seeing lorries tearing past their garden gates. They won't all be cheering then.' Ingmar suddenly threw out two great hairy hands and grabbed Digby's lapels. Digby was almost too astonished to be scared.

'This was a back-door initiative, Parkhurst; a

Civil Service operation! The politics of confusion and deceit, a nod here, a wink there. Now you've told the entire bloody world and we will have every shitty little protest group in the country on to us. Even our own wets will summon up the courage to table a question or two. There will be protests, commissions of enquiry, the whole thing will take decades, if it ever happens at all.'

'I . . . I just thought . . . a few hints, for the faithful,' muttered Digby.

'Shut up, Parkhurst,' snarled Ingmar, his big frame tensing up so that Digby thought he might be about to be punched. 'I've heard enough of your bloody girl's voice to last me a lifetime. I never want to hear it again, do you hear? For God's sake man, what came over you? Acting independently of the party line? Who do you think you are? Winston Churchill? You got the job because the Prime Minister needed a faceless bloody nobody to front up a very delicate, and secret operation, but you got delusions didn't you? You . . . you utter . . .' he struggled for a fitting expletive . . . 'turd.'

Ingmar was truly offended by Digby's stupidity. After all, if you couldn't trust a talentless, featureless, arse-kissing git with a government ministry, who could you trust? Ingmar hauled Digby almost up onto his toes and delivered the final chop.

'You've let us down, Parkhurst, and you're finished. The Prime Minister wants your resignation by midnight, all right? Now crawl away and die.'

The big man released Digby's lapels, turned on his heels and went off in search of whisky, leaving Digby stunned.

It was so brutal, so sudden. Surely he had not given away all that much of the road plans, he had only been playing to the gallery, pleasing the troops so to speak. But a couple of hours later in his hotel room, he knew, he saw the extent of his madness. His speech was the number one story of the day, it was described as 'extraordinary' and 'maverick'.

There he stood again upon the platform, 'destroy, knock down, demolish . . . Pave, concrete, tarmac,' he shouted out of the television screen, fist thumping the air. Sitting watching it Digby was forced to confess that it did sound rather radical. Worse was to come. The Prime Minister appeared extremely cross, denying everything and deliberately getting the interviewer's name wrong. For the Prime Minister to be personally involved in the Damage Control operation showed just how seriously Digby had screwed up.

The story the party were offering was that Digby was a brilliant but erratic personality. His deep sense of public duty and extraordinary political flair, had, perhaps, combined to create a slight imbalance in his political outlook. The Opposition of course were not buying it. They claimed, as did all the environmental groups that there was no smoke without fire and that the government should come clean about its plans. This time it was Ingmar

Bresslaw who appeared, admitting that of course there were road building plans, but nothing on the scale . . .

Digby would have liked to have wept for the fate of his beautiful models but he had no tears to spare, he was weeping for himself.

# THE ROAD TO RUIN

## PART OF THE FURNITURE

Back in London, Deborah's TV was tuned to the same news broadcast that Digby was weeping over. Deborah wasn't really watching it though, she was more concerned with why Geoffrey had lain down on the carpet and was tinkering with her chair.

'What are you doing Geoffrey?' enquired Deborah. 'In fact, don't tell me what you're doing, just get the hell away from my chair all right?'

Deborah was rather sensitive about people touching and fiddling with her wheelchair as if it was an ordinary piece of furniture. She had noticed in pubs and crowds that friends sometimes used it as a coat-hanger. She knew that they meant well, they wanted to show that the chair was not an issue to them and that it did not make them feel uncomfortable, but they were also glad of somewhere to put their coats while they went off to dance. Deborah hated the way she always became the receptacle and guardian of everybody's property at a disco and she knew it was the solid fact of her chair that created this position. Another thing she had noticed was that at pub gigs, whilst watching a band or perhaps a comic, if it was a crowded, standing gig, little knots of people formed behind her, the chair (and Deborah in it) providing breathing space in an otherwise crushed room. All this was OK within reason, but Deborah's chair was not a part of the furniture, it was a part of Deborah and she didn't like it being fiddled with.

'I'm measuring it, Deborah,' stammered Geoffrey, his eyes a little hurt behind his thick glasses. 'I have to, I'm going to arm it.'

'Geoffrey,' said Deborah. 'It's a wheelchair, I don't want it to have arms, they'll get stuck in doorways.'

'I don't mean arms as in "arms",' Geoffrey replied firmly, although Deborah did not really register this firmness because Geoffrey's chin was bashing against his collar-bone and she was having enough trouble following what he was saying without trying to work out the subtlety of his intonations.

'I mean arms as in arms dealer, arms race, arms treaty,' said Geoffrey.

'You mean guns?' said Deborah horrified.

'Well, guns might be difficult, but weapons certainly,' Geoffrey stuttered. 'Listen Deborah, I mean really, listen. I'm putting you in a lot of danger here, those men really did try to kill me.

Satan is dealing from a rigged deck and some sucker's going to draw the dead man's hand. I have to make sure that the sucker isn't you.'

'If you're going to keep saying "sucker" Geoffrey, go get a saucer. You can't say it without dribbling,' Deborah replied. 'Personally I think you're being melodramatic.'

'Well, maybe about Satan and the dead man's hand,' conceded Geoffrey, 'but not about the danger. It's real Deborah and it's coming for us . . .' He snapped shut his tape-measure and, using his good hand, wrote down figures in a school exercise book which he had wedged under a wheel of Deborah's chair. Of course, on reflection, Deborah didn't really think it was that melodramatic either. After all, they did both seem to have been thrust into a web of murder and deception. She supposed it was not an entirely unreasonable thing to consider protecting one's self.

'OK James Bond, so what are you going to give me, I'm all out of machine guns,' said Deborah.

'Oh there's lots of stuff around the house that I can improvise with.'

'Great,' said Deborah. 'What do I get? A mounted ballistic food processor, maybe I can blend them to death. Perhaps you could tune up the Hoover, I could suck the guns out of their hands. Listen Geoffrey, if things really are this dangerous, I think we need to make some plans here. For instance, once you've designed the engine, what then?'

'I'm going to sneak out at dead of night, maybe in a raincoat and a Homburg hat, and take it to Greenpeace or Friends of the Earth.'

'Why?' said Deborah.

'Well I just think that sneaking secret inventions around is very Dick Tracy and it's important to make the effort.'

'Not the hat and coat, why the green thing? What's it got to do with a bunch of lentil munchers?' Deborah said.

'Well, it's a pretty clear bet,' said Geoffrey conspiratorally, 'that someday soon my stolen invention is going to be introduced to the world by a part of the car industry. When that happens it's going to revolutionize private motoring. It will be worth millions to whoever claims to have thought of it.'

Deborah still couldn't quite follow the green angle.

'So what you have to do,' she insisted, 'is to reinvent it double quick and sell it to the motor industry yourself, you could do with a few million. Believe me bud, the rent on this place gets higher every minute.'

'If you do a deal with the devil,' said Geoffrey piously, 'you had better be ready to end up being impaled on fiery stakes and having your sweaty bits nibbled by his tiny crawling demons.'

'What?' enquired Deborah, not unreasonably.

'If I sold my engine to Dagenham or Detroit they

would use it on private cars and nothing but private cars and, if it's as good as I think it is, which is bloody brilliant, twenty years from now we'd just have a world clogged up with hydrogen cars instead of petrol cars.'

'So bully for the world, Geoffrey,' insisted Deborah. 'You said yourself that these engines burn cleaner. Call me an earth mother and stick my face in a vegetarian casserole if you like, but that sounds like good news to me.'

'Oh yes, and where would that leave us?' asked Geoffrey.

'Rich.' Deborah was a practical girl.

'But you'd still be a prisoner in your own city,' Geoffrey said. 'People like you and me are the best example of how too many cars isolate people. You can't use a bus, it's tough to get on a train, a lot of taxis can't take chairs, and that's because all anybody cares about is cars, cars, bloody cars.'

'Yes but I'm disabled Geoffrey, remember? Not everyone is like me.'

'Everybody is disabled by cars!' insisted Geoffrey.

'Geoffrey excuse me, but did you leave a door open in your brain here? Cars carry people around you know? They don't disable people, they *enable* them to get around – especially people like me. What's more, if you were rich you could buy me a great big car, a limmo with a chair lift and a chauffeur and a bar and a swimming pool. So just cut the philosophy OK? and hurry up and reinvent your stupid engine because the sooner I'm outta my converted Ford and into a stretch Mercedes the better.'

And with that, Deborah wheeled herself into the kitchen and filled the kettle from the hose attached to her tap. Her kettle could not move because it was attached to a clever little tilting platform that made pouring easier. Geoffrey followed Deborah into the kitchen.

'Do cars *enable* the woman with a ton of shopping waiting at the bus stop for the bus that never comes?' he shouted.

'So now he's onto Communism already,' said an exasperated Deborah, struggling with the lid of a new coffee jar that would have given Mr Universe a limp wrist. 'They tried Communism in Russia, Geoffrey, their buses were worse than ours and everybody had to eat cabbage for the rest of their lives.'

Geoffrey would not be side-tracked by red, red herrings.

'Do cars *enable* the people who live on main routes and have to listen to traffic all night? Do they enable old people who can't cross roads, or have to walk miles extra to find a crossing? Do they *enable* the five thousand people killed each year in Britain, or the forty thousand in the US? Above all Deborah, do they *enable* the hundreds of thousands of people stuck in jams every day? I mean do they really? or do people just think they do?'

Having finally got the lid off the coffee, Deborah was attempting very gently to penetrate the foil vacuum seal with her thumb. After she had done that she had to brush away all the coffee that had exploded into her lap . . . 'I think they spring-load these mothers!' she moaned before returning to the topic of the day. 'Listen Geoffrey, get real OK? People love cars, I love cars and if you manage to stop your engine being used, I'm here to tell ya, they'll just carry on making dirty old petrol ones.'

'Deborah, look at yourself,' said Geoffrey. 'You can't walk, and the reason you can't walk is because of a car that caught you at a pedestrian crossing. They called it a pedestrian crossing, but it wasn't built for people. It was built for cars, just like everything else. Whoever I sell my engine to . . .'

'Presuming you can reinvent it before these murderers get you, which isn't going to happen while you're delivering the sermon on the mount,' said Deborah. She was struggling with a milk carton and it was only after she'd had to resort to trying to chew it open that she realized that she'd been attacking the bit that says 'open other side'.

'Yes, always presuming that,' conceded Geoffrey. 'Whoever I sell it to is going to have to sign a contract saying that it will only be used to make buses . . .'

'What!' Deborah could not help but laugh.

'Or . . . or, I don't know . . . for every ten cars they make they've got to make a train coach, or at least that only one can be sold to each household, or that it can't be used in heavy freight lorries, I don't know, something. Don't you see Deborah, it's a question of beginning to change people's attitudes.'

'Look, Geoffrey,' said Deborah, deciding to have a can of Diet Coke instead. 'You can't force people to build buses. This is the free world, they can build what they like.'

'Not with my bloody engine they can't,' announced Geoffrey. 'Have you ever heard of Gridlock, Deborah?'

'Geoffrey, I come from New York, of course I've heard of Gridlock,' she snapped. Gridlocks had indeed originally been a US phenomenon. They emerged for the first time in Los Angeles in the late seventies and occur when the grids of roads (or spaghetti of roads as they are in towns like London) become jammed at a series of junctions, meaning that cars cannot escape. The jam then feeds back, blocking more junctions and hence causing further jams. The size of the Gridlock is dependent only on the number of cars feeding into the jam and how quickly the police can close the roads leading into it.

'London is heading for a super-jam,' said Geoffrey, 'so is every car city in the world. It would only take a couple of accidents to happen at the same time in peak traffic; a jack-knife on the Cromwell Road, a couple of smashes on the bridges, a pile up at the mouth of the M1 or Shepherds Bush maybe

– virtually anywhere actually. It would only take a coincidence and the whole city would be massively disabled. Just like us eh?'

'Very funny,' said Deborah.

At that point the front door slammed and a footfall was heard in the hall. 'It's only Toss, Geoffrey,' said Deborah. 'Come out from behind the sofa.'

## HIGHWAY MAN

The door opened and in walked Toss in his traffic warden uniform. 'I have to tell you guy, that I was wicked today.' He threw his traffic warden cap onto a hook and put on a baseball cap – actually he missed the hook and the cap hit the ground.

'Toss,' said Deborah, 'pick the damn hat up.'

'OK guy, it's happening, y'nah what I mean?' replied an aggrieved Toss. 'But like you know, it's only my warden lid, its not a bomb or nuffink, right Spas?'

'Right Toss,' replied Geoffrey emerging from behind the sofa. 'Personally I'm into spatial anarchy. Mess is God's way of telling us we have too much stuff.'

'Totally good point, Spas,' said Toss, getting a litre of juice from the fridge. 'You're a philosopher you know that? You should have your own show on Channel Four.'

'What am I talking to, the three wise monkeys

here? Listen Toss,' said Deborah with quiet menace, 'I have told you till my tonsils have worn out that the reason I don't want your stupid stuff on the floor is because it snags my stupid wheelchair. If you left a hat and a coat on the floor in every room of this stupid flat I would not be able to fuck'n' well move!' Deborah's voice was rising to a crescendo. 'I don't *enjoy* having to talk like I'm your fuck'n' mother, Toss! I'm only twenty-one-years-old! Twenty-one-year-olds should not have to spend their time worrying about whether little scheisters like you pick their hats up or not, but I do have to worry about it because otherwise I shall become trapped for ever in a cave made entirely of your socks and stinking underwear! So *pick things up*! Or I swear I shall personally get two shoe boxes full of wet cement and stick them on your feet when you're asleep. See how you like being anchored to the carpet!'

Toss picked up his hat, 'Nice speech Debbo, happening. I appreciate the point, although, right, it's not necessary to chuck a total mental.'

Toss was Deborah's lodger, he had been home to his mother's for the weekend, which was why he had not been there the previous night.

Deborah had taken a lodger the moment she found her place. She knew that her compensation would take years, and money was tight. Money is incredibly important to people with disabilities. You will never ever hear a person with disabilities say 'money doesn't mean much to me'. Money means mobility, money means independence and personal dignity. Yet, for a person with disabilities, money is much more difficult to come by. Toss had been a lucky find. A year younger than Deborah, he was kind and easy going.

His job had surprised Deborah at first.

'What do you do?' she had asked.

'I hang out, girl. I chill,' replied Toss.

'No, I mean for a living,' said Deborah, wondering about somebody who hung out and chilled's ability to pay the rent.

'Oh that, right? I'm a traffic warden, and I am *wicked with a ticket*, girl, all right? Just the best. Don't mess with Toss when he's got his cap on because I take no prisoners!' said Toss proudly.

'A traffic warden?' This had not been what Deborah had expected at all.

'You have a problem, girl? Are you some kind of libertarian geezer who reckons it is her democratic right to park on top of babies' heads? Is that it? Because then I am your enemy, girl, and you'd better hide right now, because the ticket of Toss has your number on it,' said Toss.

Actually, being a person who could not walk and who lived in one of the busiest cities in the world, Deborah had good reason to support those who enforced the parking laws, particularly those laws concerning disabled parking places which people often pinch. It is, however, important to remember that they do not do this out of any desire to nab a convenient space. Of course not, no, they do it out of a morally courageous desire to pay back the charlatans, scroungers and malingerers who they personally *know* to be in possession of ninety per cent of all disabled car stickers.

*Of course* they accept that there are *genuinely disabled* people and they would not *dream* of depriving them of a place, but really, sometimes, you *do wonder*. After all, are these people *really* so disabled? Lots of people get aches and pains, they don't all go putting stickers on their cars.

It was because of this type of thinking that Deborah had no objection to traffic wardens, she was merely surprised to discover that Toss was one.

'I just thought that a cool, black guy like you, would be a DJ or something,' she added.

Toss looked at Deborah slightly pityingly, as a fond uncle might look at an idiot child, or an MP might look at a constituent.

'Listen, girl, you're not thinking straight right? You have not thought this one through at all. Let me ask you this. If all the cool geezers was doing the Scratchin' and the Mixin' and the 'ooh get down-in' right? Then who would there be to get down? Who would there be to strut? No one, that's who. Check out the theory, girl, it's watertight.'

'So why a traffic warden?' asked Deborah, who could not fault Toss's disco theory.

'Because, girl, I like the streets. I like to cruise around and hang and chill and check things out.

This way I get to do it all day, *and* I get a wicked uniform, know what I mean,' and Toss laughed, 'aha ha ha.'

'Is your name really Toss?' asked Deborah who wanted to get everything sorted out at once.

'Nah, it's Tosh, Harold Wilson Tosh. But all the kids at school, right? they called me Toss. Which is understandable, y'nah what I mean? Because like Tosh to Toss is only one letter change to turn it into a wicked joke you see, girl? So I said to them, I said OK guys, you can call me Toss right, because right, and get this, because right, *I don't give a* . . . Wicked riposte, right? Aha ha ha.' Toss had clearly told this one before, and it had not improved with age.

'Quite wicked,' said Deborah rather doubtfully, and she let Toss have her spare room. That had been three years ago and Toss had not changed.

'Toss,' said Deborah, 'Geoffrey's going to have to stay here for a while. There are some people trying to kill him,' Deborah added.

'Don't worry about it, Geoffrey,' said Toss. 'You'll get used to it. I'm a traffic warden, I have people trying to kill me every day.'

'No, Toss,' said Geoffrey. 'Really trying to kill me.'

'Exactly, guy, that's what I'm saying,' replied Toss. 'I need a gun, I need armour and a gun. A traffic warden is at the *sharp end* of the twentieth century guy. When the dust settles, we *are* the enforcers, the last line of law. After us man, it's anarchy. We are *that* close to the edge,' and Toss proferred his thumb and forefinger to emphasize his point. 'They should do a film you know? it would be wicked! Clint Eastwood as a traffic warden, right? He gives this car a ticket OK? thus keeping open the city's life-lines, and letting the ambulance with the little girl in a coma get to hospital, right? Then the geezer who owns the car comes up with his portable phone and his cheese and ham croissant, and his Psion organizer . . .'

'Yeah, Toss . . .' Geoffrey attempted to interject, but Toss was on a roll.

'And the guy starts crying right? He says "Oh go on mate, let me off, I've only been gone three and a half days, I'll move it now. Go on mate, be a mate". And Clint says, "Sorry Guvnor, but it's the law. I'm really sorry, but I have to do it." And the guy says, "Well you little fucking shit, give 'em a uniform they think they're fucking Hitler. I hope you die of cancer, Cunt!" And then Clint gets out his Magnum and says, "I keep the city alive arsehole, and you're dead." Then he shoots the geezer and has his VW Golf crushed up into a tiny cube. It'd be a brilliant film, wouldn't it?'

Toss spent his entire day being either pleaded with or vilified, and, like many people in high-stress jobs, he tended to take his work home with him.

'It is mayhem out there! The minute word goes round that anything above fifteen inches of London

192

kerbstone has become vacant it is a battle zone, guy! They're all screaming "mine, mine" and spitting and snarling and throwing boiled sweets and road atlases at each other. People will *kill* to park! They will kill *themselves* to park. There are geezers out there will eat their own *testicles* to get just one wheel within a yard of the pavement, you hear what I'm saying? We are talking Conan the Barbarian in a Vauxhall Astra! He is growing horns and a forked tail here! He is a *Panzer Commander*! Left hand down, right hand down, left hand down, right hand down, left hand down, right hand . . .'

'Toss!!' said Deborah.

'Both hands down at the same time.'

'The point is, Toss,' said Geoffrey 'there's just too many private cars.'

'You telling me!' said Toss. 'It's like trying to get fifteen heads into the same hat, it *cannot be done*!!'

'Well exactly,' said Geoffrey, 'and what we as a society have to do . . .'

Deborah could stand it no longer and decided to go out for a drive.


## CAREER STALLED

Having turned off the news Digby sat alone in his hotel room for hours, until eventually steeling himself to the awful task of writing a letter of resignation – a letter that would end his meteoric political career. Wearily he crossed to the writing desk. The chocolate wafer which the maid had left beside the kettle, and was going to be his treat, seemed hollow now (it was), the neat little soaps occasioned him no glee, his life was over.

'My Dear Prime Minister,' he began, pausing to consider the correct wording for such a momentous letter. 'Deeply though I regret that our long association . . .' There was a rustle of paper. Somebody had pushed a note under his door. Digby picked it up and read it, there was not much to read.

'From the Office of the Prime Minister. Please be informed that your resignation as Minister for Transport has been accepted.'

It was the cruellest blow of all. Not even an 'I shall always appreciate your friendship'. Drink/ Drive resignations were treated more kindly than this. Tears welled up in Digby's eyes and as they dropped onto the Prime Minister's note, or rather the note from the Prime Minister's office for it was not even signed, Digby had but one thought in his head – to get Sam Turk, the man he wrongly believed had destroyed him.

Why had Turk done it? Hadn't Digby apologized enough? Why destroy him? and in such a cruel cynical manner too. Such a wicked, vicious blow to deliver; to destroy him over railways! What vindictive irony, to force Digby to sacrifice his entire career in transport over a railways announcement!

Digby could not even take any satisfaction from the thought that Turk would be as irritated, by the

spoke that Digby's improvised speech had put in the
road wheel, as Ingmar Bresslaw had been. All he
knew was that Turk's punishment of Digby for
ticking him off over the Patents Office break-in had
been terrible indeed. A huge, cruel, unjustified
punishment far in excess of Digby's crime. Digby
swore he would remember Sam Turk for what,
Digby supposed, Turk had done. And Digby did.

## CRISES IN THE BUNKER

Way way above Digby's head, in every sense of the
word, at the top of the hotel, in the Prime Minister's
penthouse bunker, a crisis meeting was in progress.
The Prime Minister and the Home Secretary were
listening to Simon Rodney Butterface in gloomy
silence. Ingmar Bresslaw was also in attendance,
plus one or two other Ministers – empty suits so
lacking in distinction that at times it was possible to
forget that they were in the room at all.

Simon Rodney Butterface was the Chairman of
the Party. He was considered an intellectual, which,
by the sad standards of the cabinet of the time,
meant that he knew who Shakespeare was. It was
Simon Rodney Butterface's job to ensure that the
party would be re-elected at the next election. A job
which, up until now, had merely involved delivering
the official pompous sneer at anything that the
Leader of the Opposition said and sending his long,
damp tongue slithering along the corridors of certain

'proudly independent' British newspapers until it located an editor's anus in which to gently insert itself. Not arduous tasks by any means, and Simon Rodney Butterface had, up until the evening in question, had plenty of time to work on a slim volume of verse he was compiling entitled *The Glory that is England*. However, tonight was different. The party was in crisis and Simon Rodney Butterface's plump face sweated under his Brylcreemed hair.

'Parkhurst's speech was a disaster, Prime Minister,' he was saying. 'As I know you are aware, we were absolutely counting on the secret Road Building Agenda to provide a short term financial stimulus in the run-up to the next election. The sort of plans we were preparing to sneak through would have provided up to half a million extra jobs. If we cancel our plans, the result will be that we will fight the next General Election with the true state of the economy obvious to the electorate, in which case of course we will lose.'

The Prime Minister visibly blanched at this gruesome reminder of political mortality.

'Oh I'm quite sure we could never lose with you at the helm Prime Minister,' slobbered one of the faceless, empty-suited Ministers on the fringe of the meeting.

'Who the hell are you?' enquired the Prime Minister, noticing the speaker for the first time.

'That is your Minister for Agriculture, Prime Minister,' murmured Ingmar Bresslaw.

'Don't shout, Ingmar,' said the Prime Minister, a murmur from Ingmar Bresslaw being something akin to a town-crier who has been given a packet of throat pastilles and a megaphone for his birthday.

The Home Secretary spoke up.

'We have to cancel the plans. They were dependent on the legislation we've been pushing through Committee on reducing the influence of the public on public enquiries. Thanks to Parkhurst everyone will be able to see that for what it is now, a transparent ploy to pave the way for unrestricted road building. Even if we force it past our lot by getting the Whips to chew a few backbench bollocks, the rural lords will junk it, they don't want motorways through their game parks . . .'

'But Prime Minister,' pleaded Simon Rodney Butterface, 'we have to press on and damn the reaction. Quite apart from the fact that if we don't there will be nothing to cover up the recession, there is the road lobby to consider. Road lobby contributions to party funds are some of the most generous we receive. I can assure you we shall lose those contributions if we renege on our sworn promise to deliver road contracts.'

'Prime Minister we have no choice!' insisted the Home Secretary. 'The public will never accept such radical plans.'

'Then the public must be forced to accept them,' said the stern voice of Ingmar Bresslaw.

'Ingmar,' replied the Home Secretary testily, 'I

bow to none in my appreciation of your power and influence, but I fear that even the mightiest mandarin in the Civil Service cannot force the British public to accept the wholesale concreting of their country.'

'I can make them plead for it, Home Secretary. And I am going to.'

'And how, may I ask, do you propose to do that?' enquired the Home Secretary.

'People have got it too damn easy at the moment,' replied Ingmar. 'What we require is a transport crisis. A transport crisis of such proportions that the apathetic public will scream for action, drowning out the shrill voices of the environmentalists.'

'So what do you propose to do?' asked the Home Secretary. 'Sit around and wait for a gridlock, hoping it falls before the next General Election?'

'Oh I think we can be more specific than that,' replied Ingmar.

## Chapter Thirteen

# SERIAL KILLER

## THE PINTO PROBLEM

Whilst Geoffrey Spasmo camped out at Deborah's place, working on the transport of the future, Sam Turk, the man who had forced him into hiding, was considering the problems of the transport of today. He was in his hotel conducting a cost evaluation exercise with his lawyers. Inwardly, of course, he knew that once he set in motion the grand plan, of which Geoffrey's engine was the centre, problems such as the one he was presently dealing with would be small fry indeed.

However, he was still head of Global Motors UK and there were appearances to be kept up.

The debate surrounded the Mark II Crappee which was to be released four years hence. Antilock, non-skid braking really should be included, but it would be expensive. What Sam wanted to know was, would Global Motors be in any way liable for the higher levels of death and injury which would inevitably follow from not fitting the brakes? and if yes, would the damages that ensued be greater or less than the enormous cost of retooling?

This simple debate Sam, who knew his motoring folklore, called the Pinto problem. The Pinto problem was first pointed out by a man named Ralph Nader who noticed that the Ford Pinto had a fuel tank located under the sill of the boot, which would turn the car into a fireball when hit by even quite gentle shunts. Ralph reasoned that, since Ford must know that they had a problem, they must be debating whether it was cheaper to change the car or let people die and fight the damages in the court.

That was the Pinto problem, and Sam was facing it again, just as he faced it with every new car launch, because, in fact, the anti-lock braking under discussion had been around for forty years. The question had always been whether it was worth putting it in. So far the answer had been 'no'. It was 'no' with the Crappee and it had been 'no' with its predecessor, the Moritz, which was why Deborah faced a lifetime without the use of her legs.

## RECYCLING

Yes, the Global Crappee had killed before and would kill again. It had been killing for years. It had not been caught and brought to book because it had committed its earlier crimes under a different name. Then it had been known as the Global Moritz.

But surely not? After all, as anyone remotely interested in cars knew, the Moritz was a classic of the old school and the Crappee a modern upstart? How could anyone possibly equate the two cars in any way, let alone suggest that they are to all intents and purposes the same car?

The Mark I Moritz had been introduced in 1965 and it was considered by those who love it to be the greatest flower in the Global garden.

The Mark II, which followed in 1971, is also held in deep affection. In some inner cities it is known as the Blackman's Rolls Royce because it is favoured by slick and cool young Blacks. The Mark III, although much more recent and hence less imbued with irrational nostalgia also has its *aficionados*. Basically, the Moritz, originally conceived as an unglamorous family car, had, with the passage of time and the adoption of second and third hand models by groovy youths, become very cool. It is certain that none of those who love and cherish the Moritz, who polish it, tune it and hang fluffy dice from the mirror of it, would be seen dead in one of these crappy new Crappees.

'Not as throaty,' they would say, 'not as gutsy,' they would add, 'no bollocks to speak of whatsoever.' Which shows just how stupid people blinded by style can be, because the Moritz and the Crappee are definitely the same car.

This fact came about as a solution to the principal problem that all mass car manufacturers encounter, which is the colossal cost of retooling their empires to produce something actually new. Consider the dilemma faced at Global Motors UK in 1971, some six years after the Moritz had crashed onto the market and established itself as the top selling family four-door in Britain, and some eighteen months since a disturbing fall in sales had first been noted. A drop of sales which strenuous market research revealed having been caused by a growing perception that the Moritz was rather old hat and very much a sixties car. The young seventies family man listening to Bowie's 'A Space Oddity' on his eight-track cartridge player was loathe to purchase the same car that his fifty-five-year-old father might own.

The solution was simple, of course: produce a new family saloon. Six years had, after all, seen definite innovations in performance and safety. Unfortunately this solution was entirely out of the question. Global Motors UK had hundreds of millions tied up in equipment and facilities that could only produce the Moritz. To start all over again with an entirely new car would mean re-equipping all their factories, and re-designing all the machinery. Faced with this horrendous prospect the Global executives decided to forget about the idea of a new car and just carry on making the old one.

And so, in 1971, came the Mark II Moritz. It looked like a new car, it was advertised as a new car, but it was in fact the same car with much more curve over the wheel arches and different shaped brake lights.

In 1977 came the Mark III, exactly the same car again, except this time, rather squarer and carrying major glove compartment innovations. This sold well until 1984 when with great fanfare Global Motors again introduced to the world exactly the same car but with radically improved rear windscreen shape and on the Ghia model, a challenging third ashtray.

Certainly there had been improvements, of course the technology surrounding cars had changed, but basically, it was the same car.

And so, after four versions of the Moritz, Global Motors UK arrived at the nineties and the momentous decision to cancel the old faithful, to put an end finally, once and for all, to a much loved motoring legend. There were nostalgic articles in the papers, an unpleasantly trendy documentary 'appreciation' on the telly, where a lot of expensively hair-cutted journos, singers and comedians established their working class credentials by going on about how much they cherished the memory of their Mark I Moritz and what 'a bleeding serious motor' the Mark II had been. All in all, there was a deal of ballyhoo and the Moritz was regretfully laid to rest never to appear again. . . . Until the following month when the Moritz Mark V was introduced, except it was called the Crappee. And what Sam Turk had to decide was, when they brought the

Crappee out again in a couple of years' time, should they fit better brakes?

## THE FRIDAY CAR

One Moritz is particularly relevant to this story. It was a blue Mark III, bought new in 1978 by a Mr and Mrs Sinclair who kept it till 1985. This particular Mark III was what they call a 'Friday afternoon car', i.e., a car that has endless niggling problems and is hence deemed to be a car made in a rush on Friday afternoon when everybody is really bored with the work and no longer gives a toss. Actually the car had been assembled on a Tuesday morning and had endless niggling problems because everybody was really bored with the work and no longer gave a toss. It was Henry Ford who invented the Friday afternoon car, and also the Tuesday morning car.

After Henry Ford, every car was built on a metaphorical Friday afternoon when everyone was really bored with the work and didn't give a toss. For it was old Hank Ford who, after deep thought and much experimentation, perfected a brilliant system whereby the life of a car worker could be rendered catastrophically boring. After years of painstaking research Henry invented a process so brilliant in reducing the quality of millions of people's working lives to crucifyingly turgid, tedious wage-slavery, that he was rewarded by becoming one of the world's richest men. True, he paid well and his assembly line methods made it possible to produce cheaper cars, hence making them widely available (a rather mixed blessing as things turned out), but the human price was considerable. With his revolutionary production line process Henry reduced his workers to being merely the most sophisticated machines on the factory floor.

Having introduced the production line, Henry, like most other car makers was surprised by the level of industrial militancy he encountered. Auto workers, over the years, have often gone on strike. Almost exclusively, these strikes have been over wage claims, causing many, not least the employers, to complain that auto workers are concerned with nothing more than money, caring not a jot for either company or product. In this complaint the employers are, of course, right. However, in expecting *esprit de corps* on the production line they are pushing it somewhat. It is too much to ask of an individual who has been deprived of every possible emotional and intellectual connection with the job he is doing that he should then take a pride in it.

## S'GONNACOSTYAGUVNA

So the Sinclairs had their Tuesday morning/Friday afternoon car for seven years, during which time it led a pretty unremarkable existence. It went to work, helped with the shopping, did Europe on four occasions and spent an inordinate amount of time at various garages where men in blue overalls would stare at it sadly, suck in their breath through pursed lips and say, as if it broke their hearts, 'S'gonnacost-yaguvna'.

Mr Sinclair had heard the phrase 'S'gonnacost-yaguvna' so often he felt it should be his epitaph. He informed his wife that when he died he wished to be cremated, for fear that any preparation for burial might involve a pimply, eighteen-year-old undertaker poking around the corpse for a while before sadly informing Mrs Sinclair that the job would take a fortnight and that he couldn't guarantee a result seeing as how the corpse had clearly been carelessly handled in the past, and above all, it was definitely gonna cost her.

## BACK SEAT WRITHING

The Sinclairs were careful drivers and during the seven years they owned the dodgy Moritz they bucked national trends by having no accidents in it at all. The car itself suffered one minor scratch at the hands of Sean, the Sinclairs' eighteen-year-old son. He was in the process of getting down to things with his girlfriend when their clumsy writhing about accidentally released the hand brake and the car rolled a few feet backwards into a tree.

This accident is important because it may serve partly to debunk one of the most enduring myths of motor transport. The myth that it is comparatively simple and also deeply desirable to have it off in the back seat. Anybody who has found themselves trying to do the business with one foot out of the window, the other one stuck in the glove compartment and the gear stick up the arse, will know that they have been conned.

In the USA where the legend began, back seat banging was once possible in comparative comfort. There was a time when Detroit turned out great football-pitch sized cars with enormous, bench-back seats and open tops to allow for the ecstatic extension of a leg. Way, way back, in the great American decade you really could do it in a Buick, get pawed in a Ford and have it away in a Chevrolet – certainly then, but not now. Sadly, you can do fuck all in a Vauxhall.

Yet the myth remains, the goal to which the whole of adolescent America seems to have aspired these four decades past, hasn't changed and, since what is teencool in the USA is by definition teencool everywhere else, the shagg'n' waggon lives. Cars are still sexy.

## TURBO CHARGED TACKLE

The great racer Stirling Moss claimed that there are two things a man will never admit he does badly, drive and make love. Which is a strange irony, because most people are not particularly good at either. None the less Stirling was probably right, it is difficult to imagine a bloke in a pub saying, 'I nearly caused an accident last night then went home and couldn't get it up'.

It isn't just adolescent dreams that connect motoring and sex. It is a reality re-enhanced through every aspect of marketing from bikini clad girls at motor shows to husband/wife power games in Renault ads. The sales people would have us believe that the connection is that, like sex, motoring involves surging, powerful rhythmic motivation, ease, space and freedom of movement. This, of course, had nothing to do with most people's experiences of driving, or indeed sex. Perhaps a more realistic explanation of why driving is like sex is because it involves an awful lot of hanging around, followed by a bit of vague shunting, a great deal of frustration, and a brief, desperate surge before grinding to a dirty, sticky halt again.

It is said that the car is a phallic symbol. It is often claimed that the shape and aerodynamics of sports and racing cars are reminiscent of the penis. Well, whoever it was who first coined this extraordinary equation must have packed something very strange indeed in his pants, or else possessed a car that was slightly banana shaped. The E-type Jaguar is reckoned by car image makers to be the most phallic of all cars. Well all right, it's longer than it is wide, but really and truly it's about as phallic as a coffee-table. When people look at an E-type, they might marvel at its slick lines and wickedly smooth contours, but it is only conditioning that would make any bloke ever say 'that looks like my nob'. In fact there has only ever been one popular (as opposed to image-created) equation between the sexual organs and a motor car and that was in the 1950s, in the USA, when Ford produced the Edsel, the greatest single failure of any car ever. Years in preparation, meticulously conceived and designed: it none the less completely flopped. Market research produced the stunning revelation that the radiator grill reminded people of a vagina and that was why they weren't buying it. No doubt, if the E-type Jag had *really* reminded people of a todger they wouldn't have bought that either. The moral of the story is that people like their sexual organs in their underwear, not in their garage.

## THE MORITZ FULFILS ITS DESTINY

Anyway, the Sinclairs had the dent, that Sean's ardour had caused, hammered out and it cost them. A year or two later, they decided to purchase the all new Mark IV Moritz, and sold their Mark III to Bob, a watch salesman. Bob already had a nice new company car. The Moritz was to be for fun, he was going to customize it, which he did, jacking up the rear end and installing a huge bendy aerial that stretched in a great loop from one end of the car to the other.

Bob was a great driver. He had had numerous prangs and near misses in his motoring life and *not one* of them had been his fault. It was an extraordinary thing but whenever he was forced to swerve, or the other bloke was forced to swerve, or brakes were jammed on, or horns were beeped, not once, ever, had it been Bob's fault.

'Did you see that stupid bastard?' Bob would say to his long suffering girlfriend, 'Chelle.

As Bob often said to his mates, he was content to drive at high speeds because he knew that he could handle a motor. What did worry him, however, was that some stupid bastard who should not be allowed on the road, might cause an accident in which Bob was involved. Bob's mates all agreed wholeheartedly with this fear, it haunted them too.

Another aspect of Bob's extraordinary powers behind the wheel was that drink did not affect them. Bob *strongly* disapproved of drinking and driving. He detested it, after all, a kiddie might be involved. Yes, he felt it was a disgusting practice, *for those who could not handle it*. If you couldn't handle your booze then you were a bloody idiot to drink and drive, that was not negotiable. Bob, however, could handle his booze, obviously not to ridiculous excess, although he would admit that he had driven completely legless on more than one occasion, but he conceded that that was naughty and he certainly did not do it any more. But two or three pints, maybe four, followed by just a half, 'because he's driving', did not affect Bob. No, if he, or his mates watched their drinking when they had the car it was simply to avoid being nicked. *No way* were they unfit to drive. In fact, Bob reckoned that he was a considerably better driver when pissed than most of the wankers on the road when sober.

Anyway Bob did the Mark III Moritz up a picture and slammed it straight into Deborah. The Sinclairs' dear old car, which had only had one scratch in twelve years, suddenly, out of the blue, crippled a young woman for life.

Of course, it wasn't Bob's fault, *no way* was it Bob's fault. This arsehole in front slammed on his anchors at a crossing, right? Even though it was green, Bob swerved to avoid him and hit this American bird who shouldn't even have been there!

In fact, what had happened was that Bob was approaching a pelican crossing which he guessed would be green by the time he arrived at it. There was a car in front stopped at the crossing, but Bob presumed that this car would be underway at any moment, thus relieving Bob of the necessity of actually stopping. Bob was hoping to do the whole thing without having to drop lower than third gear.

However, as he approached the lights, the car in front failed to move. Despite the fact that the orange signal was now flashing it remained stationary. Bob had not seen anybody step onto the crossing so why was the wanker not moving off? It was of course the old explanation, thought Bob, people were such terrible bloody drivers.

The reason Bob had seen no one start onto the crossing was that Deborah had actually begun to cross a few moments previously and she was struggling with eight new books which she had just bought. One of the great student thrills at the beginning of the first term is buying all the important looking books on the reading list. Most of the books remain unread forever of course. All ex-students have a few books on their shelves that are basically brand new, except the price on the back is 35p. None the less, it is a great buzz to buy them and feel like a real intellectual, just for a moment. Deborah having had great fun in the shop acting terribly earnest and brainy was trying to get her haul home when she dropped one of the books on the crossing and was forced to try and pick it up without upsetting all of her other purchases. This process, of course, took a few moments and by the time she had finished the little green walking man had changed to the little red standing man. However, of course, Deborah had no choice but to proceed.

Bob couldn't believe it as he neared the lights. The yellow had stopped flashing and the light was actually *green*, why did the stupid bastard not pull away? Well one thing was for certain, Bob was not going to stop just because some other wanker did not know how to drive. So he slammed the Moritz down into second, accelerated round the stationary car, just as Deborah emerged from in front of it, and broke Deborah's spine. Bob of course tried to brake but, perhaps due to the absence of an anti-lock system, only succeeded in skidding.

Deborah had only been in England for a fortnight.

## Chapter Fourteen

# THE MAN
# AND THE DOLL

## MOTOR CITY

Sam Turk took Concorde to New York and then a private Lear Jet to Detroit.

'Welcome to Motor City' a sign said, and some wag had sprayed 'Greetings honourable colleague' over the word 'welcome' in a reference to the manner in which the once mighty US motor industry now found itself desperately aping the Japanese.

Industrial dominance was a hard thing to fathom, Sam thought to himself as he took the chopper to the Global building. Why, it wasn't thirty years since the USA was such an economic power it didn't seem as if it could ever end. How do these things happen? A hundred years before, the British had been the Japanese, so to speak. After them, in the middle of the century, the people of the United States were unquestionably the Japanese. These days, perhaps rather ironically, the Japanese themselves were the Japanese. Who would be the

Japanese next thought Sam? Probably the Germans, but you can never tell.

## LIVING DOLL

From the Helipad, Sam went directly to the palatial office of his boss, Bruce Tungsten, 'Mr Automobile', the President of Global Motors.

Sam had not been expecting to be greeted with open arms and nor was he. 'Bruce, Bruce, Bruce,' he said affably, striding across the huge office to greet his long-time colleague and boss. 'Bruce, Bruce, Bruce,' he added as he continued to cross the huge office until finally, exhausted, he stood before the great oak desk that Doug Global himself had once used.

'Good to see ya, old pal,' Sam added and, leaning across the huge desk, offered his hand. Bruce did not accept it. He stared hard at Sam for a few moments through eyes that gave nothing away, and then said:

'I hear that you have allowed the first car out of Global UK since you took over to be called the Shitty.'

Sam was disappointed, he had not seen Bruce for many months and they were, after all, old friends.

'The Crappee, Bruce. If you put the emphasis on the last syllable it sounds kind of Italian.'

'Sam you couldn't make that name sound Italian if you stuck it in a gondola with a plate of spaghetti.'

Bruce was very tired. He had been boss of Global Motors for two years, having been appointed to head the dying giant by a board of receivers after old Doug Global's dissolute grandson, Karl, had brought the company to the edge of extinction. Karl's last act as President had been to insist that the wing mirrors on Global cars be fitted parallel to the road so that people could snort drugs off them.

Since that time, Bruce had been fighting to turn round the company, and indeed, since Global Motors was so big and so important, turn round the whole US motor industry. He had been banking on Sam to penetrate the European market, where import quotas still kept the Japanese vaguely at bay.

'Sam, for two years I've been working sixteen-hour days to make this company, which you and I love, a viable institution,' said Bruce wearily. 'Europe is fantastically important to us. It's a market we're already established in, with an independent British firm. We've finally sorted out our industrial trouble there and you bring me a car called Shitty.'

'Crappee, Bruce, Crappee,' Sam corrected rather defensively. 'We're hoping to get that fat opera singing guy to do the voice-overs,' and Sam attempted an exuberant Italian accent, 'You will be so ha-*pee* in a Cra-*pee*.'

Bruce Tungsten repeated the phrase, as if not quite able to believe what he was hearing. 'You will be so happy in a Crappy, Sam?'

'No Bruce,' asserted Sam. 'Ha-*pee* in a Cra-*pee*. The Global Motors Crap*pee*'.

'Global Motors,' said Bruce sadly, and clapped his hands. Instantly a little doll that he had on his desk burst into electronic laughter.

'Cute,' said Sam, 'maybe later we can have a game of Twister.'

'This isn't a toy, Sam,' said Bruce Tungsten. 'It's a challenge'.

'Yeah, I guess it must be,' Sam replied. 'Can you keep the little sucker on your desk a whole day without smashing it to pieces.'

'Did you ever hear about Henry V, Sam?' asked Bruce.

'One of the Ford boys was he?' enquired Sam. 'Let me see, there was Hank II, and Edsel, they named the car with the grid like a snatch after that loser . . .'

'Henry V of England, Sam,' corrected Bruce.

'Dagenham?'

'He didn't make cars, some people don't, you know. He was an English King, and his great rival was France, and, in order to taunt King Henry, the Dauphin of France sent him a bucket of tennis balls.'

'Nice taunt, that would have taunted the hell outa me,' said Sam.

'It was apt, because Henry was new to the crown but he was already talking big, talking about taking

217

out France altogether, busting up the whole operation. The Dauphin was showing Henry that he was just a stupid kid who should still be playing games. Do you see Sam?' enquired Bruce.

'Sure, I know history stuff,' said Sam rather huffily, 'although I ain't too sure where the dolphin fits in.'

'Dauphin, Sam, it means crown prince in French. The prince sent Henry tennis balls because he was laughing at him Sam, you understand? He was laughing at him. Well the same thing has happened to me.'

Sam was astonished.

'A French Dolphin has sent you sports equipment because he finds you funny?'

Sam suddenly felt sorry for his old friend, he had clearly flipped under the pressure.

'Listen, Bruce, I ain't no analyst, I'm a car man, grease and steel. Maybe you should see a shrink or something.'

'Two years ago I received this, Sam,' and Bruce indicated the laughing doll. 'Take a good look at it old friend and try to think of it as my balls.'

Fortunately for Sam he was not expected to answer this one for Bruce ploughed straight on with his explanation.

'It is made by the Tintandu computer-game people, who as I am sure you are aware, are part of the Hirohato group – Japan's biggest car manufacturer.'

'Those fucks don't make cars, they make toys,' Sam sneered vehemently, happy to be back on a subject he understood. 'I'd like to see a guy fence a ranch and bring home a steer in the back of a "Hirohato".' Sam put huge and contemptuous inverted commas round the very name.

'People don't want to bring home steers, they want to bring home groceries Sam and Hirohato outsell us even here at home in the States by three to one.' Bruce was angry.

'When I took over at Global I announced to the world that one day I would humble the great Hirohato giant. I said that the United States still had a great industry and, like a phoenix, it would rise again.'

'The Phoenix was a General Motors machine wasn't it? Had three tail fins I recall.'

'The Phoenix I am referring to is an allegorical fucking myth Sam. It was a bird that got barbecued but walked away from the griddle, shook off the seasoning and flew ever higher. That Sam, is what I said I would do for Global, that I would make it rise again.'

'I remember Bruce, we were all damn proud. Some of the showroom girls cried so hard they nearly slid off the bonnets of the cars.'

'Well,' continued Bruce, 'after I said that, the next day, the Hirohato people sent me this,' Bruce indicated the little doll. 'They sent it with instructions for me to say "Global Motors" and to clap my hands.'

'Little slimes. We should have dropped more bombs,' said Sam sympathetically.

'Global Motors,' said Bruce, and clapped his hands. The doll began to laugh. 'Global Motors,' said Bruce clapping his hands again and the doll laughed louder, at a third clap it laughed louder still.

'And now!' said Bruce, rising to his feet, his voice quivering with emotion whilst the doll, still laughing, added a macabre weight to his words. 'And now! My top man in Europe, a guy who goes back with Global as far as I do, brings me a car called a Shitty!!!'

'I brought you something else Bruce,' said Sam with a big smile.

'Stop grinning like that,' snapped Bruce, 'you look like the damn Jap puppet.'

'You're going to be grinning too in just a minute here Bruce. I got something that is about to turn you and me into billionaires.'

And Sam Turk explained to Bruce that he had in his possession the plans for a hydrogen engine.

## THE BIGGEST THING EVER

Bruce scarcely dared hope that what he was listening to was true. It was too extraordinary, too wonderful. It was, without doubt, the biggest thing he had ever heard. Could it be true? an engine that did not require petrol? He knew that Sam was extremely unlikely to joke about something as important as a motor engine, after all there were some things about which you just simply did not joke. None the less, there must be a catch, it was just too wonderful.

'It's true all right Bruce. I had it stolen from the British Office of Patents,' said Sam, proudly lighting a cigar.

'You stole it!' enquired Bruce. 'Was that strictly necessary?'

'Sure it was necessary. I hate to negotiate, it's demeaning.' Sam was enjoying the manner in which power had switched in the conversation.

'But what about the team who invented it?' asked Bruce. 'Have you started an industrial war here?'

'There's no team, Bruce, no industrial combines. This thing was invented by one mad professor guy, like Eddison,' said Sam. 'There ain't gonna be no war.'

'One guy! That is incredible: one guy changing the course of US industrial history. One guy.' Bruce, who was used to vast research teams, consuming even vaster budgets in order to come up with a new hub cap, could hardly believe it. 'One wonderful guy. I want to kiss him. I want to leave Maureen and marry him. Where is he?'

'He's dead, Bruce,' said Sam, 'but I'm sure he would have been touched by the offer.'

'Dead?'

'Dead or nearly dead, Bruce,' Sam assured him.

'European contractors ain't quite as efficient as the boys in Detroit, but if he's *only* nearly dead, he's *very* nearly dead.' Bruce's face was such a picture of shock and horror that Sam felt perhaps some further explanation was required. 'We stole his engine Bruce, no way was the guy going to take that lying down. What was I supposed to do?'

'Buy it off him for God's sake,' snapped Bruce. 'Couldn't you have just bought it off him like a human being? You say the guy may not have got it yet . . . ?' Bruce grabbed a phone and thrust it at Sam . . . 'Phone them, phone them now, call it off.'

'Bruce, this is the biggest thing ever, we do not need complications. Better to just take the guy's work and bump him off.'

Bruce was astounded at his old friend's coldness, but then he did not yet know the half of Sam's plan.

'Besides,' Sam continued, 'the guy would never have sold, Bruce. We checked him out, he's a public transport nut.'

Sam was trying to soothe Bruce and he had hit the right spot. Bruce was no more a lover of public transport than Sam.

'What, you mean a tram freak?' asked Bruce, relieved to hear that the condemned man was at least an evil person. 'One of those guys who wants half the damn freeway reserved for buses?'

'Exactly,' said Sam. 'Can you believe the sickoes God put on the Earth? When I get to heaven I'm gonna ask him what the fuck he thought he was doing.'

'Sam, can you imagine it?' said a very worried Bruce. 'The kind of damage a man like that could do, with all that evil engineering genius combined with his perverted communistic politics?'

'That's why I had to kill him, Bruce,' said Sam sanctimoniously. 'The guy didn't deserve to live.'

'A guy like that would have us all doing the same thing; going to the same places; looking the same; acting the same – like some kind of Chinese farm collective.'

'Exactly, and I ain't wearing no boiler suit for nobody,' replied Sam triumphantly.

Bruce was trying to convince himself that murder was justified. He did not really manage it, but the deed was done he told himself, or almost done. Besides, there was the man's legacy, his engine: the saviour of Global Motors. He would live on through his work.

'All right,' he said, 'let's forget the egghead for the moment, when can I see the engine?'

'We don't have an actual engine as such, just the plans,' replied Sam, 'and I have to tell you, they are kind of complex.'

'Then get them over here, to Detroit, right now,' said an increasingly excited Bruce. 'The sooner we get a secure lab working on producing a prototype the better.'

'A prototype,' asked Sam, rather surprised.

'Sure a prototype,' replied Bruce. 'You don't think we can build an engine without a prototype do you? Everything needs a little test. Remember when we tried to rush the Cossack? Nobody noticed the design team had drawn the wheels oval shaped to make it look slicker.'

'I was just wondering why we need to build an engine at all,' said Sam.

'What you mean franchise it!' Bruce asked, astonished. 'Let some other company produce it! What are you turning into Sam, some kind of fruit? Am I going to have to buy you a handbag here? You gonna start wearing lipstick? Franchising is the first step to wanting to go to bed with guys, Sam. We make our own fucking cars. Global Motors build 'em and Global drivers fill 'em . . .'

Sam was staring hard at his boss. 'I don't think you've grasped the full potential of this thing Bruce,' he said quietly.

'Grasped it, Sam? I can taste it!' Bruce was nearly dancing with glee, all qualms about the inventor's well-being having disappeared. 'If this engine performs the way you promise, fifteen years from now it will be the *only* engine! It will take the Japs and the Krauts easily that long to catch up. Global and the US will be on top again, and we'll be environmental heroes too! Oh my God! I love you Sam, once we've got this engine on line I'll be able to take this doll to Hirohato and tell him to stick the head in a pencil sharpener then commit *hara-kiri* with the damn thing. Laugh at us will they? I'll make them laugh!! Global Motors, ha ha,' and he clapped his hands with glee. The doll began to laugh with him . . . Global Motors' Hydrogen Engine! Ha ha.' Bruce clapped his hands again and the doll laughed louder. 'The Global Motors Hydrogen Engine, which rubbed every Japanese, every German and French nose in the mud. Yes, and Ford, and GM. Sam! Sam this is the beginning of the second age of private transport, and we'll be it Sam, we'll be it!'

Sam sat down and tugged at his cigar. He looked his friend up and down for a moment while Bruce caught his breath. When Sam did speak, he spoke gently, almost with a hint of humour.

'There ain't gonna to be no Global Motors Hydrogen Engine Bruce,' he said. 'Fact is, there ain't gonna be any hydrogen engine at all.'

'What . . . ? What are you talking about? You said . . . ' 'I know what I said Bruce,' said Sam gently, 'and there ain't gonna be no hydrogen engine. So put your stupid doll back where it was.'

Bruce stared at Sam aghast for a moment. His fists clenched.

'What is this, a joke?' hissed Bruce, 'some kind of stupid trick? You going to go down the bar and tell all the guys you sold the boss on a story about an engine that didn't drink petrol? If you've been joking Sam, I swear, I'm going to kill you, then I'm going to sack you.'

Bruce strode around his desk, the veins on his

neck standing out. He was a trim, lean looking
man, and he looked ready to bury a fist like a forty
ton truck in Sam's not inconsiderable gut.

'I ain't been kidding you, Bruce, so just wash off
your war paint, OK? The design exists, I just said
the engine ain't going to get made.' Bruce was too
stunned to speak. 'Listen old pal, what do you and
I make if we bring a radical new machine into the
corporation? Huh? One that turns round the fortunes of the whole company?'

'Well,' said Bruce thoughtfully. 'In theory, of
course, nothing. After all, it's our job to bring new
ideas into the company and I guess we're paid pretty
well as it is. But if it's money you're worrying about,
I'm sure I wouldn't be overstating things if I was to
talk in terms of million dollar bonuses.'

'Million dollar?' enquired Sam.

'Yes, I should imagine it could run as high as
that, possibly more,' Bruce assured him in his best
President of the Company manner.

'Listen Bruce, we've known each other a long
time, and I don't want to sound offensive but you're
talking like a pathetic small-minded little fuckwit,'
said Sam, not wanting to sound offensive but failing
rather badly.

'Now listen here Turk . . .' said Bruce.

'This engine is worth billions,' said Sam, 'many,
many billions. Do you hear that, Bruce, not one
million but many *thousands* of millions. The two
single largest industries in the world, motor and oil,

could be utterly destroyed by it.'

'Oil, maybe,' cried Bruce, 'and good riddance to 'em. Fuck those fat Texans and those anti-American towel-heads in the Gulf. But the motor industry! It will be the phoenix I predicted, rising out of the flames of its dead self to an even greater strength.'

'Maybe,' said Sam, 'after a minimum fifteen years of retooling, re-educating, re-equipping, fifteen years of total and utter confusion, you and I will be dead before the damn thing starts to show a profit. Christ it took compact discs nearly ten years to make any real money. Switching from oil to hydrogen will be as big a revolution as cars were in the first place.'

'So what are you saying?' said Bruce, who was beginning to guess at what Sam was saying, and it made him gasp.

'You want to know where the *real* money is in this invention? The *now* money, not the next year money. You want to know where *our* money is? Not the shareholders' of Global Motors money, but *our* money? You want to know where that is?'

Bruce knew.

'The real money is in *not* producing the engine Bruce,' said Sam, a heavenly happiness bubbling beneath his outer calm. 'That's why I need you; I need a partner with contacts a lot better than mine; a guy who I can trust to make the best deal; to help play both ends off against the centre – to grab the sale of the century. People know I'm kind of rough and ready, I need someone smooth in there, that's you, Bruce, ol' pal. Otherwise, obviously, I would have rowed you out and gone it alone.'

'Thanks Sam, I appreciate your frankness,' said Bruce. 'What's your plan? Take it to the Japs and the Krauts, tell them we got an engine that'll blow them out of the water and ask them if they want to buy it?'

'Maybe, yeah, maybe we'll put 'em in the frame, just because we're going to be rich don't mean we shouldn't be picking up the peanuts.'

'Peanuts? They'll pay billions,' protested Bruce.

'Peanuts,' said Sam firmly. 'Think bigger Bruce. This engine would score bigger losers than Honda and BMW. After all, in the end they can retool, eventually they'll pinch the design, ignore the patent, they'd come back. They've done it before haven't they? the bastards. Bavarian Motor Works wasn't worth fuck in '45 was it? No Bruce, they're the peanuts. Who really stands to lose from the hydrogen engine, old pal? Who'll never come back?'

'My God, the oil companies,' gasped Bruce. 'BP, Shell, Texaco, Esso! They'd be nothing without the petrol engine, nothing.'

'Nothing, old pal,' reiterated Sam. 'Might be a few bucks left, making fire lighters and heating town halls. Imagine it, the mighty Shell standing on the street corner selling petroleum jelly to fruits.'

'It's an incredible concept. A trillion-dollar industry, and its shirt is open, there is a big target painted on its chest . . . We could kill it Sam . . . We organize a meeting, we make 'em pool their resources – we could take them for a billion each!'

'You're right, Bruce, and we will,' answered Sam. 'But it's still peanuts old pal, it still comes dry roasted in a jar.'

'Don't be absurd,' snapped Bruce. 'A billion is not peanuts in anybody's language.'

'Oh yeah,' asked Sam. 'How about Arabic?'

'Oh my God,' said Bruce sitting down. For the first time his big chair made him look small.

'How about Venezuelan? Russian? . . . How's about Texan, yew good ol' boy yew,' said Sam in an accent which he intended to have come from Dallas but, being no actor, it could have been Scottish. Returning to his real voice, Sam returned to his original point, 'But most of all, most most of all Bruce, how about Arabic?'

'You want to hold the Gulf states to ransom?' said Bruce, and it was almost as if the room got darker as he spoke.

'I do,' said Sam. 'That is exactly what I want to do. Texas has other assets besides oil, the Russians don't even know how to pump theirs properly, but what do the Arabs have? They ain't got nothing but oil . . . Think about it, Bruce. We, the controlling figures behind America's biggest car maker, possess a secret engine, an engine that will blow those Arab kingdoms and Muslim republics all the way back to the Dark Ages. In fifteen years, if we so choose, they could be selling perfume and spices again. We could destroy their entire world. I say we *have* to be looking at a minimum of ten *billion* a piece. I guess we could be the richest men on Earth.'

The room was swimming before Bruce's eyes, after all, he had not had quite so long to adjust to the idea as Sam had. Sam was continuing his thesis . . .

'That's the real reason why I have to kill the Einstein guy. If we're asking for that kind of money, we have to be able to guarantee that, when we hand it over, those Arabs are getting the only copy in existence.'

'Sam,' Bruce tried but failed to keep the fear from his voice, 'what do you think the President would do if somebody tried to blackmail him over the entire economy of the United States?'

'Well I guess he would probably have the CIA try and bump the blackmailer off,' replied Sam.

'Yes,' said Bruce, 'and I have a kind of suspicion that that is exactly how we can expect the Gulf states to react as well.'

'Hey, hey, hey, Bruce. Who said anything about blackmail? Did I mention blackmail? You mentioned blackmail, I didn't. All I am talking about here is a simple deal, that's all. We are simply offering certain oil producing parties the first refusal to buy out the rights of a certain engine type that is in our possession. It happens all the time.'

'Well, that's true I guess,' conceded Bruce. 'But I still think they'll try and kill us.'

'Which is why there needs to be two of us. Only one of us ever goes in, the other sits tight, lays low, maybe we even tell them there's more of us. But they won't get rough, I swear it, not with Bruce Tungsten pitching them. Sure they might try and bump me off as a punk on the make, but with Mr Automobile himself they'll know it's just business. A straight deal. We have an invention which they can purchase if they wish. Listen Bruce, until they have the world rights to that engine they have to play ball, and once we have the cash what are they going to do? Mug us? The money will be the bank's problem, there'd be no point in killing us. Besides, ten billion each buys a lot of protection.'

'These people know people who blow up airplanes Sam! They take hostages! You don't know what you're getting into here . . .'

'What I am getting into is asking a group of countries to give me twenty billion dollars, minimum, so as not to destroy them. I'll tell them to think of me as a country myself if it makes it easier for them. Come on Bruce, we're big boys, I guess those kind of stakes have to be worth a little risk.'

'And if I don't want any part of it?' asked Bruce.

'Then you will never see me again. At least, when you do, it will be on the front of Business Week,' Sam replied.

'OK, I'm in. When do I get to see the plans?'

'Oh, whenever we can arrange it, ol' pal,' said Sam. 'Global Motors,' he shouted and clapped his hands at the little doll.

*Chapter Fifteen*

# HACKS AND HATCHETS

## SUPPING WITH THE DEVIL

As a politician, Digby should have realized that he who sups with the devil should use a long spoon, but Digby was rather a silly politician and he burned with fury at what he mistakenly believed had been Sam Turk's part in his political undoing. Digby had therefore decided to get back at Turk by attempting to expose him in the press. He would inform the world that the President of Global Motors UK was in the habit of stealing patents.

Digby's original idea had been to deal with what is known as a 'quality' paper. He had written a rather pompous letter, on House of Commons note paper, to the editor of a rather pompous newspaper of the type that is too large to read successfully on the lavatory – unless of course you are an expert in origami. The letter purported to be a public-spirited tip-off from a concerned MP, regarding a clear case of corporate criminality. However, the editor was a professional, expert at reading between the lines, and in the case of Digby's letter there was an ulterior motive between every one of them.

'Absolutely transparent,' the editor had remarked, describing the letter at a dinner given by his publisher. 'The spiteful little so and so's trying to smear Turk, God knows why. Must be something that happened while he was Minister. Pathetic effort, the story's unusable, nothing more than an unsubstantiated libel. Global Motors would sue us into an overdraft.'

Also present at the dinner party was Christian Corbet, the editor of another newspaper, owned by the same publisher, the *Sunday Word*. A journal of a size convenient for taking to the lavatory but for which, once there, a far better use could be found than reading it. Corbet was a man for whom the only good thing about the word 'conscience' was the first syllable.

'Would you mind if I took a look at that letter?' enquired Corbet. 'We might be able to make something of it.'

And so it was that Digby found himself in communication with the *Sunday Word*. At first he was suspicious, understandably, but Corbet (the editor himself, a point which appealed to Digby's vanity) protested such good faith and genuine interest in the story that Digby was eventually wooed. Besides, as Corbet pointed out, Digby *had* written the letter, surely he was honour bound to discuss the accusations therein, and, if possible, substantiate them. Another option, Corbet darkly hinted, might be for his newspaper to discuss the matter with Turk. The editor was forced to point out to Digby that a top motor executive suing an ex-cabinet minister for libel, also made for good copy.

Digby went to discuss his story with Corbet at the offices of the *Sunday Word* – an act comparable to a frog hopping into a French restaurant and offering to do a deal.

'So you see, Christian,' Digby was saying, as the jaws closed over him. 'Obviously the Patents Office kept me informed of any interesting developments in the field of motor engineering, and, perhaps rather foolishly, I let slip something of what I knew to Samuel Turk, the Chief Executive at Global Motors UK. Very silly of me of course. After all, careless talk costs lives and all that, aha ha ha ha, *thnn thnn thnn*.'

Digby laughed because his last comment was intended as a light witticism. It wasn't of course, but even if it had been the funniest thing since Coke tried to change their recipe, Christian would not have laughed. Being a tabloid editor, he knew that the only form of humour in the English language worthy of recognition is the pun. 'We say "peas off" to French greengrocers' for instance or, 'Trudi's no good at sums but the fellahs can tell her she's got one figure absolutely right.' Years of the ruthless pursuit of the pun had rendered Christian completely oblivious to the possibility of any other form of humour.

'Anyway,' Digby continued, oblivious to the fact that he was staring down the throat of a man who picked the likes of Digby out of his teeth at the end of the day. 'Within a very short time, the documents to which I had foolishly alluded were stolen from Whitehall. I was absolutely certain that Mr Turk had been instrumental in the theft and I confronted him furiously at party conference. He denied it of course, as any common rogue would, but he later found ways to hit back at me, demonstrating, I feel, that my accusations had found their mark. I am convinced, Mr Corbet, that a major industrial company is in the habit of breaking into government offices and I feel that despite my own unfortunate, although entirely innocent, connection with the scandal, this is a matter of which the public should be made aware.'

'Of course, Mr Parkhurst, of course,' replied Christian, through a languid, half-closed mouth, which was the way he always communicated. Some thought it was to appear relaxed and urbane, actually it was to hide his fangs . . . 'And you feel that the proof of Mr Turk's guilt in this matter is that, after you had "confronted" him, Mr Turk conspired against you personally, causing you to be severely embarrassed at party conference?'

'Yes, that is the case,' said Digby, leaping and snapping at the bright, shiny hook which Christian

Corbet dangled before him.

'How did he manage that, Mr Parkhurst, I wonder?' Christian's lips scarcely seemed to move. 'What method did he use to conspire against you and hence cause you such distress?'

'Ah . . . ah . . . now you see, I thought you'd ask that Mr Corbet,' said Digby, trying to appear wise to any journalistic tricks, but actually looking like a man with a sign on his trousers saying 'here is my arse, please kick it' . . . 'Oh yes, I was very certain that you would ask that.'

'And I did ask, Mr Parkhurst,' replied Christian.

'And I uhm, I decided that it was not relevant to the scandal I am offering you and hence have decided to say no more about it,' said Digby in his firm voice – a voice so lacking in firmness you could have spread it straight from the fridge onto fresh crusty bread.

'Oh I think it is relevant, Mr Parkhurst. I think it is the very first thing that the public will wish to know,' Christian assured Digby.

'It's really a matter of very little interest or importance to anybody,' said Digby, in a voice which was now attempting to appear relaxed but which sounded about as relaxed as a paranoid neurotic who's just sat on a box of fireworks.

'So you don't want to talk about the fact that he was blackmailing you?' said Christian.

'Blackmail! Who said anything about blackmail? It's preposterous, I never mentioned blackmail,' Digby spluttered.

'Mr Parkhurst, a week ago you were a senior minister; now, as a result of a conference débâcle, you are sat on the back benches with nobody wanting to sit next to you. He must have had something pretty juicy on you I'd have thought.'

'I can assure you that you are wrong, Mr Corbet,' said Digby. 'Now you have your story and I consider it a damn good one. So if you will excuse me, I am a very busy man.'

Digby rose to go and Christian Corbet allowed him to leave without further questioning.

'Well, well, well. Sometimes God smiles even upon us lowly hacks,' said Christian Corbet to himself, as he watched Digby's figure retreat across the mighty news floor of a great and historic British newspaper; past the top investigative teams, hard at work trying to find connections between prominent homosexuals and Aids sufferers; past the picture desks, where highly skilled graphic artists were diligently touching up the gussets on the latest pics of some minor royal with the wind up her dress; past the little corner where George Wood, 'The voice of sanity', sat twitching in his strait-jacket, waiting to be unleashed to tear off another completely barking article about lesbians being paid for by Labour councils; past all the honourable scriveners of the fourth estate – and out of the vipers' nest.

'Galton,' said Christian to his news editor, who had silently attended the interview with Digby.

'What do you think it is that I wish to know?'

Digby had hardly noticed that Galton was in the room. He was a prim, fastidious, ferretlike man, who instinctively stood in shadows and corners avoiding the light.

'I would imagine, Chief,' Galton replied, consulting the notes he had taken in his neat, precious handwriting, 'that you would like to know what it was that happened to Parkhurst, after the reported ill feeling at the road lobby reception, that would make him so radically cock-up his speech.'

'That is correct, Galton,' said Christian, and you could not have squeezed a forged fiver between his clam-like lips. 'That is exactly what I wish to know. You may unleash the pack.'


## ARMS BUILD UP

'A flame thrower! What is this, a war? Are we going to Iwo Jima? My Momma did not raise her girl to be a soldier.'

Deborah was protesting at having a canister of gas hung beneath the seat of her wheelchair.

'Listen girl,' said Toss, who was helping Geoffrey with the heavier work, 'I always reckoned the best, right, instruction in the world was one word, right? "Run", that is the world's best fight instructions, and let me tell you, if these heavy geezers ask me where Geoffrey is I'm going to say "He's over there guy, the little bloke who can't keep his head still," and then I'm going to run. But you can't run Debbo, and so if they cut up nasty, girl, you will have no alternative but to fight, and, like, I don't want to cast aspersions, but a chick in a wheelchair ain't the most scarifying sight for a ten ton thug with a meat axe and garrotting wire and an insane, maniacal grin, who enjoys inflicting pain on the helpless – know what I mean?'

'You're a very eloquent man, Toss,' replied Deborah. 'You must remind me to call you next time I need help filling out my nightmares.'

'OK, Deborah.' Geoffrey emerged from under the back of the chair like a mechanic at Brands Hatch. 'I reckon you'll be able to throw a sheet of flame about eight to ten feet from between your legs.'

'Now that is a neat trick,' said Deborah, 'and one every girl should be taught by her mom.'

'But whatever you do, make sure you spread your knees apart, otherwise, four hundred cubic centimeters of burning gas could disappear up your backside. Now Toss, help me depress the flat-iron.'

The flat-iron was exactly that, a small, old-fashioned solid flat iron welded to the jointed arm of an anglepoise lamp. Deborah, like many people, loved buying crap at markets; old fizzy pop bottles, odd cups and saucers and, in this case, a flat-iron. Toss had a great deal of trouble depressing the arm down into its niche on the inside side of the arm of Deborah's chair, because Geoffrey had replaced the springs that had been on the lamp arm with some from a Bullworker, which Toss had bought in one of those hopelessly optimistic exercise fits which occasionally consume normally rational people.

## THE BENDS

'I am going to seriously tone up my body, guy,' he had promised himself. 'I'm going to pack so much power, when I ripple a muscle, the *building* is going to shake. It is going to show up on the *Richter* scale!'

Toss was convinced, as millions had been before him, that if he bought an exercise machine, he would definitely use it, and what's more, use it every morning. He had of course used it once, and then rather unimpressively. 'Ten minutes a day' the booklet had said and Toss had grabbed up the machine with joyful enthusiasm.

After what Toss was convinced must be well over ten minutes, he glanced at the clock. To his astonishment less than two minutes had passed. 'No pain no gain, guy,' he murmured philosophically, and continued his workout. The next time he allowed himself a glance at the clock, after what seemed an eternity of pushing and pulling, scarcely another minute had passed! Toss was amazed, time seemed to be virtually standing still. He stared at the second hand on the clock, willing it on, but the more he tried, the more it appeared to be actually slowing down until eventually coming to a virtual standstill.

From Newton to Einstein there has been much fascinating discussion on the various factors that affect time. These include speed, mass, weight, distance and strange phrases like 'quantum mechanics' which scientists make up in order to sound important and convince the rest of us that we are thick. However, for some inexplicable reason, despite all this racking of the brain, no serious research has been done into the commonest and most radical 'time bender' of them all, which is, of course, exercise.

It seems that Einstein claimed that time travels more slowly at the speed of light, or he claimed something like that anyway. He made it rather difficult to be absolutely sure what he claimed, by deliberately and maliciously employing equations that nobody understood in order to put people off the scent and stop them contradicting him. Anyway, if he did claim that time travels more slowly at the speed of light, and let us presume for the purpose of argument that he did, it is difficult to see why anybody ever thought it such an earth shattering observation, because the deceleration involved pales into insignificance when compared to the rate at which time passes at the speed of an exercise bike or a gentle jog. Twenty minutes on an exercise bike can take anything up to a year of ordinary time. The seconds crawl past as if they were anchored to the clock face. A fellow might set off for a 'quick half hour run' and return to find his children grown old and his house replaced by an amusement arcade. Even then, he'll only have done twenty-six minutes and will have to fill out the remaining time with a few desultory push-ups.

The fact that exercise makes you live longer is not, as many believe, a biological circumstance, but a law of physics.

## BACK TO THE ARMS RACE

Anyway, Toss gave up exercising within three Earth minutes of beginning it. Then, a considerably older and wiser man, he hurled the machine he had bought into a corner and there it had languished ever since, staring at Toss contemptuously and whispering, 'Nice body tone, Pigeon Chest. I can't exactly feel the buildings shake'.

Finally, to Toss's delight, the Bullworker had found a purpose. He dismantled it with sadistic pleasure and gave the springs to Geoffrey, thus, providing Geoffrey with the means to propel the flat-iron through a right hook of considerable pressure.

Eventually, Toss got the arm folded down beside Deborah and the little catch Geoffrey had designed clipped over it. Geoffrey explained that, were Deborah ever to release that catch, she was to be extremely sure that there was somebody standing over her to absorb the blow. For were the iron to merely swing wildly and unchecked to the full stretch of the arm, it was most likely that the force would topple Deborah's chair.

'Great,' said Deborah, 'so this one's for putting me out of action is it? I tell the murderers not to worry, that I'll just fling myself on the ground to make their job a little easier.'

'It's for close quarters fighting, Deborah,' said Geoffrey.

'Yeah,' added Toss excitedly, 'you have to imagine that the geezer is standing over you, right. He's come across the room, right, saying, . . . "I'll waste the bitch, I'll cream her sweet arse. She is history. She is dead meat. She is . . ."'

'Yeah, OK, Toss, I'll imagine my own death if that's all right by you.'

'Just trying to get you used to heavy geezers, Debbo. Know what I mean?'

'Toss, till I was eighteen I lived in New York City. In New York if you don't get threatened occasionally you go see a therapist and ask him why you have no charisma. Where I used to live you asked someone "how was their day", they'd say it was fine, nobody shot at them. People in New York go to Beirut for a break.'

Deborah was aware that New York was not actually quite the war zone she described, but she rather enjoyed massaging the paranoid prejudices of foreigners.

'All right,' said Toss, 'we'll forget the character stuff and get to the point, right. He is standing over you with a blunt machete, saying that he's going to fillet you, dice you up and leave you marinating in a puddle of gore, unless you hand over the plans. What do you do?'

'I hand over the plans.'

'Well, yeah, that's right, but if you don't have the plans or an unexpected fit of bravery comes over you, that's when you flick the switch – but don't do it now, all right, because it packs a wicked hook.'

Geoffrey went on to explain that once the punch had been delivered, if time allowed, Deborah should put the arm across her and attach the iron end to the opposite arm of the chair so that the elbow of the jointed anglepoise arm pointed out in front of her like the prow of a ship. Having done this, there was a small wire coiled up in the end of one of the chair arms, Deborah should stretch this across and hook it onto the other arm, thus forming a draw-string to the anglepoise bow. Geoffrey had concealed two nasty looking bolt-like arrows in the uprights of Deborah's seat back.

'Stick an apple on your head, Toss,' said Deborah, 'I feel like some target practice.'

'Later,' said Geoffrey, who was behind Deborah fitting something into the back of the chair. It was a battery which Toss had pinched for him from a temporary traffic-light. Geoffrey wired this up to the handles of the chair, adding a small charge-convertor which made it possible for Deborah to deliver all the electricity in the battery in one hit, if she so desired. Geoffrey reckoned that there would be enough power to seriously scare any enemy who grabbed the handles of Deborah's chair.

'Especially if you can manoeuvre him to stand in a puddle,' Geoffrey added.

'Well, I'll sure try and remember that,' replied Deborah.

'And finally there is this,' and in danger of cutting himself and Deborah, Geoffrey put a nasty, vicious looking hatchet into a niche down by Deborah's leg.

'Oh yeah, and how does that work?' asked Deborah.

'Uhm, well, you have to grab it and chop the bloke with it,' admitted Geoffrey rather shame-facedly.

'That's OK, Geoffrey,' said Deborah. 'It can't all be Star Wars. I'm kinda pleased you left a human element in there. When I kill, I like to feel the guy die. So what about you Geoffrey? What weapons of death have you equipped yourself with?'

'Oh I'll be all right. I have to get on with the engine,' said Geoffrey. 'I wanted to see you all right first, after all I can run, sort of.'

Deborah hoped that Geoffrey was right.


## SAM'S NET CLOSES

The murderers that Sam had commissioned to find and kill Geoffrey had found a willing source of information in Denise, the woman at Geoffrey's place of work with the 'You don't have to be mad etc.' sticker on her desk. She did not know much, but what she did she was happy to divulge.

'Well, he keeps himself to himself really,' she wittered, meaning that he was generally ignored. 'A very quiet man, terribly brave. I mean if I looked like him I'm not sure I'd want to go on really, would you? being a burden and all. Anyway, we haven't seen him for a week or so, he rang in sick. Probably still hung over from Suzi's leaving do. That was the last time I saw him. He had a *lovely* time, you could tell by the way he twitched. Everyone just treated him as one of the gang. They're a wonderful lot that work here you know. Mad of course, oh yes, we're all completely potty, but wonderful. Friends? Well not really that I noticed, I think they like to be more with their own kind really, don't you? Less embarrassing for them. I did see a lady in a wheelchair come and pick him up once or twice in her car. Lovely isn't it that they can help each other like that?'

## RATTLING THE SKELETONS IN DIGBY'S CLOSET

Sam Turk's hired thugs were not the only people involved in investigations. The hack pack from the *Sunday Word* had descended on the Royal Princess Hotel, Brighton, where the upper echelons of Digby's party had stayed during conference week. Not the upper upper echelons, but Digby level echelons.

On arrival, the dedicated journos had proceeded to interview everyone, buying drinks and slipping tenners about pretty liberally.

Of course the *Word*, like all the scandal sheets, had its regular spies, whom it kept on retainers, at any venue where the famous might be found. Every hospital has its porter alert for the arrival of an overdosed sporting personality or a newsreader with a Coke bottle stuck in some important little place. All the top drinkeries have a waiter on the look out for any celebrities who seem to have a weak bladder and who always return from the toilet rather cheerful and with a small white moustache. However, regarding Digby, the regular spies at the Princess Royal knew nothing, and so the search was spread further.

'That ex-minister, Digby Parkhurst,' the hacks would ask, 'the one who resigned in disgrace. Remember anything about him the night before his speech? Anything that might have upset him?'

The hacks heard of the dressing down Digby had received over breakfast from Ingmar Bresslaw. They heard how the previous evening Digby had arrived late for the launch of the Global Crappee and how he had seemed very angry with Sam Turk. Eventually the hacks got lucky. From a receptionist, they heard that a barman knew about a maid who had a funny story about a bloke wandering the corridors of the hotel, late at night, in drag.

'I couldn't believe it, well you wouldn't, would

you?' the maid said, accepting a gin and tonic. 'I mean it was obviously a man, it's all this European influence I reckon, all the blokes are turning into poofs.'

The maid explained that the fellow had been in full drag and drunk as a lord. She had met him as she came out of the lift, it had been on the top floor where the suites are. The hacks knew already that this was the floor on which Digby had stayed. Sensing a scoop they asked the girl to describe the man in drag.

'Well, I must say, he made quite a presentable woman,' she recalled. 'Slim he was, good looking I expect, under the make-up. I remember thinking it was a shame he was a poof. I can tell you there weren't many good looking men staying in this hotel during conference. Lot of fat bastards and no mistake.'

'Anything else about the bloke?' the anxious reporters asked, 'anything to distinguish him?'

'Not really, no. Except, of course, that he was definitely Scottish.'

'Scottish,' the hacks confirmed.

'Oh definitely, he called me a wee lassie.'

## Chapter Sixteen

# OIL, ROADS AND ENGINES

## OLD FRIENDS

The elegant Dutchman was almost white with shock. Not many things in this wicked man's life had shocked him. Things that would cause a normal person to have to sit down for a minute and have a cup of tea, left Cornelius Brandt completely cold. He headed an enormous oil-based multi-national that had, for a century, abused human rights and fundamental employment practices worldwide – but Cornelius was unmoved by this. His company, Imperial Oil, had tenaciously hung on in South Africa through the worst excesses of apartheid. This, Cornelius thought merely good business. He had personally and happily dealt with Pinochet's brutal regime in Chile; he had fuelled the aircraft that had got Samosa out of Nicaragua, and never had Cornelius Brandt turned a hair, let alone been shocked. You could have crept up behind him and burst balloons in his earhole from now until the end of time and he would not have twitched – but now, Cornelius Brandt was shocked.

He gripped the arms of his chair with pale, transluscent knuckles, the bones, seemingly, trying to burst from his grasping, clawlike fingers. 'We have known each other many years, yes?' he said, in that peculiar sing-song accent with which the Dutch speak English. An accent which is normally kind and pleasant, but coming from Cornelius, it sounded like the authentic voice of a henchman of the devil.

'Sure, we go back, Cornelius,' answered Sam Turk with his usual easy charm. Sam was a bluff, straightforward Yankee who could say 'You're fired, your desk has been cleared' in such a manner that people often did not realize what had happened until they had left his office. It was this easy tone that had been in Sam's voice when he had informed Brandt that Global Motors would, without question, destroy him and Imperial Oil within an absolute maximum of fifteen years.

'We can run cars on hydrogen, Cornelius,' good ol' Sam had drawled. 'It's happened. The alternative is here, oil is history.'

'Oil is history . . .!' Tell Cornelius Brandt any three words but those! Say to him 'your wife's dead', that would be fine. 'Is it in?' Cornelius could handle at a pinch, but never 'oil is history'.

'Samuel, you and I, we have fought many good battles together, we are old and good boys, you and

I!' Cornelius was trying to sound as relaxed as Sam but the piece of concrete in his larynx was making it difficult. 'Is it thirty years since you and I lobbied congress, side by side, over the super highways?'

'Thirty-five Cornelius.'

'Don't let us be fighters to each other Sam. It would be sad, no?'

'Ain't gonna be no fight Cornelius, not unless you call putting an old hound to sleep a fight. You're the past, my old friend, you ain't got nothing to fight with.'

Cornelius dropped the Mr Nice Guy act.

'Listen, Turk, you may think you've grabbed my curly short ones, but I've got a tiger in my pants and it's going to bite you, old pal! We'll lobby to licence fee this engine out of existence. We'll push for twenty years of safety tests. We'll blow up your fuck factories . . .'

'Cornelius, once Mr and Mrs USA realize that they can drive to Alabama without paying a penny in fuel . . . Once the President realizes he ain't never going to have to kiss ass to any Arab ever again . . . Once the EEC sees the possibility of complete self-sufficiency . . . You know better than anyone how unstable the oil supply is. Every damn week there's somebody about to start a war in the Middle East. The day after we demonstrate this engine to the world, you get your death sentence, pal, and you just sit around waiting to die.'

Cornelius said nothing. Very slowly he swallowed

an aspirin, sipping from a lead crystal goblet inscribed 'stay on side, we need you,' and signed Richard Nixon.

'Of course, it doesn't have to be that way,' said Sam.

## NEW BROOM

Druscilla 'Corker' McCorkadale entered the Ministry for Transport with a firm, purposeful tread. Everything about her suggested that she had lots to do and no time to waste. This was actually an illusion because Corker had just had her car driven around for fifteen minutes until the photographers arrived. Corker had specifically asked the press office to invite some cameras, in order that her first bustling day as Minister for Transport might be duly recorded.

'Tell them it will be a super photo,' Corker had said.

'Will you be making any kind of statement, Minister?' the press officer had enquired.

'Don't be silly,' said Corker. 'What on Earth would I want to do that for?' The Prime Minister had chosen Digby's replacement well.

Just around the corner from the Ministry, Corker had her driver stop the car and remove from the boot a collapsible bicycle.

'Have you got the yellow reflector sash?' Corker whispered.

'Yes, Madam, here you are.' The driver handed it over and Corker pushed off. 'Ching ching,' went her bell. 'Shifto you chaps, I've a department to run,' she shouted cheerily, wobbling towards the hack pack on her unaccustomed steed.

'This way, Minister! Look this way please,' they shouted as the motor drives sprang into action. Corker reluctantly allowed herself to be stopped by the cameras. Ever the professional, she could not prevent a modest portion of still-shapely thigh peeping out from beneath her rising hem line, as an elegantly shod foot perched on the pedal.

Druscilla had been known as 'Corker' since the first day she entered government, when the *Sunday Word* had headlined a four-year-old photo of her in a bikini with the phrase 'Coo what a Corker!' She made a great fuss of demanding to know the source of the photograph, but colleagues suspected that she had sent it herself. Until her promotion to transport, Corker had been a junior minister at the Department for Health and, despite her relatively lowly antecedents, she was already extremely well known to the public. The reason being that she was a voracious publicity vulture. Corker had once fainted in Dixons, having hyperventilated at the sight of so many cameras.

## FISH BURGERS

It had been Corker's brilliant media intervention

that had saved the government over the great fishy beef scandal.

The feeding of fishmeal to British livestock appeared to be causing cows to go a bit scaly and spend an unhealthy amount of time sitting in puddles. This has led some scientists to propose the possibility that, since the average British teenager eats his or her weight in hamburgers every six hours, pretty soon now we might expect a few of them to start going 'glop, glop, glop', breathing through their armpits and spawning half a million eggs. Once this possibility hit the news stands ('OH COD! BEEF HAS HAD ITS CHIPS!'), there was, understandably, a degree of panic, and, for just a moment, it actually looked like the farmers might have to sell their Rolls Royces. However, at the last minute, Corker, the Junior Minister for Health, had saved the day. Not by introducing any new guidelines regarding the rearing of cattle, but by taking a posse of photographers to the Tower of London where she allowed herself to be photographed standing between two Beefeaters, eating a hamburger.

It was this genius for damage control that had led the Prime Minister to promote Corker to a senior ministerial post, in the hope that she would smile winningly whilst the Civil Service sorted out the Digby mess.

# THE ROAD TO NOWHERE

'We've got a complete environmental panic brewing, Mrs McCorkadale,' Ingmar Bresslaw had said to her during her breakfast briefing the previous week. 'Would you call that sausage cooked? I wouldn't call it cooked. What is wrong with this sodding country? Even the bloody dagoes can cook.' Ingmar took a pull at a hip flask, whilst Corker sympathized diplomatically. She knew not to get on the wrong side of Ingmar Bresslaw.

'An environmental panic, you say, Ingmar? It's not the bloody greenhouse effect again is it? I just don't understand that one. For centuries all the British have done is moan about the lousy weather, and when we *do* get the chance of a bit of sunshine everyone starts bellyaching that Southend will soon be under water. Honestly, who *cares* whether Southend is under water or not. Nobody I know lives there. Do you know anybody who lives at Southend, Ingmar?'

Ingmar admitted that he did not. Corker was very much his kind of minister; obscenely ambitious but without any particular political principles to justify that ambition. Corker simply loved being famous and she would do *anything* to get in the papers. This was a minister who would climb Churchill's statue and sit on his face for six column inches.

'No, it's not the greenhouse effect, Mrs McCorkadale,' answered Ingmar, giving his sausage the sort of bristling, eyebrowish look that made the bowels of young back-benchers dissolve and put them in severe danger of losing their deposits. 'It's roads.'

'Oh yes,' said Corker. 'That's *fascinating*,' she added, wondering how her lip gloss was holding up. There was an awful lot of it on the rim of her coffee cup, so there couldn't be much left on her.

'This government has a massive road building plan,' Ingmar was saying. 'Truly colossal. A plan that, if fully implemented, will create traffic jams well into the next century.'

'Sorry Ingmar, small point,' said Corker, grabbing a chance to show that she was listening and on the ball . . . 'You mean rid us of jams.'

'No, Minister, I mean *create* jams,' said Ingmar, lowering his voice to slightly less than its usual boom. 'The purpose of building roads is to stimulate the economy. If we were ever to arrive at a system of roads which was jam free there would be no excuse to build any more, which is the language of recession and I hope you have no wish to hear that kind of language in your ministry, Minister. Traffic jams are a necessary factor in continued economic growth.'

'You're kidding me,' said Corker.

'I am not kidding you, Minister. Why do you think motorways are constantly covered in bollards and contra-flows, restricting traffic to snail-like single lanes?' enquired Ingmar.

'Uhm . . . road-works?' Corker answered, weakly.

'When did you ever see any actual road-works being carried out behind those walls of bollards, Minister? Perhaps once a year. Is it not more common to see mile upon mile of pristine tarmac bollarded off for no apparent reason at all? The reason for that, Minister, is to create jams, jams that will persuade the public to accept further road building.'

'Coo,' said Corker, absolutely astonished. She had, of course, noticed that there has never been a major road built, ever, that did not end up constantly jammed, but she had never realized what a good thing it was . . . 'I suppose all this is a bit of a secret though, is it?' she added, trying to look professional.

'Yes, it is a secret,' said Ingmar, 'as, indeed, is our whole road strategy. There was considerable public disquiet anyway, but now that bugger Parkhurst has panicked the entire country, we are going to have to lie very low.'

'Yes, it's all off, isn't it? I heard the Prime Minister denying everything at conference. Did you have a good conference, Ingmar? I had a marvellous conference. Perhaps you saw that photo of me on a donkey? It was gruesome, I hated it,' said Corker, who had had it framed.

'Yes,' said Ingmar, pursuing his point with a weary sigh, 'As far as the public are concerned it is all off. It is your job, Mrs McCorkadale, to continue to reassure the public that we never even entertained the sort of road plans that the imbecile Parkhurst revealed at conference.'

'Right ho,' said Corker putting on her serious face. 'All off . . . never even on. Got it.'

'Until such times as you are told otherwise, the Prime Minister wishes you to present the friendly, socially aware face of our transport policy to the general public.'

'You've got the right girl, Ingmar.' Corker couldn't believe her luck, she was in the fast lane and it was easy street. Ahead of her lay years of photo calls, years of adoring profiles in the women's mags about keeping her make-up straight through a workaholic sixteen-hour day. By the time she'd finished, if she wasn't Prime Minister, she would certainly be able to get her own chat show, and that would be even better.

'In the meantime,' said Ingmar, fixing his fiery, bloodshot eyes on Corker's, in order to intimidate her with the awesome seriousness of the situation.

'The old bugger fancies me,' thought Corker, giving him a wry, flirty little smile, all subtle innuendo, with a hint of white teeth.

'In the meantime,' repeated Ingmar, 'and kindly stop grinning at me like a simpleton, Mrs McCorkadale.' Corker laughed as if to show that she knew Ingmar was only joking . . . 'In the meantime,' Ingmar continued, 'the Prime Minister wishes you to allow for the massive road building preparations to continue.'

'Uhm, which road building preparations would these be, Ingmar?' enquired Corker.

'The ones which do not exist, Minister.'

'I see.'

'The ones which have never existed and which you must deny at all times.'

'Right ho.'

'The ones which your senior Civil Servants are working on as we speak, looking to the day when the public will be persuaded to accept the necessity of thousands of new roads.'

'And how are they to be persuaded of that, Ingmar?' enquired Corker.

'Never you mind about that,' declared Ingmar. 'I shall attend to the manipulation of public opinion. I have methods.'

And by the scarily sinister way that he said it, it seemed to Corker that Ingmar was probably intending to individually torture each and every British subject until they called for the paving of the Home Counties.

'Well, that all seems pretty straightforward,' said Corker.

And thus it was that Corker McCorkadale came to be demonstrating the environmental face of government transport policy by cycling the last hundred yards to work and flashing her legs for the cameras. Whilst behind the walls of Whitehall,

Digby's precious models continued to spread across tables, over filing cabinets and out into corridors.

## MOTOR-VATION

It was hot and sweaty in Detroit that night. Bruce Tungsten was sitting up late, alone in his vast office. All the lights were out, but Bruce was occasionally illuminated by a burning flash or a shower of sparks at his window. Bruce's office overlooked the vast Global Motors works and even though everybody bought Japanese these days, the long, hot night rang to the sounds of American industry. Global Motors, an enormous corporation, dedicated to the art of making losses with out of date machinery and out of date cars. Out of date? Of course they were out of date, the Japanese innovated every five minutes, damn it.

'Global Motors,' Bruce said, and clapped his hands. The little doll that Hirohato had sent him laughed in the darkness of the night. It laughed at him, it laughed at the company he'd been with since he got out of the army, and it laughed at the United States of America.

Bruce clapped again, 'Global Motors.' He could not hear it enough even though it burnt into his soul. Again and again he clapped and the doll kept laughing. Bruce got up and strode about the office. Each time the laughter died he tormented himself anew, shouting the name of his company into the silence and clapping his hands till they were sore.

Bruce snatched up the doll.

'One day Hirohato,' he spat. 'One day soon, now, I'm going to take this little doll and stick it so far up your butt you'll need a stethoscope to hear it laugh.'

The phone rang, as Sam had said it would. Bruce picked it up and the voice on the other end spoke immediately.

'Is it true, this nightmare? Is it real? Does it exist, this damnable engine?' the voice asked, and Bruce recognized it as Cornelius Brandt's.

'Yes, it's true,' Bruce replied.

'I did not really doubt it,' said a weary Cornelius, his voice dry and choked. 'But Turk is such a gangster, I needed to hear it from you.'

'Well, you've heard it,' said Bruce, 'and now you're going to do exactly what Sam and me tell you.'

# Chapter Seventeen

# DIGBY RUMBLED

Christian Corbet and his creature, Galton, sat in Christian's office at the *Sunday Word* staring at the big television screen.

'That's it,' said Christian, freezing the video, 'best shot we're going to get. You're sure the BBC won't give us any of their tapes?'

'After what George said about them in last week's *Voice of Sanity*?' Galton shook his head. 'Of course he was right, they are nothing but raving communistic, lesbian-loving Stalinists. One day Sir, one day we shall settle scores with our television "colleagues". We shall show them that the true meaning of the word "balance" is that the scales will always tip to favour the strong and ruthless.'

'Yes, all right, Galton,' said Christian, who knew that once Galton got going it was sometimes difficult to stop him. 'Anyway, it's of no importance, this picture tells me the story plain as day.'

The image on the screen was of the moment at the party conference when Digby had stalled mid-speech. The point at which he had promised to announce government rail policy. The point just prior to his ditching his speech and ending his career with a disastrous improvisation about roads.

Galton had reported to Christian the results of the Royal Princess Hotel investigation. It seemed extremely likely that the Scottish transvestite who had been spotted near Digby's room, late on the night before the speech, was the means by which Digby believed Sam Turk had intimidated him. However, if this was the case, why was it, Christian asked himself, that Digby had appeared perfectly composed throughout the following morning, and had, indeed, delivered the first half of his speech with what was, for the average cabinet minister, considerable aplomb – meaning that he actually faced in the right direction and got the words in the right order?

'It's as if something hit him half way through his speech,' Christian had mused. 'Well, the party tittle-tattle is that it was a naked power bid, Sir,' said Galton. 'It is their belief that he felt, by exposing secret policy and gaining for it popular support, he could push the policy and himself to the forefront of the government, possibly even presenting himself as a potential leadership contender.'

'That's what they say, is it, Galton?' enquired Christian, his mouth now actually shut.

'Yes, it is presumed, Sir, that he was seething.'

'Seething?'

'Seething at the fact that Department of Transport policy had to be conducted in such an underhand manner; secret contracts; constant lobbying; the real power lying with the Civil Service. As an ambitious minister, he is deemed to have seethed, Sir, and yearned for popular approbation.'

'Galton, even Digby Parkhurst must have known that announcing plans to relocate St Paul's Cathedral behind a DIY centre in Essex would not bring him popular approbation.'

'They also think he must have been on the piss, Sir.'

But Christian knew better, he knew that something must have happened to make a dull, featureless minister screw up his career and party policy so spectacularly. This was why he had called for the video tapes of the day's events. He had watched Digby leave his hotel to be confronted by the members of the rail lobby, he had watched Digby arrive at the conference hall and he had watched Digby's speech, particularly the point of confusion. Christian had watched Digby shout, 'What this government intends to do with the railways is . . .' and he had touched the freeze-frame button. Then, taking a ruler to the screen, he attempted to follow Digby's eye line to find out what the minister had seen at that precise moment.

It was blurred, and almost off the corner of the

screen, but it was unmistakably there; a young man, standing up in the fourth row holding up a handbag.

'That's our transvestite,' said Christian. 'Bloody cheeky, eh? Fingering Parkhurst mid-speech.'

'Rather strange behaviour on Turk's part too, I feel, Sir,' added Galton. 'After all, it was the precise timing of the hit which led to Parkhurst's road speech, and the subsequent débâcle over secret government policy. Sam Turk, as a prominent road lobbyist, must be kicking himself that in bringing down Parkhurst he inadvertently brought down the biggest road building plans in British history.'

'Sam Turk had nothing whatsoever to do with the incident,' said Christian, decisively, and he called for a second television and video recorder. The equipment having arrived, he inserted into the second machine the news tape of Digby's departure from his hotel and his encounter with the rail lobby. He froze the tape at the point at which the forceful young man pushed his way through the crowd . . . Through the general babble he could be heard warning the minister not to announce the formation of BritTrak, what's more, he had a Scottish accent. Christian looked at the frozen image of the man outside the hotel. He turned to the image of the man in the fourth row, one business suit is much the same as the other, but none the less, it was clear that the two men were the same person. 'Well, well, well,' murmured Christian through a mouth that was positively imploding. 'So Digby Parkhurst got stitched by a queer train nut.'

## Chapter Eighteen

# THE ENGINE SLIPS FURTHER OUT OF REACH

## ASSEMBLING THE LAB

Toss was out traffic wardening, Deborah was at college sitting an exam and Geoffrey had the flat to himself. He was hard at work in the little work area that Toss had helped him to set up in Deborah's laundry-room. This was a partitioned area at the back of the kitchen which housed the washing machine, tumble drier and ironing stuff.

Most of what Geoffrey required to re-design his engine, was in his head. The only tool which he really needed was his home computer, a machine specially adapted to Geoffrey's needs. This, Toss retrieved from Geoffrey's flat at his first opportunity, which was the Tuesday evening after work. This meant that two days had already passed since Geoffrey had discovered that his invention had been hijacked. Toss also grabbed books, notes and whatever other stuff he was able to lay his hands on amongst the mess. This was not very much, because

Toss was forced to operate without putting on any lights. The reason for this was because it was clear to Toss, having strolled past the place a couple of times during his lunch-hour, that Geoffrey's flat was being watched.

Toss knew this, because, in the course of his years tramping about with his traffic warden cap on, he had come to know every type of loafer, trader, ne'er do well, and poser that hung out on the streets of London.

'I'm cool, guy, you understand. My eye is like an eagle and I am totally happening,' Toss had pointed out when asked by Deborah how he could be sure that the two men he had reported had actually been watching the house.

'It is my personal style to be hip to whatever is going down, yah nah what I mean?' he added. 'I know when a guy is just chillin't out right? Just catching rays, watching the fine ladies and hangin' OK? I know if he is a thief, right, a beggar, a pimp, a copper's nark. I have to tell you that I am so wicked to the street life of this city that I can tell you what people had for breakfast, yah nah what I mean! And the geezers outside of Geoffrey's flat was watching it, girl. They weren't selling chestnuts and they weren't delivering nuffink, they was watching.'

'All right already, so your cockney intuition assures us that they were watching,' said Deborah. 'I had no idea you were such a Dickensian character Toss. Anyway, the question is, what are we going

269

to do about it? Geoffrey can't exactly reshape the world with a ball point pen and pad.'

Geoffrey sat twitching on the sofa, wondering whether he should point out that greater men than he had done just that, but he couldn't be bothered to formulate the sentence.

The upshot of the conversation was that Toss had returned to the flat as dusk fell, pushing a pram. Geoffrey lived on the ground floor of a large old Victorian house, the sort where the old family living-room had been divided into six 'desirable maisonet-tes' and the understairs cupboard had been con-verted into 'a totally separate and enclosed living area suitable for a young couple'. Geoffrey was fortunate that, being a moderately well paid profes-sional person, he was able to afford a whole floor, but the great mass of bell buttons on the front door indicated that above him dwelled many souls.

'Listen, Fleur!' Toss shouted into the intercom, having pretended to push a button . . . 'It's me, doll, and I'm back for good all right. Livingstone needs his mum . . . Now don't give me that, doll, yah nah what I mean?' continued Toss, enjoying his performance. 'Just open the door and get me dinner on all right? And then you'll have to wash me shirt cos Livingstone's just pissed on it and that shirt is wicked threads, girl . . . What's that, doll?' Toss leant in, pretending to listen to the intercom . . . 'Loves yah? Course I loves yah, I fucks yah, don't I?' This triumphant bit of characterization completed, Toss leant in, to disguise his movements, and deftly unlocked the door with the key that Geoffrey had given him . . . 'Thanks doll,' Toss shouted into the uncomprehending Tannoy as he pushed the pram into the gloom of the hallway.

Having closed the door he let himself into Geoffrey's flat. He shuddered slightly to see that the white outline that the police had drawn round the body of one of the men who had been unwise enough to take on Geoffrey Spasmo, was still visible on the floor in front of the sideboard.

'That Geoffrey is a wicked geezer,' Toss said to himself, as he began to load the pram with Geoffrey's computing equipment. Toss had decided to stay the night at Geoffrey's place because he considered that the watchers might smell a rat if he emerged with his pram only half an hour after entering. A character such as the one Toss had created, would certainly stay for supper and a shag at least. It wasn't so bad. As Geoffrey had promised, there was plenty of booze in the place, so Toss got his chicken and chips out from under the pram, plus his cork-screw . . . He didn't fancy using Geoffrey's, in fact, he shuddered at the very sight of the evil spike which he knew to have inflated the bottom of the man around whose body the police had drawn their sombre line.

'Wine, food, vibes,' mused Toss, putting on his ear-phones and settling down in the darkness. 'It is time to forget the dead, and chill out.'

## REVISION CRISIS

Toss did his job of collection well and the little laboratory which Geoffrey created was sufficient to his needs, and, for a week, the little community at Deborah's place settled into a routine. Geoffrey slept on the sofa and never went out, spending almost every waking moment in his little lab, re-doing his sums on top of the washing machine, earnestly working out weight-to-power ratios in equations so long that they stretched the length of an entire ironing board and constructing anew his specifications for light-weight alloys and revolution-ary lubricants. The theory was all still in Geoffrey's head, but the retrieving of it was complex and time consuming, and, of course, there was the washing to do.

'We need to wash our stuff, Geoffrey,' Deborah protested. 'The world may be on the verge of a transport revolution, but we still need to have clean underwear.' So Geoffrey reluctantly moved all his papers and Deborah loaded the machine, swearing, yet again, that next time she really would clean out the fluff filter.

Unfortunately, Deborah's constant presence in the flat proved rather a distraction to Geoffrey's work. Despite being in danger for his life and working against the clock, he still could not help his mind wandering to the girl who was, after all, the

272

inspiration that had got him into the whole mess in the first place.

It was doubly distracting for Geoffrey because Deborah was at home much more than usual. It was the period of her final examinations, and hence her presence was not required at college. She was constantly in and out of the kitchen and whenever he heard her, Geoffrey's heart ached. Each day she thought of new things to wash, or iron. It was not that Deborah wished to distract Geoffrey, but it was the last week before her history of costume exam and Deborah was in a revision crisis.

Revising for exams is always hell. The mind wanders, panic wells up, lethargy sets in, the TV beckons. Deborah tried to concentrate, each day she tried, and yet, constantly she caught herself coming to with a start having been reading a book for five minutes and yet not having taken in a single word. Throughout the week, Deborah, who was normally so positive and so lively, mooched and slouched about the flat, made coffee, offered to make Geoffrey coffee and watched the mid-day news. She rang friends on the same course to assure them that she was not getting any work done. They rang her to assure her that they were also not getting any work done. All over the country demoralized young people were ringing each other up to assure their friends that they had managed to do no work at all, while secretly suspecting that their friends must have done loads, and loads, and loads of work.

On the third day of her torment Deborah realized, with only four days to go until the dreaded paper, that she must really pull herself together, therefore she did what all the other tormented revisers around the country did, she made a timetable. She made a detailed timetable of how best she would organize her revision time in her last four days. She drew neat squares indicating the remaining mornings, afternoons and evenings, and in these squares she neatly wrote things like 'eighteenth century French court dress' or 'work clothes as fashion', thus indicating at which time she would be revising what subject. This completed, Deborah wearily returned to the article she had been reading in *Woman's Own* about which member of the royal family had lost the most weight. Each morning Deborah read the paper from cover to cover, arguing to herself that this was a serious and legitimate use of her time. Secretly, of course, she knew that this was simply another anti-revision prevarication. Under normal circumstances, she often skimmed the paper, occasionally not even opening it at all. On revision mornings, however, she even read the situations vacant pages. Deborah was always interested in employment opportunities.

Ever since the Global Moritz had paralysed her from the waist down, she had been aware that forging a fulfilling career was going to be just that little bit harder for her than for most. Because of this, despite being currently a full time student, curiosity often led her to check out the job market. Finding out which employers claimed to be equal opportunities employers – not that that meant much because, of course, it only meant equal opportunities for human beings, not fire hazards.

'Look at this, Geoffrey,' said Deborah, breaking into the middle of some mile long equation forming in Geoffrey's mind and causing all the numbers to fly out of his ears.

'Global Motors UK are looking for graphics people in their design deparment. Maybe I should apply, do you think they'd give me special consideration seeing as it was one of their cars that put me in this chair?'

'Deborah, please,' said Geoffrey, 'I'm trying to concentrate.'

'All right already, for God's sake, one little word. I'm sorry,' Deborah snapped back. 'I have work to do too you know,' and she wheeled herself back into the sitting-room, past her lecture notes and started to watch a programme for the under-fives which asked Deborah whether she'd like to pretend to be a puppy dog along with Trudy and Sean.

## THE BELL TOLLS

Finally, the morning of Deborah's exam had dawned and she had gone off, in a rare old state, at about eleven. Toss had been gone for ages as he was on the early morning shift that week so Geoffrey briefly had the place to himself. He went through into his little workroom and prepared to concentrate his massive mind. Unfortunately for Geoffrey, he was not the only one who had been waiting for him to be alone in the house.

Blissfully unaware that terrible danger was stalking him, Geoffrey became immediately and happily engrossed in his work, so much so, that he almost did not hear when the tiny glass bell tinkled at his ear informing him that somebody was messing about at the back windows. Deborah, living as she did, on the ground floor, and being even more vulnerable than most, had done her best to make her flat secure. Toss was not always around, and, as he himself pointed out, he 'wasn't no Mohammed Ali, girl'. Hence, Deborah had had bars fitted to the rear of the flat and an alarm system installed. Geoffrey reckoned this offered him a fair degree of protection, but, as an added precaution, he had fitted an extra electronic element to the alarm, whereby, if the alarm circuit was overruled or the bell silenced by some skilled hand, the tiny little crystal bell would ring, thus informing Geoffrey that intruders were about without letting them know that their presence had been announced.

Deborah was glad that the bell had found a function, it had been one of the numerous gifts she had received whilst in hospital from relatives she scarcely knew she had. The only thing to commend the bell, in Deborah's opinion, was that it was small, unlike the six-foot teddy bear that a cousin who worked at Bloomingdales had sent. When you're in hospital for eight months people have time to send things by sea, and Deborah's relations had made good use of this service.

'Do you want to know what's embarrassing? I'll tell you what's embarrassing,' Deborah had moaned from her sick bed, in a letter to a friend. 'Being a girl from an extended Jewish family, seriously ill in hospital. I can no longer look the nurses in the eye. It ain't the treatment, having my orifices stared at in disappointment by students I can handle, peeing through a tube I'll live with, but being the cause of the postman getting a hernia, this I cannot take. The man has grown old bringing me my daily sack of presents. First he stooped a little, then he went grey and had a hernia, finally the poor guy ends up in hospital himself. They buried him last Tuesday, killed by the American shopper.'

The endless gifts had made Deborah terribly uncomfortable, not least because there are so many lonely people in hospitals, people who have no visitors and get no presents because they are old and their lives have died around them. Eventually, fortunately for Deborah, the daughter of a family of Soho/Italian restaurateurs appeared two beds up and even Deborah's family's efforts paled into insignificance – but not before she had received the bell from an aunt in the Bronx. 'Anytime, any-where, beautiful girl,' the note had said, 'you ring that bell and God will listen. You ring it, you say, let's talk, and you talk. Believe me, beautiful baby, he will be listening.'

Deborah had been rather surprised that God had so little on his hands, but she did not make this point to the kind aunt in her thank you note.

Geoffrey knew the story of the bell, and very much hoped that God was paying attention now. He knew that the intruders were attacking the back of the house, for the signal he had rigged up to the front of the house was the tiny beeping of an electric watch. Somebody, in the privacy of the back garden, was working away at Deborah's bars, and they were very good at their job, because Geoffrey could not hear a thing.

However, he trusted his warning system and so decided to institute the hiding plan.


## THE HIDING PLAN

Geoffrey, on considering what it was he should do if ever the hidden hand that pursued him were to arrive at his door, had decided that it would be unwise to try and fight. He was realistic enough to realize that on the previous occasion he had been monumentally lucky, and, it would be foolish indeed for him to go about under the impression that he was in a position to get the better of enormous, heavily armed thugs whenever he so chose. Therefore, he had prepared a hiding place behind the ironing board.

Deborah's laundry was, of course, equipped for a person who did things sitting down, a conventional ironing board was far too high for her, besides which she would have found it extremely difficult to set one up. She would, of course, not have been alone in this. Everybody finds ironing boards extremely difficult to set up. The reason for this is that they were designed by a mad octopus, the same mad octopus who designed deck chairs.

Anyway, Deborah's ironing board was set into the wall, and hinged at the bottom, so that, when it was required, it could be simply pulled down. The wall it was set into was the partition wall between the laundry and the kitchen, which had originally been a single width of reinforced hardboard. However, on Geoffrey's instructions, Toss had spent the previous Sunday morning adding a second hardboard face to the kitchen side of the wall, thus creating an eight-inch wide cavity, access to which could be gained by lowering the ironing board and climbing through the ironing-board-shaped hole.

This Geoffrey did, and not a moment too soon, for the intruders had now dealt with the bars and also the glass at the rear of the house. As Geoffrey pulled up the board behind him, he could distinctly hear somebody climbing into the back bedroom, which belonged to Toss.

It was a brilliant hiding place, the two intruders missed it completely and were very soon satisfied that the flat was empty.

'So,' said Jurgen, a German employee of Euro Despatch. 'It is a pity, yes? No sign of our quarry.'

'I don't think he's home, Fritz,' replied Noddy, who wore a bobble hat and was from Wolverhampton. Noddy had named himself after the lead singer of Slade, Wolverhampton's contribution to the rock and roll hall of fame . . . 'What we going to do? Wait?' he enquired, leaning against the clothes drier in the laundry-room.

'I think not,' said Fritz, who wore a black polo neck and wished he had a duelling scar. 'Possibly one of the other two might return first. Let me remind you that the spastic fellow is our only target. Our employers do not wish to attract any more interest than is necessary.'

'Well, let's piss off up the pub then,' said Noddy, shrugging his shoulders.

Geoffrey, in his hiding place, was of course delighted with the turn events were taking, although he knew that he would now have to find a new safe house, which would deprive him of the society of the girl he loved. Still, it might make him concentrate.

## TRAITOROUS BODY WORK

Unfortunately, Geoffrey was rejoicing too soon, for his cerebral palsy, which had saved his life on a previous encounter with the forces of evil, now let him down terribly. His head jerked and banged against the cavity wall, then it did it again and after that, a third time. Probably this rhythm solo would have gone on for some time, but at that point, Jurgen pulled down the ironing board to reveal Geoffrey twitching behind it.

'So what have we here?' said Jurgen, all icy and cool.

'I think it's the spastic bloke we're s'posed t'kill,' replied Noddy, not realizing that Jurgen had asked a rhetorical question.

Geoffrey climbed out immediately, without being told to, he knew that his chances of survival were small whatever he did, but trapped inside a wall cavity they were zero. His body was uncooperative enough without further restricting it.

The laundry was necessarily a cramped space and Noddy was leant against the drier, whilst Jurgen was in front of the washing machine. Between them and Geoffrey was the little stool Geoffrey had been sitting on while his computer sat on top of an upturned laundry basket.

Jurgen was a professional killer, and the first maxim of professional killing is, not to talk about it, but to get it over with immediately. He knew the story of how this strange little twisted fellow had already got the better of his two colleagues. Looking at Geoffrey, he found the story difficult to believe, but he was taking no chances and intended to get his job over with at once. However, pose was also important to Jurgen. He reached inside his jacket for the silenced pistol with a languid hand, the other dangling casually down beside him, limply hanging inside the open lid of the top-loading clothes washer.

## TOUGHER THAN THE REST

Geoffrey was one of the coolest people in London, he was brave as a lion, smarter than a rat and in his whole life he had never allowed himself to be beaten. If you're spastic you simply can't, because if you did you would be beaten the minute you tried to get out of bed in the morning.

Of course, nobody ever really understood just how cool Geoffrey was. Even Deborah and Toss, who knew him well and also something of his deeds, could never fully comprehend just what an extraordinary individual he was, because the social conditioning is simply too strong. No matter what Geoffrey achieved it would always be a spastic achieving it and his future potential would always be doubted because it was the future potential of a spastic. Spastics just don't look like they're up to much and when, as so often they do, they prove that they are, other people are still secretly suspicious.

Geoffrey had a matter of a second in which to act. The controls of Deborah's machinery were wall-mounted, it was Geoffrey himself who had designed this. It saved Deborah having to try to reach out of her chair and lean across the top of the machinery. Many people in wheelchairs employ concertinaed, extendable arms with grips on the end, but Deborah did not need too, she was fortunate enough to have an electronics wizard for an admirer.

Geoffrey dropped his hand down and turned on the tumble drier, it jerked and rumbled behind Noddy. For a split second both Noddy and Jurgen were distracted, it was the old 'look over there' routine, but done much more effectively with a remote-controlled clothes drier.

There was a cup of washing powder on a shelf attached to the wall in which Geoffrey had just been hiding and, in the split second he had earned himself, Geoffrey brought his good hand up to grab it. As his hand came up it flipped the washing machine onto heavy stain wash. Deborah's water heater was one of those over-enthusiastic ones that heat the water so effectively that you could virtually make tea from the hot tap. A jet of scalding water spurted over Jurgen's hand, he shouted in pain, Noddy turned to him, eyes wide with surprise, and Geoffrey flung the powder in Noddy's face.

That was it, Geoffrey had exhausted his armoury and in the momentary confusion that he had created, all he could do was run like hell, or as much like hell as his unruly body would allow him.

By the time Geoffrey was through the living-room and into the hall, Noddy had recovered, and, despite streaming eyes, had drawn his gun and was in pursuit. Geoffrey wrenched open the front door, which set off the front alarm. The clanging made

Noddy pause for a moment which allowed Geoffrey to get out into the front path. The cool air of freedom hit him, he was going to make it, the crowded street was only a few feet away. Toss was just turning in through the gate.

'Wicked, Spas, what's happening?' he enquired of the figure jerking towards him, with its head bobbing against its shoulder and one arm performing a strange modern ballet all of its own.

But then there was no head, and no arm. Both simply disappeared mid-jerk, each absorbing the terrible impact of a barrel of Noddy's double-barrelled sawn-off shotgun, which Noddy fired the moment he had reached the doorway. For a moment Geoffrey's poor twisted, now virtually headless, body remained standing. Then it collapsed.

Noddy was gone, Jurgen too, they were out of the back before Toss could even understand what had happened. He just stood there staring at the corpse of his ruined friend.

Geoffrey Spasmo was dead, and the secret of his great invention had died with him.

Now Sam Turk really did hold the only ace.

## Chapter Nineteen

# THE CASUALTIES MOUNT

## THE JOLLY GRIDDLE

Springer had been desperate for a chance to talk to Sam ever since Sam had got back from Detroit, but he had had to wait almost a week because it had been agreed that any discussion of their secret project should take place very discreetly. There should be no chance of anyone following them or overhearing or even knowing that the meeting had taken place.

To this end, Sam had arranged that they should meet at the Jolly Griddle Family Restaurant on the A40 just south of Oxford. He judged this a sufficiently anonymous venue. Travelling salesmen stopped there all the time, two men deep in discussion would certainly not be noticed. Everyone was always too busy discussing how awful the food was.

Only in Britain could the Jolly Griddle chain not only survive but prosper. Only we could eat the stuff they dish up. On the road into hell there is a Jolly

Griddle Family Restaurant, and even there, where the fires of Hades burn with a fearsome heat, the fish is still frozen in the middle when it arrives at your table.

They just can't cook *anything* at these places and one is forced to wonder whether they do it deliberately. Surely it must be as easy to microwave a portion of baked beans right, as it is to microwave it wrong, so why do the beans always arrive congealed and with a skin on them? One would have thought it would be as easy to put the bit of lemon on top of the fish *after* heating as it is to do it before, so why does the bit of lemon always arrive dried up and microwaved to death? It is *almost* as easy to shake the water out of a portion of peas before dumping them on a plate as it is not to bother, so why does one's food have to arrive floating in an eighth of an inch of water?

Is it a conspiracy? Is it a joke? Is Mr Jolly Griddle screaming with laughter in his mansion? saying to his wife, 'I don't believe it, these people will eat *anything*!! What shall I try next? I know, ring the local shoe factory and ask them for a million individual lasagnes.'

## COLD INSIDE

'I don't believe this, the fish is still cold inside,' said Sam. 'Hey kid, come here,' he motioned to a bored dispirited adolescent. 'Kid, the fish is frozen on the inside, it is hot on the outside, but frozen on the inside. Half done is not done at all. You want me to eat the breadcrumbs, is that it?'

It was absolutely clear from the lad's expression that he did not give a tiny toss what Sam did with his meal. At the end of the week he would take home less than sixty five quid, if he hadn't still been living at his mum's he would have starved.

'I'll take it back then, shall I?' he said.

'It has already been back, kid, you took it back once, but it is still cold, how can that be? Did you forget what the problem was on the way or something? It is still cold.'

'Is it?' said the waiter, 'I'll take it back then, shall I?'

'Hey Sam, why don't you just eat your French fries,' said Springer, who had been under the impression that the whole point was that they were not supposed to draw attention to themselves.

'French fries? These are not French fries, Springer, these are *English* fries, which is why they are white, bendy and soaking up water from the peas. OK kid, forget it, life's too short,' Sam motioned the waiter away.

'Sam you told me this was all hush hush,' said Springer slightly reprovingly as the waiter retreated. 'Why did we drive fifty miles to eat garbage if we are putting up a sign saying we are here?'

'Springer,' said Sam, 'look at this stuff. That kid must get asked to take back every second piece of fish he serves. If I *hadn't* have complained, now that would have drawn attention.'

This of course showed how, despite his year in the country, Sam still knew very little about the British, because the British would rather die than cause a scene. Very little food was ever sent back at Jolly Griddles. Thousands of mums and dads sit in these family restaurants, seething with anger, swearing they will say something, but, unless the fish actually bites the children, they rarely do.

Sam and Springer's conversation turned to Sam's visit to Detroit.

'So you saw Tungsten? Gosh I'll bet he freaked, I'll bet he did a back flip,' said Springer.

'Yeah, he was pretty excited,' conceded Sam.

'Excited, I'll bet he was excited. He is going to be the most important car maker since Henry Ford. The three of us are going to be American heroes! I guess even if they learnt we had to bump off the little professor they'd forgive us.'

Sam looked at Springer with the same quizzical look he had used on the beach in Brighton.

'Not that anyone's ever going to find out of course,' Springer quickly corrected himself.

'Bruce's reaction was kind of strange, Springer,' said Sam. 'He had a kind of different plan to ours. I don't know, it took me back a little I confess, but it sort of has its points.'

'What plan could there be other than to make the engine?' asked Springer, mystified.

'Well, to not make the engine of course. Bruce wants to suppress the whole thing and sell the designs to the oil people, to the Arabs. Get paid off in billions and pretend there never was a hydrogen engine.' Sam was watching Springer carefully. It took Springer a moment to reply, he was too surprised to speak.

'Why the dirty, rotten little bastard,' he said eventually. 'I can't believe this! Bruce Tungsten? Mr Automobile? I thought the guy was a car man! I thought the guy was an American! Jesus Christ, Sam, what is he? some kind of drug addict? This engine means Global is back! It means the USA is back! Big beautiful babes rolling out of Detroit and across the world. It will be like the Japs never happened! . . . I don't believe this! Jesus . . .' Springer was lost for words.

'It would mean an unimaginable amount of money,' murmured Sam.

'We make our dough from making engines, besides you couldn't spend that much. Sam, you got to talk to him.'

'Yeah, I know,' conceded Sam. 'I just felt honour bound to give you his plan, and you're sure you're not interested?'

'Hey, what do you think? Get outta here! We've made cars together for twenty years. I'm a car man.'

'Good. OK,' said Sam. 'I'll talk to Bruce, I guess he'll come round.'

They paid the bill and walked out into the car-park together.

'Nine, two, four,' said Springer, following a custom that they had observed for all their years as a team. It meant that, not including their own, there were nine cars parked, of which two were Globals and four were Japanese. Given something to stand on, Springer could do the trick almost instantly with up to a hundred cars.

'A few years from now, nine, nine, zero, huh?' said Springer, getting into his new Crappee.

'Sure thing, old pal,' said Sam. 'You got a pen?'

Springer wound down his window, Sam leant in and shot him dead.

Springer's car had been parked in the corner of the car-park, it was four whole days before anyone even noticed something was wrong. No one remembered a thing. Sam, who of course had arranged a watertight alibi, was not even questioned. What possible motive could he have for killing his old pal and trusted employee?

Sam had never meant this to happen. He cursed himself for having been so foolish as to let Springer in on the secret at all. Bruce he needed, Springer he did not. Of course, at the point he had taken Springer into his confidence, Sam had not yet fully worked out the enormity of his plan, it had just been instinct, he and Springer worked together on everything.

Sam's ruthlessness surprised even himself.

'Dough is strange stuff,' he mused to himself as he drove back to London.

## LEARNING THE HARD WAY

Digby sat down in the driving seat of his beautiful Panther Chief Executive (Kevin Class). It was the last night he would have the car, back-bench MPs are not provided with ministerial limousines and Digby had received a curt note to return his to the Westminster car pool forthwith. The chauffeur had already gone. As he turned the key in the ignition he reflected on how quickly fate can lay a person low. Only a fortnight before he had been driven down to Brighton in this very car, rehearsing a speech which he hoped might lay the foundations of a leadership bid. Now he was a disgraced back-bencher, his career in ruins. That, however, as Digby well knew was not the half of it. His current situation would appear quite idyllic once the newspapers hit the doorsteps in the morning. What's more, Digby knew that he had only himself to blame. It wasn't just his appalling naïvety in going to the press, for which he was chastising himself, it was the craven and cowardly attitude he had adopted to his whole bloody life. There was, he knew, no question that his imminent exposure in the *Sunday Word* as a homosexual (what's more a homosexual with rather camp theatrical tastes), would be rendered infinitely more cruel by the lifetime of denial which had gone before. It was not just that he had always portrayed himself as a jovially sexist rogue either, far worse was his utter failure to attempt in any way to change the prejudices of society, prejudices to which he was about to fall victim. He had not only denied the fact of his own body, he had actually conspired against it. Digby's party, despite harbouring many a closet gay, was rabidly homophobic and Digby had gone along with all the slurs and prejudices. He had snorted with laughter at the queer jokes that regularly delighted the members' bar and eagerly joined in campaigns of slander against local councils who sought more tolerant attitudes towards sexual minorities. All this was going to make Digby look pretty pathetic in the morning when four million newspapers appeared with the headline 'DIRTY DIGBY IS A RAVING WHOOPSIE'. You just don't mess with the press, that had always been the dictum. How could Digby have forgotten it?

He had learnt of the terrible consequences of his pact with the devil only that morning. Astonishingly, he had actually woken up feeling perkier than at any time since he had received the Prime Minister's acceptance of a resignation he had not then even proffered. The sun was shining, the toast was hot and as he indulged in the tiny sensual pleasure of pushing down the plunger in the coffee maker, Ingmar Bresslaw's terrible anger was beginning to fade from Digby's mind.

Contemplating life as a back-bencher again, Digby could see its good side. It wasn't a bad old life, if you had a decent sized majority and your constituency party still supported you, which Digby's did, (after all, they reasoned, better to have an ex-minister for your MP, than one who had never held real power at' all). Digby sipped his coffee, and mused, almost eagerly, on the jolly, irresponsible lot of the back-bencher. He would be able to whoop and holler and shout 'shame' and flick ink pellets at the opposition and cheek the new oiks, just as he had done before high office had dampened his high spirits. He would be able to get as drunk as he liked before debates without being in any danger of having to make a contribution, the only constraint imposed on a back-bencher's drinking being that he remains sufficiently sober to go through the right lobby at division. Yes, Digby could indulge in all the Boys' Own fun of the back of the House without that irritating anonymity which is the lot of most of the six hundred. He was an ex-minister, he would be able to strut and boast about the place posing as a rebel ('I play a lone hand, and I'm nobody's lap dog'). Having rubbed shoulders with power he would always be in demand as an after dinner speaker, people like hearing about power ('I recall once saying firmly to the Prime Minister, whilst I knew the Foreign Secretary to be listening . . .'). He was still young, he could become a socialite, dining out with celebrities, telling them what the Queen was really like ('two words: gracious lady').

Besides all this, he would be well off for the first time in his life. As an ex-minister there was no doubt he would be able to pick up numerous lucrative directorships. Already his name had been linked in the papers with Cornelius Brandt, and people were talking about him as a possible titular head of the British Division of Imperial Oil. It is a curious thing, but when ministers resign there is much press speculation about what they will do for a job. This speculation continues until, after much horse trading, they emerge as a director of British Telecom or something similar. The fact that the ex-minister in question is still an MP and, hence, already has a job, representing the tens of thousands of people in his constituency, passes without comment. This was the case with Digby. Renowned git though he was, to those in the know, he was still considered to be eminently employable. As far as the party was concerned he had resigned in disgrace, but to the public at large he was the outspoken champion of the road who had been forced out of office. There would, no doubt, be numerous petrol pumpers, car manufacturers and motoring organizations eager to improve their profiles by giving the fiery and quixotic ex-Transport Minister a position on the board.

Then the doorbell rang, shattering Digby's happy reverie forever.

Digby answered the door himself, his treasure

who 'did' for him had not yet arrived ('she is *marvellous*, I would have been *submerged* long ago without her. Can't speak a word of English, of course').

'Mr Parkhurst,' said Galton, and despite the fact that the sun was shining strongly, he did not disintegrate into a pile of dust as blood sucking vampires are supposed to do.

'Yes, Digby Parkhurst, can I help you?' replied Digby, rather stiffly.

'I see you don't remember me, Sir, that's all right, I'm used to that, Sir. We were introduced. Galton, of the *Sunday Word*, I attended the interview which you gave for Mr Christian Corbet, my editor.'

Thinking about it, Digby did recall a shadowy figure lurking in the shadows.

'Hmm, yes, well have you prepared your story?' Digby asked. 'I shall not hesitate to offer it to a rival publication.'

'Oh we've prepared it all right, Sir. Out tomorrow in fact. I wonder if I might have a few words, Mr Parkhurst. Just to clear up one or two details?'

'I really cannot see why that should be necessary,' replied Digby. 'Now if you'll excuse me, I am an extremely busy man.'

'All right Digby, boy, I'll cut the crap, shall I? We know you take it up the arse and we know that on the night before your speech one of your bum boy pals visited you in your hotel room wearing a dress and false eyelashes. We also know that the following day he blackmailed you into cocking up your career. Here's his picture. He's Scottish.'

It was moments like this that made Galton's day. Digby went from white to green. He actually gagged and croaked as his stomach turned over with fear and loathing.

'May I come in now?' enquired Galton.

'What for?' asked Digby, in a ghastly whisper.

'Well, it might be possible for us to add a slightly more favourable slant to what is, after all, a pretty seedy story, if you were able to see yourself clear to confessing everything exclusively to the *Sunday Word* and giving us the background of your queer ways, you know. Did some wicked old bugger have you when you were a kid and set you on the path to frightfulness? Very mitigating that, Digby, very mitigating.'

For a moment Digby even considered it, making up some awful fiction about being forced to be gay at school, pleading with Galton to go easy. But then a spark of sanity, perhaps even honour, bubbled its way to the surface and Digby realized that there was not a chance in hell of Galton going easy, and anyway, he had been lying for too long.

'I have nothing further to say,' replied Digby.

'We shall have to go with the story as it stands, Digby,' said Galton.

'Go to the devil,' said Digby, slamming the door, but Galton had sold his soul that way a long time before.

## CARBON MONOXIDE

The beautiful Panther Chief Executive had been running quite a while now, but Digby wasn't going anywhere. He just sat there, with the car in neutral and a hose-pipe running from the exhaust pipe in through the top of the slightly open passenger window. Digby's eyes were closed. The internal combustion engine had claimed another victim.

## Chapter Twenty

# *DOWN BUT NOT OUT*

Deborah and Toss had not spoken much in the week since Geoffrey had been murdered. Neither of them could think of anything to say, the shock was too great. Toss, who had actually seen him die, could not expunge the vision of Geoffrey's last seconds from his mind. Deborah, who had loved Geoffrey, and felt as one with him in the colossal battles of his life, was quite simply bowed down with grief.

Whilst there was still the police to deal with, they had both held up quite strongly. Deborah had tried desperately to interest the police in the disappearance of Geoffrey's invention, but since the Office of Patents vigorously asserted that they knew nothing of any invention and Deborah could not produce anything to substantiate her claims that an invention had ever even existed, the police were inclined to believe that Geoffrey lived in a world of fantasy and delusion, probably chemically induced.

'Drugs Sir, gotta be,' DC Collingwood opined to the Superintendent as they left. 'These Spasos, well, they got nothing to live for have they? Not surprising a few of them turn to the honeyed oblivion of drug induced ecstacy. The bloke couldn't pay for his trips and hits and pops, Sir, so he got done, simple as that, I reckon.'

## COMFORT IN THE LORD

Deborah had hoped that Geoffrey's funeral might provide a catalyst whereby she might come to terms a little with the dreadful mourning which haunted her, but it didn't.

'After a lifetime of struggle and torment,' the vicar had said, trying to be nice, 'our brother Geoffrey is happy in God.'

Deborah squirmed, even in death, Geoffrey was being defined by his disability. The vicar, nice bloke though he was, was offering comfort in the idea that, in a sort of way, death was a release for Geoffrey. Without saying it, he was suggesting that it must be so bloody awful being a spastic that, in a way, even having your head blown away with a sawn-off shotgun was sort of preferable. Deborah knew Geoffrey was not happy in God, he had never wanted to die. He hadn't wanted to be a spastic either, but that was beside the point. He had definitely never wanted to die. He wanted to work, write, drink, enjoy his friends and, if possible, have

299

it off occasionally. None of which, Deborah imagined, you could do with God. It just wouldn't be right.

'As we all know,' continued the vicar, 'Geoffrey rose magnificently above the burdens that God chose to place upon his shoulders. The Lord moves in mysterious ways and we can never know what purpose he had in so afflicting Geoffrey. Perhaps he understood Geoffrey's strength, and wished to use him as an example to others who were not so strong.'

'That makes sense,' thought Deborah. As tears streamed down her cheeks, her thoughts flooded with the occasions when Geoffrey's indomitable spirit and wit had proved to her how strong she could be herself, even from her chair.

'Whatever purpose God saw for Geoffrey upon Earth, it is done now,' the vicar concluded. 'For Geoffrey's struggles are over, and he is at peace.'

But Deborah knew that he wasn't. She wanted to shout. She wanted to scream to them all that Geoffrey's immortal soul was about as peaceful as Beirut. She gripped Toss's hand as anguish flooded through her. Geoffrey's work, his engine, the one he had designed for her, was gone. Gone forever. How could he ever be at peace? Everything he had dreamt of had been stolen and he wasn't there to put it right.

At the graveside they watched Geoffrey's small coffin being lowered into the grave.

'Leave plenty of room, guy,' murmured Toss

under his breath, 'because the geezer is going to be doing a lot of turning in the grave. He is going to spin.' Toss's thoughts were along similar lines to Deborah's. He knew that Geoffrey had failed, they had all failed.

## READ ALL ABOUT IT

In the days after the funeral the torment had increased. Deborah could find nothing to do with herself, nothing to occupy her mind. It was the weekend and she had decided that she would seek grief counselling on the Monday, the victims support group had been in touch and she had got the number of an analyst from a friend.

'I know it seems kinda New York to be going to an analyst,' Deborah had said to Toss, her eyes red with a week of crying. 'But I can't go on like this. It's worse than when I was crippled. He came to us for help. Now he's dead and his engine's gone and we don't know who did all this to him, Toss. We've no one to fight, no one to blame. It's the impotence that's killing me inside. If we had just one clue, Toss, just something to think about, something to do, I think I would be all right, but we don't. We've got nothing, and we never will, we're tiny people and we've been stepped on.'

That had been Saturday night, the Saturday that Digby turned the key of his ex-ministerial limmo. As Digby breathed himself to death, Deborah cried herself to sleep.

By Sunday morning Digby's suffering was long over, but for Deborah there was no relief. Often, at times of great unhappiness, a person will wake up and check themselves, wondering for a brief second, ecstatic with potential, whether the load has been lifted, only to realize a moment later, as the liquid lead runs into the stomach, that nothing has changed.

Deborah hauled herself out of bed and went through into the kitchen to make coffee, imagining, as she did every time she entered her kitchen-cum-laundry area, Geoffrey's last terrible dash for freedom.

Some people had recoiled at Deborah wanting to continue to live in a flat, in the garden of which a close friend had had his head blown off only a week before. These people had no idea what it is like to be a paraplegic. Deborah could not simply move in somewhere else. Her home was her haven. There, everything was designed as much as possible to work for her, as opposed to the exact opposite, which is how everything is designed in the outside world. Deborah needed that home, and anyway, it was hers. She would not leave it just because some evil low-life had invaded it. Toss, on the other hand, would have liked to move, but he stayed for Deborah's sake. He didn't like it, he wanted desperately to get away from the gloomy presence of tragedy and the constant reminder of the appalling moment in the garden. But he had to stay.

Toss was still asleep as Deborah made the coffee, but his paper had been delivered. He favoured the *Sunday Word*. 'Just for a laugh, know what I mean. See who's screwing who.'

Deborah always claimed to be stunned that Toss would pay good money for such drivel. However, like everybody else, she would flick through a copy herself when she got the chance.

And there it was. The clue she had been wishing for. Deborah did not realize it at first, she was merely reading with interest the surprising secret life of an ex-cabinet minister. Halfway through the article, however, she came to the meat of the matter. A sideline issue to most readers, nothing like as interesting as the stockings and suspenders, but it was life and death to Deborah.

Having got through its story that Parkhurst was being blackmailed by a Scottish transvestite railway nut, bent on hijacking the government's BritTrak scheme (probably the most accurate front page the *Sunday Word* had ever printed), the newspaper went on to explain . . .

During the *Sunday Word*'s painstaking investigations, the minister made a cowardly and dishonourable attempt to throw us off the scent. Explaining his conference cock-up by claiming that Samuel Turk, the Chief Executive of Global Motors, had been blackmailing him. The reason for this, nervous Parkhurst claimed, was that Turk had stolen plans for a 'miracle motor' from the Office of Patents, and that Parkhurst had been on to him.

The *Sunday Word* approached Mr Turk, who strenuously denied the accusation. We also contacted Deirdre Whelk, the senior Civil Servant at the Office of Patents, who denied any knowledge of a miracle motor. There had been a break-in, she admitted, but nothing had been stolen.

An hour later, when Toss wandered in wiping the sleep from his eyes Deborah had already decided what she had to do.

'Toss, the time has come to fight back,' she said, in a firm, decisive voice. He looked at her in surprise. It seemed to Toss that Deborah had been speaking in a sombre weepy monotone for so long that he had forgotten what her usual voice sounded like.

'Yo, girl,' he replied, 'what is happening with this new-found decisiveness? Has an alien with a positive attitude taken over your body?'

'Toss, I know who has Geoffrey's engine designs . . . it's all here in the paper. It's a guy called Sam Turk, an American I am shamed to say.'

'Well, they can't all be like you and the Statue of Liberty,' said Toss, kindly.

'Thanks, I hope I look as good as she does when I'm a hundred years old. Listen, this guy is the head of Global Motors, and I am going in there, and I am going to get Geoffrey's engine back.'

## Chapter Twenty-One

# *BIG DEAL*

Later that same Sunday, the unwitting target of Deborah's increasing wrath was in Geneva facing the representatives of the world's oil producers. They were a powerful crowd but Sam Turk eyeballed them without a flicker of nerves. Turk had been Global Motors' principal union-breaker back in the fifties. During those heady days, he had thought nothing of having decent men beaten and the frighteners put on their families. He had been one hundred per cent in bed with the mob, kept a baseball bat on his desk and stood as God-parent to the children of made men. Sam prided himself that it took quite something to scare him. He didn't know it, but as he sat staring down at the oil men, that something was sitting in a wheelchair in London staring at his face in a newspaper.

# THE UNION

The Union of Oil is the loose cartel by which many of those states which produce petroleum products organize their affairs and attempt, when they're not at war with one another, to prevent damaging competition.

Never had a U of O delegation been organized so quickly as the one which Bruce Tungsten and Cornelius Brandt had brought about. Even when they were fighting, Union of Oil diplomacy happened at a fairly leisurely pace. Decades of sucking out of the ground a liquid for which the whole world thirsted had led to a lack of urgency, perhaps even complacency, in its dealings. Another block to the Union operating in a time-effective manner was the disparate nature of its membership. It was made up of a mixture of feudal monarchs, military dictators and elected prime ministers. In fact, such were the differences of principle and method within the group, that everybody knew that anything the U of O decided, might, at any time, be completely ignored by one or other of the countries involved.

Not only was it extraordinary that the U of O had assembled so quickly, but it was extraordinary that it had assembled at all, because at the time of their meeting with Sam, the Union of Oil was supposed to be hopelessly divided. The conventional wisdom amongst diplomatic circles was that it would be

months, perhaps years, before they could be persuaded to even talk to each other. The problem being
that one of their number had invaded a neighbour, the
aggressor claiming that the neighbour had been
stealing its oil by means of long bendy pipes that
tunnelled deep and looped under the border.

None the less, all the member states sanctioned
this meeting, including the two belligerents whose
soldiers were at that moment locked in mortal
conflict. The reason being that when figures as
senior to Western oil interests as Bruce Tungsten,
America's Mr Automobile, and Cornelius Brandt,
the boss of Imperial Oil, shuttle red-eyed from
country to country announcing that oil will be
economically dead inside two decades unless
immediate action is taken, even the slothful U of O
gets its arse into gear.

The meeting was, of course, conducted in the
deepest secrecy. The current war had caused both
the United States and the European Community
endless diplomatic and military inconvenience. The
leaders of those powers would clearly have been
none too pleased to learn that after months of
refusing to meet, representatives of the two belligerents were now having tea together. Of course the
other, even more important, reason for secrecy was
that the meeting involved the suppression of an
invention which could bring great benefits to
humankind. The last thing anybody needed was
moral dilemmas to muddy the deal.

## A LESSON IN DIPLOMACY

Cornelius Brandt had been surprised when it was Sam Turk, not Bruce Tungsten, that he met at Geneva airport. Cornelius was extremely tense, it is never any fun having to tell the people upon whom you rely for your livelihood that they are about to get stung for a gigantic amount of cash. Of course it was not Brandt's fault, but none the less he could not help feeling that the affair, once concluded, was likely to sour his business relationships for some time to come. Perhaps it was the tension that made him so brusque.

'What are you doing here, Turk? Yes?' he snapped. 'They are expecting Tungsten, they want the master not his dog.'

If Sam was stung by this rather rude remark he did not show it.

'Well, ol' pal,' he grinned, 'I decided I needed the trip.'

In fact Bruce had also been extremely surprised when Sam had announced that he would convey a sample of Geoffrey's design to the Geneva meeting, and strike the deal himself. Bruce had argued forcefully that, since he had set up the meeting, it should be he that chaired it.

'I don't see that, Bruce,' Sam had said affably. 'Setting up the meeting was where the influence and credibility were required, but now you've done that, why it doesn't matter a damn who actually shows them the engine. Ronald McDonald could do it and the results would be the same. The engine does the talking, ol' pal.'

This had prompted Bruce to, again, make the point that he himself, as co-conspirator, had yet to set eyes on these magical designs. Sam protested that he wasn't exactly going to fax them to the States, but assured Bruce that his curiosity would be satisfied the moment he got to London. However, by the time Bruce did arrive in London, Sam had already arrived in Geneva, where he and Cornelius Brandt were getting into a limousine.

'Take us up around the lake a little,' Sam said to the driver, explaining to Brandt that he required privacy in order to offer Brandt further information. Brandt said nothing and sulked.

Soon they were amongst the countryside and Sam got out of the car.

'You go hiking if you want,' said Brandt, staying put, 'I hate trees.'

Sam walked round to the driver and gave him five thousand American dollars.

'That's to have your panel beaten out and fix your paintwork, son,' he said, before walking round to Brandt's side of the car. Brandt's look of surprise soon turned to fear as Sam dragged him out of the car by the collar, threw him face down over the bonnet of the big Mercedes and bashed his head a couple of times against the beautiful, smooth metal.

'You got yourself a bargain, kid,' said Sam to the astonished driver while still holding Brandt face down on the bonnet, 'they build these Mercs like fucking panzers. Why I don't think I've scratched it. If this had been a British car his head would be buried in the road.'

Sam pulled Cornelius Brandt round to face him, there was a huge nasty bruise on his forehead and his nose was bleeding.

'OK, listen up, little Dutchman!' said Sam, still with the same big smile and easy manner. 'Don't call me a dog, OK? Don't put me down and be mean, you understand, I hate it.'

Sam pushed Cornelius Brandt back into the car and ordered the driver to head for the private villa where the momentous deal was to be discussed.


## TEA PARTY

On arrival at the villa, Sam and Cornelius had been met by the chief technical officer of the Union of Oil. Sam presented him with a copy of Geoffrey's plans and he took them away for study by a team of top engine brains and fuel heads. After that, Sam and Cornelius waited. They knew that they would not be received by the Union representatives themselves until after the engine's credentials had been established.

The hours passed, lunch was served, and then tea. Not a word passed between Sam and Cornelius.

Conversation is always a bit stilted between two people, when one of them has recently beaten the other up. But Sam was a naturally gregarious soul and the silence really got on his nerves. As the long hours ticked away, he began to wish that he had not dealt so roughly with Brandt. Eventually he could bear it no longer.

'Hell, if I'd a'known we were gonna be sat staring at each other all day, I never would have buried your ugly mug in that car hood,' he said by way of conciliation.

Cornelius said nothing, refusing even to look Sam in the face.

'What, are you going to sulk all day?' said Sam. 'OK, so I bruised your head. Here, look, does this make you feel any better?' and with that Sam leant his big body forward and head butted the table, making all the tea things rattle. 'How was that?' he enquired, a nasty bump already rising on his forehead. Still he was received in stony silence . . . 'Oh, yeah, I forgot,' Sam continued, 'I slammed you two times didn't I?' and again Sam whacked his head down on the table, this time making the top jump off the sugar bowl.

'Mr Turk,' the Dutchman said, as if speaking to the opposite wall, 'your football yob behaviour, which is like a thug or something, yes? is not edifying, it is not smart. You disgrace yourself, yes?'

'Aw diddums,' said Sam not very cleverly. And silence returned.

Another fifteen minutes passed, it seemed like fifteen years. Sam sighed, paced about the room, sat down, drummed his fingers, sighed, got up again, whistled a couple of bars of 'Forty Second Street', accompanying it with a little shuffle, sat down again, picked up his teaspoon, sighed, then started tapping his teaspoon against his cup. Now it was Brandt's turn to be consumed with irritation.

'Don't tap please, yes?' he said through gritted teeth.

Sam stopped tapping. Then after about a minute he started again. 'Ching, ching, ching,' went the teacup. Cornelius Brandt's face grew tense, but he said nothing.

Sam kept on tapping. He tapped and tapped and tapped. Having tapped out the 'William Tell Overture' on his cup about fifty times, Sam decided he could do better than that. He stopped tapping and rolled up a little pellet of bread, which he flicked at Cornelius, making a noise like a cannon. More pellets followed.

'Enemy sighted, Sir,' said Sam, playing at being a military commander. 'Little Dutch faggot, range eight feet. OK, let's hit 'em with a thermo-nuclear, inter-continental ballistic bread pellet from Uncle Sam. Ready, aim, fire.' The pellet hit Brandt on the nose.

Sam upgraded his technology. He employed a knife to improve the force and accuracy of his projectiles. He used up all the bread on his own

313

plate in some twenty or thirty pellets. 'Peow,' he said, followed by the sound of an explosion whenever he managed to hit Brandt's head.

'Excuse me,' Sam said, leaning across, 'could I have your bread if you're not using it? Mine is all through.'

Cornelius cracked, he snatched up his teacup, which happened to be half full of cold tea, and hurled the liquid into Sam's face. Sam then emptied the contents of the pot over Cornelius, a teabag ending up perched on top of his head.

Silence fell again and not another word was said between the two men until an emissary arrived to inform them that the Union of Oil was ready to talk.

## THE DEAL

The gathering was not as large as Sam had expected. Not every country involved was individually represented and only the four largest oil companies had sent delegates. However, those in attendance had authority to speak for all, so the atmosphere was heavy with money and power.

'My science officer informs me that Mr Tungsten did not exaggerate, and nor did you Mr Brandt.'

The bearded and berobed prince was attempting to play it very calm and regal and was not doing a bad job of it. However, Sam, who had seen a hundred men bluffing in his time, could see that the oil potentate was badly shaken.

'You undoubtedly have in your possession a technological breakthrough which could, we agree, one day produce a viable alternative to the petrol engine.'

'Oh, is that so?' said Sam.

'Yes, it is, and we congratulate you,' answered the Prince.

'Well that's nice, your Highness, but congratulations, even from a big cheese like yourself, trade pretty light against the US dollar.' Sam was standing four square, a big bruise on his forehead and tea stains on his collar.

'Yes, we have no doubt that if you continue along the lines that your research has taken you so far, one day, in as little as perhaps ten years you may produce a viable prototype. A prototype which would undoubtedly put in question the long-term future of the petro dollar. We thank you most sincerely for bringing the matter to our attention.'

'Well, thank *you*, your Highness,' said Sam rather nastily.

'You were right to think that we would be interested in aquiring the world rights to the research you have conducted so far. We concur that it is essential to the Union of Oil's long-term interests that we maintain control over such developments . . .'

'Excuse me, your Highness,' Sam interrupted the Prince. The Prince was extremely surprised, having never been interrupted before. In fact, the Prince was on the verge of ordering ten lashes for impudence, but he was reluctantly forced to recognize that he did not have the authority at the present time. The Prince's surprise and irritation was to turn to anger, moments later, as Sam's tone became clear.

'I wonder if I might just dig out my big shovel here, Prince, and start to shift a little bit of this bullshit,' said Sam. Cornelius Brandt instinctively stepped away from him, half expecting a bolt of lightning to put an end to Sam's impudence. The Prince raised an elegant eyebrow.

'Explain yourself, Mr Turk. If possible without recourse to the language of the gutter,' he said.

'Oh, I'm sorry, Prince. I didn't realize a guy who would cut off a thief's hands for stealing a goat would be quite so sensitive.'

'Kindly keep your tired and unimaginative prejudices to yourself, Mr Turk, and stick to the point. What have I said that you consider to be so foolish?'

'Oh, it's just something in phrases like "one day", "in ten years", "prototype", those kind of words, Prince. Words that sort of give the impression that you're trying to bull me about how much you reckon what I got is worth.'

'On the contrary, we accept absolutely that you are in possession of a major breakthrough. We wish to acquire the rights and we are prepared to offer yourself and Mr Bruce Tungsten eight million

United States dollars each, for the world patent.'

'So long, guys,' said Sam, heading for the door. 'Get yourselves a copy of the next issue of *Scientific American*, the death warrant of your industry is going to be on the cover. You can keep those designs if you like. We're registered in the US and Bruce Tungsten will have the damn things rolling out of Detroit before you know it.'

'Mr Turk,' spluttered Brandt.

The Prince nodded a tiny nod and Sam's way was blocked by two gentlemen in suits who had been standing by the door.

'Listen, towel-head,' said Sam, spinning round. 'You know that if I don't report back to Tungsten tonight, or one of my secret partners, we go ahead with the engine.'

'Do not judge everyone by your own loathsome standards, Mr Turk. You are not in any danger,' said the Prince, and he probably meant it, although a glance round the room would quickly have informed Sam that certain other Union members might not be so considerate.

'So how come you're blocking my path?' asked Sam.

'Because I have come a long way to conduct these negotiations and I must insist that you have the courtesy to complete them,' answered the Prince.

'In which case have the courtesy not to crap me, OK? You know damn well that my engine is at production level. There ain't gonna be any more research or development. We are ready to roll, and if we do you had better buy yourself a herd of goats, because we are sure as hell gonna derail your private gravy train, Prince.'

The Prince looked about at his colleagues, all of whom were empowered to negotiate on behalf of their states. Their faces were resigned. None of them had expected the bluff to work, and it hadn't. They would have to pay.

'Twenty billion dollars you say?' enquired the Prince.

'Oh hot, damn!' said Sam. 'You see I've been working in London, England, this last year or so. I think in *pounds* these days. Have to ya see, so as I can compute how many Ecus to charge for my product!'

Cornelius Brandt shook with anger. 'You're mad, Turk. Don't ask it,' he stammered.

The Prince remained outwardly calm, but he too was shaken, everyone was. Sam had even surprised himself, he had not been planning to nearly double his demand.

'Am I to understand that your price is twenty billion *pounds*?'

Sam was a gambling man, he read the faces of the people in the game and he decided to chance raising the stakes. 'The price for the world rights in perpetuity to the Global Motors hydrogen engine is now fifty billion United States dollars. Payable in gold, securities or cash. What's more, it goes up five billion every two and a half minutes from now on,' Sam looked pointedly at his watch.

'Mr Turk,' even the ultra cool Prince was now showing his emotions. 'This is no way for civilized people to conduct negotiations.'

'I ain't civilized, your Highness,' said Sam, thumbs in waistband. 'I'm an American car man and proud of it. I wasn't born, I was beaten out of a quarter-inch steel panel in Detroit. We never set much store by being civilized down on the auto line.'

'Oh *please*,' said Cornelius Brandt.

'Now listen up, all of you, OK?' Sam barked. 'We all know that you have no choice whatsoever. Your people have checked out the plans and you know how extraordinary they are. Can't think why nobody figured out the secret before. Lucky for you they didn't, or you'd never have got as fat as you did.' This was rather rich coming from a man who himself sported a belly you could have plumped up and got cosy on. 'Maybe they did figure it out, maybe I ain't the first guy you've had to buy off. Whatever, if the engine goes into production you know that you're all peasants again. Personally, I reckon you're getting a bargain here at fifty billion. Mind you, gentlemen, I feel obliged to inform you that in about a minute the price will be fifty-five billion.'

'Mr Turk,' said the Prince, in a lifeless voice. 'The member states of the Union of Oil, in conjunction with the major petroleum refining and distribution companies' (at that Cornelius Brandt gulped) 'hereby undertake to purchase from you, Samuel Turk, managing director of Global Motors UK, the exclusive world rights, in perpetuity, to the hydrogen engine developed by the Global Motor Company. The Global Motor Company will, in their turn, undertake never to build a single unit of the said engine, or divulge the secret of the engine to any third party. The price agreed is fifty billion United States dollars.'

'Sorry,' said Sam checking his watch, 'twenty seconds too late, it's fifty-five billion.'

'What!' the Prince, so icy a moment before, positively spluttered.

'Too much pompous bullshit, Prince. All you needed to say was "deal" but you had to dress it up like some kind of fucking international treaty. Well, I warned you.'

The whole room erupted in furious protest.

'Mr Turk!' Cornelius Brandt shouted, 'this is absurd! Unjust! You cannot possibly . . .'

'I can do just what I damn well like,' barked Sam. 'Because I've got you guys over a barrel with your balls in a clamp, so don't tell me nothing, OK? Now I like you guys, and so I'm going to do you a big favour, by reminding you that in less than a minute the price goes up from fifty-five to sixty billion.'

'Deal,' said the Prince.

# NEAR TO DEATH

After Sam had gone, the Union of Oil and the big petrol pumpers had a conference. At first everyone shouted at once and the result was a confused babble. However, one thing was clear as crystal, if Sam had entertained any hopes of receiving a birthday card from the assembled group, he was going to be disappointed.

Soon it became clear that there was a distinct group who favoured direct action. The loudest voiced in this group was a tough looking man in military fatigues.

'This man cheats and insults us. He is a bully, a braggart, I am confident that General Ali will want him dead.'

General Ali was the military dictator who had invaded his neighbour, and no slouch at the bullying and braggarting game himself. A very different type of leader indeed to the people that the Prince represented, he thought nothing of using military force and terrorism to achieve his ends. All in all he was a very scary man. It was well known, about the Gulf, that you did not mess lightly with General Ali.

'Killing Turk would be pointless,' snapped the Prince.

'Oh yes?' enquired the man in fatigues. 'Then perhaps you would like to be the person who informs the General that we have just negotiated a fifty-five billion dollar pay-off and that he is expected to contribute.'

'Gladly. I will phone him now,' the Prince boldly replied.

'Why the hell not kill the man?' the hawks in the group pressed. And the doves explained that it would do no good, for some other conspirator, Tungsten for instance, would take over control of the engine.

'Well, we'll kill him as well,' announced the man in fatigues.

'We have no idea who is a party to this invention,' snapped the Prince. 'It is absurd to suppose that we would be able, with absolute certainty, to suppress it by force. The only way that we can be one hundred per cent certain that this engine will never be produced, is to own it ourselves, and the only way to do that is to purchase it legally. If we start to chase it you may rest assured that very quickly it will emerge somewhere, and then it would be unstoppable.'

There was no doubting the logic of this and the hawks sulkily agreed that the legal way was the only sure way.

'But we could kill the swine anyway,' said the General's man, hopefully, 'and deal with Tungsten.'

Fortunately for Sam, he was outvoted. Unfortunately for Sam, General Ali had never had a great respect for democracy.

## Chapter Twenty-Two

# MR AUTOMOBILE, SUPERWOMAN AND THE GENERAL

## WAITING ON THE WORD

Bruce Tungsten had been jittery ever since he got back from his mysterious trip to the Gulf, everyone had noticed. The company was in the midst of a massive catalogue update, bringing a series of new models and improved classics onto the market. By rights, Bruce Tungsten should have been at his sharpest and most involved. He wasn't though, he was preoccupied, his mind was clearly elsewhere. In vain, the top design team tried to get final approval on the results of years of labour. Particularly urgent was the new four-wheel drive, off-road Rancheroo Prairie Cruiser, it was all ready to roll off the line. The media blitz was poised and the ads had been made. The car was to be targeted at young, urbane executives and city bankers, so the advert featured a rugged cowboy gone hunting in Wyoming: lean and silent; alone by an open fire with his dog.

'Will ya just look at the final cuts boss,' they

pleaded. 'Ranger and Toytana are both snapping at our heels here. We believe Toytana are offering a four-by-four that can cross rivers up to four feet deep and Ranger have a winching line that could drag a bus out of a swamp.

'Well, those should be useful features for picking up the groceries at the Seven Eleven,' murmured Bruce, fingering the strange little doll that always stood on his desk. His staff were most surprised at this. Mr Automobile had never been cynical about a car before.

They clamoured at him to make the decisions they required, but Bruce was evasive. He was waiting for the phone to ring. Eventually it did, the secure line, Bruce knew that it was Sam Turk.

'Meeting's over, boys,' he said to his astonished employees. A collective 'but boss' was on the tip of their combined tongues, but you didn't 'but boss' Bruce Tungsten. They dutifully trooped out and Bruce spoke to Sam.

'What's the story, Sam? I had Cornelius Brandt on line an hour ago saying you were an animal, but he wouldn't tell me anything else.'

'Oh he's just a little touchy because I put a teabag on his head,' replied Sam. 'Bruce, ol' pal, we have pulled off a deal so big and so mean you could put a saddle on it and ride it in a rodeo. They had no choice pal, no choice. Guess what I stung them for, go on, guess . . . guess, you have to guess, go on, guess.'

'Sam, I have no idea,' replied Bruce. 'I haven't even seen . . .'

'Forty billion dollars.'

The phone almost fell from Bruce's hand.

'You have to be joking, Sam,' he replied, white-faced.

'Ye-e-e-e-s, I am!!!' screamed Sam Turk. 'Fifty-five billion Bruce, twenty-seven and a half each. What are you going to do huh? I think I'll just buy myself a little country in Central America and set myself up as a dictator, that way I get my own army and also I can give the President a hard time whenever the Democrats are in.'

'Sam, I've never even seen this damn engine,' said Bruce.

'No, that's right, you haven't at that,' said Sam, cheerfully, 'but you don't have to see it partner, they've seen it, and they want to buy it.'

'I want to see it, Sam,' said Bruce.

'Now listen here, Bruce. The deals have been done and you're damn lucky I'm not the kind to cheat on an old pal. It would be very easy for me to have just conveniently forgotten about any partners I might have had . . .'

'I know that, Sam,' said Bruce apologetically.

'Now, I don't know if you're having any crazy thoughts about this engine.'

'Sam, I was just curious, that's all.' Bruce was now less apologetic. 'I'm a damned car maker, and an engineer, I want to know how it works.'

'And I'll tell you sometime Bruce, believe me I will,' placated Sam. 'We'll sit down in some good old bar and I'll map the whole thing out with a couple of boxes of matches. But right now it's money that matters Bruce. We have to be in a position to receive fifty-five billion, in gold, bonds, assets and cash. And what's more, we have to do it by next Tuesday, which is when I told them I wanted to exchange.'

'That's quite impossible, Sam. The logistics would never fall into place. You can't just deposit it at a bank, it's just too much money. We are talking about the sort of assets that could destabilize an entire economy.'

'I know,' and Bruce could actually hear Sam grinning, 'isn't it beautiful?'

'Sam please, think about it. Adequately preparing to place fifty-five billion dollars on the world money markets cannot be done by two individuals in four days.'

'It has to Bruce, ol' pal. The longer we leave them to sweat over this, the more likely they are to start sticking bombs through letter boxes.'

'Sam, it can't be done.'

'Oh yes it can, least ways it had better, and it's *one* individual by the way. This is your job Bruce. I don't have the influence, or the clout to pull it off. No bank would take my word on those kind of figures. No brokerage would listen to me. So let me tell you how it's going to be Bruce. There's fifty-five billion coming in. That's two lots of twenty-seven and a half. Except the Gulf states pay on Tuesday, and what they can't unload they take back with them. So my share, ol' pal, is the *first* twenty-seven and a half they can invest on your instructions, and yours is the second, anything you can't find a home for, you lose.'

'Sam, by Tuesday!' protested Bruce. But the line was dead.

Bruce touched the intercom button.

'Michelle,' he said, 'cancel everything for the next five days.'

'But Mr Tungsten,' came the astonished reply. 'You can't possibly . . . Sir, this is the most important . . . Why the whole new range . . .'

'Cancel everything, Michelle,' said Bruce. 'A few days from now it won't matter a damn.'

## SUPERWOMAN

As Sam put the phone down on Bruce, something which he had never done before, in another part of the great Global UK building an employment officer was also putting down the phone having spoken to Deborah.

'Global Motors UK is an equal opportunities employer,' the paper had said, and as Deborah dialled the number, she wondered.

'They don't mind about murdering people with disabilities,' she said to herself, 'I'll bet they ain't so eager to give them a job.'

Paradoxically, Deborah's disability made it easier for her, on this occasion, to at least gain an interview. Global was a huge corporation, public relations were an obsession with them, the last thing they needed was some loud-mouth crip' kicking up a stink about discrimination. Always interview the cripples, that was the rule. Then, when you turn them down, you can say it's because they just aren't right for the job, nothing to do with the wheelchair.

So when Deborah rang the number, somewhat exaggerating her qualifications, and pointedly asked about disabled access, the employment officer at Global UK agreed to put her in with the first batch of interviewees to be seen the following Monday.

That evening she told Toss.

'You're mad, girl!' he exclaimed. 'Why don't you just bell the geezer and say you know all about the miracle engine and about him killing Spas and all that. He'll shit himself. I mean he'll have to see you because he doesn't know what you know, does he?'

'He doesn't care what I know either, Toss,' said Deborah. 'The guy has the designs right? What proof do we have that those designs were originally Geoffrey's? Turk can just claim he designed them himself.'

'Yeah, but I mean somebody must have known what Geoffrey was working on, and could back our story. Someone at his work, or whatever.'

'Nobody knew about Geoffrey's engine but Geoffrey. The guy was a spastic, Toss, people didn't talk to him. Besides, he kept it a secret, even from me, until it was stolen. The stupid jerk left no tracks at all. We've tried to get the police to believe the story, so did Geoffrey. Christ, Toss, it's been published in a newspaper! Nobody gives a damn and Turk knows it, he has nothing to fear. Which is why the only chance I have of getting those designs back is to tackle Turk unawares.'

'Well I have to say, girl,' said Toss, forlornly, 'at the risk of sounding negative, your chances are kind of tiny. "Infinitesimally small" are words that are not out of place here. The geezer will kill you.'

And yet again he tried to dissuade Deborah from her chosen course, as he had been doing almost continuously since the previous morning when she had read the *Sunday Word* article.

'Deborah, these people blew Geoffrey's head off! I mean they *blew it off*! It was like some sort of Robert De Niro thing, except they didn't use real ketchup, they used blood. They have no respect for - the sanctity of human life. None.'

Toss was absolutely convinced, not unreasonably, that Deborah was going to get herself killed. So fearful was he, on her behalf, that he had even, with the greatest reluctance, volunteered to attempt the mission himself. He was honest enough with himself to concede that he was relieved when Deborah said that it wouldn't work.

'This is the one time when being in a stupid wheelchair gives me the edge. Somebody has to get into the Global building right? and once in, get around it. That person is me. People don't like to *talk* to people in wheelchairs, let alone kiss them off. They're embarrassed too, so they grin weakly and ignore us instead. I have to tell you, they do not have a similar problem with young black guys. It is conceivable that you might get the job interview, but if you start wandering round their building uninvited, you are going to have the FBI and the National Guard and the Ku Klux Klan on your back in two, maybe three, seconds maximum. They will slam you against the wall, spread your legs and say hurtful things like 'Freeze Nigger mother fucker' or, seeing as how we're in London, 'Orl roit Sambo wotcha want?'

Deborah, like many Americans was rather proud of her cockney accent, which was strange because she couldn't do it at all. The American cockney accent is taught via 1940s Sherlock Holmes B movies, where actors from the Bronx sit on top of hansom cabs saying 'Cor blimey, wot a toff! Arf a crahn to roid ya to tha trine styshon.' This accent reached its glorious zenith with Dick Van Dyke's extraordinary performance as the sweep in *Mary Poppins*.

Dialect aside, Deborah's point was a forceful one. She pressed it home.

'Now little old me, on the other hand, Toss.

Who's going to press me against a wall? A poor pathetic girl in a chair? What possible danger could I be? Crippled you see, good for *absolutely* nothing. Such a shame, so young and yet so *useless*, what harm could she do?'

Toss could see the logic in this argument. But only as far as it went.

'All right, Debbo, I am happening to your point that you have got slightly more chance than me. But considering, girl, right, that neither of us have any chance whatsoever, I mean, none, right? your advantage is kind of academic.'

'That's beside the point. I have to try.'

'Listen, you're not bleeding Davy Crockett, girl, you don't have to remember the Alamo. You are going to be wheeling yourself into the lair of a killer right. And for what? So you can ask him for your engine back. Do you know what he'll say, Deborah? He'll say "no", that's what.'

But there was no dissuading Deborah, her mind was made up. Geoffrey's mission had become her mission. After all, in a way, it was *her* engine that had been stolen, Geoffrey had designed it for her. He had wanted to make her fly, and now this Turk guy had stolen her wings and she intended to get them back. What's more, she was going to demonstrate to Sam Turk that you did not deposit the heads of her friends in her flowerbeds and expect to get away with it.

It wasn't entirely personal. Since his death,

Deborah had thought hard about Geoffrey's self-imposed mission. He had intended that his engine should be used for good, that through his work transport in the next century would be prevented from destroying the planet. Deborah's backbone was always a bit stiff on account of the fact that she spent her days sitting down. At the thought of Geoffrey's dreams, however, it stiffened further, stiffened with iron resolve.

'Toss,' said Deborah, 'I am on a mission to save the world.'

## THE GENERAL

Sam was plotting with Bruce, Deborah was plotting with Toss, and the man in the battle fatigues was plotting with General Ali.

General Ali had a lot of problems. He was an army officer who had come to power via a military coup. His position had always been rather shaky. In fact, he had started up the recent war with his neighbour by way of rallying popular support. It is one of the great paradoxes of history that leaders who find themselves in difficulties at home, often start wars in order to make their people love them. Although, why anyone should feel deepening affection for someone who has exposed them to being bombed, gassed, shot at and invaded, has never been explained. However, be that as it may, the General remained in a fairly precarious position. He who rises by the coup is often condemned to fall by the coup and many terrible rumblings were to be heard in the country – although these may have had something to do with the fact that, due to war rationing, the bread was now fifty per cent sawdust.

The once beautiful city was devastated, the army was weary, its best men were gone, and the people were hungry. The last thing the General needed was to have to stump up the seven billion US dollars that the Union of Oil had designated as his country's contribution to Sam Turk's buy-off.

'We're busted, Colonel,' the General informed the man in military fatigues who had attended the Union of Oil meetings. 'Seven billion dollars? Where am I going to get it from, taxation? What is there to tax? People will say "OK General, take the rubble that used to be my house, take the food out of the empty larder." Listen, Colonel, you remember when we took power? You remember what I said?'

'You said that heads must roll because the state was bankrupt and could no longer afford to pay its soldiers or feed its babies,' the Colonel replied.

'Spot any irony?' enquired the General.

The Colonel remained silent on this one.

'You know what I think?' said the General. 'I think we can sort this out more cheaply.'

## Chapter Twenty-Three

# INGMAR'S EFFORTS

## THE EIGHTH MAN

Whilst Deborah and General Ali plotted against Sam Turk, Ingmar Bresslaw plotted to fulfil the promise he had made to the Prime Minister that he would bring the road building plans back into public favour. He was absolutely determined that the public would be persuaded, by fair means or foul, that they wanted nothing less from their government than an epoch making era of public road building.

A plan had been forming in Ingmar's mind, almost since the very moment that Digby had disgraced himself. It was an outrageous and audacious plan, requiring meticulous detail in its planning and split-second timing in its execution. Ingmar had held long and deep discussions with engineers, town planners, publicists and lobbyists and was now ready to assemble the undercover team that would be required for the job. It was for this purpose that Ingmar had gone to visit Bill 'Bogus'

Bottomley, a senior operative at MI5.

'Look, I'd love to help, Ingmar, you know I would,' said Bogus, 'but we really do try and avoid the dodgy stuff these days. Can't risk it you see. Do something dodgy, next thing you know, there's a book out about it, have to be terribly careful. Actually, I've got a book planned myself for after I retire, all the blokes have, it's terribly competitive. In fact, I've been meaning to ask you a favour on that score. You see the truth of the matter is, my book's going to be rather dull I'm afraid, never even met a Russian, let alone engaged one in a deadly game of bluff and counter-bluff. Spent my whole life listening in on students doing their year pretending to be socialists, damn dull. What I need is an edge, something to drum up a bit of interest. So I was just wondering if you could put it about that the PM thinks I might be the eighth man.'

'The eighth man?' enquired Ingmar.

'You know,' said Bogus, 'in the Burgess/Maclean, their trade is the treachery business. Nothing substantial, just a rumour, wouldn't half bump up my measly book advance.'

'Bogus,' said Ingmar, 'I require the assistance of Her Majesty's Secret Service on a very sensitive issue of grave national importance. I do not wish to discuss publishing.'

'But the Secret Service *is* publishing these days, Ingmar,' insisted Bogus. 'Nobody does anything any more without thinking about how it's going to look in their book and to be quite frank, old boy, roads won't sell, Russians do. Listen, be a sport, I can't even get a Sunday serialization, and with the Soviets going and collapsing on us, like the bastards we always knew them to be, the Burgess business will probably finally die in a year or two. I really need to get my claim in now. The Chief's bagged pretending to be the sixth man, so that's out, he's bought a couple of homosexual screen prints and a little bust of Lenin to leave lying round his flat. Damn clever, wish I'd thought of it. Then there's a chap over at MI6 who's written a book called *The Seven Dwarfs*, claiming there were seven of them, I'm certain the bastard started with the title. Even says Moscow Control was known as Snow White, and of course Penguin love that. Anyway, he's backing the Chief's claim to be the sixth man, I'm convinced money changed hands there incidentally, and he's proposing that the Queen Mum was the seventh. Not bad that, she always was a bit of a fag hag, friend of Noel Coward's etc. Anyway, I'm going for the eighth, and a hint from the PM, or even the Foreign Office would be wonderful, could put twenty-five thou' on my advance. Go on Ingmar, you could swing it.'

Ingmar Bresslaw made his excuses and left. If he wanted dirty tricks performing he would have to go elsewhere . . .

## ANGRY ALF

. . . Which was why he was to be found the next evening dining at the House of Lords with 'Angry' Alf Higgens, who had, some years before, become Lord Higgens of Hackney. Angry Alf was a trade union man born and bred, and, despite the fact that his politics had been drifting steadily rightwards all of his life, his worker credentials were something of which Alf was inordinately proud. He was the type of man who considers that the fact that his unfortunate mother was forced to bring up him and six siblings without the benefit of an indoor lavatory, imbued him in later life with an omniscient insight into the minds of working people.

'Don't tell me how to run a union,' he would instruct colleagues, 'I never had a pair of shoes until I was eight.'

Angry Alf's trade unionism was the politics of power and posture. Throughout his years of influence, he loudly boasted that his job was simply that of 'doing deals for his boys'. He gave short shrift to anyone who dared raise in his presence the broader principles of trade unionism.

'Don't give me any of that bollocks about solidarity,' he would brusquely instruct them, adding that, as a child, he had to rise at five o'clock in order to help out on a coal round before school. It was Angry Alf's narrow perspective and singleness of purpose that had made him, in his years of power, such a respected figure in the road lobby. Roads meant more work for Alf's workers and so roads had no greater champion.

Alf had long since retired, but he had kept up his connections with some senior road lobby figures and he still had influence within his old union. It was for this reason that Ingmar Bresslaw had sought him out. Ingmar's huge plan required skilful, well-motivated operatives. If MI5 could not supply them, perhaps Angry Alf could.

'The planning has already been done, your Lordship,' Ingmar assured Alf. 'All I require is the services of about twenty men. They must be of the best type of course. Utterly reliable, you understand, courageous and resourceful. Will you do it?'

Angry Alf was doubtful, life was very pleasant in the House of Lords. He had no great desire to immerse himself in Ingmar's schemes.

'I don't know, Bresslaw,' he mused. 'If we were rumbled I'd probably lose my ermine. This is social engineering you're talking about.'

'I am talking about bringing the public to their senses, Alf,' said Ingmar. 'Britain needs more roads, you know how important that is, but since Parkhurst's speech, the anti-road movement has held the moral high-ground. We have to do something now. If we're not damn careful, there won't be a square foot of tar laid in Britain for half a decade.'

Ingmar was talking a language Alf found difficult to resist.

'All right,' he said, 'I'll make a few calls, see how the land lies. But it's a dodgy game we're playing here. If we lose, or worse, get found out, they'll lynch us.'

## Chapter Twenty-Four

# MONDAY MORNING

## A COP AT THE END OF HIS ROAD

It was Monday morning and Chief Superintendent Barry Ross was completing a letter to Corker McCorkadale, the Minister for Transport. It was a very sad letter, a letter from a proud and disillusioned man. Barry Ross had controlled London's traffic for fifteen years, but he had grown old and tired in the job. This was the day he was to take premature retirement and he felt the need to explain why.

Minister, (he wrote) I have to tell you that my reason for seeking early retirement is because I am absolutely convinced that it cannot now be many months before the job I have loved will become, quite literally, impossible to perform. I am a proud police officer and will not be the man who presides over the moment when London quite simply ceases to function. Please let me assure you that this is now an inevitability. The long-feared gridlock, which has been my constant nightmare, will become my successor's reality since I see absolutely no political will to face up to the cataclysmic scale of the problem.

The problem is, of course, pure and simple. It is the private car. I have devoted my life to the rights of the private motorist and still believe in them one hundred per cent. But such rights become rather theoretical, don't you think, when traffic moves at a snail's pace and it is impossible to park? Minister, in order to protect the private motorist of the future, action must be taken now. The pollution, the road carnage and the insane inefficiency have to be dealt with. There is one answer, Minister – the rigorous promotion of public transport. Nobody has to park a bus.

Barry would be sorely missed, he was the best traffic planner in the country and had just about kept London moving, against virtually impossible odds, for years. Now he had had enough. Despite being a Monday, this was to be his last day.

## HEADING FOR TROUBLE

On that same Monday morning, Deborah and Toss left their home together and headed for the Swiss Cottage area of London, where the UK headquarters of Global Motors were located. Deborah was as sure as she could be that this was where Sam Turk was to be found. Discreet telephone enquiries during the previous week had shown Turk to be a diligent man who arrived at his office early and left late.

Deborah parked her converted car with its disabled sticker bang outside the mighty Global building. It was on a double yellow line with prominent signs about the place saying that parking was prohibited at all times. Deborah felt that she would be OK though, because riding with her was her own tame traffic warden. Toss was in uniform, and it was his job to wait by the car, ensuring it remained there, unclamped, for that ill-defined time when Deborah would be making a getaway.

'You might be hours,' complained Toss. 'I'm going to look a bit of a dickhead spending all day putting a ticket on a car, girl. I am a flash! I am lightning! Nobody books them like El Toss.'

'Listen Buster,' replied Deborah, 'you ain't the one walking into the lion's den. Just wait by the car because I got a feeling that if, and when, I get out of this place, I'm going to be in a hurry.'

And with that, Deborah wheeled herself up the ramp which Global Motors had thoughtfully provided outside their building. Unfortunately, at the top of the ramp were swing doors, and the conventional ones to either side were too stiff to open. They had dropped very slightly on their hinges and hence dragged on the metal bases as they swung. This, of course, meant that Deborah had to sit outside the building (it was now raining), trying to attract the attention of someone inside, whilst hoping someone might come along. Eventually someone did.

'I hope you ain't on the judging panel for this job,' Deborah said to the person. 'Because if you are, I just lost it.'

Once inside, Deborah found the Global building pretty well-equipped, and, having reported to reception, Deborah was escorted in a spacious lift to the appropriate floor.

'Jeez, eighth floor,' said Deborah, casually. 'I would have thought only the big boss guys got to ride this high.'

Her companion merely grinned, as if humouring an idiot. Deborah tried again. 'Maybe the great Sam Turk himself will get in. I could ask him for a job direct.'

'I don't think so,' said the girl with a patronizing smile. 'there's a private executive lift to the penthouse offices.'

Deborah had feared as much. Still, at least she knew where his office was, and hence where he was most likely to be. However, she could not strike out for it just yet. Deborah had decided that she would have to go through with the mock interview for fear that she would be missed and a sympathetic search party sent out for 'the poor stupid girl in the wheelchair.' Fortunately for Deborah, she was called first.

'Getting me out of the way early,' thought Deborah, cynically, as she was ushered solicitously into a room containing three earnest looking people, their faces a picture of heartfelt solidarity and support.

## THE CHAIR GETS INTERVIEWED

'Hi, I'm Rod. Step right in and take a seat.'

Aaaahhh! Rod wanted the floor to open and swallow him. What was he saying? What was he doing to this poor girl? just rubbing in her terrible, horrible disability.

'Sorry, stupid thing to say.'

'Pardon?' said Deborah, positioning herself next to the empty chair that had been placed in the middle of the room to accommodate interviewees.

'Uhm . . . about stepping right in . . . Uhm, stupid, silly . . . Obviously I meant wheel right in . . .'

Rod looked around for a razorblade with which to slit his wrists.

'Wheel right in!' Rod was a soggy croûton in a *faux pas* soup, a croûton going under for the third time. He was a nice, caring man, a liberal. Whilst a student he had even been a Communist for a week and a half. He just wanted to show this poor pathetic girl that he was massively aware of her catastrophic inadequacies in the leg department but, within the bounds of practicality, he would not judge her too harshly on them.

'Look, what I'm trying to say is just forget about it, all right? God knows, we certainly have.'

'Forget about what?' asked Deborah.

'Your . . . your . . .' Rod could not bring himself to use the word wheelchair. It seemed so brutal, just drawing attention to the poor girl's appalling predicament. As if she didn't have enough to put up with without insensitive oafs like him idly dropping the word 'wheelchair' about willy nilly . . .

'Your non-walking status,' he said, in a flash of particularly uninspired inspiration.

'Oh,' said Deborah. 'OK, Rod, I'll forget about it,' said Deborah.

'Will you?' said Rod, his face a picture of concern and admiration. 'Will you really?'

'Sure,' said Deborah.

'That's *super*,' said Rod, delighted at having put her at her ease.

The interview began. Deborah explained that she had just taken her examinations in graphics and design and went on to expand on how she felt that this training would provide a good grounding for work in promotions.

But Deborah knew that, as she spoke, her chair was growing. Its arms were expanding upwards to envelop her, the wheels creeping outwards across the floor. She almost seemed to be shrinking into it as the handles behind her head touched the ceiling and the foot rests crept towards the panel, and began to push against the table, behind which her three interrogators sat.

Before long the chair was as big as the room, it

was forcing Rod and his two colleagues against the wall. Such was its size and dominance that it took a great deal of concentration for them to make out Deborah at all, perched far back, as she was, in the giant seat.

Every time the interviewers attempted to shrink the chair it got bigger, backing them further and further into the corner . . . As Deborah improvised a pretty good argument as to why she would make a good promotions woman, the panel's minds raced along the myriad of problems which they saw ahead, regarding the employment of that chair. Would it fit between the desks? How would it travel to showrooms and displays? Could it get in when it got there? How many demands would it make on other workers? How would a car buyer feel confronted by a piece of transport for the lame? Would it depress people?

The answers to all these questions were depressingly negative. How else could they be, considering that the chair now filled the entire room, the foot rests sticking out of the windows and the handles cracking the plaster on the ceiling. Eventually, after what seemed like a lifetime, an acceptable twenty-three of the allotted thirty minutes had passed and Rod drew the proceedings to a close.

'Thanks, Deborah,' he gushed. 'That was marvellous, really fantastic. I mean really fantastic,' and Rod meant it. He found the fact that Deborah could talk at all, most impressive, and also very brave. 'We still have quite a few people to see but really, I mean, *really*, you were terrific.'

Rod leapt up gallantly to open the door for Deborah, attempting to imply with his body language that holding the door open for a cripple was not something he expected any gratitude for, it was just something he was happy to do as one person to another, because obviously Deborah was a person.

After Deborah had gone, the three panel members, out of a mutual sense of guilt, went through the motions of discussing *her* rather than the chair. She was a charming and intelligent girl, they assured each other, each attempting to outdo the others in demonstrating how much they had attempted to look at Deborah's candidature in a positive light.

Having done this for a moment or two, with anguished reluctance, the panel moved onto the *practicalities* of employing Deborah, addressing themselves, as they felt they must do, to whether it was fair to the company, to other employees. Rod even wondered whether it would be fair to Deborah herself, but he was never called upon to expand further on this curious worry because the intelligent nods that he received belied any further explanation.

Finally, and with the utmost reluctance, it was agreed that there was no place for Deborah at Global Motors, if for no other reason than that she was a fire hazard.

Actually, Deborah's position at Global was about to rise with remarkable speed. Her interview having concluded early, Deborah emerged from under Rod's protective arm to discover that her minder had not yet returned to escort her out of the building.

'Could you tell the lady that I made my own way out,' she enquired of the two other candidates who were sitting waiting. They promised to do this through sympathetic smiles, which hid the fact that they were thinking 'Bet she gets it because she's disabled'.

## UP IN THE WORLD

Once on the loose, Deborah set about finding the executive lift. She guessed that it would be somewhere in the same area of those lifts provided for the common herd. After all, it would be an exclusive lift indeed that had its own separate shaft. Sure enough, on returning to the lift area, Deborah spotted the discreet, unmarked sliding door beyond the stand-up ashtray and knew that there lay her only route to the penthouse offices. As Deborah had suspected, a key was required to summon the lift. Ostensibly, this was a security measure but, of course, the real reason was to avoid the pristine executive environment being polluted by the foul, rank and stinking air of non-executives.

This little example of corporate élitism is one of

the numerous ways by which the pecking orders and promotion structures are defined in commercial life. It is rather difficult to properly gauge rank and status when everyone wears much the same suit, so little signs and symbols have been devised. You can't tell a colleague how much you earn, but you can make a point of visiting the loo at the same time as he does, and then grandly disappearing into the senior management lav. This confirms your relative status. There are just as many drips on the floor of the executive bog as in the ordinary one, but the point is, they are *executive* drips.

The most meaningful badge of rank in any large company is, of course, what car they give you. The motor that you park in the company car-park tells everybody what you earn and who you can boss about. One day business people will probably dispense with confusing terms of rank such as 'under manager' and 'junior executive', and will simply define people's status by their cars.

'Well son, you'll start off as a Ford Escort, like every young lad, but if you work hard and keep your nose clean, who knows, in ten years you could be a Granada, perhaps one day even a Jaguar like me.'

This snobbery is, of course, wonderful news for the car makers who delight in endlessly producing minor variations of the same car so that the fleet managers of large companies can go mad trying to assess the career implications of awarding someone an electronic radio aerial or alloy wheels whilst his

furious colleagues only get a lockable glove compartment. This method of promotion is also a good
way of saving money, because it is possible to
honour an employee much more cheaply than by
giving him or her a pay rise. One can simply replace
his Ford Sierra with a Ford Sierra TP (Toss Pot),
thus allowing him to rush home shouting 'Darling
they've given me the tinted sun-roof!', this small
reward being much magnified by the fact that Roger
and Bill's new cars do not even have electric
windows.

## BRIEF ENCOUNTER

Anyway, the immediate upshot of this corporate
snobbery was that Deborah would require the
assistance of an executive with a key to the lift in
order to reach Sam Turk.

Deborah's first problem, of course, was to avoid
running into her minder, who would no doubt
shortly be coming to pick her up. To this end,
Deborah summoned a non-executive lift in order to
begin her mission on a different floor. The list on the
wall went 'ping' to show that a lift was coming and
Deborah prayed, as the doors opened, that the
minder would not actually be in it. Her prayers were
answered, and, struggling to conquer the fear rising
in her stomach, Deborah disappeared upwards into
the building. She decided to alight at the floor
marked 'Accountancy and Contracts'. Deborah was

seeking a floor teeming with executives anxious to use their executive lift and she felt that 'Accountancy and Contracts' sounded like the sort of activity where seniority might be required. Whilst in the lift, Deborah had donned the costume which she and Toss had prepared on the previous evening. It was hidden in the bag she kept hung behind, between the handles of her chair and consisted of a peaked cap marked 'Comet Telecommunications', a small tool bag and Deborah's laminated student union card which she clipped to her breast pocket. Close inspection of this card would, of course, beg the question of why a third year design student, who was entitled to access to all bars and leisure facilities, should necessarily be qualified to mend phones at Global Motors. However, as close inspection would require someone leaning over her and peering down her front, Deborah reckoned she would get away with it. Again Deborah was relying on her apparent helplessness to allay any suspicion. She only hoped that she would not be collared by some flustered employee saying, 'Just the person I need. Everytime I try to phone in for the cricket score I get a recorded tape about Mandy, who says she's a naughty girl and would I like to hear about her melons?'

And so Deborah sat by the lifts of the 'Accountancy and Contracts' floor of the Global Motors building and waited for an executive. Non-executives came, and non-executives went, until eventually her patience was rewarded.

'Say, listen, can you let me back in this thing?' she said as a purposeful man with a key approached the unmarked door. 'They have a fax up on the top tomatoes' floor which seems to be getting messages from Mars, and kinda enigmatic ones at that. They let me in at reception, but I goofed and got out here.'

They seemed to like their executives rude at Global. The man did not even answer Deborah, he simply nodded her into the lift and then followed her. He punched the top floor button for Deborah but himself alighted on the next floor up from accountancy and contracts. Deborah did not attempt to thank him, the man clearly was not in the mood for small talk.

## ENGINEERING A CONFRONTATION

The executive floor was rather luxuriously carpeted. This was a bit of a blow for Deborah as carpets slow wheelchairs right down, also, unless the carpet is extremely securely fitted, it is very easy to drag the thing up into a ruck whilst turning. Still, there was nothing she could do about the interior design. Deborah had a job to do and the job was to unearth Sam Turk, confront him and wrest from him Geoffrey's design. A tall order indeed, but Deborah, who regularly had to do battle in the supermarkets of Swiss Cottage, knew a thing or two about tall orders.

'Excuse me, I have to check some phone wiring in the corridor outside Mr Turk's office,' Deborah said to a passing executive-level secretary . . . 'His automatic dial keeps ringing the Finchley Road Pizza Shed and they're threatening to sue.'

'Well I haven't heard of . . .' the secretary attempted to say, but Deborah interrupted her.

'It's just in the corridor, I have to run a volto-joule reverse-current meter over it,' she said, holding up a big cooking thermometer on a spike that she used once a year for roasting the Thanksgiving turkey. Deborah always celebrated Thanksgiving. She considered herself an American (US) first and a Jew a very very long way second. The thermometer, a highly credible piece of technology, was sufficient to convince the hesitant secretary and she pointed the way to Turk's office.

It was only now that the full terror of the situation began to weigh a little upon Deborah. Shortly she was going to have to act, only a wall separated her from her prey. She felt a little like a mouse stalking a lion and an almost overwhelming desire to make a bolt for it welled up inside her.

'Courage, Deborah,' she whispered to herself. 'Courage, you schmuck. If more people would'a had courage, Hitler would'a stayed a corporal.'

All her life Deborah had been taught that those who fail to stand up for what is right share the guilt for the wickedness of the world with those who actually champion evil.

'Easy to say, Poppa,' Deborah whispered to herself as she positioned her wheelchair by an electric wall socket. 'But these people blew my pal's head off with a sawn-off shotgun. You come stand up to 'em.'

The memory of Geoffrey's demise lent an equal measure of both courage and fear to Deborah's emotions, so all in all, the memory of Geoffrey's demise was not a lot of help.

Deborah could hear discussion going on inside Sam's office, so she knew that she would have to wait. Tackling one able-bodied murderer would be difficult enough, she did not want him surrounded by henchmen. Slowly but surely, the room began to empty as earnest looking executives emerged from Sam's office door. They passed Deborah, who was earnestly waving her turkey thermometer at an electric plug socket and scratching her head with a screwdriver. They all gave her a little smile, feeling rather proud that Global, unbeknownst to them, pursued such an equal opportunities policy. Deborah prayed that Sam himself would not emerge and depart for some fifteen-course executive lunch, leaving her with the necessity of pretending to be fixing a telephone line in an electric plug socket with something that belonged up a turkey, for hours on end.

## Chapter Twenty-Five

# THE BATTLE BEGINS

## DO NOT DISTURB

Eventually, Sam's meeting seemed to be over. No one had emerged from the office for a full ten minutes and Deborah could hear no talking from within. With sinking heart she realized that Sam was alone, the time had come to do it.

'If I'm going to take this mother,' Deborah said to herself, attempting with little success to stiffen her resolve with tough talking, 'the time is now.'

She took from her bag a neat little sign that she had made. It said '**DO NOT DISTURB UNLESS YOU WANT YOUR BUTT KICKED CLEAN TO DETROIT**' and was signed, Turk. Deborah had done enough research to have a vague handle on Sam Turk's way of communicating. Very gently she hung her sign on the door handle, of course she was aware that this was not the usual method by which executives ensured that they were not disturbed. Under normal circumstances, when a top dog required absolute privacy, if for instance, they wanted to shag an employee or prise up a floorboard and count their ill-gotten tax concessions, they would bark curtly into an intercom and the door would instantly be guarded by a stern-faced private secretary with a severe bun and an armour-plated brassière. None the less, Deborah, whose whole strategy was based on bluff, thought that there was a fairly good chance that any minion, faced with her little sign, would think twice before disobeying it.

Deborah took a deep breath, reminded herself one more time that if the worst came to the worst she must remember to keep her legs apart, and opened the door.

Inside the room Sam Turk was sitting with his back to the door, and as it happened he was communicating curtly via an intercom with a stern-faced private secretary with a severe bun and an armour-plated brassière.

'If anyone from the Union of Oil turns up you send them straight through OK? No coffee, no how are yous, nothing, just send them through.'

The stern-faced private secretary in the outer office was rather surprised at this instruction. In the past she had noted that Sam was rather irritated by her stern manner. In Detroit Sam had been guarded by a blonde Californian called Farrah who gave off such a positive charge she could wipe the data off a floppy disc. Everything in Farrah's world oozed with sun-drenched enthusiasm, she could never have simply offered someone a coffee, rather she would announce that she had some *great* coffee . . .

'I also have great de-caf, plus I have sugar. I have half sweetener, or I have whole sweetener, and I promise no bitter after-taste, I use it myself. I have great cream which is in this cute jug here, but I also have great milk, skimmed, or full if you prefer. The pot's hot so just yell for more. Enjoy.'

By the time Farrah had finished offering you a cup of coffee you felt like you'd had a massage. It is a little known fact that the reason for the dramatic reversal in fortunes of the awesomely powerful US economy is that they simply let their language get out of hand. So much time is spent greeting each other, describing the coffee and sending out for 'those great chocolate-chip diet muffins they have at Bronski's', that there is no time left to keep up with the Japanese.

## THE MOUSE AND THE LION

Sam heard the door and swung round.

'What the hell do you want? My phones are fine, get out,' he barked.

'I ain't no telephone engineer, Mr Turk,' said Deborah. 'My name is Mary Hannay. I'm with the FBI.'

'Sure you are, little girl, why and I bet you have a Superwoman costume on under that cute blouse,' answered Sam, and, having no time to deal with lunatics in wheelchairs pressed the button on his intercom. 'Miss Hodges could you please . . .'

'The Bureau is kinda interested in your hydrogen engine, Mr Turk,' snapped Deborah. Sam Turk looked at her thoughtfully.

'Forget it, Miss Hodges,' he said, taking his finger from the button. Sam looked at Deborah thoughtfully some more, he did not know what to make of her. She certainly did not look like a federal agent.

'So what is the FBI doing rolling around in wheelchairs dressed up as telephone engineers?' he asked, not unreasonably.

'We have no authority in this country,' said Deborah, desperately improvising. She knew this nonsense would not lead her far, but she needed to get a little closer to him.

'I guess that's so,' said Sam, walking round to the front of his desk. He did not know who this woman was, but there was one thing of which he was already certain: she was no FBI agent. If the FBI wanted to talk to him they would knock on the door and say 'Hi, it's the FBI' and they certainly would not send a smart arse chick who looked barely out of her teens. However, as she had mentioned the engine, Sam knew that he must tread a little carefully.

'Kind of an inconvenient cover, ain't it?' he enquired, leaning against his desk. 'A wheelchair.'

'The wheelchair isn't a cover Mr Turk, I'm paraplegic. The FBI is an equal opportunities employer,' answered Deborah.

Deborah always made a habit of confronting every assumption she came across regarding the incongruity of a paraplegic being somewhere or doing something. On this occasion it was unfortunate, because Sam remembered something. 'Paraplegic' is not a word one encounters all the time, but Sam had come across it only a few days before. It had cropped up in a conversation that he had conducted over a scrambled telephone with the head of Euro Despatch after the successful conclusion of Sam's commission regarding the despatch of a certain gerbil named Geoffrey Peason. Euro Despatch were an efficient firm and they offered a degree of background information on the jobs they carried out. Sam had learnt that the gerbil Peason had eventually been discovered at the home of a young female American paraplegic student and a young black traffic warden. He even remembered her name.

'What do you want, Deborah?' Sam asked, but Deborah was too astonished to answer.

'Sure I know who you are, kid,' Sam continued. 'You're the friend of a guy I may have had a little business with recently. But you have nothing on me and you know it, or you wouldn't be here, you'd be with the law. So what do you want?'

'Well I . . .?' for a moment Deborah experienced a sensation almost unique in her experience, that of not having anything to say.

'Go home, little lady. I'll get them to order you a cab.'

Sam was acting very casual and unconcerned but that was only because he did not wish to have to have Deborah killed in his office. That would be extremely inconvenient, especially on the day before his monumental deal when the situation was tense enough. However, underneath he was hugely put out. How on Earth had this girl worked out his connection with the engine? She must also know about his connection with the death of her friend. Given time to think, Sam would probably have remembered the article in the *Sunday Word* and figured things out from that, but, for the moment, the girl in the wheelchair seemed almost clairvoyant, and terrifyingly so. Of course Sam knew that she could prove nothing, not unless she had another copy of the engine plan. None the less, the whole situation was pretty disconcerting. Sam resolved to get her out of his office immediately and then to contact Euro Despatch to arrange her murder that very afternoon.

'Miss Hodges,' said Sam again, touching the intercom button.

'I have a plan of the engine!' blurted Deborah. 'He drew up another before you had him killed, and your thugs didn't find it!' Deborah's mind was racing, she was running out of ways to stall him, she just had to get him close enough, but how?

'Forget it, Miss Hodges,' said Sam again, taking his finger off the intercom button. 'You have another copy?' he asked very quietly, all his dreams

360

of unimaginable wealth hanging on how he dealt with this girl.

'Yes, I have it right here in my blouse,' said Deborah.

Sam could scarcely contain himself, the relief was incredible. He leapt forward joyfully to tear the supposed plans from Deborah's clothing. Sam Turk never imagined that he could possibly be in any danger, but he was. He was the mouse and Deborah was the lion.

## TRUSSED TURKEY

Crack! Geoffrey's dead fist in the shape of a small Victorian flat-iron leapt out of the arm of Deborah's chair and swung hugely and horribly into the side of Sam Turk's head, the spindly anglepoise arm delivering the sort of blow that no human arm could muster – no matter how many steroids were pumped into it. Sam Turk folded up like a deck chair, i.e., in a confused heap with everything bending the wrong way.

'Jeez, Geoffrey,' muttered Deborah, addressing her dead companion at arms, 'I hope this guy has a thick skull. He's no use to me dead.'

Sam was not dead, he lay at Deborah's feet, the side of his face a throbbing purple tribute to the awesome ballistic power contained within an anglepoise lamp arm, an old flat-iron and a couple of Bullworker springs. The weapon now lay collapsed and limp across Deborah's lap. She leaned forward painfully doubling herself up over it, and stretching down in front of herself with all her might. Clutching at the turn-ups of Turk's trousers she finally managed to get a hold of his feet and pulled them up onto her lap. Producing some of the telephone cable that had played a prop part in her brilliant portrayal of the telephone engineer (she accepted that the FBI agent had been rather two dimensional, but she was proud of the engineer), Deborah proceeded to tightly secure Sam's feet. This done, she felt a little safer.

'That's evened the score a tad, bud,' she muttered to herself, perhaps a little vindictively. 'Now neither of us can walk.'

Letting Sam's feet fall from her lap, Deborah manoeuvred her chair towards Sam's hands. Of course the carpet rucked itself up under the wheels of her chair and as she struggled to free them, Sam seemed to stir. With a huge effort Deborah got herself into a position whereby she could lean forward and reach Turk's hands. First though, since she wished to tie them behind his back, Deborah had to roll the big body onto its face.

'Why didn't that clutz Geoffrey think to fit a fork-lift onto this thing?' thought Deborah, as she leant over the side of her chair and attempted to heave the unconscious Turk over without toppling herself over, which would of course mean the end of everything.

'You never hear of Jane Fonda, you bastard?' Deborah enquired of the non-comprehending Turk . . . 'It wouldn't hurt to exercise a little, maybe cut down to fifty hamburgers a day.'

Eventually Deborah got the large car maker where she wanted him, with his hands and feet firmly tied, and, what is more, his tied hands tied to his tied feet. Deborah then got herself into position and threw a jug of water at his face.

## INTERROGATION

When Sam Turk came round he could be forgiven for being a little surprised, he was in fact positively astonished. The very last thing he remembered was towering menacingly over a helpless girl in a wheelchair, and now, the very next thing, as far as he was concerned, was that he himself was being towered over. He was trussed up like the guest of honour at a sado-masochist ball, and his head appeared to have been used to stop a Network South-East train that was in danger of actually arriving on time.

More to the point, and point being the word, he was staring at the front end of the bolt on what appeared to be some kind of wheelchair-mounted crossbow. 'Don't move,' said Deborah, rather unnecessarily, considering the position that Sam Turk was in.

'Or say a word,' said Deborah, as Sam appeared

to be opening his mouth to speak. In fact he had been trying to breathe properly. In consequence of the years spent wheeling herself around, Deborah had very strong arms, and she had trussed Sam extremely tightly. His shoulders were being pulled back and down, putting a considerable strain on his chest.

Deborah stared at him across the raised arm of the anglepoise, which now served as the bow of the weapon which Geoffrey had so ingeniously designed. She had the wire, which was stretched between the arms of her chair, pulled back tightly against her chest, a short arrow, or bolt, lying gently across the bow, its point fashioned from the thin, shining spike of an electrical screwdriver, the blade of which Toss had filed down to a vicious chisel-like edge.

'Now listen to me, suckhole,' Deborah said very slowly. 'You killed my friend, OK? I know you did, so don't deny it. You killed my friend who, with one twitch of his spastic shoulder, was worth more than every beat your heart ever made. Nothing beat my friend, nothing! At least not till you, you evil little fuck! He overcame everything life ever put in his way, and that was plenty. But he couldn't overcome you, could he? and you know why? 'Cos you're too low, that's why. My friend never looked anywhere but up, and to see a slime like you, you got to look way down low. Now I'm only telling you all this so you need have no doubt that if you don't cooperate with me, I'll kill you without even thinking about it.

I mean it, I don't want anything more than to kill you and I could do it right now. Right now, do you hear! All I have to do is let go of this wire and you're dead! Nobody noticed me come in, nobody would notice me go. I'd be out of here. And I want to do it, Mr Turk, believe me, I really, desperately want to kill you. All I need is an excuse, and you can give me that any time you feel like it.'

'Why don't you then?' asked Sam, painfully.

'Shut the fuck up,' said Deborah, and Sam could see her thumb and forefinger quivering as she held back the bolt. He hoped she did not have sweaty hands. 'I told you not to say anything and I meant it. One more word, just one, unless I say so, and I'll kill you, you understand?'

Sam nodded as best he could from his difficult position.

'Now the reason I'm not killing you straight off is because I ain't a murderer, much as I'd like to be,' Deborah continued. 'Besides which, you have something that belongs to me, and I want it back. I want the designs of the hydrogen engine that Doctor Geoffrey Peason designed. He designed it for me! You understand! For me! I was his fucking inspiration! Have you ever inspired anyone Turk? Maybe to puke up, I guess, that's about the best effect you could hope to have on anyone, to make people sick. But I inspired an engine and I'm taking it back, because you are never going to use it just to put a billion more private cars on the road.'

Even in his prone state Sam felt a vague pleasure that at least there was something about him and his plans that this appalling girl did not know.

'Geoffrey wanted his engine to be part of a new way of doing things and that's exactly what it's going to be.'

Sam did not attempt to answer, he was happy to let Deborah keep talking. They would be discovered at some point and, seeing as how they were at the nerve centre of a huge industrial conglomorate in the middle of a working day, he reckoned it would happen sooner rather than later. Deborah knew this too and so she decided to get to the point.

'OK, this is what you have to do now. You have to give me your key to the executive lift and you have to tell me where the plans to my engine are. You can talk now, but only about the key and the engine.'

Sam Turk could scarcely resist a smile.

'Well, the key is right there on the desk,' he answered, indicating a key card which Deborah recognized as the same as the one which her rude companion in the lift had used . . . 'Use it, kid, get the hell out of here, by the time I get loose you'll be long gone. As to the engine, I'm afraid . . .'

'Let me save us a little time here, Turk, because we're both busy people right?' said Deborah. 'You're about to tell me that the plans ain't here, that they're somewhere else, which would be good news for you because poor old Miss Paraplegic ain't likely to get the rise on you a second time. Well, I have to tell you that I doubt that those plans are elsewhere, because I can't think of a more logical place for Sam Turk's magical new Global engine to be than in Sam Turk's office at the Global building.' Deborah was, of course, unaware that Sam did not see Geoffrey's plans as the new Global engine at all. 'Now you had better hope I'm right, Mr Turk, because either I get the plans in my hands in the next five minutes or I'm going to kill you.'

'Ah now, come on, kid . . .' Sam began to protest, but Deborah was not in a listening mood.

'I told you not to speak unless I said,' she hissed. 'One more word, just one, and the negotiations end with a bolt in your neck and I'm outta here. You ain't the only one with a stomach for murder, Turk. Now listen, this is my one chance, OK? My one chance to get back my property and to revenge my friend, right? Well believe me, if I can't do the first I will sure as hell do the second. So bite on this.'

Deborah accompanied this by leaning across her bow and, with the hand that was not holding back the bolt, flinging a scarf over Sam's head. 'Go on, I said bite on it, suck it into your puss and bite it!'

Sam had no choice but to work the scarf into his mouth as best he could without the use of his hands.

'Go on, all of it!' Deborah commanded. 'Get it in your mouth, the whole damn scarf. Do it, bastard.'

Sam sucked in the cloth until it filled his cheeks and he began to gag. He did not mind, he certainly was not going to be able to tell this stupid girl where the plans were with a scarf in his mouth.

'You biting it, Turk?' demanded Deborah. Sam nodded. 'Biting it hard?' again he nodded. 'Good,' she said and let go of the wire.

The bolt buried itself deep into the fleshy part of Sam's thigh, it was not a terribly serious wound but it was a painful and bloody one. Sam's head swam, he wanted to cry out with the shock and the pain. But of course he could not, now he understood why Deborah had made him stuff the scarf. Deborah drew the shaft of a second arrow back towards her chest.

'You want to know something, Turk?' she said, 'I wish I was in your position, I really do, because you may be hurting in your leg, but at least you can feel something. If that was me, I wouldn't feel a thing. Do you know why that is, you little scheister? You disgrace to the American flag! I'll tell you. My legs can't feel because the brakes on the Global Moritz were of the absolute minimal standard that you people could get away with at the time. Global could have fitted better brakes, but they didn't, and that's why I can't walk, and why I wouldn't feel no arrow in my leg. Now, I shot you, Turk, so that you know how serious I am. It was a hard lesson, but I guessed you have a pretty thick skin, also I am only giving you one warning so I wanted to make it good. The next arrow, you get in the face. OK, this is what happens now. I'm going to pull the cloth out of your mouth, and you ain't going to scream and you ain't going to shout. If you do, in that moment, you're dead, OK, just like my friend, you're dead, and I'm gone. The only sound you are going to make is to tell me where the plans are, and if you even hint that they ain't here, I'll kill you instantly. No further discussion, no negotiations of any kind, if they really ain't here then I lose, but you lose worse. OK, here goes.'

Keeping a firm grip on the shaft of her arrow, Deborah leant forward and, taking hold of a protruding corner of the cloth, gently pulled it out of Sam's mouth. Sam was a gambling man, but he was not foolish or impetuous. He weighed the odds of a situation carefully. In this circumstance he knew that there was a chance that if he called Deborah's bluff she would not kill him, but he could see from the bloody mess on his trousers that there was a real possibility that she would. There was also, of course, the possibility that if he gave in to her demands and gave her the plans, she would still kill him, but he didn't think so. Sam knew that his best bet was to gain more time. Deborah's position of power could not last forever, the odds would have to change soon, he had to humour her until then.

'In the safe,' he whispered. 'Seven-nine-two-zero-four – twice.'

## Chapter Twenty-Six

# THE SHIFTING BALANCE OF POWER

## THE ODDS CHANGE

Very carefully, and keeping the bound Sam in her sights the whole time, Deborah slowly reversed her chair towards the wall with the safe in it. This was a complicated process, she only had one arm for motivation, she required the other to keep tight the bolt which she was training on Sam. This meant that, to avoid simply going around in circles, Deborah was forced to continuously change hands, performing tiny arcs and thus slowly backing away.

Eventually she arrived beneath the safe. Fortunately it was set low in the wall and, reaching up, Deborah was able to shift the dial, her eyes flicking upwards to the dial and back to the prostrate Sam between each number. Click, click, click, seven-nine-two-zero-four-seven-nine-two-zero . . .'

'I got one more number Turk, if the door of this safe don't swing open, I shoot you immediately,' said Deborah. Sam nodded to show that he understood.

'Four!' The door clicked open and swung forward upon its beautiful German-made hinges. Deborah almost dropped her arrow in relief. She couldn't think what she had been expecting, some sort of booby trap perhaps, but Global Motors was a respectable business, they did not have exploding safes.

Without taking her eyes off Sam, Deborah's hand groped upwards and backwards into the safe. She could feel a sheaf of papers tied up with string. Taking a firm grip on them she dragged them out over her head and down into her lap. Reaching backwards again she discovered a couple of larger rolled up sheets, these too she awkwardly dragged out. One glance at the top page of the sheet was enough to convince her that she had struck gold, 'Notes on the Principles of Hydrogen-Powered Internal Combustion by . . .' and the name was crudely Tippexed out. 'Not even his name remains huh?' said Deborah wheeling back towards Turk. Sam tensed, why the hell had nobody disturbed them yet? What did he pay these people for? Actually, it was not so strange, it had in fact been less than fifteen minutes since Deborah had first appeared and a combination of Sam's enigmatically forestalled intercom messages to Miss Hodges, plus the sign that Deborah had put on the door had so far dissuaded everybody from risking Sam's famous wrath by disturbing him. Sam wondered what his chances would be if, bound as he was, he attempted to roll towards Deborah's chair and topple her. Deborah read the fear on his face.

'Don't worry, I ain't going to kill you, less you make me,' she assured him. 'Just you nuzzle down to the piece of cloth on the floor there and suck it back into your mouth, OK?'

Sam did as he was instructed as Deborah tortuously rolled her way back towards him, employing the same alternative thrust method that she had used to get to the safe. When her chair again stood in front of Sam, who now cut a pretty pathetic figure, bleeding and sweating and with his cheeks stuffed with cloth, Deborah produced some heavy-duty insulation tape from her prop tool-bag. Fumbling it open with one hand and her teeth, a rather difficult thing to do, she leant forward to Sam for the final time and firmly taped up his mouth.

Finally she relaxed her hold on the arrow.

'I'm going now, Mr Turk,' she said, taking up his lift key from the desk, 'and let me tell you that by tomorrow there will be a copy of my engine in the post to every environmental group in the country. Whoever makes this engine is going to consider the Earth first and profit second. I've won, you murdering schmuck.'

But Sam could not hear her, the birds were singing too loudly in his aching brain for Deborah's voice to penetrate, for behind Deborah the door had quietly opened and through it had come the one man who could ignore Sam's 'do not disturb' signs without risking the sack, Deborah's recent lift companion, Bruce Tungsten.

## CONFLICTING PLANS

Bruce strode quickly up behind Deborah and grabbed at the anglepoise arm, wrenching one end out of its clip on the arm of Deborah's chair and bending it right back, breaking the hinge on the other arm from which had been launched the first blow against Turk.

'OK, little lady,' said Bruce, grabbing Geoffrey's plans from her lap. 'Keep your hands on the arms of your chair where I can see them, don't you move them now. By the look of things around here you're a mite too resourceful for my liking.' Bruce had a pistol. Even in his state of blissful relief at being rescued in the nick of time by his co-conspirator, Sam Turk could not help wondering why Bruce had brought along a pistol.

'Well, well, well, Sam,' said Bruce, jovially, whilst none too gently pulling the tape from his mouth and allowing Sam to spit out the cloth. 'This one's going to be a barrel of laughs to tell the boys down in the locker-room. The day ol' Sam Turk got trussed up and seriously wounded by a young girl in a wheelchair.' The girl under question moved her hands slightly, she wanted to spread her knees apart and the only way she could do this was to haul them apart with her hands.

'I said keep your hands exactly still, Miss,' said Bruce waving his gun at her. 'My old pal Sam here is a very tough guy indeed, in fact he's one of the meanest men I know, and yet you got the better of him. That makes you a very formidable woman as far as I'm concerned, so just keep yourself real still OK? Or I shall be forced to tie you up like you did to Sam here.'

'Speaking of which,' grunted Sam, who it must be remembered was still lying bleeding on the floor with his arms and legs pulled backwards and bound behind him. 'For God's sake get me out of this before I bleed to death.'

Bruce ignored Sam's plea, instead he placed a little doll on top of Sam's desk.

'I have to thank you, Miss, whoever you are,' he said. 'Personally I was scared to confront old Sam here myself, I was fearful he'd get the better of me. That's why I've spent two and a half hours going to every top man in this building enquiring, hoping that one of them might have a clue as to the whereabouts of our new miracle engine. Of course it wasn't any use, none of our senior management were aware that we even had a new miracle engine. Kind of selfish of you to keep it to yourself Sam, considering it represents the entire future of our industry.'

'You can't double-cross me you bastard,' said Sam. But, of course, seeing as how he was saying it whilst trussed up and stuck to the floor with his own blood, it was palpably obvious that Bruce could do just about what he wanted. Sam changed his tack.

'Fifty-five billion bucks, Bruce,' he pleaded. 'You are holding fifty-five billion bucks in your hand, that's what the oil people will pay! You can't throw that kind of bread away just to make cars!'

Deborah could not believe her ears, the duplicity of it astonished her.

'You mean you weren't even going to make it!' she gasped. 'You were going to sell my engine to the oil people so they could put it in the trash!'

'He was, I wasn't, and keep your hands where they are!' said Bruce, noticing that yet again Deborah's hands were straying towards her knees. 'You damned idiot, Sam, did you really think I was going to let the greatest engineering breakthrough in a century just disappear? I'm a car man for God's sake, I make cars. These plans go back with me to the USA, tonight. Lord almighty man, do you have no vision at all? No soul? I'd rather be a multi-millionaire national hero than a multi-billionaire nobody, schmuck. I'm disappointed in you Sam. You need something to help you get motivated. Keep my doll, it was good for me . . . Sam Turk,' he said loudly and clapped his hands. The Doll began to laugh. It was still laughing when the windows crashed open and three masked figures in combat fatigues, balaclava helmets and carrying machine guns sailed in as if from nowhere. One knocked the pistol from Bruce's grasp, another threw him to the floor, while the third covered the room. Deborah they ignored, and she used the opportunity to haul apart her knees to the sides of her chair.

## MULTI NATIONAL ETIQUETTE

Along the corridor, in Miss Hodges' office, some of the younger girls wondered whether they should go and investigate what the noise was.

'Absolutely not,' replied Miss Hodges. She had only a few minutes before been instructed specifically by Bruce Tungsten himself, the President of the entire international group, to leave him and Turk absolutely alone.

'Gentlemen from the American mid-west often conduct business by smashing things,' she assured the nervous girls. 'I believe it's hormonal, like stags rutting and parallel walking. They must be left to get on with it or else they might take it out on their wives when they get home.'

## FOUR PARTY DISCUSSION GROUP

Inside Sam's office the balance of power had changed radically again. The chief terrorist was speaking.

'So it looks like you done half our job for us,' he said, nodding towards the prostrate Sam. 'The general wants you alive, which is bad news for you my friend, let me tell you. I don't know what you done to make him mad, but he's sure mad. You are luckier,' he said, turning to Bruce. 'You we will kill now, and the secretary.' For the first time he acknowledged Deborah. 'It is very convenient of you to be here Mr Tungsten, we did not expect to see you here at all. We thought we'd have to go to Detroit to kill you. OK, give me the plans and we'll make it quick huh?'

Bruce's mind was racing, but unfortunately he could not think of anything clever. 'Come on, come on,' said the terrorist. 'I can shoot you then take them if I like, but I don't want to get them all bloody.'

Still Bruce hesitated, his burning passion to get the better of Hirohato urging him to do anything to save those plans, throw them out of the window, try to swallow them, anything. His own life meant nothing, but he had to save the engine and pay Hirohato back for that doll. Then Deborah spoke.

'Just toss the plans over to me, pal,' she said. 'I'm a fellow American, you can trust me.'

'Shut up!' snapped the terrorist. Then, turning back to Bruce, he said, 'Give me the plans.'

'C'mon bud, you've got nothing to lose,' said Deborah quietly. 'I can get them out, somehow the thing'll get made. Trust me, I got special skills, I can do it, better I have them than him. C'mon.'

Not really knowing why, Bruce turned and tossed

the plans to Deborah. She caught them and the terrorist shot Bruce, although fortunately, because the terrorist was also turning to look at Deborah, Bruce was only winged. The other two terrorists were already moving towards Deborah to retrieve the plans. It was then that the whole room received an enormous shock, for a sheet of flame suddenly burst forth from between Deborah's legs engulfing both men in a inferno, just below the knees. Instantly their trousers were alight and both fell to the floor beating at their burning legs. Deborah revolved her chair. Suddenly she was facing an astonished and terrified terrorist chief. Again fire bounded forth from under her. Now there were three men writhing around beating their legs and searching for a vase of flowers.

'So long,' said Deborah, and wheeling her chair round, she smashed through the door.

## DECISION TO DISTURB

Down the corridor Miss Hodges was on the horns of a dilemma.

'It sounds like they're shooting at each other now,' one of the girls had said.

'Must be having an awful row,' another added.

Miss Hodges was inwardly furious, she had never warmed to Sam Turk's manners since the day he had first arrived at Swiss Cottage promising people, for some reason known only to himself, that he intended to kick their bottoms. Fortunately, in Miss Hodges' case, at least he had never carried out this threat but breaking windows and conducting shoot-outs during office hours was nearly as bad. It was such a terribly poor example to the younger girls.

She pressed the intercom connecting her to Sam's office, but there was no reply. 'Wait here,' she instructed the wide-eyed under secretaries. 'I shall enquire if they require coffee.'

Deborah was waiting by the executive lift when Miss Hodges rushed past her and into Sam's office. There she discovered a scene straight out of Dante's *Inferno*. Both the President of the company and the Chief Executive of the UK division lay wounded on the floor, one bound, and three militaristic, Middle Eastern looking gentlemen were writhing about the place desperately trying to put their trousers out.

'Mr Turk!' said Miss Hodges. 'Installing a basketball net and a golf putter in your office is one thing, but sado-masochistic orgies is quite another. I resign.'

'The girl! The girl in the wheelchair,' shouted Turk. 'For Christsake stop her!' Miss Hodges was a highly professional woman and knew full well that Sam was entitled to a month's notice of her departure. She remained therefore his senior personal assistant. Turning on her heels she rushed back into the corridor. The girl in the chair was still there, but she would not be for long. Ping! The executive lift arrived. The girl slipped a key card into the slot and the doors opened, but not before Miss Hodges had bounded down the corridor and grabbed the handles of Deborah's chair to prevent her rolling into the lift.

It was then that Miss Hodges received the shock of her life, quite literally, for Geoffrey's ghostly hand was still hovering over the woman he loved, and if there is a heaven, still loved. Deborah's hand dropped to a little switch that Geoffrey had installed, and sent the entire contents of the traffic-light battery shooting up poor Miss Hodges' arms. She wasn't standing in a puddle and it wouldn't have been a strong enough charge to do her any harm even if she had. However, it was enough to make her leap backwards in fear and surprise, and at that time Deborah disappeared into the lift and pressed ground floor.

# Chapter Twenty-Seven

# GETAWAY

## A GENUINE HAZARD

Toss was extremely glad to see Deborah emerge from the Global building (again she had had to enlist help to cope with the sticky door). Toss liked to think that he was only pleased because Deborah was still alive, but he could not deny that he was almost equally relieved that his period of guarding the car was over too. Three hours trying to look like you're booking the same car would have tested the histrionic powers of Sir Henry Irving.

None the less, it had been worth it. The getaway car was still in place and Deborah and Toss's departure was unobstructed. If Deborah had emerged a few minutes before it would have been a disaster. Toss had left his post for a moment in order to stroll up the ramp to the door of the Global building to see if he could sort of will Deborah along by meeting her half-way. When he returned, after what he considered to be a matter of seconds, busy shoppers had parked their cars to either side of Deborah's and a third had actually boxed it in. The reason that the three drivers had felt justified in this outrageous bit of attrition parking was that they had all *put their hazard lights on.*

The invention of the hazard light is one of the few genuine changes which have been introduced to cars since Benz and Daimler first realized that the explosion of volatile liquid vapours inside a piston cylinder attached to a gear system and a drive shaft, would be a wonderful way of sitting in a traffic jam. Hazard lights are, as the name suggests, a hazard. They provide certain drivers with such a combined sense of inner peace and moral justification for their actions that a casual observer might presume Jesus Christ was at the wheel.

Some people think that hazard lights excuse *anything.* If you want to stop in the middle of an urban clearway to pick up six kids and an antique kitchen dresser, no problem, bung on your hazards, that will make it all OK. Contemplating a U turn across a dual carriageway, but worried it might be a little dangerous? Not if you have four orange lights blinking simultaneously at the corners of your car, that will provide you and other road users with all the security and protection required.

There are some drivers who genuinely believe that there is no manoeuvre, no matter how dangerous, that having both indicators on at the same time will not justify. Parking on top of a bus queue, driving into the reading room of a public library, the day is surely coming when bank robbers will plead in mitigation that the getaway car had its hazards on.

Toss had given all three offending cars tickets, an action which genuinely outraged the drivers when they returned, it simply was not fair to give them tickets, they had not been gone long, besides which *they had had their hazards on.*

Anyway, by the time Deborah emerged from the Global building, the way was once again clear.

'Yo, girl, what's happening?' enquired Toss as Deborah rolled down the ramp towards him. 'So you managed to persuade him not to blow your head off then?'

'I've got it,' screamed Deborah, 'I've got it! I've got it!' She shouted, waving the plans around.

'Wicked,' said Toss, opening the driver's door for her. 'But Debbo, please try to be cool, I have a reputation in this town. Hysterical women screaming that they have "got it" at me could be misconstrued.'

'I can't believe it,' bubbled Deborah hurrying to shift herself from the chair to the driving seat. 'I went in there and I knocked Sam Turk to the ground, tied him up and tortured him until he told me where Geoffrey's plans were.'

'Cor,' said Toss, momentarily so impressed that he forgot to say anything cool. 'That's right, and I took out three guys with my flame-thrower,' Deborah continued as she leant sideways out of the car, folded up her chair and tucked it in behind her.

'Totally happening, girl,' said Toss. 'SAS-ville,' he added. Toss had regained his composure because he no longer believed a word Deborah was saying.

'Get in the car, Toss. We are on a mission to unchain the highways and byways of the world.'

As Toss got into the passenger seat a car drew up behind them. It was a big, left-hand drive, American Global, a Supreme Class Over-Cruiser.

'Here, do you think I've got time to book that flash bastard?' enquired Toss.

'I don't think so,' said Deborah, her expression suddenly changing from exuberance to fear. 'We have to move.'

Sam Turk, limping hugely, but very much on his feet, had just barged through the swing-doors, he was carrying Bruce's pistol. Sam had cut an alarming figure rushing through the building, having been untied by a deeply disturbed Miss Hodges. There was a huge blood stain on his trousers and the side of his head was swollen up like a rugby ball, the shape of the flat-iron being still clearly visible. However, when one is watching fifty-five billion dollars disappear over the horizon, it is a finicky man indeed who gives much thought to sartorial matters. Sam didn't, and his appearance would have shocked a Vietnam Vet. It certainly scared Toss.

'Girl, I dunno what you done to that geezer, but he looks well agitated. Let's scarper right now, 'cos

I don't want to meet him, girl, no way.'

'Me neither, Toss. We'd better hope his driver doesn't know London,' replied Deborah, and with that she twisted the hand accelerator and beeping wildly barged into the traffic. Looking over his shoulder Toss could see Turk running as fast as his wounded leg would allow him towards his limmo.

## MOVIE CHASE

Our entire lives are dominated by fantasy, every time we turn on the TV a deceit of one sort or another is perpetrated upon us. Mostly we recognize them as deceits and they do no real harm. We understand for instance that the 'serving suggestion' on the front of a box containing frozen food is a sort of culinary version of the picture of Dorian Gray in reverse. The more aged, putrid and dissolute the food inside is, the brighter, shinier and more delicious the picture on the box will appear. Interestingly, the 'serving suggestion' deceit was originally devised by the press office of the Kremlin prior to Gorbachev's presidency. The more utterly dead the leader became and the more his face seemed to resemble a de-frosted lasagne, the brighter and more luminous became his official portrait.

The serving suggestion trick is a fair, innocent deceit. If popping a sprig of parsley behind Brezhnev's ear made him look slightly more alive on the podium in Red Square, at least it gave the KGB something to laugh at. However, some media deceits are more dangerous, and the mournful mortality rate amongst teenage joy-riders suggests that the movie car chase is one of them.

The movie car chase is second only to back-seat shagging as the greatest car myth of all. Car chases in movies are like sex in movies, they seem to go on for ever, continually jump cutting from one completely impossible position to another and apparently involving no personal risk whatsoever.

All week people sit in traffic jams. Sometimes, on a Friday night, they go to the movies, on the way they sit in more traffic jams, they miss the first part of the movie because they can't find a parking place. Then they sit in a dark cinema and watch a man drive a car through rush-hour traffic, clear across a city at eighty miles an hour. If the man had turned into a six-foot banana we would say it was a stupid movie, but a man driving a car through a crowded city at eighty miles an hour we not only accept but remark to each other how brilliantly done the car chases were.

Nothing can stop the hero in his car. If he meets another car, he drives round it, or maybe over it, or just possibly through it. He goes on the pavement, he crosses into opposing traffic lanes, he hurtles down empty alleyways. His car can jump, his car can roll over, it is more like a performing dog than a ton and a half of lifeless metal. If you offered it a biscuit it would probably sit up and beg.

The fact that this display bears as much resembl-ance to driving as the lasagne of Dorian Gray does to food, is irrelevant. The fact that it was shot at 5.30 a.m. on four successive Sunday mornings, means nothing. The fact that if you actually tried any of that stuff for real you would not get twenty yards before ploughing into a bus queue and killing thirty innocent pedestrians, is not a part of the equation. The fact that Moses may have been able to part the Red Sea but he could not do more than ten miles an hour in London, doesn't matter. Movie car chases remind us of how much we love cars.

When the movie is over, everybody goes and sits in a jam again.

## REAL CHASE

Deborah and Toss were stuck in traffic on the Finchley Road; about thirty cars behind, Sam and his driver were also stuck.

'He had a gun,' said Toss nervously.

'I should have killed him when I had the chance,' said Deborah, causing Toss to look at his friend in a new light. A nervous silence descended. Finally Toss said 'I can't believe this traffic.'

It is a strange thing that, despite the fact that the traffic jam has become an absolute fact of modern existence, people still say 'I can't believe this traffic' whenever they find themselves in one, which is all the time. The reason for this is probably because, every now and then, very occasionally, one has a decent journey and actually gets lucky with the traffic. These journeys then exist in our memories like childhood summers in which the sun always seems to be shining. The fact that it pissed down almost continuously for most people's childhoods is irrelevant, there were wonderful summer days which stand out in our memory for their glorious unique-ness, until eventually they are all that can be recalled, it's the same with jam-free journeys.

'Can't we go any faster?' said Toss.

'Sure, Toss, sure,' snapped Deborah. 'I'll just drive right under this truck in front of us shall I?' Of course, if they had been in a movie she could have done, or perhaps instead, she would have driven through a fruit market, scattering fruit everywhere but curiously injuring no one. Or she could have simply screeched across into the other lane and woven her way forward through the bumper-to-bumper opposing traffic, causing police motor-cyclists to fall off in dramatic slides, then get up and scratch their heads.

Deborah, of course, could do none of those things, she could just sit and edge her way forward like everyone else. Back up the line, Sam Turk was in the same position, and was suffering a terrible car dilemma. Should he jump out and run up the queue on foot, and, if so, would the traffic instantly leap forward at speed, thus allowing Deborah to dis-appear into the distance? This dilemma is similar to another classic taxi dilemma, that which consumes every taxi passenger at the point at which they enter the last traffic jam of their journey, perhaps only two hundred yards from their destination. The gruesome question is, will the wait be a short one, or a long one? Would it be quicker to sit it out or pay the cabbie off and leg it? Sadly, it has been decreed that the traffic will only leap forward if the passenger leaves the cab. If he stays put, the last hundred and fifty yards will take twenty-five minutes.

'I can't believe this traffic,' said Sam.

## Chapter Twenty-Eight

# *NIGHTMARE*

Actually, the traffic was heavy even by London standards, and Toss and Sam were not the only people who could not believe it.

Chief Superintendent Barry Ross was staring at his great big flashing map, the source of so many of his grey hairs, and wondering why God hated him the way he clearly did.

Just two hours before, Ross had been a reasonably contented, if rather sad, policeman. The morning traffic had just about made it in and found somewhere to park, there had been the usual ulcer-growing half hour between eight and eight-thirty when it really did seem to Ross as if it simply would not be possible to squeeze any more cars into London – he felt that way every morning, and somehow the miracle was always achieved.

'They get there in the end, Janine,' he would say wearily to the policewoman who brought him his morning tea. 'Late, furious, double-parked and worrying about their paintwork, but they get there.'

'Yes, Sir,' said Janine.

'Apart from the casualties,' Ross continued, 'they won't get there, no I'm afraid not, they won't get there at all. Not with their mangled limbs and suchlike, and their massive internal bleeding and their being just plain, old-fashioned dead. They won't get to work at all will they? And it's my poor lads as has to scrape them off the bonnets and get their heads out of the steering wheels, what's more.'

'Yes, Sir,' said Janine, feeling a bit sick. She liked Ross, but hated it when he got morbid, which he often did, because years of being the grand orchestrator of London's single most effective killing machine had sucked the happiness out of Ross. He had become grimly familiar with death, he had forgotten the social reserve which most of us apply to the subject. Ross and his wife were seldom invited out to dinner any more because of Ross's unfortunate habit of remarking that the meat course reminded him of something his boys had hosed off the Old Kent Road that morning.

'Natural wastage, Janine, my dear, natural wastage,' Ross mused. 'The toll may be terrible, but it has been decreed acceptable by those who know about these things. We may thank our stars, Janine, that it is not you or I who are called upon to quantify an acceptable death toll. Ours not to reason why, ours but to cut them out of the bodywork.' Ross took a thoughtful cup of tea.

'Do you know that the United States of America loses nearly as many citizens each year on the roads as it lost in the entire Vietnam war?'

Janine did know, because Chief Superintendent Ross often told her this type of fact. She knew the accident frequency on almost every junction in the city, which was why she found it hard to sleep at night. Janine's mother wished that Janine would go and work in a nice flower shop or something.

'Funny that, isn't it?' continued Ross, reflecting on his Vietnam statistic. 'You'd have thought there'd be more fuss.'

'I suppose people don't fuss, Sir, because they think it's worth it,' replied Janine. 'They prefer driving their cars to fighting the Vietnam war.'

'Don't let this job make you hard, Janine,' said Ross, reprovingly. 'Don't let it sap your humanity.'

About nine-thirty Chief Superintendent Ross pulled himself out of his reverie and went for a final ride in the chopper, surveying for the last time the vast mess over which he had presided.

'Quart in a pint bottle,' he murmured to himself, as he often did when contemplating the M4 as it poured cars endlessly into West London.

'Quart in a pint bottle.'

The helicopter flew along the still chock-a-block motorway, with its queues still reaching back towards Heathrow. They followed the near-stationary line of traffic through Hammersmith and

South Kensington and up to Hyde Park Corner, and that was when they saw it. Ross's nightmare, the heart of the gridlock.

'God help us,' whispered Ross.

'You must be joking,' God whispered back.

An articulated lorry containing drums of corrosive liquid had jack-knifed whilst trying to turn into Constitution Hill, somehow it had lost part of its load. A couple of cars had been damaged by falling drums and there was a serious spill steaming and bubbling on the tarmac. The incident was perhaps forty-five seconds old, the driver of the lorry had not even got out of his cab yet, but already cars were backing up.

'Oh please, not today, please,' murmured Ross, but as God had just pointed out, it was too late for prayers. Before his very eyes, Ross could see the traffic pouring into the jam. He watched as the lines feeding back along Park Lane, Knightsbridge and Piccadilly began to freeze. Ross could actually see the movement draining out of the roads beneath.

Ross did not yet know that he had just watched the birth of a gridlock, but he knew that the situation was serious. He grabbed the radio.

'Hyde Park Corner is out, repeat out, minimum four hours. Stranded artic', looks like corrosives.'

Ross needed to give no more instructions, his team had rehearsed their techniques and plans so many times. They had a damage control exercise worked out for every possible crash in London. Ross knew that seconds after he had informed the centre, patrol cars would begin to attempt to divert traffic away from the stricken area, the BBC and commercial stations would be informed and the fire and ambulance services would attempt to pick their way up to the scene of the crash. Ross knew that all these things would be happening, he also knew that it was like putting a sticking plaster on a shotgun wound. This one stupid accident would screw up traffic in London all day, there would be long delays and huge inconvenience, it simply could not be avoided.

'Let's go home and get a cup of tea,' said Ross wearily.

'Nice retirement pressy, eh, Chief?' said the pilot. 'Block on the corner couldn't really be worse could it?' But of course it could, as they would soon find out.

## THE HORNS OF A DILEMMA

Down on the ground, in the frozen tentacles of the stricken intersection, countless human dramas were unfurling. Every car contained its degree of frustration, but some burned more agonizingly than others. The bride in the hired Daimler was assured by her father that it would be all right. He was wrong, it wouldn't be, and the embittered groom would later get drunk and, in a foolish attempt to hang his silk wedding boxer shorts on top of the church steeple, would fall and break his neck. Behind the Daimler was a fellow in a BMW who was rushing to meet a very important foreign client at Heathrow. His failure to do so put a black mark on his career ('You should have set off earlier.') which led him three years later to drive that same BMW off Beachy Head. Nearby across the countless smaller problems was a Mini in which was contained a beating heart, a beating heart that a small child lay waiting for in Great Ormond Street Hospital. That heart was destined to beat its last right there at the throbbing epicentre of the gridlock. Beeping its horn at the Mini with the heart, was an Escort van containing a plumber on his way to deal with a burst that would now sadly destroy the entire lifetime's possessions of an elderly widow. Behind the Escort, also beeping its horn, was a Mercedes containing three robbers who had just done a jewellery store near Harrods.

People's jobs, people's health, people's love affairs, people's futures were frozen in the traffic, and a great lament rose above the smoke and the growling engines, wailing in sorrow for the losses of the day. It was the hooters' chorus. In the British driving test one is informed quite clearly what the car hooter is there for, it is there to inform other road users of your presence. Well if that was what people were using their horn for around Hyde Park corner on the day of the gridlock, then they were wasting their time, everybody already knew everybody else was there, that was why no one could get anywhere. The truth is, of course, that, in the drama of the moment, people were forgetting the Highway Code and were not using their horns to say 'I am here' but were using them to say '*Why* am I here?'

Horns serve no practical purpose: they are there to alleviate personal frustration and to insult and annoy other road users. Their only real use, the one defined in the driving test as 'announcing your presence', is rendered completely useless by the fact that they are used so often to say 'fuck off' that that is the only message which other people hear. Horns are like alarm bells: one hears so many of them that it never crosses anyone's mind to take any notice of them.

## DREADFUL COINCIDENCE

When Chief Superintendent Ross arrived back at his command centre, Janine had a cup of tea ready for him.

'This is an unexpected treat, Janine,' said Ross. 'You don't normally bring me a second cup until elevenses. Is this a retirement present?'

'Oh no, Sir, that's later, we've had a whip-round . . .' Janine stopped short, Gloria was glaring at her. Gloria was the girl in traffic control with the 'You don't have to be mad to work here but it helps' sticker on her computer. She had organized a presentation for later and was anxious that Janine should not give it away.

'No, sir,' continued Janine, 'I just thought you might need a pick-me-up. There's a huge bomb scare at Holborn Circus, Sir.'

'Oh dear,' said Ross, trying to disguise how deeply shaken he was. This was another classic accident scenario location, a major junction right in the financial district. 'I suppose traffic's backing up over the river?'

'It's got as far south as Lambeth, Sir, and it's spreading back west, down the river to Waterloo.'

Ross sipped his tea.

'Have you sugared this, Janine?' he enquired.

'Oh yes, Sir, three as usual,' she replied.

'Funny,' said Ross, 'it tastes bitter.' And well it might, for Ross knew that with the Corner and Holborn Circus blocked out, there would be paralysis through the West End to the City. What a way to leave. 'You heard about old Barry,' they would say in years to come. 'London's top traffic man couldn't even get home on his last day.' Ross gripped his mug tightly, deliberately allowing it to burn his hand a little so that his whirling senses might have something to fix upon. Janine was still standing before him. He looked at her enquiringly.

'Is there something else, Janine?' he enquired.

'Yes,' she said, in a nervous squeak. 'A load of ball-bearings has come off a French lorry at the top of the Marylebone Road underpass, and a tall coach has got itself wedged at Blackwall, and . . .'

Ross raised his hand to silence Janine. He gently put down his teacup and went over to the big flashing board, the board which had been his ball and chain for so many years, and was now his executioner. The big board was flashing away like a panic full of perverts.

'Well?' he asked.

'We're trying to contain it, Sir,' said a sergeant. 'It's just there's so much traffic feeding in we can't cut it all off and so the crisis area keeps expanding.' Ross could actually watch the jam grow as new light trails snaked across the map. 'Our cars are getting blocked in as we try to turn traffic away,' the sergeant continued. 'I'm afraid this one's really come to life, Sir.'

'Four crucially positioned accidents inside an hour,' said Ross. 'There is no God.'

And God replied, 'Not in peak traffic there ain't, mate.'

## THE SHIVERING SNAKE

It was exactly an hour later that Deborah and Toss began their getaway. Central London was completely paralysed. Every escape route ended in a jam and hence became a jam itself. From the moment Ross understood the extent of his ill fortune in being presented with four crucials in one morning, he could have taken a pencil and a London streetfinder and charted the inevitable growth of the super-jam across the entire length and breadth of London. In fact, this is exactly what he did. It was a pointless exercise of course, rather like the captured Christians of Ancient Rome drawing up a detailed rota as to the order in which they would be fed to the lions, but there was little else for Ross to do. The puny defence and control initiatives which he had planned for circumstances such as these, were all in place, his officers stood bravely on the expanding edges of the grid vainly attempting to staunch the never ending feast of cars that flowed in to feed the monster's insatiable appetite, and there was nothing Ross himself could do. All morning he sat at his desk fiddling with his coloured pencils, mapping out the growth of his nightmare, struggling feebly to keep his predictions ahead of the terrible reality outside.

'Dean Street and Old Compton should be solid within the next five minutes,' he would shout to people who already knew. 'That means Soho is completely locked now.'

Then Ross would relapse into silence for a while, before shouting, 'I imagine Baker Street will be stationary by now, that means that Hyde Park and the Marylebone Road jams have officially linked.'

Perhaps the process of charting the uncontrollable gave Ross the vaguest feeling of having some control over it. If it did he was kidding himself, traffic flow has a life of its own. Occasionally Ross would attempt a positive suggestion of some sort, just for the sake of form.

'The Regent's Park ring road will be solid by now. Eventually people will take to the grass, phone the park authority to tell them to put guards on the flower-beds and warn the Zoo, maybe they could put cotton wool in the animals' ears or something.'

Ross was right, out on the streets (and on the grass) the rules were getting stretched. It takes quite a lot of provocation for most people to start breaking laws, but some cars had already been stuck for nearly two hours, and that is quite a lot of provocation.

It starts with a collectively shared paranoia that one is in the wrong lane, that the outside lane, or the inside lane, is moving whilst one's own lane is not. So, out goes an arm and a car attempts to switch lanes. Instantly the paranoias of a hundred other motorists are confirmed. 'So the other lane *is* moving faster,' and a hundred arms go out and the traffic, which is scarcely moving forward at all, attempts to make up for this by executing a pointless series of edging, bobs, slides and weaves, virtually on the spot. The effect, from the police helicopters above the turmoil, is that of a long, still, snake, shivering in its sleep.

## TO BE YOUNG AND FREE

The fruitlessness of the lane shiver, combined with the gut-wrenching tension of trying to physically drive through a taxi without scratching your paintwork, leads some of the more impetuous souls to delude themselves that the problem can be solved by more direct action.

These poor dupes, suckled on a diet of motoring images of freedom and individual triumph, convinced by generations of car makers, oil men and politicians that the car is the ultimate symbol of individual liberty and self-expression, simply cannot believe that the car is also a terrible trap. A trap which, far from confirming the individual's splendid isolation and independence, condemns the individual to a dronelike conformity of movement, or, as is increasingly the case, paralysis. Far from celebrating the freedom of the individual, more and more the private car is becoming the ultimate leveller, reducing us all to a dull conformity – identically frustrated, identically furious, identically stuck.

This hard truth is of course too much to bear for all the young Steve McQueens fuming in the jam. In their anger they decide to fight back. Surely that is what being a free individual is all about? Struggling for one's rights against impossible odds. Suddenly and completely irrationally they say, 'OK, fuck this, I'm getting out,' and with a satisfying roaring of gears drive straight up a cul-de-sac, or else, perceiving a modicum of movement in the oncoming traffic, start trying to force their way into it by attempting to execute an impossible three-point turn, thus bringing the opposite lane to a standstill as well.

# KNOCK-ON EFFECTS

Back at the control centre, Ross was fielding endless furious calls from the emergency services, who were, of course, completely unable to service emergencies. Fires were left burning out of control, the ill and injured were left to die, there was even the beginnings of some looting as enterprising souls realized that the police were having to respond to calls on foot, and anyway they were completely tied up dealing with half a million purple-faced motorists. There were calls from big businesses and financial institutions, desperately enquiring when the paralysis would lift as commerce was impossible under these conditions. Eventually there came a call from the Prime Minister's Office.

'What the hell is going on, Ross?' shouted Ingmar Bresslaw. 'The damned city's ground to a halt. The Prime Minister's trying to conduct Question Time and only six government MPs have managed to get to work! The only way we got the PM in was by police helicopter . . .'

'Yes, Mr Bresslaw . . .' attempted Ross.

'The other lot have got a hundred of their people in because half of them came by tube. The smug bastards are having a lovely time,' exclaimed a furious Bresslaw. 'Do you realize that the Prime Minister is outnumbered by a hundred to seven because of you. The opposition are desperately trying to introduce crapulent Private Member's Bills while they've got a majority. Fortunately, the Speaker's stuck on Waterloo Bridge.'

'Because of me, Mr Bresslaw?' protested Ross, who had spent years issuing fruitless warnings concerning exactly what had come to pass.

'Yes you, you clueless, clod-hopping PC Plod, damn you!' Ingmar seemed incandescent with rage. 'You're the top traffic cop. God knows what the Frogs and the Krauts will make of our efforts to be capital of Europe now. I just hope you have no aspirations to an honour Ross, because let me tell you, after this you're going to be lucky to keep your pension.'

Ingmar slammed down the phone. His voice had been filled with fury and frustration. Strangely though, as he sipped his whisky Ingmar's bloodshot old eyes were smiling.

Ross also put down the phone and looked again at his big map, the lights of which were now creeping up around Swiss Cottage and West Hampstead.

## Chapter Twenty-Nine

# IN A VERY SERIOUS JAM

For the previous five minutes or so, Deborah's little car had at least been vaguely edging forward. Toss knew this because the empty litter-bin completely surrounded by hamburger wrappers, kindly offered to the people of the Finchley Road by McDonald's, had moved from the front of the car to the back. Now, however, they had stopped completely. Both were painfully aware of the enormous danger behind them. Theirs was one of the more horrendous human dramas being played out in the gridlock that day.

'Try up towards Hampstead,' suggested Toss.

They were positioned opposite an open-right turn which the courteous driver in the other lane had left clear. The turn headed up Frognal a long, steep, quiet residential hill that pushed up from the Finchley Road to Fitzjohn's Avenue. 'It will take that Turk bloke ages to get up to the turn, girl. We'll be outa here,' he added, warming to his subject. 'We'll be dust, we'll be a memory, history baby. Don't look for us, girl, because we'll be long gone.'

'Don't call me baby, Toss,' said Deborah, 'not now, not ever.'

'It was a general expression, girl,' answered Toss.

'Oh yeah, well, I only see me and you in the car, Toss, and I ain't nobody's baby.'

Deborah was still feeling rather gung-ho after her extraordinary triumphs in Sam's office. This, combined with being completely terrified and stuck in a traffic jam, was making her rather prickly.

'Hang the left, girl,' admonished Toss. 'We have one chance, let's take it.'

But sadly there are no chances in a gridlock, no opportunities for individual initiative, no way to get lucky and beat the system. Deborah and Toss soon found that they were not alone. The first thing people do when faced with a block in the main arteries is to branch out into the rat-runs, the quiet residential streets, thus clogging up local traffic too. Within moments the road into which they had turned was hopelessly clogged, cars following Deborah in, cars appearing in front from other side streets.

'Oh for God's sake!' screamed Deborah, hammering her horn. 'We have to get away!'

She beeped, the people in front beeped, the people behind beeped, but not an inch did any of them move.

'Debbo,' said Toss, 'I think we have to do a runner.'

Deborah and Toss were about to do something that would be almost unique in that whole long desperate day. They were going to abandon their car. This is something that people find extremely difficult to do, understandably. Cars are very expensive items and most of them are only a quarter paid for. You can't just leave your most precious bit of property hanging about in the middle of the street. You have to stay with it, protect it through its time of trial. During a traffic jam the car owner is completely disabled, he cannot walk, he is incapable of movement. As the incidence of jams grows around the developed world, more and more people are choosing to voluntarily disable themselves for many hours each week, preferring to sacrifice the use of the very legs God gave them in exchange for the illusion of carefree mobility.

## MEAN WHEELS

Deborah's wheels were some of the few still rolling in London by lunch-time that day. With a considerable wrench, for as has been said, one does not abandon a car lightly, Deborah agreed with Toss that they should try to get up the hill towards Hampstead tube station.

'That geezer was real angry, right?' said Toss. 'It ain't going to take him forever to realize that he can leave his driver guy, right? Stroll up the jam, stick his gun through our window and do us in without anyone being any the wiser, right? He could do that, and I reckon he will.'

It was a persuasive argument.

'Also, I reckon if we go now, we might lose him before he gets parallel with the turn.'

They were fortunate, Deborah wrestled her wheelchair out from its position in the car while Toss stood around authoritatively, his uniform lending their actions legitimacy.

'Just popping to the lav, guys,' he shouted as people began to realize that a driverless car was about to be left in their path. Deborah got into her chair and they were off.

'Yeeha! Hi Ho Silver, away!' shouted Toss as he began pushing Deborah up the hill. They must have travelled a good hundred yards and Toss was beginning to puff when Deborah shouted for him to stop.

'We've forgotten Geoffrey's fucking plans!!' she screamed.

'Wicked girl, that's the kind of choice detail that makes the story worth telling in years to come,' observed Toss. 'Bung your brake on.'

Toss left Deborah where she was and tore back down the hill towards her abandoned car. Reaching in, he grabbed up the bundle of plans and was about to rush off again when a large fellow got out of the van that was positioned behind Deborah's car.

'Oi,' he shouted threateningly, grabbing Toss's arm, the frustration of his wrecked day fuelling his anger. 'What's the game leaving this motor then? When the traffic moves I'm sodding stuck ain't I?' Of course, the man was stuck anyway because he was in the middle of the biggest jam in history, but he wasn't to know that.

'So what's going on then, eh?' he enquired menacingly.

One or two other drivers wanted to know the same thing, and, leaving their cars, they surrounded Toss.

'I got no chance of picking up a fare with this bird's motor in my way, have I?' enquired an irate cabby, rhetorically.

'She really can't just leave her car there, and I don't care if she is disabled, I take medication myself,' said a plummy-voiced Hampstead woman, getting out of her convertible gold Mercedes. 'My husband is a Justice of the Peace,' she added.

'What is the game?' said the original van driver, fingering a nasty looking spanner.

Toss was hemmed in by aggression. He reacted magnificently, hitting back with all the authority his little peaked cap imbued him with.

'Bald tyre, guy, that is what the game is, bald tyre,' said Toss. 'Makes me weep, I mean, just totally weep. You're lucky, guy, cos I'm gonna book you and that way maybe you'll learn your lesson before you kill a little innocent child.'

'Now you listen to me, mate,' shouted the driver, veins bulging on his huge neck.

'No!' Toss shouted into his face, something which required him having to stand on tiptoes. 'You listen to me! All of you. Here on the streets I am the law! You understand? I carry a badge!'

'Yeah, a traffic warden's badge,' the taxi driver pointed out.

'Traffic warden "K" class,' shouted Toss, indicating the registration number on his shoulder which happened to end in a K. 'Do you have any idea what that means guy! It means killer traffic warden, kommando traffic warden, kung fu traffic warden! Bad driving is a disease. Meet the cure.' Toss spread his legs and stuck out his chest. 'You! Bald tyre,' Toss shouted at the van driver 'You! Cracked off-side mirror reducing visibility,' he shouted at the taxi driver. 'You! Seriously tasteless colour, reducing everybody else's visibility,' he shouted at the lady with the golden Mercedes. 'And all of you illegally jay-walking on Her Majesty's highway. Now get back to your cars or I call a chopper!' Toss took a bar of Cadbury's Dairy Milk chocolate from his pocket and held it to his ear. 'Yo! this is the Cobra, request special weapons group.'

Faced with a lunatic, Toss's inquisitors were unsure how to act next. Toss knew exactly what to do. Taking advantage of their confusion, he suddenly pushed past the big van driver and charged back up the hill towards Deborah. Sadly, by this time the advantage had been lost. Sam Turk had, as Toss predicted, decided to abandon his limmo and continue on foot. As Toss turned away from the angry motorists he saw Sam appearing at the bottom of the hill, the gun flashing in his hand.

Toss rejoined Deborah.

'Maybe we should face him out, Debbo,' he said. 'There's loads of witnesses and everything, what could he do?'

'Toss,' replied Deborah, 'he'll shoot us both and nobody will even get out of their cars. Let's go.'

The race between good and evil was fairly evenly matched. Toss was pushing a loaded wheelchair, Sam had a bloody wound in his thigh. But both teams, despite their disabilities, were making considerably better progress than any of the cars on the road, or indeed anywhere else in town. Abilities and disabilities are relative quantities.

## OBSTACLE COURSE

Hampstead is one of the highest parts of London and the approaches to it are steep. Toss's heart was pounding as he laboured to push Deborah's chair up the higher reaches of Frognal towards the village. The endless exhaust fumes from the great chain of stranded cars they were passing made him sweat and choke. Every broken paving stone, every curb was a drain on his strength. None the less, Sam too was labouring, he had been smashed in the face with an antique flat-iron and received a nasty flesh wound in the leg, he was fat, in late middle-age and now he was trying to run up a steep hill. Slowly but surely, Toss, whose muscles were toned by countless weekend raves of shaking his bottie down to the ground (and then a bit untoned again by lying around half-stoned drinking Red Stripe Crucial Brew), was increasing the distance between him and Sam.

Then human nature intervened and dealt the front runners a terrible blow. They were running up Frognal which leads to Church Row, which leads to Hampstead Village, where a tube train, or a policeman or some form of assistance, would be available. However, in order get to Church Row you have to dog leg across Frognal Road, which was of course blocked. The cars had not moved on this road for about twenty-five minutes. Actually, that is not strictly true, the cars had been moving, they just had not been getting anywhere, it was the old shivering snake again. All the drivers, for want of anything better to do, had been kidding themselves that they were making progress by shuffling their cars together, closing the gap between bumper and bumper. This always happens in queues of traffic and never a thought is given to the needs of pedestrians, let alone wheelchair users.

'Shsffllit,' said Toss. This was intended to be 'shit' but he was too knackered to speak properly.

'Don't you bastards *ever* think of people like me!!'

Deborah shouted at the drivers of the cars, for once not minding about making a scene. The drivers turned away, looked at the ceiling, stared into the distance, and did all the other things that intensely embarrassed people in cars do. They all looked as if they'd just got caught in the middle of a junction when the lights changed.

'You've gotta leave, Toss. We can't just go sideways, it's just more streets full of houses, he'll catch us in the end,' said Deborah.

'Nowahgg,' gasped Toss, which Deborah understood to mean 'no way girl'. 'He'll kill you,' Toss continued, becoming a little clearer.

'He won't, not if I don't have the plans. Why should he? Now get going!' shouted Deborah.

'I'm not leaving you!' shouted Toss.

Deborah put her brakes on. 'Get going, you fool! It's the engine that matters,' shouted Deborah, thrusting the plans at him.

'I've told you, no way, he's already killed Geoffrey,' said Toss, releasing the brakes again and beginning to push Deborah along the traffic, looking for a gap that was not there.

Sam Turk was close now, Deborah was desperate. Suddenly she remembered the vicious hatchet that Geoffrey had placed down by her leg as a low-tech part of his defence plan. She drew it, and twisting back, waved it within an inch of Toss's astonished face.

'Toss! Take the plans and *fuck off*!!' she shouted.

Toss stopped pushing. 'OK, girl, OK, there is no need to get so radical,' said Toss. He took the plans from Deborah, then spun round and fell against the bonnet of a white Mini Metro.

'Get it together, Toss, *please*,' implored Deborah.

'Hey!' shouted the irate driver of the Metro. 'That black bastard's bleeding on my bonnet! What is it? Is he having a haemorrhage? That's drugs done that to him, that is, bleeding drugs. Dirty bastard!'

Toss rolled round to look at Deborah, and a red streak appeared on the white paint work beneath his shoulder.

'Fucking hell,' said Toss, in a stunned sort of way. 'He shot me.'

## THE PLANS CHANGE HANDS

Sam had not wanted to risk gun play, but he had no choice. He was very tired anyway, and when he perceived that the young, able-bodied fellow in the uniform had grabbed the plans and hence was obviously about to ditch the wheelchair, Sam knew that he would have to act.

He knelt down on the pavement, steadied the pistol against the forearm of his non-trigger hand, and fired. It was a good shot, he did not wish to kill the lad, but he wanted to stop him. Toss took the bullet in the shoulder and was lying on the bonnet of the Metro in agony.

'Can't somebody help him?' shouted the Metro

owner. 'At least get him off my bonnet.'

Of course any movie could show us what Toss should have done. Being merely wounded in the shoulder, he should have gathered up the plans in his good arm and rushed off like an Olympic runner. Movie wounds are much like movie car chases, they are completely harmless. Real ones, however, are different, they traumatize and disable. It would be a few minutes before Toss was sufficiently collected to make any kind of move, and that was too long.

Sam staggered up, puffing, panting, bleeding and bruised, but carrying a gun. The irate owner of the Metro attempted to hide in his glove compartment. Sam leant down and snatched at the papers from the ground where Toss had dropped them, having been shot. Deborah lunged forward with her little axe, but Sam was wary of her this time. He jumped out of the way of the swinging hatchet, and, grabbing the side of Deborah's wheelchair, toppled her over onto the ground. Deborah tumbled out helplessly onto the pavement, missing the traditional English dog turd by an inch. This was, in fact, extraordinarily lucky, the chances of tipping a person out of a wheelchair on to a London pavement and not hitting a dog turd are small indeed.

Sam looked down at Deborah's immobilized form.

'What, you mean you can't fly?' Sam panted. He was feeling good, he had the plans, and he was pretty certain that anyone who realized a shot had been fired would prefer not to get involved. He was home free.

'You done good, kid,' gasped Sam. 'Makes me proud to be an American.'

'You make me sick, asshole,' replied Deborah, helpless on the ground.

Sam turned on his heel and began a leisurely jog down the hill.

## THE WHEELS OF VENGEANCE

For a moment, Toss and Deborah were alone. She on the pavement, he on the bonnet. Then one or two people from nearby cars who understood that something had happened, nervously wandered up.

'That guy!' shouted Deborah, 'that guy down the hill, he has stolen my stuff. It's very important! You have to stop him.'

It was a futile request, people were fairly happy to assist the wounded but there was no way they were going chasing gunmen to retrieve somebody's purse. Besides, how could they leave their cars?

'Can I give you a lift somewhere?' enquired one woman sympathetically, forgetting for a moment that she had now been stationary for forty-five minutes.

'I've called the police, and an ambulance on my carphone,' said a man who was clearly extremely pleased with himself for having done this.

'Get me up,' said Deborah, calmly, 'please get me

415

up and into my chair.'

'Well . . . uhm . . . how . . . ?' they all dithered, not really knowing how to manhandle a paraplegic.

'Just stand up the chair,' instructed Deborah firmly, 'Grab me by the shoulders, and haul me into it, OK?'

'OK,' they said. There was a pause.

'NOW, PLEASE!' shouted Deborah. It is difficult to be intimidating and authoritative whilst lying helpless on a pavement with a dog turd only inches from your head, but Deborah managed it. The onlookers had her back in her chair in an instant.

'Thank you,' said Deborah. 'So long, Toss,' and she pushed herself off down the hill.

'Deborah,' shouted Toss who was just coming round, but she was gone. The last chase was on.

## Chapter Thirty

# HELL ON WHEELS

Deborah's hands burned as she attempted to restrain the chair for the first part of the chase; she had a corner to turn to get back onto the main hill and she could not afford to topple over in the process. By putting her brakes on and off she traversed the thirty or so yards back to the junction with Church Row without mishap and, pushing her left hand down, as she swung round into the hill she could see the figure of Sam Turk jogging away a hundred yards or so below her. He was already halfway back down Finchley Road. Once he was down, she would have lost him for she had no speed on the flat.

It takes a pretty large measure of courage to launch yourself down a hill in a wheelchair, particularly when you will be rolling over treacherous, broken paving stones and having to negotiate terrifying kerbs, more so, even, when your final objective is a deliberate crash with an armed murderer. But Deborah was not short of courage, so she hit the wheel arches on her machine and prepared to burn rubber.

'Well Geoffrey, you wanted your engine to make me fly,' she muttered. 'Here goes.'

She gathered speed quickly, and was forced to hang heavy on the anchors as she sped past, bumping over and occasionally even managing to avoid, the great wedges of broken pavement that hurtled towards her, every one a potential grave-stone with her name on it. Sometimes a jet of water would shoot up as Deborah rolled over one of the pivoted pavements which had puddles hidden underneath. People watched amazed as Deborah sped past their windows with a grim look on her face, smoke rising from where she gripped the wheel rims. Deborah had gathered up the ends of the sleeves of her jumper in her hands in an effort to protect them, but these were quickly burning away.

There were two side streets that joined the hill down which Deborah was hurtling. The first kerb she had to negotiate was passable, the council having kindly provided a sloped stone on both sides of the road. Unfortunately, there was a car in the way. It had not been there on the way up with Toss, both the side streets had been pretty loosely packed, and it had been fairly simple to find a way between the cars. Even as Deborah started her down-hill dash to catch Turk she had seen a gap still available, but at that point frustration got the better of some pratt in a Mazda. The sleeping snake shivered, and even as Deborah headed for the precious gap, Mr Brand New Mazda rolled forward pointlessly to fill it. Deborah was by now doing about ten miles an hour, the car was only yards away, there was no way she could stop if she wanted to stay upright. It was teeth-gritting time. She shot down the kerb and slammed smash into the side of the car. With great good fortune her foot rests were high enough not to go under the Mazda, they hit it just beneath the door, thus protecting her knees. The chair tipped forward and the arm rests bashed into the car just at the level of the door handle, followed by Deborah who took the impact of the passenger window on her chest. Fortunately, the foot rests and the arm rests had taken up most of the force and, although very winded, Deborah was unhurt. She saw immediately that the Mazda had only edged forward to the stop line, there was just room in front of the car to get round between it and the stationary traffic pointing up the hill.

With a huge effort Deborah pushed herself away from the side of the Mazda, wheeled her right hand down and turned sharp left to get round the front of the car squeezing between it and the side of a Cortina, trying, by sheer lung power, to suck in the sides of her chair. As she was doing this a furious Mazda driver was jumping out of the other side.

'Now look Miss, what's the game?' he said trying to be calm. 'I hope you're insured because that was quite a thud and I'm afraid . . .'

The driver was walking around the other side of the car to meet Deborah, he intended to block her way and get the details of her vehicle. The man was in for a shock.

'Aaaaaarrrrghhh!' screamed Deborah, holding up the hatchet in classic psycho-killer pose. 'Aaaaarggghh!!'

Her hair was wild, her eyes were wild, everything about her was wild, the backs of her knees were probably wild. Understandably, the Mazda driver leapt out of the way and Deborah, slamming her arms into first gear, pushed off again, curving round the front of the Mazda, remounting the pavement on the sloped stone and powering on down.

She was closer to Turk now. Unaware that he was being followed he had slowed to an exhausted walk. Bumping and jumping, concentrating desperately, Deborah slid down the hill. She veered along hedges as a way of slowing down, throwing her torso this way and that to guide the accelerating chair past the hazards. So concentrated was she on the ground immediately in front of her, that it was nearly all over shortly after she left the Mazda. Fortunately, Deborah suddenly remembered from her trip up the hill with Toss that there had been a British Telecom obstruction on the pavement, Toss had had to squeeze her past on the road. Looking up, Deborah realized that it was almost upon her, the pavement was blocked, the kerb at that point was a good nine inches high. She was hurtling along, there was absolutely no way she could get down onto the road without a crash, Deborah had seconds to make a decision . . .

People who saw what Deborah did cheered and beeped their horns and, for once, the beeps were meant kindly: it was a magnificent manoeuvre. There was a lamp post on the pavement right by the little Telecom tent, between the lamp post and the nine-inch precipice was a further foot or so of pavement. As Deborah plunged towards the Telecom tent, she hit hard down on her right hand wheel, incinerating the last of her jumper sleeve and most of the skin on her right hand. The chair spun left and headed straight out off the kerb and into the road, but just as it appeared that Deborah and her chair would fly head first into the nearest bonnet, Deborah flung out her right arm and hooked it around the lamp post, nearly dislocating her shoulder in the process. The left wheel and most of the chair sailed out over the cliff edge, the chrome flashing in the watery sunlight, but the right wheel remained on the kerb and Deborah managed to haul the chair round with scarcely a drop in speed.

Looking down the hill, it seemed to Deborah that Sam was nearly on the Finchley Road and that all her efforts would end fruitlessly in her shooting out at the bottom and decapitating herself under a stationary articulated lorry that spanned the junction. However, Deborah could not have stopped herself at this point if she'd wanted to, so instead she spurred her chair on, removing any remaining skin on her hands in the process. The second of the two side roads loomed up before her. The gap was still there, just. With careful aiming, she could get between the cars. Unfortunately the gap was not adjacent to the ramp, if she wanted to get between the cars she would have to go off the kerb at a high point and, what is more, mount the other side at a high point too.

Deborah was now rocketing along, there was no way that she could risk a repeat of the Mazda performance. At the speed she was now doing, slamming into the side of a car could well kill her.

Deborah wiggled her body, touched the wheels and headed for the gap. As she left the kerb, flying into thin air, she leant back in order to avoid landing on her face. Even as she did this she was planning her assault on the opposite kerb, always presuming her aim was true, and she landed between the cars and managed to roll between them.

The aim was good, and it certainly was a shock to the lady in the Range Rover when a girl in a wheelchair crashed down in front of her. Deborah and the chair bounced forward under the momentum and again Deborah threw herself backwards. It was a tricky equation, she had to get her front wheels up high enough so that she would hit the far kerb with her large rear wheels and, hopefully, roll onto it, but not so far that she would topple over backwards. The kerb was not high and Deborah was on the final sprint, she had Turk in her sights and to her delight and astonishment he seemed to have stopped.

## AT BAY

By a small irony Sam had actually stopped at the point where Deborah and Toss had been forced to abandon the car. The reason for this was that even the pavement was blocked. It was blocked by the van owned by the man with the bald tyres. The frustration of the gridlock had got to the point where uptightness had completely conquered sanity and it was pavement mounting time. In the centre, where the gridlock was two or three hours older, they had already started to try and drive through shops.

The man in the van, faced with Deborah's empty car in front of him, became more and more agitated about the fact that when the jam finally cleared in his lane, if the opposing lane remained jammed, he would still be unable to move. This had weighed ever more heavily on him until it had become an obsession.

Eventually, in the jammed driver's mad desire to take some action, any action, he mounted the kerb. There was never any way he was going to get round, but at least he was doing something. Of course, the space the van vacated was instantly filled from behind, creating an endless, rippling knock-on effect as car after car shuffled forward to fill the couple of feet of tarmac that the van's partial occupation of the pavement had provided. Hours and hours later, miles away on the other side of the river, cars which had been stationary all day would suddenly find themselves with an extra few inches to travel because of that van.

However, the immediate result was that, when Sam Turk huffed and puffed his way up to it, the pavement was blocked, as was the road. The cars had shuffled so close together in the excitement caused by the huge leap forward of the van that at this point of Frognal, there was no longer even room to walk between the cars.

Sam shrugged and put his foot on the bonnet of a golden Mercedes, preparing to climb over it.

'How dare you, you filthy tramp,' screamed the posh Hampstead lady. And it has to be said that by this time Sam did look pretty much like a filthy tramp, and what's more a filthy tramp who had been in a punch-up . . . 'Get your filthy feet off my bonnet, my husband is a Justice of the Peace,' the woman continued.

The van driver, delighted for a little diversion, leant out of his cab.

'Oi, shit face! You'd better leave that lady's car alone or I'll have you.'

Sam did not want trouble, he considered waving his gun around, but he knew that waving guns around can lead to big trouble. He was now very

near the main road, movement was extremely
restricted and there were bound to be police around,
better to keep the peace, thought Sam, and look for
another way round.

'Sorry,' he said, but no one was listening any
more, they were all staring over Sam's shoulder,
back up the hill, mouths opened, transfixed.

From behind him Sam suddenly heard the long
drawn out cry. 'Baaasssttarrrd,' and he turned
around to find out who it was who had so accurately
summed him up.

## EQUALIZING

Sam never stood a chance. He managed to raise his
gun and even got off a couple of shots, but Deborah
was too close. The shots went hopelessly wide and
the gun flew out of Sam's hands as he took the full
force of a wheelchair containing an axe-swinging
woman, hurtling downhill at over twenty miles an
hour. The footrests cut his shins away from under
him and a split second later he received Deborah
plus her chair in the guts. Over the bonnet of the
Mercedes they went, with Sam on the bottom.

All three of them, the wheelchair, Deborah and
Sam landed in different places. The chair went
through the windscreen of a Datsun, Deborah
landed on the boot of the Mercedes and Sam on the
roof of an old VW next to the Merc, pointing down
hill.

As she cannoned into Sam's chest, Deborah, resourceful even in this supremely testing moment, had grabbed the plans which he had been clutching to him.

## THE PLANS CHANGE HANDS AGAIN

There was a stunned silence, the shot and the action had shut up even the posh Hampstead woman, for the moment. Deborah spoke.

'I got it, Turk! I got it! I got my engine back,' one of her arms was broken, she shoved the plans under it, with her other arm she held up the hatchet which she had managed to hang on to.

'I'm keeping them, Turk,' she shouted through the shocked silence. 'You ain't got no gun now and you come near me and I'll stick this in you! I will, I'll stick it in you.'

There was a general gasp from the observers who were, understandably, finding this dramatic stuff.

'So you could fly after all, kid,' said Sam through clenched teeth. He tried to move, but only gasped in pain, his legs would not function. Deborah's foot rests had done their work and both Sam's legs were busted. Once she understood the situation, Deborah could not resist a cry of triumph.

'My God, you're crippled! You can't walk! Is that a beautiful irony or what! Wait till I get to a phone to tell Momma I believe in God again. We're equal now Turk, and I've got the plans!'

## THE PLANS CHANGE HANDS AGAIN

The captive audience was riveted, this really was top notch Hollywood stuff. So absorbed were they, that they even forgot their fear, in fact many of them had begun to believe that the whole thing wasn't real at all, but some piece of elaborate street theatre laid on by trendy Camden Council to stop rioting during the traffic jam.

'Kid,' whispered Sam. 'In my time I've fought unions, Mafia and the United States Senate to name but a few, and you are without doubt the toughest, meanest daughter of a bitch I have ever had the misfortune to tussle with. I don't reckon there's been above fifteen minutes in this whole day when you ain't had the rise on me.'

There was even some small applause at this splendid speech.

'Fuck off, creep,' replied Deborah. And the 'tut tuts' were audible towards Deborah, whom most people now considered an ungracious victor.

In fact, Sam did admire Deborah in a way, but that was not why he was treating her to such honeyed words. The reason for this was that he was desirous of keeping her attention, having noticed Bruce Tungsten squeezing round the van behind her.

After Sam had left his office it had been a few minutes before Bruce had noticed that he had gone.

Bruce had seen Miss Hodges untie him, whilst Bruce himself tried to douse the three burning hostages and then staunch his own bullet wound, but it was not until after the security guards had arrived that he had realized Sam had gone. Bruce, at heart, was not a bad man and, faced with an office full of human torches and electrocuted secretaries, he tended to deal with the situation at hand. Sam, of course, had kept his mind on the broader issues and gone chasing the plans.

However, once relieved of his responsibilities by two old blokes in peaked caps, Bruce quickly tracked Sam down, learning over the car phone from Sam's chauffeur that the car was stuck in traffic but that Sam had disappeared on foot up Frognal. Bruce had given chase.

And there he was, unnoticed by all but Sam, standing behind Deborah. Sam was attempting to keep Deborah's attention because he far preferred Bruce to have the engine than her. If Bruce had it then Sam might yet, at least be part of things.

'I'll take these then,' said Bruce, gently leaning in and plucking the plans from under Deborah's broken arm.

'Watch out for the axe!!' cried Sam, as a shocked Deborah squirmed round on the bonnet and lashed behind her with the hatchet. This time, however, her extraordinary combative powers deserted her, and she missed.

'Oooh,' gasped the crowd.

'If you ever manage to get out of this fix, Sam,' said Bruce, 'write and tell me how you managed it, I'll be interested. You'll find me in Detroit making engines.'

'Bruce,' pleaded Sam, 'get me a lawyer, a doctor, a drink! For God's sake, you can't leave me!'

But Bruce could and he did. Without another word he turned on his heel. Although, actually, he did not get very far. Not even one step in fact, because he got smacked in the face by one of the little flashing lanterns surrounding the British Telecom tent which Deborah had avoided earlier.

'Oooh,' gasped the crowd again.


## THE PLANS CHANGE HANDS AGAIN

Toss leant down and grabbed at the plans.

'I got 'em, Debbo,' he shouted. The crowd was too riveted even to gasp. Once Toss had recovered from the shock of being shot in the shoulder, he had naturally set off after his friend. As he ran down the hill he saw the crash, and he saw a man creeping up behind the prostrate Deborah, which was why he had picked up the lantern, the only weapon that was available. It had been a good idea.

'Run, Toss, run,' shouted Deborah. 'Put them in a bank, the post office, Xerox them, stitch them to your body, but run.'

'What about you?' Toss shouted.

'Please Toss, not again, just *save Geoffrey's*

*engine.*' The appeal in Deborah's voice was sufficiently poignant to spur Toss to action. He turned
around and legged it.


## WIND POWER

Suddenly a huge beating noise filled the air,
there were shouts and a rush of wind. Up from the
Finchley Road came uniformed police. The man
with the car phone at the top of the hill had done
his job. He had reported gunfire on Church Row and
*that* the police took seriously.

Beat bobbies had run along from Swiss Cottage
Station and a helicopter of the Tactical Arms Group
had been scrambled.

Since Toss was running up the hill he did not see
the coppers behind him, and he had no time to stare
at helicopters.

What the coppers saw, of course, was a bleeding
man running away from what appeared to be a
slaughter, carrying a parcel. Clearly he was worth
having a chat with.

Toss was brought down with a neat rugby tackle
and the engine plans leapt from his hand, bursting
open on the pavement. The helicopter descended to
hover only feet above Toss and the copper.

'No!' shouted Toss.

'No!' agreed Sam, Bruce and Deborah.

But it was no use, the winds from the blades
scattered the precious plans for Geoffrey Spasmo's

hydrogen engine up and away over the vast traffic jam that used to be London. Up over the rooftops, fluttering hither and thither across the paralysed city, landing in puddles, blown into drifts of sodden leaves, stuck to the windscreens of helpless, stranded cars, until very soon there was not a word nor a single figure of Geoffrey's designs left anywhere.

## Chapter Thirty-One

# THE QUEEN'S DILEMMA

It was the day of the State Opening of Parliament, with all its inane pomp and ludicrous majesty. The strange man in the black tights had bashed on the door. The procession of the bewigged living dead (also in tights) had passed without incontinence or cardiac arrest from the Lords to the Commons – or perhaps it is the other way round. The Prime Minister and the Leader of the Opposition had walked up the aisle together conducting their one private conversation per year.

'Go fuck yourself.'

'No, *you* go fuck yourself.'

'No, *you* go fuck yourself.'

All was ready for the Queen's speech. Except her that is, the Queen was far from ready. There were no circumstances under which she would be ready, because this speech was, without doubt, the foulest and most horrible that she had ever been required by duty to utter. Prince Philip, loyal and supportive as always, reminded her that she felt this way every year. Each time she was called upon to announce some vicious, petty cut in benefits and welfare, or some further dismantling of the resources of the state, she swore that she could not do it. Each year, as the Prince reminded her, the Queen wondered if it was worth provoking a constitutional crisis by simply refusing to recite the nauseating drivel, but the Queen knew she couldn't, *noblesse oblige* and all that. The State Opening of Parliament is the time when a constitutional Monarch gets real.

'This year it's different, Philip,' she whispered backstage as they inserted the huge metal support spike in the back of her dress to hold up the great big stupid looking crown. 'I really cannot say it.'

But she knew she would, she would have to. The public outcry after the great gridlock had been horrendous. Hundreds of thousands of Londoners had been left stranded in their cars for up to three days while the jam was cleared from the outside in. The knock-on effect had shot up the motorways and down to the Channel Tunnel, causing more horrendous delays. The complete shut-down of the capital for over half a week had affected business and commerce all over the country and into Europe. Countless deals had been lost, food had rotted, looting had occurred. The whole country had been absolutely astonished to discover what Chief Superintendent Ross had known for years, which was:

that we are completely and utterly helpless in the face of motor cars, they can cripple us, any day, any time. They are a monster that we have created, we worship them, sacrifice the riches of the Earth to them and we will die for them, the moment it is demanded of us.

'Something must be done,' the people cried. 'We need more roads,' many added. It was this charged atmosphere of national disaster that had forced the Prime Minister to request Mrs McCorkadale, the Minister for Transport, to produce a radical, new, emergency road plan for Britain. By an extraordinary coincidence, the Ministry for Transport had one all ready. Digby's models were dusted off and presented to the nation. In the near hysteria that followed the gridlock, environmental objections were set aside, the country wanted roads and the government was ready to rise to the challenge.

'My government,' the Queen said, a lump rising in her throat as big as her hat, 'will begin the total rebuilding of all our major cities so that they may better accommodate the needs of the private motorist . . . This will involve the widening of all motorways . . . All B roads to become A roads . . .'

The list went on and on, and it broke the Queen's heart to read it.

Afterwards, in the Cabinet Room at 10 Downing Street, the Prime Minister spoke to Ingmar Bresslaw.

'Terrible thing that Gridlock, wasn't it, Ingmar?'